The power of the Silth

It took her ten seconds to wreck the center and slay the technicians there. Then she drove to a workshop stocking instruments she suspected of being the devices the tradermales used to neutralize the Silth.

She wrecked them all, then scooted around the base ruining anything that resembled them.

Only when that was done did she allow herself to go mad, to begin the killing.

There were so many of them that it took her half an hour. But when she finished there was not one live male inside the enclave. Hundreds had escaped, after panicking in typical male fashion. She did not expect them back . . .

Also by Glen Cook

The Starfishers Trilogy
#1: Shadowline
#2: Starfishers
#3: Stars' End

Darkwar Trilogy #1: Doomstalker*

Passage at Arms*

*Published by
POPULAR LIBRARY

DARKWAR TRILOGY·2
WARLOCK

BY GLEN COOK

POPULAR LIBRARY

An Imprint of Warner Books, Inc.

A Warner Communications Company

Popular Library books are published by
Warner Books, Inc.
666 Fifth Avenue
New York, N.Y. 10103

W A Warner Communications Company

Printed in the United States of America

First Printing: November, 1985

10 9 8 7 6 5 4 3 2 1

BOOK THREE:
MAKSCHE

Chapter Fifteen

I

Bullets hammered the north wall of the last redoubt, Akard's communications center. Mortars crumped. Their bombs banged deafeningly. Bullets leaking through the two small north windows had made a shambles of the communications gear.

Marika had done what she could to stem the nomad tide, and she had failed. She had only two regrets: that her pack, the Degnan, would go into the darkness unMourned, and that for her there would be no journey to the Reugge cloister at Maksche. For her there would be no next step on the road that might have led to the stars.

The hammer of savage weapons rose to an insane crescendo. The nomads were closing in for the last kill. Then the uproar ended. Braydic, the communications technician, whimpered into the sudden silence, "Now they will come."

Marika nodded. The last minutes had arrived. The inevitable end of the siege had come.

Marika did something never done before. She hugged the only surviving members of her pack, the huntresses Grauel

3

and Barlog. The scent of fear was heavy upon their rough fur.

Pups of the upper Ponath packs hugged no one but their dams, and that seldom after the first few years.

The two huntresses were touched deeply.

Grauel turned to the trademale Bagnel, who was teaching her to operate a firearm. His comrade, last of those who had survived last week's fall of the trademale packfast Critza, had fallen defending one of the north windows. Someone had to hold that against the savages. Grauel's heavy spear was too unwieldy.

"Wait!" Marika gasped. Her jaw went slack. "Something. . . ."

The universe of the touch, the ghost plane into which silth like Marika ducked to work their witchery, had gone mad. Some mighty shadow, terrible in its power, was raging up the valley of the Hainlin River, which this last bastion of the fortress Akard overlooked. For a moment Marika was paralyzed by the power of that shadow. Then she flung herself to a south-facing window.

Three great daggerlike crosses stormed up the frozen river. They drove into the fangs of the wind in a rigid V. That fierce and dreadful shadow-of-touch preceded them, flaying the mind with terror. Upon each cross stood five black-clad silth, one at each tip of each arm, the fifth at the axis. The incessant north wind howled around them and tore at their dark robes. They seemed to notice it not at all.

"They are coming," Marika shouted to Grauel and Barlog, who crowded her against the windowsill.

An explosion thundered out behind them. It threw them together. Marika gasped for breath. Grauel turned, pointed her rifle. It barked in unison with that of the trademale Bagnel as savages appeared in the dust swirling in the gap created by the explosion.

Marika clung to the windowsill, looking out, waiting for death.

The rushing crosses rose as they neared Akard, screaming into lightly falling snow, parting. Marika slipped through her loophole into the realm of ghosts and followed them as they plunged toward the attacking nomads, spreading death and terror.

Grauel and Bagnel stopped firing. The nomads had fled the breach. In minutes the entire besieging horde was in full flight. Two of the flying crosses harried the savages northward. The third returned and hovered over the confluence of the forks of the Hainlin, above which Akard brooded on a high headland.

Akard's pawful of survivors crowded the window, staring in disbelief. Help had come. After so long a wait. In the penultimate moment, help had come.

The cross drifted closer till the tip of its longest arm touched the fortress on the level above the communications center. Marika pushed weariness aside and went to meet her rescuers. She was only fourteen, as yet far from being a full silth sister, but was the senior silth surviving. The *only* silth surviving. Through eyes hazed with fatigue and reaction, she vaguely recognized the dark figure which came to meet her. It was Zertan, senior of the Reugge Community's cloister at Maksche.

It looked like she would get to see the great city in the south after all.

A moment after she had fulfilled the necessary ceremonial obsequiences, exhaustion overtook her. She collapsed into the arms of Grauel and Barlog.

Marika wakened after the fading of the light. She found herself perched precariously upon the flying cross. In one hasty glance she saw that she shared the strange craft with the other survivors of Akard. Grauel and Barlog were as near her as they could get—as they always were. Bagnel was next nearest. He rewarded her with a cheerful snarl as her gaze passed over him. Communicator Braydic seemed to be in shock.

The wind seemed almost still as the cross ran with it. To the left and below, the ruins of Bagnel's home, Critza, appeared. "No bodies anymore," Marika observed.

In a hard, low voice, Bagnel said, "The nomads feed upon their dead. The grauken rules the Ponath." The grauken, the monster lying so close beneath the surface of every meth. The archetypal terror of self with which every meth was intimately familiar.

The Maksche senior eyed Bagnel, then Marika from her standing place upon the axis of the cross. She pointed skyward. "It will get worse before it gets better. The grauken may rule the entire world. It comes on us with the age of ice."

Marika looked skyward, trying to forget the dust cloud that was absorbing her sun's power and cooling her world. She tried to concentrate on the wonder of the moment, to take joy in being alive, to forget the horror of the past, of losing first the pack with which she had lived her first ten years, then the silth packfast where she had lived and trained the past four. She tried to banish the terror lurking in her future.

Jiana! Doomstalker! Twice!

The voice in her mind was the voice of a ghost. She could not make it go away.

The hills of the Ponath gave way to plains. The snowfall faded. And the flying cross fled with the breath of the north wind licking behind.

II

For months Marika had seen nothing but overcast skies. Always the bitter north wind had been present, muttering of even colder times to come. But now the gale could not catch her. She mocked it quietly.

Cracks began to show in the cloud cover. One moon, then another, peeped through, scattering the white earth with silver.

"Hello, strangers," Marika said.

"What?"

The response startled Marika, for she had been enclosed entirely within herself, unmindful of her bizarre situation. "I was greeting the moons, Grauel. Look. There is Biter.

One of the small moons is running behind her. I cannot tell which. I do not care. I am just glad to see them. How long has it been?"

The huntress shifted her weapon and position gingerly. It was a long fall to the frozen river. "Too long. Too many months." Sorrow edged Grauel's voice. "Hello, moons."

Soon Chaser, the second large moon, showed its face too, so that shadows below looked like many-fingered paws.

"Look there!" Marika said. "A lake. Open water." She too had not seen unfrozen water in months.

Grauel would not look down. She clung to their transport with a death grip.

Marika glanced around.

Five strangers, five friends. All astride a metal cross the shape of a dagger, running with the wind a thousand feet above the earth and snow. Grauel and Barlog, known since birth. Bagnel, known only months, strange, withdrawn, yet with the aroma of someone who could become very close. At that moment she decided he would become an integral part of her destiny.

Marika was silth. The Akard sisters had called her the most powerful talent ever to be unearthed in the upper Ponath. Sometimes the strongest silth caught flashes intimating tomorrow.

Braydic. The only friend the exile pup had made in her four years at Akard. Marika was glad that Braydic had survived.

Finally, two pups of meth who had served the silth, holding one another, terrified still, not yet knowing their fates. She realized that she did not know their names. She had saved them, as she had saved herself, for redoubled exile. Shared terror and last-second salvation ought to account for more intimacy.

"So," she said to Grauel and Barlog. "Here we go again. Into exile once more."

Barlog nodded. Grauel merely stared straight ahead, trying to keep her gaze from taking in the long fall to the silvered snows.

The Hainlin twisted away to the west and out of sight for

a time, then swept back in beneath. It widened into a vast, slow stream, though mostly it remained concealed behind a mask of white. Time passed. Marika shook off repeated fits of bleak memory. She suspected her companions were doing the same.

Meth were not reflective by nature. They tended to live in the present, letting the past lie and allowing the future to care for itself. But the pasts of these meth were not the settled, bucolic pasts of their foredams. Their pasts reechoed with bloody hammer strokes. Their futures threatened more of the same.

"Lights," Grauel croaked. And in a moment, "By the All! Look at the lights!"

Ten thousand pinpricks in the night, like a nighttime sky descended to earth. Except that the sky of Marika's world held few stars, filled as it was with a dense, vast cloud of interstellar dust.

"Maksche," Senior Zertan said. "Home. We will reach the cloister in a few minutes."

The flying crosses pacing them suddenly swept ahead, vanished into the darkness. The lights ahead bobbed and rocked and swelled, and then the first passed below, maybe five hundred feet down. Marika felt no awe of the altitude. She exulted in the flying.

Soon the cross settled into a lighted courtyard, to a point between crosses already arrived. Scores of silth in Reugge black waited silently. The cross touched down. Zertan stepped off. Several silth approached her. She said something Marika did not catch, gestured, and stalked away. The other silth left their places at the tips of the cross.

A meth female in worker apparel approached Marika and the others. "Come with me. I have been instructed to show you quarters." She assessed them cautiously. "Not you," she told Bagnel, diffidently. "Someone from your Bond is coming for you."

Marika was amused, for she knew this meth saw only savages out of the Ponath. Even her, for all she was silth. And she knew this city meth was frightened, for savages from the Ponath had reputations for being unpredictable, irrational, and fierce.

Marika gestured. "We go. You, lead the way."

Bagnel stood aside, looking forlorn, one paw raised in a gesture of farewell.

Grauel followed the worker. Marika followed her. Barlog stayed close behind, weapon at port. Braydic and the pups tagged along at the end.

The Degnan refugees searched every shadow they passed. Marika listened with that talented silth ear that was inside her mind. She felt silth working their witcheries all around her. But the shadows were haunted by nothing more dangerous than projected fears of the unknown.

The servant led them through seemingly endless hallways, dropping first the pups, then Braydic. Marika sensed Grauel and Barlog becoming edgy. Their sense of location was confused. She grew uncomfortable herself. This place seemed too large to encompass. Akard was never so vast or tortuous that she had feared for her ability to get out.

Get out. Get out. That built within her, a smoldering panic, a dread of being unable to escape. She was of the upper Ponath, where pack meth ran free, at will.

The worker detected their mounting tension. She led them up stairs and outside, to the top of a wall at least vaguely reminiscent of the north wall at Akard, where Marika had made her away place, the place she went to be alone and think.

Each silth found such a place wherever she might be.

"It is huge," Barlog breathed from behind Marika. Marika agreed, though she knew not whether Barlog meant the cloister or city.

The Maksche cloister was a square compound a quarter mile to a side. Its outer wall stood thirty feet high. It was constructed of a buttery brown stone. The structures it enclosed were built of the same stone, all topped with steep roofs of red tile. The buildings were all very old, very weathered, and all very rectilinear. Some had corner towers rising like obelisks peaked by triangles of red.

The worker said, "A thousand meth live in the cloister,

separate from the city. The wall is the edge of our world, a boundary that is not to be passed."

She meant what she said, no doubt, but the fierceness that rose in her charges made her drop the subject. Marika growled, "Take us where we are supposed to go. Now. I will hear rules from those who make them, and will decide if they are reasonable then."

Their guide looked stricken.

Grauel said, "Marika, I suggest you recall all that has been said about this place."

Marika stared at the huntress, but soon her gaze wandered. Grauel was right. At the beginning she had best submit to the local style.

"Stop," she said. "I want to look." She did not await approval.

The cloister stood at Maksche's heart, upon a contrived elevation. The surrounding land was flat all the way to the horizons. The Hainlin, three hundred yards wide, looped past the city in a broad brown band two miles west of Marika's vantage. Neat squares of cropland, bounded by hedgerows or lines of trees, showed through the snow covering the plain.

"Not a single hill. I think it will not be long before I become homesick for hills." Marika used the simple dialect of her puphood, and was surprised when the worker frowned puzzledly. Could the common speech be so different here?

"I think so. Yes," Grauel replied. "Even Akard was less foreign than this. It is like ten thousand little fortresses, this thing called a city."

The buildings were very strange. But for Akard and Critza, every meth-made structure Marika had ever seen had been built of logs and stood under twenty-five feet high.

"I am not allowed much time away from my regular duties here," the worker said, her tone whining. "Please come, young mistress."

Marika scowled. "All right. Lead on."

The quarters assigned had been untenanted for a long time. Dust lay thick upon what tattered furniture there was.

Marika coughed, said, "We are being isolated in some remote corner."

Grauel nodded. "Only to be expected."

Barlog observed, "We can have this livable in a few hours. It is not as bad as it looks."

Feebly, the worker said, "I must take you two to ... to ..." She fumbled for a word. "I guess you would say, huntress's quarters."

"No," Marika told her. "We stay together."

Grauel and Barlog snarled and gestured toward the door with their weapons.

"Go," Marika snapped. "Or I will tie a savage's curse to your tail."

The female fled in terror. Grauel said, "Probably whelped and raised here. Scared of her own shadow."

"This is a place where shadows are terrors," Barlog countered. "We will hear from the shadow mistresses now."

But Barlog was wrong. A week passed without event. It was a week in which Marika seldom left her quarters and had no intercourse at all with the Reugge of Maksche. She let Grauel and Barlog do the physical exploration. No one came to her.

She began to wonder why she was being ignored.

The time free began as a boon. In her years at Akard she had spent most of every waking hour in study, learning to become silth. The only respite had come during summers when she had joined hunting parties stalking the nomadic invaders who brought Akard and the Ponath to ruin.

Once her quarters were clean and she had sneaked a few exploratory forays into nearby parts of the cloister, and had penetrated the rest of it riding ghosts, and had found herself in away place in a high tower overlooking the square where she had arrived, she grew bored. Even study became appealing.

She snarled her dissatisfaction at the worker who brought their meals. That was on her tenth day in Maksche.

Things seemed to move slowly in Maksche. Marika's complaints continued for a week, growing virulent. Yet nothing happened.

"Do not cause trouble," Grauel cautioned. "They are studying our conduct. It is all some sort of test."

"Pardon me if I am skeptical," Marika said. "I have walked the dark side a hundred times since we have been here. I have seen no indication that they even know we are here, let alone are watching. We have been put out of sight, out of mind, and are imprisoned in a dungeon of the soul."

Grauel exchanged glances with Barlog. Barlog observed, "All things are not seen by the witch's inner eye, Marika. You are not omnipotent."

"What is that supposed to mean?"

"It means that one young silth, no matter how strong, is not going to use her talent to see what a cloister full of more practiced silth are doing if they do not want her to see."

Marika was about to admit that that might be possible when someone scratched at the door. She gestured. "It is not time to eat. The drought must be over."

Barlog opened the door.

There stood a silth older than any Marika had encountered before. She hobbled in, leaning on a cane of some gnarled dark wood. She halted in the center of the room, surveyed the three of them with rheumy cataracted eyes. Her half-blind gaze came to rest upon Marika. "I am Moragan. I have been assigned as your teacher and as your guide upon the Reugge Path." She spoke the Reugge low speech with an intriguing, elusive accent. Or was it a natural lisp? "You are the Marika who stirred so much controversy and chaos at our northern fastness." Not a question. A statement.

"Yes." Marika had a feeling this was no time to quibble about her role at Akard.

"You may go," Moragan told Grauel and Barlog.

The huntresses did not move. They did not look to Marika for her opinion. Already they had positioned themselves so that Moragan stood at the heart of a perilous triangle.

"You are safe here," Moragan told Marika when no one moved.

"Indeed? I have your sworn word?"

"You do."

"And the word of a silth sister is worth the metal on which it is graven." She had been studying the apparel of the old sister and could not make out the significance of its decorations. "As we who were under the sworn guardianship of the Reugge discovered. Our packsteads were overrun without aid coming. And when we fled to the Akard packfast for safety, that too was allowed to be destroyed."

"You question decisions of policy about which you know nothing, pup."

"Not at all, mistress. I simply refuse to allow policy to snare and crush me in coils of deceit and broken oaths."

"They said you were a bold one. I see they spoke the truth. Very well. We will do it your way. For now." Moragan hobbled to a wooden chair, settled slowly, slapped her cane down atop a table nearby. She seemed to go to sleep.

"Who are you besides Moragan?" Marika asked. "I cannot read your decorations."

"Just a worn-out old silth so far gone she is past being what you would call Wise. We are not here to discuss me, though. Tell me your story. I have heard and read a few things. Now I will assess your version of events."

Marika talked, but to no point. A few minutes later Moragan's head dropped to her chest and she began to snore.

And so it went, day after day, with Moragan doing more asking and snoring than teaching. That day of her first appearance, she had been in one of her more lucid periods. Sometimes she could not recall the date or even Marika's name. Most of the time she was of little value except as a reference guide to the cloister's more arcane customs. Always she asked more questions than she answered, many of them irritatingly personal.

Her role, though, provided Marika with a role of her own. As a student she occupied a recognized place in cloister society and was answerable principally to Moragan for her conduct. Safely knit into the cultural fabric, Marika felt more comfortable teaching herself by exploring and observing.

Marika liked little of what she did learn.

Within the cloister the least of workers lived well. Outside, in the city, meth lived in abject want, suffering through brief lives of hunger, disease, and backbreaking labor. Everyone and everything in Maksche belonged to the Reugge silth Community, to the tradermale brotherhood calling itself the Brown Paw Bond, or to the two in concert. The Brown Paw Bond maintained its holdings by Reugge license, under complicated and extended lease arrangements. Residents of Maksche who were neither tradermale nor silth were bound to their professions or land for life.

Marika was bewildered. The Reugge possessed meth as though they were domestic animals? She interrogated Moragan. The teacher just looked at her strangely, evidently unable to comprehend the point of her questions.

"Grauel," Marika said one evening, "have you figured this place out? Do you understand it at all? That old carque Moragan cannot or will not explain anything so it makes any sense."

"Take care with her, Marika. She is more than she seems."

"She is as All-touched as my granddam was."

"She may be senile and mad, but she is not harmless. Perhaps the more dangerous for it. It is whispered that she was not set to teach you but to study you. It is also whispered that she was once very important in the order, and that she still has the favor of some who are very high up. Fear her, Marika."

"I should fear someone I could break?"

"As strength goes? This is not the upper Ponath, Marika. It is not the strength of the arm that counts. It is the strength of the alliances one forms."

Marika made a sound of derision. Grauel ignored her.

"Marika, suppose that some of them hope you try your strength. Suppose some of them want to prove something to themselves."

"What?"

"Our ears are sharp from many years of hunting the forests of the upper Ponath. When we go among the huntresses of this place—and sorrier huntresses you will never see—we sometimes overhear whispers never meant for our ears. They talk about us and they talk about you and they talk about the thinking of those around Senior Zertan. In a way, you are on trial. They suspect—maybe even know—about Gorry."

"Gorry? What about Gorry?"

"Something happened to Gorry in the final hours of the siege. There was much speculation, overheard by everyone. *We* said nothing to anyone about that, but we are not the only survivors brought out of the ruins of Akard."

Marika's heart fluttered as she thought of her one-time instructress. But she felt no remorse. Gorry had deserved the torment she had suffered, and more. All Marika felt was a heightened apprehension about being ignored. It had not occurred to her that it was that sort of deliberateness. She would have to be careful. She was in no position of strength.

Grauel watched expectantly while Marika wrapped her mind around the implications.

"Why are you looking at me that way?"

"I thought you might have some regrets."

"Why?"

"She was—"

"She was a carque of an old nuisance, Grauel. She would have done it to me if she could have. She tried often enough. She got what she asked for. I do not want to hear her mentioned again."

"As you wish, mistress."

"Have you found Braydic yet?"

"She was assigned to the communications center here, as you might expect. Students are not permitted entry there. And technicians are not allowed out."

"Why not?"

"I do not know. This is a different world. We are still feeling our way. They never tell you what is permitted, only what is not."

Marika realized that Grauel was upset with her. When Grauel was distressed, she insisted on using the formal mode of speech. But Marika had given up trying to interpret the

huntress's moods. She was exercised about something most
of the time.

"I want to go out into the city, Grauel."

"Why?"

"To explore."

"That is not permitted."

"Why not?"

"I do not know. Rules are not explained here. They are
enforced. Ignorance is no excuse."

What was the penalty for disobedience?

Marika banished the thought. It was too early to challenge constraints. Still, she felt compelled to say, "If this is
life in the fabulous Maksche cloister, Grauel, I may go over
the wall."

"Barlog and I have very little to do either, Marika. They
think we are too backward."

III

The absolute, enduring stone of the cloister became a hated
enemy. It crushed in upon Marika with the weight of mas-
sively accumulated time and alien tradition. Enforced inac-
tivity made it almost intolerable. Each day she spent more
time in her towertop away place. Each day meditation did
less to ease her spiritual malaise.

Her place overlooked nothing but the courtyard, the city,
and the works of meth. There was a constant wind, a north
wind, but it did not speak to her as had the winds at Akard.
It carried the wrong smells, the wrong tastes. It was heavy
with the sweat of industry. It was a foreign, indifferent
wind. That wind of the north had been her friend and ally.

Often she did not leave her cell at all, but lay on her pallet
and used a finger to draw stick figures in the sweat on the
cold wall.

Sometimes she went down through her loophole into the
realm of ghosts, but she found little comfort there. Ghosts
were scarce where so many silth were gathered. She sensed

a few great monsters way high above, especially in the night, but she could not touch them. She might as well reach for Biter.

There was a change in atmosphere in the cloister around the end of Marika's sixth week there. It puzzled her till Barlog showed up to announce, "Most Senior Gradwohl is coming here." Most Senior Gradwohl ruled the entire Reugge Community, which spanned the continent. "They are frantic trying to get ready."

"Why is she coming?" Marika asked.

"To take personal charge of the effort to control the nomads. Two days ago nomads were seen from the wall of the packfast at Motchen. That is only a hundred miles north of Maksche, Marika. They are catching up with us already." In a lower voice Barlog confided, "These Maksche silth are frightened. They have a contract with the tradermales that obligates them to protect traders anytime they are in Reugge territory. They have been unable to do that. Critza is just one of three tradermale packfasts that were overrun. There is a rumor that some tradermales want to register an open petition for the Serke sisterhood to intercede in Reugge territories because the Reugge can no longer maintain order."

"So?" Marika asked indifferently.

"That would affect us, Marika."

"How? We have no part in anything. We are tolerated for some reason. Barely. We are fed. And otherwise we are ignored. What do we have to fear? If no ones sees us, who can harm us?"

"Do not talk that way, Marika."

"Why not?"

"These sisters can go around unseen. One of them might hear you."

"Don't be silly. That's nonsense."

"I heard it from . . ." Barlog did not finish for fear of compromising her source.

"How much longer can you tolerate this imprisonment, Barlog? What does Grauel think? I won't endure it much longer, I promise you that."

"We can't leave."

"Says who?"

"It's not permitted."

"By whom? Why not?"

"That's just the way it is."

"For those who accept it."

"Marika, please. . . ."

"Go away, Barlog. I don't want to hear you whine." As Barlog was about to leave, she added, "They've tamed you, Barlog. Made a two-legged rheum-greater out of a once fine huntress." Use of the familiar mode made Marika's words all the more cutting.

Barlog's lips parted in a snarl of fury. But she restrained herself and even closed the door gently.

Marika went to her tower to observe the most senior's arrival. Gradwohl came in on one of the flying crosses, standing at its axis. Marika watched it drop past the tower, the silth at the tips of its arms standing rigidly with their eyes closed. There was a thrumming rhythm between them that Marika had missed during her flight south. But then she had been exhausted physically, drained mentally and emotionally, and had been interested in little but leaving a shattered fortress and life behind.

She went down inside herself and through her loophole and was astonished to find the cross surrounded by a roiling fog of ghosts, great ghosts similar to the dark killing ghosts she had ridden in the north. The sister at the tip of the longer arm controlled them. They moved the ship. The other sisters provided reservoirs of talent from which the senior sister drew. The most senior did nothing. She was but a passenger.

This, finally, was something about which Marika could get excited. How did they manage it? Was it something she could learn to do? It would be fantastic to ride above the world by night upon one of those great daggers. She studied the silth. What they were doing was different from killing, but it did not appear difficult. She touched the senior sister, trying to read what was happening, as the cross neared the ground.

Her touch distracted the silth. The cross dropped the last foot. Marika recoiled quickly. A countertouch brushed her, but was not specific. It did not return.

A great deal of pomp and ceremony followed the most senior's landing. Marika remained where she was. The most senior, her party, and those who welcomed her, vanished into the labyrinthine cloister. Marika gazed over the red rooftops at the horizon. For once the wind carried a hint of the north. That chill breath of home worsened her feeling of alienation.

Grauel found her still there near midnight, chin on arms on stone, eyes vacant, staring at the far fields of moon-frosted snow as if awaiting a message. "Marika. They sent me to bring you."

Grauel seemed badly shaken. There was something in her voice that stirred the dangerous flight-fight response within her. "Who sent you?"

"Senior Zertan. On behalf of the most senior. Gradwohl herself wants to talk to you. That Moragan was with them. I warned you to watch yourself with her."

Marika bared her teeth. Grauel was terrified. Probably of the possibility that they would get thrown out of the cloister. "Why does she want me?"

"I don't know. Probably about what happened at Akard."

"Now? They're interested now? After almost two months?"

"Marika. Restrain yourself."

"Am I not perfectly behaved before our hosts?"

Grauel did not deny that. Marika even treated Moragan with absolute respect. She made a point of giving no one cause to take offense—most of the time.

Nevertheless, she was not liked by the few sisters who crossed her path. Grauel and Barlog claimed the Maksche sisters feared her. Just as had the sisters at Akard.

"All right. Show me the way. I'll try to mind my manners."

They made Grauel stop at the door to the inner cloister, the big central structure opened only for high ceremonies and days of obligation. Marika touched Grauel's elbow lightly, restraining her. Grauel responded with a massive shrug of resignation—and, Marika thought, just the faintest hint of amusement in the tilt of her ears. It was a hint only one who knew Grauel well would have caught.

What was she up to? And where was Grauel's rifle? She had not been parted from the weapon since she had received it from Bagnel. She *slept* with it, it was so precious. Her carrying it all the time had to be cause for consternation and comment.

Almost, Marika looked back. Almost. Native guile stopped her.

Two silth led her to a vast, ill-lighted chamber. No electricity there, just tapers shuddering in chilly drafts. As must be in a place where silth worked their magics. Electromagnetic energies interfered with their talents.

This was the chamber where the most important Reugge rites were observed. Marika had been there before only as a dark-walker. Other than in its symbolic value, the place was nothing special.

Two dozen ranking silth waited, perched silently upon tall stools. Only the occasional flick of an inadvertently exposed tail betrayed the fact that anything was happening behind their cold obsidian-flake eyes. Every one of those eyes was fixed upon Marika.

She was less intimidated than she expected.

Several worker-servants moved among the silth, managing wants and refreshments. One with a tray approached Marika. She was an ancient whose fur had fallen in patches, leaving only ugly bare spots. She dragged her right leg in a stiff limp. As Marika waved her away, she was startled by the meth's scent. Something familiar. . . .

In a low voice the servant said, "Mind your manners, pup." She hitch-stepped off to the sideboard that seemed to be her station.

Barlog!

Barlog. With a limp. And Grauel's treasure was missing.

With that rifle Barlog could cut down half the silth in the room before any even thought of employing their witchery.

Marika was pleased by the resourcefulness of Grauel and Barlog. But she felt no more confident of her ability to handle the subtleties of the coming interview.

Of the silth in that room, Marika recognized only two. Zertan and Moragan. Marika faced the senior and performed the appropriate ceremonial greeting to perfection. She would show Barlog who could mind her manners.

"This is the one from Akard?" a gravelly voice asked.

"Yes, mistress."

The most senior, Marika assumed. Younger than she had expected. She was a hard, chunky, grizzled female with slightly wild eyes. Like a Gorry still sane. A sister who was as much huntress as silth, and a hungry huntress at that.

"I thought she would be older. And bigger," the most senior said, echoing Marika's own thoughts.

"She *is* young," Moragan said, and Marika noted that she was completely awake and vibrant and alive. Moragan's stool stood between those of Zertan and the most senior, an inch nearer that of the latter, subtly proclaiming her most important tie.

Senior Zertan said, "We do not know what to do with her. Her history is repellent at best. She is an astoundingly strong feral detected accidentally four years ago. Akard took her in. That was soon after the first nomadic incursions into the upper Ponath. Her hamlet was one of the first overrun. It seems that, with no training whatsoever, purely instinctively she drew to the dark and slew several savages. Her latent ability in that respect so disturbed some of our sisters that they labeled her Jiana, after the mythological and archetypal doomstalker Jiana. A sister, Gorry, who had a Community-wide reputation before the necessity for her rustification arose—"

A revenant shrieked in Marika's mind. *Jiana! Doomstalker!*

"Zertan." Most Senior Gradwohl's voice was coldly cautionary.

Zertan shifted her emphasis slightly. "Gorry had very

strong, very negative feelings about the pup. In one way of seeing, Gorry was correct. She has twice been almost the only survivor of monstrous disasters that befell those who nurtured her. Gorry was very much afraid of her, but was her teacher. Thus her training there was haphazard at best. Reliable reports do indicate that she achieved a commanding ability to reach and command the darkest of those-who-dwell."

The object of discussion was growing more irate by the moment. Barlog's cold stare helped her control her tongue.

"Zertan," Gradwohl said again. "Enough. I have seen all the reports you have, and more." For a moment the Maksche senior seemed startled. "Can you tell me anything new? Anything I do not know? How does she feel about the sisterhood?"

After a silence that began to stretch painfully, Zertan admitted, "I have no idea how she feels. But it does not matter. A pup's attitudes are the clay that the teacher—"

Gradwohl did not seize upon Zertan's clumsiness. Instead, she shifted approach. "Senior Koenic reported to me shortly before Akard fell. Among other things, we discussed a feral silth pup named Marika. This Marika, though only fourteen years old, was directly responsible for the deaths of several hundred meth. Senior Koenic was as scared of her as Gorry was. Because, as she put it, this Marika was an embryonic Bestrei or Zhorek—without the intellectual handicaps of those two dark-walkers. Senior Koenic knew Bestrei and Zhorek before *her* rustification. She watched Marika for four years. She was in a position to form an intelligent estimate of the pup."

Gradwohl eased down off her stool, surveyed the assembly. "What does it matter what a pup thinks of the Community? Consider two ideas. Trust, and personal loyalty.

"For all the backbiting that goes on, trust cements the Reugge Community. We *know* we are in no physical danger from one another. We *know* none of our sisters will *willfully* work to the detriment of the order. Our subordinates *know* we will protect and nurture them. But Marika believes none of that.

"Why? Because her hamlet and hundreds of others were overrun by savages the Reugge were pledged to repel. Because genuine attempts have been made upon her life. Because she has not been educated to see the good of the Community as paramount."

Gradwohl sounded like some windy Wise meth giving the convocation on a day of high obligation. The longer Gradwohl talked, the less closely Marika listened and the more she became wary. There was some silth game running and she was just a counter.

"About personal loyalty, few of you know a thing," the most senior continued in a hard voice. "Let us experiment. Moragan. Proceed."

Moragan got off her stool. She drew a long, wicked knife from inside her robe, presented it to Senior Zertan.

Gradwohl said, "Carry out your instructions, Zertan."

Zertan left her stool with obvious reluctance. She looked at Marika for a moment.

She flung herself forward.

Marika's response was instantaneous and instinctive. She ducked through her loophole into the ghost realm. A thought captured a ghost. A mental shout scattered the few others before any other silth could come through and seize them. She hurled her ghost at the vaguely perceived form plunging toward her.

She returned to reality while the bark of a rifle still reverberated through the chamber. Zertan was pitching forward, dropped knife not yet to the floor. Gradwohl was turning, spun by Barlog's bullet. Marika flung up a paw, restraining Barlog before she commenced a massacre.

The chamber door exploded inward. The guards posted outside tumbled through. Grauel leaped through with a Degnan ululation, shield on one arm, javelin poised for the cast. Behind her, a quivering Braydic menaced the guards with a sword she had no idea how to use.

Not one of the silth on the stools moved more than the tip of a tail.

Some silth game.

Most Senior Gradwohl recovered. The bullet had but

clipped her shoulder. She met Marika's cold stare. "I seldom miscalculate. But when I do, I do it big." Her paw went
to her shoulder, where moisture seeped into the fabric of her
robe. "I did not anticipate firearms. Halechk! See to Zertan
before she dies on us."

A silth with healer's decorations left her stool and hastened to Zertan.

Gradwohl said, "Personal loyalty. Even in the face of
certain disaster." Her teeth ground together. Her wound
had begun to hurt.

Zertan's knife had come to rest only inches from the tip of
Marika's right boot. She kicked it across the floor to the
most senior's feet.

Gradwohl's cheek began to twitch. She whispered, "Have
a care, pup. Had it been real, you *might* have gotten
through it by having surprise on your right paw."

"Had it been real, there would be only three meth alive in
this room right now." Marika spoke with conviction. She
broke eye contact long enough to glance at the knife. "We
had a saying in the Ponath. 'As strength goes.' " She had to
say it in dialect. Gradwohl did not react. Perhaps it went
past her.

"When I am manipulated or pushed, mistress, I must
push back."

Gradwohl ignored her. She surveyed the silth, still
perched upon their stools. "This assembly has served its
purpose. It is as I suspected. Someone has been remiss.
Someone allowed prejudice to overwhelm reason. Listen!
This pup ambushed and destroyed a *ranking* sister of the
Serke Community. And I promise you, that House is giving
that fact a lot more attention than this one has."

Gradwohl stared at Marika hard. Marika continued to
meet her gaze, refusing to be intimidated. Beneath, beyond
the test of wills, she sensed a kindred soul.

"This assembly is at an end," Gradwohl said, still holding
Marika's gaze. "Go. All but you, pup."

Silently, silth began filing out. Two helped carry Senior
Zertan.

Barlog and Grauel did not move.

Braydic, though, Marika noted, had disappeared. Ever cautious and timid Braydic.

Just as well, perhaps. Just as well.

Marika focused upon this meth strong enough to rule the fractious Reugge Community.

Chapter Sixteen

I

Gradwohl climbed onto a stool. "Sit if you like," she told Marika.

Marika settled crosslegged upon the floor, as had been the custom among the packs of the upper Ponath. Furniture had been unknown in her dam's loghouse.

"Tell me about yourself, pup."

"Mistress?"

"Tell me your story. I want to know everything there is to know about you."

"You know, mistress. Through your agent Moragan."

Gradwohl seemed amused. "She was that transparent?"

"Only looking back."

"Nothing substitutes for direct examination. Begin simply. Tell me your story. What is your name?"

"Marika, mistress."

"Tell me about Marika. From her birth to this moment."

Marika sketched an autobiography which included her first awarenesses of her talent, her unusually close relationship with her male littermate Kublin, her troubles with one of the Wise of her dam's loghouse, and all her troubles during her stay at the fortress Akard.

Gradwohl nodded. "Interesting. But possibly even more interesting in complete privacy."

"Mistress?"

"You have told me very little about Marika inside."

Marika grew uneasy.

"Do not be frightened, pup."

"I am not, mistress."

"Liar. I met a most senior when I was your age. I was petrified. There is no need. I am here to help. You are not happy, are you? Honestly, now."

"No, mistress."

"Why not?"

She thought she had made that clear. Perhaps their backgrounds were too alien. She rambled till Gradwohl lost patience. "Get to the point, pup. There are no ears here but mine. Even were there, your sisters would make no reprisals for what you say. I will not permit that. And do not lie. I want to know what the real Marika thinks and feels."

Irked, Marika tested the water with a few mild remarks. When Gradwohl did not explode, she continued till she had revealed most of her dissatisfactions.

"Exactly what I suspected. An absolute lack of vision from the very beginning. I was not a feral myself, but I endured similar troubles. They sense strength and power, and it frightens them. In their way, silth have minds as small as any common meth. Those who might be surpassed want to stifle you before you develop the skills to command them. It is a severe shortcoming of the society silth have developed. Now. Tell me more about Akard."

Gradwohl spoke no more of Marika's place in things, nor of her feelings. Instead, she concentrated upon a minute examination of events during Akard's final days. "What has become of the other survivors? Especially the commtech and the tradermale?" She used the Ponath dialect word tradermale as though it was unfamiliar.

Marika reflected carefully before saying, "Braydic was assigned work in the communications center here." Had the

most senior noted the sword-carrying meth who had
threatened the guards behind Grauel, keeping them from
interfering? "They will not let me see her. Bagnel vanished.
I assume he rejoined his brotherhood. They say there is a
tradermale place here in Maksche."

"Presumably I could reach him through his factors.

"Darkship, mistress?"

"The flying cross. That was you in the tower, was it not?
You touched Norgis just before we set down."

"Yes, mistress."

"What did you think?"

"I was awed, mistress. The idea of riding such a thing. . . .
I rode one coming down from Akard, but most of that
escapes me."

"You are not frightened by it?"

"No, mistress."

"You do not find those-who-dwell frightening?"

"No, mistress."

"Good. That will be all, pup. Return to your quarters."

"Yes, mistress."

"There will be changes in your life, pup."

"Yes, mistress," Marika said as she walked toward the
doorway.

Grauel went through first, surveyed the hallway, nodded.
Barlog backed out behind Marika, rifle still trained on the
most senior.

Not one word about the confrontation passed between the
three of them.

The changes began immediately. The morning following
the interview, a silth the age of Marika's dam came to her
cell. She introduced herself as Dorteka. "I am your instructress, detached from the most senior's staff for that purpose.
The most senior has ordered an individualized program for
you. We will get started now." Plainly, Dorteka did not like
her assignment, but she was careful to avoid saying so.

Marika would soon note a cloisterwide shift of attitude
toward one who had caught the most senior's interest.

That first morning Dorteka took her to a meditation

chamber. They sat upon the floor, across a table of the same stone as the cloister, in the eerie light of a single oil lamp. On Dorteka's side lay a clipboard and papers. Dorteka said, "Your education has been erratic. The most senior wants you to go back and begin at the beginning."

"I would be with pups. . . ."

"You will proceed at your own pace, independent of everyone else at every level. Where your training has been adequate, you will advance rapidly, to your limits." Dorteka straightened a paper. "What would you like to do for the sisterhood?"

Marika did not hesitate. "Fly the darkships. To the starworlds."

A trace of amusement showed in the tilt of Dorteka's ears. "So the most senior suggested. The darkship is possible. The starworlds are not."

"Why?"

"We were too late going out. We looked in the wrong places. The starworlds are all enfiefed, and they are guarded jealously by the sisterhoods who own them. Even to leave the planet now would mean an immediate challenge to darkwar. So darkwar can be our only reason for entering the dark. We will not. We have no one capable of challenging."

Puzzled, Marika asked, "What is darkwar? No one will explain."

"At your level it will be difficult to comprehend. In essence, darkwar is a bloodduel between the leading Mistresses of the Ships of Communities in conflict. The survivor wins the right of the dispute. Darkwar is rare because it usually seals the fate of an entire Community."

Bloodduel Marika understood. She nodded.

"Time enough for such things after you gain a solid foundation. You wish to become involved with the ships. Then you shall become involved, if you remain interested once you become qualified. There are never enough sisters willing to work them. You do read and write?"

"Yes, mistress."

Dorteka handed her a sheet of paper. "This is our schedule. We will adjust it as needed."

Marika looked it over. "Not much time left for sleep."

"You wish to fly darkships, you must learn to endure sleeplessness. You wish to see your friend Braydic, you will remain stubbornly devoted to your studies." Dorteka pushed a scrap of paper across the table. The notes on it were in a paw almost mechanically perfect. *"Suggested motivators for the feral subject Marika."*

"The most senior?"

"Yes."

The interest shown by the most senior was a bit intimidating.

The sheet was filled with a complicated diagram for earning the right to visit Braydic or the city.

"As you see, a visit to your friend requires you to accumulate one hundred performance points. Those are mapped out for you there. Leave to go outside the cloister will be more difficult to obtain. It is subject to my being satisfied with your progress. You will never get out if I feel you are giving less than one hundred percent."

Crafty old Gradwohl. She had speared to the heart of her and tapped forces which could *make* her learn. The thought of seeing Braydic sparked an immediate urge to begin. The opportunity to get into the city, too, stirred her, but less concretely.

"I doubt that I will permit a city visit anytime soon. Perhaps we will accumulate several opportunities for later."

"Why, mistress?"

"The streets could be dangerous for an untrained silth. We have been having a problem with rogue males. I expect the Serke are behind that, too. Whatever, silth have been assaulted. Last summer ringleaders were rounded up and sentenced to the mines, but that did little good. The brethren—those you call tradermales—may have a paw in the movement."

"The world is not so complicated on an upper Ponath packstead," Marika observed.

"No. You see the schedule and rewards. Are they acceptable?"

"Yes, mistress."

"You will become a full-time student, with no other duties. You will accept the discipline of the Community?"

"Yes, mistress." Marika was surprised to find herself so eager. Till this morning she had cared about nothing. "I am ready to begin."

"Then begin we shall."

II

Marika's education commenced before the next dawn. Dorteka wakened her and took her to a gymnasium for an hour's workout. A bath followed.

Marika's determination almost broke. She nearly broke her vow to obey and conform.

A bath! Meth—of the upper Ponath, at least—*hated* water. They never entered it voluntarily. Only when the populations of insects in one's fur became too great to stand. . . .

The bath was followed by a hurried meal prior to the first class of the day, which was an introduction to being silth. Rites and ceremonies, dogma and duties, and instruction in the secret languages of the sisterhood, which she hardly needed. She discovered that there were circles of sisterhood mysteries silth were supposed to penetrate as they became older and more skilled. Till Dorteka, she had no idea how much she had been shut out.

She ripped through those studies swiftly. They required rote learning. Her memory was excellent. Seldom did she need to be shown anything more than once.

She excelled in the gymnasium. She was her dam's pup. Skiljan had been fast, strong, hard, and tough.

The second class lay across the cloister from the first. Dorteka made her run all the way. Dorteka made her run everywhere, and ran with her. The second class was not as susceptible to rote learning, for it was mathematics. It required the use of reason. Silth naturally tended to favor intuition.

After mathematics came the history of the sisterhood, a class which Marika devoured in days. The Reugge were a minor Community with a short, uneventful past, an offshoot of the Serke that had established independence only seven centuries earlier. Sustenance of that independence was the outstanding Reugge achievement.

Silth had a history that stretched into prehistory, countless millennia back, when all meth lived in nomadic packs. The earliest sisterhoods existed long before the keeping of records began. Most silth had little interest in those days. They lived in an eternal now.

Marika's pack had maintained a record of its achievements called the Degnan Chronicle. That it had been kept in her dam's loghouse had been a source of pride to the pup. Barlog still kept it up, for she and Grauel believed that as long as it survived and remained current, the Degnan pack survived. As a historical instrument, the Degnan Chronicle was superior to any kept by the Reugge even now. For the Reugge Community, history was an oral tradition mainly of self-justification.

Broader historical studies proved no more informative. They raised more questions than they answered, as far as Marika could see. What were the origins of the meth? In olden times—as now among the nomads of the north—they were pack hunters. Physically, they resembled a carnivore called a kagbeast. But kagbeasts were not intelligent, nor did their females rule their packs. In fact, female meth did not rule the primitive packs of the southern hemisphere, where silth births were rare. There the males hunted on equal footing.

When Marika asked, Dorteka theorized, "Female rule developed because of the high incidence of silth births in northern litters. So I have heard.

"Primitive packs such as your own are structured around the strong. When the strong become weakened by time or disease, they are pushed aside. But a silth could stave off challengers even though she was weak physically, and once in command would tend to be partial to those who shared her talent. In primitive packs where breeding rights are reserved for the dominant females, silth dominance would mean especial favor to the spread of the silth strain."

Marika observed, "Then an old female like my instructress Gorry, at Akard, could stay in control till she died, yet could not lead or make rational decisions, really."

Dorteka snorted. "Which indicts the silth structure, yes. For all the most senior said about trust and whatnot in your interview—yes, I have heard all about that—we live under rule by terror, pup. The most capable do not run the Communities. The most terrible do. Thus you have a Bestrei among the Serke without a brain at all but in high station because she is invincible in darkwar. She is one of many who would not survive long if stripped of her talent."

After general history came another meal, followed by a long afternoon spent trying to harness and expand Marika's talents.

Dorteka went through everything with her, side by side. She graded herself, making herself the standard against which Marika should perform.

Marika almost enjoyed herself. For the first time since the fall of the Degnan packstead, she felt like her life was going somewhere.

The exercises, the entire program, were nothing like what she had had to suffer through with Gorry. There were no monsters, no terrors, no threats, no abuses. For silth class Marika seated herself upon a mat, closed her eyes, led herself into a trance where her mind floated free, unsupported by ghosts. Dorteka adamantly insisted she shun those-who-dwell.

"They are treacherous, Marika. Like chaphe is treacherous. You can turn to them too often, till you become dependent upon them and turn to them every time you are under pressure. They become an escape. Go inside and see how many other paths lie open."

Marika was amazed to discover that most silth could not reach or manipulate the deadly ghosts. That was a rare talent, dark-walking. The rarest and most dread talent of them all was being able to control the giants that moved the darkships—the very giants she had summoned at Akard for more lethal employment against nomads.

Her heart leapt when she learned that. She would fly!

Flight had become a goal bordering upon obsession.

"When can I begin learning the darkships, mistress?" she asked. "That is what interests me."

"Not soon. Only after you have a sound grounding in everything it takes to become true silth. The most senior would like you to become a flying sister, yes, but I feel she wants you to be much more. I suspect she plans a great future for you."

"Mistress?" At Akard there had been much talk of a great future, little of which anyone had been willing to explain.

"Never mind. Go through and see how far you can extend your touch."

"To whom, mistress?"

"No one. Just reach out. Do you need a target?"

"I always have."

"To be expected of the self-taught, I suppose." Dorteka never became exasperated, even when she had cause. "It is not necessary. Try it without."

Despite the grind, which left little time for sleep, Marika often visited her tower, sat staring at the stars, mourning the fate that had enlisted her in a sisterhood incapable of reaching them.

Dorteka's sessions could be as intense as Gorry's, if not as dangerous. Marika found herself grasping skills instinctively, progressing so rapidly she unsettled her instructress. Dorteka began to see what the most senior had intuited. That much talent in the paws of one raised to the primitive huntress world view, with its harsh and uncompromising values. . . . The possibilities were frightening.

Evenings after supper, Marika's education turned to the mundane, to the sciences as the Reugge knew them. Though they were laden with a mysticism that left Marika impatient, her progress was swift, and limited only by her ability to grasp and internalize the principles of ever more complex mathematics.

Word came down from the most senior: expand the time given math. Let the sisterhood trivia slide.

Dorteka was offended. The forms of silthdom were important to her. "We are our traditions," she was fond of saying.

"Why is the most senior doing this?" Marika asked. "I do not mind. I want to learn. But what is *her* hurry?"

"I am not sure. I am certain she would disapprove of my guessing. But I believe she may be thinking in terms of sculpting some sort of liberator for the Reugge. If the Serke keep pressing us and the winter keeps pushing south, we could be devoured within ten years. She does not want to be remembered as the last most senior of the Reugge Community. And she has begun to feel her mortality."

"She is not that old. I was surprised when first I saw her. I thought she would be ancient."

"No, she is not old. But always she hears the Serke baying behind her. However, that is not our worry. Mine is to teach. Yours is to learn. The whys are not relevant now. Time will unfold its leaves."

Marika continued to advance at a rate that shocked Dorteka. The teacher observed, "I begin to suspect that, despite themselves, our sisters at Akard taught you a great deal. At this rate you will, in every way, surpass your own age group before summer. In some ways you already exceed many sisters accounted full silth."

Much of what Marika encountered was new. She did not tell Dorteka that, afraid of frightening her teacher with the ease with which she learned.

After evening classes there was an events-of-the-day seminar conducted by the Maksche senior's second, a silth named Paustch. This took place in the hall where Marika had confronted Gradwohl, and Marika was required to attend. She kept the lowest profile possible. Her presence was tolerated only because Gradwohl insisted. No one asked her opinion. She offered none. She had no illusions about her presence there. She was the senior's marker, but she did not know in what game. She ducked out first when the seminar ended.

Thus she stayed close to the warming feud with the Serke,

with the latest on nomad predations, gained an idea of the shape of politics between sisterhoods, heard of all their squabbles, caught rumors about the explorations of distant starworlds. But mostly the Maksche leadership discussed the nomads and the ever more common problem of male sedition.

"I came into this in the middle," Marika told Dorteka. "I am not certain I understand why the problem is such a problem."

"These males are few and really only a minor irritant," Dorteka said. "Taken worldwide their efforts would not be noticeable. But they have concentrated their terrorism in Reugge territories, especially around Maksche. And a large portion of their attacks have been directed against guests of the Reugge—clearly an effort to make us appear weak and incapable of policing our fiefs. And the Serke, as you might expect, have been making the most of the situation. We have been subjected to a great deal of outside pressure. All part of the Serke maneuver against us, of course. But we cannot prove they are behind it."

"If the behavior of males here is unusual. . . . Are these rogues homegrown?" As an afterthought, she added the appropriate, "Mistress?"

Dorteka's ears tilted in mild amusement. "You strike to the heart of the matter. In fact, they are not. Our native males are perfectly behaved, though they often lend passive support by not reporting things they should. Sometimes they even grow so bold as to provide places of hiding. Certainly they sympathize with the rogues' stated goals."

Those goals were nothing less than the overthrow and destruction of all silthdom. A grand vision indeed, considering the iron grip the Communities had upon the world.

III

Marika's first attempt to visit Braydic did not go well at all. Called out of the communications center, the technician met her with evasive eyes and an obvious eagerness to be away. Marika was both amused and pained, for she recalled who it was who had held the door guards at bay in the heat of crisis.

"No one saw you, Braydic," she said. "You are safe. I doubt the guards themselves could identify you. They were on the edge of hysteria and probably recall you as being a demon nine feet tall and six wide."

Braydic shuddered and stared at the floor. Marika was disappointed, but knew what that momentary commitment had cost Braydic. She had risked everything.

"I owe you, Braydic. And I will not forget. Go, then, if you fear having me for a friend. But I promise my friendship will not falter for it."

Marika returned two weeks later. Braydic was no more sure of herself. Pained, Marika determined that she would not return again till she had attained some position of power, the shadow of which could fall upon Braydic.

She had begun to grow aware of the value and uses of power, and to think of it. Often.

That second visit, cut short, left her an hour free. She went to her away place in the tower.

Spring now threatened Maksche. The city lay under a haze from factories working overtime to fulfill production quotas before their workers had to report to the fields. Because of the shortening growing seasons, every worker now had to labor in the fields to get sufficient crops planted, tended, and harvested. Else the city would not make it through the winter.

This failing winter had been the worst in Maksche's history, though it was mild compared to those Marika had seen in the upper Ponath. But succeeding winters would be worse. The Maksche silth were now driving their tenants, their dependents, their meth property, so Maksche would be prepared for the worst when it came.

A darkship rose from the square below. The blade of the dagger turned till it pointed northward. Once it was above Maksche's highest structures, it fled into the distance.

From the date of the most senior's arrival, darkships had

been airborne every day the weather permitted, hunting nomads, tracking nomads, scouting out their strong points and places of meeting, gathering information for a summer campaign. The Reugge could not challenge the Serke directly. They had neither the strength nor proof other Communities would consider adequate. So the most senior meant to defeat their efforts by obliterating their minions.

She was tough and bloodyminded, this Gradwohl. She meant to fertilize the entire northern half of the Reugge province with nomad corpses. And if she could manage it, she would add several hundred troublesome rogue males to the slaughter.

The cloister was ahum with an anticipation Marika hardly noticed. She did not expect to become involved in Gradwohl's campaign.

How long before Dorteka allowed her to explore Maksche? She was eager to be away from the cloister, to break for a few hours from this relentless business of becoming silth.

Maksche was odd, a city of marked contrasts. Here sat the cloister, all but its ceremonial heart electrically lighted and heated. One could get water simply by lifting a lever. Wastes were carried away in a system of sewage pipes. But outside the cloister's walls few lights existed, and those only candles or tallow lamps. Meth out there drew their water from wells or the river. Their sewers consisted of channels in the alleyways, washed clean when it rained.

It had not rained all winter.

Meth out there walked, unless they were the rare, rich, favored few who could rent dray beasts, a driver, and a carriage from the tradermales of the Brown Paw Bond. Silth sisters going abroad in the town usually rode in elegant steam coaches faster than any carriage. If Dorteka allowed her out, would she be permitted the use of such a vehicle? Not likely. They were guarded jealously, for they were very expensive. They were handcrafted by one of the tradermale underbrotherhoods not part of the local Brown Paw Bond, and imported. They were not silth property.

The traders sold no vehicle outright, but leased them

instead. Lease contracts demanded huge penalty payments for damages done. Marika suspected that was motivated by a desire to keep lessees from dismantling the machines to see how they worked.

A tradermale operator came with every vehicle. Outsiders were not allowed to learn how to drive. Those males obligated to the vehicles of the cloister lived in a small barracks across the street from the cloister's main gate, whence they could be summoned on a moment's notice.

When her hour was up, Marika went to Dorteka and asked, "How many more points do I have to accumulate before I can go into the city?"

"It is not a point system, Marika. You can go whenever I decide you deserve the reward."

"Well? Do I?" She had held back nothing. Having been used as a counter in a contest she did not understand, for reasons she could not comprehend, she had gone all out to arm herself for her own survival. Dorteka could not have demanded more. There was no more she could give.

"Perhaps. Perhaps. But why go out into that fester at all?"

"To explore it. To see what is out there. To get out of this oppressive prison for a while."

"Oppressive? Prison? The cloister?"

"It is unbearable. But you grew up here. Maybe you cannot imagine freedom of movement."

"No. I cannot. At least not out there. My duties have taken me into the city, Marika. It is disgusting. I would rather not traipse around after you while you crawl through the muck."

"Why should you, mistress?"

"What?"

"There is no reason for you to go."

"If you go, I have to go."

"Why, mistress?"

"To keep you out of trouble."

"I can take care of myself, mistress."

"Maksche is not the Ponath, pup."

"I doubt that the city has dangers to compare with the nomad."

"It is not danger to your flesh I fear, Marika. It is your mind that concerns me."

"Mistress?"

"You do not fool me. You are not yet silth. And you are no harmless, eager student. A shadow lives behind your eyes."

Marika did not respond till she carefully stifled her anger. "I do not understand you, mistress. Others have said the same of me. Some have called me doomstalker. Yet I do not feel unusual. How could the city harm my mind? By exposing me to dangerous ideas? I have enough of those myself. I will create my own beliefs here or there, regardless of what you would have me believe. Or could it harm me by showing me how cruelly Reugge bonds live so we silth can be comfortable here? That much I have seen from the wall."

Dorteka did not reply. She, too, was fighting anger.

"If I must have company and protection, send my packmates, Grauel and Barlog. I am certain they would be happy to accept your instructions." Her sarcasm was lost on Dorteka.

She and Grauel and Barlog had been at odds almost since the confrontation with the most senior. The two huntresses had been making every effort to appear to be perfect subjects of the Community. Marika did not want them to surrender quite so fast.

"I will consider that. If you insist on going out there."

"I want to, mistress."

The great ground-level gate rolled back. Grauel and Barlog stepped out warily. Marika followed, surprised at their reluctance. Behind her, Dorteka said, "Be back before dark, Marika. Or no more passes."

"Yes, mistress. Come on!" She ran, exulting in her freedom. Grauel and Barlog struggled to keep pace. "Isn't it wonderful?"

"It stinks," Grauel said. "They live in their own ordure, Marika."

And Barlog; "Where are you going?" Already it was evident that Marika had a definite destination in mind.

"To the tradermale enclosure. To see their flying machines."

"I might have guessed," Barlog grumbled. "Slow down. We're not as young as you are. Marika, all this obsession with flying is not healthy. Meth were not meant for it. Marika! Will you slow down?"

Marika glanced back. The two huntresses were struggling with the cumbersome long rifles they carried. "Why did you bring those?" She knew Grauel preferred the weapon she had gotten from Bagnel.

"Orders, Marika. Pure and simple and malicious orders. There are some silth who hope you'll get killed out here. The only reason you get a pretense of a bodyguard is because you have the most senior's favor."

"Pretense?"

"Any other silth would have at least six guards. If she was insane enough to come out on foot. And they would not be so shoddily armed. They would not have let *us* come except that we are two they won't miss if something happens."

"That's silly. Nobody has been attacked since we've been here. I think all that is just scare talk. Good old grauken in the bushes."

"No one has been foolish enough to walk these streets either, Marika."

Marika did not want to argue. She wanted to see airships. She pressed ahead. The tradermales built machines that flew. She had seen them in her education tapes and from her tower in the nether distance, but it was hard to connect vision screen images and remote specks with anything real. The airfield lay too far from the cloister for examination from her tower.

An aircraft was circling as Marika approached the fence surrounding the tradermale enclave. It swooped, touched down, rolled along a long concrete strip, and came to a halt with one final metallic belch. Marika checked Grauel and Barlog for their reactions. They had seen nothing like it before. Servants of the silth saw very little of the world, and tradermale aircraft were not permitted to fly near the cloister.

They might have been watching carrion birds land upon a corpse.

"Let's get closer," Marika said. She trotted along the fence, toward a group of buildings. Grauel and Barlog hurried after her, glancing over their shoulders at the aircraft and at two big transport dirigibles resting in cradles on the far side of the concrete strip.

The advantage of being silth, Marika believed, was that you could do any All-bedamned thing you wanted. Ordinary meth would grind their teeth and endure. She breezed into an open doorway, past a desk where a sleepy tradermale watched a vision screen, dashed down a long hallway and out onto the field proper, ignoring the startled shout that pursued her. She headed for the freighters.

The nearest was a monster. The closer she ran, the more she was awed.

"Oh," Grauel said at last, and slowed. Marika stopped to wait. Grauel breathed, "All bless us. It is as big as a mountain."

"Yes." Marika started to explain how an airship worked, saw that she had lost both huntresses, said instead, "It could haul the whole Degnan pack. Packstead and all. And have room left over."

Tradermale technicians were at work around the airship's gondola. One spotted them. He yelled at the others. A few just stared. Most scattered. Marika thought that was amusing.

The fat flank of the ship loomed higher and higher. She leaned back, now as awed as Grauel and Barlog. She beckoned a male either too brave or too petrified to have fled. He approached tentatively. "What ship is this, tradermale?"

He seemed puzzled by that latter, dialect word, but got the sense of the question. "*Dawnstrider*."

"Oh. I do not know that one. It is so big, I thought it must be *Starpetal*."

"No. *Starpetal* is much larger. Way too big for our

cradles here. Usually only the smaller ships come up to the borderlands."

"Borderlands?" Marika asked, bemused by the size of the ship.

"Well, Maksche is practically the end of the world. Last outpost of civilization. Ten miles out there it turns into Tech Three Zone and just gets worse the farther you go." He tilted his ears and exposed his teeth in a way that said he was making a joke.

"I thought I hailed from the last outpost," Marika countered in a bantering tone. "North edge of the Tech Two." If she could overcome his awe, he might have something interesting to say. She did realize that most meth considered Maksche the end of the world. It was the northernmost city of consequence in the Hainlin basin, the limit of barge traffic and very border of Tech Four–permitted machine technology. It had grown up principally to service and support trade up the Hainlin, into the primitive interior of the vast and remote northern Reugge provinces. "Well, savagery is relative. Right? *We* are civilized. *They* are savages. Come, Barlog. Grauel."

"Where are you going?" the tradermale squeaked. "Hey! You cannot go in there."

"I just want to look at the control cabin," Marika said. "I will not touch anything. I promise."

"But . . . wait. . . ."

Marika climbed the ladder leading to the airship's gondola. After a moment of silent debate, Grauel and Barlog followed, shaking visibly, driven onward only by their pride. A Degnan huntress knew no fear.

Dawnstrider was a freighter. Its appointments were minimal, designed to keep down mass so payload could be maximized. Even so, the control cabin was bewildering with its array of meters and dials, levers, valves, switches, and push-buttons. "Do not touch anything," Marika warned Grauel and Barlog for the benefit of the technician, who refused to leave them unsupervised. "We do not want this beast to carry us away."

The huntresses clutched their weapons and stared around.

Marika was puzzled. They were not ignorant Ponath dwellers anymore. They had been exposed to the greater meth universe. They should have developed some flexibility.

She did not remain impressed long. *Dawnstrider* was a disappointment, though she could not pin down why. "I have seen enough. Let us go look at the little ships."

She went down the ladder behind the technician, amused by the emotion betrayed in his every movement. She was getting good at reading body language.

She did not sense the wrongness till she had moved several steps from the base of the ladder. Then it was too late.

Tradermales rushed from beneath the airship, all of them armed. Grauel and Barlog snapped their weapons to the ready, shielded Marika with their bodies.

"What is this?" Marika snapped.

"You do not belong here, silth," a male said. "You are trespassing on brethren land."

Marika's nerve wavered. Yet she stared the male in the eye with the arrogance of a senior and said, "I go where I please, male. And you mind your manners when you speak—"

"You are out of line, pup. No one comes into a brethren enclave without permission of the factors."

He had the right of it. She had not thought. There were compacts between the Reugge and the tradermales. She had overlooked them in her enthusiasm.

A stubborn something within her refused to back down, insisted that she up the risk. "You better have these males put their weapons aside. I do not wish to harm anyone."

"I have twenty rifles, pup. I count two on your side."

"You are speaking to a darkwalker. I can destroy the lot of you before one trigger can be pulled. You think about dying with your heart ripped out, male."

His lips peeled back in a snarl. He was ready to call her bluff. The set of Grauel's shoulders said that the huntress thought her mad to provoke the male so, that she would get them all killed for nothing.

Fleetingly, Marika wondered why she did provoke almost everyone who ever challenged her.

"We shall see." The tradermale gestured.

Marika felt an odd tingling, like that she experienced around high-energy communications gear. Something electromagnetic was being directed at her. She spotted a tradermale in the background aiming a boxlike device her way.

She dived down inside herself, through her loophole, snagged a ghost, and slammed it into the guts of the box. She twisted that ghost and compressed it into an ever more rapidly spinning ball, all within an instant. She watched it shred wires and glass.

She came back in time to watch the box fly apart, to hear the technician's startled yelp. He raised a bleeding paw to his mouth.

Fingers strained at triggers. The leading tradermale betrayed extreme distress. "You see?" Marika demanded.

"Hold it! Hold it there!" someone shouted from the distance. Everyone turned.

More males were running along the airstrip. In a moment Marika realized why one seemed familiar. "Bagnel," she said softly. Her spirits rose. Maybe she would escape the consequences of her own stupidity after all.

The instant she began to see hope, she started worrying about the consequences that would follow the report that would reach the cloister. There would be a complaint, surely. Tradermales were said to be militant about their rights. They had struggled for ages to obtain them. Their organization was by-the-rules where those were concerned.

Marika was mildly amazed to discover she was more afraid of Dorteka than she was of this potentially lethal confrontation.

A few tradermale weapons sagged as they awaited those approaching. Tension drooped with them. Grauel and Barlog relaxed, though they did not lower their weapons.

Bagnel rushed up, puffing. "Timbruk, what have you got here?" He peered at Marika. "Ha! Well! And I actually thought of you when they told me. Marika. Hello." He interposed himself between Marika and the male he had called Timbruk. "Can we have a little relaxation here, meth? Everybody. Put the weapons down. There is no call to get anyone hurt."

Trimbruk protested, "Bagnel, they have trespassed. . . ."

"Obviously. But no harm done, was there?"

"Harm is not the point."

"Yes. Yes. Well, Trimbruk, if they need shooting we can do that later. Put the weapons down. Let me talk. I know this sister. She saved my life in the Ponath."

"Saved your life? Come on. She is just a pup. She is the one who . . . ?"

"Yes. She is that one."

Trimbruk swallowed. His eyes widened. He looked spooked. He stared at Marika till she became uncomfortable. Twice his gaze seemed pulled toward a group of buildings at the north end of the field. Each time he jerked it back to her with sudden ferocity. Then he said, "Relax, brothers. Relax. Weapons on safety."

Marika said, "Grauel, Barlog, stand easy. Put your weapons on safe."

Grauel did not want to do it. Her every muscle was tense with a rigidly controlled fight-flight response. But she did as she was told, though her eyes continued to smolder.

Barlog merely heaved a sigh of relief.

Bagnel did likewise. "Good. Now, shall we talk? Marika, what in the name of the All did you think you were doing, coming in here like that? You cannot just walk in like you own the place. This is convention ground. Have they not taught you anything over there?

"I know. It was stupid." She stepped closer, spoke more softly. "I was just wandering around, exploring. When I saw the airships I got so excited I lost my head. I forgot everything else. I just had to look. Then these males . . ." She broke off, realizing she was about to make accusations that would be unreasonable and provocative.

Bagnel was amused. But he said, "Did you have to be so . . . I see. They have taught you—taught you to be silth. I mean, the way silth here understand being silth. Cold.

Arrogant. Insensitive. Never mind. As they say, silth will be silth. Timbruk. It is over. There is no need for you here now. This is to be forgotten. No record. No formal protest. Understand?"

"Bagnel . . ."

Bagnel ignored him. "I owe you a life, Marika. But for you I would have become meat in a nomad's belly more than once. I repay a fraction of the debt here. I forgive the trespass." In soft humor, he added, "I am sure your seniors would have a good deal to say to you if they heard about this."

"I am sure they would. Thank you."

Timbruk and his males were stalking away, some occasionally glancing back. Except for the male who had tried to use the box. Despite his wound, he was crouched over the remains, prodding them with a finger, shaking his head. He seemed both baffled and disturbed.

"Come," Bagnel said. He started toward the buildings through which Marika had made her dash.

She asked, "What are you doing here?"

"I am assigned here now. As assistant security chief for the enclave. Since I did such a wonderful job as security officer at Critza, they awarded me a much more important post." His sarcasm was thick enough to cut. Marika could not determine its thrust, though. Was he his own target? Or were the seniors who had given him the job?

"That was what you were doing up there? I always had a feeling you were not a regular wander-the-forests-with-a-pack-on-your-back kind of tradermale."

"My job was to protect the fortress and manage any armed operations undertaken in the region of its license."

"Then you were in charge of that hunting party you were with the first time we met."

"I was."

"I thought old Khronen was in charge."

"I know. We allowed you think so. He was just our guide, though. He had been in the upper Ponath all his life. I think he knew every rock and bush by name."

"He was a friend of my dam. At least as near a friend as she ever had among males."

Bagnel, daring beyond belief, reached out and touched her lightly. "The memories do haunt, do they not not? We all lost so much. And those who were never there just shrug it off."

Marika stiffened her back. "Can we look at the small aircraft on the way to the gate?"

Bagnel rewarded her with a questioning look.

"The crime is committed," she replied. "Can I compound it?"

"Of course." He altered course toward a rank of five propeller-driven aircraft.

"Stings," Marika said as they approached. "Driven by a single bank nine-cylinder air-cooled radial engine that develops eighteen hundred meth power. Top speed two hundred ten. Normal cruising speed one sixty. Not fast, but capable of carrying a very large payload. A fighting aircraft. Who do tradermales fight, Bagnel?"

"You amaze me. How did you find out? We fight anyone who attacks us. There are a lot of wild places left in the world. Even here in the higher Tech Zones. There is always a demand for the application of force."

"Are these ones here for the push against the nomads?"

"No. We may reoccupy our outposts if the Reugge manage to push the nomads out, but we will not help push."

"Why not? The Brown Paw Bond suffered more than we did, if you do not count the packs. Posts all along the Hainlin . . .

"Orders, Marika. I do not pretend to understand. Politics, I guess. Little one, you picked the wrong sisterhood at the wrong time. Strong forces are ranged against the Reugge."

"The Serke?"

"Among others. They are the most obvious, but they do not stand alone. That is off the record, though. You did not hear it from me."

"You did not tell me anything I did not know. I do wonder why, though. No one has bothered the Reugge since they split from the Serke. Why start now?"

"The Reugge are not strong, Marika, but they are rich. The Hainlin basin produces a disproportionate amount of wealth. Emeralds out of the Zhotak—those alone might be reason enough. We Brown Paw Bond traders have done very well trading junk for emeralds."

Marika harkened to younger days, when tradermales had come into the upper Ponath afoot or leading a single rheum-greater, exchanging a few iron tools, books, beads, flashy pieces of cloth, and such, for the clear green stones or otec furs. Every year Dam's friend Khronen had come to the Degnan packstead, bringing precious tools and his easy manner with pups, and had walked away with a fortune.

The Degnan had been satisfied with the trades. Emeralds were of little value on a frontier. Otec fur was of more use, being the best there was, but what it would bring in trade outweighed its margin of value over lesser furs.

Junk, Bagnel called the trade goods. And he was right from his perspective. Arrowheads, axe heads, hoes, hammers, rakes, all could be manufactured in bulk at little cost in Maksche's factories. One emerald would purchase several wagonloads here. And books, for which a pack might save for seasons, were produced in mass in the city's printshops.

"Is that why the Ponath is kept savage?"

Meth, with the exceptions of tradermales and silth, seldom moved far from their places of birth. Information did not travel well in the mouths of those with an interest in keeping it close. How angry Skiljan would have been had she known the treasures she acquired for the pack cost the traders next to nothing. She would have believed it robbery. Just another example of innate male perfidy.

"Partly. Partly because the silth are afraid of an informed populace, of free movement of technology. Your Communities could not survive in a world where wealth, information, and technology traveled freely. We brethren would have our troubles. We are few and the silth are fewer still. Between us we run everything because for ages we have shaped the law and tradition to that end."

They walked around the fighting aircraft. Marika found its presence disturbing. For that matter, the presence of

Dawnstrider was unsettling. Trade in and out of Maksche did not require a vessel so huge. There was more here than met the eye. Maybe that explained Timbruk's hostility.

"The Sting's main disadvantage is its limited range when fully fight-loaded," Marika said, continuing with the data she had given earlier.

"You are right. But where did you learn all that, Marika? I would bet only those of us who actually fly the beasts know all you have told me."

"I learned in tapestudy. I am going to be a darkship flyer. So I have been learning everything about flying. I know everything about airships, too."

"I doubt that." Bagnel glanced back at *Dawnstrider*.

"But those craft . . ." Marika indicated several low, long, ovoid shapes in the shadow of a building on the side away from the city. "I do not recognize those."

"Ground-effect vehicles. Not strictly legal in a Tech Four Zone, but all right as long as we keep them inside convention ground. You came close to catching us using them that time you first met me."

"The noise and the smell. And Arhdwehr getting so angry. Engines and exhaust. Of course."

"Every brethren station has a few for emergency use. Mainly for hurried getaways. You remember the odd tracks going away from Critza? Where I said some of our brethren got out? Ground-effect vehicles made those. They leave a pretty obvious trail in the snow." He went on to explain how the machines worked. Marika had no trouble grasping the concept.

"There is much I do not yet know, then," she said.

"No doubt. There is much we all do not know. Let me give you some advice. Try to consider the broader picture before you let impulse carry you away again."

"What?"

"There is a great deal of tension between the Brown Paw Bond and the Reugge right now. Our factors not only refused to help reclaim the provinces overrun by the nomad, they would not lease the fighting aircraft the Reugge wanted. I do not pretend to understand why. It was a chance for us to sweep up a huge profit."

"I see." Marika considered the fighting aircraft once more. It was a two-seat, open cockpit biplane with two guns that fired through the airscrew, four wing-mounted guns, and a single gimbal-mounted weapon which could be fired rearward by the occupant of the second seat. "I would love to fly one of those," she said. The tapes mentioned capabilities that could be matched by no darkship.

"It is an experience," Bagnel agreed.

"You fly?"

"Yes. If there was trouble and the aircraft had to be employed, I would be a backup flyer."

"Take me up."

"Marika!" Grauel snapped.

Bagnel was amused. "There is no limit to her audacity, is there?"

"Marika," Grauel repeated, "you exceed yourself. You may be silth, but even so we will drag you back to the cloister."

"Not today, Marika," Bagnel said. "I cannot. Maybe some other time. Come back later. Be polite at the gate, ask for me, and maybe you will be permitted entrance—without all this fuss. Right now I think you had better leave before Timbruk goes over my head and gets permission to shoot you anyhow." Bagnel strode toward the gateway buildings. Marika followed. She was nervous now. There would be trouble when she got home.

Bagnel said, "I do not think your sisters would be upset if Timbruk did you in either. You still have that smoky look. Of the fated outsider."

"I have problems with the silth," Marika admitted. "But the most senior has given me her protection."

"Oh? Lucky for you."

They parted at the gate, Bagnel with a well-wish and repeated invitation to return under more auspicious circumstances.

Outside, Marika paused to scan the field, watched Bagnel stride purposefully toward distant buildings. Her gaze drifted to those structures in the north. Cold crept down her spine. She shivered.

"Come. We are returning to the cloister right now," Grauel said. Her tone brooked no argument. Marika did not protest, though she did not want to go back. She did have to cling to the goodwill of Grauel and Barlog. They were her only trustworthy allies.

Chapter Seventeen

I

Marika went from the gate to her tower, where she sat staring toward the tradermale compound. Several dots soared above the enclave, roaming the sky nearby.

Grauel came to her there. She looked grim. "Trouble," she said.

"They have registered their protest already? That was fast."

"Not that kind of trouble. Home trouble. Somebody got into our quarters."

"Oh?"

"After we turned in the weapons they gave us, we went up to clean up. My rifle was gone."

"Anything else?"

"No. The Degnan Chronicle had been opened and moved slightly. That is all."

"The most senior should spend more time here instead of talking about spending more time here."

Marika had noted that in Gradwohl's absence she was treated far more coolly. She wished that most senior would move into Maksche in fact as well as name. Despite declarations of intent, she just visited occasionally, usually without warning.

"I will not tolerate invasions of my private space, Grauel. No one else in the entire Community has to suffer such intrusions. Back off and give me a few minutes of quiet."

She slipped down through her loophole and cast about till she found a ghost she thought sufficiently strong. She took control and began roaming the cloister, beginning in places she thought were most likely to reveal the missing weapon.

Finding it took only minutes. It was in the cloister arsenal, where some sisters argued it belonged anyway. A pair of silth were dismantling it.

Marika returned to flesh. "Come."

"You found it? That quickly?"

"It is not hidden, actually. It is in the arsenal. We will take it back."

"And I was right there a few minutes ago."

The arsenal door was closed and locked now. Marika had no patience. Rather than scratch, wait, ask permission to enter, and argue, she recalled her ghost and squeezed it down as she had done when she had destroyed the electronic box belonging to the tradermale. She shoved the ghost into the lock and destroyed the metal there.

That made enough noise to alert the silth inside. They peered at her with fear and guilt when she stalked into the room where the parts of Grauel's weapon were scattered upon a table. One started to say something. Marika brushed her soul lightly with the ghost. "Grauel. Put it back together. You. Where is the ammunition? I want it here. Now."

The sister to whom she spoke thought of arguing, eyed Marika's bare teeth, thought better of it. She collected the ammunition from a storage box. After placing it upon the table, she retreated as far as the walls would allow. She choked out, "The orders came from Paustch. You will be in grave—"

"Ask me how much I care," Marika snapped. "This is for you to remember. And perhaps even share. The next meth who enters my quarters without my invitation will discover just how vicious a savage I really am. We invented some truly fascinating tortures to get nomads to tell us things we wanted to know."

Grauel cursed under her breath.

"Is it all there?"

"Yes. But they have mixed things up. It will take me a few minutes."

Marika used the time to glare at the two sisters till they cringed.

She heard Grauel slam the magazine home and feed a round to the chamber. "Ready?"

"Ready," Grauel said, sweeping the weapon's aim across the silth. Her lips pulled back in a snarl that set them on the edge of panic. "I do suppose I should thank them for cleaning it. They did that much good."

"Thank them, then. And let us be gone."

Gradwohl might not have been present in Maksche, but her paw was firmly felt. Darkships began arriving, bearing Reugge whose accents seemed exotic. They paused only to rest and eat and further burden their flying crosses. Some of the darkships lifted so burdened with meth and gear they looked like something from the worst quarters of the city.

"Everyone that can be spared," Barlog said as she and Marika and Grauel watched one darkship lift and another slide in under it. "That is the word now. The cloister is to be stripped. They have begun soliciting workers from the city, offering special pay. I would say the most senior is serious."

There had been some silth, at the evening meetings Marika attended, who had thought Gradwohl's plans just talk meant to form the basis for rumors that would reach the Serke. Rumors that would make that Community chary of too bold interference. But the lie had been given that view. The stream of darkships was never ending. The might of the Reugge was on the move, and impressive might it was.

Mistresses of the Ship could be seen in the meal halls almost all the time. Bath—the sisters who helped fly the darkships from their secondary positions at the tips of the shorter arms—sometimes crowded Maksche silth out of the meal lines. Scores seemed to be around all the time. Marika spent all her free time trying to get acquainted with those bath and Mistresses. But they would have little to do with her. They were an order within the order, silent, separate beings with little interest in socializing and none in illuminating a pup.

Three small dirigibles, contracted to the Reugge before the Brown Paw Bond elected not to support the offensive, appeared over the cloister and took aboard workers and silth and construction equipment. The cloister began to have a hollow feel, a deserted air. A shout would echo down long, empty halls. No one was there to answer.

The dirigibles would all make for Akard, which the most senior wanted rebuilt and reoccupied. It would become the focal point of a network of satellite fastnesses meant to interdict any nomad movements southward.

"I do not think she realizes how many nomads there are," Marika told Grauel. "Or really how vast her northern provinces are. All that might is not a tenth enough."

"She knows. I believe she is counting on the nomads having spent the best they had in the past few years. I think she expects it to be a job of tracking down remnants of the real fighting bands, then letting next winter finish the rest."

"I think she would be wrong if that is the basis of her strategy."

"So do I."

"We shall see, of course. Let us hope the answer is not savages in the cloister."

The early reports from the north told of a big harvest of nomads, of kills far more numerous than anyone expected. The numbers caused a good deal of uneasiness. They implied other numbers that might prove troublesome. For everyone agreed that there would be a dozen live and concealed nomads for every one dead.

II

The dream was a nightmare Marika had not known for several years, but it was old and familiar.

She was trapped in a cold, dark, damp place, badly hurt, unable to call for help, unable to climb out.

The dream had tormented her every night since her return from the tradermale enclave. She had told no one, but Grauel and Barlog sensed that something was torturing her.

Marika wished she could go visit Braydic. The last time the dreams had come, soon after her arrival at Akard, following the destruction of the Degnan packstead, she had shared her pain with the communications technician. Braydic had been unable to interpret the dream. Eventually, she had agreed it must be Marika's conscience nagging her because the dead of the Degnan pack had not gone into the embrace of the All with a proper Mourning.

After the return of the dreams, she had asked Grauel and Barlog where they stood in regard to that unsettled debt.

"We can do nothing now," Barlog told her. "Someday, though, we will take care of it. Perhaps when you are important and powerful. The score is not forgotten, nor considered settled."

That was good enough for Marika. But meantime she had to endure the horror of her nights.

Dorteka wakened her from this dream. She was early, but Marika was too fuddled to realize that till after they had been into their gymnasium routine for some time. "Why are we up so early?" she asked.

"We have new orders, you and I. We are headed north."

"Up the river? To chase nomads?" Marika was astonished. It was the last thing she expected.

"Yes. The great hunt is in full cry. The most senior is sending everyone who has no absolute need to remain. She sent a note saying that means us especially."

Just last evening word had come round that the most

senior had ordered all patrolling darkships to destroy any
meth they found upon the ground. They were to operate on
the assumption that no locals had survived. No mercy was to
be shown.

"What is it all about, mistress?" Marika asked. "Why is
Gradwohl so determined? I have heard that winter may not
break this year, at least in the upper Ponath. That the
ground will remain frozen. No crops could be planted there.
So why fight for useless territory?"

"Someone exaggerated, Marika. There will be a summer.
Not that it matters. We are not going to send settlers into
the Ponath. We are simply validating our claim to our
provinces. In blood. Gradwohl is leading us in a fight against
the Serke, and this is the only way we can battle them.
Indirectly."

"Why are the Serke so determined, then? I am told
wealth is the reason. I know about the emeralds, and there is
gold and silver and copper and things, but nobody ever did
any mining up there. It is a Tech Two Zone. There must be
some other reason the Serke risk conflict."

"Probably. We do not know what it is, though. We just
know we cannot allow them to steal the Ponath. Them or the
brethren."

"You think the reason the tradermales will not help us is
because they want to steal the Ponath, too?"

"I expect the Brown Paw Bond would stand with us if
they could. We have been close associates for centuries. But
higher authority may have been offered a better cut by the
Serke."

"Could we not impose sanctions?"

Dorteka appeared amused by her naiveté. "Without
proof? Wait. Yes. You know, and I know, and everyone else
alive knows what is happening. Or we think we do. We
suspect that the brethren and the Serke Community have
entered into a conspiracy prohibited by the conventions. But
no Community extant will act on suspicion. The Serke have
Bestrei, and flaunt it. As long as the Reugge cannot present
absolute and irrefutable proof of what is happening, no
other Community faces the disagreeable business of having

to take sides. They would rather sit back and be entertained by our travails."

"But if the Serke get away with this, they will be a threat to everyone else. Do the other orders not see that? Armed with all our wealth, and Bestrei besides . . ."

"Who knows what is really going on? Not you or I. The other sisterhoods may be in it with the Serke. There are ample precedents."

"It all seems silly to me," Marika said. "Will Grauel and Barlog be able to go with me?"

"I am sure they will. You are a single unit in most eyes."

Marika glanced at her instructress, not liking her tone. She and Dorteka tolerated one another because the most senior insisted, but there was no love between them.

Marika, Grauel, Barlog, and Dorteka, with their gear, boarded a northbound darkship about the time Marika should have begun her mathematics class. The bath, before going to their places at the tips of the short arms, made certain the passengers strapped themselves to the darkship's frame. All gear went into bins fixed around the cross's axis.

Marika paid much more attention to the darkship and its operators this trip. "Mistress Dorteka. What is this metal? I have seen nothing like it before." It seemed almost invisible when probed with the touch.

"Titanium. It is the lightest metal known, yet very strong. It is difficult to obtain. The brethren recover it in a process similar to that they use to obtain aluminum. They fairly rob us for these ships."

"They make them?"

"Yes."

"I would think it something we would do for ourselves. Why do we let them rob us?"

"I am not sure. Maybe because to argue is too much trouble. We do buy them, I think, because their ships are better. We have been buying them for only about sixty years, though. Before that most of the orders made their own. There was a lot of artistry involved. Most of those old darkships are still in service down south, too, around TelleRai and the other big cities."

"What were they like? How were they different? And what do you mean, buy? I thought the tradermales only leased."

"Questions, questions, questions. Pup.... They do not lease darkships. We would not let them get away with that. In some ways they have us too much in their power now.

"The old ships are not much different from those you have seen. Maybe smaller, generally. They were wooden, though. A few were pretty fanciful because they were seen as works of art. They were pawcrafted from golden fleet timber, a wood that is sensitive to the touch. The trees had to be at least five hundred years old before they could be cut. They were considered very precious. The groves are protected by a web of laws even now. So-called poachers can be slain for even touching a golden fleet tree.

"Every frame member and strut in the old ships was individually carved from a specially selected timber or billet. The way I hear, a shipbuilder sister might spend a year preparing one strut. It might take a building team twenty years to complete a ship. No two darkships were ever alike, unlike these brethren products. These things are plain and all business."

All business maybe, but hardly plain. This one was covered with seals and fanciful witch signs that, Marika suspected, had something to do with the Mistress and her bath.

"You say those old ones are still around?"

"Most of them. I have seen some in TelleRai that are said to be thousands of years old. Silth have been flying since the beginning of time. The Redoriad museum at TelleRai has several prehistoric saddleships that are still taken up once in a while."

"Saddleships?" Here was something she had missed in her search for information on flying.

"In olden times that sort of silth who today would become a Mistress of the Ship usually flew alone. Her ship was a pole of golden fleet wood about eighteen feet long with a saddle mounted two-thirds of the way back. You would find the Redoriad museum interesting, what with your interest in flight. They have something of everything there."

"I sure would. I will find out about it if I ever get to TelleRai."

"You will get there soon enough if Gradwohl has her way."

"Then I suppose the reason for buying metal ships is because that is easier than making them."

"No doubt."

"Are there any artisans left? Sisters who could build darkships if necessary?"

"I am sure there are. Silth are conservative. Old things take a thousand years to die. And about darkships there are many still devoted to the old. Many who prefer the wooden ships because the golden fleet wood is more responsive than cold metal. Also, many who feel we should not be dependent upon the brethren for our ships.

"The brethren keep taking over chunks of our lives. There was a time when touch-sisters did everything comm techs do now. Their greatest bragged that they could touch anyone anywhere in the world. That far reach is almost a lost art now."

"That is sad."

The darkship was fifty miles north of the city already. Ahead, Marika could just distinguish the fire-blackened remains of a tradermale outpost. Kharg Station. It marked the southernmost flow of nomad raiding for the winter. Its fall had been the final insult that had driven Gradwohl into the rage whence this campaign had sprung. Its fall had come close to costing Senior Zertan her position, for she had made no effort to relieve the besieged outpost.

"I think so, too. We live in the moment, we silth, but many long for the past. For quieter times when we were not so much dependent upon the brethren." Dorteka eyed the ruins. "Zertan is one of those. Paustch is another."

The darkship moved north at a moderate pace. After marveling at the view of the plain and the brown, meandering Hainlin, Marika slid down inside herself. For a time she studied the subtle interplay of talent between the bath and the Mistress of the Ship. These were veterans. They drew upon one another skillfully. Fatigue would be a long time coming.

Once she thought she understood what they were doing, Marika began cataloging all she knew about her own and others' talents. She found what she was seeking. She returned to the world.

"Dorteka, could we not make our own metal darkships? Assuming we want to produce the ships quickly? We have sisters who could extract the metal from ore with their talents. It could not be difficult to build a ship if the metal was available."

"Silth do not do that kind of work."

Marika ran that through her mind, looking at it from every angle but the logical. She already knew the argument made no logical sense. She must have missed something because she still did not understand after trying to see it as silth. "Mistress, I do not understand."

Dorteka had forgotten already. "What?"

"*Why* should we not build a metal darkship if it is within our capacity? When it is all right for us to build a wooden one? Especially if the tradermales are working against us." There was some circumstantial evidence that a tradermale faction was supporting the ever more organized efforts of the rogue males plaguing the Reugge.

Dorteka could not explain in any way that made sense to Marika. She became confused and frustrated by her effort. She finally snapped, "Because that is the way it is. Silth do not do physical labor. They rule. They are artists. The wooden darkships were works of art. Metal ships are machines, even if they perform the same tasks. Anyway, we have tacitly granted that they fall inside the prerogatives of the brethren."

"We could have our own factory inside the cloister...." Marika gave it up. Dorteka was not interested in a pup's foolish notions. Marika invested in a series of mental relaxation exercises so she could clear her thoughts to enjoy the flight.

The darkship did not pursue a direct course toward Akard. It roamed erratically, randomly, at times drifting far from the river, on the off chance contact would be made with nomads. The day was far advanced when Marika began to see landmarks she recognized. "There, Grauel. What is left of Critza."

"The tradermales will not be restoring that. That explosion certainly took it apart."

Bagnel had set off demolition charges in what the nomads had left of the packfast, to deny it value to any nomads who thought to use it later.

"Now. There it is. Straight ahead," Barlog said as the darkship slipped around a bend in the river canyon.

Akard. Where Marika had spent four miserable years, and had discovered that she was that most dreaded of silth, a strong darkwalker.

The remains of the fortress were perched on a headland where the Hainlin split into the Husgen and an eastern watercourse which retained the Hainlin name. It was webbed in by scaffolding. Workers swarmed over it like colony insects. The darkship settled toward the headland.

It was a scant hundred feet off the ground when Marika felt a sudden, strong touch.

Hang on. We have a call for help.

That was the Mistress of the Ship with a warning so powerful even Grauel and Barlog caught its edges.

Marika barely had time to warn them verbally. The darkship shot forward, rose, gained speed rapidly. The robes of the Mistress and bath crackled in the rushing wind. Marika ducked down through to examine the altered relationship between the Mistress and bath. The Mistress was drawing heavily on the bath now.

The darkship climbed to three hundred feet and arced to the east, into the upper Ponath. A few minutes later it passed over the site of the Degnan packstead, where Marika had lived her first ten years. Only a few regular lines in the earth remained upon that hilltop clearing.

Marika read grief in the set of Grauel's upper torso. Barlog refused to look and respond.

The darkship rushed on toward the oncoming night. Way, way to her left Marika spotted a dot coming down from the north, angling in, occasionally spilling a crimson flash as sunlight caught it. Another darkship. Then to the south, another still. All three rushed eastward on intersecting courses.

Marika's ship arrived first, streaking over a forest where rifles hammered and heavier weapons filled the woods with flashes. A clearing appeared ahead. At its center stood an incomplete fortress of logs. It was afire. Huntresses enveloped in smoke sniped at the surrounding forest.

Something black and wicked roiled around Marika. The darkship dropped away beneath her, plunging groundward. The darkness cleared. The Mistress of the Ship resumed control of her craft, took it up. Chill wind nibbled at Marika's face.

Screams came from the forest.

The second and third darkships made passes while Marika's turned. Marika went down through her loophole, located a ghost not bearing the ship, and went riding. She located a band of wild silth and wehrlen. They were feeble but able to neutralize the three silth who commanded the besieged workers and huntresses.

A hum past her ear pulled Marika back. The Mistress was into her second pass. Rifles flashed ahead. Bullets whined past the darkship. One spanged against metal and howled away.

Marika dived through her loophole, found a steed, lashed it toward the wild silth. She allowed her anger full reign when she reached them.

She was astonished by her own strength. It had grown vastly during her brief stay at Maksche. A dozen nomads died horribly. The others scattered. In moments the nomad fighters followed.

The darkships began flying fast, low-level circles, spiraling outward from the stronghold, exterminating fugitives. Marika's Mistress of the Ship did not break off till after three moons had risen.

III

Paustch was in charge of the reconstruction of Akard. She was no friend of that uppity pup Marika or her scandalously undisciplined savage cohorts, Grauel and Barlog. She tolerated their presence in her demesne only a few days.

During those days Marika wangled a couple of patrol flights with the Mistress on whose darkship she had come north. The Mistress was not being sociable or understanding of the whims of a pup. She respected Marika's darker abilities and hoped they would help her survive her patrols.

No contact came during either flight.

On her return from the second venture, Marika found Dorteka packing. "What is happening, mistress? Have you been recalled?"

"No. *We* have been assigned the honor of establishing a blockhouse directly astride the main route from the Zhotak south into the upper Ponath, somewhere up near the Rift." The look she gave Marika said much more. It said this was an exile, and that it was all Marika's fault because she was who and what she was. It said that they were being sent out into the wilderness because Paustch wanted her both out of her fur and into a difficult position.

Marika shrugged. "I would rather be away from here anyway. Paustch and her cronies persist in aggravating me. I am long-suffering, but under the circumstances I might eventually lose my temper."

Dorteka first tilted her ears in amusement, then came near losing *her* temper. "This hole is primitive enough. Out there there will be nothing."

"The life is not as hard as you imagine, mistress. And you will have three experienced woodsmeth to show you how to cope."

"And how many nomads?"

Marika broke away as soon as she could. She did not want to argue with Dorteka. She had plenty of firm enemies already among those who had power over her. Dorteka would never be a friend, but at present she could be counted upon for support as an agent of the most senior.

She *was* pleased to be assigned to a blockhouse garrison. It meant a respite from the grinding silth life, with all its ceremony and all the animosity directed her way. She did not enjoy that, though perforce she must live with it.

Next morning a school of darkships lifted Marika, Grauel, Barlog, Dorteka, and another eight huntresses and ten workers across the upper Ponath. The assigned site overlooked the way that had been both the trade route with and invasion route for the nomads of the Zhotak. Marika did not anticipate any real danger from nomads. She believed the savages all to have left the Zhotak long since. The vast majority should be looking for easy hunting far to the south of the upper Ponath.

"Dorteka. The nomads have lived hard lives ever since I have been aware of their existence. The Zhotak was a harsh land even before the winters worsened. Before they became organized, the raids they made were all acts of desperation. Now that they are fighting everywhere, all the time, they do not seem so desperate."

"What are you driving at, pup?" They had just landed at the site, a clearing on a slope overlooking a broad, meadowed valley. There was a great deal of snow among the trees on the opposite slope yet.

"In the past they did not have time free from trying to get ready for the next winter to spend their summers attacking and plundering. Now they have that time. To me it would seem their problems getting food have lessened. But I do not see how that could be. They are hunters and gatherers, not farmers. The winters have wiped out most of the game animals. So where are they getting food? Besides from eating their dead?"

"From the Serke, I suppose. I do not know. And I do not care." Dorteka surveyed the valley, which Marika thought excitingly beautiful. "I do not see why we bother fighting them for this wasteland. If they want it so badly, let them have it."

She was in a mood. Marika moved away, joined Barlog

and Grauel, who were helping the workers unload supplies and equipment.

"We will need some sort of barrier right away," Grauel said. "I hear there are still a few kagbeasts in these parts. If so, they would be hungry enough to attack meth."

"I saw some snarltooth vines just west of here as we were coming in," Marika said. "Drive stakes and string some of those with some briars from the riverbank down there. That will do till we get a real palisade up."

"Grauel and I will work out a watch rotation. We will need big fires at night. Do we have permission to harvest live wood if there is not enough dead?"

"If necessary. But I think you will find plenty of deadwood. The winters are killing some of the less hardy trees already."

The outpost had to be built from the ground up. The task took a month. That month passed without incident, though on a couple of occasions Marika sensed the presence of strange meth on the far side of the valley. When she grabbed a ghost and went to examine them, she found that they were nomad scouts. She did not bother them. Let them prime themselves for falling into a trap.

Marika was unconcerned for her own safety, so unconcerned she sometimes wandered off alone, to the distress of Grauel and Barlog, who tracked her down each time.

Marika often joined in the physical work, too. She found it a good way to work out the frustrations she had accumulated during her months in Maksche. And in labor she found temporary surcease from concerns of the past and future.

This close to the Degnan packstead she could not help thinking often of the Mourning she owned. But there were no nightmares. Could that be because of the work? That did not seem reasonable.

After a time most of the southern huntresses joined the work, too, for all of Dorteka's disapproving scowls. There was nothing else to do but be bored.

The workers appreciated the help, but did not know what to make of it. Especially of a silth who actually dirtied her paws. Marika suspected they began to think well of her despite all the rumors they had heard. By summer's end she had most of them talking to her. And by summer's end she had begun consciously trying to cultivate their affection.

Dorteka refused to do anything but tutor Marika. That assignment she pursued doggedly, as if motivated mainly by an increasing desire to get the job over with. Their relationship deteriorated as the summer progressed, and Marika steadfastly refused to be molded into traditional silth shape.

Though the summer gave Marika a respite from her concerns and fears, she did spend a lot of time thinking about the future. She approached it with a pragmatic attitude suitable for the most cynical silth.

The only attack came soon after the blockhouse was complete. It was not a strong one, though the savages thought it strong enough. They cut through the snarltooth vine fencing and evaded the pit traps and booby traps. They used explosives to breach the palisade. Distressed, Dorteka reached out to Akard with the touch and asked for darkship support.

Marika obliterated the attackers long before the one ship sent arrived.

She deflected and destroyed the attackers almost casually, using a ghost drawn from high in the atmosphere. She had learned that the higher one could reach, the more monstrous a ghost one could find.

Afterward, Dorteka shied away from her the way she might from a dangerous animal, and never did get over being nervous when Marika was close.

Marika did not understand. She was even pained. She did not need Dorteka's friendship, but she did not want her fear.

Was her talent for the dark side that terrible? Did she exceed the abilities of other silth by so much? She could not believe that.

Soon after the first snowflakes flew, a darkship arrived bearing winter stores and a replacement silth. Marika and Dorteka received orders to return to the Maksche cloister.

"I am not going," Marika told Dorteka.

"Pup! I have had about all of your insubordination that I am going to stand. Get your coat on and get aboard that ship." Dorteka was so angry she ignored Grauel and Barlog.

"This is the last darkship that will come here till spring, barring a need for major support if the blockhouse comes under attack. Not so?"

"Yes. So what? Do you love these All-forsaken woods so much that you want to stay here forever?"

"Not at all. I want to go home. And so do these workers."

That caught Dorteka from the blind side. She could do nothing but look at Marika askance. Finally, she croaked, "What are you talking about? So what?"

"These meth were hired for the season. They were promised they would return home in time for the Festival of Kifkha. The festival comes up in four days. And no transportation has been provided them yet. You go ahead. You go south. You report to the most senior. And when she asks why I did not come back with you, you tell her why. Because once again the Reugge Community is failing to live up to a pledge to its dependents."

Dorteka became so angry Marika feared she would have a stroke. But she stood there facing her teacher in a stance so adamant it was clear she would not be moved. Dorteka went inside herself and performed calming rituals till she was settled enough to touch someone at Akard.

The workers went out next morning. From all over the upper Ponath they went, with an alacrity that said that Gradwohl herself must have intervened. Before they left, two workers very quietly told Marika where they could be reached in Makasche if ever she needed them to repay the debt. Marika memorized that information carefully. She had Grauel and Barlog commit it to memory too, protecting it through redundance.

She meant to use those workers someday.

She had plans. During that summer she had begun to look forward in more than a simpleminded, pup-obsessed-with-flying sort of way. But she was careful to mask that from everyone. Even Grauel and Barlog remained outside.

"Will your holiness board her darkship now?" Dorteka

demanded. "Is the order of the world arranged to your satisfaction?"

"Indeed. Thank you, Dorteka. I wish you understood. Those meth may be of no consequence to you. Nor are they to me, really. But a Community can only be as good as its honor. If our own dependents cannot trust our word, who else will?"

"Thank the All," Dorteka muttered as Marika began strapping herself to the cold darkship frame.

"Such indifference may well be the reason the cloister is having so much trouble keeping order in Maksche. Paustch is determined not to do right and Zertan is too lazy or too timid."

"You will seal your mouth, pup. You will not speak ill of your seniors again. I still have a great deal of control over how happy or miserable your life can be. Do I make myself understood?"

"Perfectly, mistress. Though your attitude does not alter the truth a bit."

Dorteka was furious with her again.

Chapter Eighteen

I

In most respects Marika had attained the knowledge levels expected of silth of her age. In many she had exceeded those. As she surpassed levels expected, she found herself with more and more free time. That she spent studying aircraft, aerodynamics, astronomy, and space, when she could obtain any information. The Reugge did not possess much. The brethren and dark-faring sisterhoods clung to their knowledge jealously.

Marika had a thousand questions, and suspected the only way to get the answers was to steal them.

How did the silth take their darkships across the void? The distances were incredible. And space was cold and airless. Yet darkships went out there and returned in a matter of weeks.

She ached because she would never know. Because she was stuck in a sisterhood unable to reach the stars, a sisterhood that might not survive much longer.

To dream dreams that could not be attained, that was a horror. Almost as bad as the dreams that came by night.

The nightmares resumed immediately upon her return to Maksche. They were more explicit now. Often her littermate Kublin appeared in them, reaching, face tormented, as if crying for help. She hurt. She and Kublin had been very close, for all he was male.

Most Senior Gradwohl had shifted from TelleRai to Maksche in fact as well as name while Marika was in the north. Four days after Marika's return, the wise ones of Maksche, and many others from farflung cloisters of the Community, gathered in the ritual hall. Marika was there at Gradwohl's command, though she had not as yet seen the most senior.

After a few rituals had been completed, Gradwohl herself took the floor. Meth who had accompanied her from TelleRai began setting up something electrical, much to the distress of Zertan. They tried to argue that such should not be permitted within the holy place of Maksche.

Gradwohl silenced them with a scowl. It was well-known that the most senior was not pleased with them. Though she remained outside the mainstream of cloister life, Marika had heard many rumors. Most made the futures of the Maksche senior and her second sound bleak.

The device set up projected a map upon a white screen. Gradwohl said, "This is what the north looked like at its low ebb, last winter. The darker areas are those that were completely overrun by savages.

"Our counterattack seems to have caught them unprepared. I would account the summer's efforts a complete success. We have placed a line of small but stout fortresses up the line of the Hainlin, running from here to Akard. A second line was gone in crosswise, here, roughly a hundred miles north of Maksche. It runs from our western boundary to the sea. Each fastness lies within easy touch of its neighbors. Any southward movement can be detected from these, and interdicted with support from here in Maksche.

"Akard is partially restored. It now forms the anchor for a network of fastnesses in the Ponath. They will allow us to maintain our claim there without dispute. A small fleet of darkships based there will thwart any effort to reduce the fastnesses. Work on Akard should be completed next summer.

"Next summer also, I hope to begin squeezing the savage packs from the north, south, and east, giving them no choice but to flee west into the territories of our beloved friends the Serke. Where they may do more evil than they have done. The Serke raised them up like demons. May they suffer as a witch whose demon breaks the ties that bind."

Gradwohl scanned the assembly. Nearly a hundred of the most important members of the Reugge Community were present. No one seemed inclined to comment, though Marika sensed that many disapproved of Gradwohl and her plans.

"As strength goes," Marika murmured. Gradwohl was getting her way only because she was the strongest of Reugge silth.

"Also next spring we will begin restoring several brethren strongholds that will be of use to us. Especially the fortress Mahede. From Mahede it will be possible to mount year-round darkship patrols and up the pressure on the savages even more."

Gradwohl tapped the screen with a finger. Mahede lay halfway between Maksche and Akard. She used a claw to draw a circle around Mahede. It was obvious that circles of the same size centered upon Akard and Maksche would overlap, covering the entire Hainlin rivercourse north of the city. The Hainlin was the main artery of the northern provinces.

"Meantime, this winter we will continue hunting the savages the best we can, with all the resources we can bring to bear. We must keep the pressure on. It is the only way to beat the Serke at their own game."

Several senior silth disagreed. A murmur of discontent ran through the audience. Marika scanned faces carefully, memorizing those of her mentor's opponents. They would be her enemies, too.

In the course of the discussion that followed, it began to appear that those who opposed Gradwohl's scheme did so principally because it interfered with their comfort and their abilities to exploit their own particular demesnes. Several seniors of cloisters complained because they had been stripped of their best silth and, as a result, were having trouble maintaining order among their workers. Especially among the males.

The pestilence of rebellion was spreading.

"I suspect our problems with workers are the shadows of the next Serke move against us," Gradwohl said. "It is unlikely that they expected me to collapse under pressure from the savages. The northern packs were expendable counters in their game. So will our workers be. But we will deal with that in its turn. The most critical task facing us is to make sure the northern provinces are secure no matter what troubles plague us elsewhere."

"Why?" someone demanded. The shout was anonymous, but Marika thought the voice sounded like that of Paustch.

"Because the Serke want them so desperately."

Once the grumbling faded, Gradwohl expanded somewhat. "I see it this way, sisters. The Serke appear willing to spend a great deal, and to risk even more, in order to wrest the north from our paws. They must have very powerful reasons for their behavior. If they have reasons, then we have reasons for taking every measure to retain our territories. Even though we do not know what they are.

"But I will find out what they are. And when I do, you will be informed immediately."

More grumbling.

"While I am most senior none of this is subject to debate. It will be done as I have decreed. In coming days I will speak to each of you individually and have more to say at that time. Meantime, this assembly is adjourned. Senior Zertan. Paustch. I wish to speak to you immediately. Marika. I want you to remain here. I will call upon the rest of you as I have the opportunity."

That was a dismissal. Silth rose from stools and began drifting out. Marika studied the groups they formed, identifying alliances of interest. She heard several seniors grumbling about being tied down at Maksche when they had problems at home demanding immediate attention.

Paustch and Zertan left their stools and moved forward to face Gradwohl. Marika remained upon her stool in the shadows, well away. The Maksche senior and her second did not need to be reminded of her presence.

Gradwohl said, "Mildly stated, I am not pleased with you two. Zertan. You are walking close to the line. Your problem is plain laziness compounded by indifference and maybe a dollop of malice. I will be here for some time now, watching over your shoulder. I trust my presence will lend you some incentive to become more ambitious.

"Paustch. For a number of years you have been the true moving spirit here in Maksche. You have been responsible for getting done most of what has gotten done. It is my sorrow that most of that has been negative. I have in mind several directives that you carried out to the letter but managed to sabotage in spirit. I cannot shake the feeling that I have clung too close to TelleRai since becoming most senior. My paw should have been more evident in the outlying cloisters.

"I will no longer tolerate undermining and backstabbing by subordinates. To that end, you will be transferred to TelleRai immediately. A courier darkship will be leaving at dawn. You will be aboard. When you reach TelleRai, you will report to Keraitis for assignment to duties there. Understood?"

Her entire frame shaking with rage, Paustch bowed her head. "Yes, mistress."

"You may leave us."

Paustch drew herself up, turned, marched out of the hall. Marika thought she might become trouble unless Gradwohl made further moves to neutralize her malice. Unless by its very nature her new assignment placed her where she could do no harm.

Gradwohl turned to Zertan once Paustch was outside. "Do you feel a spark or two of wakening ambition, Zertan? Do you feel you can become more productive?"

"I believe I do, mistress."

"I thought you might. You may go, too."

"Yes, mistress."

Only the sounds of Zertan's slippers disturbed the silence of the hall. Then she was gone, and Marika was alone with the most senior. Silence reigned. Lamplight set shadows dancing. Marika waited without fear, without movement.

Finally, Gradwohl said, "Come forward."

Marika left her stool and approached the most senior.

"Come. Come. Not to be frightened."

"Yes, mistress." Marika slipped into the role she assumed with every superior, that of simplicity.

"Marika, I know you, pup. Do not play that game with me. I am on your side."

"My side, mistress?"

"Yes. Very well. If you insist. How was your summer?"

"A pleasant break, mistress. Though the Ponath is colder now."

"And going to get a lot colder in years to come. Tell me about your day on the town."

"Mistress?" The debacle in the tradermale enclave had slipped her mind completely.

"You visited the brethren enclave, did you not?"

"Yes, mistress." Now she was disturbed.

Her reaction was not well concealed. Gradwohl was amused. "You had quite an adventure, I gather. No. No need to be concerned. The protest was an embarrassment, but a minor one, and a blessing as well. Am I right in assuming that the male Bagnel is the male we brought out of Akard?"

"Yes, mistress."

"And you are on friendly terms? He kept the fuss to a minimum."

"He thinks I saved his life, mistress. I did not. I was saving myself. That the others were saved was incidental."

"The fact is seldom as important as the perception, Marika. Illusion is the ruling form. Shadow signifies more than substance. Silth always have been more fancy than fact."

"Mistress?"

"It is not important whether or not you made an effort to save this male. What signifies is his belief that you saved him. Which in fact you did."

Marika was puzzled. Why the interest in Bagnel?

"You have been away for a while. Living in rather primitive, difficult circumstances. Would you like another day on the city?"

Yes, she thought excitedly. "I have studies, mistress."

"Yes. I hear you have added your own regimen to Dorteka's."

"Yes, mistress. I have been studying flying, space, and—"

"When do you sleep?"

"I do not need much sleep, mistress. I never have."

"I suppose not. I was young once, too. Are you learning anything?"

"There is not much information available, mistress. Most paths of inquiry lead to dead ends where tradermales or other Communities have invoked a privilege."

"We will find you fresh sources. About this Bagnel."

"Yes, mistress?"

"Will he accept a continued friendship?"

Warily, Marika replied, "He invited me to return, mistress. He told me I should ask for him, and he would see that there was no trouble."

"Excellent. Excellent. Then go see him again. By all means."

"Mistress? What do you want?"

"I want you to cultivate him. The brethren are supporting our enemies for reasons we do not understand. It is not like them to compromise their neutrality. You have a contact. See more of him. In time you might learn something to help us in our struggle with the Serke."

"I see."

"You do not approve?"

"It is not my place to approve or disapprove, mistress."

"You have reservations then?"

"Yes, mistress. But I cannot say what they are exactly. Except that the thought of using Bagnel makes me uncomfortable."

"It should. We should not use our friends. They are too precious."

Marika gave the most senior a calculating look. Had she meant more than she had said? Was that a warning?

"Yet at times greater issues intervene. I think Reugge survival warrants pursuit of any path to salvation."

"As you say, mistress."

"Will you pursue it? Will you cultivate this male?"

"Yes, mistress." She had decided instantly. She would, for her own purposes. For information *she* wanted. If some also fell the most senior's way, good. It would keep the cloister doors open.

"I thought you would." The most senior's tone said she knew Marika's mind. It said also that she was growing excited, though she concealed it well.

Perhaps she could read minds, Marika thought. Some silth could touch other minds and steal secrets. Was that not how a truthsaying worked? And would that not be a most useful talent for one who would command an entire unruly Community?

"I will tell Dorteka to let you out whenever you want. Do not overdo it. You will make the brethren suspicious."

"Yes, mistress."

"There is plenty of time, Marika. We will not reach the time of real crisis for many years yet."

"Yes, mistress."

Gradwohl again expressed restrained amusement. "You could become one of the great silth, Marika. You have the proper turn of mind."

"They whisper behind my back, mistress. They call me doomstalker and Jiana."

"Probably. Any of us who amount to anything endure a youth filled with distrust and fear. Our sisters sense the upward pressure. But no matter. That is all for today. Unless there is something you want to discuss."

"Why do we not make our own darkships, mistress? Why depend upon tradermales?"

"Two answers come to mind immediately. One is that most sisters prefer to believe that we should not sully our paws with physical labor. Another, and the one that is more close to the honest truth, is that we are dependent upon the brethren in too many other areas. They have insinuated tentacles into every aspect of life. If they came to suspect that we were trespassing on what they see as their proper rights, they might then cut us off from everything else they do for us.

"There is an ecological balance between male and female in our society, as expressed in silth and brethren. We are interdependent, and ever more so. In fact, I suspect an imbalance is in the offing. We have come to need them more than they need us. Nowadays we would be missed less than they."

Marika rose. "Maybe steps ought to be taken to change that instead of pursuing these squabbles between Communities."

"An idea that has been expressed often enough before. Without winning more than lip service support. The brethren have the advantage of us there, too. Though they have their various bonds and subbonds, they answer to a central authority. They have their internal feuds, but they are much more monolithic than we. They can play one sisterhood against another."

"*Find* ways to split them into factions," Marika said from the doorway. And, "We built our own ships for ages. Before the tradermales."

Gradwohl scowled.

"Thank you, mistress. I will visit Bagnel soon."

II

Grauel and Barlog were beside themselves when Marika announced another expedition to the tradermale enclave. They did everything possible to dissuade her. She did not tell them she had the most senior's blessing. They gossiped. She knew, because they brought her snippets about the

Maksche sisters. She did not doubt but what they paid in kind.

The huntresses became suspicious soon after they left the cloister. "Marika," Grauel said after a whispered consultation with Barlog, "we are being followed. By huntresses from the cloister."

Marika was not pleased, but neither was she surprised. A silth had been set upon by rogue males not a week before her return from the upper Ponath. "It's all right," she said. "They're looking out for us."

Grauel nodded to herself. She told Barlog, "The most senior protecting her investment."

"We'll be watched wherever we go," Marika said. "We have a friend."

"One is more than we did have."

"Does that tell me something?"

"Did you know that we were not supposed to come back from the Ponath?"

"We weren't?" The notion startled Marika.

"The story was whispering around the barracks here. We were sent out to build that blockhouse behind the most senior's back. We were not supposed to get out of it alive. That is why Paustch was demoted. It was an attempt to kill us."

Barlog added, "The senior councillors here are afraid of you, Marika."

"We survived."

Grauel said, "It is also whispered that nomad prisoners confessed that our blockhouse wasn't attacked once they found out who the keeper was. You have gained a reputation among the savages."

"How? I don't know any of them. How could they know me?"

"You slew the Serke silth at Akard. That has been bruited about all the Communities, they say. The one who died had a great name in her order, though the Serke aren't naming it. That would mean admitting they were poaching on the Ponath."

"I love this hypocrisy," Marika said. "Everyone knows

what the Serke are doing, and no one will admit it. We must learn the rules of this game. We might want to play it someday."

"Marika?"

Grauel's tone warned Marika that she had come too far out of her role. "We have to play the silth game the way it is played here if we are to survive here, Grauel. Not so?" She spoke in the formal mode.

"I suppose. Still . . ."

Barlog said, "We hear talk about the most senior sending you to TelleRai soon, Marika. Because that is where they teach those who are expected to rise high. Is this true? Will we be going?" Barlog, too, shifted to the formal mode.

Marika shifted back. "I don't know anything about it, Barlog. Nothing's been said to me. I don't think there's anything to it. But I will not be going anywhere without you two. Could I survive without touch with my pack?"

How could she survive without the only meth she had any reason to trust? Not that she trusted even them completely. She still suspected they reported on her to curry favor, but to do that they had to stay close and remain useful.

"Thank you, Marika," Barlog said.

"Here we are. Do not hesitate to admonish me if I fail to comport myself properly." Marika glanced back. "Any sign of our shadows?" She could have gone down through her loophole and looked, but did not care enough.

"None, Marika."

"Good." She touched the fence lightly, examined the aircraft upon the field. Today the airstrip was almost naked. One small freight dirigible lay in one of the cradles. Two Stings sat near the fence. There were a couple of light craft of a type with which she was unfamiliar. Their design implied them to be reconnaisance or courier ships.

She went to the desk in the gateway building. The same guard watched the same vision screen in the same state of sleepy indifference. He did not notice her. She wondered if his hearing and sense of smell were impaired, or if he just enjoyed being rude to meth from the street. She rapped on the desk.

He turned. He recognized her and his eyes widened. He sat up.

"I would like to speak to Assistant Security Chief Bagnel," Marika told him.

He gulped air, looked around as if seeking a place to hide, then gobbled, "Yes, mistress." He hurried around the end of his desk, down the hallway leading to the airfield. Halfway along he paused to say, "You stay here, mistress." He made a mollifying gesture. "Just wait. I will hurry him all I can."

Marika's ears tilted in amusement.

The guard turned again at the far door, called back, "Mistress, Bagnel is no longer assistant chief. He was made chief a few months ago. Just so you do not use the wrong mode of address."

"Thank you." Wrong mode of address? What difference? Unless it was something the nervous guard had let carry over from the mysteries of the tradermale brethren.

She supposed she ought to examine the relevant data—what was known—if she was going to be dealing with Bagnel regularly.

Time enough for that later. After today's encounter had shown its promise, or lack thereof. "Grauel, go down the hall and keep watch. Barlog, check the building here, then watch the street." She stepped around the desk and began leafing through the guard's papers. She found nothing interesting, if only because they were printed in what had to be a private male language. She opened the desk's several drawers. Again she found nothing of any interest.

Well, it had been worth a look. Just in case. She rounded the desk again, recalled Grauel and Barlog. To their inquisitive looks she replied, "I was just curious. There wasn't anything there."

The guard took another five minutes. He returned to find them just as he had left them. "Kentan Bagnel will be here shortly, mistress. Can I make your wait more comfortable somehow? Would you care for refreshments?"

"Not for myself, thank you. Barlog? Grauel?"

Each replied, "No, mistress," and Marika was pleased

with their restraint. In years past they would have chastised any male this bold.

"You called Bagnel Kentan. Is that a title or name?"

The guard was fuddled for a moment. Then he brightened. "A title, mistress. It denotes his standing with the brethren."

"It has nothing to do with his job?"

"No, mistress. Not directly."

"I see. Where does a kentan stand with regard to others? How high?"

The guard looked unhappy. He did not want to answer, yet felt he had to conform to orders to deal with her hospitably.

"It must be fairly high. You are nervous about him. The year has treated Bagnel well, then."

"Yes, mistress. His rise has been . . ."

"Rapid?"

"Yes, mistress. We all thought your last visit would cause him grave embarrassment, but . . ."

Marika turned away to conceal her features. A photograph graced the wall opposite the desk. It had been enlarged till it was so grainy it was difficult to recognize. "What is this place?"

Relieved, the guard came around his desk and began explaining, "That is the brethren landhold at TelleRai, mistress."

"Yes. Of course. I have never seen it from this angle."

"Marika?"

She turned. Bagnel had arrived. He looked sleek and self-confident and just a bit excited. "Bagnel. As you see, I'm behaving myself this time." She used the informal mode without realizing it. Grauel and Barlog gave her looks she did not see.

"You've grown." Bagnel responded in the same mode. His usage was as unconscious as Marika's.

Grauel and Barlog bared teeth and exchanged glances.

"Yes. Also grown up. I spent the summer in the Ponath, battling the nomad. I believe it changed me."

Bagnel glanced at the guard. "You've been grilling
Norgis. You've made him very uncomfortable."

"We were talking about the picture of the Tovand,
kentan," the guard said.

Bagnel scowled. The guard retreated behind the barrier
of his desk. He increased the volume of the sound accompanying the display on his screen. Marika was amused, but
concealed it.

"Well," Bagnel said. "You're here again."

Grauel and Barlog frowned at his use of the familiar
mode.

"I hoped I could look inside the aircraft this time. Under
supervision, of course. Nothing secret seems to be going on
now. The fighting ships and the big dirigibles are gone."

"You tease me. Yes, I suppose we could look at the light
aircraft. Come."

As they stepped outside, Marika said, "I hear you've been
promoted."

"Yes. Chief of security. Another reward for my failure at
Critza."

"You have an unusual concept of reward, I'd say."

Grauel and Barlog were displeased with Marika's use of
the familiar mode, too.

"I do?" Bagnel was amused. "My superiors do. I haven't
done anything deserving." Softly, he asked, "Do you need
those two arfts hanging over your shoulder all the time?"

"I don't go anywhere without Grauel and Barlog."

"They make me nervous. They always look like they're
planning to rip my throat out."

Marika glanced at the huntresses. "They are. They don't
like this. They don't like males who can or dare do more
than cook or pull a plow."

He gave her a dark look. She decided she had pushed her
luck. Time to become Marika the packless again. "Isn't this
a Seifite trainer?" She indicated an aircraft standing
straight ahead.

"Still studying, are you?"

"Always. When I can get anything to study. I told you I
plan to fly. I have flown three times, on darkships. Each

flight left me more convinced that flight is my tomorrow."
She glanced at several males hurrying toward them. Grauel
and Barlog interposed themselves quickly, though the males
were not armed.

"Ground crew," Bagnel explained. "They see us coming
out here, they expect us to take a ship up."

The males slowed when they discerned Marika's silth
garb. "They're having second thoughts," she said.

"You can't blame them, can you? Silth are intimidating
by nature."

"Are they? I've never seen them from the outside."

"But you grew up on a packstead. Not in a cloister."

"True. And my pack never mentioned them. I was silth
before I knew what was happening." She made the remark
sound like a jest. Bagnel tried to respond and failed.

"Well?" he asked. "Would you like to go up? As long as
you're here?"

"Can you do that? Just take off whenever you want?"

"Yes."

"In cloister we would have to have permission all the way
from the senior." She climbed a ladder to the lower wing of
the aircraft. "Only two places. No room for Grauel and
Barlog."

"Unfortunately." Bagnel did not sound distraught.

"I don't know if they'd let me."

"You're silth. They're just—"

"They're just charged on their necks with bringing me
back alive. Even if that means keeping me from killing
myself. They don't trust machines. It was a fight just getting
to come here again. The idea wasn't popular at the cloister.
Someone made a protest about last time."

"Maybe another time, then. When they understand that I
don't plan to carry you off to our secret breeding farm."

"What? Is there such a place? Oh. You are teasing."

"Yes. We recruit ragtag. Especially where the traditional
pack structures still predominate. A lot of the Brown Paw
Bond youngsters came out of the Ponath."

"I see."

Each spring newly adult males had been turned out of the

packsteads to wander the hills and valleys in search of another pack willing to take them in. They had had to sell themselves and their skills. Thus the blood was mixed.

Many, though, never found a place. A pack did not need nearly as many males as females. Marika had not wondered much about what had become of the unsuccessful. She had assumed that they died of exposure or their own incompetence. Their fates had not concerned her, except that of her littermate Kublin, the only male for whom she had ever held much regard.

"Well? Up? Or another time?"

Marika felt a longing so intense it frightened her. She was infatuated with flight. More than infatuated, she feared. She was obsessed. She did not like that. A weakness. Weaknesses were points where one could be touched, could be manipulated. "Next time," she grated. "Or the time after that. When my companions have learned to relax."

"As you wish. Want to sit in it? Just to get the feel?"

And so it went, with Marika getting a look at every ship on the field, including the Stings. "Nothing secret about them," Bagnel assured her. "Nothing you'd understand well enough to tell our enemies about."

"You have enemies?"

"A great many. Especially in the sisterhoods. Like that old silth—what was her name? Gorry. The one who wanted us thrown back to the nomads when we came to Akard asking help. Like all the other dark-faring silth have become since we joined the Serke and Redoriad in their interstellar ventures."

"What?" Why had that not been in the education tapes? "I was not aware of that. Brethren have visited the starworlds?"

"There are two ships. One is Serke, one is Redoriad. The silth move them across the void. The brethren deal on the other end."

"How is that possible? I thought only specially trained silth could stay the bite of the dark."

"Special ships. Darkships surrounded with a metal shell to keep the air in. Designed by brethren. They put in machines to keep the air fresh. Don't ask me questions because that's all I know. That is another bond entirely, and one we have no contact with."

"And the other sisterhoods are jealous?"

"So I gather. I don't know all that much. The Brown Paw Bond is an old-fashioned bond involved in trade and light manufacturing. Traditional pursuits. The only place you could get the kind of answers you want would be at the Tovand in TelleRai. I tell you, the one time I saw that place it seemed more alien than the Reugge cloister here. Those are strange males down there. Anyway, I was telling about the Serke and the Redoriad. Rumor says they asked the brethren to help them with their star ventures. That could be why the Reugge have become so disenchanted with the Serke."

"Don't fool yourself. The disenchantment did not begin with us. The Serke are solely responsible. There's something in the Ponath that they want." She studied Bagnel closely. He gave nothing away.

"The brethren won't go back to Critza, Bagnel. I thought you said trade was lucrative up there."

"When there was someone to trade with. There isn't anymore."

"Nomads?"

"What?"

"They're getting their weapons somewhere. They were better armed than ever this summer. They shot down two darkships. There is only one source for firearms."

"No. We haven't sold them weapons. Of that I'm certain. That would be a self-destructive act."

"Who did?"

"I don't know."

"They had to get them from you. No one else is allowed to manufacture such things."

"I thought you said the Serke were behind everything."

"Undoubtedly. But I wonder if someone isn't behind the Serke. No. Let's not argue anymore. It's getting late. I'd better get home or they won't let me come again."

"How soon can I expect you?"

"Next month maybe. I get a day a month off now. A reward for service in the Ponath. As long as I'm welcome, I'll keep coming here."

"You'll be welcome as long as I'm security chief."

"Yes. You owe me, don't you?"

Startled, Bagnel said, "That, too. But mostly because you break the tedium."

"You're not happy here?"

"I would have been happier had the weather never changed and the nomads never come out of the Zhotak. Life was simpler at Critza."

Marika agreed. "As it was at my packstead."

III

"Well?" the most senior demanded.

Marika was not sure what to say. Was it in her interest to admit that she suspected Bagnel had been given an assignment identical to her own?

She repeated only what she thought Barlog and Grauel might have overheard. "Mostly we just looked at aircraft and talked about how we would have been happier if we had not had to leave the Ponath. I tried to avoid pressing. Oh. He did tell me about some ships the dark-faring Serke and Redoriad had built special so the brethren could——"

"Yes. Well. Not much. But I did not expect much. It was a first time. A trial. You did not press? Good. You have a talent for the insidious. You will make a great leader someday. I am sure you will have him in your thrall before long."

"I will try, mistress."

"Please do, Marika. It may become critical down the path."

"May I ask what exactly we are doing, mistress? What plans you have for me? Dorteka keeps telling me——"

"You may not. Not at this point. What you do not know you cannot tell anyone else. When it becomes tighter tactically. . . . When you and I and the Reugge would all be better served by having you know the goal and able to act to achieve it, you will be told everything. For the present, have faith that your reward will be worth your trouble."

"As you wish, mistress."

Chapter Nineteen

I

It was the quietest time of Marika's brief life, at least since the years before the nomads had come to the upper Ponath and destroyed. The struggle continued, and she participated, but life became so effortless and routine it fell into numbing cycles of repetition. There were few high points, few lows, and each of the latter she marked by the return of her nightmares about her littermate Kublin.

She could count on at least one bout with dark dreams each year, though never at any time predictable by season, weather, or her own mental state. They concerned her increasingly. The passing of time, and their never being weaker when they came, convinced her that they had little to do with the fact that the Degnan remained unMourned.

What else, then? That was what Grauel, Barlog, and even Braydic asked when she did at last break down and share her distress.

She did not know what else. Dreams and reason did not mix.

She did see Braydic occasionally now. The comm technician was less standoffish now it was certain Marika enjoyed the most senior's enduring favor.

Studies. Always there were studies. Always there were exercises to help her expand and increase her silth talents.

Always there were frightened silth distressed by her grasp of those talents.

Years came and went. The winters worsened appreciably each seasonal cycle. The summers grew shorter. Photographs taken from tradermale satellites showed a swift accumulation of ice in the far north. Glaciers were worming across the Zhotak already. For a time they would be blocked by the barrier of the Rift, but sisters who believed themselves experts said that, even so, it would be but a few years before that barrier was surmounted and the ice would slide on southward, grinding the land.

It never ceased to boggle Marika, the Serke being so desperate to possess a land soon to be lost to nature.

The predictions regarding the age of ice became ever more grim. There were times when Marika wished she were not in the know—as much as she was. The world faced truly terrible times, and those would come within her own life span. Assuming she lived as long as most silth.

Grauel and Barlog were inclined to suggest that she would not, for she never quite managed to control her fractious nature.

The predictions of social upheaval and displacement, most of which she reasoned out for herself, were quite terrifying.

Each summer Marika served her stint in the north, from the time of the last snowfall till the time of the first. Each summer she exercised her ability to walk the dark side, as much as the nomads would permit. Each summer poor Dorteka had to endure the rustification with her, complaining bitterly. Each summer Marika helped establish a new outpost somewhere, and each summer the nomads tried to avoid her outpost, though every summer saw its great centers of conflict. She sometimes managed to participate by smuggling herself into the strife aboard a darkship commanded by a pliable Mistress.

Gradwohl's strategy of driving the nomads west into Serke territories seemed slow in paying off. The savages clung to Reugge lands stubbornly, despite paying a terrible price.

The Reugge thus settled into a never-ending and costly bloodfeud with the savages. The horde, after continuous decimation through attack and starvation, no longer posed quite so serious a threat. But it remained troublesome because of the rise of a warrior cast. The crucible of struggle created grim fighters among the fastest, strongest, and smartest nomads. Composed of both male and female fighters, and supported by ever more skillful wild silth and wehrlen, it made up in ferocity and cunning what the horde had lost in numbers.

Gradwohl's line of blockhouses north of Maksche did succeed in their mission. The final southward flow crashed against that barrier line like the sea against an uncrackable breakwater. But the savages came again and again, till it seemed they would never withdraw, collapse, seek the easier hunting to the west.

As the nomad threat waned, though, pressure against the Reugge strengthened in other quarters. Hardly a month passed but what there was not some incident in Maksche involving rogue males. And that disease began to show itself in other Reugge territories.

But none of that touched Marika. For all she was in the middle of it, she seemed to be outside and immune to all that happened. None of it affected her life or training.

She spent the long winters studying, practicing, honing her talents, making monthly visits to Bagnel, and devouring every morsel of flight- or space-oriented information Gradwohl could buy or steal. She wheedled more out of Bagnel, who was pleased to help fill such an excited, eager mind.

He was learning himself, turning his interests from those that had occupied him in the Ponath to those of the future. His special interest was the web of communications and weather satellites the brethren maintained with the aid of the dark-faring silth. The brethren created the technology, and the silth lifted the satellites aboard their void-faring darkships.

Marika became intrigued with the cycle and system. She told Bagnel, "There are possibilities that seem to have escaped everyone."

"For example?" His tone was indulgent, like that of an instructress watching a pup reinvent the wheel.

"Possibilities. Unless someone has thought of them already and these ridiculous barriers against the flow of information have masked the fact."

"Give me an example. Maybe I can find out for you."

It was Marika's turn to look indulgent. "Suppose I do have an original thought? I know you tradermales think it unlikely of silth, but that possibility does exist. Granted? Should I give something away for nothing?"

Bagnel was amused. "They make you more a silth every time I see you. You're going to be a nasty old bitch by the time you reach Gradwohl's age, Marika."

"Could be. Could be. And if I am, it'll be the fault of meth like you."

"I'd almost agree with you," Bagnel said, his eyes glazing over for a moment.

Those quiet years were heavily flavored with the most senior's favor. With little fanfare, initially, Marika rose in stature within the cloister. In swift succession she became a celebrant-novice, a celebrant-second, then a full celebrant, meaning she passed through the stages of assistanceship in conducting the daily Reugge rituals, assistanceship during the more important rites on days of obligation, then began directing rites herself. She had no trouble with the actual rituals.

There were those who resented her elevation. Of course. Traditionally, she should not have become a full celebrant till she was much older.

Each swift advancement meant someone else having to wait so much longer. And older silth did not like being left behind one who was, as yet, still a pup.

There was far more resentment when Gradwohl appointed Marika junior censor when one of the old silth died and her place among the cloister's seven councillors was taken by the senior censor. Zertan was extremely distressed. It was a cloister senior's right to make such appointments, without interference even from superiors. But Zertan had to put up with Gradwohl's interference or follow Paustch into exile.

Marika questioned her good fortune less than did Grauel or Barlog, who looked forward to a dizzying fall. Those two could see no bright side in anything.

The spring before Marika's fourth Maksche summer, shortly before she set out for her fourth season of counterattack, death rested its paw heavily upon the cloister leadership. Two judges fell in as many days. Before Marika finished being invested as senior censor, Gradwohl ordered her elevated to the seventh seat on the council.

Tempers flared. Rebellion burned throughout the halls of the ancient cloister. Marika herself tried to refuse the promotion. She had much more confidence in herself than did any of the Maksche sisters, but did not think she was ready for the duties of a councillor—even though seventh chair was mainly understudy for the other six.

Gradwohl remained adamant in the face of unanimous opposition. "What will be is what I will," she declared. "And time only will declare me right or wrong. I have decreed it. Marika will become one of the seven judges of this house."

As strength goes. There was no denying the strong, for they had the power to enforce their will.

But Gradwohl's will put Marika into an unpleasant position.

The sisters of Maksche had not loved her before. Now they hated her.

All this before she was old enough to complete her silth novitiate. Officially. But age was not everything. She had pursued her studies so obsessively that she was the equal or superior of most of the sisters who resented her unnaturally fast advancement. And that was half their reason for hating her. They feared that which possessed inexplicable strength and power.

The strengthened resentment caused her to turn more inward, to concentrate even more upon studies which were her only escape from the misery of daily cloister life. Once a month, there was Bagnel.

And always there was a touch of dread. She suspected doom lurking in the shadows always, at bay only because Gradwohl was omnipresent, guarding her while she directed the northern conflict. While she let the sisterhood beyond Maksche run itself.

Marika was sure there would be a price for continued favor of such magnitude. She believed she was prepared to pay it.

Gradwohl had plans for her, shrouded though they were. But Marika had plans of her own.

II

The summer of Marika's fourth return to the Ponath marked a watershed.

It was her last summer as a novice. On her return to Maksche she was to be inducted full silth, with all the privileges that implied. So she began the summer looking beyond it, trying to justify the ceremonies in her own mind, never seeing the summer as more than a bridge of time. The months in the north would be a slow vacation. The nomads were weak and almost never seen in the Ponath anymore. The snows up there were not expected to melt. There was no reason to anticipate anything but several months of boredom and Dorteka's complaints.

Gradwohl assigned her the entire upper Ponath. She would be answerable only to Senior Educan at Akard. She made her headquarters in a log fortress just miles from the site of the Degnan packstead. In the boring times she would walk down to the site and remember, or venture over hill

and valley, through dead forest, to Machen Cave, where
first she became aware that she had talents different from
those of ordinary packmates.

A great shadow still lurked in that cave. She did not probe
it. Because it had wakened her, she invested it with almost
holy significance and would not desecrate the memory by
bringing it out into the light for a look.

She was responsible for a network of watchtowers and
blockhouses shielding the Ponath from the Zhotak. It
seemed a pointless shield. The Zhotak was devoid of meth
life. Only a few far arctic beasts lingered there. They were
no threat to the Reugge.

That Gradwohl considered the northernmost marches
safe was indicated by Marika's command. She had twenty-
three novices to perform the duties of silth, and Dorteka to
advise her. Her huntresses and workers—commanded by
Grauel and Barlog, who had risen by being pulled along in
the wake of her own rise—were ragtag, of little use in areas
more active. Except inasmuch as the command gave her
some experience directing others, Marika thought the whole
show a farce.

The summer began with a month of nonevents in
noncountry. The Ponath was naked of meth except for its
Reugge garrisons. There was nothing to do. Even those
forests that were not dead were dying. The few animals seen
were arctic creatures migrating south. Summer was a joke
name, really. Despite the season, it snowed almost every
day.

There was a momentary break in the boredom during the
third week. One of the watchtowers reported sighting an
unfamiliar darkship sliding down the valley of the east fork
of the Hainlin, traveling so low its undercarriage almost
dragged the snow. Marika dived through her loophole,
caught a strong ghost, and went questing.

"Well?" Dorteka demanded when she returned.

"There may have been something. I could not make
contact, but I felt something. It was moving downstream."

"Shall I inform Akard?"

"I do not think it is necessary. If it is an alien darkship,

down, they will spot it soon

duled patrol."

trolled Marika's province
ported a complete absence of
mishing there was was taking
d the few nomads seen down there
radwohl wished. They were migrating
Serke country.

rumors that Serke installations had been

s like the Serke have lost their loyalty," Marika
orteka after having examined several such reports.
They have used them up. They will be little more than a
nuisance to our cousins."

"I wonder what the Serke bought them with. To have held
them so long on the bounds of death and starvation."

Dorteka said, "I think they expected to roll over us the
year they took Akard. The intelligence says they expected to
take Akard cheaply and follow that victory with a run that
would take them all the way to Maksche. Maksche certainly
could not have repelled them at the time. The glitch in their
strategy was you. You slew their leading silth and decimated
their best huntresses. They had nothing left with which to
complete the sweep."

"But why did they keep on after they had failed?"

"Psychological momentum. Whoever was pulling the
strings on the thing would have been high in the Serke
council. Someone very old. Old silth do not admit defeat or
failure. To me the evidence suggests that there is a good
chance the same old silth is still in charge over there."

"By now she must realize she has to try something else.
Or must give up."

"She cannot give up. She can only get more desperate as
the most senior thwarts her every stratagem."

"Why?"

"The whole world knows what is happening, Marika.
Even if no one admits seeing it. Our hypothetical Serke

councillor cannot risk losing face by conced
are a much weaker Community. Theoretically
ble for us to best the Serke."

"What do you feel about that?"

"I feel scared, Marika." It was a rare moment
on Dorteka's part. "This has been going on for ei
The Serke councillors were all old when it starte
must be senile now. Senile meth do things without
for consequences because they will not have to live
them. I am frightened by Gradwohl, too. She has a d
gard for form and consequence herself, without the exc
of being senile. The way she has forced you onto t
Community. . . ."

"Have I failed her expectations, Dorteka?"

"That is not the point."

"It is the only point. Gradwohl is not concerned about
egos. The Reugge face the greatest challenge of their history. Survival itself may be the stake. Gradwohl believes I
can play a critical role if she can delay the final crisis till I
am ready."

"There are those who are convinced that your critical role
will be to preside over the sisterhood's destruction."

"That doomstalker superstition haunts my backtrail
still?"

"Forget legend and superstition—though they are valid
as ways of interpreting that which we know but do not
understand. Consider personality. You are the least selfless
silth I have ever encountered. I have yet to discern a genuine
shred of devotion in you, to the Community or to the silth
ideal. You fake. You pretend. You put on masks. But you
walk among those who see through shadows and mists,
Marika. You cannot convince anyone that you are some
sweet lost pup from the Ponath."

Marika began to pace. She wanted to issue some argument to refute Dorteka and could not think of a one she
could wield with conviction.

"You are using the Reugge, Marika."

"The Reugge are using me."

"That is the way of —"

"I do not accept that, Dorteka. Take that back to Grad-wohl if you want. Though I am sure she knows."

Grauel witnessed this argument. She grew very tense as it proceeded, fearing it would pass beyond the verbal. Dorteka had been having increasing difficulty maintaining her self-restraint.

Marika had worked hard to bind Grauel and Barlog more closely to her. Again and again she tested them in pinches between loyalties to herself and loyalties to the greater community. They had stuck with her every time. She hoped she was laying the foundations of unshakable habit. A day might come when she would want them to stick with her through extreme circumstances.

For all she had known these two huntresses her entire life, Marika did not know them very well. Had she known them well, she would have realized no doubt of their loyalties ever existed.

Barlog entered the room. "A new report from Akard, Marika."

"It's early, isn't it?

"Yes."

"What is it?"

"Another sighting."

"Another ghost darkship?"

"No. This time it's a possible nomad force coming east on the Morthra Trail. Based on two unconfirmed sightings."

"Well, that is no problem for us."

The Morthra Trail was little more than a game track these days, lost beneath ten feet of snow. At one time it had connected Critza with a tradermale outpost on the Neybhor River, seventy miles to the west. The Neybhor marked the western frontier of Reugge claims in that part of the Ponath.

"Sounds like wishful thinking," Marika said. "Or a drill being sprung on us by the most senior. But I suppose we do have to pass the word. Dorteka, you take the eastern arc. I will take the western." Marika sealed her eyes, went inside, extended a thread of touch till she reached an underling in an outlying blockhouse. She relayed the information.

Two days later touch-word brought the news that Akard had lost contact with several western outposts. Darkships sent to investigate had found the garrisons dead. An aerial search for the culprits had begun.

One of the darkships fell out of touch.

Senior Educan sent out everything she had.

When found, the missing darkship was a tangle of titanium ruin. It had buried itself in the face of a mountain, evidently at high speed. The Mistress of the Ship and her bath appeared to have suffered no wounds before the crash.

"That is silth work," Marika said. "Not nomads at all, but Serke." She shivered. For an instant a premonition gripped her. Grim times were in the offing. Perhaps times that would shift the course of her life. "This must be the desperate move you predicted, Dorteka."

The instructress was frightened. She seemed to have suffered a premonition of her own. "We have to get out of here, Marika."

"Why?"

"They would send their very best. If they would go that far. We cannot withstand that. They will exterminate us, then ambush any help sent from Maksche."

"Panic is not becoming in a silth," Marika said, parroting a maxim learned at Akard. "You are better at the long touch than I am. Get Akard to send me a darkship."

"Why?"

"Do it."

"They will want to know why. If they have lost one already, they will want to hoard the ones that are left."

"Invoke the most senior if you have to."

Sighing, Dorteka started to go into touch.

"Dorteka. Wait. Find out which outposts were silenced. And where that darkship went down."

"Yes, mistress," Dorteka replied.

"Sarcasm does not become you. Hurry. Before those fools panic and run away."

Dorteka went into touch. Her strained, twisting face betrayed her difficulty getting through, then an argument ensuing. Marika told Grauel, "If those fools don't come across, I'll hike down there and take a darkship myself. Why did they put Educan in charge? She is worse that Paustch ever was. She couldn't . . . " Dorteka had come out of touch. "What did they say?"

"The darkship is coming. I had to lie, Marika. And I had to invoke Gradwohl. I hope you know what you are doing."

"What state were they in?"

"You can guess."

"Yes. Educan was packing. Grauel. Get my coats, boots, and weapons." On the frontier Marika dressed as one of the huntresses, not as silth.

Dorteka studied a map while Marika dressed. Marika glanced over her shoulder. "A definite progression, yes?"

"It does look like a developing pattern."

"Looks like? They will hit here next, then here, here, and then try Akard. No wonder Educan is in a dither. They will reach the Hainlin before dawn tommorow."

"You have that look in your eye, Marika. What are you going to do?"

No particular thought went into Marika's answer. "Ambush them at Critza." It was the thing that had to be done.

"They would sense our presence."

"Not if we use our novices to keep our body heat concealed."

"Marika". . . ."

"We will hit them on huntress's terms initially. Not as silth. They will not be looking for that. We will chew them up before they know what is happening."

"Critza is not inside your proper territory."

"If we do not do something, Educan will run off and leave us here. The Serke will not have to come after us. They can leave us to the grauken if they take Akard."

"True. But—"

"Perhaps one of the reasons Gradwohl favors me is that I am not bound by tradition. Not if form's sake means sticking my head into a kirn's den."

"Perhaps."

"Contact the outposts. We will gather everyone. Grauel. Prepare for two days of patrol for the whole force."

III

Marika kept the darkship aloft continuously, bringing huntresses to Critza, till she felt the Serke party could be within an hour of her ambush. The western outposts had fallen as she had predicted. Akard was in a panic. The leadership there had so wilted, Marika no longer bothered trying to stay in touch.

A pair of darkships raced over, fleeing south, practically dripping meth and possessions. "That," Marika observed, "is why we silth are so beloved, Dorteka. Educan has saved everthing she owns. But how many huntresses and laborers were aboard?"

Dorteka did not try to defend Educan. She was as outraged as Marika was, if not quite for the same reasons. The Akard senior's flight was indefensible on any grounds.

"Everyone in place?" Marika asked. There were no tracks in the snow, nothing to betray the ambush physically. The huntresses had dropped into their positions from the darkship. "See if you can detect anybody, Dorteka. If you do, get on the novice covering." She could detect nothing with her own less skillful touch.

Fear proved to be a superb motivator. The novices hid everyone well.

"That is it for Chaser," Marika said as the last of the major moons settled behind the opposite ridge. But there was light still. Dawn had begun to break under a rare clear sky. Long shadows of skeletal trees reached across the Hainlin. The endless cold had killed all the less hardy. They were naked of needles. Occasionally the stillness filled with the crash following some elder giant's defeat in its battle with gravity. Farther north, where the winds kept the slopes scoured of snow, whole mountains were scattered with fallen trees, like straw in a grain field after harvest.

A far hum began to build in the hills opposite Critza. "Utter silence now," Marika cautioned. "Total alertness. Nobody move for any reason. And hold your fire till I give the word. Hold your fire." She hoped it would not be much longer. The cold gnawed her bones. They had dared light no fires. The smell of smoke would have betrayed them.

A machine thirty feet long and ten wide eased down the far slope, sliding between trees. It slipped out onto the clear highway of the rivercourse, surrounded by flying snow. For a moment Marika was puzzled. It seemed like a small darkship of odd shape, floating above the surface. It made a great deal of noise.

Then she recalled where she had seen such a vehicle. At the tradermale station at Maksche.

Ground-effect vehicle. Of course.

A second slithered through the trees, engine whining as it fought to keep from charging down the slope. Marika silently praised Grauel and Barlog for having established superb discipline among the huntresses. They were waiting as instructed.

They dared not open fire till all the craft were in the open.

She could see meth inside them, ten and an operator for each of those first two. At a guess she decided two silth and eight fighters aboard each. And definitely not nomads.

What had Bagnel told her about ground-effect vehicles? Yes. They were not sold or leased outside the brethren. Ever.

This ambush would stir one hell of a stink if she pulled it off.

A third and fourth vehicle left the forest. These two appeared to be supply carriers. No heads were visible through their domes, only unidentifiable heaps.

A fifth vehicle descended the slope, and a sixth. And still those already on the river hovered, waiting.

Marika ground her teeth. How much longer could fire discipline hold among huntresses already badly shaken by what faced them?

Not long. As the eighth vehicle appeared, making four carrying meth and four carrying supplies, a rifle cracked.

The huntress responsible was a competent sniper. Her

bullet stabbed through a dome and killed an operator. The vehicle surged forward, gained speed rapidly, rose, and smashed into a bluff a third of a mile upriver. Its fuel exploded.

Long before that happened Marika's every weapon had begun thundering at the Serke. For a while the vehicles were hidden by smoke and flying snow.

Two more vehicles came down into the storm of death.

"Get that darkship up over the trail," Marika snapped at the Mistress of the Ship. "Wait. I am going with you. I do not want you following Educan. Dorteka. Keep hitting them. Get the personnel carriers first."

A vehicle broke out of the fury and scooted away north, sideslipping around the burning vehicle upstream. "That was a transport. We will catch it later. Take it up."

The darkship rose. At a hundred feet Marika could see that the remaining craft had been disabled. Huntresses had come out of some and were returning fire.

A fuel tank blew, spread fire to other crippled vehicles. The conflagration generated a battle between volatile fuel and melting snow. Burning fuel spread atop the running melt.

Marika reached with her touch and found several silth minds among the survivors, all bewildered, shocked, unready to respond. She jerked back, ducked through her loophole, grabbed the first suitable ghost she found, and hurtled down there. Slap. Slap. Slap. She dispatched three silth.

There were at least four more vehicles in the forest, all carrying silth and huntresses. They had halted. Marika flung herself that way, hammered at silth hearts and minds till she encountered one that hurled her back and nearly broke through her defenses.

She ducked back into the world long enough to order the darkship forward. The bath carried automatic weapons and grenades. She would wrestle the Serke sisters while the darkship crew demolished them with mundane weapons.

And so it went for a few minutes, the bath crippling two of the vehicles. Marika fenced the strong Serke sister, and

ducked around her occasionally, discovered that hers was
the only Serke silth mind still conscious.

On the river the survivors of the ambush were getting
organized. The Serke silth ducked away from Marika and
went to prevent Dorteka and the novices from overwhelming
her fighters.

The huntresses on the mountainside headed down to help
their sisters. They fired on the darkship as they went.

You are a strong one, the Serke silth sent. *But you will
not survive this.*

I have survived the Serke before, Marika retorted. *This is
the end of the Serke game. Here, today, you will all die.
And you will leave the Reugge the proof needed to call the
wrath of all the Communities down upon the Serke. You
have fallen into the trap.*

You are the one called Marika?

Yes. Which great Serke am I about to destroy?

None.

The silth slammed at her. Marika barely turned the blow,
interposing her ghost between herself and that ruled by the
Serke. She had made a tactical error. She had issued too
strong a challenge before fully assessing the strength of the
other's ghost. It was more powerful than hers.

Bullets hummed around the darkship. One spanged off
the metal framework. Marika wondered why the ship was
not moving, making itself a more difficult target. She
ducked into reality for a second, saw that one bath had been
wounded and another had been knocked entirely off the
darkship. The Mistress had only one bath to draw upon. She
could do little but remain aloft, a target for rifle fire.

Marika flung a hasty touch Dorteka's way. *Dorteka. Get
some mortar fire into the woods up here. Under the darkship. Before they bring us down and we are all lost.*

The Serke attacked again. She wobbled under the blow,
fought its effects, tried to locate a more powerful ghost.
There was none to be reached quickly enough. There were
some great ones high above that might have been drawn in
had she had time, but the Serke would give her no time.

She dodged another stroke, slipped back into reality.

Bombs had begun to fall on the slope below. Had she had the moment, Marika would have been amused. Those mortars were all captured weapons, taken from slain nomads. The brethren were adamant in their refusal to sell such weapons to the Reugge.

She located the Serke silth visually. The female stood beside her disabled vehicle. Marika tried a new tack, hammering at the snow in the trees above the meth.

A shower fell, distracting the silth. Marika used the moment won to stab at the huntresses firing on the darkship. She slew several. The others broke and ran.

The silth regained her composure, punched back, adding, *You do not play the game by the rules, pup.*

Marika dodged, sent, *I play to win. I own no rules.* She struck at a tree instead of the silth. The brittle trunk cracked. The giant toppled—in the wrong direction. She cracked another, then fended off the silth again.

This was not going well. The Serke was wearing her down. And the darkship had begun to settle toward the surface. For the first time she felt uncertainty. The Serke sensed it, hurled mockeries her way.

Angered, she cracked several more trees. This time the Serke was forced to spend time dodging the physical threat.

Marika used the time to unsling her rifle and begin firing. Her bullets did not touch the silth, but they forced her to keep moving, ducking, too busy evading metal death to employ her talent.

Marika hurled a pair of grenades. One fell close. Its blast threw the silth ten feet and left her stunned.

Marika took careful aim, pumped three bullets into the sprawled form, the last through the brain.

"That should do—"

The darkship began to wobble, to slide sideways, to tilt.

The Mistress of the Ship had been hit by a stray bullet.

She had wanted to fly for so long. Marika's thoughts were almost hysterical. She hadn't wanted her first opportunity at flight to come at a time like this! She grabbed at the ship with her mind, trying to put into practice what she knew only as theory, while she edged out the long arm toward the wounded Mistress.

Tree branches crackled as the darkship settled. Marika was afraid a giant would snap and in its fall sweep her and the darkship to the surface.

Without her and the darkship, the Serke would win still.

The darkship was low. She'd probably survive the fall. Still, she had to do more than survive. She had to save the darkship. She had to be available to support her huntresses, who were in a furious firefight with the Serke huntresses. She had to . . .

She reached the Mistress of the Ship. Despite the meth's salvageable condition, Marika pitched her off the position of power, ignored her cry of outrage as she fell. There was no time for niceties.

Marika closed into herself, felt for those-who-dwell, who had begun scattering, summoned them, made them stabilize the craft before it fell any farther. She drew upon the bath and willed the ship to rise.

It rose. Smoothly and easily, it rose, amazing her. This was easy! She turned it, drove it toward Critza, brought it down a little roughly just a few feet from its original hiding place.

The wounded bath died moments later, drained of all her strength. The other passed out. Marika had drawn upon them too heavily.

Marika had nothing left herself. Darkness swam before her eyes as she croaked, "Dorteka! What is the situation?"

"They have gotten dug in. There are too many of them, and they still have a few silth left. Enough to block our dark-side attacks. We dare not assault them. They would cut us apart. I am hoping the mortars will give us the needed edge. You killed the leader?"

"Yes. It was a close thing, too. I had to trick her, then shoot her. Keep using the mortars to pin them down till I recover. No heroics. Hear?"

Dorteka gave her a look that said she was a fool if she expected heroics from her teacher.

Marika drained her canteen, ate ravenously, rested.

Weapons continued to crackle and boom, but she noticed them not at all.

The Serke huntresses had gotten out of their transport with nothing but small arms. Thank the All for that. Thank the All that she had been able to think quickly aboard the darkship. Else she would be dead now and the Serke would soon be victorious.

The moment she felt sufficiently strong, she ducked through her loophole, found a monster of a ghost, flung it toward where the surviving Serke silth cowered, arguing about whether or not they should try to retreat to the two unharmed vehicles and flee.

They were terrified. They were ready to abandon their followers to their fates. The one thing that held them in place was their certain knowledge of what defeat would mean to their Community.

Marika sent, *Surrender and you shall live.*

One of them tried to strike at her. She brushed the thrust aside.

She killed them. She touched their huntresses and told them to surrender, too, then slaughtered those who persevered till she had no more strength. She returned to flesh. "The day is yours, Dorteka. Finish it. Round up the survivors."

When it was all done neither Marika nor Dorteka had strength enough to touch Akard and let the garrison there know that the threat had been averted.

Grauel started fires and began gathering the dead, injured, and prisoners inside the ruins of Critza. She came to Marika. "All rounded up now."

"Many surrender?"

"Only a few huntresses." Her expression was one of contempt for those. "And five males. Tradermales. They were operating those vehicles."

"Guard them well. They mean the end of the threat against the Reugge. I will examine them after I have rested."

Chapter Twenty

I

The moons were up, sprawling skeletal shadows upon the mountainsides. As Marika wakened, it seemed she could still hear the echoes of shots murmuring off the river valley walls. "What is it?" Barlog had shaken her gently. The huntress wore a grim expression.

"Come. You will have to see. No explanation will do." She offered a helping paw.

Marika looked at Grauel, who shrugged. "I've been here watching over you."

Barlog said, "I moved the prisoners over here, where I thought we could control them better. I did not notice, though, till one of the males asked if they could have their own fire. I spotted him when the flames came up. Before that it was like he was somebody else."

"What are you talking about?" Marika demanded.

"I want you to see. I want to know if I am wrong."

Mairka eased between fallen building stones, paused. "Well?"

Barlog pointed. "There. Look closely."

Marika looked.

The astonishment was more punishing than a physical blow. "Kublin!" she gasped.

The tradermale jerked around, eyes widening for a moment.

Kublin. But that was impossible. Her littermate had died eight years ago, during the nomad raid that destroyed the Degnan packstead.

Grauel rested a paw upon Marika's shoulder, squeezed till it hurt. "It is. Marika, it is. How could that be? Why did I not recognize him earlier?"

"We do not look for ghosts among the living," Marika murmured. She moved a couple of steps closer. All the prisoners watched, their sullenness and despair for a moment forgotten.

The tradermale began shaking, terrified.

"Kublin," Marika murmured. "How? . . . Grauel. Barlog. Keep everybody away. Don't say a word to anyone. On your lives." Her tone brooked no argument. The huntresses moved.

Marika stood there staring, remembering, for a long time. Then she moved nearer the fire. The prisoners crept back, away. They knew it was she who had brought them to this despair.

She settled onto a stone vacated by a Serke huntress. "Kublin. Come here. Sit with me."

He came, sat on cold stone, facing away from the other prisoners, who pretended not to watch. Witnesses. Something would have to be done. . . .

Was she mad?

She studied her littermate. He was small still, and appeared no stronger than he had been, physically or in his will. He would not meet her eye.

Yet there was an odor here. A mystery more than that surrounding his survival. Something odd about him. Perhaps it was something in the way the other males eyed him beneath their lowered brows. Was he in command? That seemed so unlikely she discarded the notion immediately.

"Tell me, Kublin. Why are you alive? I saw you cut down

by the nomads. I killed them . . ." But when the fighting
ended, she recalled, she had been unable to find his body.
"Tell me what happened."

He said nothing. He turned slightly, stared into the fire.
The other males came somewhat more alert.

"You'd better talk to me, Kublin. I'm the only hope you
have here."

He spat something derogatory about silth, using the dia-
lect they had spoken in their packstead. He mumbled, and
Marika no longer used the dialect even with Grauel and
Barlog. She did not catch it all. But it was not flattering.

She patted his arm. "Very brave, Kublin. But think.
Many of my huntresses died here today. Those who survived
are not in a good temper. They have designs on you prisoners. Especially you males. You have broken all the codes and
covenants. So tell me."

He shrugged. "All right."

He was never strong with her, Marika reflected. Only that
time he tried to murder Pohsit.

"I crawled into Gerrien's loghouse after dark. There was
still a fire going in the male end. I tried to get to it, but I fell
into the cellar. I passed out. I do not remember very much
after that. I kept trying to get out again, I think. I hurt a lot.
There was a fever. The Laspe found me several days later. I
was out of my mind, they said. Fever and hunger."

Marika drew one long, slow, deep breath, exhaled as
slowly. Behind closed eyes she slowly played back the
nightmare that had haunted her for so long. Being trapped
in a dank, dark place, badly hurt, trying to climb a stair that
would not permit climbing. . . .

"The Laspe nursed me back to health, out of obligation. I
must have been out of my head a long time. My first clear
memories are of the Laspe three or four weeks after the
nomads came. They were not pleased to have me around.
Next summer, when tradermales came through, I went
away with Khronen. He took me to Critza. I lived there till
the nomads came and breached the walls. When it became
obvious help from Akard would not arrive in time, the
master put all the pups aboard the escape vehicles and

helped us shoot our way out. We were sent someplace in the
south. When I became old enough, I was given a job as a
driver. My orders eventually brought me here."

A true story, Marika thought. With all the flesh left off
the bones. "That's it? That's all you can tell me about eight
years of your life?"

"Can you say much more about yours?"

"What were you doing here, Kublin?"

"Driving. That is my job."

A truth that was at least partly a lie, Marika suspected.
He was hiding something. And he persisted in using the
formal mode with her. Her. When they had been pups, they
had used only the informal mode with one another.

"Driving. But driving Serke making an illegal incursion
into Reugge territory, Kublin. You and your brethren knowingly violated age-old conventions by becoming directly
involved in a silth dispute. Why did you do that?"

"I was told to drive. Those were my orders."

"They were very stupid orders. Weren't they?"

He would not answer.

"This mess could destroy the brethren, Kublin."

He showed a little spirit in answering, "I doubt that. I
doubt it very seriously."

"How do you expect the Communities to respond when
they hear what brethren have done?"

Kublin shrugged.

"What's so important about the Ponath, that so many
must die and so much be risked, Kublin?"

He shrugged again. "I don't know."

That had the ring of truth. And he had given in just
enough to have lapsed into the informal mode momentarily.

"Maybe you don't." She was growing a little angry. "I'll
tell you this. I'm going to find out."

He shrugged a third time, as though he did not care.

"You put me in a quandary, Kublin. I'm going to go away
for a little while. I have to think. Will you be a witness for
me? Before the Reugge council?"

"No. I will do nothing for you, silth. Nothing but die."

Marika went away, amazed to find that much spirit in

him. And that much hatred of silth. So much that he would not accept her as the littermate he had shared so much with.

Marika squatted beside Grauel. She nodded toward the prisoners. "I don't want anyone else getting near them," she whispered. "Understand?"

"Yes."

Marika found herself a place beside the main fire, crowding in among her surviving novices. She did not pay them any heed.

Kublin! What was she to do? All they had shared as pups. . . .

She fell asleep squatting there. Despite the emotional storm, she was too exhausted to remain awake.

Marika wakened to the sting of cold-blown snow upon her muzzle and the crackle of small-arms fire. She staggered up, her whole body aching. "What now?"

Snow was falling, a powder driven by the wind. A vague bit of light said it was near sunrise. She could see just well and far enough to discover that yesterday's bodies and wreckage already wore a coat of white. "Dorteka! What is happening?"

"Nomads. There was a band following the Serke force. They stumbled onto the voctors I had going through the vehicles on the far slope."

"How many are there?"

"I do not yet know. Quite a few from the sound of it."

Marika moved out into the open to look across the valley. She was surprised at the effort it took to make her muscles carry out her will. She could see nothing through the falling snow. "I am still worn out. I used up far more of me than I thought yesterday."

"I can handle this, Marika. I have been unable to detect any silth accompanying them."

Marika's head had begun to throb. "Go ahead. I must eat something. I will be with you when I can."

The firing was moving closer. Dorteka hurried off into the falling snow. Marika turned, stiffly returned to the fire where she had slept, snatched at scraps of food. She found a half-finished cup of soup that had gone cold, downed it. That helped some almost immediately.

Stiffly then, she moved on to the prisoners.

Grauel sat watching them, her eyes red with weariness. "What is all the racket, Marika?"

Marika glared at the prisoners. "Nomads. Our friends here had a band trailing them, probably to take the blame." They must have known. "I wondered why the reports mentioned sighting nomads but not vehicles." She paused for half a minute. "What do you think, Grauel? What should I do?"

"I can't make a decision for you, Marika. I recall that you and Kublin were close. Closer than was healthy, some thought. But that was eight years ago. Nearly half your life. You've gone different paths. You're strangers now."

"Yes. There is no precedent. Whatever I do will be wrong, by Degnan law or by Reugge. Get some rest, Grauel. I'll watch them while I'm thinking."

"Rest? While there is fighting going on?"

"Yes. Dorteka says she can handle it."

"If you say so."

"Give me your weapons. In case they get ideas. I don't know if my talents would respond right now."

"Where are your weapons?"

"I left them where I fell asleep last night. Beside the big fire. Go on now."

Grauel surrendered rifle and revolver, tottered away.

Marika stared at the prisoners for a few minutes. They were all alert now, listening to the firing as it moved closer. Marika suspected they would be very careful to give no provocation. They nurtured hopes of rescue, feeble as those hopes might be.

"Kublin. Come here."

He came. There seemed to be no defiance left in him. But that could be for show. He was always a crafty pup.

"What do you have to say this morning?" she asked.

"Get me out of this, Marika. I don't want to die."

So. He knew how much real hope there was for a rescue by the nomads. "Will you stand witness for me?"

"No."

That was an absolute, Marika understood. The brethren had won Kublin's soul.

"I don't want you to die, Kublin. But I don't know how to save you." She wanted to say a lot more, to lecture him about having asked for it, but she refrained. She recalled how well he had listened to lectures as a pup.

He shrugged. "That's easy. Let me run. I overheard your huntresses saying there were two vehicles that weren't damaged. If I could get to one. . . ."

"That's fine for you. But where would it leave me? How could I explain it?"

"Why would you have to explain anything?"

Marika indicated the other prisoners. "They would know. They would tell when they are interrogated. You see? You put me into a terrible position, Kublin. You face me with a choice I do not want to have to make."

The firing beyond the river rose in pitch. The nomad band seemed to be very large. Dorteka might be having more trouble than she had expected.

"In the confusion that is causing, who is going to miss one prisoner? You could manipulate it, Marika."

She did not like the tone of low cunning that had come into his voice. And she could not shake the feeling that he was not entirely what he seemed.

"My meth aren't stupid, Kublin. You would be missed. And my novices would detect you sneaking toward those vehicles. They would kill you without a thought. They are hungry for blood. Especially for male blood, after what they have learned here."

"Marika, this is Critza. Critza was my home for almost four years. I know this land. . . ."

"Be quiet." Marika folded in upon herself, going away, opening to the All. It was one of the early silth lessons. Open to intuition when you do not know what to do. Let the All speak to your soul.

The dream returned. The terrible dream with the pain and the fever and the fear and the helplessness. That had been Kublin. Her mind had been in touch with his while he was in his torment. And she had not known and had not been able to help.

Grauel was right. Though he appealed to the memory, this Kublin was not the Kublin with whom she had shared the loft in their dam's loghouse. This was a Kublin who had gone his own way, who had become something.... What *had* he become?

That horrible dream would not stay away.

Perhaps her mind was not running in appropriate channels. Perhaps her sanity had surrendered briefly to the insanity of the past several dozen hours, to the unending strain. Without conscious decision she captured a ghost, went hunting her novices, touched each of them lightly, striking them unconscious.

Dorteka, though, resisted for a moment before going under.

She returned to flesh. "All right, Kublin. Now. Start running. Go. Take one of your vehicles and get out of here. This may cost me. Don't slow down for anything. Get away. I can't cover you for long."

"Marika...."

"Go. And you'd better never cross my path again, in any circumstances. I'm risking everything I've become for your sake."

"Marika...."

"You damned fool, shut up and get out of here!" She almost shrieked it. The pain of it had begun gnawing at her already.

Kublin ran.

The other prisoners watched him go, a few of the males rising, taking a pace or two as if to follow, then freezing when they saw the look in Marika's eye. Their mouths opened to protest as, slowly, as if of its own volition, Grauel's rifle turned in her paws and began to bark.

They tried to scatter. She emptied the rifle. Then she drew the pistol and finished it.

Grauel and the surviving bath sister rushed out of the snowfall. "What happened?" Grauel demanded.

"They tried to run away. I started to nod off and they tried to run away."

Grauel did not believe her. Already she had counted bodies. But she did not say anything. The bath looked studiedly blank. Marika asked her, "How do you feel this morning? Able to help me move ship?"

"Yes, mistress."

"Good. We'll start toward Akard as soon as Dorteka finishes with the nomads."

The firing was rolling toward the river quickly, Marika realized.

Then she gasped, suddenly aware of what she had done. By knocking out the novices so Kublin could slip away, she had robbed her huntresses of their major advantage in the fight. They had no silth to support them. She plunged into the hollowness inside herself, reached out, found a ghost, flogged it across the river.

She had done it for sure. The huntresses were in retreat from a nomad party that had to number more than two hundred. Most of the novices had been found and slain where she had left them unconscious.

Stupid. Stupid. Stupid.

She captured a stronger ghost. With it she hit the nomads hard, decimating them. They remained unaware of what was happening because so few could see one another through the snowfall. They came on, and they kept overtaking Marika's huntresses.

She extricated Barlog from a difficult situation, scanned the slopes, killing here and there, and by the time she returned to Barlog found the huntress trapped again.

Only a dozen of her meth made it to the river.

Only when they assembled before taking up the pursuit in the open did the nomads discover how terribly they had been hurt.

Marika ravened among them then, and they panicked, scattered.

She searched for Kublin. She found him starting up the far slope safely downstream from the action. She stayed with him till he reached an operable vehicle, silencing any nomad who came too near. Though he seemed aware of their presence almost as soon as she, and shied away. And as he had said, he knew the land and made use of its masking features.

Even so, she hovered over him while he transferred fuel to fill one vehicle's tanks, then got it going. As it began climbing the trail over which the attack had come, Marika hurried back to her proper form.

When she came out she was more exhausted than she had been the evening before.

"Marika?" Grauel asked. "Are you all right?"

"I will be. I need food and rest. Get me something to eat." The firing had stopped entirely. "Any word from over there?"

"Not yet. You went?"

"Yes. It looked awful. There were hundreds of savages. And Dorteka guessed wrong. There were silth with them. Wild silth. Most of our meth are dead, I think. Certainly most of the novices are. I could find no sign of them."

Grauel's lips twitched, but she said nothing. Marika wondered what thoughts lay behind her expressionless eyes.

Huntresses began to straggle in almost as soon as Grauel had gotten a cookfire going. Only seven showed. Marika turned inward and remained that way, loathing herself. She had fouled up about as bad as it was possible to do. That All-be-damned Kublin. Why did he have to turn up? Why couldn't he have stayed dead? Why had fate dragged him across her trail just now?

"Marika? Food." Grauel gave her of the first to come from the fire. She ate mechanically.

Dorteka staggered out of the snowfall fifteen minutes after Marika began eating. She settled beside the fire. Grauel gave her food and drink. Like all the rest of them, she ate and stared into the flames. Marika did not wonder what she saw there.

After a while Dorteka rose and trudged toward where the prisoners had been held. She was gone fifteen minutes. Marika was only marginally aware that she had gone.

Dorteka returned. She settled beyond the fire, opposite

Marika. "The prisoners tried to get away during the fighting?"

"Yes," Marika said, without looking up. She accepted another cup of broth from Grauel. The broth was the best thing for a silth who reached this exhausted state.

"One got away. A trail runs down the slope. I heard an engine over there while I was coming back. Must have been one of the males."

"I do not know. I thought I got them all." She shrugged. "If one got away he will take warning to the rest."

"Who was he, Marika?"

"I do not know."

"You helped him. Your touch cannot be disguised. You were directly responsible for the deaths of all of our novices and most of the huntresses. Who was he, Marika? What is this thing you have with males of the brotherhood? Why was the escape of this one so important you destroyed yourself?"

Was there no end to it?

Marika clutched Grauel's revolver beneath her coat. "You believe what you have said. Yes. I see that. What are you going to do about it, Dorteka?"

"You have left me no choice, Marika."

Powder burned Marika's paw. The bullet struck Dorteka in the forehead, threw her backward. She lay spasming in the snow, her surprise lingering in the air of touch.

The huntresses yelped and began to rise, to grab for weapons. Grauel and Barlog did the same, but slowed by tangled loyalties.

This would be the ultimate test of their faith, Marika thought as she slipped through her loophole, grabbed a ghost, and struck at the seven.

The last fell. Marika waited for the bullet that would tell her Grauel or Barlog had turned against her. It did not come. She returned to flesh, found both huntresses staring at her in horror. As was the bath from the darkship, who had been sleeping for so long Marika had forgotten her.

She summoned what remained of her strength and energy and rose, collected a rifle, put several bullets into each of the downed huntresses so it would look like nomads had slain them.

"Marika!" Barlog snarled.

Grauel laid warning fingers upon her wrist.

Marika said, "The snow will cover everything. We will report a huge battle with savages. We will be the only survivors. We will be stricken with sorrow. The Reugge do not Mourn their dead. There is no reason anyone should investigate. Now we rest."

Her companions radiated the sort of fear huntresses betrayed only in the presence of the mad. Marika ignored them.

She would pull it off. She was sure she would. Grauel and Barlog would say nothing. Their loyalties had passed the ultimate test. And now their fates were inextricably entwined with hers.

II

Just a few minutes more, Marika thought at the All. Just a few more miles. They had to be close.

The limping darkship was just a hundred feet up, and settling lower all the time. And making but slight headway. Snowflakes swirled around Marika. The north wind pushed at her almost as hard as she was able to push against it. When she risked opening her eyes to glance back, she could barely distinguish the bath at the girder's far end. Grauel and Barlog, riding the tips of the crossarm, were scarcely more visible.

The huntresses had little strength she could draw, but she took of them as well as of the bath. She also dredged deep into her own reserves. She knew she was not doing this right, that she was devouring far more energies than needful in her crude effort, but survival was the prize.

Only savage will kept the darkship aloft and moving.

Will was not enough. Cold gnawed without mercy. Weariness ravened as Marika rounded the last bend of the Hainlin before it forked around Akard, the ship's rear grounding strut began to drag in the loose snow concealing the river's face. Marika sucked one final dollop of strength from the bath and herself, raised the darkship a few yards, and threw it forward.

The draw was too much for the bath. Her heart exploded.

The rear of the darkship dropped into the snow. The ship began tilting left. The left arm caught. Grauel and Barlog tumbled off. The flying dagger tried to stand on its point. Marika arced through bitter air and, as snow met her, flung one desperate touch at the shadowy fortress looming above her.

III

Marika opened her eyes. She was in a cell walled with damp stone. A single candle provided weak light. She could not distinguish the features of the face above her. Her eyes refused to focus.

Had she damaged them? A moment of panic. Nothing was so helpless as a blind meth.

"Marika?"

"Is that you, Grauel?"

"Yes."

"Where are we? Did we make it to Akard?"

"Yes. Most Senior Gradwohl is on comm from Maksche. She wants to talk to you."

Marika tried to rise. Her limbs were quicksilver. "I can't. . . ."

"I'll have you carried there."

The face disappeared. Darkness and dreams returned. The dreams were grim. Ghosts wandered through them, taunting her. The most prominent was her littermate, Kublin.

She was lying in a litter when she revived. The smell of soup tempted her. She opened her eyes. Her vision was better this time. Barlog walked beside her, her gait the strained labor of a tired old Wise meth. She carried a steaming stoneware pot. Her face was as empty as that of death. The bitter chill behind her eyes when she met Marika's gaze had nothing to do with weariness.

"How did we get here?" Marika croaked.

"You touched someone. They sent huntresses out after us."

"How long ago?"

"Three days."

"That long?"

"You went too far into yourself, they say. They say they had trouble keeping you anchored in this world." Did she sound the slightest disappointed?

So many times Dorteka had warned her against putting all her trust in those-who-dwell. There were ways less perilous than walking the dark. . . . So close.

Barlog said, "They sent huntresses to Critza to find out what happened there. In case you did not make it. Their fartoucher reported by touch this morning. The most senior wanted to know when she did. She wanted you wakened when that happened. Even she was not certain you could be drawn back."

Gradwohl had taken a direct interest? Mild trepidation fluttered through Marika. But she hadn't the energy for real fear. "Give me a cup of that soup."

Barlog stopped the stretcher-bearers long enough to dole out a mug of broth. Marika gulped it down. In moments she felt a surge of well-being.

The soup was drugged. But not with chaphe. That would have propelled her back into the realm of nightmare.

Barlog said, "The most senior did not think to question simple huntresses such as Grauel and I."

Marika understood the unstated message.

Grauel met them at the comm room door. "I have placed a chair facing the screen, Marika. I will be over here, out of hearing, but watching. If you have trouble, signal me and we will develop technical difficulties." The huntress chased the technicians out. There would be no outside witnesses.

"I can handle it," Marika said, wondering if in fact she

could match her show of confidence with actions. The most senior was difficult enough to fool even when Marika had full control of her faculties.

She kept her eyelids cracked as Grauel and Barlog levered her into the chair.

The face on the screen was not that of the most senior at all, but of Braydic. Braydic looked as if she had put in some hard hours of worry. Good Braydic. She would have to be remembered in times to come.

The distant communications technician said something to someone at her end, moved out of view of the pickup.

Gradwohl replaced her. The most senior appeared concerned but neither suspicious nor angry. Maybe the effort to make it look like the nomads had wiped out the ambush had been successful.

Marika opened her eyes. "Most senior. I am here."

"I see. You look terrible."

"They tell me I did stupid things, mistress. I may have. It was a desperate and narrow thing. But I think I will recover."

"Tell me about it."

Marika told the story exactly as it had happened till the moment she had discovered Kublin. She left her littermate out of it. She left her treachery out of it. Of course. "I am not sure why the nomads were following so far behind. Maybe the Serke outdistanced them in their eagerness to reach and silence Akard before help was summoned. Whatever, I was unprepared for the advent of nomads. They surprised us while I was unconscious and my huntresses were scattered, going through the damaged vehicles. They overran everyone and crossed the river before anyone wakened me. Then the prisoners broke away and added to the confusion.

"Had the snowfall not been so heavy the savages might have been intimidated by their losses. But they could not see those. It came to hand-to-hand fighting in our camp before I managed to slay the last silth protecting them. And then I did not have the strength to finish them. All I could do was lie there while my huntresses died around me.

"Mistress, I must take responsibility for this disaster. I have betrayed you. Through my inattention I turned victory into defeat."

"What defeat, Marika? It was costly, yes. I will miss Dorteka. But you broke the Serke back. You saved the Ponath. They will not try anything like this again."

"Mistress, I . . ."

"Yes?"

"I lost my command. I lost Dorteka. I lost many valuable novices. I lost everything. This is not a thing to celebrate."

"You won a triumph, pup. You were the only one to stand her ground. Your seniors lost heart and fled before the battle was joined. And I am certain the Serke did not make it easy for you. Or you would not be in the state you are now."

"There was one of their great ones with them," Marika reiterated. "I bested her only through trickery."

Gradwohl ignored her remarks. Her voice took on a flint-knife hardness. "Educan is going to rue her male cowardice. The tall tales she told when she reached Makusche will cost her every privilege she has." A glint of humor appeared in the most senior's eye. "You would have appreciated her expression when the news came that you had saved Akard. That the garrison she abandoned there never saw hair of the invaders."

"Mistress, I fear what might happen if news of this gets out to other Communities."

"I am two steps ahead, pup. Let the villains quake and quiver. Let them wonder. What happened is not going to leave the circle of those who know now. We will let the snows devour the evidence."

Marika sighed.

"We are not ready for the upheaval going public would cause. We have years yet to go."

Marika was puzzled by what Gradwohl said. She told herself not to underestimate the most senior. That female had a labyrinthine mind. She was but a little animal being run through its maze, hoping she could keep her head well enough to use as much as she was used. "Yes, mistress. I was about to suggest that." *Let* the snows devour the evidence.

"I think we will have less trouble with the Serke now. Do you agree? Yes. They will walk carefully for a while, now. Come back to Maksche, Marika. I need you here."

Marika could think of nothing to say. Her mind refused to function efficiently.

"You flew the darkship blind, untrained, with but one bath to support you. I am impressed and pleased. You give me hope."

"Mistress?"

"It is time your education moved into new, more practical areas."

"Yes, mistress."

"That is all for the moment, Marika. We will examine this more closely after you return. When you are more fully recovered. A darkship will come for you soon."

"Thank you, mistress."

The most senior stepped off pickup. Braydic reappeared for a moment, made an encouraging gesture. Then the screen blanked.

"You ducked that one, didn't you?" Grauel asked. When Marika glanced her way, she found the huntress's back turned.

The most senior turned out the cloister in Marika's honor. Because only a very few knew the whole story, the older sisters acclaimed her only grudgingly.

"What do they want of me?" Marika asked Grauel. "No matter what I accomplish, they resent it." She was surprised that, after all these years facing the disdain of the Reugge Wise, she could still be hurt by their attitudes.

"I do not know, Marika." Grauel's voice was tired, cold, remote. "You are a heroine now. Your future is assured. Is that not enough?" She would not criticize, but censure choked her body language.

For a very long time she and Barlog would speak to Marika only when the course of everyday business required it.

Chapter Twenty-one

I

For a year the Reugge were free from outside pressures. The Serke Community assumed a posture of retrenchment that baffled the silth world. They seemed to be digging in quietly in anticipation of some great fury while overtly shifting more of their energies into offworld ventures. But nothing happened.

Some who watched the brethren closely noted that they, too, sought a lower profile. Some of the constituent bonds, especially those strongest politically within the brotherhood, also seemed to anticipate some great terror. But nothing happened.

Except that Most Senior Gradwohl of the Reugge gathered legates of the Communities at the Reugge complex in TelleRai to formally announce a major victory over the savages plaguing the Reugge northern provinces. She declared those territories officially pacified.

The savages had come to concern several other Communities whose lands bounded the Reugge and would have been threatened had the Reugge campaign been unsuccessful.

Those Communities were pleased by Gradwohl's declaration.

Gradwohl publicly announced that a young Reugge sister named Marika had engineered the end of the savages' tale.

Privately, Marika did not believe the threat to be extinct. She thought it only dormant, a weapon the Serke would unsheathe again if that seemed profitable.

TelleRai, where many silth Communities maintained their senior cloisters, simmered with speculations. What was the truth behind this bland bit of Reugge folkloring? Who was this deadly Marika, of whom there had been rumors before? Why was Gradwohl taking so little genuine note of what in fact amounted to a withering defeat for Serke intrigues? What was the Reugge game?

Already Gradwohl was a shadowy, almost sinister figure to the silth of TelleRai, known by reputation rather than by person. Her intensity and determination on behalf of a relatively minor, splinter Community, while she herself remained an enigma, were making of her an intimidating legend, large beyond her actual strength. Her spending most of her time away from TelleRai only strengthened the aura of mystery surrounding her.

Was the legend striving toward some goal greater than plain Reugge survival? Her plots were intricate, complex, though always woven within the law. . . . She made more than the Serke ruling council uncomfortable.

Once a month, on no set day, Marika left the Maksche cloister and walked to the brethren enclave. The only escort she accepted consisted of Grauel and Barlog.

"I will not be loaded down with a mob of useless meth," she insisted the first time after her return from the north. "The more I drag along, the more I have to worry about protecting."

It had become customary for a silth sister daring the streets to surround herself with a score of armed guards. Invariably there would be at least one sniping incident.

Marika wanted to get the measure of the rogue infestation. In the back of her mind something had begun to see them as potentially useful, though she had as yet formulated nothing consciously.

Silth learned to listen to their subconscious even when not hearing it clearly.

The rogues did not bother her once, though she presented an inviting target.

Grauel and Barlog invariably chided her. "Why are you doing this? It's foolish." They said it a dozen ways, one or the other, every time.

"I'm proving something."

"Such as?"

"That there is a connection between the rogue problem and the nomad problem."

"That has been the suspicion for years."

"Yes. But the Serke always get blamed for all our troubles. This is more in the nature of a practical experiment. If they feel I really burned their paws in the Ponath, maybe they'll be afraid to risk troubling me here. *I* want to be satisfied that the same strategists are behind both troubles."

She had other suspicions that she did not voice.

More than once Barlog admonished, "Do not become too self-important, Marika. The fact that we do not draw fire in the street may have nothing to do with it being you that is out there."

"I know. But I think if we are ignored often enough, it would be safe to say it's purposeful. Especially if everybody else still gets shot at. Right?"

Reluctantly, both huntresses admitted that that might be true. But Grauel added, "The Serke will now think that they have a blood debt to balance. They will want your life."

"*I* might stoop to murder to achieve my ends," Marika admitted. "But the Serke will not. That's more a male way of doing things, don't you think?"

Grauel and Barlog looked thoughtful.

Marika continued, "The Serke are too tradition-bound to eliminate an important enemy that way." She did not add that others with, perhaps, an equal interest in her death would not be bound by silth customs. Let the huntresses figure that out for themselves.

Those untraditional meth might be the ones who controlled the rogues tactically.

"You're in charge, Marika," Grauel said. "You know what you are doing, and you know the ways of those witches. But that city out there is wild country, for all its pretense to civilization. The wise huntress remains always alert when she is on the stalk."

"I will keep that in mind."

She did not need the admonition. She made each trip by a different route, carefully keeping near cover, with more wariness than even Grauel demanded. She probed every foot of the way with ghosts before she traversed it.

Not once did she divine the presence of would-be assassins.

Did that mean the Serke in fact controlled their unholy alliance with the brethren—or only that all her enemies were equally intimidated?

During that, the year of silence, Marika and Bagnel sparred carefully and subtly, each gently mining the other for flecks of information. Marika often wondered if he was as conscious of her probable mission as she was of his. She suspected he was. He was quite intelligent and perceptive. For a male.

Halfway through the year Bagnel began teaching her to fly one of the brethren's simplest trainers. His associates and hers alike were scandalized.

The visits to Bagnel relieved a growing but as yet unspoken pressure upon Marika. On returning from the Ponath she had been eligible for the final rites of silth adulthood, the passage that would admit her into full sisterhood among the Reugge. But she had not asked to be passed through the ritual. She evaded the subject however obliquely it arose, hinting that she was too busy with her duties, too involved with learning the darkship, to take out the months needed for preparation.

She did spend most of her waking time studying and practicing the methods of the silth Mistresses of the Ship, driving herself to exhaustion, trying to become in months what others achieved only after years.

II

It was not her darkship, of course, but she fell into the habit of thinking of it that way. It was the cloister's oldest and smallest, its courier and trainer. There were no other trainees and few messages to be flown. Its bath were old and drained, no longer fit for prolonged flights. They were survivors of other crews broken up by time or misfortune during the struggle with the savages. They did not mesh perfectly, the way bath did after they had been together a long time, but they did so well enough to give a young Mistress-trainee a feel for what she had to learn.

Marika had the most senior's permission to avail herself of the darkship anytime it was not employed upon cloister business. It almost never was. She had it to herself most of the time. So much so that when an occasion for a courier flight did arise, she resented having it taken from her.

She spent as much time aloft as the bath would tolerate.

They did have the right to refuse her if they felt she was using them or herself too hard. But they never did. They understood.

One day, drifting on chill winds a thousand feet above Maksche, Marika noticed a dirigible approaching. She streaked toward it, to the dismay of Grauel and Barlog, and drifted alongside, waving at the freighter's master. He kept swinging away, disturbed by silth attention.

She thought of Bagnel, realized she had not seen him in nearly two months. She had been too engrossed in the darkship.

She followed the frieghter in to the enclave.

She dropped the darkship onto the concrete just yards from Bagnel's office building. Tradermales surrounded her immediately, most of them astonished, many of them armed, but all of them recognizing her as their security chief's strange silth friend.

Bagnel appeared momentarily. "Marika, I swear you'll get yourself shot yet." He ignored the scowls his familiarity won from Grauel and Barlog.

"What's the matter, Bagnel? Another big secret brethren scheme afoot out here?" She taunted him so because she was convinced such schemes did exist. She hoped to garner something from his reactions.

"Marika, what am I going to do with you?"

"Take me up in a Sting. You've been promising for months. Do you have time? Are you too busy?"

"I'm always busy." He scratched his head, eyed her and her huntresses and bath, all hung about with an outrageous assortment of weapons. Marika refused to leave the cloister unarmed, and even there usually carried her rifle. It was her trademark. "But, then, I've always got time for you. Gives me an excuse to get away from my work."

Right, Marika thought. She grew ever more certain that *she* was his primary occupation. "I've got a better idea than the Sting. You're always taking me up in your ships. Let me take you up on mine."

Grauel and Barlog snapped, "Marika!"

The eldest of the bath protested, "Mistress, you forget yourself. You are speaking to a male." She was scandalized by Marika's use of the familiar even more than by her invitation.

"This male is my friend. This male has ridden a darkship before. He did not defile it then. He will not now. Come on, Bagnel. Do you have the courage?"

Bagnel eyed the darkship. He examined the small platform at the axis, usually shared by Grauel and Barlog. He licked his lips, frightened.

Marika said, "Grauel, Barlog, you stay here. That will give him more room."

The huntresses surveyed the unfriendly male crowd with narrowed eyes. Unconsciously, Barlog unslung her rifle. Grauel asked, "Is that wise, Marika?"

"You'll be all right. Bagnel will be my hostage for your

safety. Come on, tradermale. You claim to be the equal of any female. Can you fly with no cushion under your tail and no canopy to keep the wind out of your whiskers?"

Bagnel licked his lips and approached the darkship.

Grauel and Barlog stepped down. Marika suggested, "Use the harness, Bagnel. Don't try to show off the first time. First-timers have been known to get dizzy and fall if they aren't harnessed."

Bagnel was not too proud to harness himself. He did so carefully, under the grim gaze of the leading bath.

They were angry, those old silth. Marika expected them to resist when she tried to take the darkship up, so she lifted off before they were ready, violently, shocking them into assuming their roles for their own safety's sake.

She made a brief flight of it, stretching her capabilities, then brought the darkship down within inches of where it had settled before.

Bagnel unfastened his harness with trembling fingers. He expelled a great breath as he stepped down to the concrete.

"You look a little frayed," Marika teased.

"Do I, now? Ground crew! Prepare the number-two Sting. Come with me, Marika. It's my turn."

Grauel, Barlog, and the bath watched, perplexed, as Bagnel seated Marika in the Sting's rear seat and strapped her in.

"What's this?" Marika asked. She had worn no harness when they had flown in trainers.

"Parachute. In case we have to jump."

Bagnel wriggled into the forward seat, strapped himself in. One of the ground crew spun the ship's airscrew. The engine coughed, caught, belched smoke that stung Marika's eyes and watered her nose. The ground crew jerked the blocks away from the ship's wheels.

The aircraft bucked and roared with a power unlike any Marika had seen in the trainers. Its deep-throated growl swelled, swelled. When Bagnel let off the brakes, the ship raced down the airstrip, jumped into the air, climbed faster than was possible for any darkship.

Bagnel leveled off at one thousand feet. "All right, smart pup. Let's see about *your* courage."

The Sting tilted, dove. The airstrip swelled, spun. Buildings whirled dizzyingly. "You're getting too close," Marika said.

The ground kept coming up. *Slam!* It stopped spinning. *Slam!* Marika's seat pressed into her back hard. Her guts sagged inside her. The ground slid away ahead. The horizon appeared momentarily, then whipped upward as Bagnel dumped another fifty feet of altitude. It reappeared and rotated as Bagnel rolled the aircraft. It seemed she could pluck the frightened growls from the lips of Grauel and Barlog as the ship roared past them.

The great engine grumbled more deeply as Bagnel demanded more of it. Clouds appeared ahead—and slid away as Bagnel took the ship over onto its back. He completed the loop, resumed the climb, reached five thousand feet, and went into a stall. The ship spun and fluttered.

Bagnel turned, said, "I've been meaning to ask you about that business in the Ponath last summer. What happened anyway? I've heard so many different stories. . . ."

Marika could make no sense of what was happening outside. She clung to her courage by a thread. "Shouldn't you be paying attention to what you're doing?"

"No problem. I thought this would be a chance to talk without those two arfts hanging over your shoulder."

"I ambushed a mob of nomads. It was a tough fight. Hardly anybody got out on either side. That's all there was to it." Her eyes grew wider as the surface drew closer.

"Really? There are so many rumors. I suppose they're exaggerated."

"No doubt." He was digging. Carrying out an inquiry on instructions from his masters, she supposed. The brethren seniors would be getting nervous. They would want to know the Reugge game. That amused her mildly. She did not know the game herself. The most senior kept its strings held close to her heart.

"Looks like time to do something here," Bagnel said. "Unless you'd like to land the hard way?"

"I'd rather not."

"You're a cool one, Marika."

"I'm scared silly. But silth aren't allowed to show fear."

He glanced back, amused, then faced forward intently. He took control. The world stopped rocking and spinning. Then Bagnel went into a hard roll.

Something popped in the right wing. Marika watched a strut tear away, dragging fabric and wire. The ship staggered. The fragment spun behind, whipping at the end of a wire, threatening to pull more wing with it. "I think we might have trouble, Bagnel."

"I think you might be right. Hang on. I'll take us down."

His landing was as stately and smooth as any he had made in a trainer. He brought the wounded ship to a halt just yards from his ground crew, killed the engine. "What did you think, Marika?"

The roar in her ears began to fade. "I think you got even. Let's don't do that to each other anymore."

"Right." He unbuckled, climbed out, and dropped from the lower wing to the concrete. Marika followed. When he finished briefing the ground crew about the strut, he told Marika, "You'd better leave now. My masters won't be happy as it is."

"Why not?"

"You dropped in unannounced. Better give warning from now on. Every time."

Marika glanced at the freighter. She wondered if it really had brought in something the tradermales did not want seen by silth eyes. "All right. Whatever you say. Oh. I wanted to tell you. The most senior says it's all right if you want to visit me at the cloister. If you have time off and have nothing better to do. My time isn't as tight as it once was. I spend most of it learning the darkship. Maybe we could try another flight on one."

News of that permission had scandalized the older sisters. Already they considered her friendship with Bagnel a filthy reflection upon the cloister, a degradation, though there was nothing even a little scandalous in the relationship. When her periodic estrus threatened, Marika was scrupulous about sinter, the self-isolation of silth who had not yet completed the Toghar ceremonies leading to full sisterhood.

The pressure remained silent, but it was mounting. Her resistance was becoming more conscious.

III

Marika learned to manipulate a darkship as well as any Mistress of the Ship assigned to the Maksche cloister. And she did so in months instead of years.

She was not accepted within the select group of Mistresses, in their separate and sumptuous cloister within a cloister, though they did condescend to speak with her and give her advice when she asked it. No more was she accepted by the bath, who, in their way, formed a subCommunity even more exclusive than that of the Mistresses. They, like everyone else, had become frightened of the talent she showed.

There was nothing more she could learn from them anyway. She told herself she did not hurt for lack of their society. She had become the best again.

She received a summons to Gradwohl's presence. She believed her accomplishments were the reason for it, and felt vindicated in her belief when, after the amenities and obeisances, Gradwohl said, "If you belonged to a major Community, Marika, you would be destined for the big darkships. For the stars. There are moments when I hurt because the Reugge are too small for you. Yet, there *is* tomorrow."

In private Gradwohl seemed partial to such cryptic remarks. "Tomorrow, mistress?"

"You once asked why we do not build our own darkships anymore. When the brethren announced that they would no longer replace darkships lost by the Reugge, I started looking into that. I located sisters willing to soil their paws on the Community's behalf. I found more of them than I expected. We are not as far gone in sloth and self-importance as one like yourself might think. I have them hidden away now, with a good crew of workers to help them. They have begun to report modest successes. Extracting the titanium is more difficult than we expected.

"But there are several golden-fleet groves within the Reugge territories. Those most immediately threatened by the advancing ice I have ordered harvested. Old shipwrights with the ancient skills promise me that we do not need to be fancy, and that wood can be substituted many places even in the brethren designs.

"So we will no longer be dependent. May a curse fall upon all male houses. If this works out the way I expect, we may even be able to build our own void darkships."

Marika arrayed her face in a carefully neutral expression. Now she understood the additional, intensified silth exercises she had been assigned on her return from the Ponath.

There was little more she could learn from teachers available at Maksche. Indeed, she seemed to have exhausted the Reugge educational resources. Her responsibilities as a councillor took up very little time. She was free to pursue private studies and to expand her silth capacities. Gradwohl insisted she do the latter, feeling she was especially weak in her grasp of the far touch.

The far touch was a talent increasingly rare because the use of telecommunications was so much easier. One side of Marika was lazy enough to want to ignore the talent—just as that lazy side throughout the Reugge Community was responsible for the talent's diminution. She rebelled against that laziness, hammered away at learning. And at times was very amused at herself. She, the outsider, the cynic about silthdom's traditional values, seemed to be the Community's most determined conservator of old ways and skills.

Often she wrestled the question of why Gradwohl wanted her to become the complete silth when what she really wanted was to create a Mistress of the Ship able to darkwar for the Reugge.

In one of her more daring moods, Marika asked the most senior, "Is Bestrei getting old, mistress?"

"You cannot be fooled, can you? Yes. But we all age. And

the Serke, knowing how much their power depends upon their capacity for darkwar, have other strong darksiders coming up behind Bestrei."

"Yet you believe I will be able to conquer them."

"In time, pup. In time. Not now. I have never encountered anyone with your ability to walk the dark side. Not even Bestrei herself. And I have met her. But you are far from ready for such a confrontation. The Reugge must survive till you have been tempered, and hardened in your heart, and till we have built ourselves a true voidfaring darkship, and assembled bath who can fare the dark with you."

"So that is why you have been avoiding confrontation when you knew you could force it and probably win the backing of the other Communities."

"Yes. I am playing this game for the biggest stakes imaginable."

Marika put that aside. She said, "I have had an idea for a device I think would be useful. To test it I would need someone from communications to modify one of the receivers for taking signals off the satellite network."

"You are zigging when I am zagging, Marika." Gradwohl appeared mildly baffled.

"I want to try to steal the signals of other sisterhoods, mistress. From what Bagnel has said, doing so should not be difficult. Just a matter of altering one of the receivers so it will accept signals other than our own."

Gradwohl reflected for a moment. "Perhaps. The males would be most incensed if ever they discovered the fact." Like mechanized transport, communications equipment came from the brethren on lease. Only minor repairs were permitted the lessees.

"They will not find out. I will use receivers we took away from the nomads."

"All right. You have my permission. But I suspect you will find it more trouble than it is worth. Any messages of importance will be couched in the secret languages of the Communities sending them. And in code besides, if they are critical. Still, much could be learned from the daily chatter between Serke cloisters."

Marika was more interested in intercepting data returned from tradermale research satellites, but she could not have interested the most senior in that. Gradwohl was an obsessive, interested only in defeating the Serke and augmenting Reugge power. "We might even find out what is so important about the Ponath," Marika said. "If we knew that we might become a more powerful Community simply by possessing the knowledge."

"That is true." Gradwohl did not seem much interested in pursuing the thought, though. Something else was on her mind. Marika had a glum suspicion. Gradwohl said, "Let us get to the point, Marika. To the reason I called you here."

"Yes, mistress?"

"Utiel is about to retire."

"Mistress?" Marika knew what was coming. Utiel was fourth on the Maksche council. Only first chair, or senior, held more real power.

"I want to move you to fourth chair, Marika."

"Thank you, mistress. Though there will be protests from —"

"I can quiet the egos of those passed over, Marika. Or I could if I did in fact move you up. I said I want to move you. I cannot. Not the way things stand."

Marika slipped into her cautious role. "Mistress?" She controlled her emotions rigidly. Fourth chair she wanted badly. It could become her springboard into the future.

"Fourth chair is understudy for third as well as being responsible for cloister security, Marika."

She knew that well. In the security responsibility she saw opportunities that seemed to have evaded those who had held the chair before.

Gradwohl continued, "Third chair is liaison with other cloisters, Marika. A coordinating position. A visible, public position. As fourth, understudying, you would be expected to begin making contacts outside the Maksche cloister. As fourth you would become known to the entire sisterhood as my favorite. As fourth you would be seen to have ambitions beyond Maksche.

"For all those reasons your behavior and record would be subjected to the closest scrutiny by those who hope to place obstacles in your path.

"From fourth chair, Marika, it is only a step to an auditor's seat at conventions of the Reugge seven at TelleRai."

"I understand, mistress."

"I do not think so, Marika."

"Mistress?"

"Never has one so young sat upon the Maksche council. Or any other cloister council, except in legend. But the sisters here accept your age, if grudgingly, because of your demonstrated talent, because of all you have done for the Community, and especially because you have my favor. They can brag about you before sisters from other cloisters. You have helped put a remote cloister upon the map, so to speak. But there are limits to what their pride and my power can force them to swallow."

"Mistress?"

"They would revolt before they permitted you to assume a position in which you would represent this cloister elsewhere, pup."

"You have lost me, mistress."

"I doubt that. I doubt that very much. You know exactly what I am talking about. Don't you? I am talking about Toghar, Marika. You have been eligible for the ceremony since you returned from the Ponath. You have put it off repeatedly, calling upon every excuse you can muster."

"Mistress. . . ."

"Listen, Marika. I am speaking of roads to the future opened and closed. If you continue to evade the ceremony you will not only not rise any higher than you are now, you will begin to slide. And there will be nothing I can do. Tradition must be observed."

"Mistress, I—"

"Marika, you have many dreams. Some I know, some I infer, and some must be entirely hidden. You are one moved by dreams." The most senior stared at her intently. "Listen, pup. Marika. Your dreams all live or die with that ceremony. No Toghar, no stars. And the darkship will go. We cannot invest so much of the Reugge in one who will not invest of herself in the Community."

She awaited an answer. None came.

"Pay the price, Marika. Demonstrate your dedication. So many smaller, weaker, less dedicated silth have done so before you."

Still Marika did not respond.

She had witnessed the Toghar ceremonies. They were not terrible, just long. But the cost. . . . The price of acceptance as an adult silth, with full privileges. . . .

She had no plans to birth pups, ever. She did not wish to be burdened with trivial, homey responsibilities. Yet to surrender the ability to dam them . . . it seemed too great a price.

She shook her head. "Mistress, do you have any idea what Grauel would give to possess the ability you are asking me to surrender? What she would *do?* We came out of the Ponath, mistress. I carry the burden of ten years of living with and accepting those frontier values that—"

"I know that, pup. The entire cloister knows. That is why I am being pressed to push your ceremonies. There are those who hope you will stumble upon that early training."

She had already. When she had released her littermate Kublin. Where was he now? There had been none of the terrible nightmares since that day on the Hainlin. Had she laid some ghosts?

"Make up your mind, Marika. Will you be silth? Or will you be a Ponath huntress?"

"How long do I have, mistress?"

"Not long. There are pressures I cannot resist forever. So make it soon. Very soon."

Smug bitch, Marika thought. She was sure what the decision would be. She thought she had Marika's every emotional end tied to a puppet string.

"But enough of that now, Marika. I also want your

thoughts on the rogue situation. Did you hear that there was another factory explosion last night?"

"At another place belonging to someone friendly to us?"

"It was at the tool plant. That pushes the brethren down the list of suspects, does it not?" When she spoke in council, Marika always insisted the brethren were connected with the rogues.

"No."

There had been a series of explosions lately, all of which had damaged meth bonded to the Maksche cloister. One bomb had gone off in a farm barracks during sleeping hours, killing twenty-three male field workers. Rumor blamed disaffected males. As yet there had been no captures of those responsible.

Marika, like everyone else in the cloister, believed the Serke were responsible. But unlike everyone else, she believed the rogues were drawing support from within the tradermale enclave. Were, perhaps, striking from there, and thus remaining unseen.

"There is no such evidence, Marika," the most senior argued. "Males are naturally foolish, I admit, but there are few fools among the Brown Paw Bond—with whom we have had an understanding for centuries."

"There is no evidence because no one is trying to collect it, mistress. Why is it that Utiel cannot catch the males responsible for these explosions? Is she not trying? Or is she just inept? Or could it be that she still does not believe the rogues to present a threat worth taking seriously? Do they have to start throwing bombs over the cloister wall before we take direct action? I have heard that several of the Communities have begun watching us here."

"Do not lecture me, pup. Utiel has tried. She is old and has her faults, I admit, but she has tried. She has been unable to detect them. It is almost as if the rogues have found a way to hide from the touch."

"So must we be so dependent upon our talents? Must we be wholly committed to one method of looking? We cannot assume a reactionary stance and expect to handle this sort of threat."

"You have a better idea?"

"Several. Again, does Utiel take all this seriously enough? I do not believe she does. Old silth grumble about rogues but just go on about their business. They say there are always a few rogues. It is a pestilence that will not quite go away. But this is a disaffection that has been growing for years. As you know. And it is clear that there is organization behind it. Organization and widespread communication. It is worst here in Maksche, but the same shadow falls upon a dozen other Reugge cloisters. I think we would be fools to just try waiting it out. Before long we would be watching the Educans run away when reality closes in."

"You will not forgive her, will you?"

"I lost a lot of meth because of her. If she had not lost her nerve, we could have devoured the nomads and Serke before they knew what hit them."

The most senior looked at her hard. Marika was sure Gradwohl had not swallowed her whole story about what had happened at Critza. But she was equally certain that the most senior did not suspect the truth.

She hoped Kublin had had sense enough to keep his mouth shut.

"I would have had her shot, mistress. Before the assembled cloister."

"Perhaps. You think you can do better with the rogues? You think you can handle the security function of fourth chair? Then take charge."

"Mistress?"

"It is fourth chair's responsibility."

"Will you assign me the powers I will need to get the job done?"

"Will you take the Toghar rites?"

"Afterward."

Gradwohl eyed her coldly. "This is your watershed, pup. You had better. There will be no more bargaining. Be silth, or be gone. You can have whatever you need. Try not to walk on too many toes."

fugitives from the law, were seen enterin
ay."
d back in an unconscious snarl, and sh
of the strain that had him so edgy.
ght the orders necessary for their removal
. They have a future in the mines."
be some mistake."
ever, Bagnel. Each of these meth has been
rt, on evidence presented by confederates.
een passed. Each was seen entering here.
photographs of them doing so? I will have to
ister for them." She ran a spur-of-the-
d bluff with that remark. Photo surveillance
her only in retrospect.
job you do, by now you have heard about
wn. I presume your staff were involved in
r back." Give him a ready-made excuse.
this list fled here. They are here still. No
t the enclave. You have two hours to deliver
and Barlog. If you do not, you will be
lation of the conventions and your charter."
aghast.
Barlog waited outside with a dozen armed

Bagnel's tone was plaintive. "Marika, that
reat."
have a copy of the charter negotiated before
ssumed control of this enclave. I have added
personal information."
ined the map first. "I do not understand."
speech in the formal mode.
te that it shows your enclave surrounded
belonging directly to the Reugge Commu-
me they assumed control, the Brown Paw
rcraft. Now they do. You must know that the
that no aircraft of any sort may be flown
without direct permission of the sisterhood

Paw Bond have never obtained that permis-

Chapter Twenty-two

I

Marika moved quickly, drafting every silth and huntress she respected. Two nights after receiving the most senior's blessing, she began moving small teams into every site she believed to be a potential rogue target. She followed the dictum of the ancient saw, "The night belongs to the silth." She moved in the dark of the moons, by low-flying darkship, unseen even by those who managed the places she chose to protect.

She was certain there would be an attack soon. Some show of strength. She had written Bagnel bragging about her appointment, transparently implying that she suspected his bond of being behind the rogues.

If he was what she believed, and reported the contents of her letter to his factors, there should be a move made in an effort to show nothing so simple would frighten them off. Or to make it appear the Brown Paw Bond really had no control over the rogue group.

She hoped.

Her planted teams kept themselves concealed from those who worked and dwelt in and around the potential targets.

Marika herself shifted to a nighttime schedule, remaining aloft on the trainer darkship she had made her own.

The rogues waited four days. Then they walked into it. It could not have gone better for Marika had she been giving the villains their orders.

Three were slain and two captured in an action so swift no shots were fired. Marika lifted the captives out quietly and carried them to the cloister aboard her darkship.

One of those two managed to poison himself. The other faced a truthsaying.

He yielded names and addresses.

Marika threw teams out aboard every darkship the cloister possessed, ignoring all protests, invoking the most senior where she had to. By dawn seven more prisoners had been brought into the cloister. Five lived long enough to be questioned.

A second wave of raids found several rogues forewarned or vanished completely. This time there was some fighting. Few rogues were taken alive.

Even Marika was surprised at how many rogues Maksche boasted.

The third wave of raids took no prisoners at all. Few rogues were found. But weapons and explosives enough for an arsenal were captured, along with documentary evidence of rogue connections in TelleRai and most cities where the Reugge maintained cloisters.

Marika had the captured arms laid out upon the cloister square. The dead rogues joined them.

"Very good, Marika," Gradwohl said as she and the Maksche councillors inspected the take. "Very impressive. You were right. We were too passive, and even I underestimated the scale and scope of what was happening. No one could see this and remain convinced that we are dealing with the usual scatter of malcontents. I will order all the Reugge cloisters to —"

"Excuse me for interrupting, mistress. It would be too late for that. The rogues will have vanished everywhere. Posting rewards might help a few places, if they are large enough. A point that I have to make, over and over till

everyone understand
sentiments, and all th
almost everywhere, t
the Reugge."

"Noted," Gradwo
Marika. The Serke ar
rogues themselves wo

"They did not whe
"Where did they g
Marika felt certain
was about to give—an

"You did not collec
know this. So where
resigned to a great ur

"Into the traderma
watched. As a sort o
rapidly after we bega
round. Almost no one

"So they are safe fi
"Safe? Mistress? A
ties? Is there no mecl
convention territories?

"We shall see." Gra
of the council. "Come

"If there is no mecha
softly.

The most senior gav
would, pup." A few pa
care. Sometimes this
different from that of t
the better path to winr

"You didn't let me kr
plained. "How come yo
around." He looked ab
under a strain.

"Official business th
clipboard she carried,
numbers by heart. She

"These meth, al
this gate yester

His lips peele
knew the cause

"I have broug
from the enclav

"There must
"None whatso
convicted in cou
Sentence has b
Would you like
send to the clo
moment, inspire
had occurred to

"Holding the
the ruckus in to
this behind you

"The males on
airships have le
them to Graue
considered in vi

Bagnel looke
Grauel and
huntresses.

"Marika . . .
sounds like a tl

"No. Here I
your brethren a
a map for your

Bagnel exam
He couched his

"You will n
entirely by land
nity. At the ti
Bond had no ai
conventions say
over silth lands
involved."

"Yes, but—
"The Browr

sion for the Maksche enclave, Bagnel. They have never applied. The enclave is in violation of the conventions. Overflights will cease immediately. Otherwise sanctions will be applied."

"Sanctions? Marika, what in the world is going on here?"

"Any aircraft or airship attempting to leave this enclave will be destroyed. Come." She led him to the doorway, showed him three darkships slowly circling the enclave.

Bagnel opened and closed his mouth several times, said nothing.

Marika presented a fat envelope. "This contains a formal notice of the Reugge Community's intent to cancel all Brown Paw Bond charters that now exist within Reugge territories."

"Marika...." Bagnel began to get hold of himself. "These fugitives. You really want them that badly?"

"Not really. Not personally. It would not matter now if you did sneak them out. They are dead. Bounties have been posted on them—very large bounties. As you once noted, the Reugge are a very wealthy Community. No. What is at stake is a principle. And, of course, my future."

Bagnel looked puzzled. She had come at him hard, from unexpected directions, and had managed to keep him off balance.

"I have reached a position of substance within my sisterhood, Bagnel. I am very young for it. My age alone has made me many foes. Therefore I have to consolidate my position and fashion a springboard to a greater future. I have chosen to do that in my usual way, by taking the offensive against enemies of the Community. My opponents inside the sisterhood are unable to fault that." A pause for effect. "Those who get in my way can expect the worst."

"You intend to climb over *me?*"

"If you get in my way."

"Marika, I am your friend."

"Bagnel, I value you as a friend. I have treasured your friendship. Often you were the only one I could turn to."

"And now you are so strong you do not need me anymore?"

"Now I am so strong I do not need to blind myself to what

you are doing. Nor was I ever so weak as to allow crimes to be committed simply because a friend was involved."

"Involved?"

"Drop the act, Bagnel. You know the brethren are backing the Serke effort to steal the Ponath from us. You know the brethren have been sponsoring the terrorism practiced by disaffected males. It is another ploy against us. You use criminals now that there are no more nomads to be your proxies. You even flew in males from outside because Maksche did not produce enough villains of its own. Now, is that something I should ignore simply because one of the behind-scenes movers is a friend?"

"You are mad, Marika."

"You will stop. Cease. Give me my prisoners and do nothing more. Or I will see the Brown Paw Bond torn apart like an otec rent by kagbeasts."

"You are totally insane. They have given you a taste of power and it has gone to your head. You begin imagining nonexistent plots."

"Phoo! Think, Bagnel. I struck near the mark, yes? Insofar as you know? Naturally, you have not been trusted with full knowledge. You deal with me. You traffic with silth. Can they trust you? When they hoard knowledge the way old Wise females hoard metal in the Ponath? You recall my great triumph up there, so called? Did you know that nomads had very little to do with it? Did you know that what I defeated was actually an invasion carried out by Serke and armed brethren, with a few hundred nomads along for show? If you do not know these things, then you have been used worse than I suspect."

Almost out of pity she stopped hitting him. She could see that he was hearing much of this for the first time. That, indeed, he had been used. That he did not want to believe, yet his faith was being terribly tested.

"Enough of that. Friend. When you report to your factors, as inevitably you must before you dare yield the criminals I want, tell them for me that I can produce thirteen burned-out ground-effect vehicles, with their cargoes and the corpses of their drivers and passengers, anytime I feel inclined to assemble delegates from the various Communities."

Bagnel composed his features, but could not help staring.

"You do not have to believe me, Bagnel. Just tell them what I said. Nice word, 'driver.' It is from the brethren secret speech, is it not? Not everyone aboard those vehicles died in the ambush."

"What is this madness you're yammering?"

He was innocent of guilty knowledge, she was now sure. A tool of his factors. But he had heard so many wild rumors that she now had him on the edge of typical male panic. Composed as he kept his face, his eyes glittered with fear. His hackles had risen and his head had dropped against his shoulders. She wanted to reach out to him, to touch him, to reassure him. To tell him she did not hold him personally responsible. She could not. There were witnesses. Any softening would be perceived as weakness by those who were not here and did not know them.

"The message will register once you pass it along, Bagnel. Tell them the price of silence is their desertion of the Serke. Tell them they can tell the Serke that if they want to do us in, henceforth they must come at us directly, without help."

He began to understand. At least, to understand what she wanted him to understand. He whispered, "Marika. As a friend. Not as Bagnel the tradermale or Bagnel the security chief of this enclave. Don't push this. You'll get rolled under. I know nothing of the things you have talked about. I do know that you cannot withstand the forces that are ranged against the Reugge. If you really have the sort of evidence you claim, and I report it, they will kill you."

"I suspect they'll be reluctant to try, Bagnel." She spoke in a whisper herself, and pointed to one of the circling darkships, to make those watching think she was talking about her threats. "Their force commander in the Ponath was the Serke number four. Stronger than anyone but Bestrei herself. She's dead. And I'm here."

"There are other ways to kill."

Marika rested a paw upon the butt of her rifle. "And I know them. They may have their way with the Reugge. But they will pay in blood. And pay and pay and pay. We have just started fighting, Gradwohl and I."

"Marika, please. You're too young to be so ruled by ambition."

"There are things I want to do with my life, Bagnel. This struggle with the Serke is a distraction. This scramble is something I want to get over early. If I sound confident of the Reugge, that's because I am. In the parlance of your brethren, I believe the hammer is in my paw. I'd rather you and your silth allies just went away and left us alone. I'd rather not fight. But I am ready to bring on the fire if that is the way they want it. You may tell them that we Reugge believe we have very little to lose. And more to gain than they can imagine."

Bagnel sighed. "You always were headstrong and deaf to advice. I will tell my factors what you've said. I'll be very much interested in their response myself."

"I'm sure you will. As you walk over there, keep one eye on the darkships up top. Keep in mind that they have orders to kill anyone who tries to leave the enclave. You can shoot them down if you like. But I don't think even the Serke will tolerate that."

"I hope you know what you're doing, Marika. I really do. I think, though, that you don't. I think you have made some grave and erroneous accusations, and based serious miscalculations upon them. I fear for you."

She *was* making a long bet, setting the price of protecting the rogues so high the brethren factors would have no choice but to surrender them. A success would cement her standing within the Community.

She did not care if the silth liked her, so long as they respected and feared her.

"I intend to be very careful, Bagnel. I give these things more thought than you credit me for. Go. Grauel and Barlog will be waiting here at the gate." She walked through the building beside him, halted at the door to the airstrip, counted silently while he walked fifteen steps. "Bagnel!"

"What?" he squeaked as he whirled.

"Why is the Ponath worth risking the very existence of the brethren?"

An instant of panic betrayed him. If he did not know, he had firmly founded suspicions. Perhaps because the tradermales of Critza had been involved from the beginning?

"The plan is for the brethren to betray the Serke after they take over, isn't it? The brethren think they have some way to force the Serke out without a struggle."

"Marika. . . ."

"I questioned some of the drivers who were with the Serke invaders, Bagnel. What they didn't know was as interesting as what they did."

"Marika, you know very well I do not know what you are howling about. Tell me. Does Most Senior Gradwohl know what you are doing here?"

"The most senior has ambitions greater than mine."

That was not a direct answer, but Bagnel nodded and resumed walking, his step tentative. He glanced at the circling darkships only once. His head lowered against his shoulders again.

She had rattled him badly, Marika knew. Right now he was questioning everything he knew and believed about his bond. She regretted having had to use him so harshly. He *was* a friend.

Given her victory, the day would come when things would balance.

When she returned to the street outside the enclave, Grauel asked, "Are they going to cooperate?"

"I think they will. You can put anything over on anybody if you sound tough enough and confident enough."

"And if they are guilty as charged?"

"That will help a lot."

Barlog looked at one of the darkships. "Did you really order . . . ?"

"Yes. I could not run the bluff without being willing to play part of it out. They might test me."

Barlog winced, but said nothing.

II

Grauel received the rogue prisoners within the deadline. "But nine of them were given over dead, Marika," she reported.

"I expected that. They resisted being turned over, did they?"

"That is what Bagnel told me."

"Want to bet the dead ones could have connected the brethren of the enclave with their movement?"

"No bet. They had to get their weapons and explosives somewhere. Bagnel slipped me a letter, Marika. A personal communication, he said."

"He did?" She was surprised. After what she had put him through? "Let's see what he has to say."

Bagnel said much in few words. He apologized for his brethren having betrayed the conventions. He had not believed her at the gate, but now he had no choice. He was ashamed. As his personal act of contrition, he appended two remarks. *"Petroleum in the Zhotak. Pitchblende in the western Ponath."*

Petroleum she understood instantly. She had to go to references to make sense of the other.

She hurried to Gradwohl's quarters. "My cultivating the male Bagnel has finally paid a dividend, mistress," she reported. She did not mention the brethren yielding the criminals. Gradwohl's meth would have reported all that already. "He has told me what is so important about our northern provinces."

"You broke him down? How? I had begun to think him as stubborn as you."

"I shamed him. I showed him how his factors had been making a fool of him, using him in schemes he would not have touched had they asked him directly. But no matter. He has turned over the rogues, and he has given me the reason behind all the years of terror.

"Petroleum and pitchblende. Our natural resources. Considering what they were willing to risk, the deposits must be huge."

"Petroleum I understand." It was a scarce commodity, very much in demand in the more advanced technological zones farther south. "But what is pitchblende? I have never heard of it."

"I had to look it up myself," Marika admitted. "It is a radioactive ore. A source of the rare heavy elements radium and uranium. There is very little data available in our resources, but there is at least the implication that the heavy elements could become an energy source far more potent than petroleum or other fossil fuels. The brethren already use radioactives as power sources in some of their satellites."

"Space. I wonder.... Now I wonder why the Serke would.... ?"

"Yes. Suddenly, it looks like we have seen everything backward, does it not? For a long time I thought the Serke were using the brethren. Now I think the brethren have been using the Serke the way the Serke used the nomads. The Serke promised a great prize and secret support. The savages had little real choice, pressed as they were by the onset of the ice age. The brethren in turn baited their snare with the petroleum of the Zhotak. And the Serke leapt on it like an otec onto the scraps of greasy bread huntresses use in their traps along the side creeks. I am sorry. The brethren. I believe they are interested in the pitchblende."

"You have evidence?"

"Only intuition at this point."

Silth accepted intuition as a reliable data base. Gradwohl nodded. "Can you guess what their motives might be?"

"I think that brings us full circle, back to the problem that put me in a position to learn what I have. I think their ultimate goal is the destruction of the silth. Not just the Reugge, a minor Community, but all silth everywhere."

"That is stretching intuition into the wildest conjecture, Marika. Into implausible conjecture."

"Perhaps. Yet there were those who said that about the connection between the rogues and the enclave brethren. And there is no evidence to the contrary. Nothing to show any great tradermale love for silth. Not so? Who does love us? We even hate ourselves."

"I will not permit that kind of talk, Marika."

"I am sorry, mistress. Sometimes I grow bitter and am unable to contain myself. May I proceed upon my assumptions?"

"Proceed? It seems to me that you have handled the situation." Gradwohl glared suspiciously, sensing that Marika wanted to cling to power momentarily gained. "Now it is time we started planning your Toghar ceremonies."

"There will be more incidents, mistress. The brethren have been allowed to create an alternative society. One with far greater appeal to the mass of meth. One in which silth are anachronistic and unnecessary. In nature, the species that is unnecessary soon vanishes."

"I am becoming fearful for your sanity, Marika. Intuition is a fine thing, but you persist in going far beyond intuition, into the far realms of speculation, then treating your fantasies as though they are fact. That is a dangerous habit."

"Mistress, the brethren have created a viable social alternative. Please think about that. Honestly. You will see what I mean. Their technology is like a demon that has been released from a bottle. We have let it run free for too long, and now there is no getting it back inside. We have let it run free so long that now it nearly possesses the power to destroy us. And we have no control over it. They have cunningly held that in their own paws so long that tradition now has the virtual force of law. Our own traditions of not working with our paws cripple us."

"My head understands your arguments. My heart insists you are wrong. But we cannot listen to our hearts always. I will reflect."

"We cannot confine ourselves to reacting to threats only, mistress. As in the old folklore, devils spawn devils faster than they can be banished. They will keep on gnawing off little chunks of us unless we go straight after the demons who raise the demons."

Gradwohl set aside a traditionalist silth's exasperation with ideas almost heretical. That, more than her grasp of silth talents, was the ability that had fueled her rise to the first position among the Reugge. "All right, Marika. I will accept your arguments as a form of working hypothesis. You will be replacing Utiel soon. By stretching the imagination, the problems you conjure will fall within the purview of fourth chair. You may pursue solutions. But be careful who you challenge. It will be years yet before the Reugge are in any position to assert independence from the brethren."

Marika controlled her features carefully. She exulted inside. Saying that, Gradwohl revealed far more than she knew. She did believe! And somehow, though she did not want it known, she was moving to loosen the chains of tradermale technology.

"As you wish, mistress. But let us not remain so enamored of our comforts that we allow ourselves to be destroyed for fear of losing them."

"The ceremonies, Marika. All your arguments, all your desires, all your ambitions are moot without Toghar. Will you stop ducking and changing the subject? Are we going to secure your future? Or deliver it into the paws of those who would see you fail?"

Marika sighed. "Yes, mistress."

"Can we set a date, Marika? Sometime soon?"

Fear twisted Marika's guts. What was the matter with her? Toghar was simple. Countless silth had survived it. None that she had heard of had not. It was less to be feared than facing down the brethren over a few dozen criminals. Why could she not overcome her resistance? "Yes, mistress. I will begin my preparations immediately."

Maybe something would come up to delay it.

III

"Grauel. . . . I'm terrified."

"Thousands have been through it, Marika."

"Millions have been through birthing."

"No one has ever died." Hard edge to Grauel's words. The birthing remark was the wrong thing to say before her two packmates. "It's not that. I don't know how to explain. I'm just scared. Worse than when the nomads came to the packstead. Worse than when they attacked Akard and we all *knew* we were not going to get out alive. Worse than when I was bluffing Bagnel about attacking brethren aircraft if they tried to leave the enclave."

"You were not bluffing."

"I guess not. I would have done it if he had forced me. But I didn't want to. And I don't want to do this."

"I know. I know you're scared. When you're genuinely terrified, you can't shut up."

Startled, Marika asked, "Really? Do I give myself away so easily?"

"Sometimes."

"You will have to educate me. I can no longer allow myself to be easily read."

Barlog stepped around Grauel, held out the white undershift that was the first of the garments Marika would don. She appeared less empathetic than did Grauel. But when Marika leaned forward to allow her to slide the shift over her head, Barlog hugged her.

Each huntress, in her own way, understood well the price of becoming silth. Grauel, who never could bear pups, and Barlog, who had not been allowed since accepting the Reugge bond. Barlog said, "It isn't too late to leave, Marika."

"It's too late, Barlog. Far too late. There's nowhere we could go. Nor would they tolerate us trying. I know too much. And I have too many enemies, both within and outside the Community. The only way out is death."

"She's right," Grauel said. "I've heard the sisters talking. Many hope she won't go through with it. There is a powerful faction ready to take all our heads."

Marika walked to a window, looked out on the cloister. "Remember when we rated nothing better than a cell under Akard?"

"You've come a long way," Grauel admitted. "You've done many things of which we couldn't approve. Things I doubt we can forgive, even knowing what moved you. There are moments when I can't help but believe what some say, that you're a Jiana. But I guess you've only done what the All demands, and that you've had no more choice than we do."

"There's always a choice, Grauel. But the second option is usually the darker. Today the choice is Toghar or die."

"That's why I say there really isn't any choice."

"I'm glad you understand." She turned, let Barlog pull the next layer of white over her head. There would be another half-dozen layers before the elaborate outer vestments went into place. "I hope you'll understand in future. There will be more evil choices. Once I fulfill Toghar, my feet will settle onto a path from which there will be no turning aside. It is a path into darkness, belike. A headlong rush, and the Reugge dragged right along with us, into a future not even the most senior foresees."

Grauel asked, "Do you really believe the tradermales want to destroy the silth? Or is that just an argument you're using to accumulate extraordinary powers?"

"It's an argument, Grauel, and I'm using it that way. But it also happens to be true. An obvious truth to which the sisters have blinded themselves. They refuse to believe that their grasp is slipping. But that's of no moment now. Let's move faster. Before they come to find out why I'm taking so long."

"We're right on time," Barlog said, arranging the outer vestments.

Grauel slipped the belt of arft skulls around her waist. Barlog placed the red candidate's cap upon her head. Grauel passed her the gold-inlaid staff surmounted by a shrunken kagbeast head indistinguishable from a meth head in that state. In the old days it would have been the head of a meth she had killed.

Grauel brought the dye pots. Marika began staining her exposed fur in the patterns she had chosen. They were not traditional silth or Reugge. They were Degnan patterns meant for a huntress about to go into single, deadly combat. She had learned them as a pup, but never had seen them worn. Neither had Grauel or Barlog, nor anyone of the pack that they could recall. Marika was confident none of today's witnesses would understand her statement.

She stared at herself in a mirror. "We are the silth. The pinnacle of meth civilization."

"Marika?"

"I feel as barbaric as any nomad huntress. Look at me. Skulls. Shrunken head. Bloodfeud dyes." For weeks she had done nothing but prepare for the ceremonies. She had gone into the wild to hunt arfts and kagbeasts, wondering how other candidates managed because the hunting skills were no longer taught young silth.

The hunt had not been easy. Both arfts and kagbeasts were rare in this winter of the world. She had had to slay them, to bring the heads in, and to boil the flesh off the arft skulls and to shrink the head of the kagbeast. Grauel and Barlog had assisted only to the limits allowed by custom. Which was very little.

They had helped more preparing the dyes and sewing the raiments. They were better seamstresses than she, and the sewing had been done in private.

"Do you want to go over your responses again?" Grauel asked. Barlog dug the papers out of the mess on Marika's desk.

"No. Any more and it'll be too much. I'll just turn off my mind and let it happen."

"You won't have any problems," Barlog prophesied.

"Yes," said Grauel. "Overstudy. . . . I studied too hard when they made me take the voctor exams." "Voctor" was the silth word that approximated the Degnan "huntress," though it also meant "guard" and "one who is trusted in the silth presence bearing weapons." "There were questions where I just went blank."

Barlog said, "At least you got a second chance at the ones you missed. Marika won't."

It did not matter terribly, insofar as the outcome of the ceremonies proper, if Marika stumbled occasionally. But to be less than perfect today would lend her enemies ammunition. They would use any faltering as a sign that she was less than wholly committed to the silth ideal.

Appearances, as always, were more important than substance.

"Barlog. Are you still keeping the Chronicle?"

"Yes."

"Someday when I have the free time I'd like to see what you have said about what has happened to us. What would Skiljan and the others have thought if they could read what you've written, only fifteen years ago? If they'd had that window into the future."

"They would have stoned me."

Marika applied the last daub of vegetable dye. Gathering the dyes had been as difficult as collecting the animal heads. There had been no choice but to purchase some, for the appropriate plants were extinct around Maksche, destroyed by the ongoing cold.

Marika went to the window again, stared north, toward her roots. The sky was clear, which was increasingly rare. The horizon glimmered with the intensity of sunlight reflected off far snowfields. The permanent frostline lay only seventy miles from Maksche now. It was expected to reach the city within the year. She glanced at the heavens. The answer lay up there, she believed. An answer being withheld by enemies of the silth. But there would be nothing she could do for years. There would be nothing she could do, ever, unless she completed today's rites.

"Am I ready?"

"On the outside," Grauel said.

"We haven't forgotten a thing," Barlog said, referring to a checklist Marika had prepared.

"Let's go."

Turmoil twisted into hurricane ferocity inside her.

The huntresses accompanied Marika only as far as the doorway to the building where the ceremonies would be held. The interest was such that Gradwohl had set the thing for the great meeting chamber. Novices turned the huntresses back. Ordinarily the Toghar rites were open to everyone in the cloister. Only those involved and their friends turned out. But Marika's ceremonies had drawn the entire silth body. She was no ordinary novice.

Her enemies were there in hopes she would fail, though novices almost never did so. They were there in hopes their presence would intimidate her into botching her responses, her proper obeisances. They were there in hopes of witnessing a stumble so huge that it could not be forgiven, ever.

Those who were close to Gradwohl, and thus to the most senior's favorite, were there to balance the grim aura of Marika's enemies.

The enemies made sure no nonsilth were present. Marika was more popular among the voctors, whom she had given victories, whom she treated as equals, and who liked the promise of activity she presented.

Marika stepped through the doorway and felt a hundred eyes turn upon her, felt the disappointment in enemies who had hoped she would not show. She took two steps forward and froze, waiting for the sisters not yet seated to enter the hall and take their places.

Fear closed in.

It was not a proper time. Gradwohl and Dorteka both repeatedly had tried to tell her not to place all her trust in those-who-dwell. Even knowing she should not, she slipped down through her loophole, into that otherworld that overlapped her own, and sought the solace of a strong dark ghost.

She found one, brought it in, and used it to ride through the chamber ahead, reassuring herself that the ceremonies would proceed in the usual way. It was a cold world out there, with the ghosts. Emotion drained away. Fear dribbled into the ether, or whatever it was through which the ghosts swam. The coldness of that plane drained into her.

She was ready. She had control. She could do it now. She could forget what it would cost her, could forget all her nurture as a huntress-to-be, dam-to-be, of the Degnan pack. She released the ghost with a stroke of gratitude, pulled back to the world of everyday, of continuous struggle and fear. She scanned the hall ahead with cold eyes. All the sisters had taken their places.

Coolly, she stepped forward, standing straight, elegant in her finery. She paused while two novices closed the door behind her. She faced right and bent to kiss the rim of an ancient pot that looked like a crucible used till it had had to be discarded. She dipped a finger in, brought thick, sweet daram to her lips and tongue.

That pot was older than the Reugge. Older, even, than the dam Community, the Serke. Its origins had been lost in the shadows of time. Its rim had been worn by the touch of countless lips, its interior crusted by residue from the tons of daram that had filled it over the ages. It was the oldest thing in the Reugge world, an icon-link that connected the Community with the protosilth of prehistory, the symbolic vessel of the All from which silth were granted a taste of infinity, a taste of greater power. It had been the kissing bowl of seven gods and goddesses before the self-creation of the All.

The glow of the daram spread through Marika, numbing her as chaphe would, yet expanding her till she seemed to envelope everyone else in the hall. They, too, had tasted daram. Their mind guards were down a fraction. Touch leaked from everyone, pulling her into a pool of greater consciousness. Her will and personality became less sharply defined and singular. It was said that in the ancient lodges, before civilization, silth had melded into a single powerful mind by taking massive doses of daram.

That part of her, the majority, which remained wholly Marika, marveled that hidden beyond this welcoming glow there could be so much fear, spite, enmity, and outright irrational hatred.

Her sponsor Gradwohl and the chief celebrants waited at the far end of the hall. She spoke her first canticle, the novice requesting permission to approach and present her petition for recognition. A silth somewhere to her right asked a question. She replied automatically, with the proper response, noting in passing that her primary interrogator would be Utiel, the old female she would replace in fourth chair. All the Maksche councillors seemed to have assumed roles in the ceremonies, even the senior, who had been all but invisible since falling out of favor with Gradwohl.

Before she realized what was happening, the initial interrogatory ended. She approached the celebrants. Again there were questions. She did not become involved on a conscious level. She responded crisply, automatically, made her gestures at the exact appropriate instant. She felt like a dancer perfectly inserted into her dance, one with the music, leaping, twisting, turning with absolute grace, the thing itself instead of an actor, the ultimate and ideal product of a perfect sorcery. Her precision, her *artistry*, fed back to the celebrants so that they, too, fell into her matchless rhythm.

The slight tension brought on by the presence of enemies faded from the shared touch of the daram, expunged by the experience of which she was heart. That experience began to swell, to grow, to drown everything.

And yet, deep within her, Marika never wholly surrendered to the commitment the rite was supposed to represent.

The celebrants completed the final interrogatory. One by one, Marika surrendered her staff, her belt of skulls, her cap, her ceremonial raiments to the kettle of fire around which the celebrants stood. Noisome smoke rose, filled the hall. In moments she stood before the assembly wearing nothing but her dyes.

Now the crux. The stumbling stone. The last hope of those who wished her ill. The truly physical part, when they would stretch her on the altar and a healer sister would reach into the ghost realm and summon those-who-dwell, lead a ghost into her recumbent form, and destroy forever her ability to bear young.

Marika met Gradwohl's eye and nodded. The most senior stepped around the smoking kettle, presented the wafer. Marika took it between her teeth.

And added her bit of style, her own fillip to the ceremony. She faced the assembly before biting down, chewing, swallowing. She felt the stir in the entwined touch, the slight, unwilling swell of admiration.

The wave of well-being came over her as concentrated chaphe spread through her flesh. The celebrants stepped around the kettle and allowed her to settle into their arms. They lifted her to the altar. The healer sister loomed over her.

That reluctant something tried to wriggle forth, tried to scream, tried to will her to move, break away, flee. She stifled it.

She felt the ghost move inside her. Felt her ovaries and tubes being destroyed. There was no pain, except of the heart. There would be little discomfort later, she had been promised.

She turned inward, felt for the ghost world, fled there for several moments.

It was all over when she returned. The observers were filing out. The celebrants and their assistants were cleaning up. Gradwohl stood over her, looking down. She seemed pleased. "That was not so bad, was it, Marika?"

Marika wanted to say the hurt was all in her mind, but she could not. The daram and chaphe held her. She reflected momentarily upon a pack still unMourned and wondered if their spirits would forgive her. Wondered if she could ever forgive Gradwohl for forcing her into this crime against herself.

It would fade. The heart's pains all faded.

"You did very well, Marika. It was a most impressive Toghar. Even those who dislike you had to admit that you are extraordinary."

She wanted to protest that they never had denied that, that that was the reason they feared her, but she could not.

Gradwhol patted her shoulder. "You are fourth chair now. Utiel officially announced her retirement the moment the ceremony was complete. Please use your power wisely. Your two voctors will be in to help you shortly. I will tell them to remind you that I want to see you after you have recovered." Gradwohl touched her gently, almost lovingly, in a fashion her own dam never had managed. For a moment Marika suspected there might be more to her patronage than simple interest in the fate of the Reugge.

She forced that out of mind. It was not difficult with the chaphe in her blood.

"Be well," Gradwohl murmured, and departed.

Grauel and Barlog appeared only several minutes after the last of the silth departed. Marika was vaguely amused as she watched them prowl the chamber, peering into every shadow. They, who believed silth could render themselves invisible with their witchcraft. Finally, they came to her, helped her down off the altar.

"How did it go?" Barlog asked. She seemed under a strain.

"Perfectly," Marika croaked through a throat parched by drugs.

"Are you all right?"

"Physically, I'm fine. But in my soul I feel filthy."

Again both huntresses scanned the shadows. "Can you speak business? Are you too disoriented?" Grauel asked.

"I can. Yes. But take me away from here first."

"Storeth found those workers," Grauel told Marika, after they had taken her to her quarters. "She reported while you were in that place. They were reluctant to talk, but she convinced them she came from you. They acknowledged their debt. They knew very little, but they did say there is a persistent rumor that the rogues have found themselves a powerful wehrlen. One who will be able to defeat silth at their witchcraft when he is ready. So the thing is not done. As you thought."

In the questioning of all the rogues taken, there had been that thread of belief in something great about to befall the criminal movement. Marika had not been able to identify it clearly. In the end she had decided to seek out two Maksche workers who had served her in the Ponath years ago, workers who had vowed they would repay an imagined debt.

"Warlock," she murmured. "And a great one, of course. Or he would not be able to inspire this mad hope."

She had not mentioned anything of this to the most senior. Intuition told her this was a thing best kept to herself. For the present, at least.

"We must find him. And kill him, if he cannot be used."

For once Grauel and Barlog concurred in a prospective savagery.

They remembered the wehrlen who first brought the nomads out of the Zhotak.

BOOK FOUR:
TELLERAI

herself, closed her eyes, allowed herself to sink into the All.
She waited for intuition to fuel her thoughts.

She came out to find Barlog poised near the doorway,
waiting, doing nothing to disturb her. "Barlog?"

"Is there to be an answer to the message, Marika? The
messenger is waiting."

"Indeed? Then tell him to tell Bagnel that I will be there
an hour after midnight." She consulted her calendar. "An
hour and thirteen minutes after, to be precise."

The major moons would attain their closest conjunction of
the month at that time. The tides would rise high enough to
halt the flow of the Hainlin. The hour would be one considered especially propitious to the silth. Bagnel would understand. She was sure he had been studying everything known
about the silth with as much devotion as she studied everything known about flying and space. He might not be wholly
ware of the part he was playing in this game, but he was as
dicated as she. A pity he could not become her prime
ponent. He would make a good one. The tension of their
ndship would add spice.

rom Bagnel she shifted thought to the rumored wehrlen.
that anything but wishful thinking by rogues? She
catch the odor of nothing even remotely concrete. Her
ces were inadequate.

minutes before she was due at the enclave, Marika
d her position at the tip of the dagger of her dark-
e had elected to fly to avoid the chance of rogue
She did not fear ambush, but it would be too much
raction.

and Barlog accompanied her, standing at the axis
ss. Marika and they carried their weapons. She
bath go armed. The moment they were airborne
d a portable transceiver to contact the tradermale
She followed procedures identical to those Bag-
landing approaches.
ought that amusing. Especially if the brethrer
ome wickedness.
t the darkship down near Bagnel's headquar

Chapter Twenty-three

I

Barlog relayed the message that had been left at the cloister
gate. "A communication from Bagnel, Marika. And I wish
you would do as the most senior suggests and move to
quarters more suitable to one of your status. I am growing
too old to be scampering up and down stairs like this."

"Poo. You're only as old as you think, Barlog. You're still
in your prime. You have a good many years ahead of you.
What is it?"

"But are they all years of up stairs? I don't know what it
is. It's sealed."

"So it is." Marika opened the envelope. It was a large
one, but contained only a brief note.

"Well?"

"He wants a meeting. Not a visit. A meeting." She
pondered that. It implied something official. Which further
implied that the tradermales were aware of her official
elevation to fourth chair and her brief for dealing with rogue
males. She had not wanted the news to get out of the cloister
so quickly. But outside laborers would talk. "I guess a

month of secrecy is enough to ask. Barlog. I want to talk to Braydic. In person. Here. Don't let her give you any of the usual excuses."

Ever since the confrontation in the main ceremonial hall, Braydic had bent every effort to avoid compromising herself further by avoiding Marika.

"Yes, mistress."

Braydic's evasions had done her no good. Marika had made her head of a communications-intercept team. Like it or not. And Braydic did not.

Marika did not quite understand the communications technician. From the first a large part of her friendship for the refugee pup had been based upon her belief that Marika would one day become powerful and then be in a position to do her return favors. But now she was afraid to harvest what she had sown.

Braydic was too conservative. She was not excited by new opportunities and new ideas. But she carried out her orders and did so well. In the nine days since she had gotten the intercept system working, she had stolen several interesting signals.

Marika paced while waiting. She was not sure where she was going now. There had been a time when she thought to displace Gradwohl and head the Reugge Community in her own direction. But Gradwohl seemed to be steering a course close to her own ideal, if sometimes a little cautiously and convolutedly, and not seizing control of the sisterhood meant not having to deal with the flood of minutiae which swamped the most senior.

She lamented having so few trustworthy allies. She could not do everything she wanted herself, yet there was no one she could count on to help move the sisterhood in directions she preferred.

Was she getting beyond herself? Looking too far down the path?

She went to a window, stared at the stars. "Soon," she promised them. "Soon Marika will walk among you."

She returned to her desk and dug out the file containing outlines of Braydic's reports.

The critical notation to date was that Braydic had identified signals from more than one hundred orbital satellites. Though the spacefaring sisterhoods did not announce an orbiting, the available data suggested that they had helped boost no more than half that number into orbit. Which meant that the brethren had somehow put the rest up on their own, trespassing upon silth privilege by doing so. The space codicils to the conventions specifically excluded the brethren from the dark, except as contract employees of t[he] sisterhoods.

Intriguing possibilities there.

Braydic entered tentatively. "You sent for me, mistr[ess]"

"Yes. I want to know what you have intercepted re[cently]. Especially today."

"I sent a report not two hours ago, mistress."

"I know, Braydic. A very long, thick, dull re[port] would take forever to get through. It will take [me] you just tell me if there was anything worth [note]. Especially from our male friends at the encla[ve]."

"There has been heavy traffic all day, mistr[ess]. been in cant or in the brethren cult languag[e] been able to decipher much of it, but we[ ] expecting an important visitor."

"That would make sense," Marika mu[sed].

"That is all?"

"All we could determine without an[ ] expect me to unravel the content of the[ ] going to have to give me interpreters [ ] discovering the meaning of the secre[t] nor any of my team are capable."

"I will see what I can do about [ ] please me, too, if we could und[erstand] said. Thank you for taking tim[e] want you to know I appreciate [ ]"

"You are welcome, mistres[s] network has also been carryin[g]"

"There might be a chanc[e]. Thank you again. This call[ ]"

ters. Barlog and Grauel dismounted quickly and took their places to either paw. One bath went ahead of Marika, two followed. The party bristled with weapons. Marika herself carried a revolver and automatic rifle taken from enemies in the Ponath. She hoped the tradermales would see the symbolism.

Bagnel handled her irregular arrival well. She wondered if she could surprise him anymore. He greeted her pleasantly. "Right on time. Come into the back."

Marika was startled. Never before had he offered her entrance to his private quarters.

"Is all the hardware necessary?" Bagnel asked.

"That remains to be seen. We live in strange times. I don't believe in taking needless chances."

"I suppose." He sounded as though he thought his honesty had been questioned.

"It's not personal, Bagnel. I trust you. But not those who use you. I want to be able to shoot back if somebody shoots at me. More sporting than obliterating them with a blow from the touch. Don't you think?"

"You've developed a bloodthirsty turn, Marika."

She wanted to tell him it was calculated. But even with him there were truths best kept close to the heart. So she told him an incomplete truth. "It's my upbringing. I spent so much time getting away from meth who wanted to eat me. What did you expect anyway? This can't be social. You've never invited me over in the middle of the night. That would be an impropriety."

Marika gestured. Grauel, who retained the sensitive nose of a Ponath huntress, stepped up and sniffed the fruit punch Bagnel had begun preparing. The tradermale eyed her with a look of consternation.

"I didn't think you'd be fooled," he said. "Knowing you, you have it half figured out."

"You want me to meet someone who is going to try to bribe me or twist my arm. I trust that you were a good enough friend to warn them that their chances of success are slight."

"Them?"

"I expect there will be more than one, and at least one will be female, of exalted rank, representing the Serke."

A door opened. Marika glimpsed a sleeping room. Bagnel had spartan tastes in private as well as public. She credited him with a point to his account of positives. He worked to fulfill his tasks, not to acquire a more luxurious life.

Several meth came out of the sleeping room. None were armed and none were of low status. Their trappings reeked of power and wealth. Marika's party seemed incongruous in their presence, all of them clad for the field, all armed, the bath and Grauel and Barlog nearly fight-alert against the walls.

Marika had hit near the mark. There were two silth and two males. The males were so old their fur had a ratty, patchy look. Both exuded a strong presence seldom seen even in females. She recognized neither, but there were few photographic records of those who were masters among the brethren.

One of the males stared at her in a fashion she found too bold. Too much like a butcher sizing up livestock.

"Marika," Bagnel said, stirring the punch, "I want to be on record as having arranged this meeting under orders. I don't know what it's about, so don't blame me personally if you don't like the way it goes."

"I know that, Bagnel. It would be unreasonable to expect thieves to give any consideration to friendship. Few of them are aware that it exists. I'll bet the word does not occur in the Serke secret tongue, or even in your tradermale cant." She turned. "Greynes. Natik. Korth. Guard the outside. One of you take the hall doorway. The other two patrol around outside. I doubt you will see anyone, as these bandits will not want it known what they are doing and orders will have been given keeping everyone away from here. But, just in case, shoot first and ask questions later."

The moment the door closed behind the bath, she asked, "What are you going to offer?" She brought her gaze ripping across four sets of hard but mildly unsettled eyes.

The silth looked back blankly, careful students of their art. Marika judged them to be high in their order. Almost certainly from the Serke controlling council itself. They would want a close look at the Reugge youngster who had slain two of their number.

The tradermales remained blank, too.

None of the four spoke.

"But surely you have something to offer. Some way of getting me to betray my Community so you can work your wicked wills. Think of the prizes at stake. Our Reugge provinces are floating on oil. Those parts that are not sinking beneath the weight of rare heavy elements." She revealed her teeth as she tilted her ears in a contrived expression of amusement. "But look at you, crinkling around the corners of your eyes and wondering what is this creature? It is just me. The troublesome savage Marika. The shin-kicker who forestalls the conspiracies of thieves. Trying to drive a wedge between you."

Teeth began to show. But for some reason they had made it up to allow her all the initial talking. Perhaps a test?

"Yes. I am forthright. I tell you right out front that I am going to put you at one another's throats. No proxies and no lies. Sisters, did your friends here ever tell you about the pitchblende in the western Ponath?"

One of the tradermales jerked upright, lips peeling back in an unconscious snarl. The silth did not miss that. Grauel and Barlog snapped their rifles down, aimed at his chest.

"Pitchblende is a source of radioactives, rare and dangerous heavy metals. They have very limited technological applications at the moment—primarily as power sources in satellites. But it takes no imagination to see that major surface installations could be built by an advanced technology. I suspect the brethren could have something operating within ten years. Sisters, do look up radium and uranium when you get back to Ruhaack, or wherever. While you are checking things, see if you can get an accurate count on the number of satellites orbiting our world. Compare that number with the number that the dark-faring Communities have lifted."

Marika faced the tradermales. "I am perfectly transparent, am I not? It is your turn. You, of course, have been anticipating Serke treachery from the beginning. That is the way those witches are. You have been preparing for the scramble for the spoils. But suppose we could short-circuit the process? Lovely technical term, short-circuit. Suppose you did not have to deal with the Serke at all? Suppose I offered you a Reugge license allowing you access to all the pitchblende you want? Without your having to sneak through the wilds outside the law, hoping you can survive the malice of your accomplices."

The males exchanged looks.

"There? You see? I have been perfectly obvious, and yet I have given you much on which to think. Why not get what you want the cheaper and safer way? I understand you better than you think. I know what moves you." She shifted her gaze to the silth. "You, though, remain enigmas. I do not know if I will ever fathom your motives for committing such hideous crimes."

She settled into the one chair standing on her side of the room, waiting. A shaken Bagnel hovered in no-meth's land. He sped Marika a look of appeal.

"I am waiting," she said after half a minute of silence.

They had found their strategy wanting, though they took its failure well. One of the males finally said, "Not long ago you placed the brethren in a tight position. You tied us up so we had no choice but to do something we considered despicable."

"That is just beginning, old-timer. If you persist in arming, training, sending out criminals to attack silth, you are going to find yourselves in even tighter places. You will find the Reugge have so many criminals under sentence we will be selling their sentences to Communities that have a shortage of condemned laborers."

Her confidence rattled the male for a moment. But he recovered, held unswervingly to what had to be a prepared line of argument. "We have decided to do unto you as you did unto us."

"Really? Why do I get the feeling I am about to witness the unfolding of a grand delusion?"

"We do not delude ourselves!" he snapped. She could almost hear him thinking, *You silth bitch.*

"*Arrogant* silth bitch," she corrected aloud. "Come ahead, then. Try me."

For the first time the Serke looked genuinely uncertain. The appearance of confidence becomes confidence, Marika reminded herself.

The male who had not yet spoken did so now. From several glances he had thrown Bagnel's way, Marika inferred that he must somehow be her friend's superior. He said, "Some time ago you ambushed a joint force in the Ponath. You once threatened to make the circumstances public. We would like it noted that the same event can be used to *your* detriment. If you refuse to cooperate with us."

Marika was not surprised. She had expected that Kublin would come back to haunt her eventually. But she had let the matter float, hoping she could do the right thing intuitively when he did.

The male suggested, "You might want to send your guards outside."

"I might not. There are two Serke of exalted status here. I might not be able to kill both of them quickly enough to keep you from sticking a knife into me. Go ahead with your threats."

"As you wish. You allowed a littermate to escape that ambush. Surrounding circumstances suggest that you did more than that to assure his safety. Suppose that were made known?"

The one thing Marika *had* done about the matter was to send a group of huntresses, picked by Grauel, to Critza. They were under instructions to lie low and capture any snoopers. So she controlled the physical proofs. "Go ahead. If that is your best."

"What we have in mind is presenting the evidence to your most senior. She, I believe, is your principal anchor within the Reugge Community."

Marika shook her head, honestly less worried by the moment. "Go with it. See what it gets you. While you are at it, though, why not up the stakes? Why not try to buy me somehow?"

That caused more consternation.

"We *will* present Most Senior Gradwohl with the evidence."

"I said go ahead. You will have assembled a fair file on me by now. You know I do not bluff."

"We know your bluff has not been called. We know you are young. A characteristic of youth is that it takes long risks, betting that older, more cautious heads will not hazard stakes as dangerous."

"Play your stakes," Marika said. "Grauel, our presence here seems pointless. Tell the bath to ready the darkship."

"Wait," one of the silth said. "You have not heard what we want."

"To tell the truth, I do not care what you want. It would not be anything in my interest, or in the interest of the Reugge Community."

"You could become most senior of the Reugge if you cooperated."

"I have no wish to become most senior. That is a job that would distract me too much from those things that do interest me."

"Is there any way to reach you?"

"Almost certainly. We all want some things so badly we will befoul ourselves to get them. Witness yourselves. But I cannot think of anything that is within your power to offer. At least nothing I cannot take for myself. I suggest you stop trying to steal the Ponath. Accept the fact that the Reugge control it. Deal for the petroleum and pitchblende. Frankly, I find it impossible to comprehend your frenzy for outright control."

Marika looked at the tradermales, hoping they would understand that she actually had no trouble at all understanding. "I will go now. You four squabble over the ways you may have planned to stab one another in the back."

With Grauel and Barlog covering her, she backed to the doorway. She paused there, added, "The most senior is away this month, as she often is. You will not be able to contact her for some time. However, she will return to Maksche for a two-week period beginning the fifth day of Biter—if you feel compelled to present *your* evidence. My own proofs are held by a trusted sister at TelleRai, under seal. She is under bond to break the seal in the event of my death or prolonged disappearance." She left. But after she had taken a few steps, she turned back to add, "After me, my fine thieves, the end of the world. At least for you and yours."

Her feet flew as she dashed to the darkship. She had gotten away with yanking their whiskers. Very nearly with yanking them out by the roots. She had left them completely at a loss.

It was wonderful.

It was the sort of thing she had wanted to do to some of her elders almost from the time she had grown old enough to reason.

She took the darkship up, on a long flight, pursuing the rogue orbit of a small retrograde moon. She pushed hard, glorying in the cold air's rush through her fur.

After the crude joy began to fade, she halted, floated high, where the air was thin but cut like knives of ice. She looked southward. Far, far down there were the great cities of the world. Cities like TelleRai, which spawned the Gradwohls and silth like the Serke she had faced tonight. And thousands of miles farther still lay the equator, over which orbited many of the tradermale satellites.

The ice was advancing because the world had cooled. The world had cooled because not enough solar radiation impinged upon it now that it had entered the interstellar cloud. To halt the ice required only an increase in the amount of solar energy reaching the surface of the planet.

Someday, and perhaps not that long now, she would begin throwing more coals on the fires of the sun—as it almost had to be said in the dialect of her puphood, naked as it was of technical and scientific terms.

II

Marika had won again, apparently. Neither the Serke nor brethren appeared inclined to test her.

A quiet but busy year passed.

Three months after the confrontation in Bagnel's quarters, third chair came open. Gradwohl moved her up. Marika clung to those security functions pertaining to the rogue male problem. She continued to expand them as much and as often as she dared, though she operated with a more delicate paw than had been her custom. With more to lose and more to gain, she invested much thought before making more enemies.

Third chair meant having to monitor meetings of the Reugge council at TelleRai. Tradition insisted third chair accompany first chair, or senior, at each such gathering. Marika refused to attend in person, though Gradwohl herself often urged her to make herself known to the sisters of the ruling cloister.

She audited the meeting electronically. She did not feel comfortable leaving the heart of the network she had begun building.

She spent seven months in third chair, then second came open. The All was a persistent taker during those years at Maksche, an ally almost as valuable as Gradwohl herself, hastening her rise till it rattled her almost as much as it did her detractors.

At every step of her elevation she was the youngest ever to hold her position.

Gradwohl moved her into second chair. And within the month her ally the All passed its shade across the order's ruling council itself. Gradwohl appointed her seventh chair, a step which shook the entire Community. Never before had an order-wide chair been held by one less than a cloister senior. Never before had two chairs been held by sisters from the same cloister.

Marika ignored the grumbles and uproar. Let the most

senior deal with it if she insisted on elevating her favorite over others who felt themselves more deserving.

Again the most senior urged her to make herself known at TelleRai. Her arguments were basic and irrefutable. One day she would have to deal with those meth regularly. She should get to know them now, while they could yet become comfortable with her.

Again she demurred, wishing to remain near the root of a growing political power.

She did not have to be in TelleRai to know what they were saying down there. It was the same old thing, on the larger scale of the sisterhood. They did not like one so young, from the wilds, acquiring so much power within the Community. They were afraid, just at the sisters of Maksche and Akard had been afraid. But the resistance down in TelleRai was even more resistance of the heart than of the mind. They did not know her at all. Only a few had encountered her during the campaigns in the Ponath. The silth there recognized her accomplishments. They were not as bitter as the silth at Maksche. Even those silth gave her very little real trouble, preferring to hate her in their hearts and minds while hoping she set herself up for a fall.

Marika slept very little that year. She pushed herself hard, developing her antirogue force, making of it a personal power base she insinuated into every Reugge cloister. Cynically, she made strong use of the rumors about a great wehrlen lurking among the rogues. If Gradwohl understood what she was doing, she said nothing.

With Braydic's reluctant help Marika developed stolen technology into tools suited to her tasks. Her finest became a listening device she planted in the quarters of those she suspected of trying to thwart her. Toward the end of the year she began having such devices installed in the quarters of anyone she thought might someday get in her way.

The listening devices, unknown outside her circle, gave her a psychological edge on her enemies. Some of her more superstitious sisters came to believe that she could indeed become invisible as in old silth myth. Her revenges were subtle but emotionally painful. Before long all Maksche lived in fear of offending her. The terror of her sisters remained mainly a terror of what she might become, not a fear of what she was.

Each such tiny triumph of intimidation strengthened her. In building her power base she switched back upon her past, in other cloisters, and tried to recruit the most reactionary silth to manage the rogue program.

Her efforts in that direction yielded results sufficient to convince the most doubting silth that there was a grand conspiracy against the sisterhoods, with the Reugge the chosen first victim. Every criminal male taken and questioned seemed to provide one more fragment fitting into a grand mosaic of revolution.

The warlock began to take substance, if only as a dreadful shadow.

Marika's first contacts outside her own Community came not as a result of her place on the council at TelleRai but because several of the more friendly sisterhoods became interested in creating their own rogue-hunting apparatus before the problem in their territories swelled to the magnitude of that in the Reugge. They came to Marika for advice.

The parade of outsiders impressed the Maksche sisters. Marika made of that what she could, gradually silencing more of her strongest critics.

Yet silence bought nothing. The more widely known she became, the more hated she became by those who had chosen to stand against her in their hearts.

There was no conquering irrationality. Especially not among silth.

There were nights when she lay awake with the pain of unwarranted hatred, vainly consoling herself with the knowledge that all silth who attained any stature did so at the cost of hatred. Few of the Maksche council were well liked. No one liked Gradwohl. Were the most senior there more often, instead of away doing what no one knew what, she might have absorbed some of the hatred directed her favorite's way.

Often when Marika did sleep she fell into a strange dream wherein she rode a surrealistic, shifting beast across a night infested with stars, without a wind stirring her robes and fur, without a planet below. There was peace in that great star-flecked void.

Mornings afterward she would waken with her determination refreshed, no longer caring if anyone loved her.

She was alive for the sake of a creature called Marika, not for anyone else. She would salvage the freedom of the Reugge if she could. She owed the Community something. If she succeeded, so much the better. If she did not, she would not much care.

She would help the Serke if there were no other way of opening her pathway into the great dark.

She was second chair, yet Gradwohl tinkered with it in a manner that there were no duties for her at Maksche. In time her campaign against the rogues was so successful she had little to do but monitor reports of ever-dwindling criminal activity. She began to find herself with time on her paws. That left her time to brood. She began to feel hemmed in, pressured, restless.

III

It was the anniversary of Marika's confrontation in Bagnel's quarters. She had extended her morning exercises by an hour, but they had done nothing to stay her restlessness. A call to Bagnel had proven fruitless. He was tied up, unable to entertain her. She faced a long and tiresome day of poring over stolen texts, searching for something she did not already know; of skimming reports from Braydic's intercept teams and plant listeners, finding the same old things; of scanning statements from informants seeking rewards for helping capture members of the rogue movement.

She had had all she could stand of that. She wanted to be free. She wanted to fly.

"This is not what I want to do with my life. How do they get anyone to take first chairs? Barlog! Tell the bath to prepare my darkship."

"Marika?"

"You heard me. I am sick of all this. We're taking the darkship up."

"All right." Barlog disapproved. She had found herself a niche, helping direct the movement of information, which suited her perfectly. And she did not like Marika's laying claim to the ship. It was not yet assigned her formally. It still belonged to the cloister generally, though no one else had used it all year. Barlog was becoming very conscious of place and prerogative. "Where will you be going?"

"I don't know. I'll just be going. Anywhere away from all this. I need to feel the wind in my fur."

"I see. Marika, we have come no nearer finding the warlock."

Marika stifled a sharp reply. She was tempted to believe the warlock a product of rogue wishful thinking. "Inform Grauel. She'll need to find a sub if she has cloister duty today."

"Do you expect to be up long?" Barlog looked pointedly at a heap of reports Marika had yet to consider.

"I think so. I need it this time." She had done this before, but only for brief periods. Today, though, demanded an extended flight. The buildup of restlessness and frustration would need awhile to work off.

"As you command." Barlog departed.

Marika scowled at her back. For one who had come to set so much stock in place, Barlog was getting above herself. She shuffled papers, looking for something that might need immediate attention.

For no obvious reason she recalled something Dorteka had said. About a museum in TelleRai. The Redoriad museum? Yes.

TelleRai. Why not? She was secure enough now. Both in her power and within herself.

She summoned one of the novices assigned to run and fetch for her. "Ortaga, get me some medium-scale maps of the country south of here. The Hainlin to the sea, the coast, and everything west to and including the air corridor to TelleRai. As far south as TelleRai."

"Yes, mistress."

The maps arrived before Barlog returned. Marika laid out a flight path that would pass over outstanding landmarks she had heard mentioned by bath and Mistresses of the Ship with whom she had spoken. She told the novice, "I will be gone all day. I expect to return tonight. Have the other novices sort the papers the usual way. Tag any that look important."

"Yes, mistress."

"Barlog. At last. Is the darkship ready?"

"It will be a short time yet, mistress. The bath told me that they will want to fulfill the longer set of rites if you intend an extended flight."

"I see." Marika did not understand the bath. They had their own community within the greater Community, with private rites they practiced before every flight. The rites apparently amounted to an appeal to the All to see them through unscathed.

There were Mistresses, like Bestrei of the Serke, who considered their bath in the same class as firewood. They cared not at all for them as meth. They drew upon them so terribly they burned them out.

Even lesser and more thoughtful Mistresses had been known to miscalculate and destroy their helpers.

Marika took some coin from her working fund, then donned an otec coat. Otec fur was rare now. The coat was her primary concession to the silth custom of exploiting one's status. Otherwise she lived frugally, dressed simply, used her position only to obtain information. Any sort of information, not just news about rogue males or about the space adventures of the dark-faring Communities. She had accumulated so much data she could not keep track of it all, could not keep it correlated.

Grauel joined her as she and Barlog reached the grand court where the darkships came and went. Workers were removing hers from its rack. It was so light only a half dozen were needed to lift it down and carry it to the center of the square. They unfolded the short arms and locked them into place. Marika eyed the line of witch symbols painted on shields hung along the main beam.

"Someday I will have a darkship all my own. I will have it painted all in black," she said to no one in particular. "So it can't be seen at night. And we will add Degnan symbols to those of the Reugge."

"The tradermales could still follow you with their radar," Grauel said. "And silth could still find you with the touch."

"Even so. Where are they? Do their rituals take so long? Barlog, where are your weapons? We don't go anywhere without our weapons." She herself carried the automatic rifle and revolver captured in the Ponath. She carried a hunting knife that had belonged to her dam, a fine piece of tradermale steel. She never left her quarters unarmed.

Grauel still carried the weapon Bagnel had given her during the siege of Akard. It remained her most precious treasure. She could have replaced it with something newer and more powerful, but she clung to it superstitiously. It had served her well from the moment it had come into her paws. She did not wish to tempt her fates.

Barlog was less dramatically inclined. Marika often had to remind her that they were supposed to be living savage roles. Marika *wanted* other silth to perceive them as terribly barbaric. It amused her that those with the nerve sometimes asked why she did not wear ceremonial dyes as well as always going armed.

She never bothered telling them that the daily dyeing of fur was a nomad custom, not one indigenous to the Ponath. For all there had been a deadly struggle of years, most of the Reugge could not understand the difference between Ponath and Zhotak meth.

There was a chill bite to the morning wind. It made her eager to be up and away, running free, riding the gale. Someday she wanted to take the darkship up during a storm, to race among growling clouds and strokes of lightning. Other Mistresses thought her mad. And she would never be able to try it. The bath would refuse to participate. And they had that right if they believed a flight would become too dangerous.

Marika had worked long and hard to develop and strengthen her natural resistance to electromagnetic interference with her silth talents. But in her more realistic moments she admitted that even she would be overwhelmed by the violent bursts of energy present in a thunderstorm. Flight among lightnings would never be more than a fantasy.

Barlog came hustling back armed as though for a foot patrol against the nomad. She even carried a pod of grenades. Marika ignored the silent sarcasm, for the bath appeared at the same time, each with her formal greeting for the Mistress of the Ship. All bath seemed to be very much creatures of ceremony.

Each of the bath was armed as a huntress. They knew Marika's ways.

They did not like serving with her, Marika knew. But she knew it was nothing personal. The Reugge bath did not like any of the Reugge Mistresses of the Ship. It was part of their tradition not to like anyone who held so much power over their destinies.

"Positions," Marika said.

"Food?" Grauel asked. "Or have I guessed wrong? Will it be a brief flight?"

"I brought money if we need it. Board and strap, please."

The bath counted off the ready. "Stand by," Marika called, and stepped onto her station. Unlike the bath, she often disdained safety restraints. This was one of those times when she wanted to ride the darkship free, in the old way, as silth had done in the days of slower, heavier wooden ships.

"Be prepared!"

Marika went down inside herself, through her loophole, and sent a touch questing. Ghosts were scarce around the cloister. They did not like being grabbed by silth.

She knew the cure for that. A whiff of the touch, like the sense of one of their own calling. A lure laid before them and drawn slowly closer. They were not smart. She could draw in a score at a time and bind them, and reach for another score.

The grand court was aboil within a minute with more ghosts than any other Mistress could have summoned. There were far more than Marika really needed to lift and move the darkship. But the more there were, the safer she would be. The more there were, the farther she could sense and see through that other level of reality. And the higher and faster she could fly—though speed was determined mainly by her ability to remain aboard the darkship in the face of the head wind of her passage.

She squeezed the ghosts, pressed them upward. The darkship rose swiftly. Grauel and Barlog gasped, protested, concerned for her safety. But Marika always went up fast.

She squeezed in the direction she wished to travel. The titanium cross rushed forward.

She rose as high as she dared, up where the air was cold and rare and biting, like the air of a Ponath winter, and maintained control of the ghosts with a small part of her mind while she gazed down on the world. The Hainlin was a wide brown band floating between mottled puzzle pieces of green. From that height she could not make out the flotsam and ice which made river travel hazardous. The dead forests of the north were coming down, seeking the sea. She glanced at the sky overhead, where several of the smaller moons danced their ways through the sun's enfeebled light. She again wondered why the tradermales did nothing to stay the winter of the world.

She would, one day. She had mapped out a plan. As soon as she had garnered sufficient power. . . . She mocked herself. She? A benefactor? Grauel and Barlog would be astonished if they knew what she had in mind.

Well, yes. She could be. Would be. After she had clambered over scores of bodies, of sisters, of whoever stood in her path. But that was far away yet. She had to concentrate upon the present. Upon the possibilities the Serke-brethren conspiracy presented. She had to get back to them, to sound them out. There might be more there than she had thought.

IV

Marika followed the Hainlin for a hundred miles, watching it broaden as two mighty tributaries joined it. She was tempted to follow the river all the way to the sea, just to see what the ocean looked like. But she turned southward toward the Topol Cordillera, not wishing to anger anyone by trespassing upon their airspace. She was not yet in the position of a Bestrei, who could fly wherever and whenever she wished. That lay years in the future.

Quietly, she admonished herself against impatience. It all seemed slow, yes, but she was decades ahead of the pace most silth managed.

The Topol Cordillera was a low range of old hills which ran toward TelleRai from the continent's heart. The airspace above constituted an open, convention corridor for flights by both the sisterhoods and the brethren. The hills were very green, green as Marika recalled from the hills of her puphood. But even here the higher peaks were crowned by patches of white.

The world was much cooler. The waters of the seas were being deposited as snow at an incredible rate. "And it need not be," she murmured. She wondered that meth could be so blind as to miss seeing how the ice could be stopped. Never did she stop persisting in wondering if they did see, know, and do nothing because that was to their advantage. Whose?

The tradermales', of course. They were the technicians, the scientific sort. How could they help but see?

Who would hurt most? The nomads of the polar regions first. Then the pack-living meth of remote low-technology areas. Then the smaller cities of the far north and south, in the extremes of the technologized regions. The great cities of the temperate zones were only now beginning to catch the ripple effect. They would not be threatened directly for years.

But the silth who owned them and ruled from them drew

their wealth and strength from all the world. They should *try* to do something, whether or not anything could be done.

Ordinary meth would direct their anxieties and resentments toward the sisterhoods, not toward the brethren, who were careful to maintain an image as a world-spanning brotherhood of tinkerers.

The real enemy. Of course. Always it added up when you thought in large enough terms. The brethren pursued the same aim as the rogues. Secretly, they supported and directed the rogues.

Then they had to be broken. Before this great wehrlen came out of the shadows.

Her ears tilted in amusement. Great wehrlen? What great wehrlen? Shadow was all he was. And break the brethren? How?

That was a task that could not be accomplished in a lifetime. It had taken them generations to acquire the position they held. To pry them loose would require as long. Unless the Communities were willing to endure another long rise from savagery.

The mistake had been made when the brotherhood had been allowed to become a force independent of the Communities. The attitude that made it unacceptable for a sister to work with her paws had become too generalized. The brethren's secrets had to be cracked open and spread around, so silth-bonded workers could assume those tasks critical to the survival of civilization.

Her mind flew along random paths, erratically, swiftly curing the world's ills. And all the while the darkship was driving into the wind. The world rolled below, growing greener and warmer. Ghosts slipped away from the pack bearing the darkship. Others accumulated. Marika touched her bath lightly, drawing upon them, and pushed the darkship higher.

The Cordillera faded away. A forested land rolled out of the haze upon the horizon, a land mostly island and lake and very sparsely inhabited. The lakes all drained into one fast watercourse which plunged over a rift in a fall a mile wide, sprinkled with rainbows. The fall's roar could be heard even from that altitude. The river swung away to Marika's left, then curved back beneath her in a slower, wider stripe that, after another hundred miles, left the wilderness for densely settled country surrounding TelleRai. TelleRai was the most important city on the continent, if not on the meth homeworld.

The silth called this continent the New Continent. No one knew why. Perhaps it had been settled after the others. None of the written histories went back far enough to recall. Generally, though, the cities on other continents were accepted as older and more storied and decadent. Several were far larger than TelleRai.

The outskirts of the city came drifting out of the haze, dozens of satellite communities that anchored vast corporate farms or sustained industrial enclaves. Then came TelleRai itself, sometimes called the city of hundreds because its fief bonds were spread among all the sisterhoods and all the brethren bonds as well. It was a great surrealistic game board of cities within the city, looking like randomly dropped pieces of a jigsaw puzzle, with watercourses, parks, and forests lying between the cloisters.

Marika slowed the darkship and came to rest above the heart of the city, a mile-wide circle of convention ground enfiefed to no Community, open to everyone. She harkened to the map in her mind, trying to locate the skewed arrowhead shape of the Reugge cloister.

She could not find it.

She touched her senior bath. *Greynes. You have been here before. Where is our cloister?*

Southwest four miles, mistress.

Marika urged the darkship southwestward at a leisurely pace. She studied the city. It seemed still and lifeless from so high above. Till she spied a dirigible ascending. That must be one of the tradermale fastnesses there.

Now she saw the Reugge cloister. Even from close up it did not resemble the picture she had had in mind. She took the darkship down.

From a lower altitude the cloister began to look more as it should. It had tall, lean spires tapering toward the sky.

Almost all its structures were built of a white limestone. It was at least three times the size of the Maksche cloister and much more inviting in appearance.

The city itself looked more pleasant than Maksche. It lacked the northern city's grim, grimy appearance. It did not suffer from the excessive, planned regularity of Maksche. And the poverty, if it was there, was out of sight. This heart of the city was more beautiful than Marika had imagined could be possible.

Meth scurried through the visible cloister as the darkship descended. Several startled touches brushed Marika soon after it became obvious her darkship would land. She pushed them aside. They would not panic. They could see the Reugge ensignia upon the underframe of the darkship.

She drew on Greynes for word of the proper landing court, drifted forward a quarter mile, completed her descent as silth and workers rushed into the courtyard.

The landing braces touched stone. Marika relaxed, released the ghosts with a touch of gratitude. They scattered instantly.

Grauel and Barlog were there when she was ready to step down. The three bath positioned themselves a step behind. "A beautiful flight, sisters," she told the bath. They seemed fresher than she was.

The eldest bowed slightly. "You hardly drew upon us, Mistress. It was a pleasure. It is seldom we get a chance to see much of the country over which we travel. If from ever so high." She removed her gloves and rubbed her paws together in a manner meant to suggest that Marika might refrain from going up into such chill air.

Several silth rushed to Marika, bowed according to their apparent status. One said, "Mistress, we were not informed of your coming. Nothing is prepared."

"Nothing needs to be prepared," Marika replied. "It was an impulse. I came to visit the Redoriad museum. You may arrange that."

"Mistress, I am not sure—"

"Arrange it."

"As you command, mistress."

They knew who she was. She smelled the fear in the courtyard. She sensed a subtle flavor of distaste. She could read their thoughts. Look at the savage. Coming into the mother cloister under arms. With even her bath carrying weapons. Carrying mundane arms herself. What else could be expected of a feral silth come from the northern wilderness?

"I will view the highlights of the cloister while arrangements are being made."

The level of panic did not subside. More silth arrived, including several of the local council. They appeared as distressed as their lesser sisters. One asked, "Is this a surprise inspection, Marika?" The name stuck in the silth's throat. "If so, you certainly have taken us off our guard. I hope you will forgive us our lack of ceremony."

"I am not interested in ceremony. Ceremony is a waste of valuable time. Send these meth back to work. No. This is not an inspection. I came to TelleRai to visit the Redoriad museum."

Her insistence on that point baffled everyone. Marika enjoyed their confusion. Even the senior silth did not know what to make of her unannounced arrival. They went out of their way to be polite.

They knew she had the favor of the most senior, though. And the most senior's motives were deeply shadowed. They refused to believe this a holiday excursion.

Let them think what they would. The most senior was not around to set them straight. In fact, she was not around much at all anymore. Marika often wondered if that did not bear closer examination.

"How *is* the most senior?" one of the older silth asked. "We have had no contact with her for quite a long time."

"Well enough," Marika replied. "She says she will be ready to begin what she calls the new phase soon." Marika hoped that sounded sufficiently portentous. "How soon will a vehicle be ready?"

"The moment we obtain leave from the Redoriad. Come this way, mistress. You should see the pride of the cloister."

Marika spent the next hour tagging after various old silth,

leaving a wake of staring meth. Her reputation had preceded her. Even the lowliest of workers wanted to see the dangerous youngster from the north.

A novice came running while Marika's party was moving through the most senior's private garden, where fountains chuckled, statues stood frozen in the midst of athletic pursuits, and flowers of the season brightened the soft, dark soil beneath exotic trees.

Marika said, "I cannot see Gradwohl having much taste for this, sisters."

The eldest replied, "She does not. But many of her predecessors liked to relax here. Yes, pup?" she snapped at the panting novice.

"The Redoriad have given permission, mistress. Their gate has been informed. Someone will be waiting."

Marika's companions seemed surprised. She asked, "You did not expect them to allow me to see their museum?"

"Actually, no," one of the old silth said. "The museum has been closed to outsiders for the last ten years."

"Dorteka did not mention that."

"Dorteka?"

"My instructress when I first came to Maksche. She reminisced fondly of a visit to the Redoriad museum when she was a novice herself."

"There was a time, before the troubles began, when the Redoriad opened their doors to everyone. Even bond meth and brethren. But that has not been true since rogue males tried to smuggle a bomb inside. The Redoriad have no wish to risk their treasures, some of which date back six and seven thousand years. After the incident they closed their gates to outsiders."

Another silth explained, "The Redoriad take an inordinate interest in the past. They believe they are the oldest Community on the New Continent."

"May we go, then?" Marika asked. "Is a car ready?"

"Yes." The old silth seemed displeased.

In a merry tone, Marika said, "If you really want to be

inspected, I can come back later. I must become acquainted with this cloister, as I no doubt will be moving here soon."

Deep silence answered that remark. The older silth started walking.

"Why are they this way?" Grauel asked. "Feeling hateful, but being so polite?"

"They fear that I'm Gradwohl's chosen heir," Marika replied. "They don't like that. I am a savage and just about everything else they don't like. Also, my being heir apparent would mean that they would have no chance of becoming most senior themselves. Assuming I live a normal life span, I will outlast them all."

"Maybe it's a good thing we arrived unannounced, then."

"Possibly. But I doubt they would go to violent extremes. Still, be alert when we get into the streets. There has been time for news of our arrival to have gotten out of the cloister."

"Rogues?"

"And the Serke. They aren't pleased with me either."

"What about these Redoriad? They are the other major dark-faring Community. Might not their interests parallel those of the Serke? Getting into their museum so easily. . . ."

"We'll find out. Just don't let them move me out of your sight."

"That has not needed saying for years, Marika." Grauel seemed almost hurt by the reminder.

Marika reached out and touched her arm lightly.

Chapter Twenty-four

I

The vehicle selected for Marika's use proved to be a huge steam-powered carriage capable of carrying twelve meth in extraordinary comfort. Silth began climbing aboard. Marika snapped, "Leave room for my companions. Barlog, you sit with the driver."

She hustled the bath and Grauel inside, climbed aboard herself. The coach's appointments were the richest she had ever seen. She waited indifferently while the silth jockied for seats. She intervened only to make certain her TelleRai deputy in the antirogue program found a place. She confined her conversation to business while the coach huffed along TelleRai's granite-cobbled streets at a pace no faster than a brisk walk. Grauel watched the world outside for signs of any special interest in the coach. Marika occasionally did the same, ducking through her loophole to capture a ghost. She would flutter with it briefly, trying to catch the emotional auras of passersby.

She detected nothing that warranted excessive caution.

The Redoriad were the largest of all sisterhoods as well as

the oldest upon the New Continent. Their cloister showed it. It was a city in itself in an ornate, tall architectural style similar to that of the Reugge cloister.

The steam vehicle chugged to a gate thirty feet high and nearly as wide. The gate opened immediately. The vehicle pulled through, halted. Silth in dress slightly different from the Reugge formed an honor guard. An old female with the hard, tough look of the wild greeted Marika as she descended from the coach.

"They told me you were young. I did not expect you to be this young."

"You have a beautiful cloister. Mistress . . . ?"

"Kiljar."

Marika's local companions made small sounds of surprise.

"You honor me, mistress." She was surprised herself. The Kiljar whose name she knew would be second or third of the Redoriad, depending upon one's information source.

"You know me, then?"

"I am familiar with the name, mistress. I did not expect to be snowed under with notables on a simple visit to a museum."

"Simple visit?" The Redoriad silth began walking. Marika followed, staying just far enough away to allow Grauel and Barlog room. Kiljar was not pleased but pretended not to notice. "Do you really expect anyone to believe that?"

"Why not? It is true. I wakened this morning feeling restless, recalled an old instructress's wonder at the Redoriad museum, decided to come see it for myself. It was sheer impulse. Yet everyone is behaving as though my visit has some sort of apocalyptic portent."

"Perhaps it does not, after all. Nevertheless, the name can be the thing. What is expected is what is believed. Recent times have made it seem that the fate of the Reugge Community may revolve around you. Your name has become known and discussed. Always twinned with that of Most Senior Gradwohl, as strange and unorthodox a silth as ever became a most senior."

"I will agree with that. A most unusual female."

Kiljar ignored that remark. "Young, ambitious silth everywhere are militating for agencies similar to that you created within the Reugge. Old silth who have had brushes with you or yours follow your every move and wonder what each means. Brethren beg the All to render you less a threat than you appear."

Marika stopped walking. The column of Reugge and Redoriad halted. She faced Kiljar. "Are you serious?"

"Extremely. There has not been a day in months when I have not heard your name mentioned in connection with some speculation. Usually it is on the order of, 'Is Marika the Reugge behind this?' Or, 'What is Marika the Reugge's next move?' Or, 'How does Marika the Reugge know things as though she were in the room when they were discussed?' "

Marika had had some success with her signal intercepts, but not that much. Or so she had thought. Penetrating the various secret languages was very difficult, with the results often unreliable. "I am just one young silth trying to help her Community survive in the face of the most foul conspiracy of the century," she replied. She awaited a response with both normal and silth senses alert.

"Yes. To have a future you must have a Community in which to enjoy it. But I have heard whispers that say the Serke made a proposal in that regard."

Marika did not miss a step or feel a flicker of off-beat heart, but she was startled. Word of her encounter with the Serke and brethren had gotten out? "That is not quite true. The Serke approached me once, in their usual hammer-fisted way. They tried to compel me to turn upon my sisters. Nevertheless, the Reugge are stronger today, and the Serke are more frightened."

"Do they have cause?"

"Of course. A thief must be ready to pay the price of getting caught."

"Yes. So. But these are thieves with considerable resources, not all of which have entered the game yet."

"Bestrei?"

"Especially Bestrei."

"Bestrei is getting old, they say."

"She can still deal with any two Mistresses of the Ship from any other Community."

"Perhaps. Who can tell? But that is moot. The Reugge will not challenge her. And how could the Serke challenge us? Would that not amount to a public admission that the Reugge have a right to leave the surface of this planet? I would so argue before the convention on behalf of all those sisterhoods denied access to space." Carefully, Marika admonished herself. This old silth speaks for a Community of darkfarers at least as powerful as the Serke.

"There is that. This thing you have about rogue males. This campaign you have undertaken in the rural territories. I wish to understand it better. In modern times the Redoriad have concentrated their attention offworld. We have leased our home territories to other sisterhoods and paid little attention to what is happening here."

"Are the Redoriad still calling for censure because the Reugge allow such flouting of the law within their provinces?" Marika lifted her upper lip enough to make it clear she was being facetious.

"Hardly. Today there is a fear that you may be going too far in the opposite direction. That you may be drawing the brethren in. Particularly since several Communities have begun emulating you."

"With less success."

"To be sure. But that is not the point. Marika, some of the Communities have become very uneasy with this."

"Because all paths lead one way?"

"Pardon?"

"Because each path through the rogue tangle eventually leads to a brethren enclave?"

"Exactly." Kiljar seemed reluctant to admit it.

"They are trying to destroy the sisterhoods, Mistress Kiljar. Nothing less than that. There is no doubt about it, much as so many would blind themselves to the fact. There is ample evidence. Even this winter that is devouring the world has become a weapon with which they weaken silthdom. They are manipulating the Communities, trying to bring on feuds like the one the Reugge have smoldering with the Serke. They are trying to gain control of natural resources properly belonging to the sisterhoods. They are doing everything within their power, if subtly, to crush us. We would be fools not to push back."

"The brethren are—"

"Essential to society as we know it? That is one of their weapons, too. That belief. They think that belief will stay our paws till it is too late for us. Come into the museum with me, Mistress Kiljar. Let me show you what you Redoriad have had here all the time. Nothing less than proof that silth can exist without the brethren."

"Marika. . . ."

"I do not propose that they be destroyed. Not at all. But I believe they should be disarmed and controlled before they destroy us."

"Mistress?" Grauel said from behind Marika. "May I speak with you a moment? It is important."

Surprised, Marika dropped back. Barlog dropped even farther, to prevent the column from drawing close enough to overhear. "What? Have you seen something?"

"I have heard something. You are talking too much, Marika. That is not Barlog or myself, or even the most senior. That is the second of the Redoriad, a Community whose interests are not identical to those of the Reugge."

"You are right. Thank you for reminding me, Grauel. She's crafty. She knew just how to goad me. I'll watch my tongue." She overtook Kiljar. "My chief voctor reminds me that I did not come here to lay bare the Reugge breast. That we came entirely unofficially, to examine old darkships."

"I see." Kiljar seemed amused.

"May we proceed, and perhaps save the discussion for a time when I feel more comfortable with the Redoriad?"

"Certainly. I will remind you, though, that the Redoriad are no friends of the Serke."

"Mistress?"

"The Serke have been the next thing to rogue among silth for centuries. They have gotten away with it because they have always had a strong champion. They have become intolerable since they developed Bestrei. No sisterhood dares challenge them. There are many of us who follow the Reugge struggle with glee. You have embarrassed them many times."

"That is because we avoid confronting their strengths. We let them hurt themselves. The most senior is a crafty strategist."

"Perhaps she outsmarts herself."

"Mistress?"

"She is preparing a challenger for Bestrei. Buying time till you are ready. Do not argue. What is evident is evident. Certainly, it is possible that when you attain your full strength Bestrei will have aged so much she can no longer best you. It is said you are as strong as she was at your age. Perhaps stronger, because you have a brain and more than one talent. It is whispered that twice you have slain Serke who came from their ruling seven."

"Mistress, that is not—"

"Do not argue. These things are whispered but they are known. Let me tell you a thing I know. You are alive today only because you belong to a sisterhood without access to space. Because, as you mentioned, there would be extensive legal ramifications to a challenge."

Marika waited patiently through a long pause while Kiljar ordered her thoughts. They were on the doorstep of the museum. The door was open. She was eager to see what lay beyond, but waited while the old silth found what she wanted to say.

"You cannot hope to best Bestrei at her most senile without learning the ways of the dark, Marika. Handling a darkship out there is not the same as handling one on-planet. You are Reugge. You have no one to teach you those ways. You dare not teach yourself. The Serke will know if you go out on your own. And they will challenge immediately because you will in effect have challenged the sisterhoods who hold the starworlds. They will make it a challenge for the existence of the Reugge. And Bestrei will devour you."

Involuntarily, Marika glanced at the sky. And sensed the truth of what Kiljar said. She had not thought the situation through.

Had Gradwohl?

"I have a solution," Kiljar said. "But we will save that for another time. Today you came here only to look at old darkships." There was a light touch of mockery in her voice.

II

The Redoriad museum was as marvelous as Dorteka had claimed. Marika breezed through most of it, eager to reach the darkships, having saved them for last. She had done that with treats as a pup.

She did stop once to ask about a set of wooden balls. "What are these?"

"In primitive times one test for the presence of silth talents was juggling. All female pups were taught. Those who showed exceptional talent early often were managing the balls unconsciously. They were tested further. Today we have more subtle methods."

"May I touch them?"

"They are not breakable."

"I was a very good juggler. My littermate Kublin was, too. We would put on shows for the huntresses when they were in a mood to tolerate pups." She tossed a ball into the air, then a second and a third. Her muscles no longer recalled the rhythms. Her mind stepped in, made the balls float in slowed motion. She kept them moving for half a minute, then fumbled one and immediately lost them all. "I am a little out of practice." She returned the balls to the display.

Memories came back. Kublin. Her dam, Skiljan. The Degnan packstead. Juggling. Flute playing. She had been very good with the flute, too. She had not picked one up since fleeing Akard for Maksche. Maybe that deserved some attention. Playing the flute had been as relaxing as flying the darkship or fleeing into the realm of ghosts.

Enough. Thought could be too painful. In this instance it reminded her that her pack remained unMourned.

She went for her treat.

There were a dozen darkships, arranged to show stages of evolution. First a quarter scale model of a darkship similar to the newest flown by the Reugge. Then another, similar yet different. The plaque said it was aluminum. There was only one more metal ship, also of aluminum, incredibly ornate.

"This one never got off the ground," Kiljar said. "The brethren created an exact copy of a famous golden-fleet darkship of the period, but it would not fly. It takes more effort to lift metal, even titanium, than it does golden-fleet wood. Even though the wood is heavier. There is power in the wood itself. It pleases those-who-dwell. With the metal ships they come only under compulsion."

"Then why use brethren darkships? Why use a vessel less effective and made by someone we do not control?"

"Because building a wooden darkship, even in its most rudimentary, functional form, is a long and difficult process. Because the brethren can produce all we want almost as fast as we want them. Consider the Reugge experience with the nomads. My sources tell me you lost six darkships in the fighting. In the old days you could not have replaced those in two generations. Generations during which other sisterhoods might have devoured you. These days when you lose a darkship you just order another. The brethren take it out of stock."

"Sometimes. If you happen to be in favor."

"That is right. They would not replace yours. That is on the agenda for the next convention. They will be required to defend that decision."

"They could refuse all the Communities."

"The convention will sort it out."

"If there is one." It took a majority of sisterhoods agreeing one was needed before a convention could actually convene.

Marika moved along the line of darkships. The next was wooden, similar in style to the brethren ship that would not fly. It was a work of art, almost grotesque in its ornateness. She noted almost thronelike seats for the Mistress and bath.

The wooden darkships grew simpler and more primitive, ceased to be crossed. The last three were saddleships, also declining in complexity. The latest looked like an animal with an impossibly elongated neck. The oldest was little more than a pole with fletching at its rear.

Kiljar indicated the fanciest. "In this period silth imitated life. There was an animal called a redhage which was used as a riding beast. It has become extinct since. Saddleships of the period are stylized imitations with the neck elongated. The longer a saddleship was, the more stable it was in flight. As you can see, the oldest were stabilized the same as an arrow."

"But an arrow spins in flight."

"So it does. It may have been a clumsy way to travel. We do not know now for certain. The redhage type still gets taken up occasionally, though. Some of our Mistresses enjoy them. And they are much faster than anything in common use. The Mistress can lie on its neck and cut loose. The weakness of the darkship being the obvious: the Mistress is limited by her own endurance."

"Bath are that important?"

"That important. Well? Are you satisfied?"

"I think so. I have seen what I came to see. I should get back. There is no end to the work that awaits me at Maksche."

"Think on what I have said about the Serke, Bestrei, and learning the ways of the void. Mention it to Most Senior Gradwohl. Mention that I am interested in speaking with her."

"I will."

"There is, by the way, a voidship that belongs to the museum. An early one, now retired, but still far too big to bring inside. Would you like to see it?"

"Of course."

Marika followed Kiljar out a side door, into a large

courtyard. Barlog and Grauel followed alertly, shading their eyes against the sudden change in lighting, searching for signs of an ambush. Marika reached through her loophole and checked. She made a gesture telling the huntresses all was well.

She stopped cold when she saw the void darkship. Her hopes for walking among the stars almost died. Yes. There was no way she was going to challenge a Bestrei anytime in the near future. "That is a small one, you say?" It was three times the size of the largest Reugge darkship.

"Yes. The voidships the Redoriad use today are twice this size. And the voidship we run in concert with the brethren is bigger still."

"If it is so difficult to move metal ships, how . . . ?"

"Out there those-who-dwell are much bigger, too. And much more powerful. That is one thing you would have to learn before you dared face a Bestrei. How to manipulate the stronger ghosts."

"Thank you." Marika closed in upon herself, squeezing a knot of disappointment down into a tiny sphere. "I think I had best be off for Maksche. I have let my duties slide long enough."

"Very well. Do not forget to tell Gradwohl that Kiljar of the Redoriad wishes to speak with her."

Marika did not respond. With Grauel and Barlog and her train of bath and TelleRai silth keeping pace, she strode back to the steam coach. She climbed aboard, settled into her seat, and closed in upon herself again.

This required a lot of thinking. And rethinking.

III

It was very late when Marika returned to the Reugge cloister. She dismissed her bath with a grunt instead of the usual thank-yous, went straight to her quarters. Grauel and Barlog followed and stayed near, but she did not take advantage of their unspoken offer. She went to bed immediately, exhausted from the day's flights.

She had the dream again, of whipping through a vast darkness surrounded by uncountable numbers of stars. It wakened her. She was angry, knowing it to be false. She would not walk the stars.

Asleep again, she dreamed once more. And this time the dream was a true nightmare, a littermate of the one she had had soon after fleeing the overrun Degnan packstead. But in this dream a terrible shadow hunted her. It raced across the world like something out of myth, howling, slavering, tireless, faceless, murderous. It hunted her. It would devour her. It drew closer and closer, and she could not run fast enough to get away.

This time she wakened shaken, wondering if it were a true dream. Wondering what the shadow could represent. Not Bestrei. There had been a definite male odor to it. An almost familiar odor.

Warlock! something said in the back of her mind. Certainly it was a presentiment of sorts.

The rogue problem, which had seemed close to solution, took a dramatic turn for the worse. In places, outlying cloisters were surprised and suffered severe damage. It almost seemed her return from TelleRai signaled a new and more bitter phase in the struggle, one in which the rogue leadership was willing to sacrifice whatever strength it had left.

For a month it made no sense whatever. And nothing illuminating came off the signal networks of the Serke or brethren. Then the most senior returned to Maksche, making one of her ever more infrequent and brief visits.

"Think, Marika. Do not be so provincial, so narrow. You visited the Redoriad," Gradwohl said. "There are times you are so naive it surpasses belief. The Redoriad are in harsh competition with the Serke among the starworlds. The competition would become fiercer if there were a champion capable of challenging Bestrei. Your visit was no secret. Your strength is no secret. You have slain two of their best. It is no secret that the Reugge have no access to the void, and only slightly less well known that we covet an opportunity out there. If you were Serke, unable to see what transpired within the Redoriad cloister, had suffered several embarrassing setbacks at the paw of a Marika, what would you suspect?"

"You really believe the Redoriad want to train me?" It was a revelation, truly.

"Just as the Serke suspect."

Much of what Kiljar had said without saying it in so many words, and much of the attitude of the silth during her TelleRai excursion, became concrete with that reply. "They all thought—"

"And they were right. As you suggested, I got in touch with Kiljar. And that is exactly what she had in mind. An alliance between Reugge and Redoriad. Marika, you have to *think*. You have become an important factor in this world. Your every move is subject to endless interpretation."

"But an alliance...."

"It is not unprecedented. It makes sense on several levels. In fact, it is an obvious stratagem. So obvious that the Serke —yes, all right, and the brethren, too—must make some effort to counter or prevent it. Thus rogues who will devour your time while they hatch something more grim. Be very careful, Marika. I expect you will be spending a great deal of time in TelleRai soon. TelleRai will be far more dangerous than Maksche."

"And you?"

"I am fading away, am I not?" Gradwohl seemed amused.

"If you are trying to slip me the functions of most senior without having to rejoin the All, I want you to know that I do not want them. I have no intention of assuming that burden ever. I do not have the patience for the trivial."

"True. But patience is something you are going to have to learn anyway, pup." No one else called her "pup" these days. No one dared.

"Mistress?

"Consider a Reugge sisterhood without a Most Senior

Gradwohl. It would not much benefit you without your
being in charge. Would it?"

"Mistress. . . ."

"I am not immortal. Neither am I all-powerful. And
there are strong elements within the sisterhood who would
not scruple to hasten my replacement, if only to prevent
your becoming most senior. That danger is partly why I
have made myself increasingly inaccessible."

"I thought you were spending all your time with the
sisters trying to build us darkships of our own."

"I have been. In a place completely isolated. My bath are
the only meth outside who know where it is. And there are
times when I do not trust them to remain silent."

The bond between Gradwohl and her bath was legendary.

Marika said, "I did get the feeling that the TelleRai
council are disturbed by your lack of visibility. One sister
went so far as to hint that I might have done away with
you."

"Ah?" Again Gradwohl was amused. "I should show
myself, then. Lest someone get silly notions. I could adopt
your approach. Go armed to the jaw."

Now Marika was amused. "They would accuse me of
having acquired an unholy influence over you."

"They do that already." Gradwohl rose, went to a window, slipped a curtain aside. It was getting dark. Marika
could see one of the smaller moons past the most senior's
shoulder. "I believe it is time, " Gradwohl mused. "Yes.
Definitely. It is time. Come with me, pup."

"Where are we going?"

"To my darkship manufactory."

Marika followed the most senior through the cloister, to
the courtyard where the darkships landed. She felt uneasy.
Grauel and Barlog were not with her.

Gradwohl's bath were waiting. Her darkship was ready
for flight. Marika's uneasiness grew. Now it surrounded the
most senior. Gradwohl had made this project her own. Her
revealing it implied that she feared she might not be around
much longer.

Had she had an intuition? Sometimes silth of high talent caught flashes of tomorrow.

Gradwohl said, "We are doing this on the sly, pup. No one is to know we are leaving the cloister. They may wonder why we do not appear for ceremonies, but I do not think our failure will make anyone suspicious. If we hurry. Come. Step aboard."

"I could use a coat."

"I will stay low. If the wind is too much for you, I will slow down."

"Yes, mistress."

In moments they were airborne, over the wall, heading across the snowbound plain.

Gradwohl became another person while flying, a Mistress of immense vigor and joy. She flew with the verve of a Marika at her wildest, shoving the darkship through the night at the greatest speed she dared. The countryside whipped away below, much of it speckled silvery with patches of snow-reflected moonlight.

The flight covered three hundred miles by Marika's estimate. She had the cold shakes when they arrived at their destination. She had not yielded to weakness and touched the most senior with a request that she slacken the pace.

Gradwohl's goal proved to be an abandoned packfast well north of the permanent snowline, far to the west, on the edge of Reugge territory. Even from quite close it appeared empty of life. Marika could detect no meth presence with her touch. She could smell no smoke.

But thirty sisters turned out for the most senior's arrival. Marika recognized none of them. None were from Maksche. Too, some wore the garb of other Communities, all minor orders like the Reugge. She was surprised.

She said nothing, but Gradwohl read her easily enough. "Yes. We do have allies." Amused, "You have been my chosen, but there is much that I have not told you. Come. Let me show you the progress we have made here."

They went down deep into the guts of the old fortress, to a level that had been dug out after its abandonment, to a vast open area lighted electrically. Scattered about were the frames of a score of partially assembled darkships.

"They are wooden!" Marika exclaimed. "I thought—"

"We discovered that while sisters could extract titanium as you suggested, the process was slow and difficult. With modern woodworking machinery, we could produce a wooden darkship faster. Not elegant ships like those of the high period before the brethren introduced their imitations, but functional and just as useful as anything they produce. Over here are the four craft we have completed so far. We are learning all the time. Using assembly-line techniques, we expect to produce a new ship each week once we are into production. That means that soon no sisterhood will be dependent upon the brethren for darkships. We expect to produce a large reserve before circumstances force us to reveal ourselves. Come over here."

Gradwohl led Marika to a large area separate from the remainder. It was empty except for a complex series of frameworks. "What is this?" Marika asked.

"This is where we will build our voidship. Our Reugge voidship."

"A wooden one?"

"Why not?"

"No reason, I guess."

"None whatsoever. And it would not be a first. Over here. Not exactly a darkship, but something I had put together for you. I thought it might prove useful."

"A saddleship."

"Yes."

"It is gorgeous, mistress."

"Thank you. I thought you would appreciate it. Want to try it?"

"On, yes."

"I thought you might take it back to Maksche."

"But mistress. . . ."

"I will follow you in case you have trouble managing it. It is not difficult, though. I learned in minutes. You just have to get used to not having bath backing you."

"How do we get it out of here?"

"It disassembles. All these ships come apart into modules. We thought it would be useful to be able to take them inside, where they would be safer."

Marika thought of the brethren's airships and nodded. "Yes. All right. Let us do it."

Half an hour later she was riding the wooden steed through the night a thousand feet up, racing the north wind toward Maksche. She found the saddleship far more maneuverable and speedy than the conventional darkship, though more tiring.

The experience filled her with elation. Gradwohl had to press her to take the saddleship down before the cloister began rising for the day. The most senior wanted her to keep its existence secret. "Use it only when you are certain you will not be seen. It is for emergencies. For times when you have to go somewhere swiftly and secretly. Which I will be talking to you about more later."

Chapter Twenty-five

I

Most Senior Gradwohl's "later" came just two weeks after she gifted Marika with the saddleship.

Those two weeks saw rogue pressure rise markedly. Marika sent three hundred prisoners to the Reugge mines. The sisters responsible for managing them protested they could feed no more, had work for no more. And still the rogue movement found villains willing to risk silth wrath.

They came from everywhere, and though few recalled how they had come to Reugge territory, it was obvious they had been transported. They spoke openly, almost bragging, of the great wehrlen who was their champion. But Marika could learn nothing about him. Could not even gain concrete evidence of his existence as more than a legend being used to motivate the criminals.

The rogues succeeded in killing a number of silth. They overran one small, remote cloister and slaughtered everyone within. Marika was distressed. She could not understand how those attackers could have been so successful. Unless they had been led by this wehrlen himself.

The rogues were active elsewhere, too, for the first time, though to a lesser degree. But whomever they struck, wherever, friends of the Reugge Community were hurt.

Even the Redoriad suffered.

There was one assassination right in TelleRai.

The Serke hardly pretended noninvolvement anymore. Marika intercepted a message in which a rumor was quoted. It claimed a senior sister of the Serke had said in public that anyone who stood with the Reugge could expect to suffer as much as did they.

Marika remained baffled by the Serke determination. And angry. She had to ask Grauel to keep reminding her to control her temper. At one point she nearly flew off on a one-meth mission to destroy a Serke cloister in retaliation.

Two weeks after receiving her saddleship, she began to get less sleep.

Gradwohl visited her. She was direct. "I have spoken with Kiljar, Marika. An arrangement has been made. Each third night you will fly to TelleRai, directly to the Redoriad cloister, where you will meet Kiljar. Your first few visits will be devoted to teaching you to pass as a Redoriad sister. When she is satisfied that you can do that, you will be introduced to the voidships."

Marika had seen it coming. Her furtive late night flights aboard her saddleship, which she could assemble and slip out the largest window of her quarters, had shown her it was capable of velocities far beyond those of a standard darkship. If she used the saddle straps, and lay out upon the saddleship's neck, and bundled herself against the chill of passing air, she could reach TelleRai in two hours. Obviously, the most senior had had something in mind when she had the saddleship built.

"To the world's eye you will remain here, pursuing your normal routine. Only the most reliable silth on either end will be aware of what is happening. We hope the Serke and brethren will be lulled."

"I do not believe they will be, mistress. That is, they may not see what we are doing, but they already see the possibil-

ity. Otherwise they would not have resumed pressing so
hard."

"That will come up at the convention. The Serke are
trying to avoid one, but they will not be able to stall for long.
They have made themselves immensely unpopular. Their
behavior is no longer a matter of strictly parochial interest."

Marika went into TelleRai that night undetected, and
joined Kiljar in her private quarters. She discovered that the
Redoriad seniors lived very well, indeed. She did not learn
much else that trip, except that she had limits. She barely
had the strength to keep the saddleship aloft long enough to
return to Maksche. She slept half the following day.

She returned to her work groggy of mind and aching in
her joints. That she did not understand, for there had been
nothing physical in her night.

The experience repeated itself each time Marika flew
south, though each trip became easier. Developing endurance for flying was easier than developing it for running.

She had let her morning gym sessions lapse once Dorteka
was no longer there to press her. She resumed those now.

Grauel caught on during Marika's third absence. Marika
returned to her quarters to find her packmates awake and
waiting. They eyed the saddleship without surprise. Marika
disassembled it and concealed the sections. Still they said
nothing.

"Does anyone else know? Or guess?" Marika asked.

"No," Grauel replied. "Even we do not know anything
certain. It just seemed strange that you should be so tired
each third day. Each time you looked like you had not had
much sleep."

"I should learn to bar my door."

"That might be wise. Or you might have someone guard
it from within. If there was anyone you could trust to do so."

Marika considered the huntresses. "I suppose I do owe
you an explanation. Though the most senior would not
approve."

Grauel and Barlog waited.

"I have been flying down to TelleRai. To train with the

Redoriad silth. As soon as I can pass as a Redoriad sister I will begin learning the ways of their voidships."

"It is what you wanted," Barlog said.

"You sound disappointed."

"I am still a Ponath huntress at heart, Marika. Still Degnan. I was too old when I came to the silth. All this flying, this feuding, this witchcraft, this conspiring and maneuvering, they are foreign to me. I am as frightened now as I was when we arrived at Akard. I would as soon be back at the packstead, for all the wonders I have seen."

"I know. But we have been touched by the All. The three of us. We have no choice of our own."

"Touched how?" Grauel asked. "There are mornings when I rise wondering if it might not have been better had the nomads taken us all at the beginning."

"Why?"

"Things are happening, Marika. The world is changing. Too much of that change centers upon you, and you never seem fully aware of it. There are times when I believe those sisters who feared you as a Jiana sensed a truth."

"Grauel! Don't go superstitious on me."

"We will stand by you as long as we survive, Marika. We have no choice. But do not expect us to give unquestioning approval to everything you do."

"All right. Accepted. I never expected that. Did anything interesting happen while I was away?"

"It was a quiet night. I suspect you were right when you predicted the rogues would give up on Maksche. You'd better rest now. If you still plan to go flying with Bagnel this afternoon."

"I forgot all about that."

"You want to cancel?"

"No. I see him so seldom as it is."

Despite all else, she maintained her relationship with Bagnel. He maintained his end as well, despite hints that it was no longer fashionable with his superiors. He was, she felt, her one true friend. More so than Braydic, for he asked only that she be his friend in return. He stayed as close as

Grauel and Barlog, in his way, without being compelled by their sense of obligation.

"Yes. Definitely. I'll be going. I wish I could show him the saddleship. Maybe someday. Waken me when it's time."

Thenceforth Grauel and Barlog watched her quarters while she was away.

II

Marika had just come to the end of her seventh visit. She asked, "How much longer do you think, mistress? I am getting impatient."

"I know. Gradwohl warned me you would be. Next time we will go aloft. The Mistress of the Ship and her bath will be preoccupied with the ascent. They should not notice your peculiarities. What they do note can be explained by telling them that you are from the wilderness. We will pass you off as a junior relative of mine. I come from a rural background myself, though I went into cloister younger than you did. We Redoriad keep a better watch on our dependents."

"Three days, then."

"No. Five this time. And find a reason for being out of sight longer. We will not be able to make an ascent and return in time to get you home in one night."

"That may be difficult. Maksche keeps a close eye on Marika."

"If you do not appear I will know that you were unable to make the arrangements."

"I will manage it. One way or another."

She did so by feigning ill health. She began three days early, pretending increasing discomfort. Grauel and Barlog aided in the deception. She received offers of help from the healer sisters, of course, but she put them off. Before departing, she told Grauel, "They will want to treat me when you tell them I am not feeling well enough to come out. If only so they can report my condition to my enemies. Stall them. I expect to be tired enough to look thoroughly ill when I get back. We can let them at me then. I'll make a swift recovery."

"Be careful, Marika." Grauel was both in awe and dread of what Marika was about to do. "Come back."

"It isn't that dangerous, Grauel." But, of course, she could not convince the huntress of that. Grauel was only a few years past not even being able to imagine walking among the stars.

Marika began assembling her saddleship, eager to be airborne, eager to be free of her mundane duties, eager to mount the voidship, and more than a little frightened. Her insides were tight with anticipation.

"This coming and going. . . ." Grauel started, then tailed off.

"Yes?"

"I think some of the sisters are suspicious. You move at night, but the night is the time of the silth. Even at night there are eyes to see strange things moving above Maksche's towers. There has been talk about strange visions in the moonlight. Whenever strange things happen they somehow become attached to the name Marika, despite the evidence. Or lack of it. I may not be able to keep the sisters from entering if—"

"You may go to any extreme but violence. This has to be kept quiet as long as possible. A leak could bring both the Reugge and Redoriad into direct confrontation with the Serke. That would mean the end of us."

"I understand."

Marika finished assembling the saddleship. She bestrode it, strapped herself into a harness she had modified, lay down behind the windscreen she had installed. Windscreen and harness adaptations made it possible to fly at great speeds.

She reached for ghosts. The saddleship lifted and drifted through the window, brushing its stone frame. She glanced back once to wave to Grauel, and saw Barlog come rushing into her apartment. What did she want?

No matter. Nothing could be more important than tonight's flight.

She set her ghosts to work with a vengeance, raced away.

She thought she heard a far voice call her name, but decided it was just a trick of the air rushing around the windscreen.

Snow-splattered earth whipped past below.

III

Softly, Kiljar said, "Just stand there on the axis, the same as any passenger on any darkship."

"Will we get cold? Marika asked question after question, all of which she had asked before and had had answered. She was too nervous to control her tongue. She recalled Grauel or Barlog telling her, long ago, that she betrayed her fear because she talked too much when she was frightened. She tried to clamp down.

The senior bath left the Mistress of the Ship and came to Marika and Kiljar carrying a pot like a miniature of the daram cauldron that stood inside the doorway to the grand ceremonial hall at Maksche. She held it out to Kiljar. The Redoriad took it and drank. The bath then offered it to Marika, who sipped till Kiljar said, "That is enough."

"It tastes like daram, but it is not as thick."

"There is essence of daram in it. Several other drugs as well. They make it possible for the Mistress to draw fully upon everyone aboard. You will see."

A feeling of peace crept over Marika, a feeling of oneness with the All. She turned into herself, went down through her loophole, watched as the Mistress gathered ghosts and drew upon her bath. The giant cross lifted slowly. Marika sensed the strain required to elevate so massive a darkship. She was tempted to help, overcame that temptation. Kiljar had admonished her repeatedly against doing anything but remaining an observer. There would be ample opportunity for participation later. First she had to experience being separated from her birth world, to explore a new realm of those-who-dwell.

The darkship rose straight toward Biter, which stood at zenith, glowing down from his pockmarked face. Higher and higher. For a time Marika did not realize how high, for there was no change in temperature nor of the rarity of the air she breathed.

Then she could see all TelleRai spread below her. She had flown very high aboard her saddleship, but never so high that she could see all the city and its satellites in their entirety. The satellites lay scattered over hundreds of square miles. To the west, clouds were moving in, rolling over the islands of light.

The Mistress of the Ship was surrounded by a golden glow. Turning, Marika saw that the same glow surrounded each of the bath. It was not intense, but it was there. She could detect nothing around Kiljar or herself.

She started to ask a question.

Touch, Kiljar sent. *Use nothing but the touch.*

Yes. The glow. What is it?

The screen that restrains the void. What some sisters call the Breath of the All.

We are surrounded, too?

We are. Watch now. Soon you will begin to see the horizon curve. Soon you will see the moonlight shining off the snow in the north. No. Not tonight. It is snowing there again. Off the backs of the clouds, then.

It is a rare night when it is not snowing north of Maksche, mistress. The darkship was gaining velocity rapidly. *What is that glow along the horizon?* The horizon had developed a definite bow.

Sunlight in the atmosphere and dust cloud.

Marika lost herself in growing awe. She could see almost all the moons. More than she had seen at one time before. She could discern a score of the satellites put up by the brethren and dark-faring sisterhoods. They were brilliant dots moving against the darkness.

What is that? She indicated a bright object rising from the glow along the edge of the world. It was too small to be a moon, yet larger than any satellite.

The Serke-brethren voidship Starstalker. *Just in from*

*the dark this week. We will pass near it. By design. The
Redoriad ship is out, but* Starstalker *is similar.*

Won't they . . . ?

*Be upset? Perhaps. But they have no basis for a protest.
We can look. Inside Biter orbit is convention space.*

Marika glanced back at the world—and was startled. The
Mistress had reoriented the voidship. The planet was down
no longer. The darkship was moving very fast now.

She was in the void. If the glow she could not see failed
her, she would die quicker than the thought.

All sense of motion vanished, yet the world continued to
grow more curved. The bright spark of the voidship *Starstalker* drew closer, though the ship upon which Marika
stood seemed at rest.

She looked upon the naked universe, sparklingly bright,
clearer than ever she had seen it from the surface, and
surrendered to awe.

Kiljar touched her. *Over there. The darkness where there
are almost no stars at all. That is the heart of the dust
cloud. The direction our sun and world are traveling. It will
become more dense before it clears. It will be five thousand
years before we finish passing through.*

That is a long winter.

*Yes. We are getting close to the voidship. Do nothing to
attract attention to yourself. They will be displeased
enough as it is.*

The darkship turned till its long arm indicated a piece of
sky ahead of the swelling voidship. It began to move, though
Marika could tell only because the voidship skewed against
the fixed stars. As they approached the shining object, she
detected lesser brightnesses moving around it. Closer still.
The voidship resolved into something more than a bright
glow. Looking over her shoulder, Marika saw that the sun
had risen above the edge of the world. The world itself,
where it was daytime, was extremely bright—especially at
the upper and lower ends of the arc of illumination. The
snowfields, she supposed. The cloud cover looked heavier
than in any photograph she had seen. A quick query to

Kiljar, though, told her that it was a phenomenon of the moment.

It was impossible to discern the shapes of continents and islands. This world looked like no globe she had seen.

Turning to *Starstalker,* she found that the voidship had swollen into an egg shape. The surrounding sparks had become smaller ships. They looked like none she had seen before. Two were moving away, one of them well ahead of the other. Two were moving in. Another waited idly, matching orbit. Several were nosed up to the voidship like blood-sucking insects. Marika asked no questions for fear her touch would leak over and be detected.

But Kiljar looked as puzzled as was she. Marika felt a leak-over as she touched the Mistress of the Ship. Their approach slowed. Then the Redoriad darkship began to turn away. Marika looked at the Redoriad with her question plain upon her face.

Something is happening here that should not be, Kiljar sent. *Those little ships are like nothing I have ever seen, and I have been in space for three decades. They may be in violation of the conventions. Oh-oh. They have noticed us.*

Marika felt the questioning touch, felt it recoil in surprise, alarmed because the darkship was not Serke.

The touch returned. *Stop. Come here immediately.*

Kiljar waved at the Mistress of the Ship. *Starstalker* began to dwindle.

A spear of fire ripped through the great night, coming from one of the small ships. It touched nothing. Marika had no idea what it was, but felt the deadliness of it. So did the Mistress. She commenced a turn to her left and dove toward the planet.

What is happening? Marika asked.

I do not know. Do not distract me. I am trying to touch the cloister. They must know about this in case we do not survive.

Fright stole into Marika's throat. She stared back at the dwindling voidship. Another spear of light reached for the Redoriad darkship, came no closer than the last. The Mistress skewed around and took the darkship another direction, like a huntress dodging rifle fire.

Flames bloomed around one end of one of the small ships attendant upon *Starstalker*. It came after the darkship, its lance of light probing the darkness repeatedly. Behind it another such ship blossomed flame and joined the chase,.

Marika nearly panicked. She hadn't the slightest notion of what was happening, except that it was obvious someone wanted to kill them. For no apparent reason.

Another spear of fire. And this one grazed the pommel end of the dagger that was the darkship. A silent scream filled Marika's head. The rear bath drifted away, tumbling. She disappeared in the great night, her glow gone.

Kiljar ran along the titanium beam to the spot where the bath had stood. And in her mind, Marika felt, *Use that vaunted talent for the dark side, Reugge. Use it!*

Marika had begun to get a grip on herself. Down through her loophole she went—and froze, awed.

They were huge out here! Not nearly so numerous as down below, but more vast even than the monsters she sometimes detected above while flying high in the chill upon her saddleship. Bigger than imagination.

Another beam snapped through the dark. The Mistress of the Ship was in the shadow of the planet now, trying to hide as she would from another darkship. But her maneuver proved more liability than asset. The pursuers had vanished into the darkness, too, but seemed able to locate the darkship, and had the muscle to keep after it.

A thousand questions plagued Marika. She shoved them aside. They had to wait. She had to survive before she dared ask them.

She grabbed the nearest ghost. She felt a definite, startled response to her seizure. Then she had it under control and began searching for a target.,

A flare from one of the pursuing ships gave her that. She hurled the ghost, marveled at the swift cold way it dispatched the tradermales inside the ship.

Tradermales. That ship was crewed entirely by brethren. It was wholly a machine. Rage filled Marika. She clung to its fire and hurled her ghost toward another flare. Again brethren died.

All the ships around *Starstalker* were in the chase now, strung out in a long arc back around the planet's horizon. Only one more seemed to be close enough to reach the darkship with its deadly spear of light. Marika hurled her ghost again.

This time, after she finished its crew, she lingered over the ship's interior. Within minutes she understood its principles.

She explored its drive system. Brute force supplied by what Bagnel called rocket engines. She used her ghost, compressed to a point, to drill holes in a liquid-oxygen tank, then into another that carried a liquid she did not recognize, but which seemed to be a petroleum derivative.

The rear of the ship exploded.

She did the same to the other two vessels, though the last was difficult, for it was far away. She might die here in the realm of her dreams tonight, but she would make of it an expensive victory for the brethren.

She ducked back into reality to find the planet expanding below and the darkship headed back in a direction opposite that it had been flying when she went down. High above there were flares as brethren ships changed course. *Was that good enough, mistress?* she asked Kiljar.

More than adequate. A terrible awe informed the Redoriad's thought. *Now let us get down and start raising a stink.*

IV

It was not that easy. The tradermales came down after them. They plunged into atmosphere far faster than the Mistress of the Ship dared do. Spears of light ripped past the falling cross. But it fluttered and swayed in the wisps of air, making a difficult target.

Marika went back through her loophole and destroyed another two brethren ships. These proved more difficult. The tradermales were prepared for silth attack, and were very good flyers.

Nevertheless, she took them, blew them, and fragments of them raced past the darkship, beginning to glow.

Then she sensed something coming up from below. Several somethings, in fact, but one something far stronger than the others, rising on a fury like that of something elemental.

She slipped back into reality, saw that the darkship was over TelleRai now, at perhaps 250,000 feet. *Kiljar. Darkships are coming up. At least five of them.*

I know. I completed touch. The cloister is sending everyone able to come.

But it was not a Redoriad voidship that appeared moments later, shoved past, dropped like a stone, and matched fall. It bore Serke witch signs.

Marika tried to make herself small. She did not have to be told who was riding the tip of that dagger. The power of the silth reeked through the night.

Bestrei.

Bestrei, who was the destiny Gradwohl had determined for her. Bestrei, who could eat her alive right now. Bestrei, who made her feel tiny, vulnerable, without significance.

The darkship continued to fall.

Marika felt a leak of touch as something passed between Kiljar and the champion of the Serke. She was unable to read it. The ship fell, and she unslung her rifle, feeling foolish, doubting she could hit anything in her unsettled state, aware recoil might throw her off the darkship.

Another darkship materialized, coming out of the night below, not so much rising as not falling as fast till Bestrei and the Redoriad darkship caught up. It slid beneath the other darkships and took station on Bestrei's far side. Marika could not make out its witch signs, but felt it was friendly. Then another slid out of the deeps of night and fell in behind Bestrei.

Marika sensed the tension slipping away. Below, the clouds began to have a touch of glow as the lights of TelleRai illuminated them from beneath. She guessed they were below one hundred thousand feet now, falling fast, but not as fast as before. The witch signs aboard her ship had begun to wobble as though in the passage of a high wind. At that altitude the air had be extremely rare, so the ship had to have a great deal of velocity left.

She leaned back to stare at the night above. *Starstalker* had passed beyond the horizon. The surviving brethren ships had gone with it. No more danger there.

Another Redoriad darkship had appeared, was on station below Bestrei. And now Marika could sense at least a score more darkships in the sky, all closing slowly, trying to match their rapid fall. They had to have come from half a dozen Communities, for none of the dark-faring sisterhoods had so many unoccupied.

Bestrei's voidship surged forward, out of the pocket formed by the Redoriad, tilted, went down like a comet, outpacing everyone.

We are safe, Kiljar sent.

She did not do anything, Marika responded. *Why?*

Bestrei may be stupid and vain, but she has a sense of honor, Kiljar returned. *She is very old-fashioned. There was nothing in what we did deserving of challenge. She was angry with those who wakened her and sent her up. I think she will cause a stir among her sisters today. They will talk her out of it, of course. They always do. But by then it will not matter. We will be long safe, and you will be on your way back to Maksche.*

Puzzled, Marika made a mental note to investigate Bestrei more closely. *Did she recognize me?*

I think not. I did my best to distract her. It was not wise of you to start waving a rifle. There is no known silth but Marika the Reugge who flies around armed like a voctor.

What now?

Now we return to the cloister. You rest till nightfall, then hasten home. Meanwhile, the Communities will get into a great fuss about what happened. You lie low till you hear from me. There can be no more lessons till less attention is turned toward the void. I think, after this, that the Serke will have great difficulty blocking the convening of a con-

*vention. And the brethren themselves will have some long
explaining to do once that happens.*

We must find out why they are so anxious.

Of course.

The darkship plunged into the clouds, slipped through.
Another layer of clouds lay below, lighted more brightly by
the city. The Mistress plunged down through it and into the
night a few thousand feet above TelleRai.

. The entire city was in a state of ferment. Touch scalded
the air.

Chapter Twenty-six

I

Marika wakened suddenly, completely, as though by alarm, two hours before sunset. The flight into the void returned. She shuddered. So close. And that Bestrei! The sheer malignant power of the witch!

Something called her from the north. An impulse to be gone, to head home? Now? Why so intense? That was not like her.

The urge grew stronger, almost compulsive.

She completed a rapid toilet and went to her saddleship. She was eager to get back to Braydic. There would have been a great many signals today. Braydic was bound to have intercepted something that would illuminate the behavior of the Serke and brethren. There had to be some outstanding reason for their having been so touchy about having their voidship observed.

She was supposed to wait for darkness, but she could not. The compulsion had grown overwhelming. She told herself that no one would notice one tiny saddleship ripping through the dusk.

As she flitted out the window, she sent a touch seeking
Kiljar. Something came back, anxious, but by then Marika
had attained full speed and was rushing away north too fast
for Kiljar to catch the moving target.

The region of lakes appeared and fell behind. The Topol
Cordillera passed below, speckled golden and orange in the
fading light. She reached the Hainlin and turned upstream.
Seventy miles south of Maksche she passed over a squadron
of brethren dirigibles plowing along on a westward course.
Seven? Eight? What in the world? The setting sun made
great orange fingers of them. Some were as big as the first
airship she had ever seen. What did that mean?

Minutes later she began to suspect.

The light of the setting sun painted the westward face of a
pillar of smoke that rose in a great tower far ahead, leaning
slightly with the breeze, vanishing into high cloud cover.
The reverse face of the pillar was almost black, so dense was
the smoke. As she drew nearer, she began to pick out the
fires feeding it.

Maksche. All Maksche was aflame. That could not be.
How? . . .

She forced her ghosts to stretch themselves, plowed down
through thicker air so swiftly it howled around her.

She roared right through the smoke, so shocked she
barely maintained sense enough to stay above the taller
towers. The cloister was the heart of it. The Reugge bastion
had been gutted. The main fires now burned among the
factories and tinderbox homes of Reugge bonds.

Meth still scampered around down there, valiantly fighting the flames. They fought in a losing cause. Back over the
cloister Marika passed, and saw scores upon scores of bodies
scattered in the sooty courts, upon the blackened ramparts.
She dropped lower, though the heat remained intense. The
stone walls radiated like those of a kiln. She let her touch
roam the remains, found nothing living.

She had not expected to find anything. Nothing could
have lived through the inferno that raged down there.

Up she went, and across the city, touch-trolling, pain
filling her. She hurt as she had not hurt since the day the

nomads had crossed the packstead wall and left none but herself and Kublin living. And Grauel and Barlog.

Grauel! Barlog! No! She could not be alone now!

Touch could not find one silth mind.

She heard shooting as she rocketed over the tradermale enclave, certain it had had something to do with the disaster.

She went down, saw tradermales behind boxes and bales and corners of buildings firing at the gatehouse. Rifles barked back at them. Outside the gatehouse lay two dead meth in Reugge livery. Voctors. They had attacked the enclave.

She read the situation instantly. The huntresses were survivors of the holocaust. They had decided to die with honor, storming the source of their grief.

Tradermales in great numbers were closing a circle around the gatehouse. Machine guns yammered away, slowly gnawing at the structure. None of the brethren looked up.

They might not have seen her in the treacherous firelight anyway.

Marika lifted her saddleship a hundred feet, detached one large ghost, and sent it ravening while her conveyance settled toward the runway. By the time the carved legs of the wooden beast touched concrete, the male survivors were in full flight, headed for the one small dirigible cradled across the field.

Marika dismounted, sent the ghost after them. They died swiftly.

The firing from the gatehouse had ceased. Because the huntresses there were dead? Or because they had recognized her? She started that way.

A badly mauled Grauel slipped out a doorway, stood propped against the building. There was blood all over her.

Marika ran to her, threw her arms around her. "Grauel. By the All, what happened? This is insane."

Weakly, Grauel gasped into her ear, "Last night. During the night. The warlock came. With his rogues. Hundreds of them. He had a machine that neutralized the silth. He attacked the cloister. Some of us decided to break out and circle around. One of the sisters thought they had come in on tradermale dirigibles because a whole flight of airships dropped into the enclave after sunset."

"Where's Barlog?"

"Inside. She's hurt. You'll have to help her, Marika."

"Go on. Tell me the rest." She thought of that westbound squadron she had seen during her passage north. The same? Almost certainly. She had been within a few thousand feet of the warlock, that she had thought an imaginary beast.

"They destroyed the cloister. Surely you saw."

"I saw."

"Then they destroyed everything that belonged to the Reugge and Brown Paw Bond. The fires got out of control. I think they would have killed everyone in the city just so there would be no witnesses, but the fires drove them off. They left a couple of hours ago, just leaving the one airship load to finish up. I think they may have wanted to search the ruins after the fires died down, too."

"Come inside. You have to rest." Marika supported Grauel's weight. Inside she found most of a dozen huntresses. The majority were dead. Barlog was lying on her side, a froth of blood upon her muzzle. Only one very young voctor was uninjured. She was in a state bordering on hysteria.

Bagnel lay among the casualties. He had been bound and gagged. Marika leapt toward him.

He was not dead either, though he had several bullets in him. He regained consciousness briefly as she pulled the gag from his mouth. He croaked, " I am sorry, Marika. I did not know what was happening."

She recalled Grauel saying the raiders had destroyed Brown Paw Bond as well as Reugge properties. "For once I believe you. You are an honorable meth, for a male. We will talk later. I have things to do." She turned. "Grauel. You're in charge. Get this pup settled down and have her do what she can. And, Grauel? When I get back I want to find Bagnel healthy. Do you understand?"

"Yes. What are you doing, Marika?"

"I have a score to balance. This is going to become painfully costly for those responsible."

"You're going after them?"

"I am."

"Marika, there were hundreds of them. They had every sort of weapon you can imagine. And they had a machine that can keep silth from walking the dark side."

"That is of no import, Grauel. I will destroy them anyway. Or they will destroy me. This marks the end of my patience with them. And with anyone who defends them. You tell me the one called the warlock was with them. Did you see him?"

"He was. I saw him from very far away. He did not move far from the airships. We tried very hard to shoot him, but the range was too great. He was very strong, Marika. Stronger than most silth."

"Not stronger than I am, I am sure. He will pay. The brethren will pay. Though I be declared an outlaw, though I stand alone, this is the first day of bloodfeud between myself and them. Stay here. I'll be back."

"And if you're not?"

"You do what you have to do. Sooner or later someone will come."

"And maybe not, Marika. Before we lost the signals section, we heard that they were attacking several other cloisters as well."

"That figures." Where did they gather their strength? She had been killing and imprisoning them for years.

"Braydic did have some advance warning, Marika. She tried to tell us. But you flew off to TelleRai too fast."

Marika recalled Barlog rushing into her quarters as she went out the window.

This was her fault, then. If she had waited a moment . . . Too late for regrets. It was time to give pain for pain received.

"Good-bye, Grauel." She stalked out of the gatehouse, and shut everything behind her out of mind, out of her life. Bloodfeud. There was nothing but the bloodfeud. From this moment till death. A short time, perhaps.

An entire squadron of dirigibles. How did one go about destroying them? Especially when they had some device capable of rendering a silth's talent impotent?

Worry about that in its time. First she had to find them again. She strapped herself on to her saddleship and rose into the night, raced to the southwest, cutting a course that would cross that last seen being made by the dirigibles.

II

Marika did not spare herself. In less than an hour she found the squadron, still doggedly flying westward, chasing the vanished sun. The ships were down low, hugging a barren landscape. They did not want to be seen.

She hung above them a few minutes, way up in the rare air. She was tempted to strike then, but desisted. She even refrained from probing, certain the wehrlen would detect her. Then she found her appropriate idea.

They had attacked silth using a device that stole the silth talent. She would requite them in similar coin.

Maps slipped through her mind. Yes. A major, remote brethren enclave lay nearly two hundred miles ahead. Their destination? Probably. There were no neighbors to witness what villainy was being launched from the enclave. She headed there as swiftly as she could, dropping to treetop level as she approached, flying slower because of the denser air and reduced visibility.

She hedgehopped because she was not sure her saddleship would be invisible to tradermale radar. What she had learned from Bagnel suggested she would not be seen, but now was no time to make such bets. Now she wanted to play the longer odds her own way.

She supposed she was an hour ahead of the dirigibles when she reached the edge of the enclave. There were hundreds of lights burning there, lots of activity. Yes. The base expected the raiders. Doubtless it had been the staging ground for all the attacks. The sheer number of males suggested something of vast proportion being managed from there. There were thousands of males. And the enclave bristled with weaponry. Whole squadrons of fighting aircraft sat upon the runway. Half a dozen dirigibles rested in the enclave's cradles, and there were cradles enough to take another score.

She gave herself ten minutes to rest, then she ducked through her loophole. Her anger was such that she wanted to go ravening among these brethren, killing all she could, but she did not yield to the red rage. She scouted instead, and was astounded by the magnitude of what she had found.

She did not let numbers intimidate her.

Once she was certain she knew where everything lay, she came back, checked the time, went out, and collected the most awesome monster of a ghost she could reach. She took it to the tradermale communications center.

It took her ten seconds to wreck the center and slay the technicians there. Then she drove the ghost to a workshop stocking instruments she suspected of being the devices the tradermales used to neutralize the silth. They resembled the box she had destroyed during the first confrontation on the airstrip at the Maksche enclave.

She wrecked them all, then scooted around the base, ruining anything that resembled them.

Only when that was done did she allow herself to go mad, to begin the killing.

There were so many of them that it took her half an hour. But when she finished there was not one live male inside the enclave. Hundreds had escaped, after panicking in typical male fashion. By now they were well on their ways to wherever they were trying to run. She did not expect them back.

She came back to her flesh, checked the time again. The dirigibles should arrive soon. Maybe fifteen minutes. By now they should be alert because they could make no radio contact.

She wanted to rest, to bring herself down from the nerve-wrecking high of the bloodletting, but she had no time. She trotted forward, catching a ghost once more and using it to slice a hole through the metal fence surrounding the enclave. She slipped through and raced toward the combat aircraft.

Every one was fully fueled and armed. The Stings even carried rockets. The males had been ready. Ready for anything but her. She examined several aircraft quickly, as Bagnel had taught her, and selected the one that looked soundest. Into it she climbed.

It was a well-maintained ship. Its starter turned over, and its engine caught immediately. She warmed it as Bagnel had taught her, a part of her blackly amused that one of the brethren had taught her to use the one weapon that would be effective for what she planned.

Eight minutes, roughly. They should be in sight soon. She jumped out of the aircraft, kicked the chocks away, piled back inside, harnessed herself, closed the canopy, and shoved forward on the throttle. Down the runway she rolled, and whipped upward into the night, without moonlight to help or hinder. Night was the time of the silth.

This would be a surprise for them. They seldom flew by night. Too dangerous. But they did not have the silth senses she did. Except for one.

Up. Up. Eight thousand feet. Where were they? They were showing no running lights. She caught a ghost, took it hunting.

There. The dirigibles were several minutes behind the schedule she had estimated. They were running more slowly than before. Perhaps they were concerned about the enclave's lack of response.

Down. Full throttle. Bagnel said you should fight at full throttle, though no one he knew ever had been in actual aerial combat. The brethren pilots skirmished with themselves, practicing.

She found the safeties for the guns and rockets. She was not quite sure what she was doing with those. Bagnel had not let her fire weapons.

A dark sausage shape appeared suddenly. She yanked back on the stick as she touched the firing button. Tracers reached, stitched the bag, rose above it. She barely avoided a collision.

Back on the throttle. Lesser speed and turn. At the speed she had been making there was no time to spot and maneuver.

Up and over in a loop. Grab a ghost during the maneuver. Use it to pick a target. Close in. Tracers reaching as she ran in from behind, along the airship's length, the belly of the Sting nearly touching it.

Still too fast. And doing no special damage.

She sideslipped between two dirigibles and came up from below, firing into a gondola, felt the pain of males hit, saw the flash of weapons as a few small arms fired back. Could they see her at all?

She felt the brush of one of the talent suppressors. For an instant it seemed half her mind had been turned off. But it did not bother her as much as she expected.

In the early days, at Akard, she had somehow learned to get around the worst effects of proximity to electromagnetic energies. This was something of the sort, and something inside her responded, pushing its worst effects away.

She turned away, found a ghost as soon as she could, reached in to study the airships more closely. This was not quite the same as seeing drawings in books.

She slammed the throttle forward and went after the airship out front.

Which ship carried the warlock? Would he respond to her attack?

She came in from the flank and fired a rocket. It drove well into the gasbag before blowing its warhead. Deeply enough to pass through the outer protective helium bag and reach the bigger hydrogen bag inside.

The brethren used hydrogen only when they wanted to move especially heavy cargoes. For this raid they had used hydrogen aboard all the airships, inside, where Reugge small arms could not penetrate.

She rolled under the dirigible as it exploded. The Sting was buffeted by the explosion. She fought for control, regained it, climbed, turned upon the rest of the squadron.

She glanced over her shoulder, watched the airship burn and fall, meth with fur aflame leaping from its gondola.

"One gone," she said aloud, and found herself another ghost. She used it to spot another target.

This time the neutralizing weapon met her squarely. Its effect was like a blow from a fist. Yet she gasped, shook its worst effects, fired a rocket, climbed away. Small arms hammered the night. The very air was filled with panic. She came around and swept through the squadron, firing her guns, felt them firing back without regard for where their bullets might be going.

Back again. And again. And again. Till the Sting's munitions were exhausted. Five of the airships went toward the ground, four of them in flames, the fifth with gasbags so riddled it could no longer balance the leaks.

Now she was at risk. If she wished to continue attacking, she would have to go take another aircraft. If they came after her . . .

But they did not. Their vaunted warlock seemed as panicked as the rest. The survivors shifted course.

Marika put the Sting down fast and hard. She threw herself out of the cockpit even before it stopped rolling, hit the concrete running, and picked a second aircraft. In ten minutes she was aloft again, pursuing the remnants of the airship squadron.

One after another she sent them down and continued to attack till each had burned. She went back for the one that had descended for lack of lift, used her last two rockets to fire it.

Where was the warlock? Why did he not fight back? Was he staying low, sacrificing everything, because he knew the certain destruction he faced if he gave himself away? Or had he been killed early?

She returned to the enclave. And this time when she crawled into a cockpit, she went to sleep.

She did not have much left. They could have taken her then, easily.

She wakened before dawn, startled alert. Someone was

nearby. She reached for a ghost rather than raise her head and betray herself.

Some of the males from the airships had found their way to the base. They were standing around stunned, unable to believe what had happened.

Marika's anger remained searing hot. Not enough blood had been spilled to quench the flames. She took them, adding them to the hundreds of corpses already littering the enclave. Then she started the Sting and went aloft, and in the light of dawn examined the wreckage of the dirigibles she had downed. She could not believe she had managed so much destruction.

She strafed survivors wherever she found them, like a pup torturing a crippled animal. She could have slaughtered them with her talent easily, but she was so filled with hatred that she took more pleasure in giving them a slow, taunting death, letting them run and run and run till she tracked them down.

But by midday that had lost its zest. She returned to the enclave and settled into a more systematic, businesslike revenge. After spending a few hours demolishing the base, she went to her saddleship and resumed hunting survivors again.

The brethren and rogues would not soon forget the cost of their treachery.

She wondered if she ought not to try taking a few prisoners. Questions really ought to be asked about the fate of the wehrlen. If he had existed at all, his survival might well keep the rogue movement alive despite her fury.

Toward sundown she suffered a horrible shock.

She was circling above woods where a dirigible had gone down, and . . . two things happened at once. She detected a small force of dirigibles approaching the enclave from the north, which fired her hatred anew, while below her she detected a moving meth spark that was all too familiar.

Kublin!

III

Kublin. More killer airships. Which way to throw herself?

Those airships would not be able to flee fast enough to escape her. She could catch them later. Kublin might vanish into the forest.

Down she went, among the trees, pushing through branches till her saddleship rode inches off the ground. She stalked him carefully, for he seemed quite aware that he was being hunted. He moved fast and quiet, with the skill of a huntress. Once, when she drew close, he sent a burst of automatic weapons fire so close one bullet nicked the neck of her saddleship.

Kublin. The treasured littermate for whom she had risked everything. Here. With the killers of her cloister.

Even now she did not want to harm him, though she remained possessed of a virulent hatred. She seized a small, feeble ghost and went hunting him, found him, struck quickly, and touched him lightly.

He brushed the ghost aside and threw a stronger back at her, almost knocking her off her saddle.

What?

Wehrlen!

Kublin?

Another blow as ferocious as the last. Yes. It could not be denied.

She dodged his blows and collected a stronger ghost, struck hard enough to knock him down. He struggled to fight off the effects.

He did have the talent, though he was no stronger than a weak sister.

In a way, it made sense. They were of the same litter, the same antecedents. He had shown a feel for the talent as a pup, a strong interest in her own early unfoldings of silth talents.

She grounded the saddleship, rushed him before he could recover, hit him physically several times, then slowly, forcibly, nullified his talent, reaching inside to depress that center of the brain where the talent lived.

Her attack left him too groggy to answer questions.

She sat down and waited, studying the uniform he wore.

She had seen its like several times before. The rogues wore uniforms occasionally. She had examined enough prisoners to have learned their uniform insignia.

Either Kublin had adopted insignia not properly his or he was very important among the rogues. Very important, indeed. If his insignia could be believed, he was a member of their ruling council.

She should have killed him in the Ponath. Before she asked the first question, she had the dark feeling the Maksche raid would not have occurred had she finished him there.

She ached inside. He was still Kublin, her littermate, with whom she had shared so much as a pup. He was the only meth for whom she had ever felt any love.

He recovered slowly, sat up weakly, shook the fuzziness from his mind, felt around for his weapon. Marika had thrown it into the brush. He seemed puzzled because it was not there beside him. Then his glance chanced upon Marika, sitting there with her own rifle trained upon him.

He froze. In mind and body.

"Yes. Me again. I did all that last night. And I have just begun. When I have finished, the brethren and rogues will be as desolate as Maksche. And you are going to help me destroy them."

Fear obliterated Kublins's defiance. He never did have much courage.

"How does a coward rise so high among fighters, Kublin? Ah. But of course. You rogues and brethren are all cowards. Stabbers in the back. Friends by day and murderers by night. But the night is the time of the silth.

"No! I do not want to hear your rationale, Kublin. I have heard it all before. I have been feeding on rogues for years. I am the Marika who has taken so many of your accomplices that we no longer have room for laborers in the Reugge mines. You know what I am doing with them now? Selling

them to the Treiche. They have a hard time maintaining an
adequate work force in their sulfur pits. The fumes. They
use up workers quickly. I do not think it will be long before
the Treiche have all the methpower they can handle."

"Stinking witch," he muttered, without force.

"Yes. I am. Also an enraged, bloodthirsty witch. So
enraged I will destroy you brethren and your proxies, the
rogues and this warlock, even if I die in the process. Now it
is time for you to sleep. I have more airships to destroy.
Later, I will return and ask you about this great warlock,
this great cowardly murderer who animates you rogues so."

He gave her an odd look.

She continued, "This is the base from which the whole
filthy thing was launched. It is fitting that the villains die
here. I will wait here and slaughter your accomplices as they
return." She snagged a ghost and touched him, left him in a
coma.

She slew the crews of two airships. The others drove her
off with the talent suppressors. She had made a mistake,
destroying everything at the enclave. The Sting remained
the best weapon against airships.

Later, she decided. She would find more fighting aircraft
somewhere else.

The madness had begun to pass. She could not get her
whole heart into the fight. It was time to move on. Time to
take Kublin in and drain him of knowledge. Time to find the
most senior and join her in assessing the damage to the
Reugge Community.

Time to rest, to eat, to recover. She was little stronger
than a young pup.

She returned to Kublin.

He had wakened and gnawed at his wrists in an effort to
kill himself. Her touch had left him too groggy to succeed.
She was astonished that he had had the will and nerve to
try. This was her cowardly Kublin? Maybe his courage was
selective.

She bandaged him with strips torn from his clothing, then
threw him across the neck of her saddleship. She clambered
aboard, called up ghosts, rose from the woods. Airships

quartered the wind to the west, searching for those who had destroyed the enclave and attacked them. She bared her teeth in bitter amusement. Never would they believe that all that damage had been done by a single outraged silth.

"Have to be more careful next time," she mused. "The time after that for sure. They will be ready for any kind of trouble then."

As the saddleship limped eastward, slow and unstable with Kublin aboard, she fantasized about the Tovand, the main brethren enclave in TelleRai. A major strike there would make a dramatic statement. One that could not be misinterpreted. She imagined herself penetrating its halls by night, stalking them like death itself, leaving a trail of corpses for the survivors to find come sunup. Surely that would be something to make the villains think.

Chapter Twenty-seven

I

Marika's passage eastward was a slow one. The extra burden of her littermate added geometrically to her labor. And she had been expending her reserves for days.

Each fifty miles she descended for an hour of rest. One by one, the moons rose. She considered Biter and Chaser and a point that might be the Serke voidship *Starstalker*. The weather seemed better lately. Did clear skies signal a change for the better? Or just a brief respite?

It took her awhile to recall that it was the tail end of summer. In a month the storm season would arrive. The snows would return. Below, scattered patches threw back silvery glimmers. Despite the season and latitude. It would get no better.

As Marika neared the Hainlin she sensed something ahead. It was little more than a premonition, but she took the saddleship down. Kublin whimpered as the bottom dropped out.

Too late. That something had sensed her presence, too. It moved toward her.

Silth.

She dropped to the surface, skipped off the saddleship, slithered into the brush, checked her rifle and pistol, ducked through her loophole to examine the ghost population. "Damn," she whispered without force. "Damn. Why now, when I'm too tired to face a novice?" The All laughed in the secret night.

She did her best to make herself invisible to silth senses.

The silth did miss her on her first passage, sliding over slightly to the north. Marika extended no probes, for she did not want to alert the hunting Mistress or her bath.

She felt the silth halt at the edge of perception, turn back. "Damn it again." She slipped the safety off her rifle, then collected a strong ghost.

She would not use the ghost offensively. She was too weak. She would fend attacks only, and use the rifle when she had the chance. Few silth expected rifle fire from other silth.

Not once did it occur to her that the prowler might be friendly.

The silth approached cautiously. Marika became more certain her intentions were unfriendly. And she was a strong one, for she masked herself well.

Almost overhead now. Low. Maybe she could get a killing burst off before . . . A shape moved in the moonlight, dark, low, slow. . . .

That was no darkship! That was a saddleship like her own.

Marika?

There was no mistaking the odor of that touch. Gradwohl! A flood of relief. *Here, mistress. Right below you.* She left the brush and walked toward her own saddleship as the most senior descended.

"What are you doing here, mistress?"

"Looking for you. What have you been doing?"

"I went after the raiders. Have you been to Maksche, mistress?"

"I came from there."

"Then you know. I got them, mistress. All of them. And

many more besides. Perhaps even their warlock. They have paid the first installment."

Gradwohl remained astride her saddleship, a twin of Marika's. Marika mounted her own. Gradwohl indicated Kublin. "What is that?"

"A high-ranking prisoner, mistress. Probably one of the leaders of the attack. I have not yet questioned him. I was considering a truthsaying after I have recovered my strength."

She felt rested after the few minutes down, despite the tension. She was eager to get back to Grauel and Barlog. She lifted her saddleship. Gradwohl followed, hastened to assume the position of honor. They rose into the moonlight and drifted eastward at a comfortable pace.

I want you to drink chaphe when we get back, Gradwohl sent. *I want you to rest long and well. We have much to discuss.*

Marika considered that thoroughly before she responded. Between them she and Gradwohl had seldom shifted from the formal mode, yet tonight there was an unusually odd, distant aroma to the most senior's sending. She was distressed about something.

What is wrong, mistress?

Later, Marika. After you have rested. I do not want to go into it when you are so exhausted you may not be in control of all your faculties.

Marika did not like the increased distance implied by the sending's tone. *I think we had best discuss what must be discussed now. In the privacy of the night. I sense a gulf opening between us. This I cannot comprehend. Why, mistress?*

If you insist, then. The Reugge have been crippled, Marika. This is what is wrong. This is what we must discuss. The Reugge have been hurt badly, and you want to make the situation worse.

Mistress? The Reugge have been hurt, that is true, but we have not been destroyed. I believe the cornerstones of our strength remain intact. We can turn it around on the brethren and—

We will turn it around, but not in blood. All the world knows what happened. No one believes rogues made the raids on their own, unsupported. Those, and Kiljar's experience with the Serke voidship, have been enough to cause a general clamor for a convention. Even by some elements within the brethren. The Brown Paw Bond nearly ceased to exist because of the raids. Their enemies within the brotherhood tried to exterminate them along with us. The Redoriad are going to demand dismemberment of the Serke and the banning of all brethren from space for at least a generation. Already some among the brethren are crawling sideways, whimpering as they try to bargain for special consideration for their particular Bonds. They have imprisoned a number of high masters, saying they acted on their own, without approval, in a conspiracy with the Serke. We have won the long struggle, Marika. At great expense, yes, but without resort to challenge or direct bloodletting— other than that in which you have indulged yourself. It is time now to back away and let the convention finish it for us.

You will accept that? After all these years? After all the Reugge have suffered? You will not extract payment in blood?

I will not.

Marika reflected a moment. *Mistress, will I be continuing my education with Kiljar?*

Gradwohl seemed reluctant to respond. Finally, she sent, *There will be no need, will there? Bestrei will have been disarmed by the dispersal of her Community.*

I see.

I am not sure you do. Your focus is sometimes too narrow. That is why I want you to rest under the influence of chaphe. To become totally recovered before we examine this in detail. I want you able to see the whole situation and all the options. We will be headed for a period of delicate negotiations.

What will become of Bestrei? She could not imagine a sisterhood being dismantled. But there were precedents. The

Librach had been disbanded by force after a convention four
centuries earlier, after considerable bloodshed.

*She will be adopted into another Community. If she
wishes.*

And the Serke assets?

They will be dispersed according to outstanding claims.

*The Reugge will possess the strongest of those. Yes? And
because the brethren will pretend to have been used, and to
be contrite, and will sacrifice a few factors, they will get off
with a wrist slap. And in a generation, before you and I are
even gone, they will be back stronger than ever, better
prepared, more thoroughly insinuated into the fabric of
society.*

*Marika. I told you you should rest before we discuss
this. You are becoming unreasonably emotional.*

*I am sorry, mistress. I remain a Ponath bitch at heart.
When I see bloodfeud directed my way, I have difficulty
letting the declarer beg off if he sees that he is going to lose.
Particularly when he will return as soon as he feels strong
enough to try again.*

The brethren were manipulated by the Serke.

*You are a fool if you believe that, mistress. The brethren
were the manipulators. You have seen the evidence. They
used the Serke, and now I see them starting to use you even
before they have shed their previous victims.*

*Marika! Do not anger me. You have been brought far in a
very short time. You are a member of the ruling council of
the Reugge, soon to be one of the major orders.*

At the price of honor?

*Do not harp on honor, pup. Yours remains indicted by the
existence of the male lying before you.*

Mistress? Coldness crept into Marika.

Would you subject him to a truthsaying? Really? Now?

*It would provide the final proof of the villainy of the
brethren.*

Perhaps. And what would it prove about you?

Mistress?

*You accuse me, Marika. By your tone you accuse me of
crimes. Yet I have forgiven you yours. Dorteka was pre-*

cious to me, pup, yet I forgave even that. For the sake of the Community.

You know?

I have known for more than a year. The Serke presented the evidence. You saved a littermate in the Ponath. The result was what has happened these past few days. But even that I can forgive. If you will shed the role of Jiana.

Jiana? And, You engineered this holocaust? This is where you were headed all along? You had no intention of challenging Bestrei? Of breaking into the void? I was just your distraction?

I pursued both goals equally, Marika. The success of either would have satisfied me. My mission is to preserve and strengthen the Reugge. I have done that. I will not permit you to diminish or destroy what I have won.

You called me Jiana. I do not like that.

There are times when you seem determined to fill the role.

Mistress?

Everywhere you go. Maksche is just the latest.

I had nothing to do with that. I was in TelleRai when—

You were. Yes. And that is the only reason you survived. The rhythm of your visits altered. The only reason the brethren attacked was to destroy you. You, Marika. The other attacks were diversions meant to keep aid from rushing to Maksche. But you were not there. You went off to TelleRai off schedule. You did not have the decency to perish. Accept, Marika. Do not continue to be a doomstalker.

I am no doomstalker, mistress.

Destruction walks in your shadow, pup.

This is foolishness, mistress.

First your packstead, Marika. Then your fortress, your packfast, Akard. Now Maksche. What has to happen before you see? The end of the world itself?

Marika was baffled. Gradwohl had been sound of mind always, spurning such superstitious nonsense. This made no sense. *All these things would have happened without me, mistress. The brethren and Serke began their game long before anyone ever heard of Marika.* •

The All knew you. And the All moved them.

Marika gave up. No argument could change a closed, mad mind. She peered down at moonlight reflected off the Hainlin. That was as much of the void as she might see. *I want the stars, mistress.*

I know, Marika. Perhaps we can get something for you in the settlement.

I will not accept perhaps, Most Senior.

This is not the time to—

This is the time.

This is what I feared. This is why I did not want to discuss this with you now. I knew you would be unsettled.

When will this convention set the silth stamp of approval on the treacheries of the brethren?

The first session will meet as soon as I reach TelleRai. I will take my saddleship south as soon as I have won your promise to support me.

I cannot give you that, mistress. My conscience will not permit it. There is bloodfeud involved. You would betray all those sisters who have perished.

Damned stubborn savage. Put aside your primitive ways. We are not living in the upper Ponath. This is the real world. Allowances and adjustments have to be made.

Wrong.

I did not want it to come to this, pup.

Marika felt the otherworld stir. She was not surprised, nor even much frightened. The moment seemed destined.

She did not try her loophole. It was too late for that. She did what silth never seemed to expect. She squeezed the trigger of the rifle she had not returned to safety. The entire magazine hammered the air.

Gradwohl separated from her saddleship and tumbled toward the river.

Marika! Damn you, Jiana! Then the sensing of Gradwohl vanished into a fog of pain. And then that spark went out.

Marika circled twice, fixing the spot in her mind. Then she went on, composing herself for Maksche.

II

Marika had nothing left when she brought the saddleship down on the airstrip near Bagnel's quarters, Kublin still limp across its neck. Someone came out, recognized her, shouted back inside. In a moment Grauel limped forth. She reached out feebly, far too slowly, as Marika slipped off and fell to the concrete. "You're still here," Marika rasped.

"Yes." Grauel tried to lift her to her feet, could not. More meth gathered around. Marika recognized faces she had not seen last visit. Somehow, Grauel had assembled some survivors. "The most senior told us to remain."

"Gradwohl. Where is she?"

"She went looking for you."

"Oh. I got them, Grauel. Every one of them."

"Take her inside," Grauel told the others. "Where did you find him?" She indicated Kublin.

"With them. He may have been one of their commanders."

"Oh."

"Yes."

"Give her the chaphe," Grauel ordered as they entered the building.

"Grauel. . . ."

"The most senior's orders, Marika. You get two days of enforced rest."

Marika surrendered. She did not have the strength to resist.

Several times she wakened, found Grauel nearby. She told the huntress about the brethren base in snatches. Grauel did not seem much interested. Marika allowed the enforced rest to continue, for she had stretched herself more than she had realized. But the third night she refused the drug. "Where is the most senior? Enough is enough. Things are happening and we are out of touch."

"She has not returned, Marika. I have become concerned. Sisters from TelleRai were here this morning, seeking her. I had thought she might have gone there."

"And?" Time to be cautious. Time to have a care with Grauel, who persisted in using the formal mode.

"They flew west, seeking some trace. I believe they called for more darkships to join in the search. They were very worried."

"Why?"

"The . . . You do not know, do you? A convention of the Communities has been called to bring the Serke and brethren to account. The most senior must be there. The Reugge are the principal grievants."

Marika struggled up from her cot. "That's happening? Gradwohl is missing? And you've kept me drugged? Grauel, what . . . ?"

"Her orders, Marika."

"Orders or not, that's over. Bring me food. Bring me fresh clothing. Bring me my weapons and prepare my saddleship."

"Marika. . . ."

"I have to go to TelleRai. Someone has to represent the most senior's viewpoint. Someone has to be there if the worst has happened. If the brethren have slain her and the wrong sisters hear of it first, her whole dream will die. Get me out of here, Grauel. I'll send for you as soon as I get there."

"As you command."

Marika did not like Grauel's tone. She let it slide. "How is Barlog doing?"

"Recovering. The most senior was able to save her."

There was an accusation behind those words. "I am sorry, Grauel. I was not myself that day."

"Are you ever, Marika? Are you now? Have you slaked your blood thirst yet?"

"I think so."

"I hope so. They say this convention is an opportunity to

end what has been happening. I would not want to see it fail."

"How are Bagnel and Kublin doing?"

"Bagnel is recovering nicely. The most senior treated him, too, inasmuch as he seems to be the sole surviving Brown Paw Bonder from this enclave. Kublin is in chains. There were those who wanted to do him injury. I have protected him."

"Maybe you shouldn't have. I'm not sure why I brought him in. When the darkship comes, bring him to TelleRai. He may prove useful during the convention."

"Perhaps."

"What is the matter, Grauel? I feel . . ."

"I fear you, Marika. Since you returned from this vengeance, even I can see the look of doom upon you. And I fear you the more because Gradwohl is not here to temper your ferocity."

"Be about your business, Grauel." Marika stood. Her legs were weak. She ducked through her loophole to check her grasp of the otherworld, fearful she might not be strong enough to get to TelleRai in time.

She would manage. She was not weak in her grasp of the dark.

She visited Bagnel briefly. He apologized again. "It was despicable," she agreed. "But I think we're about to conclude that era. Keep well, Bagnel." Outside, as she prepared to mount her saddleship, Marika told Grauel, "Bring Bagnel, too."

"Yes, mistress."

Marika looked at Grauel grimly. She did not like it when the huntress took the formal mode. It meant Grauel did not approve.

Irked, she lifted the saddleship without another word.

She sped southward, paused briefly where Gradwohl had gone down. She found no trace of the most senior's body. She did find Gradwohl's saddleship, broken, in a tree. She dragged it out, dismantled it, threw the pieces into the river. Let them become driftwood, joining other flotsam come down from the dying north.

The sisters at TelleRai were not pleased with her advent. Many had hoped she had perished in the raid. More feared the most senior had perished sometime afterward. They dreaded the chance the savage northerner would lay claim to the most senior's mantle.

As strength goes. They were convinced none could challenge the outlander.

"I will not replace the most senior," Marika told anyone who would listen. "It has never been my wish to become most senior. But I will speak for Gradwohl till she returns. Her mind is my mind."

Word of what had happened at the enclave in the wilderness had reached TelleRai. Though Marika did not claim responsibility and no one made direct accusations, there were no doubts anywhere who had been responsible for the slaughter. Terror hung around her like a fog. No one would dispute anything she said.

Grauel and Barlog, Kublin and Bagnel arrived a day after Marika, near dawn, with the first group of survivors brought out of the ruins of Maksche. Marika had insisted that every survivor, including workers and Reugge bonds, be evacuated south. That earned her no friends, for it would strain the resources of the TelleRai cloister.

Barlog was somewhat recovered. She was not pleasant at all when Marika visited her.

There was a small fuss when Marika insisted Bagnel be assigned guest quarters. She had Kublin imprisoned. She did not visit him.

Grauel and Barlog retired to their new quarters to rest, or to hide. Marika was not certain which. They were attached to Marika's own, where she paced outside their door, wondering what she could do to recover their goodwill.

Someone knocked on the apartment door. Marika answered it, found a novice outside. "Yes?"

"Mistress, second Kiljar of the Redoriad wishes to speak with you."

"Is she here?"

"No, mistress. She sent a messenger. Will there be any reply?"

"Tell her yes. The second hour after noon, if that is convenient. In the usual place. She will understand what I mean."

"Yes, mistress."

Shortly after the novice departed, sisters Cyalgon and Tascil, the order's sixth and third chairs, in TelleRai for the convention, came calling. Marika knew Cyalgon. She had been with the party that had gone to the Redoriad museum. She presumed upon that now. After the appropriate greetings, Marika asked, "To what do I owe the honor of your visit?"

Cyalgon was direct. "First chair. You say you would refuse it. We wish to know if this is true or just a ploy."

"I have made no secret of the fact that I have no wish to bury myself in the petty details that plague a most senior. But for that I would not mind having a Community behind me."

"Perhaps something might be arranged."

"Oh?"

"Someone might assume the weight of detail."

"I will not become a figurehead in any task I assume. In any case, I would prefer being the power behind. I am young, mistress. I still have dreams. But this whole discussion is moot. The Reugge have a most senior."

"It begins to appear that Gradwohl is no longer with us."

"Mistress?"

"Even experts at the long touch cannot detect her."

"Perhaps she is hiding."

"From her own sisters? At a time like this? She would have responded if she could. She must be dead."

"Or possibly a prisoner? Suppose the brethen captured her. Or the Serke. They could have lifted her off-planet. She could be alive and there be no way to touch her."

"Amounts to the same thing."

"I fear it does not. I fear I do not want to be party to what could later be interpreted as an attempt to oust a most senior who has been very good to me. I think I would like stronger proof that she is not with us. But I will give the matter some thought. I will speak to you later."

They had not gotten what they wanted. They departed with shoulders angrily stiff.

"Starting to line up for a grab-off," Marika snarled after they departed. "I suppose I will hear from them all. I wish I knew them better."

She was speaking to herself. But a voice from behind said, "Perhaps if you had paid more attention to your duties here. . . ."

"Enough, Grauel. I am going out. Take the names of any who ask to see me. Tell them I will contact them later."

"As you command, mistress."

Irked, Marika began assembling her saddleship.

III

Marika swept in over the Redoriad cloister as fast as she dared, hoping to remain unnoticed. Vain hope. There was an inconvenient break in the cloud cover. Her shadow ran across the courts below, catching the eyes of several Redoriad bonds. By the time she reached Kiljar's window, meth were running everywhere.

"You came," Kiljar said.

"Of course. Why not?"

"I received your message but doubted you would make it. My sources suggested there is a lot of maneuvering going on inside the Reugge."

"I have been approached," Marika admitted. "But only once. I will tell them all the same thing. First chair is not open. If it were, I would not take it. Though I do want someone philosophically compatible to be most senior. I am busy enough with the brethren and Serke."

"That is what I wanted to discuss with you."

"Mistress?"

"Do not become defensive, Marika. It is time you assessed your position. Time you shed this hard stance."

Marika's jaw tightened.

"Were you not satisfied with what you wrought at that brethren enclave?"

"No, mistress. That was not sufficient at all. That was an insect's sting. I am going to devour them. They destroyed a city. Without cause or justification. They will pay the price."

"I do not understand you, Marika. Victory is not enough. Why do you make this a personal vendetta?"

"Mistress?"

"You are not killing for the honor or salvation of your Community. You are more selfish than the run of silth. No! Do not deny it. For you your order is a ladder to climb toward personal goals. Gradwohl was crafty enough to use you to the benefit of the Reugge. But now Gradwohl is gone. We all fear. . . ."

"Why does everyone insist that? For years Gradwohl has been in the habit of disappearing. Sometimes for months."

"This time it is for good, Marika."

"How can you know that?" A blade of ice slashed at her heart.

Kublin might know what had become of Gradwohl. That had not occurred to her before. Suppose he had not been unconscious throughout the whole flight? Indeed, all he needed to know was that she and Gradwohl had met.

"Come." Kiljar led her to another room. "Look." She indicated fragments of wood. Some retained bits of gaudy paint. "Parts from a saddleship not unlike yours. Some of our bonds found them drifting in the Hainlin yesterday. I have heard of only one saddleship other than yours. The one Gradwohl was flying when last seen."

Marika settled into a chair uninvited. "Does anyone else know?"

"My most senior. Do you accept this evidence?"

"Do I have any choice?"

"I think it is close enough to conclusive. It seems obvious Gradwohl went down in the Hainlin. How we may never know. What stance will you take now, Marika? Will you think of someone besides yourself?"

"Oh. I suppose. Yes. I have to." Was Kiljar suspicious?

"You had best reconsider your position on the Serke, the brethren, and the convention, then."

"But . . ."

"I will explain. I will show you why it can be in our interest to see the convention through to the conclusion you abhor. Let me begin with our passage near *Starstalker*."

"Mistress?"

"We were attacked. Without provocation. Unprecedented. Have you not wondered why? And the how was so startling."

"Those ships."

"Exactly. Nothing like them has been seen before. Yet they could not have been created overnight. And, sneaky as they are, the brethren could not have built them without the project having come to my attention."

"The brethren have done many things without attracting attention, mistress. Including putting satellites into orbit without the help or license of any Community."

"Yes. I know. They used rockets half as big as TelleRai, launched from the Cupple Islands. For all the organizing you have done, I have resources that you do not. The brethren are not monolithic. Some bonds can be penetrated with the wealth at my command. There are no secrets from me in TelleRai."

Kiljar paused. Marika did not care to comment.

"The brethren did not build those ships here. They came here aboard *Starstalker*. We were not supposed to see them because the brethren did not build them at all."

Startled, Marika asked, "What?"

"The brethren did not build them. It took great pressure upon my contacts and the spreading of much Redoriad largess, but I wormed out an amazing truth. A truth which has been before us all for years, unseen because it was so fantastic."

"You are toying with me, mistress."

"I suppose I am. Marika, the fact is, *Starstalker* crossed starpaths with another dark-faring species fifteen years ago. A species without silth. They are like the brethren, only more so. The Serke were unable to comprehend them, so they enlisted the help of those bonds with whom they had operated closely before. And the brethren took control. Much as you have claimed."

Marika could not keep her lips from peeling back in a snarl.

"At first only a few dark-faring bonds were in it with the Serke. Thus, overall brethren policy was inconsistent. The Serke began trying to seize Reugge territories because of advantages they hoped to gain from these aliens. Their ally bonds helped. At the same time the Brown Paw Bond, being uninformed, were battling the nomads the Serke and other brethren had armed. Do you follow?"

"I think I see the outline. Bagnel once said—"

"After Akard and Critza fell, but before you defeated the force near the ruins of Critza, the dark-faring bonds gained ascendancy over all the brethren. A smaller faction inimical to silth controlled *them*. Though you Reugge suffered, there was much quiet feuding among the bonds in private. Increasing bitterness, failure of communication, and outright disobedience on the part of a few highly placed individuals resulted in the ill-timed, ill-advised, much too massive attempt to kill you at Maksche."

"To kill me? They destroyed an entire city just to get me?"

"Absolutely. There was one among them who was quite mad."

"The warlock. We have been hearing about him for some time."

"The warlock. Yes. He engineered the whole thing. My contacts say he had an insane fear of you. Insanity bred insanity. And when it went sour it all went sour. His madness caused the overthrow of the dark-faring brethren. They have been replaced by conservatives who favor traditional relationships with the Communities. Now."

"Mistress?"

"Now is the time you must *listen* and *hear*. Timing is important now. If the convention moves fast the rogue faction can be disarmed forever. What the Serke found, and hoped to use to our detriment, can be exploited for the benefit of all meth. If we do not move fast the dark-faring brethren may regain their balance and attempt a counter-move. I have gotten hints that they received fearsome weapons and technologies from the aliens."

Marika left the chair, began to pace. She recalled once naively telling Dorteka or Gradwohl that the Reugge ought to try creating factions within the brethren.

"The pitchblende. These aliens wanted it?"

"The brethren believed so. Apparently they use it in power plants of the sort you once predicted in one of our discussions. It seems the Ponath deposit is a rich one indeed. It was because of it that the dark-faring brethren took control of all the brethren. They believed they could use the ore to buy technology. And thus the power to destroy all silth. But for you they might have succeeded."

"Me?"

"You have a friend among the brethren. You were open with him apparently, even when relationships were most strained. The brethren, like silth, are able to extract a great deal from very little evidence. Like the Serke and Gradwohl and everyone else who paid attention to you, they saw what you might become."

"Bestrei's replacement."

"Exactly. With a strong conservative bent and a tendency to do things your own way. The brethren foresaw a future in which they would lose privileges and powers. Also, you are more than Bestrei's potential successor. You have a reasonable amount of intelligence and a talent for intuiting whole pictures from the most miniscule specks of evidence. That you insisted on isolating yourself in a remote industrial setting only further disturbed those who feared you. You recall the stir at the time of your first visit here? You recall me remarking that everyone was following you closely? Had you spent more time in TelleRai you might have been more aware of what you are and how you are perceived."

"Such talk mystifies me, mistress. I have heard it for years. It always seems to be about someone else. I think I know myself fairly well. I am not this creature you are talking about. I am no different from anyone else."

"You compare yourself to older silth, perhaps. To sisters who have risen very high, but who are in the main within a few years of death. They have passed their prime. You have your whole life ahead of you. It is what you might become that scares everyone. Your potential plus your intellectual orientation. That can frighten meth who, to you, may seem unassailable."

Marika looked inside herself and did not find that she felt special. "Where do we stand now? Where are we headed? You wished specifically to know about my position on the convention."

"Yes. It is critical that none of us holds a hard line. We must not give the dark-faring brethren excuses to recapture control. We must be satisfied with recapturing yesterday. The ruling brethren are eager to please right now."

"They attacked—"

"I know what they did, pup! Damn you, *listen*! I know bloodfeud. I come from a rural background. But you cannot make enemies of all brethren. That will give the wicked among them ammunition. In that you risk defeat for all silth."

Marika moved toward her saddleship, suddenly aware that Kiljar was unusually tense. There was a threat implicit in her plea.

"Yes," Kiljar said, reading her well. "If you sustain your stance, you will find yourself very unpopular. It is my understanding that some elements within the Reugge have sent out feelers seeking aid in removing you."

"I see. And if I bend? If I go along? What is in this for me?"

"Probably anything you want, Marika. The Communities want to avoid further confrontation. You could name your price."

"You know what I want."

"I think so."

"That is the price. I will put it to the convention formally."

Kiljar seemed amused. "You will do nothing the easy way, will you?"

"Mistress?"

"The dark-faring Communities will shriek if you demand extraplanetary rights for the Reugge."

"Let them. That is the price. It is not negotiable."

"All right. I will warn those who should know beforetime. I suggest you present a list of throwaway demands if you wish to make them think they have gotten something in return."

"I will, mistress. I had better return to the cloister. I must shift my course there, too. Immediately."

Kiljar seemed puzzled.

Marika slipped astride her saddleship and took flight. She rose high above TelleRai and pushed the saddleship through violent, perilous maneuvers for an hour, venting her anger and frustration.

Chapter Twenty-eight

I

Marika told the gathered council of the Reugge Community, "I have changed my mind. I am laying claim to first chair. I have seen that there is no other way for the Community to properly benefit from the coming convention."

None of the sisters were willing to challenge her. Many looked angry or disappointed.

"I have been to the Redoriad cloister. They showed me evidence, collected upon their estates, that Most Senior Gradwohl is no longer with us. Despite my claim, however, my attitude toward the most senior's position has not altered. I intend to retain first chair only long enough to win us the best from the convention and to set our feet upon a new, star-walking path. Once I succeed, I will step aside, for I will have a task of my own to pursue."

Blank stares. Very blank stares. No one believed.

"Does anyone wish to contest my claim? On whatever grounds?"

No one did.

"Good. I will leave you, then. I have much to do before

tomorrow morning. As long as you are all here, why not consider candidates for seventh chair?" She thought that a nice touch, allowing them an opportunity to strengthen themselves by enrolling another of her enemies in the council.

She truly did not care. Like Gradwohl before her, her strength was such that she could do what she liked without challenge.

She departed, joined Grauel, who had awaited her outside the council chamber. "Gradwohl's darkship crew is here in the cloister somewhere. Assemble them. We have a flight to make."

Grauel asked no questions. "As you command, mistress." She persisted in her formal role.

"Have Kublin and Bagnel brought to the darkship court. We will take them with us. And have someone you trust care for Barlog. Most of the Maksche survivors have arrived now, have they not?"

"Yes, mistress,"

"Go."

Marika hurried to her quarters, quickly sketched out what she would demand from the convention. Space rights for the Reugge. Serke starworlds for the Reugge. The void-ship *Starstalker* for the Reugge. The other orders could squabble over Serke properties on-planet.

Bar the brethren from space forever, not just for a generation. Disarm the brethren except in areas where weapons were necessary to their survival. Allow them no weapons exceeding the technological covenants for any given area, so that brethren in a region like the Ponath, a Tech Two Zone, must carry bows and arrows and spears like the native packs. Demand mechanisms for observation and enforcement.

There would be screams. Loud and long. She expected to surrender on most all the issues except Reugge access to space and a Reugge share of Serke starholdings. As Kiljar had said, let them think they had won something.

"Ready, mistress," Grauel said from the doorway. "The bath were not pleased."

"They never are. They would prefer to spend their lives loafing. Kublin and Bagnel?"

"They are being transferred to the courtyard. I told the workers to break out a darkship. Everything should be ready when we arrive."

The flight was uneventful, though early on Marika had to lose a darkship following her at the edge of sensing. She crossed the snowline and continued north, and by moonlight descended into the courtyard of Gradwohl's hidden darkship factory. "Good evening, Edzeka," she said to the senior of the packfast. "Have you been following the news?" The fortress could send no messages out, except by touch, but could collect almost everything off almost every network. Gradwohl had established one of Braydic's interception teams there. She would miss Braydic more than anyone else who had died at Maksche.

"Yes, mistress. Congratulations. Though I was unhappy to hear that Most Senior Gradwohl has left us for the embrace of the All."

"There will be no changes here, Edzeka. We will continue to do what we can to make the Communities independent of the brethren. We will expand our operations when we can."

Edzeka seemed pleased. "Thank you, mistress. We were concerned when it seemed you would forego first chair."

"There is a great deal of pressure on me to abandon the ideals that drew Gradwohl and me together, and you to her. I may have to present the appearance of abandoning them. It will be appearance only. The fact that you continue your work will be my assurance that I have not changed in my heart."

"Thank you again, mistress. What can we do for you?"

"I need one of the new darkships. Tomorrow I must speak for the Reugge before a convention of the Communities. I thought I might make an unspoken statement by arriving aboard one of your darkships."

"You have males with you."

"Yes. Two very special males. The one who is not bound is a longtime friend, one of the few survivors of a bond friendly to the Reugge, who may be at risk in these times. I wish to keep him safe. He is to be accorded all consideration and honor."

"And the other?"

"A prisoner. One of the commanders of the attack upon Maksche. He is to be assigned to the communications-intercept section to translate messages out of the brethren cant. Do what you need to to enforce his cooperation. Otherwise do not harm him. I may have a use for him. Now. May I have one of the new ships?"

"Of course. I will give you the one prepared for the most senior."

"Good. I cannot spend time here, unfortunately, for I have to be back in TelleRai early. I will need to borrow bath as well. Mine need rest. I will need a Mistress of the Ship also, if I am to get any rest myself."

"As you wish."

"And something to eat."

"Never any problem there, mistress. Come down to the kitchen."

II

Grauel wakened Marika as the darkship approached Tel-leRai. She checked the time. Edzeka had not given her the strongest of Mistresses. It was later than she had hoped. There would be no time to pause at the cloister. She touched the Mistress, told her to proceed directly to convention ground. The convention would meet there despite the weather, which threatened snow.

The flight south had encountered patch after patch of snowfall, the Mistress being unwilling to climb above the clouds. She was young and unconfident.

It smelled like another hard winter, one that would push farther south than ever before.

A victory today, Marika reflected, and she would be in a position at last to do something about that.

The sky over TelleRai was crowded. Every darkship seemed to set a course identical to Marika's. She edged up to the tip of the wooden cross, touched the Mistress, took over.

The moment the silth reached the axis, Marika took the darkship up five thousand feet, well above traffic, and waited in the still chill till it seemed the crowd should have cleared. Then she dropped a few hundred feet at a time, feeling around in the clouds.

If something was to be tried, this was the time.

So many enemies.

She glanced over her shoulder. Grauel was alert, her weapon ready. She checked her own rifle, then allowed the darkship to sink till it had cleared the underbellies of the clouds.

Still a fair ceiling. The snow might hold off awhile.

The air was less crowded. In fact, the few darkships aloft seemed to be patrolling.

She let the bottom fall out.

Startled touches bounced off her, then she was swooping toward the heart of convention ground as faces turned to look. The glimpses she caught told her they were thinking of her as that show-off savage, making a late, flashy entrance.

Exactly.

She touched down fifty feet from the senior representatives of the Communities. Kiljar was the only silth she recognized. The Redoriad came toward her, skirting a small pond.

Tall, slim trees surrounded the area, winter-naked, probably dying. The heart of convention ground centered upon a group of fountains surrounded by statuary, exotic plantings, and benches where silth came to meditate in less exciting times. A dozen Serke waited near the trees in silence, eyes downcast, resigned. On the opposite side of the circle stood a larger group of males, most of whom were old. Marika spied the tradermales from Bagnel's quarters among them. She raised a paw in mocking greeting.

The males were sullen and hateful.

They were resigned, too, but theirs was not the resignation of the Serke. Marika sensed an undercurrent, something resembling the odor of triumph.

Was there something wrong here? A truthsaying might be in order.

"I had begun to be concerned," Kiljar said. "Where were you? Your cloister told me you were away." She eyed Marika's darkship. While not as fancy as those of times past, it was large and ornate. "Where did you get that?"

"Sisters made it. That was Gradwohl's legacy. A first step toward independence for the brethren."

"You might avoid that subject."

"Why did you wish to contact me?"

"Shortly after you announced you would become first chair of the Reugge, there was a rebellion among the brethren of the Cupple Islands. They have taken control there. What they do next depends upon what you say now."

"I see."

"I hope so."

"I thought it was foregone what would happen. Dismember the Serke and ban the brethren from space for a while."

"Essentially. But the details, Marika. The details. Your past attitude toward the brethren is well-known."

"These prisoners. They are the sacrificial victims?"

"You could call them that."

"The males are old. Those who will replace them are all younger?"

"I would not be surprised."

"Yes. Well. To be expected, I suspect. I have brought a list. As I said, I will negotiate on everything but a Reugge interest in the void."

"Understood. Come. I will introduce you. We will get into the details, then go to the convention for approval. Simply a matter of form, I assure you."

Marika scanned the encircling trees. Here, there, curious faces peeped forth. Silth by the hundred waited in the greater park outside. "Have those meth no work?"

"This is the event of the century, Marika. Of several centuries. I will gather everyone. Tell them what is on your mind."

Marika watched Kiljar closely, wondering about her part in the game. She was behaving as though there was some special alliance between herself and the new most senior of the Reugge.

Random snowflakes floated around. Marika glanced at the overcast. It would not be long.

"Speak, Marika," Kiljar told her. And in a whisper, "Demand what you like, but avoid being belligerent."

Marika spoke. The silth listened. She became uncomfortable as she sensed that they were trying to read into her tone, inflexion, and stance more than was there. She was too young to deal with these silth. They were too subtle for her.

Her speech caused a stir among the trees. Many silth hastened away to tell others farther back.

Kiljar announced, "The Redoriad endorse the Reugge proposal." More softly, she said, "Remember, Marika, this is an informal discussion, not the official convention. Do not take to heart everything that is said."

"Meaning your endorsement is a maneuver."

"That, and that some unpleasant attacks may be made by those opposed. Those who speak against will not be declaring bloodfeud."

The various representatives responded individually. Some felt compelled to do so at great length. Marika seated herself on a bench. She felt sleepy. Sitting did not help. She caught herself nodding.

The breeze became more chill. The snowflakes became more numerous, pellets of white that swirled around the heart of the park. They caught in the grass and whitened it till it looked like the fur of an old female. Kiljar settled beside Marika. "That fool Foxgar will never shut up."

"Who is she?"

"Second of the Furnvreit. A small Community from the far south with limited holdings in the outer system. In a convention the smallest order speaks with a voice equaling that of the largest. Unfortunately. She may be stalling in hopes her vote will be bought."

"Do the Furnvreit have any claim on the Serke?"

"None whatsoever. Few Communities do. But they all

want a share of the plunder. And they will get it. Otherwise the convention will go nowhere."

"Wonderful."

A slith came from the trees, hastened to Kiljar, whispered. Kiljar looked grim.

"What is it?" Marika asked. A bad feeling twisted her insides.

"Somebody relayed your opening terms to the Cupple Islands. Those ships we saw around *Starstalker*. A great many of their type are lifting off, packed with brethren."

Marika's bad feeling worsened.

III

An old silth appeared, too excited to retain her cool dignity. "The darkships are leaving the cloister at Ruhaack! The Serke are . . . are . . ."

"You would deal with brethren!" Marika snapped at Kiljar. She raced to her darkship. "Grauel! Get aboard. Bath! Mistress! Get it airborne."

The remaining silth stood bewildered for a moment, then scattered.

Marika was well away before anyone else lifted off. She touched the Mistress of the Ship. *The Reugge cloister. Hurry.*

"What is it, Marika?" Grauel asked. She kept turning, weapon ready, seeking something she could not find.

"I don't know. But I don't like this. I have a bad feeling. A premonition. I don't want to be caught on the ground. We'll pick up Barlog, then head for Ruhaack." She was as confused as any of the silth aboard the darkships swarming up below.

Any course of action had to be positive.

The enemy was on the move.

She touched the Mistress of the Ship again, showed her where to go as Grauel protested, "Marika, Barlog is in no condition to—"

"I don't care. I want her with me till we see what's going to happen."

The Mistress of the Ship brought the darkship to rest beside the window to Marika's quarters. Marika gestured violently. The Mistress rotated the darkship, brought one arm into contact with the windowsill. "Hold it there!" Marika ordered. "We'll be back in a minute. Grauel, break that window."

Grauel tottered along the beam, eased past the bath at its tip, smashed glass with her rifle butt. She jumped through. Marika followed. "What now?" Grauel asked.

"Barlog." In her mind a clock was ticking, estimating the time it would take the brethren fugitives to rendezvous with *Starstalker*.

Intuition began shrieking at her. "Hurry!" she barked.

They found Barlog sleeping, still partially immobilized by the healer sisters. They pulled her out of bed and hustled her to the window. Marika leapt out onto the arm of the darkship. It sank beneath her weight. "Hold it steady!" she yelled. "All right, Grauel. Push her up. Come on, Barlog. You have to help a little."

Barlog was no help at all. Marika pulled, balanced the huntress upon her shoulder. For a moment she became conscious of the long plunge that awaited her slightest misstep, froze. Never before had she been particularly cognizant of the danger of falling. She turned carefully, gestured the bath to duck, eased past. "Come on, Grauel."

Grauel, too, was conscious of the emptiness beneath the darkship. She was slow about boarding and slower crossing to the axis. Marika had Barlog strapped down by the time she arrived. "Strap up fast," Marika said. "Mistress! Take us up! Go high and head toward Ruhaack."

Marika became aware that she was being observed from a darkship poised just beyond the boundary of the cloister. Kiljar. She waved, pointed. Kiljar's darkship rose.

The clock in Marika's mind told her the tradermale lifters would have reached *Starstalker*. She touched Kiljar. *I am going to the Ruhaack cloister. With any luck those left behind may be cooperative.*

Do not forget Bestrei.

How can I? Would you care to bet that she was not aboard the first voidship up?

Behind them, above the city, darkships swarmed like insects on a warm morning. Touches of panic fluttered the otherworld. There had been collisions and deaths by falling.

Marika reached, touched every sister she could, told them to get higher, to get away from the city.

She felt for the sky, for the Serke voidships, and to her surprise she found them. They were clustered, more than a dozen of them, and they were much higher than she could rise in pursuit. They were on the edge of the void and hurrying outward.

Marika felt *Starstalker* rise from behind the rim of the world. There was a deadly feel to the voidship, as though it had metamorphosed into something terrible. It radiated a threatening darkness. It climbed the sky rapidly.

It lost its deadly aura as it approached zenith, as Marika hurried to TelleRai's southwest, toward Ruhaack. That modest city, where the Serke made their headquarters, lay a hundred miles away. Its supporting satellites brushed those of greater TelleRai.

Why did *Starstalker* seem less black? Marika opened to the All. There! The deadliness remained, but it had separated from the voidship.

Kiljar. They have sent something down against us.

That something came down fast. Very fast. Streaks of fire burned the upper sky and backlighted the clouds. Thunder hammered the air.

They were forty miles from TelleRai when the first sword of fire smote the world.

The first flash blinded Marika momentarily. There were more flashes. A grisly globe of fire rolled upward above the city. Shuddering, fur bristling, Marika felt the thundering wind, the first shock wave raging toward her.

Another great flash illuminated the mushroom cloud.

The Mistress of the Ship lost control. The darkship twisted toward the ground.

Praise for *New York Times* and
#1 international bestselling author

CHRISTINA LAUREN

"This is without a doubt the best in Lauren's Beautiful series thus far. Hanna and Will are both fully formed characters and, for once, the alternating his and her POVs don't diminish the story. Readers will enjoy watching this friends-to-lovers relationship unfold and, aside from some awkward flirting, will find the chemistry between Hanna and Will electrifying. Not to mention Hanna's nerdy banter will charm anyone who can't resist a geek-girl heroine."

—*RT Book Reviews* on *Beautiful Player*

"Christina Lauren is my go-to author when I'm looking for sexy and sweet."

—Jennifer L. Armentrout, #1 *New York Times* bestselling author

"At turns hilarious and gut-wrenching, this is a tremendously fun slow-burn."

—*The Washington Post* on *Dating You / Hating You* (A Best Romance of 2017 selection)

"Delightful."

—*People* on *Roomies*

"A passionate and bittersweet tale of love in all of its wonderfully terrifying reality . . . Lauren successfully tackles a weighty subject with both ferocity and compassion."

—*Booklist* on *Autoboyography*

"In our eyes, Christina Lauren can do no wrong."

—*Bookish*

"Lauren brings her characteristic charm to the story. Holland's tale is more than an unrequited crush; it's about self-expectations, problematic friendships, unconventional family, and the strange power of love."

—*Booklist* on *Roomies*

"Christina Lauren hilariously depicts modern dating."

—*US Weekly* on *Dating You / Hating You*

"Perfectly captures the hunger, thrill, and doubt of young, modern love."

—*Kirkus Reviews* on *Wicked Sexy Liar*

"A crazy, hilarious, and surprisingly realistic and touching adventure . . . One of the freshest, funniest, and most emotionally authentic erotic romances."

—*RT Book Reviews* on *Sweet Filthy Boy*
(the *Romantic Times* 2014 Book of the Year)

"Truly a romance for the twenty-first century. A smart, sexy romance for readers who thrive on girl power."

—*Kirkus Reviews* (starred review)
on *Dating You / Hating You*

"Deliciously steamy."

—*Entertainment Weekly* on *Beautiful Bastard*

"Smart, sexy, and feminist, *Dating You / Hating You* will delight contemporary romance fans."

—*Shelf Awareness*

"No one is doing hot contemporary romance like Christina Lauren."

—*Bookalicious*

"Full of expertly drawn characters who will grab your heart and never let go, humor that will have you howling, and off-the-charts, toe-curling chemistry, *Dark Wild*

Night is absolutely unforgettable. This is contemporary romance at its best!"

—**Sarah J. Maas, author of *Throne of Glass***

"Smart, sexy, and satisfying . . . destined to become a romance classic."

—**Tara Sue Me on *Beautiful Bastard***

"[Christina Lauren] have fast become my go-to for sexy, honest contemporary erotic romance."

—*Heroes and Heartbreakers*

"Funny, feminist, and a great example of a modern romance . . . Evie is amazing and will go down in history as one of the best heroines I've read."

—*Smart Bitches, Trashy Books* on *Dating You / Hating You*

"Smart and sexy . . . Lola can't believe that someone as wonderful as Oliver (he is rather wonderful) would ever love her, and Lauren captures her insecurities in a powerful way that will hit close to home for many."

—*The Washington Post* on *Dark Wild Night*

"Fresh, hip, and energetic, *Wicked Sexy Liar* layers earthy sexiness with raw, honest dialogue to create a page-turning keeper."

—*BookPage*

"I blushed. A lot."

—*USA Today* on *Sweet Filthy Boy*

"Christina Lauren is back in top form in this light, funny, and unflinchingly honest stand-alone novel about growing up, standing up, and falling in love."

—*RT Book Reviews* **(top pick)** on *Dating You / Hating You*

"A sexy, sweet treasure of a story. I loved every word."

—**Sylvia Day on *Sweet Filthy Boy***

CHRISTINA LAUREN

BEAUTIFUL PLAYER

POCKET BOOKS

NEW YORK • LONDON • TORONTO • SYDNEY • NEW DELHI

Pocket Books
An Imprint of Simon & Schuster, Inc.
1230 Avenue of the Americas
New York, NY 10020

This book is a work of fiction. Any references to historical
events, real people, or real places are used fictitiously. Other
names, characters, places, and events are products of the author's
imagination, and any resemblance to actual events or places or
persons, living or dead, is entirely coincidental.

First Pocket Books paperback edition June 2018

POCKET and colophon are registered trademarks
of Simon & Schuster, Inc.

For information about special discounts for bulk purchases,
please contact Simon & Schuster Special Sales at 1-866-506-1949
or business@simonandschuster.com.

The Simon & Schuster Speakers Bureau can bring authors
to your live event. For more information or to book an event,
contact the Simon & Schuster Speakers Bureau at 1-866-248-3049
or visit our website at www.simonspeakers.com.

Manufactured in the United States of America

10 9 8 7 6 5 4 3 2 1

ISBN 978-1-5011-9840-3
ISBN 978-1-4767-5141-2 (ebook)

Prologue

We were in the ugliest apartment in all of Manhattan, and it wasn't just that my brain was especially programmed away from art appreciation: objectively these paintings were *all* hideous. A hairy leg growing from a flower stem. A mouth with spaghetti pouring out. Beside me, my oldest brother and my father hummed thoughtfully, nodding as if they understood what they were seeing. I was the one who kept us moving forward; it seemed to be the unspoken protocol that party guests should make the circuit, admire the art, and only *then* feel free to enjoy the appetizers being carried on trays around the room.

But at the very end, above the massive fireplace and between two garish candelabras, was a painting of a double helix—the structure of the DNA molecule—

and printed across the entire canvas was a quote by Tim Burton: *We all know interspecies romance is weird.*

Thrilled, I laughed, turning to Jensen and Dad. "Okay. *That* one is good."

Jensen sighed. "You *would* like that."

I glanced to the painting and back to my brother. "Why? Because it's the only thing in this entire place that makes any sense?"

He looked at Dad and something passed between them, some permission granted from father to son. "We need to talk to you about your relationship to your job."

It took a minute before his words, his tone, and his determined expression triggered my understanding. "Jensen," I said. "Are we really going to have this conversation *here*?"

"Yes, here." His green eyes narrowed. "It's the first time I've seen you out of the lab in the past two days when you weren't sleeping or scarfing down a meal."

I'd often noted how it seemed the most prominent personality traits of my parents—vigilance, charm, caution, impulse, and drive—had been divided cleanly and without contamination among their five offspring.

Vigilance and *Drive* were headed into battle in the middle of a Manhattan soiree.

"We're at a party, Jens. We're supposed to be talking about how wonderful the art is," I countered, waving vaguely to the walls of the opulently furnished living room. "And how scandalous the . . . something . . . is." I had no idea what the latest gossip was, and this little white flag of ignorance just proved my brother's point.

I watched as Jensen tamped down the urge to roll his eyes.

Dad handed me an appetizer that looked something like a snail on a cracker and I discreetly slid it onto a cocktail napkin as a caterer passed. My new dress itched and I wished I'd taken the time to ask around the lab about these Spanx things I had on. From this first experience with them, I decided they were created by Satan, or a man who was too thin for skinny jeans.

"You're not just smart," Jensen was telling me. "You're fun. You're social. You're a pretty girl."

"Woman," I corrected in a mumble.

He leaned closer, keeping our conversation hidden from passing partygoers. Heaven forbid one of New York's high society should hear him giving me a lecture on how to be more socially slutty. "So I don't understand why we've been visiting you here for three days and the only people we've hung out with are *my* friends."

I smiled at my oldest brother, and let my gratitude for his overprotective hypervigilance wash over me before the slower, heated flush of irritation rose along my skin; it was like touching a hot iron, the sharp reflex followed by the prolonged, throbbing burn. "I'm almost done with school, Jens. There's plenty of time for life after this."

"*This* is life," he said, eyes wide and urgent. "*Right now.* When I was your age I was barely hanging on to my GPA, just hoping I would wake up on Monday and not be hungover."

Dad stood silently beside him, ignoring that last remark but nodding at the general gist that I was a loser with no friends. I gave him a look that was meant to communicate, *I get* this *coming from the workaholic scientist who spent more time in the lab than he did in his own house?* But he remained impassive, wearing the same expression he had when a compound he expected to be soluble ended up a goopy suspension in a vial: confused, maybe a little offended on principle.

Dad had given me *drive,* but he always assumed Mom had given me even a little *charm,* too. Maybe because I was female, or maybe because he thought each generation should improve upon the actions of the one before, I was meant to do the whole career-life balance better than he had. The day Dad turned fifty, he'd pulled me into his office and said, simply, "The people are as important as the science. Learn from my mistakes." And then he'd straightened some papers on his desk and stared at his hands until I got bored enough to get up and go back into the lab.

Clearly, I hadn't succeeded.

"I know I'm overbearing," Jensen whispered.

"A bit," I agreed.

"And I know I meddle."

I gave him a knowing look, whispering, "You're my own personal Athena Poliás."

"Except I'm not Greek and I have a penis."

"I try to forget about that."

Jensen sighed and, finally, Dad seemed to get that this was meant to be a two-man job. They'd both come down to visit me, and although it had seemed a strange combination for a random visit in February, I hadn't given it much thought until now. Dad put his arm around me, squeezing. His arms were long and thin, but he'd always had the viselike grip of a man much stronger than he looked. "Ziggs, you're a good kid."

I smiled at Dad's version of an elaborate pep talk. "Thanks."

Jensen added, "You know we love you."

"I love you, too. Mostly."

"But . . . consider this an intervention. You're addicted to work. You're addicted to whatever fast track you think you need your career to follow. Maybe I always take over and micromanage your life—"

"Maybe?" I cut in. "You dictated everything from when Mom and Dad took the training wheels off my bike to when my curfew could be extended past sunset. And you didn't even live at home anymore, Jens. I was *sixteen*."

He stilled me with a look. "I swear I'm not going to tell you what to do just . . ." He trailed off, looking around as if someone nearby might be holding up a sign prompting the end of his sentence. Asking Jensen to keep from micromanaging was like asking anyone else to stop breathing for ten short minutes. "Just call someone."

" 'Someone'? Jensen, your point is that I have no friends. It's not *exactly* true, but who do you imagine I should call to initiate this whole get-out-and-live thing? Another grad student who's just as buried in research as I am? We're in biomedical engineering. It's not exactly a thriving mass of socialites."

He closed his eyes, staring up at the ceiling before something seemed to occur to him. His eyebrows rose when he looked back to me, hope filling his eyes with an irresistible brotherly tenderness. "What about Will?"

I snatched the untouched champagne flute from Dad's hand and downed it.

⁂

I didn't need Jensen to repeat himself. Will Sumner was Jensen's college best friend, Dad's former intern, and the object of every one of my teenage fantasies. Whereas I had always been the friendly, nerdy kid sister, Will was the bad-boy genius with the crooked smile, pierced ears, and blue eyes that seemed to hypnotize every girl he met.

When I was twelve, Will was nineteen, and he came home with Jensen for a few days around Christmas. He was dirty, and—even then—delicious, jamming on his bass in the garage with Jensen and playfully flirting away the holidays with my older sister, Liv. When I was sixteen, he was a fresh college graduate and lived with us over the summer while he worked for my father. He exuded such raw, sexual charisma that I gave my virginity to a fumbling, forgettable boy in my class, trying to relieve the ache I felt just being near Will.

I was pretty sure my sister had at least *kissed* him—and Will was too old for me anyway—but behind closed doors, and in the secret space of my own heart, I could admit that Will Sumner was the first boy I'd ever wanted to kiss, and the first boy who eventually drove me to slip my hand under the sheets, thinking of him in the darkness of my own room.

Of his devilish playful smile and the hair that continually fell over his right eye.

Of his smooth, muscled forearms and tan skin.

Of his long fingers, and even the little scar on his chin.

When the boys my age all sounded the same, Will's voice was deep, and quiet. His eyes were patient and knowing. His hands weren't ever restless and fidgety; they were usually resting deep in his pockets. He licked his lips when he looked at girls, and he made quiet, confident comments about breasts and legs and tongues.

I blinked, looking up at Jensen. I wasn't sixteen anymore. I was twenty-four, and Will was thirty-one. I'd seen him four years before at Jensen's ill-fated wedding, and his quiet, charismatic smile had only grown more intense, more maddening. I'd watched, fascinated, as Will slipped away into a coatroom with two of my sister-in-law's bridesmaids.

"Call him," Jensen urged now, pulling me from my memories. "He has a good balance of work and life. He's local, he's a *good guy*. Just . . . get out some, okay? He'll take care of you."

I tried to quell the hum vibrating all along my skin when my oldest brother said this. I wasn't sure *how* I wanted Will to take care of me: Did I want him to just be my brother's friend, helping me find more balance? Or did I want to get a grown-up look at the object of my filthiest fantasies?

"Hanna," Dad pressed. "Did you hear your brother?"

A waiter passed with a tray of full champagne flutes and I swapped out the empty one for a full, bubbly glass.

"I heard him. I'll call Will."

Chapter One

One ring. Two.

I stopped pacing long enough to pull back the curtain and peek out the window, frowning up at the sky. It was still dark out, but I reasoned it was bluer than black and starting to smudge pink and purple along the horizon. Technically: morning.

It was three days after Jensen's lecture and, fittingly, my third attempt to call Will. But even though I had no idea what I would say—what my brother even *expected* me to say—the more I thought about it, the more I realized Jens had been right: I was almost always at the lab, and when I wasn't, I was home sleeping or eating. Choosing to live alone in my parents' Manhattan apartment instead of somewhere closer to my peers in Brooklyn and Queens didn't exactly help my social options. The contents of my refrigerator consisted of the odd vegetable, question-able takeout, and frozen dinners. My entire life to this point had revolved around finishing school and launching into the perfect research career. It was so-bering to realize how little I had outside of that.

Apparently my family had noticed, and for some reason, Jensen seemed to think the solution to saving me from impending spinsterdom was Will.

I was less confident. Much less.

Our shared history was admittedly scant, and it was entirely possible he wouldn't remember me very well. I was the kid sister, scenery, a backdrop to his many adventures with Jensen and his brief fling with my sister. And now I was calling him to—*what*? Take me out? Play some board games? Teach me how to . . .

I couldn't even finish that thought.

I debated hanging up. I debated climbing back into bed and telling my brother he could kiss my ass and find a new improvement project. But halfway through the fourth ring, and with the phone clenched so tightly in my hand I'd probably still feel it tomor-row, Will picked up.

"Hello?" His voice was exactly how I remembered, thick and rich, but even deeper. "Hello?" he asked again.

"Will?"

He inhaled sharply and I heard a smile curl through his voice when he said my nickname: "Ziggy?"

I laughed; of course he'd remember me that way. Only my family called me that anymore. No one really knew what the name *meant*—it was a lot of power to give then-two-year-old Eric, nicknaming the new baby sister—but it had stuck. "Yeah. It's *Ziggy*. How did you—?"

"I heard from Jensen yesterday," he explained. "He told me all about his visit and the verbal ass-kicking he gave you. He mentioned you might call."

"Well, here I am," I said lamely.

There was a groan and the whispering rustle of sheets. I absolutely did not try to imagine what degree of naked was on the other end of the line. But the butterflies in my stomach flew into my throat when I registered he sounded tired because *he'd been asleep*. Okay, so maybe it wasn't technically morning *yet.* . . .

I chanced another look outside. "I didn't wake you, did I?" I hadn't even looked at my clock, and now I was afraid to.

"It's fine. My alarm was about to go off in"—he paused, yawning—"an hour."

I bit back a groan of mortification. "Sorry. I was a little . . . anxious."

"No, no, it's fine. I can't believe I forgot you lived in the city now. Hear you've been holed up over at P and S, pipetting in a safety hood for the past three years."

My stomach flipped slightly at the way his deep

voice grew husky with his playful scolding. "You sound like you're on Jensen's side."

His tone softened. "He's just worried about you. As your big brother, it's his favorite job."

"So I've heard." I returned to pacing the length of the room, needing to do something to contain this nervous energy. "I should have called sooner . . ."

"So should I." He shifted, and seemed to sit up. I heard him groan again as he stretched and closed my eyes at the sound. It sounded exactly, precisely, and distractingly like *sex*.

Breathe through your nose, Hanna. Stay calm.

"Do you want to do something today?" I blurted. So much for calm.

He hesitated and I could have smacked myself for not considering that he'd already have plans. Like work. And after work, maybe a date with a girlfriend. Or a wife. Suddenly I was straining to hear every sound that pushed through the crackling silence.

After an eternity, he asked, "What did you have in mind?"

Loaded question. "Dinner?"

Will paused for several painful beats. "I have a thing. A late meeting. What about tomorrow?"

"Lab. I already scheduled an eighteen-hour time point with these cells that are really slow-growing and I will legitimately stab myself with a sharp tool if I mess this up and have to start over."

"Eighteen hours? That's a long day, Ziggs."

"I know."

He hummed before asking, "What time do you need to go in this morning?"

"Later," I said, glancing at the clock with a wince. It was only *six*. "Maybe around nine or ten."

"Do you want to join me at the park for a run?"

"You run?" I asked. "On purpose?"

"Yes," he said, outright laughing now. "Not the I'm-being-chased running, but the I'm-exercising running."

I squeezed my eyes closed, feeling the familiar itch to follow this through, like a challenge, a damn assignment. Stupid Jensen. "When?"

"About thirty minutes?"

I glanced out the window again. It was barely light out. There was snow on the ground. *Change*, I reminded myself. And with that, I closed my eyes and said, "Text me directions. I'll meet you there."

⌐═══════⌐

It was cold. Ass-freezing cold would be a more accurate description.

I reread Will's text telling me to meet him near the Engineers Gate at Fifth and Ninetieth in Central Park and paced back and forth, trying to stay warm. The morning air burned my face and seeped through the fabric of my pants. I wished I'd brought a hat. I wish I'd remembered it was February in New York and only crazy people went to the park in February in New York. I couldn't feel my fingers and I was legitimately worried the cold air combined with the windchill might cause my ears to fall off.

There were only a handful of people nearby: over-achieving fitness types and a young couple huddled together on a bench beneath a giant spindly tree, each clasping to-go cups of something that looked warm, and delicious. A flock of gray birds pecked at the ground, and the sun was just making an appearance over the skyscrapers in the distance.

I'd hovered on the edge between socially appro-priate and rambling geek most of my life, so of course I'd felt out of my element before: when I got that research award in front of thousands of parents and students at MIT, almost anytime I went shopping for myself, and, most memorably, when Ethan Kingman wanted me to go down on him in the eleventh grade and I had absolutely no idea how I was supposed to do so and breathe at the same time. And now, watching the sky brighten with each passing minute, I would have gratefully escaped to any one of those memories to get out of doing this.

It wasn't that I didn't want to go running . . . actually, yes, that was a lot of it. I *didn't* want to go running. I wasn't even sure I knew how to run for sport. But I wasn't dreading seeing Will. I was just *nervous.* I remembered the way he'd been—there was always something slow and hypnotic about his attention. Something about him that exuded sex. I'd never had to interact with him one-on-one before, and I worried that I simply lacked the composure to handle it.

My brother had given me a task—go live your life more fully—knowing that if there was one way to ensure I'd tackle something, it was to make me think I was failing. And while I was pretty sure it hadn't been Jensen's intent that I spend time with Will to learn how to date and to, let's face it, get *laid*, I needed to get inside Will's head, learn from the master and be more like him in those ways. I just had to pretend I was a secret agent on an undercover assignment: get in and out and escape unharmed.

Unlike my sister.

After seventeen-year-old Liv had made out with a pierced, bass-playing nineteen-year-old Will over Christmas, I'd learned a *lot* about what it looks like when a teenage girl gets hung up on the bad boy. Will Sumner was the definition of that boy.

They all wanted my sister, but Liv had never talked about anyone the way she talked about Will.

"Zig!"

My head snapped up and toward the sound of my name, and I did a double take as the man in question walked toward me. He was taller than I remembered, and had the type of body that was long and lean, a torso that went on forever and limbs that should have made him clumsy but somehow didn't. There'd always been *something* about him, something magnetic and irresistible that was unrelated to classically symmetrical good looks, but my memory of Will from even four years ago paled in comparison to the man in front of me now.

His smile was still the same: slightly crooked and always lingering, lending a constant sense of mischief to his face. As he approached, he glanced in the direction of a siren and I caught the angle of his stubbly jaw, the length of smooth, tan neck that disappeared beneath the collar of his microfleece.

When he got to me, his smile widened. "Morning," he said. "Thought it was you. I remember you used to pace like that when you were nervous about school or something. Drove your mom nuts."

And without thinking, I stepped forward, wrapped my arms around his neck, and hugged him tight. I couldn't remember ever being this close to Will before. He was warm and solid; I closed my eyes when I felt him press his face to the top of my head.

His deep voice seemed to vibrate through me: "It's so good to see you."

Secret Agent Hanna.

Reluctantly, I took a step back, inhaling the way the fresh air mixed with the clean scent of his soap. "It's good to see you, too."

Bright blue eyes looked down at me from beneath a black beanie, his dark hair tucked haphazardly beneath it. He stepped closer and placed something on my head. "Figured you'd need this."

I reached up, feeling the thick wool cap. Wow, that was disarmingly charming. "Thanks. Maybe I'll get to keep my ears after all."

He grinned, stepping back as he looked me up and down. "You look . . . different, Ziggs."

I laughed. "No one but my family has called me that in for*ever*."

His smile fell and he searched my face for a moment as if, were he lucky enough, my given name would be tattooed there. He'd only ever called me Ziggy, just like my siblings—Jensen, of course, but also Liv and Niels and Eric. Until I left home, I'd *always* just been Ziggy. "Well, what do your friends call you?"

"Hanna," I said quietly.

He continued to stare. He stared at my neck, at my lips, and then took time to inspect my eyes. The energy between us was palpable . . . but, no. I had to be completely misreading the situation. This was precisely the danger of Will Sumner.

"So," I started, raising my eyebrows. "Running."

Will blinked, seemed to realize where we were. "Right."

He nodded, reaching up to pull his hat down farther over his ears. He looked so different than I remembered—clean-cut and successful—but if I looked close enough, I could still see the faint marks where his earrings used to be.

"First," he said, and I quickly pulled my attention

back to his face. "I want you to watch out for black ice. They do a good job of keeping the trails clear but if you're not paying attention you can really hurt yourself."

"Okay."

He pointed to the path winding around the frozen water. "This is the lower loop. It surrounds the reservoir and should be perfect because it only has a few inclines."

"And you run this every day?"

Will's eyes twinkled as he shook his head. "Not this one. This is only a mile and a half. Since you're just starting out we'll walk the first and last bit, running the mile in the middle."

"Why don't we just run your usual route?" I asked, not liking the idea of him slowing down or changing his routine for me.

"Because it's six miles."

"I can totally do that," I said. Six miles didn't seem like that many. It was just under thirty-two thousand feet. If I took big strides, that was only maybe sixteen thousand steps . . . I felt my mouth turn down at the corners as I fully considered this.

He patted my shoulder with exaggerated patience. "Of course you can. But let's see how you do today and we'll talk."

And then? He winked.

So apparently I wasn't much of a runner.

"You do this every day?" I panted. I could feel a trickle of sweat run from my temple down my neck and didn't even have the strength to reach up and wipe it away.

He nodded, looking like he was just out enjoying a brisk morning walk. I felt like I was going to die.

"How much farther?"

He looked over at me, wearing a smug—and delicious—grin. "Half a mile."

Oh God.

I straightened and lifted my chin. I could do this. I was young and in . . . reasonably good shape. I stood almost all day, ran from room to room in the lab, and always took the stairs when I went home. I could totally do this.

"Good . . ." I said. My lungs seemed to have filled with cement and I could only take tiny, gasping breaths. "Feels great."

"Not cold anymore?"

"Nope." I could practically *hear* the blood pumping through my veins, the force of my heartbeat inside my chest. Our feet pounded on the trail and, no, I definitely wasn't cold anymore.

"Other than being busy all the time," he asked, breath not even the slightest bit labored, "do you like the work you're doing?"

"Love it," I gasped. "I love working with Liemacki."

We spoke for a while about my project, the other people in my lab. He knew my graduate advisor from his reputation in the vaccine field, and I was impressed to see that Will kept up with the literature even in a field he said didn't always perform the best in the venture capital world. But he was curious about more than my job; he wanted to know about my *life*, asked about it point-blank.

"My life is the lab," I said, glancing at him to gauge his level of judgment. He barely blinked. There were a few graduate students, and an army of post-docs cranking out papers. "They're all great," I explained, swallowing before taking in a huge gulp of air. "But I get along best with two that are both married with kids, so we aren't exactly going to go hit the pool tables after work."

"I don't think the pool tables are still open after you're done with work anyway," he teased. "Isn't that why I'm here? Big-brothering—getting you out of your routine kind of thing?"

"Right," I said laughing. "And although I was pretty annoyed when Jensen flat-out told me I needed to get a life, he's not exactly *wrong*." I paused, running a few more steps. "I've just been so focused on work for so long, and getting over the next hurdle, and then the next one, I haven't really stopped to enjoy any of it."

"Yeah," he agreed quietly. "That's not good."

I tried to ignore the pressure of his gaze, and kept my eyes pinned on the trail in front of us. "Do you ever feel like the people who mean the most aren't the people you *see* the most?" When he didn't respond, I added, "Lately I just feel like I'm not putting my heart where it matters."

From my peripheral vision I saw him glance away, nodding. It took forever for him to reply, but when he did, he said, "Yeah, I get that."

A moment later, I looked over at the sound of Will laughing. It was deep, and the sound vibrated through my skin and into my bones.

"What are you *doing*?" he asked.

I followed his gaze to where my arms were crossed over my chest. I winced inwardly before admitting, "My boobs hurt. How do guys do this?"

"Well, for one, we don't have . . ." He waved vaguely to my chest region.

"But, what about the other stuff? Like, do you run in boxers?" *Holy hell, what is wrong with me? Problem number one: no verbal filter.*

He looked over at me again, confused, and almost tripped on a fallen branch. "What?"

"Boxers?" I repeated, making the word into three full syllables. "Or do you have things that keep your man parts from—"

He interrupted me with a loud barking laugh that echoed off the trees in the frigid air. "Yeah, no boxers," he said. "There'd be too much stuff moving around down there." He winked and then looked forward at the trail, wearing a flirty half-grin.

"You have extra parts?" I teased.

Will threw me an amused look. "If you must know, I wear running shorts. Form-fitted to keep the boys safe."

"Guess girls are just lucky *that* way. No stuff down there to just"—I waved my arms around wildly—"flop all over the place. We're compact down below."

We reached a flat part of the trail, and slowed to a walk. Will laughed quietly next to me. "I've noticed."

"You *are* the expert."

He threw me a skeptical look. "What?"

For a split second my brain attempted to hold back what I was about to say, but it was too late. I'd never been particularly good at censoring my thoughts—a fact my family was more than happy to point out whenever the chance arose—but here it felt like my brain was stealing this rare opportunity to let it all out with the legendary Will, as if I may not get another chance. "The . . . *pussy* expert," I whispered, all but mouthing the P-word.

His eyes widened, his steps faltering a bit.

I stopped, bending to catch my breath. "You said so yourself."

"When would I ever have said I was the 'pussy expert'?"

"Don't you remember telling us that? You said Jensen was good with the saying. You were good with the doing. And then you wiggled your eyebrows."

"That is *horrifying*. How in the world do you re-member all this?"

I straightened. "I was twelve. You were a nineteen-year-old hot friend of my brother who joked about sex in our house. You were practically a mythical creature."

"Why don't I remember any of this?"

I shrugged, looking past him at the now-crowded trail. "Probably for the same reason."

"I don't remember you being this funny, either. Or this"—he took a moment to covertly look me up and down—"grown-up."

I smiled. "I wasn't."

He reached behind him, pulling his sweatshirt up and over his head. For a brief moment, his shirt underneath was pulled up with it, and a long stretch of his torso was exposed. I experienced a full-body clench at the sight of his flat stomach and the dark hair that trailed from his navel down into his shorts. His running pants hung low enough for me to see the carved lines of his hips, the enticing suggestion of man parts, and man legs and . . . holy crap Will Sumner's body was unreal.

When he tugged the hem of his shirt back down, he broke my trance and I looked up to take in the rest of him, arms now bare below the short sleeves of his shirt. He scratched his neck, oblivious to the way my eyes moved over his forearm. I had a lot of memories of Will from the summer he'd lived with us while working for Dad: sitting on the couch with him and Jensen while we watched a movie, passing him in the hallway at night wearing nothing more than a towel around his hips, inhaling dinner at the kitchen table after a long day at the lab. But only from the evil influence of dark magic could I have forgotten about the tattoos. Seeing them now, I could remember a bluebird near his shoulder, a mountain and the roots of a tree wrapped up in vines on his bicep.

But some of these were new. Swirls of ink formed a double helix down the center of one forearm, the etching of a phonograph peeked out from beneath his sleeve on the other. Will had grown quiet and I looked up to find him smirking at me.

"Sorry," I mumbled, smiling sheepishly. "You have new ones."

His tongue darted out to lick his lips, and we turned to start walking again. "Don't be sorry. I wouldn't have them if I didn't want people to look."

"And it's not weird? With the business job and everything?"

Shrugging, he murmured, "Long sleeves, suit jackets. Most people don't know they're there." The problem with what he said was it didn't make me think about the *most people* who remained ignorant to his tattoos. It made me wonder about the ones who knew each and every line of ink on his skin.

The Danger of Will Sumner, I reminded myself.

*Everything he says sounds filthy, and now you're think-
ing of him naked. Again.*

I blinked away, searching for a new topic. "So what
about *your* life?"

He eyed me, wary. "What do you want to know?"

"Do you like your job?"

"Most days."

I acknowledged this with a smile. "Do you get
to see your family often? Your mom and sisters are
in Washington, right?" I remembered that Will had
two much older sisters who both lived close to their
mother.

"Oregon," he corrected. "And yes, a couple of
times a year."

"Are you dating anyone?" I blurted.

He furrowed his brows as if he hadn't quite understood what I'd asked. After a moment he answered,
"No."

His adorably confused reaction helped me forget
how inappropriate my question had been. "Did you
have to really think about it?"

"No, smart-ass. And no, there is no one I would
introduce to you by saying, 'Hey Ziggy, this is so-and-
so, my *girlfriend.*'"

I hummed, studying him. "What a very specific
evasion."

He pulled his hat from his head, running his fingers through his hair. It was damp with sweat and
stuck up in a million directions.

"No one woman has caught your eye?"

"A few have." He turned his eyes on me, refusing to shrink from my interrogation. I remembered this about Will; he never felt the need to explain himself, but he didn't shy away from questions, either.

Clearly he was the same Will he'd always been: often with women, and never with just one. I blinked down, looking at his chest as it widened and retracted with his slowly-steadying breaths, at his muscular shoulders leading to a smooth, tan neck. His lips parted slightly and his tongue peeked out to wet them again. Will's jaw was carved and covered in dark stubble. I had a sudden and overwhelming urge to feel it on my thighs.

My eyes dropped to his toned arms, the large hands relaxed at his sides—*holy shit what those fingers probably knew how to do*—his flat stomach, and the front of his running pants that told me Will Sumner had plenty going on below the belt. Good sweet baby Jesus, I wanted to bang the smirk off this man.

Silence ticked between us and awareness trickled in. I wasn't living behind a damn two-way mirror and I'd never had a poker face. Will could probably read every single thought I'd just had.

His eyes darkened in understanding, and he took one step closer, looking me over from head to foot as if inspecting an animal caught in a trap. A gorgeous, deadly smile tugged at his mouth. "What's the verdict?"

I swallowed thickly, closing my fists around sweaty hands, saying only, "Will?"

He blinked, and then blinked again, stepping back and seeming to remember himself. I could practically see the realizations tick through his mind: *this is Jensen's baby* sister . . . *she's seven years younger than I am . . . I made out with Liv . . . this kid is a dork . . . stop thinking with your dick.*

He winced slightly, saying, "Right, sorry," under his breath.

I relaxed, amused by the reaction. Unlike me, Will had an infamous poker face . . . but not *here*, and apparently not with me. That understanding sent a jolt of confidence through my chest: he might be nearly irresistible and the most naturally sensual man on the planet, but Hanna Bergstrom could handle Will Sumner.

"So," I said. "Not ready to settle down, then?"

"Definitely not." His smile pulled up one corner of his mouth and he looked *completely* destructive. My heart and lady bits would not survive a night with this man.

Good thing that's not even an option, vagina. Stand down.

We'd circled back around to the beginning of the trail, and Will leaned against a tree. "So why are you diving into the world of the living *now*?" He tilted his head as he turned the conversation back to me. "I know Jensen and your dad want you to have a more active social life, but come on. You're a pretty girl, Ziggs. It can't be that you haven't had offers."

I bit my lip for a second, amused that *of course* Will would assume that, for me, this was about getting laid. The truth was . . . he wasn't entirely wrong. And there was no judgment in his expression, no weird distance around such a personal topic.

"It's not that I haven't dated. It's that I haven't dated *well*," I said, remembering my most recent, completely bland encounter. "I know it might be hard to tell behind all this smooth charm but I'm not very good in those kinds of situations. Jensen's told me stories. You managed to get through your doctorate with top honors and what sounds like a whole lot of fun. Here I am, in a lab with people who seem to consider social awkwardness a field of study. Not really that many jumping in the boat, if you know what I mean."

"You're young, Ziggs. Why are you worrying about this now?"

"I'm not *worried* about it, but I'm twenty-four. I have functioning body parts and my mind tends to go to interesting places. I just want to . . . explore. You weren't thinking about these things when you were my age?"

He shrugged. "I wasn't stressing over it."

"Of course you weren't. You'd lift an eyebrow and panties would hit the floor."

Will licked his lips, reaching to scratch the back of his neck. "You're a trip."

"I'm a *scientist*, Will. If I'm going to do this I need to learn how men think, get inside their head." I took a deep breath, watched him carefully before saying, "Teach me. You told my brother you'd help me, so do that."

"Pretty sure he didn't mean *Hey, show my kid sister the city, make sure she isn't paying too much for rent, and, by the way, help her get laid.*" His dark brows pulled together as something seemed to occur to him. "Are you asking me to set you up with a friend?"

"No. *God*." I wasn't sure whether I wanted to laugh or crawl into a hole and hide for the rest of *forever*. Despite his DEFCON 1 degree of hotness, what I needed was for him to help me bang the smirk off *other* men. Maybe then I'd be properly degeeked and socialized. "I want your help to learn . . ." I shrugged and scratched my hair beneath the hat. "*How* to date. Teach me the rules."

He blinked away, looking torn. "The 'rules'? I don't . . ." He shivered, letting his words fall away as he reached up to scratch his jaw. "I'm not sure I am qualified to help you meet guys."

"You went to Yale."

"Yeah, and? That was years ago, Ziggs. I don't think they offered this in the course catalog."

"And you were in a band," I continued, ignoring that last part.

Finally, amusement lit up his eyes. "What's your point?"

"My point is that I went to MIT and played *D&D* and *Magic*—"

"Hello, I was a fucking *D&D* pro, Ziggs."

"My point," I said, ignoring him, "is that Yale-attending, lacrosse-playing former bass players might have ideas about how to improve the dating pool options of bespectacled, nerdtastic geeks."

"Are you fucking with me right now?"

Instead of answering, I crossed my arms over my chest and waited patiently. It was the same stance I'd adopted back when I was supposed to be rotating through several labs to help decide what type of research I wanted. But I didn't want to do lab rotations for my entire first year of graduate school; I wanted to get started on my research with Liemacki, immediately. I'd stood outside his office after explaining why his work was perfectly positioned to move away from viral vaccine research into parasitology, and what I thought I could work on for my thesis. I'd been prepared to stand like that for hours, but after only five minutes he'd relented and, as the chair of the department, made an exception for me.

Will looked off into the distance. I wasn't sure if he was considering what I was saying, or deciding whether he should just start running and leave me wheezing in his snow-dust.

Finally, he sighed. "Okay, well, rule one of having a broader social life is never call anyone except a cab before the sun is up."

"Yeah. Sorry about that."

He studied me, eventually motioning to my outfit. "We'll run. We'll go out and do stuff." He winced, waving vaguely at my body. "I don't really think you need to do anything but . . . fuck, I don't know. You're wearing your brother's baggy sweatshirt. Correct me if I'm wrong, but I have a feeling that's pretty standard attire, even when you're not jogging." He shrugged. "Though it is kind of cute."

"I am not dressing like a hoochie."

"You don't have to dress like a *hoochie*." He straightened, messing up his hair before tucking it beneath his beanie again. "*God*. You're a ballbuster. Do you know Chloe and Sara?"

I shook my head. "Are those some girls you're . . . *not dating*?"

"Oh, hell no," he said with a laugh. "They're the women who have my best friends by the balls. I think they'd be good for you to meet. Swear to God you'll all probably be best friends at the end of the night."

CHAPTER TWO

"So wait," Max said, pulling out his chair to sit down. "Is this Jensen's sister you shagged?"

"No, that's the other sister, Liv." I sat across from the Brit and ignored both the amused grin on his face as well as the uncomfortable twist in my stomach. "And I didn't *shag* her. We just hooked up a little. The youngest sister is Ziggy. She was only a kid that first time I went home with Jensen for Christmas."

"I still can't believe he took you home for Christmas and you made out with his sister in the backyard. I'd kick your ass." He reconsidered, scratching his chin. "Ah fuck that. I wouldn't have given a shit."

I looked at Max, felt a small grin pull at my mouth. "Liv wasn't there when I came back a few years later for the summer. I behaved myself the second time around."

All around us, glasses clinked and conversation

carried on in a quiet murmur. Tuesday lunch at Le Bernardin had become a routine for our group in the past
six months. Max and I were usually the last ones to
the table, but apparently the others had been held up
in a meeting.

"I suspect you want an award for that," Max said,
studying his menu before closing it with a snap. Truth-
fully, I'm not sure why he even bothered to open it in
the first place. He always got the caviar for his first
course, and the monkfish for the main course. I'd recently surmised that Max kept all of his spontaneity for
his life with Sara; with food and work, he was a quiet
creature of habit.

"You just forget what *you* were like before Sara," I
said. "Stop acting like you lived in a monastery."

He acknowledged this with a wink and his big, easy
smile. "So tell me about this little sis."

"She's the youngest of the five Bergstrom kids,
and in grad school here at Columbia. Ziggy's always
been this ridiculous brain. Finished undergrad in three
years, and now works in the Liemacki lab? The one
who does the vaccine work?"

Max shook his head and shrugged as if to say, *The
fuck are you talking about?*

I continued, "It's a very high-profile operation over
at the med school. Anyway, last weekend in Vegas
when you were off chasing your pussy to the blackjack
tables, Jensen texted to let me know he was coming
to visit her. I guess he gave her a *Come-to-Jesus* about

not living among the test tubes and beakers for the rest of her life."

The waiter came by to fill our water glasses, and we explained that we were waiting on a few more people to join the table.

Max looked back to me. "So you have plans to see her again, yeah?"

"Yeah. I'm sure we'll go out and do something this weekend. I think we'll run together again."

I didn't miss the way his eyes widened. "Letting someone in your private little running headspace? That seems like it would be more intimate than sex to you, William."

I waved him off. "Whatever."

"So it was fun then? Catching up with the little sis and all?"

It *had* been fun. It hadn't been wild, or even anything all that special—we'd gone for a run, of all things. But I still felt a little shaken by how unexpected *she* had been. I'd gone in thinking there had to be a reason for her isolation, other than her long work hours. I'd expected she would be awkward, or hideous, or the poster child for inappropriate social behavior.

But she'd been none of those things, and she definitely didn't seem anything like someone's "little sister." She was naïve and a bit unfiltered at times, but really she was simply hardworking and had found herself trapped in a set of habits she didn't enjoy anymore. I could relate.

I'd first met the Bergstroms over Christmas, my sophomore year in college. I hadn't been able to afford to fly home that year, and Jensen's mother had such a fit at the idea of me staying alone in the dorms that she drove down from Boston two days before Christmas to pick me up and bring me home for the holidays. The family was as loving and loud as one would expect with five kids spaced almost exactly two years apart.

True to form for that stage in my life, I'd thanked them by secretly fooling around with their oldest daughter in the shed out back.

A few years later I'd interned for Johan, and lived at the Bergstrom house. Most of the other kids had moved out or stayed near college for the summer, so it was just me and Jensen, and the youngest daughter, Ziggy. Theirs had come to feel like a second home to me. Still, even though I'd lived near her for three months, and had seen her a few years ago at Jensen's wedding, when she'd called yesterday, it had been hard to even remember her face.

But when I saw her at the park, more memories than I realized I'd had came flooding in. Ziggy at twelve, her freckled nose hidden behind books. She'd offer only the occasional shy smile across the dinner table, but otherwise avoided contact with me. I'd been nineteen and nearly oblivious anyway. And I remembered Ziggy at sixteen, all legs and elbows, her tangled hair cascading down her back. She spent her afternoons wearing cutoff shorts and tank tops, reading on a blanket in the backyard while I worked with her father. I'd checked her out, like I'd checked out every female at the time, as if I were scanning and cataloging body parts. The girl was curvy, but quiet, and obviously naïve enough about the art of flirting to earn my scornful disinterest. At the time, my life had been full of curiosity and kink, younger and older women who were willing to try anything once.

But this afternoon, it felt as though a bomb had gone off in my head. Seeing her face was—strangely—like being home again, but also like meeting a beautiful girl for the first time. She didn't look anything like Liv or Jensen, who were towheaded and gangly, almost carbon copies of one another. Ziggy looked like her father, for better or worse. She had the paradoxical combination of her father's long limbs and her mother's curves. She inherited Johan's gray eyes, light brown hair, and freckles, but her mother's wide-open smile.

I'd hesitated when she stepped forward, wrapped her arms around my neck, and squeezed. It was a comfortable hug, bordering on intimate. Other than Chloe and Sara, I didn't have a lot of females in my life who were strictly *friends*. When I hugged a woman like that—close and pressing—there was generally some sexual element. Ziggy had always been the kid sister, but there in my arms it fully registered that she wasn't a kid anymore. She was a twenty-something woman with her warm hands on my neck and her body flush to mine. She smelled like shampoo and coffee. She smelled like a *woman,* and beneath the bulk of her sweatshirt and pathetically thin jacket, I could feel the shape of her breasts press against my chest. When she stepped back and looked me over, I'd immediately *liked* her: she hadn't dressed up, hadn't put on makeup or expensive workout gear. She wore her brother's Yale sweatshirt, black pants that were too short, and shoes that definitely looked like they'd seen better days. She wasn't trying to impress me; she just wanted to *see* me.

She's so sheltered, man, Jensen had said when he'd called a little over a week ago. *I feel like I let her down by not anticipating she had Dad's work-obsession genes. We're going down to visit her. I don't even know what to do.*

I blinked back into awareness when Sara and Bennett approached the table. Max stood to greet them, and I looked away as he leaned over to kiss Sara just beneath her ear, whispering, "You look beautiful, Petal."

"Are we waiting on Chloe?" I asked once everyone was seated.

Bennett spoke from behind his menu. "She's in Boston until Friday."

"Well, thank fuck," Max said. "Because I'm starving and that woman takes forever to decide what she wants."

Bennett laughed quietly, sliding his menu back on the table.

I was relieved, too, not because I was hungry but because I was fine occasionally having a break from the role of fifth wheel. My four coupled-up friends were two steps away from Smug and had *long* ago skipped past Overly-Invested-in-Will's-Dating-Life. They were convinced that I was two breaths away from having my heart ripped out by the woman of my dreams and were eager for the show.

And, only increasing this obsession, upon returning from Vegas last week, I'd made the mistake of casually mentioning that I was feeling detached from my two regular lovers, Kitty and Kristy. Both women were happy to meet regularly for no-strings fucking and didn't seem to mind the existence of the other—or the occasional new fling I might have—but lately I felt like I was just going through the motions:

Undress,

touch,

fuck,

orgasm,

(maybe some pillow talk),

a kiss good night,

and then I was gone, or they were.

Had it all become too easy? Or was I finally getting tired of just sex—sex?!

And why the fuck was I thinking about all of this again, *now*? I sat up, scrubbed my face with my hands. Nothing in my life had changed in a day. I'd had a nice morning with Ziggy, that's it. That was *it*. The fact that she was disarmingly genuine and funny and surprisingly pretty shouldn't have thrown me so dramatically.

"So what were we discussing?" Bennett asked, thanking the waiter when he slid a gimlet on the table in front of him.

"We were discussing Will's reunion with an old friend this morning," Max said, and then added in a stage whisper, "a *lady* friend."

Sara laughed. "Will saw a woman this morning? Why is this news?"

Bennett held up his hand. "Wait, isn't tonight Kitty? And you had another date this morning?" He sipped his gimlet, eyeing me.

In fact, Kitty was the exact reason I'd suggested to Hanna that we meet up this morning instead of tonight: *Kitty* was my late meeting. But the more I thought about it, the idea of spending my usual Tuesday with her seemed less and less appealing.

I groaned, and both Max and Sara burst out laughing. "Is it weird that we all know Will's Weekly Hookup Calendar?" Sara asked.

Max looked over at me, eyes smiling. "You're thinking of canceling plans with Kitty, aren't you? Think you're going to pay for that one?"

"Probably," I admitted. Kitty and I dated a few years back, and it ended amiably when it came out that she wanted more than I did. But when we met up again in a bar a few months ago, she said this time she just wanted to have fun. Of course I'd been game. She was gorgeous, and willing to do almost anything I wanted. She insisted our just-sex arrangement was fine, fine, fine. The thing was, I think we both knew she was lying: every time I had to ask for a rain check, she would become insecure and needy the next time we were together.

Kristy was almost the complete opposite. She was more contained, had a fetish for being gagged that I didn't share, but wasn't against indulging, and rarely stayed beyond the moment of our shared release.

"If you're interested in this new girl, you should probably end it with Kitty," Sara said.

"You guys," I protested, digging into my salad. "There isn't a thing with Ziggy. We went *running*."

"So why are we still talking about it?" Bennett asked with a laugh.

I nodded. "Exactly."

But I knew we were talking about it because I was tense, and when I was tense I wore it like a neon sign. My brows pulled together, my eyes got darker, and my words came out clipped. I turned into an asshole.

And Max *loved* it.

"Oh, we're talking about it," the Brit said, "because it's getting William riled up, and that's my favorite fucking thing. It's also very bloody interesting how pensive he's being today after a morning with this little sis. Will doesn't usually look like he's thinking so hard it hurts."

"She's Jensen's youngest sister," I explained to Sara and Bennett.

"He snogged the older sister when they were teens," Max added helpfully, overplaying his accent for dramatic effect.

"You are such a shit-stirrer," I said, laughing. Liv was a short blip; I could barely remember much about what had happened other than some heated kissing and then my easy evasion when I'd returned to New Haven. Compared to some of my relationships at the time, what happened with Liv barely registered on the sex meter.

Our entrées came and we ate in silence for a little bit. My mind started to wander. Partway through our run, I'd given up and just outright stared at Ziggy. I stared at her cheeks, at her lips, at the soft hair that had fallen free from her messy bun and lay straight against the soft skin of her neck. I'd always been open about my appreciation for women, but I wasn't attracted to every woman I saw. So what was it about this one? She was pretty but definitely not the prettiest girl I'd ever seen. She was seven years younger than I was, green as an apple, and barely came up from her work to breathe. What could she possibly offer me that I couldn't find somewhere else?

She'd looked over and caught me; the energy between us was palpable, and confusing as fuck. And when she smiled, it lit up her whole face. She looked as open as a screen door in the summer, and despite the temperature, something warmed in my veins. It was an old, yet familiar hunger. A desire I hadn't felt in forever, where my blood filled with adrenaline and I wanted to be the only one to discover a particular girl's secrets. Ziggy's skin looked sweet; her lips were full and soft, her neck looked like it had never been marked with teeth or suction. The beast in me wanted to look more closely at her hands, at her mouth, at her breasts.

I looked up when I felt Max watching me, chewing thoughtfully.

He lifted his fork, pointed it at my chest. "All it takes is one night with the right girl. I'm not talking about sex, either. One night could change you, young m—"

"Oh, stop," I groaned. "You're such a fucking asshole right now."

Bennett straightened, joining in. "It's about finding the woman who gets you thinking. *She'll* be the one who'll change your mind about everything."

I held up my hands. "It's a nice thought, you guys. But Ziggy really isn't my type."

"What's your type? Walks? Has a pussy?" Max asked.

I laughed. "I guess she just feels young?"

The guys hummed and nodded in understanding, but I could feel Sara watching me. "Out with it," I said to her.

"Well, I'm just thinking you haven't found anyone who makes you *want* to delve deeper. You're choosing a certain type of woman, a type you know will fit into your structure, your rules, your limits. Aren't you bored yet? You're saying this sister—"

"Ziggy," Max offered.

"Right," she said. "You're saying Ziggy isn't your type, but last week you said you were feeling detached from the women who happily screw you without strings attached." She forked a bite of her lunch and shrugged as she started to lift it to her mouth. "Maybe you should reevaluate *your type*."

"Illogical. I can be losing interest in my lovers and it doesn't have to mean that I need to overhaul the whole system." I continued to poke at my food. "Though actually, I do have a favor to ask."

Sara swallowed, nodding. "Of course."

"I was hoping maybe you and Chloe could take her out? She doesn't have any real girlfriends here and you guys—"

"Of course," she said again quickly. "I can't wait to meet her."

I glanced at Max from the corner of my eye, unsurprised to see him biting his lip and looking like the cat that had caught the canary. But Sara must have picked up a thing or two from Chloe and had him by the balls beneath the table, because, for once, he was uncharacteristically quiet.

Do you ever feel like the people who mean the most aren't the people you see the most? Lately I just feel like I'm not putting my heart where it matters.

Her voice and wide, honest eyes when she'd said

this had made me feel full and hollow all at once, like the ache was so heavy I couldn't tell if it was pain or pleasure.

Ziggy wanted me to show her how to get out and date, how to meet people she wanted to get to know . . . and the reality was I wasn't even doing that myself. I might not be the one sitting in my apartment alone, but that didn't mean I was happy.

Excusing myself to the men's room, I pulled my phone from my pocket and typed a text to the mobile number she'd given me.

```
Project Ziggy still on your mind?
If so, I'm in. Running tomorrow,
plans this weekend. Don't be late.
```

I stared at the phone for a few seconds but when she didn't reply right away I returned to my lunch, my friends.

But later, when I left the restaurant, I noticed there was a single message now and I laughed, remembering that Ziggy mentioned an old flip phone she barely ever used.

```
Aw3esome!Icantfindthespacekey=butI
willcallyou.
```

Between Ziggy's, Chloe's, and Sara's crazy schedules, the three of them couldn't get together until the weekend. But thank God they finally made it work, be-cause watching Ziggy run every morning with her arms crossed across her chest was actually staring to make *my* boobs hurt.

That Saturday afternoon, Max was sitting at a table at Blue Smoke when I arrived, panting from my six-mile run and famished. As always seemed to happen with this group, a plan was formed without any of my help, so I woke to a text from Chloe that I was supposed to have Ziggy meet them for breakfast and shopping, meaning I'd be running by myself for the first time in days.

It was fine. *Good*, even. And even though my run felt silent, and strangely dull, Ziggy needed to get out and get some *things*. She needed running shoes. She needed running clothes. She could even stand to get some regular clothes if she was serious about dating, because most guys were shallow dicks and relied on the shorthand of first impressions. Ziggy wasn't very strong in this department, but part of me didn't want to push too much on her. I liked looking at well-dressed women, but oddly enough, with Ziggy, what was most intriguing was that she wasn't really concerned with any of that. I figured we should probably stick with what was already working for her.

Without even looking up, Max moved the stack of newspaper pages from my chair and waved to the wait-ress to come take my order.

"Water," I said, using the paper napkin to wipe my

brow. "And maybe just some peanuts for now. In a little bit I'll have some lunch."

Max took in my clothes and went back to his paper, handing me the Business section of the *Times*.

"Weren't you out with the girls earlier?" he asked.

I thanked the waitress when she put my drink down in front of me, and took a big gulp. "I dropped Ziggs off this morning. I wasn't sure she would be able to navigate her way around anything past the Columbia campus."

"Such a loving mother hen, you."

"Oh, in that case I should lovingly let you know that Sara accidentally texted a picture of her ass to Bennett." There was virtually nothing I loved more than giving Max shit about his and Sara's kinky photo obsession.

He looked at me over the top of his paper and his face relaxed when he saw that I was kidding. "Tosser," he mumbled.

I flipped through the Business section for a few minutes before turning my attention to Science and Technology. Behind his wall of newspaper, Max's phone rang. "Hey, Chlo." He paused, putting the paper down on the table. "No, 's just me and Will here getting a bite. Maybe Ben's on a run?" He nodded and then handed the phone to me.

I took the call, surprised. "Hey . . . everything okay?"

"Hanna is adorable," Chloe said. "She hasn't bought new clothes since college. I swear we aren't treating her like a doll, but she's the cutest thing I've ever seen. Why didn't you bring her around sooner?"

I felt my stomach tighten. Chloe hadn't been at the lunch where we discussed Ziggy. "You know she's not a girlfriend, right?"

"I know, you're just banging, whatever, Will—"

I started to interrupt but she continued on.

"—just wanted to let you know we're all good. She looks like she would get lost in this Macy's if we didn't keep track of her."

"That's exactly what I said."

"Okay, that's all I got. Was just calling to see if Max knew where Bennett was. More shopping."

"Hey wait," I said before I really considered what I was about to ask. I closed my eyes and remembered jogging with Ziggy the past few days. She was relatively slim but damn, there was a lot up front.

"Hmm?"

"If you're shopping, make sure Ziggs gets some . . ." I glanced up at Max, confirming he was absorbed in his newspaper before I whispered, "Make sure she gets some bras. Like, for jogging? But maybe also . . . just . . . regular ones, too. Okay?"

I felt rather than heard the silence on the other end of the line. It was leaden, and pressed down on my chest as the awkwardness grew. And grew. When I chanced a look up, Max was staring at me, wearing an enormous shit-eating grin.

"You are so lucky I'm not Bennett right now," Chloe

said, finally. "The amount of crap I would give you is on the planetary scale."

"Don't worry, Max is here and I can tell he's enjoying this enough for the both of them."

She laughed. "We're on it. Bras to support the supple breasts of your nongirlfriend. God, you're a pig."

"Thanks."

She hung up and I handed the phone back to Max, avoiding his eyes.

"Oh, *Victoria*," he said, giddy. "Do you have a *Secret*? Do you have a fondness for helping women find well-fitting ladywear?"

"Fuck off," I said through a laugh. His expression was as if Leeds United had just won the fucking World Cup. "She's been joining me on my morning run, and she wears these . . . whatever. They're not sports bras. And her bras do that . . ." I gestured to my chest. "That weird four-boob thing up front? I just figured if they were out shopping already . . ."

Max leaned his chin on his fist and smiled at me. "Christ you're precious, William."

"You know how I feel about breasts. It's no joking matter." And, I didn't add, Ziggy was stacked like a pinup girl.

"Indeed not," he agreed, lifting his paper again. "I just like how you're pretending you wouldn't cream your panties for a girl with four tits."

———

About half an hour later, the door behind Max opened and I looked up as a tangle of shiny hair and shopping bags careened toward our table. Max and I stood, helping Ziggy unload her loot on one of the chairs.

She wore a pale blue sweater, dark fitted jeans, and green flats. She wasn't dressed like she was coming off a runway, but she looked comfortable, stylish. Her hair was . . . different. I narrowed my eyes, studying it as she slipped her messenger bag from her shoulder. She'd cut it, or maybe it was that she just had it down instead of confined to her trademark messy bun. It fell past her shoulders, thick, and straight and smooth. But despite the changes in her clothes and hair, she, fortunately, still looked like *Ziggy*: a tiny bit of makeup, bright smile, sun-kissed freckles.

She reached her hand out for Max's, smiling. "I'm Hanna. You must be Max."

Grasping her hand, he said, "Nice to meet you. I trust you had a good morning with the two crazy women?"

"I did." She turned to me, wrapped her arms around my neck, and I tried not to groan when she squeezed. I both loved and hated her hugs. They were tight, almost smothering, but disarmingly warm. When she let go, she collapsed into a chair. "That Chloe likes her lingerie, though. I think we spent an hour in that section alone."

"Let me find my surprised face," I murmured, discreetly checking out Ziggy's chest as I sat back down.

The girls looked fantastic: full and high. Just perfectly in place. She must have purchased some lingerie herself.

"On that note . . ." Max stood, slipping his wallet into his back pocket. "I think it's time for me to find the Petal and see how successful *her* shopping ventures were. Nice to meet you, Hanna." He patted my shoulder, winking at her. "Have a nice lunch."

Ziggy waved to Max, and then turned to me, eyes wide. "Wow. He's . . . *hot*. I met Bennett earlier, too. You guys are like the Hot Men's Club of Manhattan."

"I don't think that's a thing. And anyway, do you really think we'd let Max in?" I said, grinning. "You look great, by the way." Her head shot to me, eyes surprised, and I quickly added, "I'm glad you didn't let them cover you up with makeup. I would miss your freckles."

"You would miss my *freckles*?" she asked in a whisper and I winced inwardly at how forward I sounded. "What man says that? Are you trying to make me have an orgasm right now?"

Whoa. I no longer felt like *I'd* been too forward. I worked very hard to not look at her chest again when she said that. I was still getting used to the way she seemed to let out every thought she had. Glancing down at her shopping bags, I softly redirected, "I . . . uh, it looks like you bought plenty of running shoes."

Bending, she rummaged through a few things and I blinked up to the ceiling, ignoring the view of her full cleavage. "I think I got *everything*," she said. "I've never shopped like that. Liv is probably going to pop some champagne when she hears." When I finally looked back down, her eyes were scanning my face, my neck, my chest as if she were just now seeing me. "Did you go for a run this morning?"

"And a bike ride."

"You're so *disciplined*." She leaned forward with her hands on her chin and batted her lashes at me. "It does really nice things for your muscles."

Laughing, I told her, "It calms me. Keeps me from . . ." I searched for words, feeling my neck heat. "From being stupid."

"That isn't what you were originally going to say," she said, sitting up. "It keeps you from what? Like getting into bar fights? Release of tension and man angst?"

I decided to test her a little. I had no idea where the urge came from, but she was a confusing mix of inexperienced and wild. She made me feel reckless, and a little drunk. "It keeps me from wanting to fuck all the time."

She barely skipped a beat. "Why would you want to run instead of fuck?" She tilted her head, considering me for a beat. "Besides, exercise increases testosterone and blood flow. I think, if anything, you're having better sex *because* you exercise."

Talking about this with her felt dangerous. It was tempting to look at her a little too long, and Ziggy didn't shrink under my inspection. She would look right back at me.

"I have no idea why I told you that," I admitted.

"*Will*. I'm neither a virgin nor a woman trying to get into your pants. We can discuss *sex*."

"Hmmm, I'm not sure that's such a good idea." I lifted my juice to my lips, taking a sip while I watched her drink some of her water, her eyes locked on mine. She wasn't trying to get into my pants? Not even a little?

The air between us seemed to hum quietly. I wanted to reach forward, run my finger over her lower lip. Instead, I put my juice down and curled my hands into fists.

"I'm just saying," she said, "there's no need to sugarcoat with me. I like that you're not a guy who talks around things."

"Are *you* always this open with people?" I asked.

She shook her head. "I think this might be you-specific. I say a lot of things, really, but I especially feel stupid around you, and I can't seem to shut up."

"I don't want you to shut up."

"You've always been so obviously sexual and open about it. You're this hot, player guy who doesn't apologize for enjoying women. I mean, if I noticed that about you when I was twelve, it was *obvious*. Sex is natural. It's what our bodies *do*. I like that you are who you are."

I didn't respond, didn't know what to say. She liked the thing about me that every other woman wanted to tame, but I wasn't sure I liked that this was her primary impression of who I *was*.

"Chloe said you asked them to take me bra shopping."

I looked up to catch her eyes as they flickered away from my mouth.

Her smirk curled into a playful smile. "How thoughtful, Will. So nice of you to think about my boobs."

I bent to take a bite of my sandwich, murmuring, "We don't need to discuss that conversation. Max already gave me an appropriate amount of shit."

"You're a mysterious man, Player Will." She lifted the menu, skimming the choices before putting it back down. "But, fine. I'll change the subject. What should we talk about?"

I swallowed, watching her. I couldn't imagine this wild young thing with the intense and poised combination of Chloe and Sara. "Whatever you ladies talked about today," I suggested.

"Well, Sara and I had a fun conversation about what it feels like to be almost revirginized after not having sex for so long."

I almost choked, coughing loudly. "Wow. That's . . . I don't even know what that is."

She watched me, amused. "Seriously though. I'm sure it's not like that for guys. But for girls, after a while, you're like . . . does the virginity grow back? Is it like moss over a cave?"

"That is a disgusting image."

Ignoring me, she sat up straighter, excited now.

"Actually this is perfect. You're a scientist so you'll totally appreciate this theory I recently developed."

I pressed back farther into my chair. "You just ended with a moss over a cave analogy. Honestly, I'm a little scared."

"Don't be. So, you know how a girl's virginity is considered kind of sacred?"

I laughed. "Yes, I've heard of this concept."

She scratched her head, her freckled nose wrinkling a little. "My theory is this: Cavemen are making a comeback. Everyone wants to read about the guy who ties the girl up, or gets all violently jealous if—God forbid—she wears something sexy outside the bedroom. Women supposedly like that, right? Well, I think the new fad is going to be revirginization. They'll want their man to feel like he's their first. And can you imagine how women will do this?"

I watched her eyes grow increasingly excited as she waited for me to attempt an answer. Something about her sincerity, her earnest consideration of this topic tightened an invisible band beneath my ribs. "Um, with lies? Women always assume we can read braille with our cocks. What's that about? I honestly probably wouldn't know a girl was a virgin unless she—"

"With surgery first, probably. Let's call it 'hymen restoration.' "

Dropping my food, I groaned. "Jesus Christ, Ziggs.

I'm eating brisket. Can you just hold off on the hymen talk for like—"

"And then"—she drummed her hands on the table, building suspense—"everyone is waiting to see what stem cells can do for us. But spinal cord injury, Parkinson's . . . I don't think that's where they'll start. You know what I think the big splash will be?"

"Edge of my seat," I deadpanned.

"I bet it will be a restoration of the maidenhead."

I coughed again, loudly. "Dear God. 'Maidenhead'?"

"You said no 'hymen,' so—but am I right?"

Before I could answer and tell her the theory was actually pretty good, she barreled on. "Stupid amounts of money are spent on this kind of thing. Viagra for boners. Four hundred different shapes of fake boobs. Which filler feels the most natural? It's a man's world, Will. Women won't stop to think that you're putting *actively growing cells* in their *vagina*. Next year, one of your nongirlfriends will get her hymen regenerated, and she'll give her new virginity to you, Will."

She leaned down, put her lips around her straw, and sucked, her gray eyes locked on mine. And with that lingering, playful look, I felt my cock harden slightly. Releasing the straw, she whispered, "To *you*. And will you appreciate what a gift that is? What a sacrifice?"

Her eyes danced and then she tilted her head back and burst out laughing. Holy fuck, I liked this girl. I liked her a lot.

Leaning forward on my elbows, I cleared my throat.

"Ziggy, listen up because this is important. I'm about to impart some wisdom."

She sat up, her eyes narrowing conspiratorially.

"Rule one we've already covered: don't ever call someone before the sun is up."

Her lips twitched into a guilty little smile. "Right. Got that one."

"And rule two," I said, shaking my head slowly. "Don't ever discuss hymen regeneration over lunch. Or . . . like, ever."

She dissolved into giggles and then moved out of the way when the waitress brought her food. "Don't be so quick to mock it. That's a billion-dollar idea, money-man. If that comes across your desk soon, you'll thank me for the heads-up."

She dug into her salad, taking an enormous bite, and I tried not to study her. She wasn't like any of the girls I knew. She was pretty—actually, she was beautiful—but she wasn't poised or contained. She was silly, and confident, and so much her own person it almost made the rest of the world seem monochromatic. I had no idea if she even took herself seriously, but she certainly didn't expect me to.

"What's your favorite book?" I asked, the question bubbling up out of nowhere.

She sucked her bottom lip into her mouth and I blinked down to my sandwich, picking at the tiny pieces of crispy meat at the edges.

"This is going to sound cliché."

"I sincerely doubt that, but hit me."

She leaned forward, and whispered, *"A Brief History of Time."*

"Hawking?"

"Of course," she said, almost offended.

"That's not cliché. Cliché would be if you said *Wuthering Heights* or *Little Women*."

"Because I'm a woman? If I asked *you*, and you said Hawking, would you be cliché?"

I considered this. I imagined saying that book was my favorite, and getting a few *Dude, of course*'s from my grad school friends. "Probably."

"So that's bull, for it to be cliché for you and not me just because I have a vagina. But anyway," she said, shrugging and popping a small bite of lettuce into her mouth, "I read it when I was twelve, and—"

"Twelve?"

"Yeah, and it just blew me away. Not so much what he said—because I don't think I understood everything then—but more that he thought that way. That there were people out there who spent their lives trying to figure these things out. It opened up a whole world for me." Suddenly she closed her eyes, taking a deep breath, and smiled a little guiltily when she opened them again. "I'm talking your ear off."

"Yes, but lately you're *always* talking my ear off."

With a little wink, she leaned forward to whisper, "But maybe you kind of love it?"

Unbidden, my mind flooded with the fantasy of her

neck arched, her mouth open in a hoarse plea while I
licked a line from the hollow of her throat to her jaw.
I imagined her nails digging into my shoulders, the
sharp sting of pain . . . and blinked, standing and pushing my chair back so quickly that it hit the chair behind
me. I apologized to the man seated there, apologized
to Ziggy, and practically sprinted to the restroom.

Locking the door behind me, I wheeled around on
my reflection. "What the actual *fuck* was that, Sumner?" I bent to splash a handful of cold water over my
face.

Bracing my hands on the sink, I met my own eyes
in the mirror again. "It was just an image. It wasn't
anything. She's a sweet kid. She's pretty. But, one:
she's Jensen's sister. Two: she's Liv's sister, and you
practically dry-humped Liv in a shed when she was seventeen. I think you cashed in your single Bergstrom-
Sister-Hookup Card already. And three . . ." I bent
my head, took a deep breath. "Three. You wear track
pants around her way too often to be having sexual
fantasies without her getting wise. Put a lid on it. Go
home, call Kitty or Kristy, get some head, call it a day."

When I returned to the table, Ziggy had nearly pol-
ished off her salad and was watching people move
down the sidewalk. She looked up when I sat down,
concern etching her features. "Stomach troubles?"

"What? No. No, I . . . had to call someone."

Fuck. That sounded douchey. I winced, and then
sighed. "I actually should probably go, Ziggs. I've been

here for a couple of hours, and was planning to get a few things done this afternoon."

Damnit. That sounded even douchier.

She pulled her wallet from her purse and put down a few fives. "Of course. God, I have a ton to do, too. Thanks so much for letting me meet you here. And thanks so much for hooking me up with Chloe and Sara." With one more smile she stood, hitched her bag over her shoulder, collected her shopping bags, and walked to the door.

Her sandy hair shone and fell most of the way down her back. Her spine was straight, her gait steady. Her ass looked fucking amazing in the jeans she wore.

Holy fuck, Will. You are so goddamn screwed.

Chapter Three

This running thing really wasn't getting any easier.

"This running thing will get easier," Will insisted, looking down at where I sat, slumped over in a whiny pile on the ground. "Have some patience."

I pulled a few blades of brown grass from the frost, mumbling to myself exactly what Will could do with his patience. It was early, the sky was still dull and gray and not even the birds seemed willing to venture out into the cold. We'd run together almost every morning for the past week and a half, and I was sore in places I didn't even know I owned.

"And stop being a brat," he added.

Looking up at him, eyes narrowed, I asked, "What did you say?"

"I said get your ass up here."

I stood, lagging behind a few steps before jogging

to catch up. He glanced over at me, assessing. "Still stiff?"

I shrugged. "A little."

"As stiff as you were on Friday?"

I considered this, rolling my shoulders and stretching my arms over my head. "Not really."

"And does your chest still feel like—how did you put it—like someone doused your lungs in gasoline and lit them on fire?"

I glared at him. "No."

"See? And next week it'll get easier. And the week after that you'll crave running the way I bet you sometimes crave chocolate."

I opened my mouth to lie but he quieted me with a knowing look.

"This week we'll call and get you with someone who'll keep you on track and before you know it—"

"What do you mean 'we'll get me with someone'?" We moved into a jog and I lengthened my stride to match his.

He gave me a brief glance. "Someone to run with you. Like a trainer."

The bare trees seemed enough to insulate us because, though I could see the tops of buildings and the skyline in the distance, the sounds of the city felt miles away. Our feet pounded over fallen leaves and bits of loose gravel in the path, and it narrowed just enough that I had to adjust my steps. My shoulder brushed against his and I was close enough to smell him, the scent of soap and mint and a hint of coffee clinging to his skin.

"I'm confused, why can't I just run with you?"

Will laughed, drawing an arc with his hand as if the answer were suspended in the air around us. "This isn't really running for me, Ziggs."

"Well, of course not; we're barely *jogging*."

"No, I mean I'm supposed to be training."

I looked at our feet and up at his face, my eyes full of meaning. "And this isn't training?"

He laughed again. "I'm doing the Ashland Sprint this spring. It'll take more than a mile-and-a-half run a few days a week to get me ready."

"What's the Ashland Sprint?" I asked.

"A triathlon just outside Boston."

"Oh." The rhythm of our steps echoed in my head and I felt my limbs warm, could almost feel the blood pumping through my body. It wasn't entirely unpleasant. "So I'll just do that with you."

He looked down at me, eyes narrowed and a smile pulling at the corners of his mouth. "Do you even know what a triathlon is?"

"Of course I do. It's the swim, run, shoot a bear thing."

"Good guess," he deadpanned.

"Okay, so enlighten me, Player. Exactly how long is this triathlon of manliness?"

"Depends. There's sprint distance, intermediate, long course, and ultra-distance. And no bears, dumbass. Swim, run, *bike*."

I shrugged, ignoring the steady burn in my calves as we reached an incline. "So which one are you doing?"

"Intermediate."

"Okay," I said. "That doesn't sound too bad."

"That means you swim about a mile, bike for twenty-five, and then run the last six."

The petals of my blooming confidence wilted a little. "Oh."

"And that's why I can't stay over here on the bunny trail with you."

"Hey!" I said, shoving him hard enough that he stumbled slightly.

He laughed, steadying himself before grinning over at me. "Has it always been this easy to get you worked up?"

I raised my brows and his eyes widened.

"Never mind," he groaned.

⁂

The sun finally broke through the gloom by the time we slowed to a walk. Will's cheeks were pink from the cold, the ends of his hair curling up from beneath his beanie. A hint of a beard covered his jaw and I found myself studying him, trying to reconcile the person in front of me with the guy I thought I remembered so well. He was such a *man* now. I bet he could shave twice a day and still have a five o'clock shadow. I looked up in time to catch him staring at my chest.

I ducked to catch his gaze but he ignored my attempt to redirect his attention. "I hate to ask the obvious, but what are you looking at?"

He tilted his head, studying me from a different angle. "Your boobs look different."

"Don't they look awesome?" I took one in each hand. "As you know, Chloe and Sara helped me pick out new bras. Boobs have always been sort of a problem for me."

Will's eyes widened. "Boobs are never a problem for anyone. Ever."

"Says the man without a pair. Boobs are functional. That's it."

He looked at me with genuine fire in his eyes. "Fucking right they are. They get the job done."

I laughed, groaning. "They aren't functional for *you*, frat boy."

"Wanna bet?"

"See, the problem with boobs is if you have big ones, you can never look thin. You get these burns on your shoulders from bra straps, and your back hurts. And unless you're using them for their intended purpose, they're always in the way."

"In the way of *what*? My hands? My face? Don't you blaspheme in here." He looked up to the sky. "She didn't mean it, Lord. Promise."

Ignoring him, I said, "That's why I had a reduction when I was twenty-one," which is when his expression morphed into one of horror.

You'd have thought I told him I made an amazing stew from tiny babies and puppy tongues.

"Why on earth would you do that? That's like God giving you a beautiful gift and you kicking him in the nuts."

I laughed. "God? I thought you were agnostic, Professor."

"I am. But if I could motorboat perfect tits like yours I might be able to find Jesus."

I felt my blush warm my cheeks. "Because Jesus totally lives in my cleavage?"

"Not anymore he doesn't. Your boobs are now too small for him to be comfortable in there." He shook his head, and I couldn't stop laughing. "So selfish, Ziggs," he said, grinning so widely that I actually stumbled a little.

We both snapped around at the sound of a voice. "Will!"

I glanced from the perky redhead jogging toward us, to Will, and back again.

"Hey!" he said awkwardly, waving as she passed.

She turned to run backward, calling out to him, "Don't forget to call me. You owe me a Tuesday." She gave him a flirty little smile before continuing down the path.

I waited for an explanation but none came. Will's jaw was tight, his eyes no longer smiling as he focused on the trail ahead of us.

"She was pretty," I offered.

Will nodded.

"Was she a friend?"

"Yeah. That's Kitty. We . . . hang out."

Hang out. *Right.* I spent enough time on college campuses to know that ninety-five percent of the time the phrase *hanging out* was boy-code for *doing it.*

"So, not someone you would introduce as a girlfriend."

His eyes shot to mine. "No," he said, looking almost as if I'd offended him. "Definitely not a girlfriend."

We walked in silence for a few moments and I looked back over my shoulder, understanding dawning. She was a nongirlfriend. "Her boobs were . . . *wow.* She clearly knows Jesus."

Will completely cracked up and wrapped his arm around my shoulders. "Let's just say finding religion cost her a lot of money."

⟳

Later, when we were done, and Will was stretching on the ground next to me, reaching for his toes, I peeked over at him and said, "So I have this thing tonight." And then I winced.

Beneath his track pants I could see the pop of muscles in his thigh and so almost missed it when he repeated, "A thing?"

"Yeah. It's sort of a work . . . thing? Well, not really. Like, a social mixer, an interdepartmental thing. I never go to these, but in the spirit of not dying alone surrounded by feral cats, I figured I'd give it a go. It's Thursday night so I'm sure it's not going to be *that* wild."

He laughed, shaking his head as he switched his position.

"It's at Ding Dong Lounge." I paused, chewing my lip. "Seriously, is that a made-up name?"

"No, it's a place over on Columbus." Reaching up, he scratched his stubbly jaw, thinking. "Not far from my office actually. Max and I go there sometimes."

"Well, a bunch of my coworkers are going, and this time when they asked if I was going I said I was, and now I realize that I totally have to at least pop in and see what it's about, and who knows, maybe it could be fun."

He peeked up at me through his thick lashes. "Did you even breathe during that entire sentence?"

"Will." I stared him down. "Will you *come* tonight?"

He snickered, shaking his head as he looked down, stretching.

It took me a beat to understand why he was laughing. "Ugh, *pervert*." I groaned, shoving his shoulder. "You know what I mean. Will you come with *me*?"

He looked up at the sound of me smacking my forehead.

"Oh my God, that's worse. Just text me if you're interested in coming." I winced, turning to walk down the trail toward my apartment building and basically wanting the trail to crack open and transport me to Narnia. "Forget it!"

"I like it when you ask me to come!" he called after me. "I can't wait to come tonight, Ziggy! Should I come around eight? Or do you want me to come around ten? Maybe I'll come both times?"

I flipped him the bird, and kept moving away down the trail. Thank God he couldn't see my smile.

CHAPTER FOUR

My legs burned from sitting at my computer all day, and beyond that I had a wild itch to get to the Ding Dong Lounge—never thought I'd say that—pull up beside Ziggs at the bar and just . . . relax. It had been a long time since I'd had so much fun with a woman without getting naked.

Unfortunately for me, the more time I spent with Ziggy, the more I wanted it to morph into something that involved being naked. Which felt like a cop-out, like my brain and body wanted to fall back on the familiar comfort of sex over emotional depth. Ziggy pushed me, even if she didn't know it; she made me think about everything from why I did my job to why I kept sleeping with women I didn't love. It had been forever since I'd felt like I wanted to take over someone's sexual history, completely overwrite it with my hands and dick and mouth. But with Ziggy, I couldn't tell if that was because sex would somehow be easier than the way she had my brain all twisted, or if it was because I wanted her to twist me in other ways entirely.

So I stayed away until around ten, wanting to push her to socialize and spend time with friends from her lab. When I arrived, I spotted her at the bar without too much trouble, and slid up next to her, bumping her shoulder with mine. "Hey, lady. Come here often?"

She beamed at me, eyes lit with happiness. "Hey, Player Will." After a pause pregnant with some strange, mutual inspection, she said, "Thanks for com . . . *showing up.*"

Biting back a laugh, I asked, "Did you have dinner?"

She nodded. "We went to a seafood place down the street. I had mussels for the first time in years." When I made a face, she shoved me playfully. "You don't like mussels?"

"I hate shellfish."

She leaned closer, whispering, "Well, they were *delicious.*"

"I'm sure they were. All floppy and chewy and tasting like dirty ocean water."

"I'm happy to see you," she said, abruptly changing the subject. But she didn't shrink away from the proclamation when I looked over at her. "Outside of running, you know."

"Well, I'm happy to be seen."

She looked at my eyes, my cheeks, my lips for a long moment before meeting my eyes again. "Your smoldering might eventually kill me, Will. And the best thing is I think you have no clue that you look at women this way."

I blinked. "My *what*?"

"What can I get for you?" the bartender asked, startling us both when he slapped two cardboard coasters down in front of us and leaned closer. It seemed like Ziggy's lab friends had left, and the Ding Dong was uncharacteristically quiet; usually the bartenders here took my drink order from halfway down the bar, while pouring someone else's beer.

"Guinness," I said, then added, "And a shot of Johnny Gold."

The bartender looked to Ziggs. "Something else for you?"

"Another iced tea, please."

His eyebrow rose and he smiled at her. "That all you want, sweetheart?"

Ziggy laughed, shrugging. "Anything stronger and I'll be asleep in fifteen minutes."

"I'm pretty sure there are plenty of strong things back here that could keep you up for hours."

What he said made me draw back, look over at Ziggy to assess her reaction. If she looked horrified, I might have to kick this guy's ass.

She laughed, oblivious and embarrassed for having been called out on being square in a bar, and spun her coaster in front of her. "You mean a coffee with Bailey's or something?"

"No," he said, resting on his elbows right in front of her. "I had something else in mind."

"Just the iced tea," I cut in, feeling like my blood pressure had gone up about seven thousand millimeters. With a smirk, he stood and left to get our drinks.

I could feel Ziggy watching me, and I grabbed a cocktail napkin in order to have something to studiously shred.

"What's with the stern tone, William?"

I blew out a breath. "Did he not see me sitting here with you? He was all over you. What a dick."

"Taking my drink order?" she asked, giving me a baffled stare. "What a *jerk*."

"Innuendo," I explained. "Surely you speak it."

"Surely you're kidding."

" 'Something strong behind the bar that could keep you up for hours'?"

Her mouth formed a tiny O as she seemed to figure it out, and then she grinned. "Isn't that the point of our little project? To get some more innuendo in my life?"

The bartender returned and set our drinks in front of us, winking at Ziggy before walking away.

"I suppose," I grumbled, sipping my beer.

Beside me, I saw her sit up a little straighter and turn on her stool to face me. "Not to change the subject, but I watched some porn last night."

I coughed, putting my beer down on the rounded edge of the bar, then barely catching it before it spilled all over me. Even so, some of it slopped over the lip of the glass, and onto my lap. "Christ, Ziggs, you have *zero* filter." I grabbed a small pile of cocktail napkins and wiped my pants.

"Don't you watch porn?"

I stared at my shot of whiskey and downed it, before admitting, "Sure."

"So why is it weird that I did?"

"It's not weird that you watched it. It's weird that it's the start of a conversation. I just . . . I'm still getting used to this. Before Project Hot Chick, I just knew you as the dorky little sister. Now you're this . . . porn-watching woman who had a breast reduction and develops theories about hymen restoration. It's an adjustment."

That, and I find you almost irresistible, I thought.

She waved me off. "Anyway, I have a question."

I looked at her out of the corner of my eye. "Okay?"

"Do women really make those noises in bed?"

I stilled, grinning over at her. "*What* noises, Ziggy?"

She didn't seem to realize I was completely fucking with her, and she closed her eyes, and whispered, "Like, 'Oh, oh, Willll, I need your cock' and 'Harder, harder, oh God, fuck me, big daddy' . . . and so on." Her voice had gone soft, and breathy, and I was horrified to feel my dick lengthen. Again.

"Um, some do."

She burst into laughter. "It's ridiculous!"

I fought a smile, loving her natural confidence even

on a topic I suspected she had little experience with. "Maybe they *do* need my cock. Wouldn't you like to want someone so much you *need* their cock?"

She took a long pull on her iced tea, considering this. "Actually, yeah. I don't think I've ever wanted someone so much I would beg for it. A cookie? Yes. A cock? No."

"That would have to be one hell of a cookie."

"Oh, it was."

Laughing, I asked, "What movie was it?"

"Um." She looked up at the ceiling. Not blushing, not even a little embarrassed. "*Frisky Freshmen*? Something like that. A lot of college girls having sex with a lot of college guys. It was kind of fascinating, actually."

I fell quiet, losing my thoughts down a weird trail from college coeds, to Ziggy at work in the lab, to Jensen's hope that she would make new friends, to the bartender hitting on her right in front of me, to my still-lengthened cock.

"What are you thinking about?" she asked.

"Nothing, really."

She put her tea down, and turned on her stool to stare at me. "How is that possible? How can men say they're not thinking about anything?"

"I'm not thinking about anything of substance, how's that?" I clarified.

"We're talking about porn and you're not even thinking about sex?"

"Strangely, no," I said. "I'm thinking about how na-ïve and sweet you are. I'm wondering what I've agreed to do here, when I said I would help you figure out the whole dating world. I'm worried I'm going to make you into the most vulnerable bombshell in the history of the planet."

"You were thinking of *all* of that just now?"

I nodded.

"Wow. *That's* something of substance." Her voice had gone quiet, and soft. Kind of like her pretend porn voice, but with real words, and real emotion. But when I looked over at her, she was staring out the window. "I'm not naïve and sweet, though, Will. I know what you mean, but I've always been kind of obsessed with sex. Mostly the mechanics of it. Why different things work for different people. Why some people like sex one way, and others like it another. Is it anatomy? Is it psychology? Are our bodies really organized that differently? Things like that."

I had literally no idea how to respond to this, so I just drank. I'd never thought about these things, had instead preferred to just try anything and everything that a given woman wanted, but I found that I really liked that Ziggy pondered all of this.

"But lately, I'm kind of figuring out what *I* like," she admitted. "That's fun, but it's hard not having a way to figure it out firsthand. Hence, porn."

She took a long drink and then grinned over at me. Two weeks ago if Ziggy had said something like this to me, I would have been secondhand embarrassed for her to be so open in her inexperience. Now I found that I wanted to protect it, just a little.

"I can't believe I'm encouraging this conversation, but . . . I worry porn might give you a false sense of what sex should be like."

"How so?"

"Because the sex you see in porn isn't very realistic."

Laughing, she asked, "You mean most men don't have a Pringle can in their pants?"

This time I didn't choke. "That's one difference, yes."

"I have had sex before, Will. Just not much variation. Porn is a good way to see what rings the old bell, if you know what I'm saying."

"You surprise me, Ziggy Bergstrom."

She didn't respond for several long beats. "That isn't my name, you know."

"I know. But it is what I call you."

"Will you always call me 'Ziggy'?"

"Probably. Does it bother you?"

She shrugged, swiveling on her stool to face me again. "A little maybe? I mean, it doesn't really fit me anymore. Only my family calls me that. Not, like, friends."

"I don't think you're a kid, if that's what you're worried about."

"No, that isn't what I'm worried about. Everyone

grows up being a kid, and learns how to be a grown-up. I feel like I've always known how to be a grown-up, and am just learning how to be a kid. Maybe Ziggy was my grown-up name. Maybe I want to let loose a little."

I tweaked her ear, and she squealed, pulling away. "So you start to let loose by watching porn?"

"Exactly." She studied the side of my face. "Can I ask you some personal things?"

"You need my permission now?"

She giggled, shoving my shoulder. "I'm serious."

I slid my empty pint glass down the bar a little and turned to meet her eyes. "You can ask me anything you want if you buy me another beer."

She raised her hand, catching the bartender's attention immediately. Pointing, she said, "Another Guinness," before turning back to me. "Are you ready?"

I shrugged.

Leaning forward, she asked, "Guys really like the anal, don't they?"

I closed my eyes for a beat, holding in a laugh. "It's just called anal. Not *the* anal."

"Don't they?" she repeated.

Sighing, I rubbed my face. Did I even want to go there with her? "I guess? I mean, yeah."

"So you've done it?"

"Seriously, Ziggy?"

"And you don't think about how you're in—"

I held up a hand. "No."

"You don't even know what I was going to say!"

"I do. I know you, Ziggs. I know *exactly* what you were going to say."

She made a face, turning back to the television above the bar, where the Knicks were killing the Heat. "Guys can just turn off their brains. I don't even get that."

"Then you haven't had sex worth turning off your brain for."

"I think *you* turn your brain off even for mediocre sex."

Laughing, I admitted, "Probably. I mean, you had mussels for dinner. That's like . . . sinewy, chewy sea shit. But still, you could give me a blow job and I wouldn't be thinking about how you just swallowed mussels."

I detected a hint of a blush beneath her cheeks. "You'd be thinking about my awesome blow job skills."

I stared at her. "I . . . what?"

She started laughing, shaking her head at me. "See? You're already speechless and I haven't even done anything yet. Men are so easy."

"It's true. Guys would fuck every orifice they could."

"Every *fuckable* orifice."

Turning on my seat to face her, I asked, "What?"

"Well, not every orifice is fuckable. Like a nose. Or an ear."

"You obviously haven't heard 'The Man from Nantucket.' "

"No." She wrinkled her nose, and I glanced at her freckles. Tonight her lips seemed especially red, but I could tell she wasn't wearing makeup. They were just . . . flushed.

"*Everyone* has heard this. It's a dirty limerick."

"With me?" She pointed to her chest, and I struggled to not look down. "This doesn't increase the odds."

" 'There once was a man from Nantucket. Whose dick was so long he could suck it. He said with a grin with some come on his chin, if my ear was a cunt I could fuck it.' "

She regarded me steadily. "That's . . . kind of gross."

I loved that *this* was her first reaction. "Which part? The come on his chin or the ear fucking?"

Ignoring that, she asked, "Would you suck your own dick if you could?"

I started to say there is no way in hell, but then reconsidered. If it was even possible, I probably would at least once, just out of curiosity. "I guess . . ."

"Would you swallow?"

"Jesus, Ziggs, you're really making me think here."

"You have to *think* about it?"

"I mean, I would sound like an asshole if I said there is no way I would swallow, but there is really no way I would swallow. We're talking about a hypothetical situation where I'm sucking my own dick, and I like it when *girls* swallow."

"Not every girl swallows, though."

My heart picked up, not only faster but harder, as if it were punching me from the inside. This conversation felt like it was careening quickly out of control. "Do *you*?"

Ignoring *that,* she asked, "But guys don't really like going down on girls, do they? I mean, if you're being totally honest."

"I like going down on some girls. Not everyone I'm with, and not for the reason you're thinking. It's intimate, and not every woman is totally relaxed about it, which makes it hard to have fun. I don't know, for me a blow job is like a hand job, but feels way better. But giving a girl head? I feel like that's a little farther into a relationship. It requires trust."

"I've never done either. They *both* seem pretty intimate to me."

I stopped, quietly thanked the bartender when he put the beer down in front of me, but had no idea how to restrain the weird victory surging in my blood. What was that even about? It wasn't like I was going to be her first head. It wasn't like I could go there with her. Besides, Ziggy was so up front about what she wanted . . . with a tightening of my gut I realized that if she wanted me that way, she probably would have already said it. She would have walked up to me, put her hand on my chest, and said, *"Would you fuck me?"*

"See?" she asked, leaning closer to grab my attention. "What are you thinking about *now*?"

Tilting my bottle to my lips, I said, "Nothing."

"If I was a violent woman, my palm would be smacking your cheek right now."

This made me laugh. "Fine. I was just thinking that it's a little . . . unusual for you to have had sex before but not given anyone oral sex, or been on the receiving end."

"I mean," she started, leaning back a little on her bar stool, "I guess I kind of gave this one guy a blow job, but I literally had no idea what I was doing, so I ended up just going back up to the face zone."

"Guys are pretty easy: you stroke up and down and we shoot."

"No, I mean . . . I get that. I just mean for *me*. How to do it and breathe, and not worry that I would bite him? Have you ever walked through a china section at a fancy store and you have that panicked moment where you're totally sure you're going to flail suddenly and break all of the Waterford crystal?"

I leaned over, laughing. This girl was fucking *unreal*. "So you're worried when you have a dick in your mouth you're just going to . . . bite?"

She started laughing, too, and then before I knew it we were doubled over at the prospect. But almost at the same time, we died down a little and I realized she was staring at my mouth.

"Some guys *like* teeth," I said quietly.

" 'Some guys' . . . like you?"

Swallowing, I admitted, "Yeah. I like girls to be a little rough."

"Like, scratching and biting and stuff?"

"Yeah." A charged thrill ran through me just hearing her say those words. I swallowed heavily, wondering how long it would be before I'd be able to get the image of her *doing* those things out of my head. "How many guys have you been with?" I asked.

She took a sip of her iced tea before answering. "Five."

"You've never given head but you've had sex with *five guys*?" My stomach dropped into an abyss, and although I knew my irritation was wildly hypocritical, I couldn't rein it in. "Holy shit, Ziggs, *when*?"

She rolled her eyes, actually laughing at me. "I lost my virginity when I was sixteen. The summer you worked with my dad, actually." Covering my mouth with her hand when I started to protest, she added, "Don't even start on me, Will. I know you probably lost yours when you were thirteen."

I closed my mouth, sat up. She'd guessed right.

With a knowing smile, she continued. "And *please*. I'm sure you've had sex with hundreds of women. Five is not that many. I slept with a few guys over the next couple of years and then decided I was doing it wrong. It wasn't very interesting. I had one boyfriend in college for a little while but . . . I feel like I'm broken. Sex is kind of fun until the actual sex part. Then I'm like, 'Hmmm, wonder if I have enough cells plated to run the dose response curve with the tool compound tomorrow.'"

"That's pathetic."

"I know."

"Sex is *not* boring."

She studied me, and then shrugged. "I don't think it's *supposed* to be boring. I think it's boring because most guys my age have no idea what to do with the female body." She looked away, and I almost told her to come back. I was growing addicted to the buzz I felt when she was looking directly at me. "I'm not blaming them. That's some complicated stuff down there." She waved a hand over her lap. "It's just been so long since I met anyone who made me want to see what the big fuss is about." She looked at my lips before blinking away and studying the wall of draft beers on tap.

I blinked down to my beer in front of me, turned it in little circles on the coaster. Of course she was right, and so many women I knew had sex for reasons other than getting off. Kitty once told me she felt close to me after we fucked. She said it right as I'd begun mentally cataloging my fridge. I felt so much closer to Hanna right now than I'd ever felt to Kitty before, during, or after sex.

Something about her made me feel hungry, like I wanted to be as honest and calm about everything in my life as she was. I wanted to know Hanna, to hear her thoughts on *everything*.

I paused, my fresh beer partway to my lips, and registered that I'd thought of her as Hanna. It sort of felt like letting out a long-held breath.

Ziggy was Jensen's sister. *Ziggy* was the kid I never knew.

Hanna was this uninhibited, self-possessed woman in front of me who I was pretty sure was going to effectively wreck my world.

Chapter Five

I'd come to a decision: if I was going to monopolize Will's time and insist on training with him, then I would have to actually . . . you know . . . *train* for something.

I'd decided to get serious, to stop thinking of it as a game and start really treating it like an experiment. I started going to bed at a decent hour so I could get up and run with him and still get to the lab early enough for a full day of work at the bench. I expanded my running wardrobe to include some quality workout gear and an extra pair of shoes. I stopped thinking of Starbucks as a food group and cut back on the complaining. And with much flailing on my part and much reassurance on his—we signed up for a half-marathon in mid-April. I was terrified.

But it turned out Will was right: it *did* get easier.

Just a few weeks in and my lungs had stopped burning, my shins had stopped feeling like they were made of brittle sticks, and I no longer felt like vomiting by the time we reached the end of the trail. In fact, we'd actually been able to increase our distance and move to his normal trail along the outer loop. Will said if I could handle the six miles a day and get up to eight-mile runs twice a week, he wouldn't need to train additionally without me.

It wasn't just that it started to feel good. I'd started to *see* a difference, too. Thanks to genetics, I'd always been relatively thin, but never what you'd call *fit*. My stomach was a tad soft, my arms did that weird jiggle thing when I waved, and there was always this damn little pooch over the top of my jeans if I didn't keep that shit sucked in. But now . . . things were changing, and I wasn't the only one who noticed.

"So what's happening here?" Chloe asked, eyeing me from inside my closet. She pointed a finger at me and swept it around. "You look . . . different."

"Different?" I asked.

The point of Project Ziggy actually wasn't to spend as much time as possible with Will—even though he was quickly becoming my favorite person—but to help me find balance, to have a life outside the lab. In the past couple of weeks, Chloe and Sara had become an important part of the effort, dragging me out for dinner or coming over to just hang for a few hours at my apartment.

This particular Thursday evening they'd brought takeout and we'd somehow migrated into my room, where Chloe had taken it upon herself to go through my closet, deciding what could stay and what absolutely had to go.

"Different good," she clarified, and then turned to Sara, who was stretched across my bed, thumbing through some sort of financial file for work. "Don't you think so?"

Sara looked up, eyes narrowing as she considered me. "Definitely good. Happy, maybe?"

Chloe was already nodding. "Was just going to say that. There's definitely some kind of glowy thing happening in your cheeks. And your ass looks *amazing* in those pants."

I looked at my reflection, checked out the front and turned to see the back. My ass did look pretty happy. My front wasn't too bad, either. "My pants are a little loose," I noted, checking the size. "And look, no muffin top!"

"Well, that's always a plus," Sara said with a laugh, shaking her head, then going back to her documents.

Chloe started putting things on hangers, shoving others into plastic bags. "You're toning up. What have you been doing?"

"Just running. And lots of stretching. Will is big on the stretching. He added sit-ups to our routine last week, and let me be clear on how much I hate those." I continued to study my reflection, adding, "I can't remember the last time I had a cookie, and that feels like a crime."

"Still training with Will, huh?" Chloe asked, and I couldn't miss the look that passed between her and Sara. The look that said I'd just dropped a giant nugget of awesome in their lap and they were going to talk it to death and then dissect it until I begged for mercy.

"Yeah, every morning."

"Will trains with you *every* morning?" Chloe asked. Another look exchanged.

I nodded, moved to pick up a few errant things lying around. "We meet at the park. Did you know he does triathlons? He's in great shape." I snapped my mouth shut, realizing it probably wasn't safe to be as obliviously unfiltered with Chloe as it was with Will. I knew her well enough at this point to know she didn't let very many things slide.

And indeed, she lifted a brow and reached up, pushing a thick wave of dark hair behind her shoulder. "So, about William."

I hummed, folding a pair of socks together.

"Do you see him outside of this daily running date?"

I could feel their attention like heated laser beams on the side of my face so I nodded, not looking over at either of them.

"He's very handsome," Chloe added.

Danger danger, my brain warned. "He is."

"Have you seen each other naked?"

My eyes shot to Chloe's. *"What?"*

"Chloe," Sara groaned.

"No," I insisted. "We're just friends."

Chloe snorted, moving to the closet with a handful of clothes draped over her arms. "Right."

"We run in the mornings, meet up for coffee sometimes. Maybe breakfast," I said, shrugging and ignoring the way my honesty meter seemed to flare into the red zone. Lately we'd been having breakfast together almost every morning, and talked at least one other time during the day. I'd even started to call him for advice on my experiments when Liemacki was traveling or just busy . . . or just because I valued his scientific opinion. "Just friends." I glanced at Sara. Her eyes were trained on her papers but she was smiling, shaking her head.

"Bullshit," Chloe all but sang. "Will Sumner doesn't have any women in his life that are *just* friends, outside of family and the two of us."

"This is true," Sara reluctantly agreed.

I didn't say anything, just turned and began searching through my drawers for a sweater. I could feel Chloe watching me, though, could feel the pressure of her gaze against the back of my head. I'd never had a lot of female friends—and I'd definitely never had one like Chloe Mills—but even I was smart enough to be a little afraid of her. I got the distinct impression that even *Bennett* was a little afraid of her.

I found the cardigan I'd been hunting for and slipped it over my favorite *Firefly* T-shirt, doing my best to keep my expression neutral and my head free of anything Will-related that ventured outside of the friend zone. Something told me these two would see through that in a second.

"How long have you guys known each other?" Sara asked. "He and Max go way back, but I've only known him since I moved to New York."

"Same here," Chloe added. "Spill, Bergstrom. He's too smug and we need some ammo."

I laughed, grateful for the semi-shift in topic. "What do you want to know?"

"Well, you knew him when he was in college. Was he a giant dork? Please say he was in the chess club or something," Chloe said, hopeful.

"Ha, *no*. I'm pretty sure he was the guy who turned eighteen and all of the moms wanted to bang." I frowned, considering. "Actually, I think I might have heard that exact story from Jensen. . . ."

"Max said something about him dating your sister?" Sara asked.

I chewed on my lip and shook my head. "They hooked up once over a holiday, but I think they just made out. He met my oldest brother, Jensen, on their first day of college, and then he lived with us and worked with my dad after graduation. I'm the youngest, so I didn't really hang around with them that much other than at meals."

"Stop evading," Chloe said, narrowing her eyes. "You have to know more."

I laughed. "Let's see, he's the youngest, too. He has two sisters who are way older than him, but I've never met them. I get the feeling he was sort of mothered a lot. I remember hearing him talk one time about how his parents are both physicians, and they divorced long before he was born. Years later, they met up at a medical conference, got drunk, and reconnected for one night . . ."

"And boom. Will," Sara guessed.

I nodded slowly. "Yeah. But his mom raised him. So, his sisters are twelve and fourteen years older than he is. He was their little baby."

"Well, that would explain why he thinks women were put on this earth to cater to him," Chloe added, flopping on the bed next to Sara.

That didn't sit right with me, and I sat down, shaking my head. "I don't know if it's that. I think he just really, *really* likes women. And they seem to like him, too," I added. "He grew up surrounded by women so he knows how they think, what they want to hear."

"He definitely knows how to play the game," Sara said. "God, some of the stuff Max has told me."

I thought back to Jensen's wedding and watching Will slip off, otherwise unnoticed, with two women at once. I was pretty sure that wasn't the first or last time something like that had happened.

"Women have always loved him," I said. "I can remember overhearing some of my mom's friends talk about him when he worked for Dad. Jesus, the things they would have done to that boy."

"Cougars!" Chloe squealed, delighted. "I *love* it."

"God, every girl was in love with him." I pulled a pillow to my chest, remembering. "I had a few girl-friends in school—I was twelve the first time he came home with Jensen—and they would find all these crazy reasons to need to come over. One of them pre-tended like she had to return my sweater on Christ-mas Eve, and it was *her* sweater she gave me. I mean, picture Will now but as a nineteen-year-old guy, play-ful, clearly wise to the ways of the female body, and with that damn cheeky smile. He was in a band, had tattoos . . . he was walking sex. Then when he lived with us over the summer? He was twenty-four and I was sixteen. It was unbearable. It was like it offended him to wear a shirt in the house and he had to show off all that smooth, perfect man skin."

I broke out of my memory to see both of them grinning at me.

"What?"

"Those were some very lascivious descriptions, Hanna," Sara said.

Glancing over at her, I asked, "Did you just use the word *lascivious*?"

"She most certainly did," Chloe said. "And I agree. I feel like I just watched something dirty."

I groaned, getting up off the bed.

"So, clearly, teenage Hanna had a bit of a crush on Will," Sara said. "But, more importantly, what does twenty-four-year-old Hanna think of him now?"

I had to think on this for a beat, because to be honest, I thought about Will a lot, and in every possible way. I thought about his body and his dirty mouth and of course all the things he could do with them, but I also thought about his brain, and his heart. "I think he's surprisingly sweet, and he's absurdly smart. He's a total player but underneath that, a genuinely good guy."

"And you haven't thought about banging him at all?"

I stared at Chloe. "What?"

She stared right back at me. "*What* what? You're both young and hot. There's a history there. I bet it'd be incredible."

Hundreds of images flashed through my mind in only a few seconds, and even though I thought about *banging* him more than I should probably even admit to myself, I forced the words out: "I am absolutely *not* having sex with Will."

Sara shrugged. "Not yet, maybe."

I turned to her. "Aren't you supposed to be the demure one?"

A laugh burst out of Chloe's mouth and she shook her head, giving Sara a playfully scolding look. "*Demure*. It's always the ones who *seem* sweet and innocent, trust me."

"Well, regardless," I said, "Will thinks of me as a little sister."

Chloe sat up, pinning me with a serious expression. "I can tell you that when a man meets a woman, he puts her in one of two categories: unequivocal friend, or possible banging candidate."

"Doesn't he have scheduled booty calls?" I asked, wrinkling my nose. I liked the idea of dating, but I got the impression that Will was more structured in his relationships than just a conversation about keeping things casual. To have regular nights scheduled the way he seemed to? I wasn't sure I could get behind that kind of boundary regarding something as fluid and shapeless as sex.

Sara nodded. "Lately, Kitty is Tuesday nights, Kristy is Saturday evening." She hummed thoughtfully and added, "I don't think he's seeing Lara anymore, but I'm sure others make cameos here and there."

Chloe shot her a look and Sara stared back. I blinked away, letting them have their little showdown in private.

"I'm not suggesting she fall in love with him," Chloe said. "Just bang the hell out of him."

"I'm only making sure everyone knows the score," Sara answered, a challenge in her eyes.

"Well," I started, "it doesn't matter anyway. Given that he's my brother's best friend, I think we can pretty safely assume I am in unequivocal friend territory."

"Has he talked about your boobs?" Chloe asked.

I felt the heated blush crawl up my neck. Will talked about, stared at, and seemed to idolize my chest. "Um, yes."

Chloe smiled, smug. "I rest my case."

———

The next morning, I'm sure Will was convinced I was on some sort of mood-altering medication . . . or needed to be. I was distracted during our run and kept going over my conversation with Sara and Chloe in my mind. Not only was I thinking about how often Will looked at my boobs, gestured to my boobs, and *spoke* to my boobs, I was unfortunately thinking about Will with the other women I knew were in his life: what he did with them, how they felt when they were with him, and if they had as much fun with him as I did. Plus the fact that he was probably naked with women . . . a lot.

This, of course, led to me thinking about Will naked, which did nothing to help my focus, or my ability to go in a straight line down the path in front of me.

I forced my thoughts away from the man running in easy silence beside me, and to the work I had waiting at the lab, the report I needed to finish, the exams I needed to help Liemacki grade.

But later, when Will leaned over me, stretching my right leg after I'd basically crumpled on the trail from a leg cramp, he stared at me so intently, his eyes mov-

ing slowly over my face, every thought I'd tried to
banish came rushing back. My stomach twisted and a
delicious heat spread from my chest and down to the
neglected ache between my legs. I felt like I was melting into the cold ground.

"You okay?" he asked quietly.

I was only able to nod.

His brows drew together. "You're so quiet this
morning."

"Just thinking," I murmured.

His sexy little smile appeared and I felt my heart
trip and then begin to hammer in my chest. "Well, I
hope you're not thinking about porn or blow jobs or
how you want to experiment with sex, because if you
think you're keeping that shit to yourself, you're in
trouble. We have a rhythm now, Ziggs."

I took a particularly long shower after that run.

＊

I'd never been a texter—in fact, before Will, my only
texts had consisted of one-word responses to my family or coworkers.

Are you still coming? Yes.

Can you pick up a bottle of wine? Sure.

Are you bringing a date? Ignore.

Until a week ago—when I'd finally unwrapped the
iPhone Niels had given me for Christmas—I still used
a flip phone Jensen teased was the first cell phone ever
made. Who had time to type a hundred messages

when I could call and get it over with in less than a minute? It definitely didn't seem very efficient.

But with Will it was fun, and I had to admit, the new phone made it easier. He would text me random thoughts throughout the day, send me pictures of his face when I made a particularly bad joke or a photo of his lunch when the chicken breast he'd been served was shaped like a penis. So, after my . . . relaxing shower, when my phone buzzed in the other room, I wasn't surprised to see it was Will.

What I was surprised by however, was the question: What are you wearing?

I felt my brows pull together in confusion. It was random but by far not the weirdest thing he'd ever asked me. We were meeting for breakfast in a half hour and maybe he was worried I would show up looking, as he liked to say, like a graduate student hobo.

I looked down at the towel around my otherwise naked chest and typed, Black jeans, yellow top, blue sweater.

No, Ziggy. I mean *insert innuendo* WHAT ARE YOU WEARING.

Now I really was confused. I don't get it, I typed.

I'm sexting you.

I paused, looked down at the phone for a few more seconds before responding with What?

He typed so much faster than I did, and his response appeared almost immediately. It's not nearly as hot when I have to explain it. New rule: you need to be at least border-line competent in the art of sexting.

Understanding went off like a lightbulb in my head. Oh! And ha! "Sexting." Clever, Will.

While I appreciate your enthusiasm and the fact that you think I'm witty enough to have come up with that, he replied, I didn't invent the term. It's been around in popular culture for quite some time, you know. Now, answer the question.

I paced the room, thinking. *Okay. An assignment, I could do this.* I tried to think of all the sexy innuendo I'd ever heard in movies and of course, in the moment, could not think of a single thing. I thought back on every pickup line I'd heard my brother Eric use . . . and then shuddered, reconsidering.

I drew a total blank.

Well, actually I'm not dressed yet, I typed. I was standing here trying to decide if it's against the rules to go without underpants because I think my skirt shows all the lines but I hate wearing thongs.

I stared at the phone as the little dots indicated he was replying. Shit that was pretty good kid. But don't say underpants. Or blouse. Never sexy.

Don't make fun of me. I don't know what

to say. I feel like an idiot standing here naked texting you.

I waited.

A few moments passed before my phone lit up again. OK. So you've obviously gotten the hang of it. Now say something dirty.

Dirty?

I'm waiting.

Oh God. Did I have time to google something? No. I searched my mind and typed the first semi-dirty thing I could think of: Sometimes, when we're running and you're controlling your breathing and lost in the rhythm of it, I wonder what noises you make during sex.

So maybe that was a bit more than semi-dirty, and for what felt like an eternity, he didn't reply. *Oh God.* I put my phone down, convinced that Will was going to walk away and not reply ever again. He probably wanted something playful and not so . . . *honest.*

I walked into the bathroom, pulled a brush through my wet hair, and then piled it into a knot on top of my head. In the other room, I heard my phone buzz on the desk.

WHOA, was the first message.

The second message: Way to just . . . dive on in there. OK I'm gonna need a minute. Or five.

OMGIMSOSOEEY I typed, with stupid fumbling

fingers and completely ready to climb into a hole and die. I MEAN SORRY I CANTBELIEVEISAIDTHAT

You're kidding me, he replied. That was like Christmas. Clearly I need to up my game. Hold on, I might need to stretch first.

I rolled my eyes. Waiting.

Your tits looked great today.

That's all you got? I typed. Honestly, he'd said more perverted things to my face. To my *boobs*. Did he really think he was schooling me in being sexy right now?

Really? You're completely unimpressed?

Zzzzzzzzzz, I wrote back.

Can I SEE your tits next time?

Well. I felt a little warmth in my cheeks but there was no way I was admitting that.

Yawn. I smiled like an idiot at my phone.

The little text bubble appeared in the window to show that he'd started typing. I waited. And waited. Finally, Can I touch them? Taste them?

I hitched my towel up higher over my breasts and swallowed, shaking. My face wasn't the only thing that was warm now. I replied, That was a little better.

Can I lick them and then fuck them?

I dropped my phone, and scrambled to pick it up. Pretty good, I typed with shaking hands. I closed my eyes, struggling to push away the image of Will's hips moving over my chest, his cock sliding over the skin between my breasts.

I could almost feel his determination through the phone when he said, Let me know when you need a minute of ALONE time. Are you ready?

No. Absolutely not. Yes.

You were wearing this shirt the other day, the pink one. Your tits looked fucking phenomenal. Full and soft. I could see your nipples when the wind picked up. All I could think about was what you'd feel like in my hands, your nipples against my tongue. What my cock would look like against your skin and how it would feel to come all over your neck.

Holy shiiiit. Will? Can I just call you?

Why?

Because it's hard to type with one hand.

He didn't reply for a minute and I let myself imagine he'd dropped *his* phone this time. But then he replied: YES! Are you touching yourself??

I laughed, typing, Gotcha, and then threw my phone to the side and closed my eyes.

Because yes, I absolutely was.

⌐━━━━━⌐

Since at the end of our run I'd agreed to meet Will for breakfast at Sarabeth's, after I finished "thinking" about his texts, I hurried to dress and ran out the door. Despite the temperature and the snow starting to fall, I felt the heat of my blush all the way to Ninety-third, and wondered if it was possible to sit across from him and not have him figure out I'd just masturbated to his texts. Things felt like they were veering off course, and I tried to remember when it had happened. Was it the run earlier this morning when he'd hovered over my body, looking as if he were climbing on top of me? Or was it a couple of weeks back, at the bar when we'd started talking about porn and sex? Maybe it was even before that, the first day we went running together and he'd slipped a hat on my head, giving me a smile that made me feel like I'd just been fucked against a wall?

This was not going well. *Friends,* I reminded myself. *Secret agent assignment. Learn the ways of the Ninja, and escape unharmed.*

I kept my head down as I crunched through the thin layer of snow, cursing the March weather, as snowflakes tangled in my loose hair. A young couple was just leaving the restaurant, and I managed to slip in through the open door as they passed.

"Zig," I heard, and looked up to see Will smiling down at me from the loft seating area. I waved before I walked to the stairs, taking off my hat and scarf as I went.

"Fancy seeing you again," he said, standing as I neared the table.

I found myself becoming irrationally annoyed by his good manners, even more so by his still-damp hair and the way his sweater clung to his unending torso. He had a white shirt underneath and, with the sleeves pushed up his forearms, the lines of his tattoos peeked out from beneath the folded cuffs. Gorgeous *asshole*.

"Morning," I said back.

"A little grumpy? Maybe a little tense?"

Scowling, I said, "No."

He laughed as we each took a seat. "I ordered your food."

"What?"

"Your breakfast? The lemon pancakes with berries, right? And that flower juice thing?"

"Yeah," I answered, eyeing him from across the table. I picked up my napkin and unfolded it, laying it across my lap.

He bent to meet my eyes, looking a little anxious. "Did you want something else? I can get the waitress."

"No . . ." I took a deep breath, opened my mouth, and closed it again. It was such a small thing—the food I always ordered, the type of juice I liked, the fact that he'd known exactly how to stretch me this morning—but it felt big, important somehow. It made me feel a little bad that he'd been so sweet and I couldn't seem to keep my head out of his pants. "I just can't believe you remembered that."

He shrugged. "No big deal. It's breakfast, Zig-zag. I'm not donating a kidney here."

I forced away the unreasonably bitchy attitude that flared up at that. "Well, it was just really nice. You surprise me sometimes."

He looked somewhat taken aback. "How so?"

I sighed, deflating somewhat into my chair. "I just assumed you'd treat me more like a kid." As soon as I said this, it was clear he didn't like it. He sat back in his chair and let out a slow breath, so I continued on, rambling, "I know you're giving up your peace and quiet to let me run with you. I know you've canceled plans with your nongirlfriends and had to rearrange things to make time for me, and I just . . . I want you to know that I appreciate it. You're a really great friend, Will."

His brows drew together and he stared down at his ice water instead of looking at me. "Thanks. Just, you know, helping out Jensen's . . . baby sister."

"Right," I said, feeling my irritation flare up again. I wanted to take his water and dunk it over my own head. What was with the hot temper?

"Right," he repeated, blinking up to me and wearing a playful little smile that immediately defused my crazy and made my girl parts perk right back up. "At least that's the story we'll tell everyone."

CHAPTER SIX

Something had changed, some switch had flipped in the past few days, and there was a leaden weight between us now. It had started a few mornings ago, on our run when she was quiet and distracted and had fallen to her side when her leg cramped up. Afterwards at breakfast, she'd clearly been irritated, but that was easy to read: she was fighting something. She was annoyed in the same way I was, as if we should be able to wrestle against this magnet that seemed intent on pulling us to a different place.

A non-friend-zone place.

My phone buzzed on the coffee table and I jerked upright when Hanna's picture lit up the screen. I tried to ignore the warm hum of levity I felt simply because she was calling.

"Hey, Ziggs."

"Come to a party with me tonight," she said simply, completely bypassing any traditional greeting. The classic sign of a nervous Hanna. She paused, and then added more quietly, "Unless . . . shit, it's Saturday. Unless you have an otherwise-platonic regularly-scheduled-sex-partner over."

I ignored the elaborate implied second question and considered only the first, imagining a party in a conference room at the Columbia biology department, with two-liter bottles of soda, chips, and grocery store salsa.

"What kind of party?"

She paused on the other end of the line. "A house-warming party."

I smiled at the phone, growing suspicious. "What kind of *house*?"

On the other end of the line, she let out a groan of surrender. "Okay, fine. It's a grad student party. A guy in my department and his friends just moved into a new apartment. I'm sure it's a shithole. I want to go, but I want you to come with me."

Laughing, I asked, "So it's going to be a grad school *rager*? Will they have kegs and Fritos?"

"Dr. Sumner," she sighed. "Don't be a snob."

"I'm not being a snob," I said. "I'm being a man in his early thirties who finished grad school years ago and considers it a wild night when he goads Max into spending over a thousand dollars on a bottle of scotch."

"Just come with me. I promise you'll have an awesome time."

I sighed, staring at a half-empty bottle of beer on my coffee table. "Will I be the oldest person there?"

"Probably," she admitted. "But I know for a fact you'll also be the hottest."

I laughed at this, and then considered my night without this option. I'd canceled on Kristy, and I still wasn't really sure why.

That was a lie. I knew exactly why. I felt weird, like maybe I was being unfair to Hanna by being with other women when she seemed to be giving so much of herself to me. When I told Kristy I needed a rain check, I knew she heard something else in my voice. She didn't question why or try to reschedule, the way Kitty would have. I suspected I wouldn't be sleeping with that particular blonde again.

"Will?"

Sighing, I stood and walked over to where I'd left my shoes near the front door. "Okay, fine, I'll come. But wear a shirt that shows off your tits so I have something to entertain me if I get bored."

She let out a small, breathy laugh, managing to sound both girlish and seductive. "You have yourself a deal."

It was exactly what I'd expected: a serial renter to poverty-level graduate students, and an entirely familiar scene.

I was hit with a small wave of nostalgia as we stepped inside the cramped apartment.

The two couches were droopy futons, with stained, drab covers. The television was propped on a board balanced between two milk crates. The coffee table looked like it had seen better days, before having some very bad days, and *then* had been given to these guys to trash further. In the kitchen, a horde of bearded, hipster grad students huddled around a keg of Yuengling and there were assorted half-full bottles of cheap booze and mixers on the counter.

But from the look on Hanna's face you'd think we just stepped into heaven. Beside me, she bounced a little and then reached for my hand, squeezing it. "I'm so glad you came with me!"

"Seriously, have you actually ever been to a party before?" I asked.

"Once," she admitted, pulling me deeper into the mayhem. "In college. I drank four shots of Bacardi and barfed on some guy's shoes. I still have no idea how I got home."

The image made my stomach twist. I'd seen that girl—wide-eyed, trying out *wild*—at virtually every party I'd been to in college and grad school. I hated to think of *that girl* ever being Hanna. In my eyes she was always smarter than that, more self-aware.

She was still talking, and I leaned in to catch the rest of what she said. ". . . wild nights were mostly spent playing *Magic* in our dorm lounge and sipping ouzo. Well, everyone else would be drinking ouzo. I can barely smell it without wanting to puke." She looked back at me over her shoulder, clarifying, "My roommate was Greek."

Hanna introduced me to a group of people, mostly guys. There was a Dylan, a Hau, an Aaron, and what I think was an Anil. One of them handed Hanna a cocktail made with a trendy plum sake and fizzy soda water.

I knew Hanna wasn't much of a drinker, and my protective instincts kicked in. "Would you rather have something nonalcoholic?" I asked her, loud enough for the others to hear me. What dicks, just assuming she wanted booze.

They all waited for her to answer, but she sipped the drink and made a quiet cooing noise. "This is *good*. Holy crap!" Apparently she liked it. "Just make sure I only have the one," she whispered to me, sliding closer into my side. "Otherwise I can't be held responsible for my actions."

Well, fuck. With that one line she managed to derail my plans to be the good, big-brother figure for the evening.

Hanna drank her cocktail faster than I expected and her cheeks grew rosy, her smile lingered. She met my eyes and I could see her happiness there, lighting her up. *Christ, she's pretty,* I thought, wishing she and I were alone at my place watching a movie, and making a mental note to make that happen soon. I looked around the room and realized how many more people had joined the party. The kitchen was growing crowded. Another graduate student joined our little circle partway into a conversation about the craziest professors in the department and introduced herself to me, stepping between me and Dylan on my right. To my left, I could feel Hanna watching my reaction. I felt hyperconscious around her, seeing myself through her eyes. She was right when she said I noticed women, but while this other woman was pretty, she did nothing for me, especially not with Hanna so nearby. Did Hanna really think I made a habit of having sex with someone every single time I went anywhere?

I met her eyes and gave her a scolding look.

Hanna giggled, mouthing, "I know you."

"You really don't," I murmured. And fuck it, I let it all out: "There's still so much you could learn."

She stared up at me for several long, loaded beats. I could see her pulse in her neck, see the way her chest rose and fell with her quickened breathing. She looked down, put her hand on my bicep, and ran her fingertips over the tattoo of the phonograph I'd had done when my grandfather died.

In unison, we stepped away from the group, sharing a secret little smile. *Fuck, this girl makes me feel unhinged.*

"Tell me about this one," she whispered.

"I got that a year ago when my Pop died. He taught me how to play the bass. He listened to music every second he was awake, every day."

"Tell me about one I've never seen before," she said, attention moving to my lips.

I closed my eyes for a beat, thinking. "I have the word NO written just over my smallest rib on my left side."

Laughing, she stepped closer, close enough for me to smell the sweet plum drink on her breath. "Why?"

"I got it when I was drunk in grad school. I was on an antireligion kick and didn't like the idea that God made Eve out of Adam's rib."

Hanna threw her head back, laughing my favorite laugh, the one that came from her belly and took over her entire body.

"You're so fucking *pretty*," I murmured, without thinking, running my thumb over her cheek.

She jerked her head back upright, and, with a lingering glance to my mouth, pulled me out of the kitchen, a small, devilish smile on her face.

"Where are we going?" I asked, letting her lead me down a narrow hall lined with closed doors.

"Shh. I'll lose my nerve if I say it before we're there. Just come with me."

Little did she know I'd follow her down this hallway even if it caught fire. I'd come to this dirty bohemian party with her after all.

At a random closed door, Hanna stopped, knocked, and waited. She pressed her ear to the wood, smiled up at me, and when we heard nothing, turned the knob, letting out a cute, nervous squeak.

The room was dark, blessedly empty, and still relatively sterile from the recent move. A bed was freshly made in the middle of the room, and a dresser was pressed tight in a corner, but the far wall was still lined with boxes.

"Whose room is this?" I asked.

"I'm not sure." Reaching around, she flipped the lock at my back, and then stared up at me, smiling. "Hi."

"Hi, Hanna."

Her mouth dropped open and her beautiful eyes went wide. "You didn't call me Ziggy."

Smiling, I whispered, "I know."

"Say it again?" Her voice came out husky, as if she was asking me to *touch* her again, to *kiss* her again. And maybe when I'd called her Hanna it felt like a kiss. It certainly had to me. And part of me—a very large part of me—decided I didn't care anymore. I didn't care that I'd kissed her sister twelve years ago and her brother was one of my closest friends. I didn't care that Hanna was seven years younger than I was, and, in many ways, very innocent. I didn't care that I'd probably fuck it up, or that my past would bother her. We were alone, in a dark room, and every inch of my skin felt like it was buzzing with my need for her to touch me.

"Hanna," I said quietly. The two syllables filled my head, hijacked my pulse.

She smiled a secretive little smile and then looked at my mouth. Her tongue slipped out, wetting her bottom lip.

"What's going on, Mystique?" I whispered. "What

are we doing in this very dark bedroom, exchanging flirty eyes?"

She held up her hands, her words coming out in a breathless tumble. "This room is Vegas. Okay? What happens here stays here. Or, rather, what's *said* here stays here."

I nodded, mesmerized by the soft curve of her bottom lip. "Okay . . . ?"

"If it's weird, or if I cross a friendship boundary that by some force of magic I haven't yet crossed, just tell me, and we'll leave, and it will be the same level of ridiculous it was before we walked in."

I whispered, "Okay," again, and watched as she took a deep, shaky breath. She was tipsy, and nervous. Anticipation pricked along the back of my neck, and down my spine.

"I'm so wound up around you," she said quietly.

"Just me?" I asked, smiling.

She shrugged. "I want you . . . to teach me things. Not just about how to be around guys but how to . . . be *with* a guy. I think about it all the time. And I know you're comfortable doing this stuff without being in a relationship, and . . ." She trailed off, looking up at me in the dark room. "We're friends, right?"

I knew with absolute certainty where this was going, and murmured, "Whatever it is, I'll do it."

"You don't know what I'm asking."

Laughing, I whispered, "So *ask*."

She stepped a little closer, put her hand on my

chest, and I closed my eyes as her warm palm slid down to my stomach. I wondered for a beat if she could feel my heart hammering all the way down my torso. *I* felt my pulse everywhere, slamming through my chest and all along my skin.

"I watched another movie," she said. "A porny one."

"I see."

"Those movies are actually pretty bad." She said this quietly, as if she was worried she might be offending my male, porn-loving sensibilities.

With a quiet laugh, I agreed, "They are."

"The women are so over-the-top. Actually," she said, considering, "so are the guys for most of it."

"*Most* of it?" I asked.

"Not at the end," she said, her voice dropping to barely a decibel. "When the guy came? He pulled out of her and did it *on* her." Her fingers moved beneath my shirt, tickling over the line of hair that went from my navel and beneath the waist of my pants. She sucked in a breath, running her hand up higher and over my pectorals, exploring.

Fuck. I was so worked up I could barely keep my hands from reaching for her hips. But I wanted her to lead this conversation. She'd pulled me in here, started this. I wanted her to get it all out before she turned it over to me. And then I wouldn't hold back.

"That's pretty common in porn," I said. "The guys don't come inside the women."

She looked up at me. "I *liked* that part."

I felt myself grow rigid in my pants, and swallowed thickly. "Yeah?"

"I liked it because it felt *real*. I feel like I'm just figuring these things out. I haven't really tried before . . . or maybe I haven't wanted to explore it with the guys I've been with. But ever since I started hanging out with you, I can't stop thinking about these things. I want to figure out what I like."

"That's good." I winced in the dark room, wishing I hadn't answered so quickly, sounded so desperate. I wanted more than anything for her to ask me to carry her over to the bed and fuck her so loud the entire party knew where we'd gone and what she was getting.

"I don't really know what feels good to men. I know you say guys are easy, but they aren't. To *me*, they aren't." She took my hand, and with her eyes trained on my face, she brought it to her breast. Beneath my palm, she was exactly how I'd imagined a hundred fucking times. So full and soft, all lush curves and creamy skin. It was all I could do to keep from lifting her, and crushing her between my body and the wall.

"I want you to show me how," she said.

"What do you mean 'show you how'?"

She closed her eyes for a beat, swallowing. "I want to touch you, and make you come."

I took a deep breath and glanced over at the bed in the middle of the room. "Here?"

She followed the path my eyes had taken, and shook her head. "Not there. Not a bed yet. Just . . ."

She hesitated and then very quietly asked, "Are you saying yes?"

"Um, of course I'm saying yes. I'm not sure I could say no to you even if I should."

She bit back a smile, slid my hand down to her hip.

"You want to give me a hand job? Is that what you're asking?" I bent my knees to look her in the eyes. I felt like an asshole being so blunt, and this whole conversation felt *completely* surreal, but I had to be clear what was actually happening before I let go of my tenuous self-control and took it too far. "I'm just making sure I understand."

She swallowed again, suddenly shy, and nodded. "Yeah."

I stepped closer and when the light botanical smell of her shampoo hit me, I grew aware of how amped up I was. I'd never been nervous before, but right then I was terrified. I didn't care so much about how good it was for me—it could be awkward and fumbling, too slow or fast, too soft or too hard—I knew I'd fall apart in her hands. I just wanted her to keep feeling this open with me, every second. I wanted sex to be *fun* for her.

"It's okay to touch me," I told her, trying to carefully balance my need to be gentle with my tendency to be demanding.

She reached for my belt, unfastening it, and I moved my fingers from her hips, sliding up her waist to the top button of her shirt. Her smile was giddy, and she tried to duck her head to hide it but failed. I had no idea what I looked like, but I imagined my eyes were wide, mouth parted, hands shaking on her tiny buttons. Slipping her shirt from her shoulders, I noticed the way she hesitated on my fly, fingers unsure, before she moved away to let her shirt fall to the floor.

She stood in front of me in a simple white cotton bra. I reached behind her, meeting her eyes for permission before I unclasped it and slid it from her arms.

I'd been unprepared for the sight of her naked chest, and stood staring, dumbly.

"Just so you know," she whispered, "you don't have to do anything to me."

"Just so *you* know," I said, just as quietly, "keeping my hands to myself would be impossible right now."

"I want to pay attention. You might . . . distract me."

I groaned; she was killing me. "Such a good student," I said, leaning to kiss the juncture of her shoulder and neck. "But there's no way I can stand here and not look at these. You may have noticed I'm a bit obsessed with your chest."

Her skin was soft and smelled amazing. I opened my mouth, bit her gently, testing. She gasped and pressed into me, the *best* fucking reaction. My mind flooded with images of her nails digging into my back, my mouth open and pressing hard and hungrily into her breast as I rocked over her.

"Touch me, Hanna." I lifted the weight of her breast in my hand, pushed it higher, squeezing. *Holy fuck, she's edible.*

She'd moved her hands back to my fly, but they remained there, unmoving. "Show me how to do this?"

It was probably the hottest thing I'd ever heard a woman say. Maybe it was the tone of her voice, a little hoarse, a lot hungry. Maybe it was knowing how accomplished she was, and this one task felt so far out of her comfort zone but she'd asked *me* to help. Or maybe it was simply that I was wild for her, and showing Hanna how to pleasure me made me feel like I was telling the universe, *This one belongs to me.*

I moved her hands to the waist of my jeans, and together we worked them and my boxers down my hips, freeing my cock between us.

I let her look at me while I lifted both hands to slide her hair behind her neck, leaning in to kiss her throat. "You taste so fucking good." I was so hard I felt my pulse hammering along my length. I needed relief from this tension. "Shit, Hanna, wrap your hand around me."

"*Show* me, Will," she pleaded, running both hands over my stomach and down, just barely touching where the tip of my cock strained, erect. We looked down the length of our bodies and swayed slightly in unison.

I took her warm hand, wrapped it around the middle of my shaft and slid it down and then back up, groaning a long, drawn-out *"Fuuuck."*

She moaned quietly—a tight, excited sound—and I almost broke. Instead, I squeezed my eyes shut, leaned down again to kiss a line up her neck, and guided her. It was so slow. I hadn't had a hand job in forever, and would take head or sex over a hand one hundred percent of the time, but this, right here, was perfect.

Her lips were so fucking close to mine. I could feel her breath, could taste her candy-sweet plum drink.

"Is it weird that I'm touching you here and we haven't even kissed yet?" she whispered.

I shook my head, looking down to where her fingers wrapped around me. I swallowed, could barely think. "There's no right or wrong here. No rules."

She lifted her eyes from where she'd been staring at my mouth. "You don't have to kiss me."

I gaped at her. I'd wanted to kiss her for weeks now. "Shit, Hanna, yes. I do."

Her tongue slipped out to wet her lips. "Okay."

I bent low, hovering so close, moving her hand up and down my length, and just taking her in. Her lips were a breath away from mine, her little sounds coming out whenever she reached the head of my cock and I let out a grunt. It felt too good to be just a hand job. And all of this was suddenly too intimate to be *just friends*.

I looked at her eyes, and then her mouth, before moving that last inch to kiss her.

She was so fucking sweet and warm, our first kiss

was unreal: just a slide of my lips over hers, asking: *Let me do this. Let me do this and be gentle and careful with every part of you.* I kissed her a few times, full lips, careful kisses so she knew I'd take this as fucking slowly as she needed me to.

When I opened my mouth just enough to suck on her bottom lip, a thrill ran through me at the sound of her tight moan. *Christ,* I wanted to lift her up, fuck her mouth with my tongue, and take her against the wall, with the party raging outside and my eyes on her face, watching her process every single sensation.

When she pulled back, she studied my mouth, my eyes, my forehead. She studied *me;* I couldn't tell if it was a general fascination with what she was learning, or specific to this moment, to me. But nothing would have pulled me out of my trance. Not fireworks outside, or a fire in the hall. My need to someday be inside her—to completely possess her—spiked through me and planted beneath my ribs, pressing.

"You'll tell me if this is lame, right?" she asked, voice quiet.

I laughed, wheezing. "Oh, it's not lame. It's so fucking good, and it's just your hand."

Looking unsure, she asked, "Do . . . others not do this?"

I swallowed thickly, hating the mention of other women right now. Before, I'd almost wanted them to be a lingering presence, a reminder to all parties what was and wasn't happening in a moment like this. With

Hanna, I wanted to wipe their shadows from the wall. "Shh."

"I mean, do you usually just have sex?"

"I like what *we're* doing. I don't want something else right now; will you just focus on the dick in your hand?"

She laughed, and I pulsed in her palm, loving the sound. "Fine," she whispered. "I just have to start with the basics."

"I like that you want to learn how to touch me."

"I like touching you," she murmured against my mouth. "I like that you're showing me."

We were moving faster together now; I showed her how hard to squeeze, letting her know it was okay to hold on tight and that I needed it to start getting faster and harder than she'd expected.

"Squeeze it," I whispered. "I like it pretty hard."

"It doesn't hurt?"

"No, it's fucking *killing* me."

"Let me try." She gently pushed my arm away with her free hand.

It freed me to cup her breasts, and I bent down to suck one nipple into my mouth, blowing lightly over the peak.

She moaned, her rhythm slowing for a moment before she sped up again. "Can I keep doing this until you finish?" she asked.

I laughed quietly into her skin. She had me practically vibrating, struggling to not lose it every time she slid her hand down and over the head of my cock. "I was kind of counting on that."

I sucked on her neck, closing my eyes and wondering if she'd let me mark her there, so I could see it tomorrow. So everyone could. All around me the world seemed to spin. Her hand felt good, of course, but the reality of *her* absolutely rocked me. The smell and taste of her smooth, firm skin, her sounds of pleasure simply from touching me. She was sexual and responsive and curious, and I wasn't sure I'd been this turned on in a long, long time.

The familiar tension built deep in my belly, and I began to rock forward in her grip. "Hanna. Oh, shit, just a little faster, okay?" The words felt so much more intimate this way: spoken into her skin, my breath ragged.

She faltered for only a second before responding, pulling harder and faster, and I was close—embarrassingly soon—and I didn't give a single fuck. Her long, slim fingers wrapped tight around me and she let me suck on her bottom lip, her jaw, her neck. I knew she would taste good *everywhere*.

I wanted to show her how it felt to be fucked.

With that thought, of falling over her and into her, making her come with my body, I leaned into her, begged her to bite me, bite my neck my shoulder . . . *anything*. I didn't care how it sounded; somehow I knew that she wouldn't balk, or recoil from the reality of this admission.

Without hesitation, she leaned in, opened her mouth on my neck, and pressed her teeth sharply into me. My thoughts blurred, everything flashed hot and wild; for a moment it felt like every synapse in my body had rewired, unplugged, gone off. Her hand slipped over me fast, my orgasm barreling down my spine and I came with a quiet groan, the heat crawling up my spine and pouring from me into her hand and over her bare stomach.

Just when I needed her to, she stopped moving but didn't let go. I could feel her eyes on where she held me in her hand, and I jerked when she moved down my length again, experimentally.

"No more," I gasped, my voice tight.

"Sorry." She slid the thumb of her free hand over where I'd come on her palm, rubbed it over her hip, eyes wide and fascinated. She was breathing so hard her chest jerked with the movement.

"Holy shit," I exhaled.

"Was it . . . ?" The room seemed full with her unfinished question and the sound of my heavy breathing. I felt a little dizzy, and wanted to pull her down onto the floor with me and pass out.

"That was fucking unreal, Hanna."

She looked up at me, almost triumphant with discovery. "I was right—you made the best noise when you came."

The world dropped into an abyss when she said

that, because here I was, growing soft in her hand, and all I wanted was to find out whether doing that to me had made her wet.

I bent forward and asked, "Is it my turn now?" into the soft skin of her neck.

With a trembling breath, she whispered, "Yes, please."

"Do you want my hands?" I asked. "Or do you want something else?"

She let out a little nervous laugh. "I'm not really ready for more, but . . . I don't think hands work on me."

I leaned back enough to give her my most skeptical look, unbuttoning the top button of her jeans and just daring her to stop me.

She didn't.

"I just mean I don't know if I can get off with fingers, like, just inside," she clarified.

"Well, of course you can't get off just with fingers inside. Your *clit* isn't inside." I slid my hand beneath her cotton underwear and froze at the sensation of soft, bare skin. "Uh, Hanna? I did not peg you as a waxer."

She wiggled a little, embarrassed. "Chloe was talking about it. I was curious. . . ."

I slipped a finger between her lips—holy *fuck*, she was drenched. "Jesus Christ," I groaned.

"I like it," she admitted, her mouth pressed against my neck. "I like how it feels."

"Are you fucking kidding? You're so fucking soft; I want to lick up and down every part of this."

"*Will* . . ."

"I'd have my mouth on you in two seconds if we weren't in some random guy's bedroom."

She shivered under my touch, letting out a quiet moan. "I can't tell you how many times I've imagined that."

Holy hell. I felt myself lengthen between us again, already. "I think you'd melt like sugar on my tongue. What do you think?"

She laughed a little, holding on to my shoulders. "I think I'm melting now."

"I think you are. I think you're going to melt all over my fucking hand and I'll lick it off after. Are you loud, little Plum? When you come are you wild?"

A tiny choking sound escaped before she whispered, "By myself I'm not loud."

Fuck. That's what I wanted to hear. I could build fantasies for a decade just thinking about Hanna, legs spread on her couch or while she was lying in the middle of her bed, touching herself.

"By yourself, what do you do? Just the clit?"

"Yeah."

"With a toy or . . . ?"

"Sometimes."

"I bet I can make you come like this," I said, and slid two fingers carefully inside, feeling her squeeze me. I brushed my nose against hers. "Tell me. Do you like my fingers here? Fucking you?"

"Will . . . you're so *dirty.*"

I laughed, nibbling at her jaw. "I think you *like* dirty."

"I think I'd like your dirty mouth between my legs," she said softly.

I groaned, moved my hand faster and harder into her.

"Do *you* think about it?" she asked. "Kissing me there?"

"I have," I admitted. "I think about it and wonder if I'd ever come up for air."

So wet. She was wiggling all over my hand, making these little desperate sounds I wanted to eat. I pulled my fingers out, ignoring her angry little growl, and with them painted a wet line up her chin and across her lips, following almost immediately with my tongue, covering her mouth with mine.

Fuuuck.

She tasted all woman, soft and heady, and her tongue was still sticky sweet from her girly drink. She tasted like plum, ripe and soft and small in my mouth, and I felt like a fucking king when she begged me to touch her *more, again, please Will I was close.*

Returning to her, I shoved her pants and underwear all the way down her legs, waiting as she stepped out of them. She was completely naked and my arms were shaking with the need to slide inside her perfect, warm heat.

She reached for my wrist, pulling my hand back between her legs.

"Greedy girl."

Her eyes went wide, embarrassed. "I just—"

"Shh." I quieted her with my mouth on hers, sucking on her lip and licking her sweet tongue. Pulling back, I whispered, "I like it. I want to make you explode."

"I will." She jerked in my hand when I slid my fingers between her legs and over her clit. "I've never felt this."

"So wet."

Her mouth opened in a sharp gasp when I slid my fingers back inside her. She stared at my lips, my eyes, my every reaction. I loved that she was so curious she couldn't even look away.

"Do me a favor," I asked. She nodded. "When you're close, tell me. I'll know, but give me the words."

"I will," she gasped. "I will, I will, just . . . please."

"Please what, Plum?"

She weaved slightly against me. "Please don't stop."

I slid my fingers deeper, faster, pressing my thumb up against her clit and working it right there in tighter, smaller circles. *Yes. Holy shit, she's so close.*

I was hard again, rubbing over her bare hip where I'd already come on her only minutes ago, and close again myself.

"Grab my dick, okay? Just hold on. You're so fucking wet and your sounds . . . holy fuck, I . . ."

And then she was there, holding on to me tight

enough to fuck her fist, and every thought became about how smooth she was around my fingers and the fruit plumpness of her lips and tongue.

She started to dissolve, her body completely losing it. She was quietly gasping the same thing over and over—*Oh my God*—which I was thinking, too.

"Say it."

"I'm going . . ." She hiccupped, tightened her hold on my length as I fucked her fist.

"Fucking *say it*."

"Will. My God." Her thighs started to shake and I wrapped my free arm around her waist to keep her from falling. "I'm coming."

And with a wild jerk of her hips she did, shaking and wet. Her orgasm rippled along the lengths of my fingers as she cried out, digging her nails into my shoulders. It was exactly what I needed—*how did she fucking know*? With a low groan, I felt my second orgasm surge forward, hot and liquid into her hand.

Fuck. My legs shook and I leaned into her, pinning her to the wall.

We'd been loud. Too loud? We were far down the hall, separated from the raging party by a number of rooms, but I still had no sense what the outside world had done while mine had melted in Hanna's arms.

Her breath came out warm and sweet on my neck and I carefully pulled out my fingers, rubbing along her sex to relish in her warm, sensitive skin.

"Good?" I murmured into her ear.

"Yeah," she whispered, wrapping her arms around my shoulders and pressing her face into the crook of my neck. "*God,* so good."

I left my hand where it was, my mind reeling as I gently ran my fingers up her clit, down back to her entrance and along the soft crease of her pussy. It was quite possibly the best first time I'd ever had with a girl.

And it had only been our hands.

"We should probably get back out to the party," she said, her voice muffled by my skin.

Reluctantly, I pulled my hand away, and immediately winced as she turned on the light switch behind her back. As I pulled up my pants, I stared at her, completely naked in the bright room.

Well, fuck. She was smooth and toned, with lush breasts and gently curved hips. Her skin was still flushed from her orgasm, and I relished the sight of the blush that spread up her neck and across her cheeks as I studied the moisture on her stomach from my orgasm.

"You're staring," she said, bending to reach for a box of tissues on the dresser. She looked down, cleaning herself up and then tossing the tissue into a trash can.

I buckled my belt and then sat at the edge of the bed, watching her put her clothes back on. She was unbelievably sexy, and she had no fucking idea.

The room smelled like sex, and I knew she could

feel my attention on her but she didn't rush. In fact, she seemed perfectly content to let me look at every angle, every curve as she slid on her panties, shimmied into her pants, put her bra on, slowly buttoned her shirt.

Looking over at me, she licked her lips and my heart tripped as I registered she could taste herself from my fingers. I wondered if I'd be remembering her taste until the end of time.

"What now?" I asked, standing.

"Now"—she reached for my arm, tracing the double helix from my elbow to my wrist—"we go back out there and have another drink."

My blood cooled a bit, hearing her voice return to steady. No longer breathy and excited, no longer tentative and hopeful. She was back to her regular bubbly self, the same Hanna everyone else saw. No longer mine.

"Works for me."

She looked at my face for several long moments, at my eyes and cheeks, chin and lips. "Thanks for not being weird."

"Are you kidding?" I bent down and kissed her cheek. "What's there to be weird about?"

"We just touched each other's private parts," she whispered.

I laughed, fixing the collar of her shirt. "I noticed that."

"I think I could totally do the friends-with-benefits thing. It feels so easy, so relaxed. We're just going to head back out there," she said, grinning widely up at me. With a little wink, she added, "And we're the only ones who know you just came all over my stomach and I just came all over your hand."

She turned the knob, opened the door, and let in the roar of the party. No way would anyone have heard us. We could pretend it didn't even happen.

———

I'd done this before, scores of times. Hooked up with a woman and then returned to the throes of a party, blending into the room and losing myself in another form of fun. But despite the genuinely nice crowd of people, I couldn't ever lose track of where Hanna was and what she was doing. In the living room, talking to the tall Asian guy I remembered as Dylan. Heading down the hall, waving to me before ducking into the restroom. Filling her plastic cup with water in the kitchen. Looking over to me across the room.

Dylan found Hanna again, smiling as he bent and said something to her. He had a wide smile, clothes that suggested he got out enough to be on the cutting edge of grad student chic, and seemed genuinely fond of her. I watched her smile grow, and then turn a little unsure. She hugged him, and watched him head into the kitchen. I had no idea what was happening; I loved seeing her have a good time. But the itch for something else started to spread across my skin, and after two hours of partying post–hand job, I realized I wanted to take her home where we could feel each other for real for the remainder of the night.

I slid my phone from my pocket, typing a text to her. Let's get out of here. Come to my place tonight and stay with me.

I moved my thumb to the SEND button before I noticed that she was also typing in our iMessage window. I paused, waiting.

Dylan just asked me out, she said.

I stared at my phone before looking up to meet her anxious eyes across the room.

Deleting what I'd written, I typed instead, What did you tell him?

She looked down when her phone buzzed in her hand, and then replied, I told him we could figure it out on Monday.

She was looking for guidance, maybe even looking for permission. Only a month ago I was regularly having sex with two to three different women every week. I had no idea where my head was concerning Hanna; my own thoughts were too jumbled and complex to help her translate hers right now.

My phone buzzed again and I glanced down. Is this really weird after what we just did?? I don't know what to do, Will.

This is what she needs, I told myself. *Friends, dates, a life outside of school. You can't be the only thing in it.*

For once I was looking for complicated, and she was trying on simple.

Not at all, I typed back. This is called dating.

Chapter Seven

If I'd ever wondered what a cat in heat sounded like, now I knew. The noises—the meows, the whining, the howls—had started about an hour ago and had only gotten worse until the sexually frustrated animal was practically screeching outside my bedroom window.

I knew exactly how it felt. Thanks, Life, for giving me the living, breathing metaphor for how I was feeling.

With a groan, I rolled to my stomach, reaching blindly for a pillow to drown out the sound. Or to use to smother myself. I hadn't decided. I'd been home from my date with Dylan for three hours and hadn't gotten even a few minutes of sleep.

I was a mess, having tossed and turned since I'd climbed into bed, staring up at the ceiling as if the secret to all my problems lay hidden in the mottled plaster overhead. Why did everything feel so complicated? Wasn't this what I'd wanted? Dates? A social life? To have an orgasm in the company of another person?

So what was the problem?

The way Dylan tripped my *only-a-friend* vibe was the problem. The fact that we'd gone to one of my favorite restaurants and I'd been completely zoned out, thinking about Will when I should have been swooning over Dylan, was an even bigger one. I wasn't thinking about Dylan's smile as he'd picked me up, the way he'd opened my door and the adoring way he'd looked at me all through dinner. Instead, I was obsessing over Will's teasing smile, the look on his face as he'd watched me touch his cock, his flushed cheeks, how he'd told me exactly what to do, the way he'd sounded when he came, and how it had looked on my skin.

Annoyed, I flopped onto my back and kicked off the blankets. It was March, light snow had been falling all day, and I was *sweating*. It was two o'clock in the morning and I was wide awake and frustrated. Really, *really* frustrated.

The hardest part to wrap my head around was how sweet Will had been at the party, how gentle and caring, and how I knew without a doubt how easily all of that would translate into sex. He'd been encouraging, saying everything I'd needed to hear, but never pushing, never asking for more than I'd been willing to give. And holy shit he was hot . . . those hands. That mouth. The way he sucked on my skin, kissing me as if he had years of pent-up need and it was finally unleashed. I wanted him to fuck me, probably more than I ever wanted anything, and it was the most logical next step in the world: we were both there, it was dark, he was worked up and God knows I'd been ready to explode, there'd been a bed . . . but, it hadn't felt right. I hadn't felt ready.

And he hadn't pushed. In fact, when I expected it to be weird, it wasn't. When he'd been the only person I wanted to talk to about Dylan, he'd encouraged me. On the taxi ride home he'd told me I needed to go out, have fun. He told me he wasn't going anywhere, and what we'd done was perfect. He told me to explore, and be happy. *God*, it just made me want him even more.

Deciding this was a losing battle and I would never get to sleep now, I sat up and went into the kitchen. I stared into the fridge, closing my eyes as the cool air floated along my heated skin. I was slick between my legs and even though it had been six days since Will had touched me there, I *ached*. I'd seen him every day for our run, and we'd had breakfast afterward on three of those days. It had been easy; with Will, it was *always* easy. But each time he was near, I wanted to ask if he could touch me again, if I could touch him. I could still feel the echo of every stroke of his fingers, but I didn't trust my memory. It couldn't possibly have been so good as all that.

I walked into the living room and looked out the window. The sky was dark but silver-gray, the rooftops glittering with frost. I counted the streetlights and calculated how many of them there were between his apartment building and mine. I wondered if there was even a chance he was awake, too, feeling even a fraction of the want I felt now.

My fingers found the pulse in my neck and I closed my eyes, feeling the steady thrum beneath my skin. I told myself to go back to bed. Maybe this was a good opportunity to sample the brandy Dad always kept in the living room. I told myself that calling Will was a bad idea and that there was absolutely no way that anything good could come from this. I was smart and logical and thought everything through.

I was so tired of thinking.

Ignoring the warning inside my head, I grabbed my things, stepped outside, and started walking. The lingering snow had been stomped down during the day and formed a thick crust along the sidewalk. My boots crunched with every step and the closer I got to Will's apartment, the more the chaos in my thoughts settled into a steady hum in the background.

When I looked up, I was standing in front of his building. My hands shook as I pulled out my phone and found his picture, typing the only thing that came to mind: Are you awake?

I almost dropped the phone in surprise when an answer came only a few seconds later. Unfortunately.

Let me in? I asked, and honestly, did I want him to say yes? Or send me home? At this point I didn't even know.

Where are you?

I hesitated. In front of your building.

WHAT. Down in a sec.

I'd barely had time to consider what I was doing, turning to look back in the direction I'd come, when the front door flew open and Will stepped outside.

"Holy shit, it's freezing!" he yelled, and then looked behind me to the empty curb. "For fuck's sake, Hanna, did you at least take a cab here?"

Wincing, I admitted, "I walked."

"*At three a.m.*? Are you out of your goddamn mind?"

"I know, I know. I just . . ."

He shook his head and pulled me inside. "Get in here. You're crazy, you know that? I want to strangle you right now. You don't just walk around Manhattan alone at three in the morning, Hanna."

My stomach twisted with warmth when he said my name, and I knew I'd stand out in the cold all night if it meant he'd say it again. But he shot me a warning look, and I nodded as he led me to the elevator. The doors closed and he watched me from the opposite wall.

"So did you just get home from your date?" he asked, looking far too sleep-rumpled and sexy for my current state of mind. "The last you texted, you were getting in the cab to meet Dylan at the restaurant."

I shook my head and blinked down to the carpet, trying to understand what exactly I'd been thinking when deciding to come here. I hadn't been thinking, that was the problem. "I got home around nine."

"Nine?" he asked, looking completely unimpressed.

"Yes," I challenged.

"And?" His tone was even, his face impassive, but the speed of his questions told me he was worked up about something.

I shifted from foot to foot, not sure exactly what to say. The date hadn't been a complete disaster. Dylan was sweet and interesting, but I'd been totally checked out.

I was saved from answering when we reached Will's floor. I followed him out of the elevator and down the long hallway, watching his back and shoulders flex with every step. He wore blue pajama bottoms and the outlines of some of his darker tattoos were visible through his thin white T-shirt. I had to push down the urge to reach out and trace them with my fingertip, to take off his shirt and see them all. There were obviously more than there had been all those years ago, but what were they? What stories hid beneath the ink on his skin?

"So are you going to tell me?" he asked.

He'd stopped in front of his door and my eyes shot up to his. "What?" I asked, confused.

"Date, Hanna."

"Oh," I murmured, blinking away and trying to make some order of the chaos inside my head. "It was dinner and blah blah blah, I took a cab home. You're sure I didn't wake you?"

He sighed long and deep, gesturing for me to lead us inside. "Unfortunately, no." He tossed me a blanket from the back of the couch. "I haven't been able to fall asleep yet."

I wanted to pay attention, but I was suddenly surrounded by so many pieces of Will's life. His apartment was one of the newer buildings in the area, and it was modern, but modest. He flipped a switch to a small fireplace against one wall, and the flames bit to life with a soft whoosh, washing the honey-colored walls in flickering light.

"Warm up while I get you something to drink," he said, motioning to the rug in front of the hearth. "And tell me more about this date that ended at *nine*."

The kitchen was visible from the living room and I watched as he opened and closed cupboards, filling an ancient-looking kettle before setting it to heat on the stove. His place was smaller than I'd have imagined, with wood floors and bookcases packed to the brim with dog-eared novels, thick genetics texts, and an entire wall dedicated to what looked like a rather impressive collection of comic books. Two leather couches dominated the living room and simple framed art lined the walls. There were magazines in a basket on the floor, a stack of mail tucked into the mantel, a glass full of bottle caps resting on a shelf.

I tried to focus on what he was asking, but every object in his apartment was a fascinating puzzle piece to the story of Will. "There's really not much to tell," I said distractedly.

"Hanna."

I groaned, taking off my jacket and folding it over the back of a chair. "My head just wasn't in the game, you know?" I said, and stopped at the expression on his face. His eyes were wide, his mouth open as his gaze moved slowly down my body. "What?"

"What are you . . ." He coughed. "You came all the way over here in *that?*"

I looked down and if possible, became even more mortified than I'd been before. I'd gone to bed in shorts and a tank top, only taking time to throw on a pair of pajama pants, my fuzzy boots, and Jensen's giant old coat. My shirt left nothing to the imagination and my nipples were hard, completely visible beneath the thin material.

"Oh. Oops." I crossed my arms over my chest, trying to hide the fact that it was obviously very, *very* cold outside. "I probably should have paid more attention but I . . . I wanted to see you. Is that weird?

It's weird isn't it? I'm probably breaking about twelve of your rules right now."

He blinked. "I, uh . . . I think there's a clause in there to make an exception for any rule-breaking while wearing an outfit like that," he said, managing to pull his eyes from my chest long enough to finish up in the kitchen. There was an unfamiliar sense of power in being able to fluster him, and I tried not to look too smug as he walked out, carrying two steaming mugs.

"So why was this date so uneventful?" he asked.

I sat on the floor in front of the fire, legs stretched out in front of me. "Just had other things on my mind."

"Like?"

"Liiiiiike . . ." I said, dragging the word out long enough to decide if I really wanted to go there. I did. "Like the party?"

A moment of long, heavy silence stretched between us. "I see."

"Yeah."

"Well, in case you hadn't noticed," he said, glancing over at me, "I wasn't exactly sound asleep here."

I nodded and turned back to the fire, not sure how to proceed. "I've always been able to control where my mind went, you know? If it's time for school I think about school. If it's work, I think about work. But lately," I said, shaking my head, "my concentration is crap."

He laughed softly next to me. "I know exactly how you feel."

"I can't focus."

"Yeah." He scratched the back of his neck, looking up at me through dark lashes.

"I'm not sleeping very well."

"Same."

"I'm so fucking wound up I can hardly sit still," I admitted.

I heard the sound of his exhale, a long, measured breath, and only then did I realize how close we'd gotten. I looked up to see him watching me.

His eyes searched every inch of my face. "I don't know . . . if I've ever been this distracted by someone," he said.

I was *so close,* close enough to see each of his eyelashes in the firelight, close enough to make out the tiny scattering of freckles along the bridge of his nose. Without thinking I leaned in, brushing my lips over his. His eyes widened and I felt him stiffen, frozen for only a moment before his shoulders relaxed.

"I shouldn't want this," he said. "I have no idea what we're doing."

We weren't kissing, not really, just teasing, breathing the same air. I could smell his soap, a hint of toothpaste. Could see my own reflection in his pupil.

He tilted his head and closed his eyes, moving in just enough to kiss me once, lips parted. "Tell me to stop, Hanna."

I couldn't. Instead I reached up, cupping the back of his neck to bring him closer. And then it was he who pushed forward, harder, longer, and I had to grip his shirt to keep myself steady. He opened his mouth, sucking on my lower lip, my tongue. Heat pulsed low in my belly and I felt like I was dissolving, melting until I was nothing more than a racing heart and limbs that twisted with his, pulling us both to our sides and down to the floor.

"I don't . . ." I started, breath tight. "Tell me what I should do."

I felt the shape of him hard against my hip and I wondered how long he'd been that way, if he'd been thinking about this as much as I had. I wanted to reach down and touch, watch him fall apart like he had at the party, the way he did in my mind every time I closed my eyes.

His lips moved over my jaw, down my throat. "Just relax, I'll make it good. Tell me what you *want* to do."

My hand moved under his shirt and I felt the solid strength of muscle in his back, his arms as he rolled us over to hover above me. I said his name, hating how weak and unfamiliar my voice sounded, but there was something new there, something raw and desperate, and I wanted more.

"I used to imagine what it'd be like to have you on top of me," I admitted, not sure where the words were coming from. He rested his body more fully on mine, his hips settling between my open legs. "When you were lounging in the living room with my brother. When you'd take your shirt off outside to wash the car."

He moaned, moving a hand to my hair, his thumb drawing a path along my face and pressing into the skin along my jaw. "Don't tell me that."

But it was *all* I could think about: how I remembered him from those years, and the reality of him *now*. I couldn't possibly count the number of times I wondered what he would look like without his clothes, the sounds he'd make when he was chasing his release. And here he was, heavy on me, hard between my legs, beneath his clothes. I wanted to catalog every tattoo, every line of muscle, every inch of his carved jaw.

"I used to watch you from my window," I said, gasping as he shifted so that the length of him pressed directly over my clit. "God, when I was sixteen you starred in every one of my dirty dreams."

He pulled back just enough to meet my eyes; he was clearly surprised.

I swallowed. "Should I not have told you that?"

"I . . ." he began and licked his lips. "I don't know?" He looked dazed and conflicted. I couldn't look away from his mouth. "I know I shouldn't think that's hot but Christ, Hanna. If I come in my pants you have no one to blame but yourself."

I could do that? His words lit a fuse in my chest

and I wanted to tell him everything. "I would touch myself, under the covers," I admitted in a whisper. "Sometimes I could hear you talking . . . and I would pretend . . . wonder what it would be like if you were there. I used to make myself come and pretend it was you."

He swore, dipping back down to kiss me again, deeper and wetter, his teeth dragging along my bottom lip. "What would I say?"

"How good I felt and how much you wanted me," I said into his kiss. "I wasn't very creative at the time, and I'm pretty sure your mouth is way filthier in reality."

He laughed, the sound so low and rough it was a physical pressure on my neck where he breathed. "So let's pretend you're sixteen, and I just snuck into your room," he said, moving his mouth just over mine, his voice coming out the slightest bit unsure. "We don't have to take our clothes off if you aren't ready."

And I wasn't sure what to say because *yes*, I wanted to be completely bare under him, to imagine what it would feel like to have him naked and over and inside me. But *actual* sex with Will tonight felt too fast, too soon. Too dangerous.

"Show me?" I asked, "I don't know how to with clothes on." I paused, adding in a whisper, "Or even off, I guess. I mean obviously."

He laughed, kissing over to my ear and growling quietly as he nipped at my earlobe. The way his hands moved over me, the way his lips slid across my skin . . . touching like this seemed as second-nature to Will as breathing.

He exhaled into my neck, groaning quietly. "Move under me. Find what feels good for you, okay?"

I nodded, shifting beneath him and feeling the hard press of his cock between my legs.

"Can you feel that?" he asked, pressing meaningfully against my clit. "Is that where it feels good?"

"Yeah." I moved my hands to his hair and pulled hard, hearing him hiss in a breath as he rocked against me, faster and faster.

"Fuck, Hanna." He pushed my tank top up over my ribs, bunching it above my chest. And then he bent, gripped my breast, plumping it, and sucked a nipple deep into his mouth. The air left my lungs, my hips pressed up from the floor, searching. I scratched at his skin, and was rewarded each time with a mumbled curse or groan.

"That's it," he said. "Don't stop." His mouth followed his hands everywhere and I closed my eyes, feeling the heat of his tongue as it moved over me. He kissed my lips, my throat. The ache between my legs grew and I could feel how wet I was, how empty, how much I wanted his mouth against me, his fingers inside. His cock. We slid along the floor and I felt something wedge beneath my back, but didn't care. All I wanted was to chase down this feeling.

"So close," I gasped, surprised to find him looking down at me, lips parted and hair falling across his forehead.

His eyes widened, blazing with thrill. "Yeah?"

I nodded, the rest of the world blurring as the feeling between my legs grew, becoming hotter and more urgent. I wanted to claw at my skin and beg him to take off my clothes, to fuck me, to make me beg.

"Fuck. Don't stop what you're doing," he said, rocking his hips forward against me, the perfect drag of heat and pressure exactly where I needed. "I'm almost there."

"Oh," I said, my fingers twisting in the thin fabric of his shirt as I felt myself start to fall, closing my eyes as my orgasm moved down my spine to explode between my legs. I cried out, calling his name and feeling him speed up as he moved against me. His fingers pressed tightly into my hips as he pushed once, twice, grunting into my neck as he came.

Feeling seeped back into my body one limb at a time. I felt heavy and limp, suddenly so exhausted I could hardly keep my eyes open. Will collapsed against me, his breath hot on my neck, his skin damp with sweat and warmed by the fire.

He pushed up onto his elbows and looked down at me, his expression drowsy and sweet and a little timid. "Hi," he said, a crooked smile sliding into place. "Sorry for sneaking into your bedroom, teenage-Hanna."

I blew the bangs from my forehead and smiled back. "You're welcome there anytime."

"I . . . uh," he started, and laughed. "I don't mean to rush off but I sort of . . . need to clean up."

The absurdity of the entire situation seemed to bubble up out of nowhere and I started to laugh. We were on his floor, I think I had a shoe or something lodged under my back, and he'd just come in his pants.

"Hey," he said. "Don't laugh. I said it'd be your fault."

I was suddenly so thirsty and licked my lips. "Go," I said, patting his back.

He kissed me softly, twice on the lips before pushing himself to stand and walking into the bathroom. I stayed there for a moment, sweat drying on my skin and heart rate slowly returning to normal. I felt both better and worse. Better because I was actually tired, but worse because the new echo of Will's cock moving between my legs was infinitely more distracting than the memory of his fingers.

I called a taxi, then walked into the kitchen to splash some cool water on my face and get a drink.

He came back into the room wearing different pajamas, and smelling of soap, and toothpaste.

"I called a cab," I assured him, giving him the *don't-worry* look. His face fell—or it seemed to—but it happened so fast that I wasn't sure I believed my eyes.

"Good," he murmured, walking over to me and handing me my coat. "I actually think I'll be able to sleep now."

"Just needed the orgasm," I said, grinning.

"Actually," he said, voice deep, "I'd tried that a few times already tonight. It hadn't worked so far. . . ."

Holy shitballs. Any drowsiness I'd felt immediately evaporated. I was going to imagine what it would be like to watch Will get himself off for the rest of the night. I wasn't sure if I'd ever be able to sleep again.

He walked me downstairs, kissed my forehead at the door, and stood watching as I walked to the curb, climbed into the cab, and drove off.

My phone lit up with a text from him: Tell me when you get home.

I lived only seven blocks from him; I was home in minutes. I climbed into bed, curling into my pillow before answering, Home safe.

CHAPTER EIGHT

The promise of crowds was always a reality, living near the Columbia campus, but, mysteriously, the Dunkin' Donuts nearest my building always seemed busiest on Thursdays. Even during a slow stretch, though, I probably wouldn't have recognized Dylan in line, just ahead of me.

So, when he turned, eyes widening in recognition, and let out a friendly "Hey! Will, right?" I startled.

I blinked, feeling caught off guard. I'd just been daydreaming about taking things with Hanna in a different direction than I had two nights ago, when she'd come to my apartment in the middle of the night and ended up beneath me, both of us coming with our clothes on. The memory of that night was a current favorite, one I'd pulled out in almost every quiet moment since, to play with, take down a different path, warm my blood.

It had been years since I'd dry-humped a girl, but fuck, I'd forgotten how dirty and forbidden it felt.

But the sight of this kid in front of me—the guy Hanna was *dating*—felt like an ice bucket dumped over my head.

Dylan looked like every other Columbia student in the place: dressed down to the point he was toeing the line between pajama-clad and hobo.

"Yeah," I said, extending my hand to shake his. "Hi, Dylan. Good to see you again."

We stepped forward as the line moved ahead, and the awkwardness hit me slowly. I hadn't realized at the party how young he looked: he had that silently vibrating, feet-bouncy thing going on, where he seemed constantly excited about something. He nodded a lot, looked at me as if I was someone to be treated as a superior.

Looking between us, I registered how much more formal I looked in my suit. Since when was I the guy in a suit? Since when did I have little patience for stupid, twenty-something grad students? Probably the same day Hanna jacked me off in the back room of a grad student party and it was the best sex I'd ever had, I reminded myself.

"Did you have fun at Denny's?"

I stared at him for a long moment, trying to remember when I had last been to Denny's. "I . . ."

"The party, not the restaurant," he prompted, laughing. "The apartment belonged to a guy named Denny."

"Oh, right. The party." My mind immediately went to the image of Hanna's face as I slid my fingers beneath her underwear and across her bare skin. I could remember with perfect clarity her expression just before she came, like I'd done something fucking *magical*. She looked like she was discovering sensation for the first time. "Yeah, the party was pretty great."

He fidgeted with his phone, looking up at me, and seemed to be working up to something.

"You know," he said, leaning in a little, "this is the first time I've run into someone who's sort of dating the same girl I'm sort of dating. Is this really weird?"

I bit back a laugh. Well, he certainly had blunt-force honesty in common with Hanna. "What makes you think I'm dating her?"

Dylan immediately looked mortified. "I just assumed . . . because of how it seemed at the party. . . ."

Giving him a sly smile, I chided him, "And yet you asked her out anyway?"

He laughed as if he, too, couldn't believe his own audacity. "I was so drunk! I guess I just went for it."

I wanted to punch him. And I registered that I was the world's biggest hypocrite. I had absolutely no right to feel so indignant about any of this.

"It's fine," I said, calming down. I'd never been on this side of a conversation before, and for a beat wondered if any of my lovers had ever run into each other in places like this. How awkward. I tried to imagine what Kitty or Lara—all sparkles and sunshine—and

Natalia or Kristy—who would barely crack a smile even in the best of moods—would do if they were put in this kind of situation.

Shrugging, I told him, "Hanna and I go way back. That's all."

He laughed, nodding as if this answered all of his unasked questions. "She said she's just dating right now. I get that. She's a really fun girl, I've been wanting to ask her out for ages, so I'll take whatever I can get, you know?"

I stared at the cashier, silently begging her to ring up customers just a little faster. Unfortunately, I knew exactly what he meant. "Yeah."

He nodded again and I was tempted to tell him the rule of silence: *sometimes an awkward silence is actually far less awkward than forced conversation.*

Dylan stepped up to order his coffee and I could return to the safety of distraction via smartphone. I didn't meet his eye again as he paid and walked away, but I felt like my gut was made of lead.

What the fuck was I doing?

With every step to my office, I felt more and more uncomfortable. In the past near-decade, the lines were drawn with each of my sexual partners before the sex even happened. Sometimes the conversation occurred as we left an event together, other times it came up organically when they asked if I had a girlfriend and I could simply say, "I'm dating, but not seeing one person exclusively right now." In the few cases when the sex turned into something more, I'd always made a point to be clear about where I stood, find out where they stood, and discuss—openly—what we both wanted.

I hadn't registered how blindsided I'd been by the appearance of Dylan—in my world, and, more importantly, in Hanna's. For the first time ever, I'd made the assumption that when she pulled me to that back bedroom, she would want to explore sex with me . . . and *only* me.

Karma was clearly a bitch.

———

That morning, I dove into work, burning through three prospectuses and a stack of bullshit paperwork I'd been putting off for the past week. I followed up on calls, arranged for a business trip to the Bay Area to check out a few new biotechs. I barely stopped to breathe.

But when the afternoon rolled around, and I hadn't eaten anything for hours and my caffeine rush had long since tapered, Hanna pushed her way back into my thoughts.

My office door opened and Max walked over, tossing an enormous sandwich on my desk before sinking into the chair across from me. "What's going on, William? You look like you just found out DNA is a right-handed helix."

"It *is* a right-handed helix," I corrected him. "It just turns to the left."

"Like your dick?"

"Exactly." I pulled my sandwich toward me, unwrapping it. I hadn't realized until it was in front of me, smelling delicious, just how hungry I was. "Just thinking too much."

"Why do you look mental, then? Thinking too much is your fucking superpower, mate."

"Not about this it isn't." I rubbed my face, opting for honesty over jokes. "I'm kind of confused over something."

He took a bite, studied me. After several long moments, he asked, "This is about Tits, isn't it?"

I looked up at him, expression flat. "You *can't* call her that, Max."

"'Course I can't. Not to her face anyway. I mean, I call my Sara 'Tongue' after all, but she doesn't know it."

Despite my angst-ridden mood, I laughed at this. "You do not."

"No, I don't." His smile gave way to a frown of mock contrition. "That would be tacky, wouldn't it?"

"*Very* tacky."

"I can't help but notice that Hanna does have a fantastic pair, though."

Laughing again, I murmured, "Maximus, you have no idea."

He sat up straighter in his chair. "No, I don't," he said. "But it sounds like *you* do. Have you seen them? I wasn't aware things had progressed beyond your dating-mentoring bullshit."

When I looked up at him, I knew he could see it all in my face: I was in deep with Hanna. "I have. Things . . . uh . . . *progressed* the other night. And then again a couple of nights ago." I picked at my sandwich. "We haven't had sex, but . . . Alas, tonight she's going on another date with this one guy."

"Doing the 'dating' thing she was so keen on, eh?"

I nodded. "Seems like it."

"Does she know you're walking around under a lovesick rain cloud?"

I took a bite of my sandwich and threw him a look. "No," I mumbled. "Dick."

"She seems pretty great," he hedged carefully.

I wiped my mouth on my napkin and leaned back in my chair. *Great* didn't seem to cover it with Hanna. I hadn't known a girl like her, maybe ever. "Max, she's the entire package. Funny, sweet, honest, beautiful . . . I just feel so out of my depth on this." As soon as the words were out of my mouth, I could sense how foreign they sounded coming from me. A strange ringing silence filled the room, and I knew the wave of mockery was coming straight at me. It was evident in the little twitch of Max's lips.

Fuck.

He stared at me a beat longer before holding up a finger for me to wait, and pulling his phone out of his jacket pocket.

"What are you doing?" I asked, wary.

He shushed me, hitting speaker so we could both

hear the call ringing. Bennett's voice answered on the other end: "Max."

"Ben," Max said, leaning back in his chair with a giant grin. "It's finally happened."

I groaned, resting my head on my hand.

"You got your period?" Bennett asked. "Congratulations."

"No, you twat," Max said, laughing. "I'm talking about Will. He's gone arse over tits for a girl."

A loud slap sounded in the background and I imagined Bennett's desk had just received a very enthusiastic high-five. "Fantastic! Does he look miserable?"

Max pretended to study me for a beat. "As miserable as they come. And—*and!*—she's going on a date with another bloke tonight."

"Oooh, that's rough. What's our boy up to?" Bennett asked.

"Looking like a sad sack of shite, is my guess," Max answered for me, and then raised his eyebrows as if I was allowed to answer now.

"Just hanging at home," I said. "Watching the Knicks. I'm sure Hanna will tell me all about her date. Tomorrow. When we go running."

Bennett hummed on the other end of the line. "I should probably inform the girls."

I groaned. "Don't *inform* the girls."

"They'll want to come over and mother-hen you," Bennett said. "Max and I have a dinner meeting anyway. We can't leave you alone in this pathetic state."

"I'm not pathetic. I'm fine! Jesus," I muttered, "why did I say anything?"

Ignoring me, Bennett said, "Max, I'll take care of this. Thanks for letting me know." And the line went dead.

———

Chloe pushed past me, into my apartment. Her arms were full of bags of takeout.

"Having some people over at my place tonight?" I asked. She threw me a look over her shoulder and disappeared into my kitchen.

Behind her, Sara lingered in the hall, holding a six-pack and some sparkling water. "I was hungry," she admitted. "I made Chloe order one of everything."

I pushed the door open wider to let her in and followed her into the kitchen, where Chloe was busy unpacking enough food for seventeen people.

"I already ate," I admitted, wincing. "I didn't realize you were bringing dinner."

"How can you think we weren't bringing dinner? Bennett said you were a hot mess. Hot mess means pad thai, chocolate cupcakes, and beer. Besides, I've seen you eat," she said, pointing to the cabinet where I kept my plates. "You can eat more."

Shrugging, I grabbed three plates, some silverware, and a beer. I eased back to the living room and set up our plates on the coffee table. The girls joined me, Chloe sitting on the floor, Sara curling up next to me on the couch, and we all dug in. We sat and ate in front of the television, watching basketball in comfortable, intermittent conversation.

After all of it, I was glad they were here. They didn't bother me with a thousand questions about feelings; they just came, ate with me, kept me company. Kept me from getting too lost in my own head. I was fairly certain it wasn't the first time someone I was dating was out on a date with someone else, but it was the first time it even occurred to me to care.

I was happy Hanna was out, having fun. That was the weirdest part of all of it—I wanted her to have what she wanted. I just wanted her to want only me. I wanted her to come over tonight, admit that she would prefer to just fuck me and quit this dating nonsense, and that would be that. It was ridiculous, and I was the world's biggest asshole for thinking it, especially since in the past I'd made a hundred girls feel just like I did now, but it's what I wanted.

And, fuck, I was restless. As soon as I finished eating, I began obsessively checking my phone, checking the clock. Why hadn't she texted? Didn't she even have one question she needed answered? Didn't she even want to say "hi"?

God I hated myself.

"Have you heard from her?" Chloe asked, correctly reading my fidgeting.

I shook my head. "It's fine. I'm sure she's fine."

"So what did Kitty and Kristy say?" Sara asked, putting her glass of water down on the table.

"To what?" I asked.

Silence filled the space between us and I blinked, confused. "To what?" I asked, again.

"When you *ended* things with them," Sara prompted.

Fuck. Fuuuuuuck.

"Oh," I said, scratching my jaw. "I haven't technically ended things."

"So, you're hung up on Hanna, but you haven't let your other two lovers know that you have sincere feelings for someone else?"

I picked up my beer, stared down into it. It wasn't just the hassle of going through the awkward let's-end-this conversation with Kitty and Kristy. If I was honest with myself, it was also partly about the security of the distraction they could provide if this whole thing with Hanna went downhill. That sounded like a dick move even to me.

"Not yet," I admitted. "It's all so casual. Who knows if a conversation is really needed?"

Chloe leaned forward, setting her bottle down and waiting until I looked her in the eye. "Will, I love you. I really do. You are going to be a part of our wedding; you will be a part of our family. I want the best things in the world to happen to you." She narrowed her eyes at me, and I felt my balls crawl up into my body. "But I still wouldn't tell a girlfriend of mine to take a chance with you. I'd tell her she should let you fuck her brains out, but keep her emotions out of it because you are a clueless little shit."

I winced, kind of chuckled, and shook my head. "That's refreshingly honest."

"I'm being serious. Yes, you're always open with your sex buddies. No, you don't have anything to hide. But what's your thing against relationships?"

Throwing my hands in the air, I said, "I don't have anything against relationships!"

Sara jumped in, saying, "You assume from day one that you won't want anything more than convenient sex," before continuing more gently, "and let me tell you, from a woman's point of view? When you're younger you want the boy who knows how to play the game but when you're older you want the man who knows when it's not a game anymore. *You* don't even know that yet, and you're, what? Thirty-one? Hanna may be young in years, but she's an old soul, and she's going to quickly figure out that your model isn't the right one for her. You're teaching Hanna how to balance multiple lovers but you should be teaching her what it feels like to be *loved*."

I smiled at her, and then rubbed my face with both hands, groaning, "Did you guys come over here to lecture me?"

Sara said, "No," at the same time that Chloe said, "Yes."

Finally, Sara laughed and said, "Yes." She leaned

forward to put her hand on my knee. "You're just so clueless, Will. You're like our adorable, derpy mascot."

"That is awful," I said, laughing. "Don't ever repeat that."

We all turned back to the basketball game. It wasn't awkward. I didn't feel defensive. I knew they were right; I just wasn't sure what I could actually do about any of it, seeing as how Hanna was out with fucking *Dylan*. It was fantastic for me to be able to admit that I wanted more with her, and that I didn't want her out with another guy, but it one hundred percent did not matter as long as Hanna and I were on different pages about it. And the truth was, I wanted her to fuck only me, but I didn't really want things between us to change.

Did I?

I picked up my phone, checking to see if I'd somehow missed a text from her in the past two minutes.

"Jesus, Will. Just fucking *text* her!" Chloe said, throwing a napkin at me.

I stood abruptly, less to comply with Chloe's bossy shit and more to just *move*. What was Hanna doing right now? Where were they? It was almost nine. Shouldn't they be done with dinner by now?

Actually, given his track record, she was probably at home . . . unless they were at his place?

I felt my eyes go wide. Was it possible she was in his bed? Having sex with him? I closed them just as fast, jaw bulging as I remembered how she felt beneath me, her curves, the feeling of her knees pressed to my sides. And to think she might be with that weaselly kid? *Naked?*

Fuck that.

Turning, I walked down the hall toward my bedroom, stopping when my phone buzzed in my palm. I don't think even my knee-jerk reflex was as fast as my reaction to the lit screen. But it was only Max.

Your girl is here at the restaurant with me and Ben. Nicely done on the Project Hanna, Will. She looks bloody hot.

I groaned, leaning against the wall in my hallway as I typed. Is she kissing the kid?

No, Max replied. She keeps checking her phone though. Stop texting her, you little shit. She's "exploring life" right now, remember.

Ignoring his obvious attempt to rile me, I stared at the text, reading it again, and again. I knew I was the only person who regularly texted Hanna, and I hadn't sent her anything all night. Was it possible she was checking her phone as obsessively as I'd been checking mine?

I moved down the hall, slipping into the bathroom under the ruse of actually using it for its intended purpose and instead sitting on the edge of my tub. It *wasn't* a game with her. Sara was wrong there; I *knew* it wasn't a game. It wasn't even fun right now. My time away from Hanna oscillated wildly between exhilaration and obsessive anxiety. Is this what it was about? Taking this kind of risk, opening up and gambling on someone else's ability to tread carefully with your feelings?

My thumbs hovered over the letters for several pounding heartbeats and then I typed a single line, reading it over, and over, checking it for diction, tone, and the overall *no-big-deal-I'm-not-obsessing-about-your-night-or-anything* vibe of it. Finally, I closed my eyes, and hit SEND.

Chapter Nine

I was not going to text Will.

". . . and then maybe live abroad someday . . ."

I was not going to text Will.

". . . maybe Germany. Or, maybe Turkey . . ."

I blinked back to the conversation and nodded to Dylan, who sat opposite me and who had basically trekked the entire globe during our conversation. "That sounds really exciting," I said, smile stretched wide across my face.

He looked down to the linen tablecloth, cheeks slightly pink. Okay, so he was pretty cute. Like a puppy. "I used to think I'd want to live in Brazil," he continued. "But I love visiting there so much, I don't want it to ever feel familiar, you know?"

I nodded again, doing my best to pay attention

and rein in my thoughts, to focus on my date and not the fact that my phone had been silent all night.

The restaurant Dylan had chosen was nice, not overly romantic but cozy. Soft lighting, wide windows, nothing heavy or too serious. Nothing that screamed *date*. I'd had the halibut; Dylan had ordered a steak. His plate was practically empty; I'd hardly touched mine.

What had he been saying? A summer in Brazil? "How many languages did you say you spoke again?" I asked, hoping I was close enough to the mark.

I must have been because he smiled, obviously pleased I'd remembered this detail. Or at least that such a detail existed.

"Three."

I sat back a little, genuinely impressed. "Wow, that's . . . that's really amazing, Dylan."

And that wasn't even stretching the truth. He *was* amazing. Dylan was good-looking and smart and everything an intelligent girl would be looking for. But when the waiter stopped at our table to refill our drinks, none of those things kept me from glancing quickly down to my phone again, and frowning at the blank screen.

No messages, no missed calls—nothing. Damn.

I swiped a finger over Will's name, and reread a few of his texts from earlier in the day. Random thought: I'd like to see you stoned. Pot amplifies personality traits so you'd probably talk so much your head would explode, though I don't know how you could possibly say even crazier things than you do now.

And another: Just saw you on 81st and Amsterdam. I was in a cab with Max and watched you cross the street in front of us. Were you wearing panties under that skirt? I plan on filing that away in the old spankbank so whatever you do, just say no.

The time stamp on his last message was just after one this afternoon, almost six hours ago. I scrolled through a few more before pressing the box to type, my thumb hovering over the keyboard. What could he possibly be doing? The phrase *or who* crept into my thoughts and I felt my frown deepen.

I started typing out a message and deleted it just as quickly. *I will not text Will,* I reminded myself. *I will not text Will. Ninja. Secret agent. Get the secrets, and get out unharmed.*

"Hanna?"

I looked up again; Dylan was watching me.

"Hmm?"

His brows drew together for a moment before he laughed a small, uncertain sound. "Are you okay tonight? You seem a bit distracted."

"Yeah," I said, horrified to have been caught. I lifted the phone from my lap. "Just waiting for a text from my mom," I lied. Horribly.

"But everything's good?"

"Absolutely."

With a small, relieved sigh, Dylan pushed his plate away and leaned forward, resting his forearms on the table. "So what about you? I feel like I've done nothing but talk. Tell me about the research you're doing." For the first time all night, I felt the grip on my phone lessen. This I could do. Talk about my work and school and science? Hell yes.

We'd just finished dessert and my explanation of how I was collaborating with another lab in our department to engineer vaccines for *Trypansoma cruzi* when I felt a tap on my shoulder, and turned to see Max standing behind me.

"Hey!" I said, surprised to see him here.

He was about ten feet tall and yet when he bent to kiss my cheek, he didn't look awkward at all. "Hanna, you look absolutely smashing tonight."

Damn. That accent was going to kill me dead. I smiled. "Well, you can pass your compliments to Sara; she's actually the one who picked out this dress."

I wouldn't have thought it possible for him to get even more attractive, but the proud grin that stretched across his face did just that. "I'll do that. And who is this?" he said, turning to Dylan.

"Oh!" I said, turning back to my date. "Sorry, Max, this is Dylan Nakamura. Dylan, this is Max Stella, my friend Will's business partner." The two men shook hands and chatted for a moment, and I had to talk myself out of asking about Will. I was on a date, after all. I shouldn't be thinking of him in the first place.

"Well, I'll just leave you two to it, then," Max said.

"Tell Sara I said hi."

"Absolutely. Enjoy the rest of your evening."

I watched Max walk back to his table, where a group of men were waiting for him. I wondered if he was out for a business dinner, and if so, why hadn't Will gone with him? I realized I didn't know much about his job, but didn't they do this kind of stuff together?

A few minutes later, just as the bill came, my phone vibrated in my lap.

How's your night, Plum?

I closed my eyes, feeling that word vibrate through me like an electrical current. I thought back on the last time he'd called me that and felt my insides liquefy.

Fine. Max is here, did you send him to check on me?

Ha! As if he'd ever do that for me. And he just messaged. Said you look pretty hot tonight.

I'd never known I was much of a blusher before Will, but I felt the heat as it flashed through my cheeks. He looked pretty hot himself.

Not funny, Hanna.

You home? I hit SEND and then held my breath. What would I do if he said no?

Yes.

I was really going to have a talk with myself; knowing Will was home and texting me should not have made me quite so damn happy. Running to-morrow? I asked.

Of course.

Quickly wiping the smile from my face before Dylan noticed, I tucked my phone away. Will was home and I could rest easy and attempt to enjoy the rest of my night.

———

"So how was your date?" he asked, stretching beside me.

"Good," I said. "Fine."

"Fine?"

"Yeah." I shrugged, unable to get it up for a more enthusiastic response. "Fine," I said again. "Good." I felt decidedly worse about my Will codependency this morning than I did last night. I would need to get my act together and remember: *Secret agent. Like a Ninja. Learn from the best.*

He shook his head. "What a glowing review."

I didn't respond, instead walking to retrieve the water bottle I'd stowed against a nearby tree. It was cold—so cold the water had turned to slush and sloshed around as I tried to force it open. We were at the post-workout stage of our run, where Will would give me a pep talk and say something inappropriate about my boobs, and I would complain about the cold or the lack of easily accessible bathrooms in Manhattan.

And I really wasn't sure I wanted to have this conversation today, or admit that while I actually liked Dylan, I didn't daydream about kissing him or sucking on his neck or watching him come on my hip, like I did a certain someone else. I didn't want to tell him I was constantly distracted on our dates and having a hard time becoming invested. And I also refused to admit that I was failing at this whole dating thing, and might never learn how to keep things casual, enjoy life, be young, and experience things the way Will could.

He ducked to meet my eyes and I registered that he was repeating a question. "What time did you get back?"

"A little after nine, I think?"

"Nine?" he said, laughing. "Again?"

"Maybe a little later. Why is that so funny?"

"Two dates in a row end at nine o'clock? Is he your grandfather? Did he take you out for the early bird special?"

"For your information I had to run into lab early this morning. And what about your wild night, Player? Partake in any orgies? Maybe a rave or two?" I asked, intent on changing the subject.

"Kind of did the Fight Club thing," he said, scratching his jaw. "Except without the guys or the punching." At my confused stare, he clarified, "Basically, I had takeout with Chloe and Sara at my place. Hey, you sore today?"

I immediately remembered the delicious ache his fingers had left me with after Denny's party, and the way my pelvic bone felt almost bruised from grinding against him on the floor of his apartment.

"Sore?" I repeated, blinking quickly back to him.

He smiled knowingly. "Sore from yesterday's *run*. Jesus, Hanna. Get your mind out of the gutter. You were home by nine—what else *could* I possibly have been talking about?"

I took another pull from my water bottle, and winced at the cold on my teeth. "I'm good."

"Another rule, Plum. You can only use the word *good* so many times in a conversation before it becomes disingenuous. Find better adjectives to describe your state of mind post-dates."

I wasn't exactly sure how to handle Will this morning. He seemed a little edgy. I'd thought I had him figured, but my thoughts, too, seemed to be all over the place, a growing problem when we were together. Or judging by last night, when we were apart, too. Did he care at *all* that I'd been out with Dylan?

Did I want him to care?

Ugh. This dating thing was way too complicated, and I wasn't even sure whether Will and I were technically dating. It seemed to be one of the only questions I *couldn't* ask him.

"Well," he said, sliding his gaze to me with a teasing little smile. "Just so you're clear on the meaning of the word 'dating', maybe you should go out with someone else. Just to see how it all works. What about another one of the guys at the party? Aaron? Or Hau?"

"Hau has a girlfriend. Aaron . . ."

He nodded encouragingly. "He seemed pretty fit."

"He's fit," I agreed, hedging. "But, he's sort of . . . SN2?"

Will's brows pulled together in confusion. "'SN2'?"

"*You* know," I said, waving my hands awkwardly. "Like when the C-X bond is broken, and the nucleophile attacks the carbon at one hundred-eighty degrees to the leaving group?" The words came out in a breathless rush.

"Oh, my God. Did you just use an O-chem reference to tell me Aaron looks better from the back than the front?"

I groaned and looked away. "I think I just broke some sort of nerd record."

"No, that was amazing," he said, sounding genuinely awed. "I wish I thought of that about ten years ago." His mouth turned down at the corners when he considered this. "But honestly, it's awesome when you say it. If I said it, I would just sound like a giant dick."

I swallowed, most definitely *not* glancing down at his shorts.

Despite the dropping temperatures and early hour, more people than usual had decided to brave the cold. A cute pair of college guys kicked a soccer ball back and forth, dark beanies pulled down over each of their heads and Styrofoam cups of rapidly cooling coffee in the grass nearby. A woman with a giant stroller power-walked by us, and a handful of others ran along the various trails. I looked over just in time to see Will bend in front of me, reaching to tie his shoe.

"I've got to hand it to you. I'm really impressed with how hard you're working," he said to me over his shoulder.

"Yeah," I mumbled, moving to stretch my hamstrings the way he'd taught me, and most definitely not look at his ass. "Hard."

"What was that?"

"Hard work," I repeated. "Really hard."

He straightened and I followed the movement, forcing myself to blink away before he turned.

"Not going to lie to you," he said, stretching his back. "I was surprised you didn't punk out that first week."

I should have glared and been annoyed that he'd assumed I'd give up so quickly, but instead I nodded, attempting to look pretty much everywhere other than that strip of stomach that showed when he stretched his arms over his head or the line of muscle that cut down both sides of his abdomen.

"Might even place in the top fifty at the race if you keep it up."

My eyes darted across that small sliver of skin, and the landscape of muscle beneath it. I swallowed, immediately recalling what it felt like under my fingertips. "Definitely keeping it up," I mumbled, giving up and staring outright at his exposed skin.

Clearing my throat, I turned away from him and began walking back down the trail because honestly, that body was just *obscene*.

"So what time's your date tonight?" he asked, jogging to catch up.

"Tomorrow," I said.

He laughed beside me. "Okay, what time's your date *tomorrow*?"

"Um . . . six?" I scrunched my nose, trying to remember. "No, eight."

"Shouldn't you be sure?"

I slid my eyes to him, giving a guilty smile. "Probably."

"Are you excited?"

I shrugged. "I guess."

Laughing, he wrapped his arm around my shoulder. "What does he do again?"

"Drosophila stuff," I mumbled. He'd given me an opening to talk about science and I couldn't even get it up for that this morning. I was a mess.

"A genetics man!" he said in a playfully booming voice. "Thomas Hunt Morgan gave us the chromosome, and now labs across the country give other labs tiny, escapee fruit flies all over the building." He was trying to be jovial, but his voice was so deep and sexual, even when he geeked out, he only made my bones rattle, my limbs go all liquid. "And Dylan is nice? Funny? Great in bed?"

"Sure."

Will stopped, his look thunderous. *"Sure?"*

I looked up at him. "I mean, of course he is." And then his words sunk in. "Well, except the great in bed part. I haven't sampled the goods."

Will turned to keep walking, staying silent, and I chanced another look over at him. "Speaking of which, can I ask you a question?"

He glanced at me from the corner of his eye, wary. "Yes," he said slowly.

"What exactly is third-date etiquette? I googled it—"

"You *googled* it?"

"*Yes,* and the consensus seems to be that the third date is the sex date."

He stopped and I had to turn to face him. His face had gone red. "Is he pressuring you to have sex?"

"What?" I stared at him, bewildered. Where did he get that idea? "Of course not."

"Then why are you asking about sex?"

"Calm down," I said. "I can wonder what the expectations are without him having to be pushy about it. Good Lord, Will, I just want to be *prepared*."

He exhaled and shook his head. "You drive me insane sometimes."

"Likewise." I stared off into the distance, thinking out loud. "It just seems there's like some sort of progression chart. Dates one and two seemed pretty much the same. But how does one go from that to sex date? A cheat sheet would definitely make this less confusing."

"You don't need a cheat sheet. Jesus." He pulled his beanie from his head, pushed his hair back, I could practically see the wheels turning in his head. "Okay, so . . . the first date is sort of like the interview. He's scanned your resume"—he looked at me meaningfully and lifted his brows, eyes moving directly to my chest—"and now it's time to see if you live up to that. There's the field trip portion, the Q and A, the *could this person be a serial killer?* thought process, and of course, the *do I want to have sex with this person?* elimination decision. And let's be honest, if a man has asked you out he already wants to have sex with you."

"Okay," I said, eyeing him skeptically. I tried to imagine Will in this scenario: meeting a woman, taking her out, deciding if he wants to have sex with her or not. I was ninety-seven percent sure I didn't like it. "And date two?"

"Well, the second date is the callback. You've passed the preliminary screening—so the other party obviously likes what you bring to the table—and now it's time to follow up. To take it to human resources and see if your charming answers and sparkling personality were all just a fluke. And also to see if they still want to have sex with you. Which again . . ." he said, and shrugged as if to say *duh*.

"And the third date?" I asked.

"Well, this is where shit gets real. You've gone out twice and obviously still like the other person; they've met all your requirements so this is where it's all put to the test. You're compatible on some level and usually this is where you get naked, to see if you can 'work well together.' Guys usually up the stakes: flowers, compliments, romantic restaurant."

"So . . . sex."

"Sometimes. But not always," he stressed. "You don't have to do anything you don't want to, Hanna. *Ever*. I will remove the balls of any man who pressures you."

My insides went warm and fluttery. My brothers had said almost the same thing to me on different occasions and I can assure you, it sounded very different coming out of Will Sumner's mouth. "I know that."

"Do you *want* to have sex with him?" he asked, attempting to sound casual but failing miserably. He couldn't even look at me, and instead stared down where he was pulling at a string in the hem of his shirt. I felt a shiver move down my spine at the hint that he wasn't entirely okay with this.

I took a deep breath, thought about it. My first instinct was to rush to an automatic no, but instead, I just shrugged, noncommittal. Dylan was cute and I'd let him kiss me good night at my doorstep, but it was *nothing* compared to what I'd experienced with Will. And that was one hundred percent of my problem. I was pretty sure the reason Will made me feel good was that he was experienced. But that was exactly why he was off-limits.

"Honestly," I admitted. "I'm not even sure. I guess I'll just have to see how I feel when the time comes."

Any doubts I may have had about Will's third-date protocol were quickly put to rest as soon as Dylan and I stepped inside the restaurant I had chosen.

Dylan had wanted to take me somewhere I'd never been before—not hard considering I'd been in New York three years and barely left the lab to eat. He smiled proudly when the cab pulled up and deposited us at Daniel, at Park and Sixty-fifth.

If I'd been asked to draw you a picture of a romantic eatery, it would have looked exactly like this: cream walls, silvery grays and chocolate browns, arches and Grecian columns that skirted the main dining area. Round tables draped in sumptuous linens, vases of greenery everywhere and all of it set beneath giant glass light fixtures. The complete opposite of our second-date place. The stakes had been raised.

I was not prepared.

Dinner started off well enough. We selected appetizers and Dylan ordered a bottle of wine, but it had gone downhill from there. I'd promised myself that I wouldn't text Will but near the end when Dylan excused himself to go to the bathroom, I caved. I think I'm failing third date 101.

He answered almost immediately. What? Impossible. Have you seen your teacher?

He ordered some expensive wine and then seemed insulted when I didn't want any. You never care that I don't drink, I typed.

The icon appeared to show that he'd entered text—quite a bit of it if the amount of time it took was any indication—so I waited and looked around to make sure Dylan wasn't headed back my way.

That's because I'm a genius and can do basic math: I pour you half a glass, you pretend to drink it all night, and so the rest of the bottle's for me. Boom, smartest man alive.

Pretty sure he doesn't see it that way, I typed.

So tell him you're much more fun when you're actually awake and not drooling into your soup. Why are you texting me, btw? Where's Prince Charming?

Bathroom. We're leaving.

A full minute elapsed before he answered, Oh?

Yeah, my place. He's coming back, I'll let you know how it goes.

⌐━━━━⌐

The ride back to my apartment was awkward. Stupid dating rules and expectations and Google, and stupid Will for getting in my head in the first place.

I didn't understand what was happening. I didn't really *want* Will. Will had a program of lovers and a shady past. Will didn't want attachments or relationships, and I at least wanted to be open to it. Will wasn't an option or part of the plan. I liked sex; I wanted to do it with another person again soon. Wasn't this how it happened? Boy meets girl, girl likes boy, girl decides to let boy in her pants. I was definitely ready to let someone into my pants. So where was the rush, the feeling of heat climbing up my legs and settling in my stomach, the ache I'd felt at the very *idea* of pulling Will into that bedroom? The feeling that had sent me out into the snow at 3 a.m. and the thought that I might explode the moment his hands found my skin?

I most certainly didn't feel that now.

The snow had just started to fall outside by the time we reached my building. Upstairs in my apartment, I switched on the lamp and Dylan hovered near the front door awkwardly for a moment before I invited him in. I was moving on autopilot. My stomach was in knots and the white noise in my head was so loud I wanted to turn on the most obnoxious music I could find just to block it out.

Should I? Shouldn't I? Do I even want to?

I offered him a nightcap—I actually said "nightcap"—to which he said yes. I moved to the kitchen, pulled down some glasses and poured a tiny bit for me, a large drink for him, hoping maybe it would make him sleepy. I turned to hand him his glass and was surprised to find him right there, completely in my space. A strange sense of wrongness seeped into my chest.

Dylan wordlessly took the glass from my hand and set it back on the counter. Soft fingertips brushed along my cheeks, over my nose. He took my face in his hands. His first kiss was tentative, slow and exploring. A small peck before he came back in for another. I closed my eyes tight at the first touch of his tongue, felt the racing of my heart and wished it had something to do with longing and lust, and not this clawing sense of panic that had started to build in my throat.

His lips were too soft and tentative. Pillow lips. His breath tasted like potatoes. I was aware of the ticking clock above the stove, the sound of someone yelling in an apartment nearby. Did I notice anything when I kissed Will? I noticed the way he smelled, the way his skin felt beneath my fingertips and the way it felt like I might explode if he didn't touch me *there* and deeper. But never anything as commonplace as the garbage trucks rumbling outside.

"What's wrong?" Dylan said, taking a step back. I touched my lips; they felt fine, not swollen or abused. Not thoroughly ruined.

"I don't think this is going to work," I said.

He was quiet for a moment, eyes searching mine, obviously confused. "But I thought—"

"I know," I said. "I'm sorry."

He nodded, taking another step back before running his hands through his hair. "I guess . . . If this is about Will, well, tell him congratulations."

I closed the door behind Dylan and turned, pressing my back to the cool wood. My phone felt heavy and leaden in my pocket and I pulled it out, found the name of He Who Effectively Hijacked My Brain, and started to type.

I started and erased a dozen different messages before finally stopping on one. I typed it and waited just a moment before I pressed SEND.

Where are you

CHAPTER TEN

Honestly, I had no idea what I was doing. I was walking—walking like I had somewhere to be. But in reality, I didn't have to be anywhere, and I *really* didn't need to be headed directly to Hanna's apartment building.

```
Yeah, my place. He's coming back,
I'll let you know how it goes.
```

My hands formed fists at the memory of the text—the words were burned onto my brain—and the image of her in there, with Dylan. It made my chest literally ache. And I kind of wanted to break everything I saw.

It was cold; so cold I could see my breath, and my fingertips were growing numb even shoved deep into my pockets. As soon as I got her text, I'd run out of the house, no gloves, a too-light jacket, and running shoes, no socks.

For the span of seven city blocks, I was furious with her for doing this to me. I'd been fine until she came fumbling into my life with her chatterbox mouth and mischievous eyes. I'd been *fine* before she pushed her way into my easy routine, and I half wanted Dylan to get the fuck out of her apartment so I could go upstairs and tell her what a pain in the ass she was, how pissed I was at her for pulling the very stable, predictable ground out from under me.

But as I approached, and saw lights on in her window, saw the shadows of bodies upright and moving around, I felt only relief that she wasn't already prone on her bed, beneath him.

Pulling my hat farther down over my head, I growled through my teeth, looking along the street for a coffee shop, or something else to do. But there were only more apartment buildings, retail shops that had long since closed, and, in the distance, a little bar. The last thing I needed right now was alcohol. And if I was two blocks away from her apartment, then I might as well be home.

How long would I wait here? Until she texted me again? Until morning, when they emerged together, rumpled and smiling over their shared memories of the night before—of Hanna's perfection and Dylan's lame inexperience?

I groaned, looking up just in time to see a man leaving the apartment building, head bent into the wind, collar up. My heart tripped. It was definitely Dylan, and although my veins filled with the warm hum of relief, the fact that I could so easily recognize him from a distance made me feel like the creepiest asshole of all time. I waited to see if he was going to return, but he kept moving down the block, never slowing his pace.

That's it, I told myself. *You've crossed a line and need to find your way back to the other side.*

But what if she needed me? I should probably stay to make sure she was okay before walking home. I stared at my phone, brows drawn. If I left here, I was going for a run. I didn't care that it was almost eleven at night and freezing out; I was going to run for fucking miles. I was so buzzed with relief, and frustration, and nervous energy that I could barely steady my thumb long enough to click on the icon and open our text thread.

I exhaled when I saw that she was already typing something to me.

It felt like minutes, entire *minutes* during which I gripped my phone, staring intently and waiting for her message to appear. Finally it delivered, and instead of the paragraphs I was expecting, it said only, Where are you

I laughed, dragging my hand through my hair, and took a deep breath. OK, don't kill me, I typed. I'm outside your apartment.

────

Hanna came out of the building wearing a heavy down jacket over a silky blue dress, bare legs, and Kermit the

Frog slippers. She shuffled toward me and I couldn't move, could barely breathe.

"What are you doing here?" she asked, stopping in front of where I sat, perched on a fire hydrant.

"I don't know," I murmured. I reached for her, pulling her closer and spreading my hands over her hips.

She winced a little when I squeezed—*what the fuck is going on with me?*—but instead of stepping away, she leaned closer. "Will."

"Yeah?" I asked, finally looking up at her face. She was fucking *beautiful*. She'd put on the smallest amount of makeup, had let her hair dry in soft, loose curls. Her eyes were heavy with the same look I'd seen when I'd been braced over her on the floor of my living room, or when I'd slid my fingers over the soft rise of her clit. When my attention focused on her mouth, her tongue peeked out, wetting her lips.

"I *really* need to know why you're here."

Shrugging, I leaned forward, resting my forehead against her collarbone. "I wasn't sure you were really into him, and it was bothering me knowing he came back here with you."

She slid her fingers under the collar of my jacket, stroking the back of my neck. "I think Dylan thought we were going to have sex tonight."

Without meaning to, I dug my fingers deeper into the flesh just above her hips. "I'm sure he did," I mumbled.

"But . . . and I don't know how to handle this, because it should be easy, right? It should be easy to enjoy being with people I like. I mean, I find him attractive. I have fun with him! He's nice, and thoughtful. He's funny, and he's good-looking."

I remained silent, trying not to howl.

"But when he kissed me? I didn't feel lost in him the way I get lost in you."

Pulling back, I looked up at her face. She shrugged, looking almost apologetic. "He was nice to me tonight," she whispered.

"Good."

"And he didn't even seem mad when I asked him to go."

"*Good,* Hanna. If he gave you grief I swear to God—"

"*Will.*"

I closed my mouth, calmed by her interruption, and waiting to hear what she needed. I would do anything she wanted, even if she asked me to crawl. If she asked me to leave, I would. If she asked me to help her zip her jacket, I'd do that, too.

"Come upstairs with me?"

My heart climbed into my throat. I watched her for a few seconds more, but she didn't take it back by breaking eye contact, or laughing at herself. She just studied me, waiting for my answer. I stood, and she moved back to give me space, but not too much space, because I was almost pressed against her once I was upright. She ran her hands down my sides, letting them come to rest on my hips.

"If I go up with you . . ." I started.

She was already nodding. "I know."

"I don't know if I can be slow."

Her eyes darkened and she pressed against me. "I *know*."

———

A light was out on one side of the elevator, casting the space in a strange half shadow. Hanna leaned into the corner, watching me from where she stood at the dark end.

"What are you thinking?" she asked. Always such a little scientist, trying to dissect me.

I was thinking *everything*: wanting everything, and panicking, wondering if I was cutting the last thread of control I had over my emotions. I was thinking about what I was going to do to this woman when we got up to her bed. "A lot of things."

Even in the shadows, I could see her smile. "You want to be more specific?"

"I don't like that that guy came up to your apartment tonight."

She tilted her head, assessing me. "I thought that was part of dating. Sometimes guys will come up to my apartment."

"I get that," I murmured. "But you did ask what I was thinking. I'm telling you."

"He's a nice guy."

"I'm sure he is. He can be a nice guy who doesn't get to kiss you."

She stood up a little straighter. "Are you *jealous*?"

I stared at her, nodded.

"Of *Dylan*?"

"I don't relish the thought of anyone else having you."

"But all this time you're still seeing Kitty and Kristy."

I didn't bother to correct her yet. "What were you thinking when you were with him tonight?"

Her smile faded a little. "I was mostly thinking about you. Wondering if you were with someone."

"I wasn't with anyone tonight."

This seemed to throw her and she fell silent for what felt like forever. We reached her floor, the doors opened, hovered, and then closed with a small ding. The elevator car fell quiet and wouldn't move again until it was called.

"Why?" she asked. "It's Saturday. That's your night with Kristy."

"Why do you even *know* that?" I asked, tamping down the white-hot frustration with whoever told her this information. "And I was with you the last *two* Saturdays."

She looked down at her feet, thinking for a beat, and then back at me. "Tonight, I thought about what I wanted you to do to me," she said, adding, "and what I wanted to do to *you*. And how I didn't want any of those things with Dylan."

I took a step closer into the darkness, ran a hand up her side and over the curve of her breast. "Tell me what you want now. Tell me what you're ready for me to do."

I could feel the rise and fall of her chest as she breathed faster. I ran the pad of my thumb over the tight peak of her nipple.

"You go down on me," she said, voice shaking a little. "You do it until I come."

"Obviously," I whispered, laughing a little. "When I do it, you'll come more than once."

Her lips parted, and she wrapped her hand around my wrist, pressing my palm more firmly against her breast. "You lean over me on the couch, jerking off, and come on my chest."

I was already so hard and *fuck*, that was a good visual. "What else?"

Shaking her head, she finally shrugged and looked away. "*Everything* else. Sex in all kinds of places on my body. How you like me to bite you, and how good it feels to do it. We're having sex and I'm doing everything you want and it isn't just good for me, it's good for you, too."

I lost my words for a beat, surprised by this. "Does that worry you? That I'm somehow *humoring* you?"

She looked up, met my eyes. "Of *course*, Will."

I stepped even closer so I was pressed against her and she had to tilt her head back to maintain eye contact. Angling my hips, I pushed the rigid shape of my erection into her stomach.

"Hanna. I don't know if I've ever wanted something

more than I want you. I really don't think I have," I said. "I think about just kissing you, for fucking *hours*. Do you know that kind of kissing? Where it's enough for so long you don't even think of doing anything else?"

She shook her head, breath coming out against my neck in short, sharp bursts.

"I don't know about that kind of kissing, either, because I've never wanted just that before."

Hanna slid her hands under my jacket and beneath my shirt. Her hands were warm, and the muscles of my abdomen jumped and tensed beneath her fingers.

"I think about having you spread over my face," I said. "And taking you on the floor just inside my apartment because I can't wait long enough to get us anywhere more comfortable. I don't want to be with anyone else lately, and it means I spend an awful lot of time going for runs at random hours, or with my hand on my own dick wishing it was yours instead."

"Let's get out of the elevator," she said, pushing me gently through the opening doors and into the hallway.

She fumbled slightly with the key to her place and my hands shook as I reached for her sides, ran my palms from her waist to her hips. It took every ounce of self-control I had left to not take it from her and shove it into the lock myself.

When she finally got the door open, I pushed her inside, slamming it closed behind us and pressing her into the wall just a few steps in. I bent, sucking her neck, her jaw, running my hands under the skirt of her dress to feel the smooth skin of her thighs.

"You're going to have to tell me to stop if I move too fast."

Her hands shook as she slid them into my hair, dug her nails into my scalp. "I won't."

I kissed up her chin to her mouth, sucking and licking, tasting every millimeter of her soft lips and sweet hungry tongue. I wanted her to lick me, suck marks into my chest and feel the bite of her teeth on my hips, my thighs, my fingers. I felt a little like a criminal unchained, sucking and biting at her, stepping away from her only long enough to pull our jackets off, tug my own shirt over my head, unzip her dress, and push it to the floor. With a flick of my fingers her bra came undone and she shrugged out of it, stepping into my arms. Her breasts pressed against my skin and I just wanted to rub on her, wild and fucking *inside* her already.

She pushed me back, taking my hand and leading me down the hall to her bedroom, throwing me a little smile over her shoulder.

Her room was tidy, sparse. A king bed was positioned against one wall, which, other than Hanna, was basically all I saw. She stood in only her panties, hair loose and soft around her shoulders as she looked from my chest, up my neck, to my face.

The room seemed to tick in the silence.

"I've thought about this so many times," she said, hands running up my stomach and then lightly tickling through the hair on my chest. She traced the patterns of the tattoo on my left shoulder, trailed her fingers down my arm. "God, it feels like I've been thinking about this forever. But actually having you here . . . I'm nervous."

"You have no reason to be nervous."

"It helps me when you tell me what to do," she admitted in a small voice.

I cupped her breast, lifting it and bending my head to suck the tight peak into my mouth. She gasped, hands sliding into my hair. I smiled into a sharp bite at the full curve below her nipple. "You could start by taking off my pants."

She unfastened my belt, tugged the buttons free on my jeans. I'd grown obsessed with the memory of the way her hands shook when she was excited like this, a little nervous, too. I studied her almost-naked body in the dim street light filtering in from outside: her neck and breasts, the dip of her waist, curved hips and long, soft legs. I reached forward, ran two fingers down her navel and between her thighs, gliding over the fabric of her underwear.

Sliding a knuckle beneath the lace and through the heady slickness there, I whispered, "I love your skin, love feeling your wet."

"Step out of your pants," she said, coyly. "You can touch me all night."

I blinked, realizing my jeans were pooled around my ankles and I stood only in my boxers. She hadn't taken those off; whether she was nervous still, or just wanted one more chance to remove something, it was all fine with me. I pulled my feet free and walked her backward to her bed, urging her down. She inched back, pushing toward the headboard as I crawled over her. Hanna's gray eyes were wide and clear—my thrilled, breathless prey.

Her panties were light blue, accentuating the creamy color of her skin, making her look like she was made of blown glass. Only the tiny freckle on her navel hinted that she was even remotely real.

"Did you wear these for him?" I asked before my brain had time to think better of it.

She looked down at the lace, and I moved my eyes up to her full, plump breasts as she said, "I didn't even let him take my shirt off. So, I don't think I wore them for him."

I kissed down her belly to the elastic hem of her underwear. Hanna had never been timid, or flighty, but this was all new. She was propped on her elbows, watching. Beneath where I was braced over her, she was trembling, her heart beating so fast I could see the trip of her pulse in her neck. This didn't feel like our standard game of How to Play Sexbomb, didn't have that veneer. This felt too real, and Hanna looked too perfect lying almost naked in front of me. I'd kick my own ass for an eternity if I ever fucked this up. "Well, then I'll pretend that you wore them for me."

"Maybe I did."

I pulled at the elastic with my teeth, releasing it with a sharp snap against her hip. "And I'll pretend that whether you're naked or clothed, you're always thinking about me."

She looked up at me, gray eyes wide and searching. "Lately, I think I am. Does that worry you?"

Looking up the length of her body, I asked, "Why would it worry me?"

"I know what this is about, Will. I don't expect you to be anything you're not."

I had no idea what she meant; in truth I had no idea what this could or couldn't be, and for once I didn't want to define it before it even started. Inching up so my face hovered just over hers, I bent to kiss her, whispering, "I don't know where to start."

I felt wild and a little rough, wanting to eat her and fuck her and feel those lips around me. I had a flash of fear that this was all a fleeting moment, a single night, and I had to find a way to condense everything into a few hours. "I'm not going to let you sleep."

Her eyes widened, and she gave me a tiny smile. "I don't want to sleep." Tilting her head, she said, "And start with the first thing I told you in the elevator."

I kissed my way down her neck, chest, ribs, stomach. Every inch of her was tight and smooth and twitching under my lips, *wanting*. She never closed her eyes, never once. I'd been with women who watched, but it had never felt like this, so fucking intimate and connected.

As I got closer to the space between her legs, I could see her muscles tense, heard her breath hitch. I turned my head, sucked on her inner thigh. "I'm going to lose my fucking *mind* with my mouth on you."

"Will, tell me what to do," she said, her voice tight. "I've never . . ."

"I know. You're perfect," I told her. "You like watching?"

She nodded.

"Why, Plum? Why do you watch everything I do?"

She hesitated, holding back some truth in a little swallow. "You know how to . . ." She let the words trail away, ending the thought with a one-shouldered shrug.

"You mean you like to watch me because I know how to make you come?"

She nodded again, eyes widening as I pulled at her panties, sliding them down over her hips.

"You can make yourself come with your hand. Do you watch your hand when you touch yourself?"

"No."

I pulled her underwear the rest of the way down her legs, tossing them behind me and onto the floor before returning to the stretch of mattress between her spread legs.

"You have a vibrator?"

She nodded, eyes dazed.

"*That* can make you come. Does looking at your vibrator make you this wet?" I dipped a finger inside, raising myself up and over her again, slipping the same fingertip into her mouth. She moaned, sucking hard and pulling me closer to kiss her instead. Her lips tasted like sex and heat and, *fuck,* I wanted to taste her directly. "Is it because you like watching me do this to you?"

"Will . . ."

"Don't go shy on me now." I kissed her, sucking on her bottom lip. "Are you being a little engineer, watching the mechanics of how a man would lick your pussy? Or is it the image of *my* mouth doing it?"

She ran her hands down my chest and wrapped them around my cock through my boxers, giving me a slow, hard squeeze. "I like watching *you.*"

Groaning, I managed to say, "I like when you watch me. I can't think straight when you have those crazy gray eyes on me."

"Please . . ."

"Now let go so you can watch my mouth."

"Will," she said, voice shaking.

"Yeah?"

"After this? Please don't break me."

I paused, searching her expression. She'd sounded scared, but her face was only hunger.

"I won't," I said, kissing down her neck, over her breasts, sucking, nipping. I moved farther down her body, and her thighs shook as I pushed them apart, blowing a soft stream of air across her heated flesh.

She propped herself up on her elbows again, and I gave her one more smile before dipping my head and opening my mouth over her sweet slide of skin. My eyes rolled closed at the heat of her, and I groaned, sucking gently.

With a shaky cry, her head fell back, hips arching from the bed. "Oh *God*."

I smiled into her, licking up one side and down the other before covering her clit with my tongue, circling over and over and over.

"Don't stop," she whispered.

I wouldn't. I *couldn't*. I added my fingers, sliding them lower to where she was wettest and sweetest, and the heavy drag of my touch as I pushed two fingers into her caused her to fall back, reach blindly for the headboard. As I watched, she turned her head, pulled the pillowcase between her teeth, tugging. Tiny sounds of pleading misery and pleasure slipped from her lips and I did everything I could to not let up on the intensity of it for a single fucking second.

She was right there, hovering at the edge. Fucking her with two fingers, I pushed them deep, sucking her so hard my cheeks hollowed, staring up the length of her body at her fucking perfect breasts and long neck. With a twist of my wrist, she arched off the mattress, pushing into my mouth. Hanna let out a cry again and again as she contracted around my fingers.

One.

I was so hard I was practically fucking the mattress, and I could feel the tightening of the tendons in her thighs, relished the way her sounds became strained and higher and her hands reached down, threading into my hair and *fuck,* she started to rock into me, legs wide and hips fast, unself-consciously fucking my face for several long, perfect minutes. Oral sex had never felt so much like *fucking* as it did with this woman, and I gave into it, wild and wide open, roughly devouring her.

With a cry she came again, sweet and hot, her hands pulling so hard on my scalp I thought I might come right along with her. I couldn't close my eyes, couldn't for one second look away from the sight above me on the bed. I sucked and sucked on the silk of her skin, completely fucking lost in the feel of her.

"Please," she gasped, legs shaking and eyes as dark and heavy as I'd ever seen them. She pushed up on one elbow, leaving the other pulling at my hair. "Come up here."

I pushed my boxers down, dragging the weight of my cock against her leg as I slid up her body, tasting, licking the dip of her belly button, the rise of her breasts, the tight pull of her nipples.

I wanted to fuck every part of her: the valley between her breasts and the sweet fullness of her mouth, her round backside, and her soft, capable hands. But right now I wanted only to slide into the warmth of her sex. Her legs spread wider as she reached for her bedside table, for a box of condoms. I stared at the flush blooming across her chest, absently pulling along the length of my cock, until I registered she was extending the box to me.

"Let's just start with one." I chuckled.

Pushing the box into my hand, she nodded, eyes wide and pleading.

"So get one out," I growled.

"I don't know how to put it on," she whined sweetly, fingers fumbling to open the packaging. She opened it messily, cardboard ripping wide open, and a snake of condoms spilled out onto her stomach.

I tore a single packet from the train and handed it to her, pushing the others onto the bed beside her. "It's not complicated. Take it out, roll it down my dick."

Her hands shook, and I hoped it was anticipation rather than nerves but I was quickly relieved when she reached for me, hungrily, and covered the head of my cock with latex.

But I knew immediately it was on the wrong way; it wouldn't unroll.

She realized it after several painful seconds, tossing it away with a little growl and a "damnit!" before grabbing another packet.

I was hard and swollen and so fucking ready I could feel my teeth grinding as she pulled the second condom out, studying it closely, and this time put it on the right way. Her hands were warm and her face was so close to my cock, I could feel her excited breath on my thighs.

I needed to fuck her.

She unrolled it awkwardly, fingers too tentative and light, and the whole process seemed to take an eternity. She slid it over me in tiny increments as if I were made of glass and not about to fuck her so hard the bed would drop into the apartment below us.

When she reached the base of my cock, she exhaled in relief, lying back and pushing her hips to me. But with an evil smile, I pulled the condom off and tossed it away.

Gritting my teeth through my agony, I told her, "Again. Don't be so tentative. Put the condom on my dick so I can *fuck* you."

She stared up at me, silver eyes full of confusion. And finally, they cleared as if she'd been able to hear my thoughts: *I don't want you to have a single second of uncertainty. I am as hard as I have ever been in my life, I just sucked your pussy until you were screaming, and I'm not fucking delicate.*

With her eyes on mine, she lifted the package to her teeth, tore it open, and pulled out the roll of latex. Feeling the shape, she turned it in her hand, rolled it down my length smoothly, quickly, giving me a rough squeeze at the base. She slid her hand down lower, pulled gently on my balls, and then slid her hand to my inner thigh.

"Good?" she whispered, stroking the sensitive skin there, no smile, no frown, simply needing to know.

I nodded, reaching to run my thumb over her cheek. "You're perfect."

With a relieved smile she leaned back and I followed, sliding through the heat of her sex, teasing her, teasing myself, and *fuck,* I was dizzy with how much I wanted her. My hips were tense, ready to arch and thrust, spine already itching with the need to explode inside this woman.

I was unprepared for the feeling of my bare chest fully over hers, her thighs slipping around my hips. It was too much. *Hanna* was too much.

"Put me inside you."

She gasped, slipping her hand between us; I hadn't given her much space. I was lying heavily on her, warm skin to warm skin, but she found me, guided me up until I could feel the dip of her entrance, and then she led me higher, slipping and teasing my cock over the slick rise of her clit, the soft warm folds of her sex.

"I might be rough."

She exhaled a burst of air, breathlessly telling me, "Good. Good."

Pushing onto my hands, I watched as she rubbed me over her skin. Her eyes fell closed and a small moan slipped from her. "It's just . . . it's been a while," she whispered.

I pulled my eyes up to her face, watching her lick her lips, her lashes flutter open so she could look down at the space between us, watch herself play with me.

"How long?" I asked.

She blinked back up at me again, her hand stilling between us. "About three years." Her forehead wrinkled slightly as she said, "I've had sex with five guys but probably only had sex about eight times. I *really* don't know what I'm doing, Will."

I swallowed, bending to kiss her jaw. "Maybe I won't be so rough then," I whispered, but she laughed, shaking her head.

"I don't want you to be gentle, either."

I looked at her breasts, her belly, where she held me between her legs. I wanted to feel her bare skin on my cock. I'd never in my life had sex without a condom and wanted to feel her so much it hardened me further. "I'll make it good," I spoke into the skin of her neck. "Just let me feel you."

Hanna jerked beneath me, pressing me into her opening, her eyes fluttering closed as I shifted forward.

A hot flush crawled up her neck and her lips parted in a sweet sigh. It was overwhelming for me to watch her process what we were about to do, and I could see the moment when it happened, when it *really* hit her that we were about to have sex. She opened her eyes again, and her gaze fell to my lips and went softer, calmed momentarily from the frenzy. She ran her hands up my chest and cupped my neck, whispering, "Hey."

That look, that tenderness in her eyes, made me realize for the first time what was happening to me: I was falling in love.

"Hey," I rasped, bending to kiss her.

It was a relief so enormous it wrung the air from my lungs, and I deepened the kiss, wondering whether she could feel from my touch that I had just put a name to what we were doing—making love—or if she simply tasted her sex on my tongue, and didn't understand that my entire world had just spun free of its programmed orbit.

I pulled my face back but pushed my hips forward, aching to feel the softness of her body fully pressed to mine; I just wanted to get inside her and stay deep.

Fuck.

Good, hot, holy fuuuck.

She looked up at me as I slid deeper, but she no longer seemed to be able to see my face. Her eyes were glazed, overwhelmed, and tiny little inward gasps accompanied her every inhale. A tight twinge of pain passed over her face. I was only a few inches in, and it was tight, but it was so fucking good.

I heard my own voice come out but it sounded faraway: "Open up for me, Plum. Move with me."

Hanna relaxed, lifting her legs higher up her sides so I slid in deeper, and we both let out a taut moan. She gave her hips an experimental roll, pulling me fully inside, and the sensation of her warm thighs pressed to my hips caused me to let out a loud grunt.

"I can't believe we're doing this," she whispered, stilling below me.

"I know." I kissed her jaw, her cheek, the corner of her lips.

She nodded, pushing up, unconsciously telling me with her body that she needed me to move.

I pulled back, starting an easy rhythm, getting lost

in the feel of her warmth. I would pick up my pace, sucking savagely on her neck, growing wild and heated and then slow, and eventually stop, kissing her deeply, relishing the way her hands explored my back, my ass, my arms, my face.

"You okay?" I asked, moving—but slowly—again. "Not too sore?"

"I'm good," she whispered, turning into my hand when I swept some damp hair off her forehead.

"You look so fucking perfect under me."

I wanted to build the need in her, make her go off like a bomb when she finally came with me inside her like this. She started to shake when I sped up, but growled in tight frustration when I slowed again. But I knew she trusted me, and I wanted to show her how fucking good it could be if there was no rush, no need to do anything but this for hours, and *hours*.

I kissed her, sucked on her tongue, stole every one of her sounds into my mouth, swallowing them like a greedy fucking bastard. I loved her hoarse noises, how often she said *please*, how much she let me drive what we were doing. The reality of *her*, sweaty and pliable beneath me, ate away at my calm, and I shifted from lazy pushing into quicker, hungrier thrusts. She answered with mirrored movements of her hips, arching into me, and I knew this time she was close and I couldn't stop or slow.

"Feel good?" I ground out, pressing my face to her neck.

She nodded, unable to answer, hands gripping my ass and fingernails digging sharply in my flesh. I pulled her leg up, pushing her knee to her shoulder and let go, fucking her as fast and hard and close to her body as I could.

It was wild, unreal, *explosive* the way her orgasm built beneath her skin first as a flush, and then a tightening of her muscles until she was shaking, and sweaty and begging unintelligible words beneath me, preparing to come.

"That's it," I whispered, struggling to hold back my own release even as it itched low in my belly. "Fuck, Plum, you're right there . . ."

I watched her eyes squeeze closed, her mouth open, and her body bow off the bed as she screamed in climax. I moved through it, giving her every single second of pleasure I could possibly wring from her body.

Her arms fell away, leaden, and I propped myself up on my hands, looking down at where I moved in her, feeling her eyes on my face.

"Will," she exhaled, and I heard the languid glee in her voice. "My *God*."

"Fuck, it's so good. You're so wet."

She reached up, slid her finger into my mouth so I could taste her sweetness. I moved one hand between us, rubbing her clit, knowing she was going to be sore soon, but needing to feel her come around me one more time.

After only a few minutes she arched, hips rocking faster with me. "Will . . . I . . ."

"Shh," I whispered, watching my hand move over her, my cock slide in and out. "Give me one more."

I closed my eyes, my mind diving down into pure sensation: her quivering thighs all around me, the rhythmic tightening of her pussy as she came again with a hoarse, surprised cry. I cut the last chain of my self-control, hitting deeper and harder, prolonging her release with my thumb pressed to her clit. Hanna's head was thrown back into the pillow, hands on my ass, pulling me forward while she rocked up into me. Her eyes were squeezed shut, lips parted, and all around her head, her hair was a wild mess on her pillow. I'd never seen anything more beautiful in my life.

She dragged her nails up my back, watching my face, fascinated. The sensation was too much: her rough touch, soft body beneath, and her wide-eyed, fascinated study.

"Tell me it feels good," she whispered, lips swollen and wet, cheeks flushed, hair matted with sweat.

"So good," I hissed in a rush. "I can't . . . I can't fucking think straight."

Her nails pushed down, in a rough pinch and in a flash I knew with the pain of her nails and sweet pleasure of her body wet and squeezing me, I wasn't going to last. Pleasure flooded my veins, hot and frantic.

"Harder," I begged.

She curled into me, biting down my shoulder to my

chest. "Come," she gasped, dragging her nails possessively down my back. "I want to *feel* you come."

It was as if I'd been plugged into an outlet, every inch of my skin alive and buzzing with heat. I stared down at her: breasts moving with the force of my thrusts, skin sweaty and perfect, angry red bite marks from my teeth all over her neck, shoulders, and jaw. But when I looked up and met her eyes, I lost it. She was staring at me and it was her—*Hanna,* this girl I saw every morning and fell in love with a little bit more every single time she opened her mouth.

It was so fucking *real.* With a loud shout, I collapsed on her, bucking wildly and flooded with a pleasure so intense I barely registered the warmth of her arms around my shoulders, the press of her kiss to my neck when I stilled on top of her, or the way she whispered, "Stay on top of me like this forever."

"Don't ever stop being so fucking *open,*" I murmured, pulling my gaze to her face. "Don't stop asking for what you want."

"I won't," she whispered. "I got you tonight, didn't I?"

And just that simply, I was claimed.

Chapter Eleven

I woke to the shifting of the mattress, the sound of springs as Will climbed out of bed.

Dim, blue light seeped through the window and I blinked into the darkness, trying to make out the shape of objects nearby—the doorway, my dresser, his silhouette disappearing through the bathroom door.

Without switching on a light, I heard the water start, the shower door opening and closing again. I considered joining him but seemed unable to move: my muscles felt like rubber, my body heavy and sinking into the mattress. There was a deep, unfamiliar ache between my legs and I stretched, squeezing my thighs together to feel it again. To remember. Now my room smelled of sex and Will and I could feel myself grow dizzy from it, from his proximity and the thought of so much of his naked skin just on the other side of the wall. Arms, legs, a stomach like granite. What exactly was the protocol here? Was I lucky enough that he'd come back and we'd do it all over again? Is that how this worked?

My thoughts drifted to Kitty and Kristy and I wondered whether last night was just like all the other nights he'd spent with numerous other women. If he held them the same way, made the same sounds, offered the same promises of how good he'd make them feel. Will didn't spend every night with me, but we did spend a lot of them together. When did he see them? A part of me wanted to ask, so I could know the specifics of how he slotted all of us into his life. But a bigger part of me didn't, not really.

I ran my hand through my tangled hair and thought of last night: of Dylan and our disastrous date, of Will, and how it felt to realize he'd been just outside my apartment. Worrying. Waiting. Wanting. Of the things we'd done and how he'd made me feel. I'd never known sex could be like that: both hard and soft and alternating between the two for what felt like *forever*. It was wild; his hands and teeth left me deliciously bruised, and there were moments I thought I might break into a million pieces if I couldn't get him even deeper into me.

The familiar squeak of the faucet sounded above the pounding spray and I turned my head toward the door. The water slowed before the shower fell silent, and I listened as he stepped out, pulled a towel from the rack on the wall, and dried himself off.

I couldn't pull my eyes away as he walked out, his naked body moving through a slice of moonlight. Sitting up, I crawled to the edge of the bed. He stopped just in front of me, his cock lengthening as I stared.

Will reached up, running his fingers carefully through my tangled hair before drawing a line down the side of my face and, finally, tracing my lips with his fingertip. He didn't duck down to look me in the eye. It was as if he knew I was studying him. As if he *wanted* me just to look.

I swear I could hear my heart hammering in my ears. I wanted to touch him. I wanted, more than that, to *taste* him.

"You look like you want to put your mouth on me," he said, his voice thick and hoarse.

Swallowing heavily, I nodded. "I want to see how you taste."

He slid his hand down his length and he took another step closer, sweeping the head of his cock across my lips, painting me with the bead of moisture there. When my tongue darted out to taste it—and him—he let out a low groan, letting his hand slide up and down the base as I slipped my mouth around the tip, licking a little.

"Yeah," he whispered. "That's so . . . *so* good."

I don't know what I was expecting but it wasn't this, to be so turned on by the actual act, or how empowering it was to be the person who made this gorgeous man unravel. His hands moved to my hair and I closed my eyes. His breaths were ragged as I moved my mouth farther and farther onto him. Finally, I heard him swallow and then gasp with a shaky inhale.

"Stop, stop," he said, and took a step back. He sounded like he'd been running a marathon. "You have no idea how much I'd love to let you play with me like this, your tongue and fuck, those lips, Hanna." His thumb brushed over my chin. "But I want to be careful with you the first time you take me in your mouth, and right now I feel too wild, and too fucking greedy."

I knew exactly how he felt. My body hummed, my pulse hammered in my neck, and I squeezed my thighs together again, feeling the sweet, impatient ache grow with every second.

He leaned down, kissed me, and whispered, "Roll over, Plum. I want to fuck you facedown."

I could only nod, moving to lie on my stomach, my mind too hazy to even come up with a response. The bed dipped and I felt him behind me, settling between my parted legs. His hand moved along the back of my thighs, over my ass. He gripped my hips, fingerprints burning into my skin as he pulled me to my knees and farther down the bed, closer to where he wanted. I could feel how wet I was, feel it on his fingers as he moved them against me, on my thighs. My heart hammered in my chest and I tried to shut out everything but the heat of his skin, the brush of his lips and hair along my back.

I'd always understood why women wanted Will in the first place. He wasn't beautiful in the same way Bennett was, and he wasn't tender like Max. He was visceral and imperfect, dark and *knowing*. He gave the sense that he looked at a woman and in an instant read every need she had.

But now I knew why women truly lost their mind over him. Because in the end, he *did actually* know every need a woman had, that I had. He'd ruined me for any other man, even before the first touch. And when he leaned in behind me, dragging his lips across the shell of my ear—not a kiss, not exactly—and asked, "You think you'll scream when you come this time, too?"—I was *lost*.

He reached across me, pulling a condom from the pile. I heard the foil tear, the sound of it as he rolled it over himself. I could still remember what it looked like, that thin piece of rubber stretched impossibly tight around the length of him. I wanted him to hurry. Needed him to hurry and fuck me, make this ache go away.

"I can go deeper this way," he said, bending to kiss my back again. "But tell me if I hurt you, okay?"

Nodding frantically, I pushed back into his hands, wanting him to quell the frantic hunger inside me.

His palm was surprisingly cool and I gasped in surprise when he pressed it to my lower back, steadying me. Was I shaking? In the darkness I could see my hand against the stark white of the sheet, see the fabric twisted in my grasp, wound tight just like every part of me. "You just feel," he said as if reading my thoughts, his voice so deep it was more vibration than sound. "I just want to *take* right now, okay?"

I felt the solid muscle of his legs moving between mine, the tip of his cock as he positioned himself. With every slide of our skin across each other, I arched back, lifting my ass to change the angle and hoping that this time, *this time* he might slip inside.

I felt his mouth along my shoulder, down my back and around my ribs. It was still early, still cold in my room, and I shivered as the air landed on skin he'd just kissed, tasted, scraped with his teeth.

And when he whispered against the shell of my ear how amazing I looked from his vantage, how badly he needed me, it seemed like my heart might burst through my ribs. It was so different like this, when he was behind me, out of sight. I couldn't rely on his overwhelmed expressions and the reassurance of his steady gaze on my face. I had to close my eyes and pay attention to his hands, how they shook, how rigid he felt when he slid forward across my clit. I listened to his choppy breathing and tiny grunts, pressed back into him and felt my chest twist in pleasure when the contact between his thighs and my ass made him moan.

He was so thick, so *stiff*, and my breath caught as

he shifted back so he could position himself against my tender skin, and—*finally*—slowly inch inside.

"*Oh,*" I said, a sound that felt like it must have been torn from my throat because it was the only word I could think.

Oh I didn't know it would feel like this.

Oh it hurts but in the most delicious way.

Oh please don't ever stop. More, more.

As if I'd said those words aloud, Will nodded against my skin, moving slower, deeper. We'd only just started but it was already too good, too perfect. I felt the drag of him deep inside, so close to that place that brought me to the edge of a tiny explosion.

"Okay?" he asked, and I nodded, overwhelmed. He started to move, small stabs of his hips that pushed me farther up the mattress, pushed me closer to that point where everything inside me threatened to shatter. "Fuck, look at you."

I felt his hand on my shoulder and then in my hair, fingers wrapping in the strands to brace me, keep me just where he wanted. "Spread your legs wider," he grunted. "Drop to your elbows."

Immediately I did what he said, crying out at the depth of the position. Heat settled in my stomach and between my legs at the idea of him using my willing body to get off. I was positive I'd never felt sexier in my entire life.

"Knew it would be like this," he said, and I couldn't even comprehend the words. I felt like I might collapse and I slid my arms down farther, face pressed to the pillow and my ass in the air as he continued to fuck me. The fabric was cool against my cheek and I closed my eyes, tongue darting out to wet my lips as I listened to the sounds of our bodies moving together, his uneven breaths. He was so good, and I straightened my arms over my head, the tips of my fingers brushing along the headboard and my body stretched so fully beneath him that I felt like I'd been hammered too thin. Like I might snap in half when I finally came.

His damp hair tickled along my back and I imagined what he must look like: hovering above me, arms supporting his weight as he leaned over my shaking body, pushing into me again and again, the bed rocking beneath us.

I remembered when I used to hide under my blankets and imagine this very thing, touching myself, tentative and unpracticed until I came. It felt the same—every bit as dirty and forbidden but even better now, better than all the fantasies and all the secret dreams combined.

"Tell me what you want, Plum," he managed to say, his voice so hoarse it was almost inaudible.

"More," I heard myself say. "Go *deeper*."

"Touch yourself," he rasped. "I'm not going without you."

I slipped my hand between the mattress and my sweaty body and found my clit, smooth and swollen. He was so close to me, close enough that I could feel the heat of each exhale and the slick of his skin. I could feel the tremble of muscle, note the way his breath changed and his sounds grew louder as he shifted the angle of his hips, drove so deep my spine arched sharply, involuntarily.

"Fucking *come* for me, Hanna," he said, hips speeding up.

It took only a moment, a few more circles of my fingers before I was coming, choking on sounds that got stuck in my throat and swallowed by a wave that hit me so hard I swore my bones were vibrating.

White noise filled my ears but I felt the slap of his skin against mine and the way he stiffened behind me, muscles growing tense before he groaned, low and long into my neck.

I was exhausted; limbs loose and joints feeling as if they might come apart at the seams. My skin was prickly with heat and I was so tired I couldn't bring myself to open my eyes. I felt Will reach for the base of the condom, grabbing it securely before pulling out. There was a shuffle before he climbed from the bed and moved to the bathroom, and then the sound of water again.

When the mattress dipped and the heat of him returned, I was barely conscious.

I opened my eyes to the smell of coffee, the sound of the dishwasher opening and the clank of dishes. I blinked up to the ceiling, the final remnants of sleep slipping from my brain as the reality of last night hit me.

He's still here, was my first thought, followed by *What the hell happens now?*

Last night had come easily; I'd shut off my brain and done what felt good, what I'd wanted. What I'd wanted was *him* and somehow, he'd wanted me in return. But now, with the sun pouring through the windows and the world awake and breathing outside, I was filled with uncertainty, unsure what our boundaries were or where we stood.

My body was stiff, sore in the most random places. I felt like I'd done a thousand sit-ups. My thighs and shoulders ached. My back was stiff. And between my legs I was throbbing and tender, as if Will had driven into me for hours and hours in the black of night.

Imagine that.

I eased myself off the bed, tiptoed to the bathroom, and carefully closed the door, hissing at the way the latch seemed to click too loudly.

I didn't want things to be weird between us, or to ruin the easy comfort we'd always had. I didn't know what I'd do if we lost that.

So with my teeth brushed and hair smoothed, I slipped into a pair of boy shorts and a tank and made my way out to the kitchen, intent on letting him know I could do this and that things didn't have to change.

He was standing in front of the stove in nothing but black boxers, his back to me, flipping what looked to be pancakes.

"Morning," I said, crossing the room and making a beeline straight for the coffeepot.

"Morning," he said, grinning down at me. He leaned over and twisted the fabric of my shirt in his hand, using it to pull me toward him for a quick kiss on the lips. I ignored the tiny, girlish flutter in my stomach and reached for a mug, careful to keep a long stretch of counter between us.

My mother had cooked breakfast for us every Sunday we spent on vacation in this kitchen, and had insisted the room be large enough to accommodate her ever-expanding family. The space was twice the size of any other in the building, with gleaming cherry cabinets and warm tile. Wide windows that overlooked 101st Street took up one wall; a large counter with enough stools for all of us filled another. The wide marble expanse of counter had always felt too big for the apartment, and a waste of space now that it was just me using this as a home. But with the memory of last night playing on a loop in my head, and with so much of his perfectly naked skin on display, I felt like I was in a shoe box, like the walls were closing in and pushing me closer and closer in this strange, sexy man's direction. I definitely needed some air.

"How long have you been up?" I asked.

He shrugged, the muscles of his shoulders and

back flexing with the movement. I could see the edge of the tattoo that wrapped around his ribs. "A while."

I glanced at the clock. It was early, too early to be awake on a Sunday with no plans, especially after the night we'd had. "Couldn't sleep?"

He flipped another pancake, placed two others on a plate. "Something like that."

I poured my coffee, eyes trained on the dark liquid as it filled the mug, the steam as it twisted through a beam of sunlight. The counter was set, placemats and a plate for each of us, glasses of orange juice off to the side. I had a flash of Will with one of his *not girl-friends* and couldn't help but wonder if this was part of the well-honed routine: making his ladies breakfast before leaving them in their empty apartments with wobbly legs and dopey smiles.

With a small shake of my head I replaced the carafe, and straightened my shoulders. "I'm glad you're still here," I said.

He smiled, and scraped the last bit of batter from the bowl. "Good."

We stood in comfortable silence while I added sugar and cream, then moved with my coffee to a stool on the other side of the counter. "I mean, I would have felt ridiculous if you'd left. This is easier."

He flipped the last pancake and spoke to me over his shoulder. "Easier?"

"Less awkward," I said with a shrug. I knew I needed to keep this casual, keep it from becoming a *thing* between us. I didn't want him to think I couldn't handle it.

"I'm not sure I'm getting you, Hanna."

"It's just easier to do this part now, the awkward *I've seen you naked part,* rather than later when we're trying to remember how we interact with our clothes on."

I watched him pause, staring down into the empty pan, obviously confused. He hadn't nodded or laughed, hadn't thanked me for saying it before he'd had to. And now I was the one clearly confused.

"You don't think all that highly of me, do you?" he said, finally turning to face me.

"Please. You know I think you practically walk on water. I don't want you freaking out or thinking I expect you to change anything."

"*I'm* not freaking out."

"I'm just saying that I know last night meant different things for each of us."

His brows pulled together. "And what was it to you?"

"Amazing? A reminder that even though I failed miserably with Dylan, I can have fun with a man. I can let go, and enjoy it, I know it probably didn't change who you are, but it feels a little like it changed me. So, thank you."

Will's eyes narrowed. "And who exactly am I, do you think?"

I walked over to him and stretched to kiss his chin.

His cell phone buzzed where it sat on the counter, the name *Kitty* lighting up the screen. So that answered *that* question. I took a deep breath, gave myself a moment for all the pieces to line up in my head.

And then I laughed, nodding to where it continued to vibrate across the counter. "A man who's good in bed for a reason."

He frowned, reaching for the phone and shutting it off. "Hanna," he said, pulling me back toward him. He placed a lingering kiss on my temple. "Last night—"

I sighed at how easily we slotted together, at how perfectly my name was shaped by his mouth. "You don't have to explain, Will. I'm sorry I made it weird just now."

"No, I—"

I pressed two fingers to his lips, wincing. "God, you must hate the postsex processing and I don't need it, I swear. I can handle all of this."

His eyes searched my face and I wondered what he was looking for. Did he not believe me? I reached for his jaw and kissed him softly, feeling the tension slip from his body.

His hands came to rest on my hips. "I'm glad you're okay with this," he said finally.

"I am, I promise. No weirdness."

"No weirdness," he repeated.

CHAPTER TWELVE

The only reason I ever skipped a run was if I was deathly ill or on a plane headed somewhere. So Monday morning, I hated myself a little for shutting off my alarm and rolling back over into the pillow. I just had no interest in seeing Hanna.

But as soon as I had the thought, I had to consider its accuracy. I didn't want to see *Ziggy*, bouncing and chatting away as if she hadn't blown me apart two nights ago with her body and words and needs in the guise of *Hanna*. And I knew if Ziggy showed up this morning, acting like Saturday night never happened, it would wreck me a little.

I'd been raised by a single mother, with two older sisters who didn't give me any choice but to understand women, know women, *love* women. In one of the two serious relationships in my life, I'd talked to my girlfriend about the possibility that this comfort with women worked out pretty well for me when I hit puberty and ended up wanting to have sex with every girl I met. I think that girlfriend had been trying to not-so-subtly hint that I manipulated women by pretending to listen. I didn't probe the issue much; we broke up pretty soon after that.

But whatever my comfort with the opposite sex, it didn't seem to help me at all with Hanna. She felt like a separate creature, a separate *species*. She threw all my experience out the window.

Somehow, when I fell back asleep I started dreaming about fucking her on a giant pile of sports equipment. A lacrosse stick dug into my back but I didn't care. I just watched her rock on top of me, eyes clear and locked to mine, her hands moving up and around my chest.

My phone buzzed beneath me, wedged into my spine, and I woke with a start. Glancing at my clock, I realized I'd overslept; it was nearly eight thirty. I answered without looking, assuming it was Max asking me where the fuck I was for our Monday morning meeting.

"Yeah, man. I'll be there in an hour."

"Will?"

Fuck. "Oh, hey." My heart squeezed so tightly beneath my ribs that I groaned, and ran a hand over my mouth to stifle it.

"You're still asleep?" Hanna asked. She sounded out of breath.

"I *was*, yeah."

She paused, and the wind on the other end whipped through the phone line. She was outside *and* out of breath. She'd gone running without me. "Sorry to wake you."

I closed my eyes, pressing a fist to my forehead. "Don't worry about it."

She stayed quiet for a few long, painful seconds and in that time we had several different conversations in my head. One where she told me I was being a dick. One where she apologized for implying that I could be so cavalier about the intense night we had. One where she prattled on about nothing in particular, Ziggy-style. And one where she asked if she could come over.

"I went running," she said. "I thought you'd started and maybe I'd see you on the trail."

"You thought I started without you?" I asked, laughing. "That would be rude."

She didn't answer and I realized too late that what I had done—not shown up, not even bothered to call—was just as bad.

"Shit, Ziggs, I'm sorry."

She sucked in a sharp breath. "So I'm Ziggy today. Interesting."

"Yeah," I mumbled, and then hated myself immediately. "No. *Fuck,* I don't know who you are this morning." I kicked away my sheets, willing my groggy brain to wake the fuck *up* already. "It messes with my head to call you Hanna."

It makes me think you're mine, I didn't add.

Laughing sharply, she started walking again, the wind whipping even louder through the receiver. "Get over your man-angst, Will. We had sex. You're supposed to do this kind of thing better than anyone. I'm not asking for a key to your apartment." She paused, and my heart dropped into my stomach as I understood how my distance was coming across to her. She assumed I was brushing her off. I opened my mouth to backpedal, but her words came out faster: "I'm not even asking for a repeat, you egomaniacal jerk."

And with that, she hung up.

———

I requested we move our regular group lunch from Tuesday to Monday on the basis that I'd lost my balls and my mind, and no one argued. It seemed that I'd reached a level of moony lovesickness that made giving me shit a lot less fun for my friends.

We met at Le Bernardin, ordered whatever we always ordered, and life seemed to move on as it had for the past nine months. Max kissed Sara until she batted him away. Bennett and Chloe pretended to hate each other over the salad she insisted they split for lunch, in some confusing form of flirty foreplay. The only thing that seemed different was that I drank my alcoholic lunch beverage in less than five minutes and then earned a raised eyebrow from our regular waiter when I ordered another.

"I think I'm the Kitty," I said once the waiter left. When conversation came to a screeching halt, I registered that my friends had been happily babbling on about whateverthefuck while my brain was practically melting next to them.

"With Hanna?" I clarified, searching each of their faces for any sign of understanding. "*I'm* the Kitty. I'm the one saying I'm fine with just fucking around, but I'm not. I'm the one saying I'll be happy to fuck only on the third Tuesday of odd-numbered months just so I can be with her. She's the one who's like, 'Oh, I don't need to hook up again.'"

I was met with Chloe's flat palm held up in my face. "Hold up, William. You're *fucking* her?"

I sat up straight, eyes wide and defensive. "She's twenty-four, not thirteen, Chloe. What the *hell*?"

"I don't care that you're fucking her—I care that you've fucked her and she didn't call one of us immediately. When did this happen?"

"Saturday. Two days ago; settle down," I mumbled.

She sat back, expression softening somewhat.

Relaxing, I reached for my new drink almost as soon as the waiter put it in front of me. But Max was faster, pulling it out of my reach before I could get it. "We have an afternoon meeting with Albert Samuelson and I need you sharp."

I nodded, bending to rub my eyes. "I hate all of you."

"For being right?" Bennett correctly surmised.

I ignored him.

"Have you actually ended things with Kitty and Kristy?" Sara asked gently.

Fuck. This again.

I shook my head. "Why should I? There's nothing going on with Hanna."

"Except you have *feelings* for her," Sara pressed, eyebrows drawn together. I hated her disapproval. Of any of my friends, Sara only gave me shit when it was fully deserved.

"I just figure why create more drama right now," I reasoned, lamely.

"Has Hanna actually said that she doesn't want anything more with you?" Chloe asked.

"It's pretty obvious from the way she acted Sunday morning."

Already nodding, Max added, "I hate to state the obvious, mate, but why haven't you had the Will Sumner sit-down with her? Aren't you sort of proving the long-suffering point you always throw at us regarding your hookups: that it's better to discuss things up front than leave questions?"

"Because," I explained, "it's easy to have that convo when you know what you want and don't want."

"Well, what *do* you know?" Max asked, shifting to the side so the waiter could place his food down in front of him.

"I know I don't want Hanna fucking anyone else," I growled.

"Well," Bennett began wincing slightly, "what if I told

you I saw Kitty clearly hooking up with someone else the other night?"

Relief inundated me. "Did you?"

He shook his head. "No. But your reaction sure is telling. Fix things with Hanna. Figure your shit out with Kitty." Picking up his fork, he said, "And now shut up so we can eat."

———

I was up at five fifteen the next morning, waiting outside Hanna's apartment building. I knew that now that she had a taste for running she wouldn't miss a day. I had to fix things with her. . . . I just wasn't sure how to do it yet.

She drew up short when she saw me, eyes widening before she put on a calm, unaffected mask. "Oh, hi, Will."

"Good morning."

She started to walk past me, eyes straight ahead. Her shoulder brushed mine as she passed, and I could tell from the way she winced that it had been unintentional.

"Wait," I said, and she stopped but didn't turn around. "Hanna."

She sighed. "And today it's Hanna again."

I walked to where she stood, turning to face her and putting my hands on her shoulders. I didn't miss the way she shivered slightly. Was it anger or the same thrill at contact I felt? "It's *always* been Hanna."

Her eyes darkened. "It wasn't yesterday."

"Yesterday I fucked up, okay? I'm sorry I didn't show for our run, and I'm sorry I came off like a dick."

She watched me, eyes wary. "An *epic* dick."

"I know I'm supposed to be the one who knows what I'm doing here, but I'll admit that Saturday night was different for me." Her eyes softened, shoulders relaxing. I continued, my voice quieter, "It was intense, okay? And I realize that this sounds insane, but I was a little taken aback when you were so casual about it the next day."

I let go of her shoulders, stepping back to give her space.

She looked at me as if I'd sprouted the head of a lizard from my forehead. "How was I *supposed* to be? Weird? Angry? In *love*?" Shaking her head, she said, "I'm not sure what exactly I did wrong. I thought I handled it pretty well. I thought I acted just like *you* would have told me to if it was anyone else I'd had sex with." She blushed, hotly, and I had to push my hands into the pockets of my hoodie to keep them to myself.

I took a deep breath. This was the moment I could tell her, *I have feelings for you I haven't had before. I've been struggling with them since the first second I saw you, weeks ago. I don't know what these feelings mean, but I want to find out.*

But I wasn't ready for that. I looked up at the sky. I was clueless and had no idea what I was doing. For all I knew, this was nothing more than what I'd feel if

I were having sex with anyone whose family I'd known forever; a protectiveness, a yearning to take caution with both of our feelings. I needed more time to sort things out.

"I've known your family for so long," I said, turning back to her. "It isn't the same as hooking up with some random person, no matter how much we want it to be casual. You're more to me than just someone I want to be sexual with, and . . ." I ran my hand over my face. "I'm just trying to be careful, okay?"

I wanted to punch myself. I was pussing out. Everything I'd said was true, but it was a flimsy half-truth. It wasn't only just about knowing her for so many years. It was wanting to know her, like this, for so many more.

She closed her eyes for a beat, and when she opened them, she was looking to the side, to some unknown point in the distance. "Okay," she murmured.

"Okay?"

Finally she looked up at me and smiled. "Yeah." Tilting her head in indication that we should get moving, she turned and soon our feet were slapping the pavement in an easy, steady rhythm, but I had no idea what conclusion we'd just reached.

It was gorgeous out, for the first time in months, and even though it was probably still under forty degrees, it felt like spring. The sky was clear, no clouds or gray shadows, just light, and sun and crisp air. Only three blocks from her house, I grew too warm, and I slowed slightly, pulling my long-sleeved thermal up and over my head and then tucked it into the back of my track pants.

I heard the sound of a toe butting into pavement, and before I knew what was happening, Hanna was sprawled out on the sidewalk, the wind knocked from her in a forceful gust.

"Holy crap, are you okay?" I asked, kneeling next to her and helping her sit up.

It was several long seconds before she could inhale and when she did, it was loud and desperate. I hated that sensation more than almost anything, getting all of the air knocked out of my lungs. She'd tripped on a large crack in the sidewalk and landed hard, her arms pressed to her ribs. Her pants were torn at one knee, and she was holding on to her ankle.

"Owwww," she groaned, rocking.

"Shit," I murmured, reaching behind her knees and around her waist, picking her up. "Let's get you home and ice that."

"I'm fine," she managed, struggling to keep me from lifting her.

"Hanna."

Swatting at my hands, she begged, "Don't carry me, Will, you'll break your arms."

I laughed. "Hardly. You're not heavy, and it's three blocks."

She gave in, wrapping her arms around my neck.

"What happened?"

Hanna was quiet, and when I ducked my head to catch her eye, she laughed. "You took off your shirt."

Confused, I murmured, "I had another shirt on, you goof."

"No, I mean, the tattoos." She shrugged. "It's been cold. I've only seen them a couple of other times, but I saw a *lot* of them on Saturday, and it made me think . . . I looked over just now . . ."

"And *fell*?" I asked, laughing despite my better judgment.

Groaning, she whispered, "Yes. Shut up."

"Well, you can stare at them while I carry you," I told her. "And feel free to nibble on my earlobes while we walk," I whispered, smiling. "You know I like your teeth."

She laughed, but not for long, and as soon as I'd caught up with her and realized what I'd said the tension grew into a heavy *thing* between us. I moved down the sidewalk to her building and with every step in silence, the monster tension only grew. It was the unspoken *oh, right,* the way I'd so casually referenced how she knew what I liked in bed, the reality of where we were heading—her apartment, where we'd had sex all night long Saturday.

I dug around inside my head for what to say, but the only words that bubbled right near the surface were words about *us,* or that night, or her, or my own fucked-up brain. I put her down when we reached the elevator and I had to hit the up button. It arrived with a quiet ding, and I helped Hanna limp inside.

The doors closed, I hit the button for the twenty-third floor, and the lift jerked with the initial ascent. Hanna settled into the same corner she'd been in the last time we were in here together.

"You okay?" I asked quietly.

She nodded, and everything we'd said right here two nights ago filled the elevator car like smoke rising from the floor. *You go down on me. You do it until I come.*

"Can you move your ankle?" I asked in a rush, my chest tightening with how much I wanted to step closer, kiss her.

She nodded again, eyes locked to mine. "It's sore, but I think it's okay."

"Still," I whispered. "We should ice it."

"Okay."

The gears of the elevator creaked; something just above us in the elevator shaft slid into place with a loud thunk.

You lean over me on the couch, jerking off, and come on my chest.

I licked my lips, finally letting my eyes move to her mouth, my mind wander to the memory of how it felt to kiss her. The echo of her words was loud enough in my head that it was as good as if she'd said them aloud: *Sex in all kind of places on my body. How you like me to bite you, and how good it feels to do it.*

I stepped closer, wondering if she remembered saying, *We're having sex and I'm doing everything you want and it isn't just good for me, it's good for you, too.* And, if she did, I wondered if she could see in my eyes that it *had* been good, so good for me; it was making me want to kneel at her feet right now.

We arrived at her floor and I relented as she insisted on limping down the hall, needing to break the tension somehow. Inside her apartment, I grabbed a bag of frozen peas from the freezer and guided her to the bathroom, making her sit down on the toilet seat while I dug around under her sink for Bactine or some type of antiseptic. I settled for water and hydrogen peroxide.

Her pants were only ripped on one knee, but the other was scuffed enough to tell me that both knees were probably pretty scraped. I rolled up each pant leg, ignoring the way she swatted my hands away at the sight of the mild stubble on her legs.

"I didn't know you would be touching my legs today," she said, laughing a little.

"Oh, stop."

Dabbing at the cuts with a wet cotton ball, I was relieved to see they weren't too bad. They were bleeding, but there wasn't anything that wouldn't heal in a few days, and without stitches.

Finally, she looked down, straightening one leg as I cleaned up the other. "I look like I was walking around on my knees. I'm a *mess.*"

I grabbed a couple of clean cotton balls and dabbed

her cuts with hydrogen peroxide, trying—but failing—to tamp down a smile.

She leaned down to get a better look at my face. "You are such a pervert, smiling at my scraped knees."

"*You're* such a pervert, knowing why I'm smiling."

"You like the idea of getting my knees all scraped up?" she asked with a growing smile of her own.

"I'm sorry," I said, shaking my head with absolute insincerity. "I *really* do."

Her smile dissolved slowly and she ran a finger over my chin, studying the little scar there. "How did you get this?"

"Happened in college. A woman was giving me head and freaked out and bit down on my dick. I slammed my face into the headboard."

Her eyes widened in horror: her worst oral sex nightmare realized. "*Really?*"

I burst out laughing, unable to keep up the story any longer. "No, not really. I was hit in the face with a lacrosse stick in the tenth grade."

She closed her eyes, pretending she wasn't amused, but I could see her swallow a laugh. Finally, she looked back down at me. "Will?"

"Mmm?" I put down the last cotton ball and screwed the cap back on the hydrogen peroxide bottle as I blew gently across the cuts. Once I had it all clean, I didn't even think she would need a Band-Aid.

"I heard what you said about wanting to be careful

because of our history. And I'm sorry that I came off as too casual."

I smiled at her, absently running my hand slowly down her calf, before realizing how familiar that was.

She sucked on her bottom lip for a beat before whispering, "I've thought about Saturday night almost constantly since."

Outside a horn blared, cars sped down 101st, and people rushed off to work. But in Hanna's apartment it fell completely silent. She and I just stared at each other. Her eyes grew anxious and wide, and I realized she was getting embarrassed the longer I took to reply.

I couldn't push any air past the tangle in my throat. Finally, I managed, "Me, too."

"I never thought it could be like that."

I hesitated, worrying she wouldn't believe me when I said, "Me, either."

Her hand lifted at her side, pausing before reaching out. Sliding her fingers into my hair, she followed forward with her body, eyes wide open as she slid her mouth over mine.

I groaned, and my heart slammed against my sternum, skin growing hot as my cock lengthened; every part of me felt tight and stiff.

"Okay?" she asked, pulling back, eyes anxious.

I wanted her so fiercely I was worried I wouldn't be able to be gentle. "Fuck yes, it's okay. I was worried I wouldn't ever have you again."

She stood on wobbly legs, reaching for the hem of her shirt and pulling it up and over her head. Her skin shone with a thin sheen of sweat, and her hair was a mess, but I wanted nothing else than to bury myself in her and feel her give in to me for hours.

"You're going to be late to work," I whispered, watching as she pulled off her sports bra.

"So are you."

"Don't care."

She shimmied out of her pants. With a little ass wiggle, she turned and hopped on one foot to her bedroom.

I stripped as I walked, pulling off my shirt, kicking off my pants—and leaving it all in piles in the hallway. I found Hanna on her bed, lying on top of the covers.

"Do you need more first aid?" I asked, smiling as I climbed over her, kissing my way up her belly to her breasts. "Does anything else hurt?"

"One guess," she said on an exhale.

Without needing to ask, I stretched, reaching for the drawer where she'd kept her condoms. Wordlessly, I tore one from the pack and handed it to her. Her hand was already extended expectantly.

"Fuck. We should fool around a little first," I said into her neck even as I felt her begin to roll the condom down my length.

"We've been fooling around in my head since Sunday morning," she whispered. "I don't think I need more warm-up."

She was right. When she positioned me and then reached for my hips, pulling me deep in one, slow move, she was wet and ready, quickly pulling on my ass to get me moving fast, and hard.

"I like when you're hungry like this," I murmured into her skin. "I feel like I can't get my fill of you. Just like this, against me, under me."

"Will . . ." She pushed into me, sliding her hands over my shoulders.

I could hear the rustle of the sheets as we moved, the slick sounds of our lovemaking, and nothing else. The rest of the world seemed to have fallen away, been put on mute.

She was quiet, too, staring, fascinated, down at where I moved in and out of her.

I slid a hand between us, played with her body, loving the way her back arched off the bed, her hands reached above her head, seeking anchor on the headboard.

Fuck.

With my free hand, I reached up, pinning her wrists and letting myself dissolve into her, mindless and warm, the rhythm of our bodies working together, rolling and wet with sweat. I sucked and bit at her chest, pressing down on her wrists and feeling the familiar build of my orgasm grip me somewhere between my hips, low in my spine. I jerked over her, going faster and hard, relishing the sounds of my hips slapping her thighs.

"Aw fuck, Plum."

Her eyes opened, burning with understanding and the wild thrill of seeing my pleasure unfolding.

"Almost," she whispered. "I'm right there."

I circled her clit faster, three fingers flat and rubbing, her little hoarse cries growing louder and tighter, the telltale flush spreading up her neck. She struggled, pulling her wrists apart from my grip in abandon, and then she went off with a sharp cry, hips bucking wild and body coiling and sucking all around me.

I held on by a fucking thread, moving hard and fast until she went limp and soft, and then let go, rasping, "Coming . . ."

I pulled out, jerking the condom off and tossing it away before gripping my cock, squeezing as I stroked up my length.

Hanna's eyes flamed with anticipation, and she propped herself on her elbows, staring intently down at where my hand flew over my length between us. Her attention, how much she clearly enjoyed watching . . . it overwhelmed me.

Heat burned up my legs and down my spine and my back arched in a sharp jerk. My orgasm pulsed through me unbelievably strong, tearing a loud groan from my throat as I came. Stuck in my head were images of Hanna, thighs spread under me, skin slick, her eyes open and telling me without words how good it felt. How good I made her feel.

Pulsing, pulsing, *pulsing* heat . . . and my entire body let go.

My hand slowed, and I opened my eyes, dizzy and breathless.

Her eyes burned, dark gray and fascinated as she ran her fingers over her stomach and stared at my orgasm on her skin.

"Will." My name came out of her mouth in a purr. No way were we done here.

I propped one hand on the pillow beside her head, staring down at her. "Did you like that?"

She nodded, her bottom lip trapped viciously between her teeth.

"*Show* me. Touch yourself for me."

She initially looked uncertain, but then it transformed into determination. I watched as she ran her hand down her torso, reaching briefly for my still-erect cock, her fingers first on me and then herself. She slid two fingers down over her clit, arching into her touch.

I ghosted my hand up her side and over her breast, bending to suck at the tight peak, before telling her, "Make yourself come."

"Help me," she said, eyes heavy.

"I'm not there when you do this alone. Show me what you do. Maybe I like to watch, too."

"I want you to watch while you *help*."

She was still so warm from the friction of our sex; flesh soft and so fucking wet. With my fingers inside and hers out, we found a rhythm—she stroked up as I pushed in—and fuck if it wasn't the most amazing thing to see her so unchained and intense, alternating between staring down at where I'd come on her and where I was growing hard again between us.

It didn't take long to get her there, and soon she was pushing into my hand, her legs pulled up tight to her sides and lips parted as she grew tense, and then fucking exploded with a scream.

She was beautiful when she went off, skin flushing and nipples tight; I couldn't help but taste her skin, nibbling the underside of her breast and slowing my hand in her as she came down.

She took stock of our appearance: covered in sweat and, on her stomach, my orgasm.

"I think we need a shower."

I laughed. "I think you may be right."

———

But we didn't. We started to get up, but then I would kiss her shoulder, or she would bite mine, and each time we would just slide back onto the mattress, until eventually it was nearly eleven in the morning, and we'd both long since given up on the idea of going in to work.

After the kissing escalated again, and I took her while she was bent over the edge of the bed, collapsing over her, she rolled onto her back and stared up at me, playing with my sweaty hair. "Are you hungry?"

"A little."

She started to get up but I pushed her back down, kissing her stomach. "Not hungry enough to get up yet." I spotted a pen on her bedside table and reached for it without thinking, murmuring, "Stay still," as I pulled the cap off with my teeth and pressed the tip to her skin.

She'd left the window near her bed open a crack, and we listened to the sounds of the city outside as I drew on the smooth skin just beside her hip. She didn't ask what I was doing, didn't even really seem to care. Her hands slid through my hair, down over my shoulders, along my jaw. She carefully traced my lips, my eyebrows, down the bridge of my nose. It was the way she might touch me if she were blind, trying to learn how I fit together.

When I finished, I pulled back, admiring my handiwork. I'd written a fragment of my favorite quote in tiny script, from her hipbone to just above her bare pubic bone.

All that is rare for the rare.

I loved the dark ink on her. Loved seeing it in my handwriting even more. "I want to tattoo this on your skin."

"Nietzsche," she whispered. "Overall a good quote, actually."

" 'Actually'?" I repeated, rubbing my thumb over the unmarked skin below, considering all the things I could put there.

"He was a bit of a misogynist, but came out of it with a few decent aphorisms."

Holy fuck, the brain on this woman.

"Like what?" I asked, blowing across the drying ink.

" 'Sensuality often hastens the growth of love so much that the roots remain weak and are easily torn up,' " she quoted.

Well. I looked up in time to catch her teeth release her lip, her eyes shining with amusement. That was interesting. "What else?"

She ran a fingertip across the scar on my chin, and studied my face carefully. " 'All that glitters is not gold. A soft sheen characterizes the most precious metal.' "

I felt my smile falter a little.

" 'In the end one loves one's desire and not what is desired.' " She tilted her head, running her hand through my hair. "Do you think that one is true?"

I swallowed thickly, feeling trapped. I was too wrapped up in my own tangled thoughts to figure out whether she was selecting meaningful quotes about my past or just quoting some classic philosophy. "I think it's sometimes true."

"But all that is rare for the rare . . ." she said quietly, looking down at her hip. "I like it."

"Good." I bent to even out one letter, darken another, humming.

"You've been singing that same song the entire time you wrote on me," she whispered.

"I have?" I hadn't realized I'd even made a noise.

I hummed a few more bars of it, trying to remember what it was I'd been singing: "She Talks to Angels."

"Mmmm, an oldie but a goodie," I said, blowing a stream of air on her navel to dry the ink.

"I remember hearing your band cover it."

I looked up at her, searching for her meaning. "A recording? I don't even think *I* have that."

"No," she whispered. "Live. I was visiting Jensen in Baltimore the weekend your band covered it. He said you guys always covered a different song at every show so you'd never play it again. I was there for that one." There was something restrained behind her eyes when she said this.

"I didn't even know you were there."

"We said hi before the show. You were onstage, adjusting your amp." She smiled, licking her lips. "I was seventeen, and it was right after you came to work for Dad, over fall break."

"Oh," I said, wondering what seventeen-year-old Hanna had thought of that show. It was one I still thought about, even just over seven years later. We had played tight that night, and the crowd had been amazing. It was probably one of our best shows ever.

"You were playing bass," she said, drawing small circles with her fingers on my shoulders. "But you sang that one. Jensen said you didn't often sing."

"No," I agreed. I wasn't much of a singer, but with that one I didn't care. It was more about emotion anyway.

"I saw you flirting with this Goth girl up front. It was funny, how I felt jealous then when I never had before. I think it was because you'd lived in our house, I felt a little like you belonged to us." She smiled down at me. "God, that night I wanted to be her so bad."

I watched her face as she walked through the memory, waiting to hear how this night ended for her. And me. I couldn't remember seeing Hanna when I lived in Baltimore, but there were a million nights like this, at a bar with the band, some Goth girl or preppy girl or hippie chick up front and, later in the night, under or over me.

She licked her lips. "I asked if we were meeting up with you later, and Jensen just laughed."

I hummed, shaking my head and trailing my hand up her thigh. "I don't remember what happened after that show." Too late, I realized how awful it sounded, but the reality was, if I wanted to be with Hanna, she would eventually know the truth of just how wild I'd been.

"Was that the kind of girl you liked? 'She paints her eyes as black as night now'?"

I sighed, climbing up her body so we were face-to-face. "I liked all kinds of girls. I think you know that."

I'd tried to emphasize the past tense, but realized I'd failed when she whispered, "You're such a player."

She said it with a smile but I hated it. I hated the tight edge to her voice and knowing that was exactly how she saw me: fucking anything that moved, and now *her,* in this conglomeration of limbs and lips and pleasure.

In the end one loves one's desire and not what is desired.

And I had no defense; it had been mostly true for so long.

Rolling closer, she wrapped her hand around my semi-erect cock, stroking up, squeezing. "What's your type now?"

She was giving me an out. She didn't want it to be true anymore, either. I leaned in, kissed her jaw. "My type is more along the lines of a Scandinavian sex bomb named Plum."

"Why did it bother you when I called you a player?"

I groaned, rolling away from her touch.

"I'm serious."

I threw my arm over my eyes, trying to collect my thoughts. Finally, I said, "What if I'm not that guy anymore? What if it's been twelve years since I was that guy? I'm open with my lovers about what I want. I don't *play* anyone."

She pulled back a little and looked at me, wearing an amused smile. "That doesn't make you receptive and deep, Will. No one says a player has to be an asshole."

I rubbed my face. "I just think the word 'player' has a connotation that doesn't fit me. I feel like I try harder than that to be good to the women I'm with, to talk about what we're doing together."

"Well," she said. "you haven't talked to *me* about what you want."

I hesitated, my heart exploding in a wild gallop. I hadn't, and it was because it felt so different with her from every other time I'd been with a woman. Being with Hanna wasn't just about intense physical pleasure; it also made me feel calm, and thrilled, and *known*. I hadn't wanted to discuss this because I hadn't wanted either of us to have the chance to limit it.

Taking a deep breath, I murmured, "That's because with you, I'm not really sure if what I want is *sex*."

She pulled away, sat up slowly. The sheets slid off her body and she reached for a shirt at the end of the bed.

"Okay. This is . . . awkward."

Oh, shit. That hadn't come out right. "No, no," I said, sitting up behind her and kissing her shoulder. I pulled her shirt from her hands, dropping it on the floor. I licked down her spine, slipping my hand around her waist and sliding up, resting my palm over her heart.

"I'm trying to find a way to say I want it to be *more* than sex. I have feelings for you that go way past sexual."

She stilled, growing completely frozen. "You don't."

"I don't?" I stared at her rigid back, my pulse picking up from anger rather than anxiety. "What do you mean I *don't*?"

She stood, wrapping the sheet around her body. Ice slid into my veins, cooling every part of me. I sat up, watching her. "Are you—what are you doing?"

"I'm sorry. I just—I have some stuff to do." She walked over to the dresser, began pulling things from a drawer. "I need to get to work."

"Now?"

"Yes," she said.

"So I tell you I have feelings and you're kicking me out?"

She spun around to face me. "I need to go right now, okay?"

"I can see that," I said, and she limped into the bathroom.

I was humiliated and furious. And I was terrified this was it. Who would have thought I'd fuck it up with a girl by falling for her? I wanted to get the hell out of there, and I wanted to climb out of the bed, pull her back. Maybe we both needed to think about a few things.

Chapter Thirteen

I closed the door behind me and took a few deep breaths. I needed some space. I needed a minute to wrap my head around what the hell was going on. This morning I thought I'd been discarded like one of Will's many conquests, and now he was saying he wanted more?

What the fuck?

Why was he complicating this? One of things I loved about Will was that people always knew where they stood with him. Good or bad, you always knew the score. Nothing about him had ever been complicated: sex, no complications. End of story. It was easier when I didn't have the option to consider more.

He'd been the bad boy, the hot guy my sister fooled around with in a shed in the backyard. He'd been the object of my earliest fantasies. And it wasn't that I'd spent my youth pining over him—the opposite, in fact—because knowing I could lust for him, but never *actually* stood a chance, made it easier somehow.

But now? Being able to touch him and have him touch me, hearing him say that he wanted more when there was no way he could actually mean it . . . complicated things.

Will Sumner didn't know the meaning of *more*. Hadn't he admitted to never having even a single long-term monogamous relationship? Having never found anyone who kept him interested long enough? Didn't he get a text from one of his nongirlfriends the *morning after we first had sex*? No thanks.

Because as much as I loved spending time with him, and as fun as it was to pretend I could learn from him, I knew that I would never be a player. If I let him into more than my pants—if I let him into my heart and fell for him—I would *submerge*.

Deciding I actually did need to get to work, I started the shower, watching as steam filled the bathroom. I moaned as I stepped under the spray, letting my chin drop to my chest and the sound of water drown out the chaos in my thoughts. I opened my eyes and looked down at my body, at the smeared black ink on my skin.

All that is rare for the rare.

The words he'd drawn so carefully across my hip were now bleeding into each other. There were marks where the ink had rubbed off onto his hands, and touches that alternated between pressing bruises and feather-light caresses had left a necklace of smudged fingerprints between my breasts, over my ribs, lower.

For a moment I let myself admire the gentle curve of his handwriting, remembering the determined expression on his face while he'd worked. His brows had knitted together, his hair fell forward to cover one eye. I was surprised when he didn't reach up to push it back—a habit I'd come to find increasingly endearing—but he was so focused, so intent on what he'd been doing he'd ignored it and continued meticulously inking the words across my skin. And then he'd ruined it by losing his mind. And I'd freaked out.

I reached for the loofah and covered it in way too much body wash. I began scrubbing at the marks, half of them gone already from the heat and pressure of the spray, the rest dissolving into a sudsy mess that slipped down my body and into the drain.

With the last traces of Will and his ink washed from my skin and the water growing cold, I stepped out, dressing quickly and shivering in the cool air.

I opened the door to find him pacing the length of the room, running clothes back in place and a beanie on his head. He looked like he'd been debating leaving.

He whipped off his hat and spun to face me. "Fucking finally," he muttered.

"Excuse me?" I said, temper flaring again.

"You're not the one who gets to be mad here,"
he said.

My jaw dropped. "I . . . you . . . *what?*"

"You left," he spit out.

"To the next room," I clarified.

"It was still fucked-up, *Hanna.*"

"I needed space, *Will*," I said, and, as if to further
illustrate my point, walked out of the bedroom and
down the hall. He followed.

"You're doing it again," he said. "Important rule:
don't freak out and walk away from someone *in your
own house.* Do you know how hard that was for me?"

I stopped in the kitchen. "*You?* Do you have any
idea what kind of a bomb that was to drop? I needed
to think!"

"You couldn't think there?"

"You were naked."

He shook his head. "What?"

"I can't think when you're naked!" I shouted.
"There was too much." I motioned to his body but
quickly decided that was a bad idea. "It was just . . . I
freaked, okay?"

"And how do you think I felt?" He glared at me,
the muscles of his jaw flexing. When I didn't answer,
he shook his head and looked down, shoving his
hands into his pockets. That was a bad idea. The waist
of his track pants slipped lower, the hem of his shirt
moved up. And *oh.* That little slice of toned stomach
and hipbone was most definitely not helping.

I forced myself back into the conversation. "You just told me you don't know what you want. And then you said you had feelings that went past sexual. I have to be honest, it doesn't seem like you have a very good grasp on anything that's going on here. The first time we had sex you basically brushed me off, only to now tell me you want *more*?"

"Hello!" he yelled. "I didn't brush you off. I told you, it was jarring to have you be so cavalier—"

"Will," I said, voice firm. "For twelve years I've lived with the stories of you and my brother. I saw the aftermath of you hooking up with Liv—she was hung up on you for *months* and I bet you had no idea. I've seen you sneak off with bridesmaids or disappear at family gatherings and *nothing's* changed. You've spent the majority of your adult life acting like a nineteen-year-old guy, and now you think you want more? You don't even know what that means!"

"And *you* do? Suddenly you know everything? Why would you assume that I knew this thing with Liv was so monumental? Not everyone discusses their feelings and sexuality and whatever comes to mind as openly as you do. I've never known a woman like you before."

"Well, statistically speaking, that's really saying something."

I didn't even know where all this was coming from, and the minute the words left my mouth I knew I'd gone too far.

All at once the fight seemed to leave him and I watched his shoulders fall, the air leave his lungs. He stared at me for a long beat, eyes losing their heat until they were just . . . flat.

And then, he left.

———

I paced the old rug in the dining room so many times I wondered if I was wearing a track in it. My head was a mess, my heart wouldn't stop pounding. I had no idea what had just happened, but all along my skin and into my muscles I felt tight and tense, afraid that I had just chased off my best friend, and the best sex of my entire life.

I needed something familiar. I needed my family.

The phone rang four times before Liv picked up.

"Ziggy!" my sister said. "How's the lab rat?"

I closed my eyes, leaning into the doorway between the dining room and kitchen. "Good, good. How's the baby maker?" I asked, quickly adding, "And I·was most definitely not talking about your vagina."

Her laugh burst through the line. "So the verbal filter hasn't grown in yet. You're going to confuse the hell out of some man one day, you know that?"

She didn't know the half of it. "How're you feeling?" I asked, steering the conversation to safer waters. Liv was married now and very pregnant with the first, oft-heralded Bergstrom grandchild. I was surprised my mother ever left her alone for more than ten minutes at a time.

Liv sighed, and I could imagine her sitting at the dining room table in her yellow kitchen, her giant black Labrador moving to lie down at her feet. "I'm good," she said. "Tired as hell, but good."

"Kiddo treating you okay?"

"Always," she answered, and I could hear the smile in her voice. "This baby's going to be perfect. Just wait."

"Of course it is," I said. "I mean, look at its aunt."

She laughed. "My thoughts exactly."

"You guys picked a name yet?" Liv was thoroughly set on not knowing the sex of their incoming package until it was born. It made spoiling my new niece or nephew a lot more difficult.

"We may have narrowed it down."

"And?" I asked, intrigued. The list of gender-neutral names my sister and her husband had come up with was bordering on comical.

"Nope, not telling you."

"What? Why?" I whined.

"Because you always find something wrong with them."

"That's ridiculous," I gasped. Though . . . she was right. So far her name choices were terrible. Somehow she and her husband Rob had decided that tree names and types of birds were gender-neutral and fair game.

"Now what's new with you?" she asked. "How has your life improved since your epic showdown with the boss man last month?"

I laughed, knowing of course she meant Jensen, and not Dad, or even Liemacki.

"I've been running, and getting out more. I mean, we came to sort of a . . . compromise?"

Liv didn't miss a beat. "A compromise. With Jensen?"

I'd spoken to Liv a few times in the past weeks, but had steered clear of my growing friendship, relationship, *whatever*ship with Will. For obvious reasons. But now I needed my sister's thoughts on all of it, and my stomach clenched into a giant ball of dread.

"Well, you know Jens suggested I go out more." I paused, running my finger around a swirling pattern carved into the antique hutch in the dining room. I closed my eyes, wincing as I said, "He suggested I call Will."

"Will?" she asked, and a beat of silence passed in which I wondered if she was remembering the same tall, gorgeous college-aged lad that I was. "Wait— Will *Sumner*?"

"That's the one," I said. Even talking about him made my stomach twist.

"Wow. Was not expecting that."

"Neither was I," I mumbled.

"So did you?"

"Did I *what*?" I asked, instantly regretting the way it came out.

"*Call* him," she said, laughing.

"Yeah. Which is sort of why I'm calling you today."

"That sounds *deliciously* ominous," she said.

I had no idea how to do this, so I started with the simplest, most innocuous detail there was. "Well, he lives here in New York."

"I thought I remembered that. And? I haven't seen him in ages, sort of dying to know what he's been doing. How's he look?"

"Oh, he looks . . . good," I said, trying to sound as neutral as possible. "We've been hanging out."

There was a pause on the line, a moment where I could almost see the way Liv's forehead would furrow, her eyes narrowing as she tried to find the hidden meaning in what I'd said.

" 'Hanging out'?" she repeated.

I groaned, rubbing my face.

"Oh my God, Ziggy! Are you banging *Will*?"

I groaned, and laughter filled the line. Pulling back, I looked at the phone in my hand. "This isn't funny, Liv."

I heard her exhale. "Yes, it totally is."

"He was your . . . boyfriend."

"Oh, no, he wasn't. Not even a little. I think we made out for like ten minutes."

"But—girl code!"

"Yes, but there's some sort of time limit. Or base limit. Like, I think we barely shanked it down the first base line. Though, at the time, I was completely prepared to let him enter the batter's box, if you know what I'm saying."

"I thought you were devastated after that holiday."

She started cracking up. "Take it down a notch there. First of all, we were never together. It was a horny fumble behind Mom's gardening tools. Jesus, I barely remember."

"But you were so upset, you didn't even come home the summer he worked with Dad."

"I didn't come home because I'd fucked around all year and needed to catch up on credits over the summer," she said. "And I didn't tell you because Mom and Dad would have found out and killed me."

I pressed my hand to my face. "I am so confused."

"Don't be," she said, her tone changing to concerned. "Just tell me, what's actually going on with you guys?"

"We've been hanging out a lot. I really like him, Liv. I mean he's probably my best friend here. We hooked up and then he was weird the next day. Then he started talking about feelings, and it just seemed like he was using me as a test subject in some sort of weird emotional-expression experiment. He didn't exactly have the best track record with Bergstrom girls."

"So you ripped him a new one because in your twelve-year-old memories he was the man of my dreams and left me, brokenhearted and alone."

I sighed. "That was part of it."

"What was the rest of it?"

"That he's a whore? That he doesn't remember a fraction of the women he's been with and less than twenty-four hours after brushing me off, he's telling me he wants more than just sex?"

"Okay," she said, considering. "Does he? Do *you*?"

I sighed. "I don't know, Liv. But even if he did—if *I* did—how could I trust him?"

"I don't want you to be an idiot, so I'm going to do a little overshare here. Ready?"

"Not even a little bit," I said.

She went on anyway: "Before I met Rob he was a *giant* slut. I swear to God his penis had been everywhere. But now? Different man. Worships the ground I walk on."

"Yes, but he wanted to get married," I said. "You weren't just banging him."

"When we first got together it was definitely just banging. Look, Ziggy, a lot of stuff happens to a person between the ages of nineteen and thirty-one. A lot changes."

"I'll believe *that*," I mumbled, imagining Will's even-deeper voice, his expertly wicked fingers, his broad, solid chest.

"I'm not just talking about the developing male body, you know." She paused, adding, "Though that, too. And now that I think of it, you should totally send me a picture of Will Sumner at thirty-one."

"Liv!"

"I'm kidding!" she laugh-yelled through the phone and then paused. "No, I'm serious, actually. Send me a picture. But I really would hate for you to pass up a chance to spend time with him just because you expect him to always act like a nineteen-year-old man-whore. The truth is, don't you feel like you've changed a lot since you were nineteen?"

I didn't say anything, just chewed on my lip and continued to trace the carving on my mother's antique hutch.

"And that was only five years ago for you. So think how he feels. He's thirty-one. There's a lot of wisdom to be gained in twelve years, Ziggs."

"Blerg," I said. "I hate when you're right."

She laughed. "I assume your logical brain has been using all this as some sort of a force field against the Sumner charm?"

"Not very well, apparently." I closed my eyes and leaned back against the wall.

"Oh God, this is amazing. I'm so fucking happy you called today. I'm giant and pregnant and nothing about me is interesting right now. This is awesome."

"Isn't this weird to you at all?"

She hummed, considering. "I guess it could be, but

honestly? Will and I . . . he was the first boy I fell in lust with, but that's pretty much it. I got over that two seconds after Brandon Henley got his tongue pierced."

I pressed my hand over my eyes. "Oh *gross*."

"Yeah, I didn't tell you about that one because I didn't want to ruin you, and I didn't want you to ruin it for *me* by researching how the piercing affected the contractility of the muscle or whatever."

"Well, this has been a scarring conversation," I said. "Can I go now?"

"Oh stop."

"I really made a mess of things," I groaned, rubbing my face. "Liv, I was a total dick to him."

"Looks like you have some ass to kiss. Is he into that sort of thing now?"

"Oh my God!" I said. "Hanging up!"

"Okay, okay. Look, Zig. Don't see the world from the eyes of a twelve-year-old. Hear him out. Try and remember that Will has a penis and this makes him an idiot. But a sweet idiot. Even you can't deny that."

"Stop making sense."

"Impossible. Now go put on your big-girl panties and fix things."

⸺

I spent the entire walk to Will's apartment trying to dissect every memory I had of that Christmas, trying to reconcile them with what Liv had told me.

I'd been twelve and fascinated by him, fascinated

by the idea of him and my sister together. But now that I'd heard Liv's version of events of that week and what had come after, I wondered how much of it had been real, and how much my overdramatic brain had manufactured. And she had a point. Those memories had made it so much easier to shove Will into a man-whore-shaped box, and almost impossible to imagine him out of it. Did he want more? Was he capable of it? Did I?

I groaned. I had a lot of apologizing to do.

He didn't answer the door when I knocked; he didn't answer any of the messages I sent standing there.

So I did the only thing I could think, and resorted to texting him bad dirty jokes.

What's the difference between a penis and a paycheck? I'd typed. When there was no reply, I continued. A woman will always blow your paycheck.

Nothing.

What did one boob say to the other? And when no answer came: You're my breast friend. Jesus these were bad.

I decided to try one more. What comes after sixty-nine?

I'd used his favorite number, and hoped this might be enough to lure him out.

I almost dropped my phone when the word What popped up on my screen.

Mouthwash.

Oh for fucks sake, Hanna. That was terrible. Get up here before you embarrass us both.

⟶————⟵

I practically sprinted to the elevator.

His door was unlocked, and when I walked in, I saw he'd been in the middle of cooking dinner, pots boiling on the stove, the counter colored in produce. He was wearing an old Primus T-shirt and faded, ripped jeans—looking good enough to eat. He didn't glance up when I entered, but kept his head down, his eyes on the knife and the cutting board in front of him.

Unsure feet took me across the room and I stood at his back, pressed my chin into his shoulder. "I don't know why you put up with me," I said.

Breathing in deeply, I wanted to memorize the smell of him. Because what if I'd really done it—what if he'd had enough of silly Ziggy and her idiotic questions and fumbling sexual encounters and jumping to conclusions? I would have kicked me to the curb ages ago.

But he surprised me by putting down his knife, and turning to face me. He looked miserable, and guilt twisted my stomach.

"You might have had the details wrong about Liv," he said, "but that doesn't mean there weren't others. Some I don't even remember." His voice was earnest, apologetic, even. "I've done some things I'm not proud of. It's all sort of catching up with me."

"I think that's why the idea of you wanting more terrified me," I said. "That there have been so many women in your past and I can tell you have *no* idea how many hearts you've broken. Maybe no idea how to *not* break them. I like to think I'm too smart to join those ranks."

"I know," he said. "And I'm sure that's part of your charm. You're not here to change me. You're just here to be my friend. You make me think more about the decisions I've made than I ever have before, and that's a good thing." He hesitated. "And I'll admit I got a little wrapped up in our post-coital moment . . . I just got carried away."

"It's okay." I stretched to kiss his jaw.

"Just friends is good for me," he said. "Friends who have sex is even better." He pulled me back to meet my eyes. "But I think that's a good place to stay for now, okay?"

I tried to read his expression, understand why he seemed to be so carefully considering every word he spoke.

"I'm sorry about what I said," I told him. "I panicked and said something hurtful. I feel like an idiot."

He reached out, hooked a finger into my belt loop, and pulled me to him. I went willingly, feeling the press of his chest against mine.

"We're both idiots," he said, and his eyes dropped

to my mouth. "And just so you know, I'm about to kiss you."

I nodded, pushing up onto my toes to bring my mouth to his. It wasn't really a kiss, but I wasn't sure what else to call it. His lips brushed against mine, each time with just a bit more pressure than the time before. His tongue licked out softly, barely touching before he pulled me closer, deeper. I felt him tuck his fingers beneath the fabric of my shirt and stay there, resting on my waist.

My mind was suddenly spinning with ideas of what I wanted to do to him, how much closer I needed to be. I wanted to taste him, all of him. I wanted to memorize every line and muscle.

"I want to go down on you," I said, and he pulled back, just enough to gauge my expression. "For real this time. Like, making you orgasm and everything."

"Yeah?"

I nodded, brushing my fingertips over the line of his jaw. "Show me how to be awesome at it?"

Laughing, he said, "*Christ*, Hanna," quietly into another kiss.

I could feel him already hard against my hip and I slid my hand down his body to palm him. "Okay?" I asked.

Eyes wide and trusting, he took my hand, leading me to the couch. He hesitated for a moment before sitting. "I might pass out if you keep looking at me like that."

"Isn't that the point?" I didn't wait for an invitation and kneeled on the floor between his legs. "Tell me how you want me to do it."

His eyes grew heavy, staring down at me. He helped me with his belt, helped push his pants down his hips, and watched as I bent and kissed the tip.

He paused for a moment when I sat back up, and gauged my expression. And then he gripped his cock at the base. "Lick from base to tip. Start slow. Tease me a little."

I bent, drawing my tongue up the underside of his length, along the thick vein, and slowly over the tightness of the crown. He leaked a little at the top and it surprised me with its sweetness. I kissed the tip, sucking for more.

He groaned. "Again. Start at the bottom. And suck it a little at the top again."

I kissed his cock, whispering, "So specific," with a smile.

But he seemed unable to smile back; his blue eyes turned stormy with intensity. "*You* asked," he growled. "I'm telling you step by step what I've imagined a hundred times."

I started again, loving it, loving to see him like this. He looked a little dangerous, and at his side, his free hand had formed a fist. I wanted him to unleash himself, digging hands into my hair, and start pushing hard into my mouth.

"Now suck."

He nodded as I surrounded him with my lips, then my mouth, using my tongue to stroke a little.

"*Suck* more. Hard."

I did what he asked, closing my eyes for a beat and trying not to panic at the thought of choking on him and losing control. Apparently, I did it right.

"Oh fuck yes, like that," he groaned when I sealed my lips around him. "Be sloppy . . . use a little teeth on the shaft." I looked up at him for confirmation, before letting my teeth graze his skin. He grunted, hips jerking so he hit the back of my throat. "That's it. Jesus. Everything you do feels so *fucking* good."

It was just the compliment I needed to take over, suck him harder and let go, unleash *myself*.

"Yes, oh . . ." His hips moved harder, rougher. His eyes were fixed on my face, his hands pushed into my hair just the way I'd wanted. "Show me how much you like it."

I closed my eyes, humming around him, sucking in earnest now. I could feel small noises escaping my throat and all I could think was *yes*, and *more*, and *fall apart*.

His deep grunts and choppy breaths were like a drug to me, and I felt my own ache build as his pleasure grew and grew. We fell into a rhythm, my mouth and fist working him in tandem with the movements of his hips, and I could tell he was holding back, making it last.

"*Teeth*," he reminded me in a hiss, and then groaned in relief when I complied.

With one hand, he used his fingertip to trace my lips around him, and the other hand remained threaded in my hair, guiding me and, eventually holding me in place while he carefully thrust up. Against my tongue, he swelled and his hand in my hair formed a tight fist.

"Coming, Hanna. Coming." I could feel the muscles of his stomach jump and tighten, his thighs tensing. I gave his cock one last long suck before I pulled off, taking him in my hands and, sliding up fast and rough, gripping him the way he liked, squeezing.

"Oh fuck," he warned, hissing in a breath as he came, warm on my hands. I worked him through it, continuing to pull in slow drags until it was too much and he batted me away, smiling as he pulled me up to him.

"Fuck, you're a fast learner," he said, kissing my forehead, my cheeks, the corners of my mouth.

"Because I have an excellent teacher."

He laughed, pressing his smile to mine. "I can assure you I didn't learn *that* from experience." He pulled away, eyes traveling over every inch of my face. "Stay and have dinner with me?"

I curled into his side and nodded. There wasn't anywhere I'd rather be.

CHAPTER FOURTEEN

It had been so long since I'd cuddled on my couch with a woman, I forgot how awesome it was. But with Hanna, it was borderline blissful to simultaneously enjoy a beer, a basketball game, some nerdy science talk, and nice lady with curves at the ready. I finished my drink with a long swallow and then looked over at Hanna, her eyes glazed as if she was on the cusp of a nap.

I was disappointed that I'd backpedaled after seeing her reaction this morning. But as I was quickly learning, I'd do anything for her. If she wanted to keep things casual, then that's what we'd do. If she wanted us to be friends with benefits, I could pretend. I could be patient, I could give her time. I only wanted to be with her. And as pathetic as it sounded, I'd take what I could get.

For now, I was okay being the Kitty.

"You good?" I murmured, kissing the top of her head. She nodded, humming, and wrapping her hand more firmly around the beer bottle in her lap. Hers was still mostly full and, at this point, probably pretty warm, but I liked that she had one anyway.

"Don't like the beer?" I asked.

"This one tastes like pinecones."

Laughing, I pulled my arm out from behind her neck and leaned forward to put my empty down. "That's the hops."

"Is that like what they make marijuana clothes from?"

I bent over farther, laughing harder. "That's hemp, Hanna. Holy shit you're amazing."

When I looked over at her, she was smiling and I realized, of course, she'd been fucking with me.

She patted my head patronizingly and I shrugged away from her hand, saying, "I like how I forgot for a minute there that you've probably memorized the name of every plant, ever."

Hanna stretched, her arms shaking slightly over her head as she hummed in pleasure. Naturally I took the opportunity to check out her chest. She also happened to be wearing a totally badass Doctor Who shirt, I hadn't even noticed earlier.

"Are you looking at the goods?" she said, opening one eye and catching me, slowly lowering her arms.

I shook my head. "Yes."

"Are you always such a boob man?" she asked.

In what was clearly becoming a pattern, I ignored the implied question about other women, deciding I wasn't going to address anything about that entire taboo conversation again . . . for now. Beside me, she grew still and I knew she felt the same unspoken question settle back between us: *is this conversation over?*

We were saved by the bell, or in this case the buzzing of my phone on the coffee table. A text from Max lit up my screen.

Headed to Maddie's for some pints. Coming?

I showed the phone to Hanna, in part wanting her to see that it wasn't a woman texting me on a Tuesday night, and in part to see if she'd be up for coming along. I raised my eyebrows in silent question.

"Who's Maddie?"

"Maddie is a friend of Max's, who owns and runs *Maddie's,* a bar in Harlem. It's usually pretty empty, and it has great beer. Max likes it for the horrible British pub food."

"Who's going?"

Shrugging, I said, "Max. Probably Sara." I stopped, considering. It was Tuesday, so Sara and Chloe would probably be testing to see if I was with Kitty. It was all probably a quasi-causal ruse to check up on me. "I'm betting Chloe and Bennett are coming, too."

Hanna tilted her head, studying me. "Do you guys go out to bars on weekdays a lot? Seems strange for all of these serious business career people."

I sighed, standing and pulling her up with me. "I think they're trying to track my sex life, to be honest." If she knew Saturdays had been my nights with Kristy, then she may also know Tuesdays were usually reserved for Kitty. May as well be up front with her about how meddling my friends could be.

Her expression remained unreadable, and I couldn't tell if she was irritated, jealous, nervous, or maybe even just listening neutrally. I wanted so much to know what was going on in her head, but I couldn't possibly start the talk again and have her freak out. I was a man; a man perfectly capable of accepting sex from a woman even under the murkiest of emotional circumstances. Especially when that woman was Hanna.

I bent to pick up both beer bottles.

"Will it be weird if I'm there? Do they know about us?"

"Yes, they know. No, it won't be weird."

She looked skeptical, and I put my hands on her shoulder. "Here's a rule: things are only weird if you let them be."

———

As the bar was roughly fifteen blocks from my apartment building, we decided to walk. Late March in New York was either gray and cold, or blue and cold, and luckily the snow had finally disappeared and we were having a pretty decent spring.

Only a block from my apartment, Hanna reached for my hand.

I threaded my fingers with hers, and pressed our palms together. I'd somehow always expected love to be primarily a mental state, so I still felt unaccustomed to the physical manifestation of my feelings for her: the way my stomach would grow tight, my skin would start to feel hungry for her touch, the way my chest would press in, my heart pounding blood hard and fast through my arteries.

She squeezed my hand, asking, "Do you actually like doing sixty-nine? I mean, really."

I blinked over to her, laughing and *fuck*, falling even harder for her. "Yeah. I love it."

"But, and I know you're going to hate what I'm about to say—"

"You're going to ruin it for me, aren't you?"

She looked up at me, tripping slightly on a crack in the sidewalk. "Is that even possible?"

I considered this. "Probably not."

Opening her mouth, she started to speak and then closed it again. Finally, she blurted, "Your face is basically in someone's ass."

"No, it isn't. Your face is on someone's cock or someone's pussy."

She was already shaking her head. "No. Let's say I'm on top of you, and—"

"I like this hypothetical." I kept waiting for her to

take charge and ride me. In fact, I wanted it so much that as soon as I pictured it, I had to take a moment to discreetly adjust myself in my jeans with my free hand.

Ignoring my hint, she continued, "So that means you're under me. My legs are spread over your face, so my ass is . . . it's like *eyeball* level."

"Fine with me."

"It's my *ass*. By your *eyes*."

I let go of her hand and reached up to tuck a stray hair behind her ear. "This won't surprise you, but I have zero aversion to asses. I think we should try it."

"It's not awkward?"

Pulling up short, I turned her to face me. "Have we done anything yet that feels awkward?"

Her cheeks went pink, and she blinked down the street, mumbling, "No."

"And you believe me when I say I'll make *everything* good for you."

She looked back up at me, eyes soft and trusting. "Yeah."

I took her hand in mine again, and we continued walking. "It's settled then. There will be some sixty-nine in your future."

We walked in silence for several blocks, listening to the birds, the wind, the sound of traffic in bursts organized by the streetlights.

"You think I'll ever teach *you* something?" she asked just before we reached the bar.

I smiled down at her, growling, "Without a doubt."

And then I opened the door to Maddie's for Hanna, gesturing that she lead us inside.

My friends, seated at a table just to the side of the little dance floor, saw us as soon as we walked in. Chloe, facing the door, noticed us first, her mouth forming a tiny, surprised O that she almost immediately tucked away. Bennett and Sara turned in their seats, each of them deftly hiding any reaction. But fucking Max had an enormous shit-eating grin spreading from ear to ear.

"Well, well," he said, standing to walk around the table and give Hanna a hug in greeting. "Look who's here."

Hanna smiled, greeting everyone alternately with little hugs and waves, and then pulled up a chair to the end of the table. I made Max move down so I could sit next to her, and didn't miss his amused laugh, and under his breath, a guffawed "Smitten."

Maddie herself approached our table, tossing down a couple more coasters in front of us and asking what we wanted to drink. She listed the beers on tap, and because I knew she wouldn't like any of them, I leaned close to tell Hanna, "They also have regular bar drinks, or sodas."

"Soda is expressly forbidden," Max chided. "If you don't like beer, there is whiskey."

Hanna laughed, making a face. "Would you drink a vodka and 7-Up?" she asked, anticipating our usual routine where she ordered the drink and I was the one who actually drank it.

I shook my head and made a face, leaning into her, our foreheads practically touching. "Probably not."

Humming, she thought about it some more. "Jack and Coke?"

"I'd drink that." I looked up at Maddie and said, "Jack and Coke for the lady, and I'll have a Green Flash."

"Ooh, what's that?" Hanna asked.

"It's a really hoppy beer," I told her, kissing the corner of her mouth. "You wouldn't like it."

Once Maddie left us, I pulled away from Hanna and glanced around the table, finding four very interested faces looking back at us.

"You two look rather cozy," Max said.

With a little wave of her hand, Hanna explained, "It's our system: I'll only have a few sips of my drink and then he'll finish it. I'm still learning what he orders."

Sara squeaked out a tiny, thrilled noise and Chloe smiled at us as if we had turned into a photograph of two cuddling baby sloths. I shot them a warning look. When Hanna asked where the restrooms were, then headed in that direction, I leaned in toward the group, meeting each of their eyes.

"This is not going to be the Will and Hanna show, you guys. We're in a weird place. Just act normal."

"Fine," Sara said, but then narrowed her eyes. "But for the record, you two look really cute together and since we all know you guys have been hooking up, she's really brave for coming out with the entire group tonight."

"I know," I mumbled, lifting my beer when Maddie

had delivered it and taking a sip. The sharp bite of the hops mellowed almost immediately into a warm, malty finish. I closed my eyes, moaning a little while the others began chatting.

"Will?" Sara said, quieter now, so only I could hear her. She turned, looking behind her before turning back to me. "Please only do this with Hanna if you know it's what you want."

"I really appreciate the meddling, Sara, but stop meddling."

Her face straightened and I registered my mistake. Hanna was a bit older than Sara had been when she started dating the douchebag congressman in Chicago, but I was exactly the same age he had been: thirty-one. Sara probably felt it was her duty to look out for other women who could fall into the same situation she was in for so long.

"Shit, Sare," I said. "I get the meddling. Just . . . it's different. You know that, right?"

"It's always *different* at first," she said. "It's called infatuation, and it will make you promise anything."

It wasn't as if I hadn't been infatuated with a woman before; I had. But I'd always kept my head about me, knowing how to let myself take as much as I could physically, while taking the emotional side more slowly, or pushing it aside entirely. What was it about Hanna that made me want to shed that model and dive straight to the bottom, where things were the most tender and terrifying?

Hanna returned, smiling at me before sitting down and taking a sip of her drink. She coughed and looked up at me, eyes wide and watery as if her throat were on fire.

"Right," I said, laughing. "Maddie makes the drinks on the strong side. I should have warned you."

"Keep drinking," Bennett advised. "It gets easier once your throat is numb."

"That's what he said," Chloe quipped.

Max's laugh boomed across the table, and I rolled my eyes, hoping Hanna stayed oblivious to their banter.

She seemed to be, taking another sip and coming out of it with a more normal reaction. "It's fine. I'm fine. Holy crap, you guys must feel like you're watching someone have her first drink. I promise you I drink sometimes, just—"

"Just not very capably," I finished, laughing.

Below the table, Hanna's palm covered my knee and slid up to my thigh. She found my hand there and curled her fingers around it.

"I remember the first drink I ever had," Sara said, shaking her head. "I was fourteen, and I went up to the bar at my cousin's wedding. I ordered a Coke, and the woman next to me ordered a Coke but with some kind of booze in it. I accidentally took hers and went back to my table. I had no idea what was wrong with my drink and why it tasted so funny, but let me tell you it was the first time this white girl ever tried to bust out some break-dancing moves."

We all laughed, particularly of the image of sweet, reserved Sara doing the robot or some spin drunk. Once our humor died down, it seemed as though our thoughts all drifted to the same topic, because we all turned to Chloe almost in unison.

"How's the wedding planning going?" I asked.

"You know, Will," she said, wearing a sly smile. "I think that's the first time you've ever asked about the wedding."

"I spent four days in Vegas with these sad bastards." I nodded to Bennett and Max. "It's not like I don't know it's happening. Do you want me to tie ribbons on the flower arrangements or some shit?"

"No," she said, laughing. "And the planning is going . . . fine."

"Mostly," Bennett muttered.

"Mostly," Chloe agreed. They shared a knowing look and she started laughing again, leaning into his shoulder.

"What does that mean?" Sara asked. "Is this about the caterer again?"

"No," Bennett said, before taking a sip of his beer. "The caterer is settled."

"Thank God," Chloe interjected.

Bennett continued, "It's just unbelievable the things that families do around weddings. All kinds of drama comes out of the woodwork. Swear to God, if we manage to pull this off without a quadruple homicide we will both deserve a fucking medal."

Reflexively, I gripped Hanna's hand tighter.

After a small pause, she squeezed back, turning to look at me. Her eyes searched mine, and then lightened into a little smile.

I was thinking about her, and me. I was thinking about her family, and how, over the past twelve years, they'd become my surrogate east coast family, and how in this tiny desperate breath I could even see this future—falling in love, getting married, deciding to start a family—for myself down the road.

I released her hand rubbing my palm on my thigh and feeling my pulse explode in my neck. *Holy fuck, what happened to my life?* In only a couple of months, almost everything had changed.

Well, not everything. My friends were still the same, my finances were fine. I still ran (almost) daily, still caught basketball on TV whenever I could. But . . .

I'd fallen in love. How often does anyone see that coming?

"You okay?" she asked.

"Yeah, I'm good," I whispered. "Just . . ." I couldn't say anything. We'd agreed on just-friends. I'd told her it was what I wanted, too. "It's just crazy to see friends going through this," I said, gesturing to Chloe and Bennett, covering myself up that way. "I totally can't relate."

And with that, everyone was looking back to us, eyes soft and fucking *invested* in every single look or touch that passed between me and Hanna. I glared at each of them quickly and then stood. My chair squeaked across the floor, making my awkwardness even more evident. I was okay with being the center of attention within this group, whether I was teasing one of them or the other way around. But this felt different. I could laugh off the jokes about my scheduled hook-ups or colorful past with women, but right now I felt fucking *vulnerable* in this new place with Hanna, and wasn't used to being on this side of the knowing looks.

I wiped my sweaty palms on the thighs of my jeans. "Let's . . . I don't know." I looked around the bar helplessly. We should have just stayed on my couch, maybe fucked again out there in my living room. We should have stayed put until things were slightly less up in the air between us.

Hanna looked up at me, amused expression in place. "Let's . . . ?"

"Let's dance."

I jerked her out of her chair and out to the empty dance floor, realizing when we got there that it would be even worse than what I was escaping. I'd taken us from the pack-safety of the table and onto what was essentially a *stage*. She stepped close to me, pulling my arms around her waist and running her hands up my chest and into my hair.

"Breathe, Will."

I closed my eyes, taking a deep breath. I'd never felt more awkward in my life. Come to think of it, I'd never really felt awkward at all before.

"You're a mess," she said, laughing into my ear

when I pulled her close. "I've never seen you so dis-combobulated. I have to admit, it's really kind of cute."

"It's been a really fucking weird day."

Maddie was playing some mellow indie shit, and this particular song was only instrumental. It was sweet, almost a little melancholy, but just the right speed for the kind of dancing I wanted to do with Hanna: slow, pressing. The kind of dancing where I could pretend to dance but really just stand and hug her for a few minutes away from the table.

On a slow spin, I turned and could see that my friends weren't even looking at us anymore; they had returned to their conversation. Chloe was speaking animatedly about something, arms flapping above her head and I was almost positive she was reenacting some wedding-related fiasco. Now that the weird Will Inspection moment had cleared, I was torn between staying put, here with Hanna, and heading back to the table so I could be kept up to date on the increasing number of shenanigans Bennett and Chloe were dealing with. I could only imagine they were pretty epic.

"I like being with you," Hanna said, breaking back into my thoughts. Maybe it was the lights in the bar, or maybe it was her mood, but her eyes had more blue in them today than they normally did. It made me think of spring being released full bore into New York City. I wanted winter gone. I think I needed everything around me to transition so it didn't feel like I was the only one going through something.

She paused, and her eyes focused on my lips. "I'm sorry about earlier."

Laughing, I whispered, "You said that already. You apologized with words. And then with your mouth on my dick."

She laughed, tucking her head into my neck, and I could pretend we were alone, just dancing in my living room, or bedroom. Only, if we were there, we wouldn't be dancing. I clenched my jaw, trying to keep my body from reacting to this fresh reminder that she was pressed against me, had given me the blow job of my life earlier, and that it might be possible to convince her to come back to my place again later. Even if she just wanted to curl up and sleep, I'd be completely down for that. After all the drama of the day, I didn't really want her to go home after this.

"I guess I don't really know what to do," she admitted. "I know we talked earlier but things still feel kind of weird."

I sighed. "Why is it complicated, though?" The lights from the dance floor ran shadows across her face, and she looked so fucking beautiful, I felt like I was losing my mind. The question filled my throat like smoke until I felt too full. "Isn't *this* good?" I smiled so she might think I knew it was; maybe she would believe for a second that I didn't actually need the reassurance.

"It's actually amazing how good it is," she whispered. "I feel like I didn't know you at all before, even though I *thought* I did. You're this brilliant scientist, with these really amazing, meaningful tattoos. You run triathlons and have this close, sweet relationship with your sisters and your mom." Her nails scratched lightly down my neck. "I know you've always been sexual, *really* sexual. From the first time I met you when you were nineteen, to now, twelve years later. I really like spending time with you for that reason, too, because you're teaching me things I didn't know about my body, and what I like. I think what we have right now is actually really perfect."

I was a second away from kissing her, running a hand up her side to feel the shape of her ribs and her spine. I wanted to pull her down onto the floor and feel her under me. But we were at a bar. *Fucking idiot, Will.* I looked away, and inadvertently over at my group of friends behind her. All four of them were back to watching us. Bennett and Sara had actually turned their chairs so they could see us without having to crane their necks, but as soon as they noticed I had noticed them, they snapped their attention elsewhere: Max to the bar, Sara up at the ceiling, Bennett down at the watch on his wrist. Only Chloe continued to stare, a big smile on her face.

"This was a bad idea, coming here," I said.

Hanna shrugged. "I don't think so. I think it was good to get out of the house and talk a little."

"Is that what we did?" I asked, smiling. "Talked about how we don't need to talk about it?"

Her tongue peeked out to wet her lips. "Sure. But I

think I just want to go back to your place and *do* things while we talk."

———

I pulled my keys from my pocket, sifting through them to locate the right one. "You're not coming up here to grab a cup of tea and then head home."

She nodded. "I know. But I do need to go to lab tomorrow. I don't think I've ever just not shown up like I did today."

I unlocked my front door, pushing it open and letting her lead us inside. She headed straight for the kitchen.

"Wrong way."

"I won't leave after tea," she said over her shoulder. "But I do want some. That drink made me sleepy."

"You had *two sips*." We'd left her mostly full Jack and Coke on the table while Bennett and the rest did their best to convince us to stay and not only finish the one, but have another.

"I think there was the equivalent of seven shots in those two sips."

Stepping up to the stove, I grabbed the kettle and then turned to fill it with water. "Then you're a pretty boring drunk. If I had seven shots I would have been stripping on the table."

She laughed, opening my fridge, rooting around, and finally pulling out a carrot. She walked over to my counter and hopped up on it, swinging her legs. Even though this was so new, it seemed like she'd been coming over here for years.

Her hair had started to come undone and a few pieces fell in small curls next to her face and down the back of her neck. The warmth of the bar, or maybe the two sips of her drink, had left her cheeks flushed, her eyes bright. She blinked slowly as she looked over at me and I smiled.

"You look pretty," I said, leaning against the counter beside her.

She snapped into the carrot. "Thanks."

"Think I might fuck you senseless in a few minutes."

Shrugging and pretending to look nonchalant, she murmured, "Okay."

But then she reached out with her legs and pulled me closer, between her thighs. "Despite that whole 'work' thing I mentioned, I think you could probably keep me up all night again, if you really wanted."

I reached forward with one hand and slipped the top button of her shirt free. "What do you want me to do to you tonight?"

"Anything."

I lifted an eyebrow. "Anything?"

She reconsidered, whispering, "Everything."

"I love this," I said, stepping closer and running my nose up the column of her neck. "This kind of sex where I get to learn everything you like. I discover all of your sounds."

"I don't know . . ." She trailed off, waving her carrot in a vague circle next to my head. "Isn't sex with someone you've been with forever the best kind, though? Like she's in bed, falls asleep, he comes in, and she just instinctively rolls to him, you know? And it's like, her face in his warm neck and his hands all up and down her back, then her pants come off and he's pushing inside her before her shirt is even off. He knows what's under there. Maybe he can't wait to be inside her first. He doesn't have to take things off in order anymore."

I pulled back and stared at her as she snapped another bite of her carrot. She had quite the vivid image of such a moment. I personally would never have said familiar sex is the best kind. A good kind, sure. But the way she said it—the way her voice dropped and her eyes kind of closed—fuck, yes, it sounded like the *best* kind. I could see that life with Hanna, where we shared a bed, and a kitchen, and finances and fights. I could see her getting angry with me, and me coming to find her later and making it up to her in whatever sneak-attack ways I had learned over time because she was mine and, being Hanna, she couldn't help but let every thought and desire slip out of her mouth.

Damn. She wasn't sexy in any of the ordinary ways. She was sexy because she didn't care if I was watching her chow down on a carrot, or that her hair was in this half-assed ponytail she hadn't bothered to fix since we were lounging on the couch earlier. She was so comfortable in her skin, so comfortable being *watched*—I'd

never known a woman like her. She would never assume I was staring and judging. She assumed I was
staring because I was listening. And I was. I would listen to her ramble about familiar sex and anal sex and
porn films forever.

"You're looking at me like I'm food." She held out
her carrot, grinned wickedly. "Want some?"

I shook my head. "I want you."

She moved her hands up, unbuttoning her shirt
now, and slid it off her shoulders.

"Tell me what you like," I said, stepping even closer
and kissing the hollow of her throat.

"I like when you come on me."

I let out a quiet laugh into her neck. "I know *that*.
What else?"

"When you watch where you're moving in me."

Shaking my head, I said, "Tell me what you like that
I do *to* you."

Hanna shrugged a little, running her fingertips
down my chest before reaching for the hem of my shirt
and pulling it up and over my head. "I like when you
throw me around a little, have your way with me. I like
when you act like my body is yours."

The teakettle whistled, screeching in the quiet
kitchen, and I moved away just long enough to grab her
mug and pour some hot water over a tea bag. "When
I'm touching you," I told her, putting the kettle down,
"your body *is* mine. Mine to kiss, and fuck, and taste."

She lifted her eyebrow and smiled at me. "Well,

when *I'm* touching *you*, your body is mine, too, you know."

My mind went completely, directly into the gutter when she leaned across the counter, reached for the honey, and drizzled some into the mug.

Taking the honey wand from her, I swiped some excess on the lip of the jar then ran the stickiness across the top swell of her breast. She watched me, her tea apparently forgotten.

"So take control," I told her, kissing her jaw. "Tell me what to do next."

She hesitated for only a beat. "Suck it off."

I groaned at the quiet command, licking across the honey before sucking her skin into my mouth with such force I left a small, red mark. "What else?"

Her hands slipped behind her, unlatching her bra just as I ran my tongue over her skin. I moved to her nipple, blowing lightly across the peak before sucking her into my mouth. Gasping, she whispered, "Make it wet."

I leaned forward, doing exactly what she asked, licking her breasts, sucking them deeply, laving her skin with my tongue until it glistened. "These will be fucked soon."

"Teeth," she whispered. "Bite me."

With a groan, I closed my eyes, biting small circles into the swell of her breasts, finding small traces of honey remaining on her skin. My hands slid lower, to her jeans, and I worked them and her underwear down her hips so she could kick them to the floor.

Her hands ran over my shoulders, legs spread open. "Will?"

"Mmmm?" I teased down her ribs, lifting both breasts in my hands. I knew her tone; knew what she was about to beg me to do.

"Please."

"Please what?" I asked, pressing my teeth carefully into her nipple. "Please hand you your tea?"

"Touch me."

"I *am* touching you."

She let out an angry little growl. "Touch me between my legs."

I dipped my finger into the small bowl of honey, and pressed it against her clit, rubbing it across her skin as I pressed my teeth into the delicate flesh of her breast. She moaned, head falling back, and pulled her feet up onto the counter, legs spread wide.

Crouching, I ran my tongue over her, not teasing, not even able to. The honey was warm from her skin, and tasted fucking amazing. "Holy fuck," I whispered, sucking gently on her small fold of nerves.

Her hand ran into my hair, pulling, but not for pleasure. She raised me up to her face, leaning forward to kiss me. She'd put honey on her tongue, too, and I knew in a hot pulsing heartbeat that I would now associate this flavor with Hanna forever.

Her quiet little moans filled the space between our lips and our tongues, echoing mildly, growing tighter when I reached between us, slid my fingers over her skin, playing where she was slippery and hot. The counter was a little higher than my hips, but I could make it work if she wanted to fuck in the kitchen.

"Let me get a condom."

"Okay," she said, pulling her fingers from my hair.

I turned, padding in bare feet down the hall, unbuttoning my jeans. I pulled a packet out of the box in my drawer and moved to return to the kitchen, but Hanna was standing just inside my bedroom.

She was completely naked, and without saying anything, walked over to my bed and climbed to the middle. Resting back on her heels, she sat with one hand on her knee. Waiting for me.

"I want to be in here."

"Okay," I said, pushing my jeans down my hips.

"On your bed."

I got it, I thought. *It's pretty obvious you want to have sex on my bed, what with the nakedness and condom in my hand.* But then I realized she was actually asking me something. She was wondering whether my bed was off-limits, whether I was that kind of playboy, who never brought girls home and took them into the inner sanctum of the bedroom.

Would it always be like this? Her unspoken questions, uncertainty about what I was giving her that was new and special? Wasn't it enough that I was secretly giving her the chance to break my heart?

I joined her on the bed, beginning to tear the condom packet open with my teeth before she reached up and took it from me.

"Fuck," I mumbled, watching her duck down to run a tentative tongue across the tip of my dick. "Holy hell. I just love your fucking mouth."

She kissed the tip, running her tongue up and over me. Drawing me into her mouth.

"I like watching you," I babbled. I was so fucking tight and the vision of her doing this . . . I wasn't sure I could hold out. "I feel like I'm going to come."

"I'm barely touching you," she said, clearly proud of herself.

"I know. I'm just . . . it's a lot."

She took the condom and rolled it over me, laid back on the bed. "Ready?"

I hovered over her, looking down the length of our bodies before I positioned myself to slide into her. She was so warm, so slippery, and I wanted to last, draw this moment out just a tiny bit longer. I pulled my hips back slightly, tapping my cock gently against her clit.

"Will," she whined, hips arching up.

"Do you realize how wet you are?"

With a shaky hand, she reached between us, touching herself. "Oh God."

"Is that because of me? Plum, I don't know if I've ever been this hard." I felt my pulse reverberating down my length, pounding.

She gripped me then, and inhaled sharply, whispering, "Please."

"Please what?"

Her eyes opened and she whispered, "Please . . . inside."

I smiled, enjoying her sweet, urgent agony. "Does your pussy ache a little?"

"Will." Beneath me, she moved, searching with her hands and hips. I brought her fingers to my mouth, sucked each into my mouth to taste her sweetness.

Then I reached between us, circling a finger around her slick opening. "I asked you, does it ache right here?"

"Yes . . ." She tried to push up, to get even my finger inside but I slid it up and over her clit, making her moan loudly. I dragged my finger back down, dipping into the unbelievable wetness. "Does it ache in your thighs? Are these sweet little petals right here—" I bent, sucking her nipple into my mouth and playing a little with my tongue. "Are they tight and aching, too?" *Fuck,* her breasts. So fucking soft and warm. "God, Plum," I whispered, feeling desperate. "I'm going to make it so good tonight. I'm going to make you feel so *fucking* good."

She arched off the bed, hands in my hair, down my neck, scratching along my back.

Drawing my finger down across her pussy and lower, I pressed it against her backside. "I bet I could make you do anything right now. I could fuck you right here."

"Anything," she agreed. "Just . . . please."

"Are you . . . begging me?"

She nodded urgently and then blinked up to my face, eyes wide and wild. Her pulse thrummed in her throat. "Will. Yes."

"So those girls in the porn movies you so love," I whispered, smiling as I rocked my hips. We both groaned when the crown of my cock slid over the taut rise of her clit. "The ones who beg. Say they *need* it . . ." I tilted my head, jaw tight as I resisted the urge to sink into her, pound her into the bed. "Would you say right now *you* need it?"

She groaned, fingernails digging into my chest just below my collarbones and dragging down so roughly she left a trail of fire-red marks from my sternum to my navel. "I'll do whatever you want tonight, just make me come first."

Unable to tease any longer, I rasped, "Put me inside."

Her hands flew to my cock, wrapping around me and rubbing over herself before sliding me inside, pushing her hips off the bed to take me deeper. My skin flushed warm, and with a grunt, I met her movements, sinking in deep and pushing her legs to her sides so I could press all the way in, so I could rub her right where she needed it.

I closed my fists around the sheets on either side of her shoulders, struggling to control myself. She was so wet. She was so *fucking* warm. I squeezed my eyes closed, blood thundering in my veins as I pulled back and pushed in again, and again, hard and deep.

Her noises—sweet moans and growls that it was good, *so good*—made me want to dive deeper, press harder, make her come over and over until she could never imagine feeling anyone else inside her like this. She knew now I would go all night, and it wasn't just that first night we shared. I would *always* keep her up for hours. With Hanna, I would rarely let it to be over quickly.

She was perfect, and gorgeous, and wild—hands on my face, thumb in my mouth, begging me with little noises and her wide, pleading eyes.

But when those eyes rolled closed I stopped, groaning loudly and rasped, "Watch me. I'm not going to be gentle tonight."

She looked up at my face—not down at my cock—so I let her see every single sensation as it passed over me: the way it wasn't enough even with my punishing thrusts and savage hands rasping over every inch of her skin; the way I relished how she began to jut up into me, and it started to be just right, *just fucking right,* and I laughed through a growl, watching her chest flush and her first orgasm sneak up on her, tearing from her screaming and frenzied; the way I wanted to slow down, enjoy the long drag of my cock in her, the warm, perfect hum in my blood, run my finger between her breasts and feel her sweat, slow down enough to make her beg again.

She pulled at my shoulders, begging for *faster*.

"So demanding," I whispered, pulling out and flipping her over to lick down her back, bite her ass, her thighs. I left a pattern of red marks across her skin.

I pulled her down to the edge of the bed, bending her over the mattress, and sank back into her, so goddamn deep it made us both cry out. I closed my eyes, needing that sense of distance. Before, with every woman, I had watched everything. I'd needed that layer of visual stimulation when I was ready to come. But with Hanna, it was too much. *She* was too much. I couldn't watch her when I was close like this, the way her spine arched, or how she'd look at me over her shoulder, eyes full of question and hope and that sweet adoration that spiked me right between my ribs.

I felt her begin to tighten around me, and lost myself in the way she got even wetter when I gripped her hair, roughly gripped her breasts in my hungry hands, and smacked her ass to hear a sharp crack, which was followed by her eager moan. Her sounds morphed from sharp cries to tiny gasps of breath as I bit her shoulder and told her to *fucking come, Plum*. And when she started to, I tried to hold on, tried to block out the image of us together, the way we must look. My hand tightened on her hip, the other on her shoulder as I pulled her forcibly onto me with every thrust until I was so close, could feel it barreling down my spine.

She said my name, pushed back into me and suddenly it felt like I was falling, spinning into darkness.

My eyes flew open, both my hands gripping her tightly for support as I came, filling the condom with a groan. I continued to thrust into her, fucking her through her orgasm as my head swam, my legs on fire. I felt like I was made of rubber and could barely hold myself up.

I pulled out and discarded the condom, watched as she slid down onto the mattress. She looked so fucking perfect in my bed, her hair a mess, her skin bite-marked and flushed and sweaty, a glint here and there from the honey that still clung to her. I climbed on the bed, collapsing behind her and wrapping my arms around her waist. There was something so familiar about this. It was the first time she'd slept in my bed and yet it felt like she'd always been there.

Chapter Fifteen

I woke the next morning to the feel of unfamiliar sheets and the smell of Will still clinging to my skin. The bed was a disaster. The sheets were dislocated from the mattress and twisted around my body; the pillows had been shoved to the floor. My skin was covered in bite marks and fingertip bruises, and I had no idea where my clothes were.

A glance at the clock told me it was just after five, and I rolled over, pushing the tangled hair from my face and blinking into the dim light. The other side of the bed was empty and bore only the telltale indentation of Will's body. I looked up at the sound of footsteps to see him walking toward me, smiling and shirtless, carrying a steaming mug in each hand.

"Morning, sleepyhead," he said, setting the drinks on the bedside table. The mattress dipped as he sat next to me. "You feel okay? Not too sore?" His expression was tender, a smile curving the corners of his mouth, and I wondered if I'd ever get used to the reality of him looking at me so intimately. "I wasn't particularly easy on you last night."

I took the mental inventory: in addition to the marks he'd left all over my body, my legs were weak, my abdomen felt like I'd done a hundred sit-ups, and, between my legs, I could still feel the echo of his hips pounding into me. "Sore in all the right places."

He scratched his jaw, letting his eyes move over my face before dropping to my chest. Predictably. "That is now my favorite thing you've ever said. Maybe you could text that to me later tonight. If you're feeling generous, you could include a picture of your tits."

I laughed, and he reached for a mug, handing it to me. "Someone forgot their tea last night."

"Hmmm. Someone was distracted." I shook my head, motioning for him to put it back down. I wanted both hands free. Will was predatory and seductive every minute of the day; but in the morning, he should be *illegal*.

He grinned in understanding, slowly brushing his hands through the ends of my hair, smoothing it down my spine. I shivered at the emotion in his eyes, how his fingers set off sparks that settled warm and heavy between my thighs. I wished I knew what exactly it was I saw there: friendship, fondness, something more? I bit back the question that continued to rise up in the back of my throat, not sure either of us was ready to have an honest conversation so soon after the last, disastrous one.

The sky that peeked through the window was still purple and hazy, making each inked line across his skin seem sharper, each tattoo stark against his skin. The bluebird looked almost black; the words that wrapped around his ribs seemed as if they'd been carved there in delicate script. I reached to touch them, to press my thumb into the groove formed by his obliques, the flat planes of his stomach and lower. He hissed in a breath when I slipped a finger just under the waistband of his boxers.

"I want to draw on you," I said, and blinked quickly back to his face to gauge his reaction. He looked surprised, but more than that, he looked *hungry*, his blue eyes heavy and hidden in shadow.

He must have agreed, because he leaned over to search the small table next to the bed, and returned with a black marker. He climbed over me and lay down on his back, stretching out long and sculpted in the middle of his bed.

I sat up, feeling the sheet slip down my body, the cool air reminding me just how completely naked I was. I gave myself no time to think about what I was doing or how I looked as I crawled over and straddled him, my thighs bracketing his hips.

The air in the room seemed to condense, and Will

swallowed, eyes wide as I took the marker from him and removed the cap. I could feel the length of him starting to harden against my backside. I bit back a moan at the way he flexed his thighs and rocked his hips upward the tiniest bit in an attempt to rub against me.

I looked down, not even sure where to start. "I love your collarbones," I said, brushing my fingers along them to the little hollow below his throat.

"Collarbones, huh?" he asked, voice warm and still raspy.

I ran my fingers down his chest, biting back a triumphant smile over the way his breathing spiked, jagged and excited, under my touch.

"I *love* your chest."

He laughed, murmuring, "Likewise."

His was perfect, though. Defined, but not bulky. His chest was broad, with smooth skin leading from his muscular shoulders to his pectorals. I traced a line with my index finger. He didn't shave or wax his chest like the men in magazines or on my rare night zoning out in front of mindless television. Will was a *man*, with a smattering of dark hair on his chest, smooth bare stomach, and the soft trail leading from his navel to his . . .

I bent down, dragging my tongue down his happy trail.

"Good," he grunted, shifting impatiently beneath me. "Oh, God yes."

"And I love this spot right here," I said, veering my mouth away from where he wanted me and over to his hip. Pulling his boxers down just an inch, I drew an *H* just inside his hipbone, a *B* below. I sat back to examine it, smiling wide. "I like that."

He lifted his head to see where I'd written my initials on his skin and blinked up to me. "Likewise."

I remembered the smudged words and drawings I'd scrubbed from my body the other day, and brought the marker to my thumb, scribbling across the pad until it was wet with ink. I pressed it to his skin, right below where his hipbone jutted out, pushing hard enough that he sucked in a breath, and then pulled my hand away, leaving my thumbprint.

I sat back and admired it.

"Fuck," he hissed, eyes fixed on that black mark. "That's probably the hottest thing anyone's ever done to me, Hanna."

His words plucked at something raw inside my chest, a resurfacing of the knowledge that there were others: others who had done *hot* things, others who made him feel good.

I blinked away from his pressing gaze, not wanting him to see the thoughts that simmered steadily in the back of my mind—the nongirlfriend thoughts. Will had been good for me. I felt sexy and fun; I felt *wanted*. I wouldn't bog it down with worries of what happened before me, or inevitably, what would happen after. Hell, what probably happened on those days we weren't together. He'd never said anything about ending things with the other women. I saw him most nights of the week, but not *every* night. If I knew anything about Will, it was that he valued variety, and was pragmatic enough to always have a backup plan.

Distance, I reminded myself. *Secret agent. In and out, unharmed.*

Will sat up beneath me, sucking on my neck before moving his mouth to the shell of my ear. "I need to fuck you."

I let my head fall back. "Didn't you do that last night?"

"That was *hours* ago."

Goose bumps exploded across my body, and my tea was forgotten again.

———

The air was still cool but it was starting to feel like spring. There were leaves and blossoms, birds chattering in trees, and the blue-skied promise of better weather to come. Central Park in the spring always rocked me; it was amazing how a city of such size and industry could hide a jewel of color, water, and wildlife in its very heart.

I wanted to think about what I had to do that day, or the upcoming Easter weekend, but I was sore, and tired, and having Will running beside me was proving only more distracting with time.

The rhythm of his feet on the pavement, the cadence of his breath . . . all I could think about was sex. I could remember the hard bunch of muscle beneath my hands, the quiet teasing way he asked me to bite him, as if he was doing it for me, knowing I needed to tear something loose in him, too, and that maybe I'd find it buried beneath his skin. I could remember how he breathed near my ear in the middle of the night, in a rhythm, holding himself back for what felt like hours as he made me come, and then again, and again.

He lifted his shirt and wiped his forehead as he continued to run, and my mind flashed hot and sharp back to the way his sweat felt on my stomach, his come on my hip at the party.

He dropped his shirt, but I couldn't seem to tear my eyes from where he'd just exposed his stomach. "Hanna."

"Hmm?" Finally, I managed to snap my eyes to the trail in front of us.

"What's up? You have this sort of glazed look on your face."

I took a gulping breath and squeezed my eyes shut for only a beat. "Nothing."

His feet stopped, and the cadence of sex and his hips thrusting over and into me halted abruptly. But the tenderness between my legs didn't go away at all when he bent to meet my gaze. "Don't do that."

I filled my lungs, the words escaping with my exhale, "Fine, I was thinking about you."

Blue eyes scanned my face before taking stock of the rest of me: nipples pebbled beneath his too-big T-shirt I wore, stomach in tangles, legs on the verge of collapsing and, between them, muscles coiled so tight, I clenched harder just to relieve the ache.

A tiny smile skittered across his face. "Thinking of me how?"

This time, when I closed my eyes, I kept them closed. He said my strength was in my honesty, but it was really in how he made me feel when I told him everything. "I've never been distracted by someone like this before." I'd always only been *drive*. Right now, I was *lust, want, desire, insatiable student.*

He was quiet for too long and when I looked again, I found him watching me, considering. I needed him to joke or tease, to say something filthy and bring us back to the baseline of Hanna and Will. "Tell me more," he whispered, finally.

I opened my eyes, looked up at him. "I've never had a hard time focusing before, staying on task. But . . . I think about you—" I stopped abruptly. "*Sex* with you all the time."

Never before had my heart felt like such a thick organ, beating with heavy, squeezing pulses. I loved these reminders he gave me that my heart was a muscle and my body was made, in part, for being raw and animalistic, fucking. But not emotions. Definitely not those.

"And?" he pressed.

Fine.

"And it's scary."

His lip twitched in a suppressed grin. "Why?"

"Because you're my friend . . . you've become my *best* friend."

His expression softened. "Is that bad?"

"I don't have a lot of friends and I don't want to screw things up with you. It's important."

He smiled, brushing a strand of hair away from where it clung to my sweaty cheek. "It is."

"I'm scared that this whole friends-who-bang thing will, as Max says, 'go tits up.'"

He laughed, but didn't say anything in response to this.

"Aren't you?" I asked, eyes searching his.

"Not for the same reasons you are, I don't think."

What did that even mean? I loved Will's ability to remain contained, but right now I wanted to throttle him.

"But is it weird that even though you're my best friend, I can't stop thinking about you naked? Me naked. *Us* naked together and the way you make me feel when we're naked? The way I hope *I* make you feel when we're naked? I think about that a lot."

He took a step closer, resting one hand on my hip and the other on my jaw. "It's not weird. And Hanna?"

When he swept his thumb down over the pulse in my neck, I knew he was trying to tell me that he knew how much this scared me. I swallowed, whispering, "Yeah?"

"You know it's important for me to be up front about things."

I nodded.

"But . . . do you want to talk about this now? We can if you want but," he said, squeezing my hip in reassurance, "we don't have to."

A tiny spike of panic went through me. We'd had this conversation before and it hadn't gone well. I'd panicked and he'd taken it back. Would it be different this time? And how would I respond if he said he wanted me, but he didn't want *only* me? I knew what I would say. I would tell him it wasn't working for me anymore. That eventually . . . I'd walk away from this.

Smiling, I shook my head. "Not yet."

He tilted his head, his lips moving to the shell of my ear. "Fine. But in that case I should tell you: *nobody* makes me feel like you do." He said each word carefully, as if each one were placed on his tongue and he had to inspect them before he could let them go. "And I think about sex with you, too. A *lot*."

It wasn't exactly that it surprised me he thought about sex with me; that was fairly clear, given his ongoing commentary. But I suspected he wanted to be with me in some clarified, almost contract-oriented way as he did with all of his women, where it was discussed, and laid out in some sterile mutual agreement. I simply wasn't sure whether for Will that meant committed fucking, or . . . less-committed fucking. After all, if nobody made him feel the way I did, then obviously someone else was out there trying, right?

"I realize you may have . . . *plans* for this weekend," I started and his brows pulled together in frustration or confusion, I couldn't tell, but I barreled on: "But if you do but you don't want to have plans, or if you don't have plans but would *like* to have plans, then you should come home with me for Easter."

He pulled back just enough to see my face. "What?"

"I want you to come home with me. Mom always does an amazing Easter brunch. We can head up Saturday and head home Sunday afternoon. *Do* you have plans?"

"Uh—no," he said, shaking his head. "No plans. You're serious?"

"Would it be weird for you?" I asked.

"Not weird. It would be great to see Jensen, and your folks." Mischief lit up his eyes. "I realize we probably won't be telling the family about our recent sexcapades, but do I get to see your boobs while I'm there?"

"In private?" I asked. "Maybe."

He tapped his chin, pretending to consider this.

"Hmm . . . This is going to make me sound totally creepy, but . . . in your room?"

"My *childhood* room? You *are* a pervert," I said, shaking my head. "But perhaps."

"Then I'm in."

"That's all it took? Boobs? You're *that* easy?"

He leaned in, pressed a kiss to my mouth, and said, "If you have to ask, then you still don't know me very well."

━━━━━━━◦━━━━━━━

Will showed up at my apartment Saturday morning, having parked an ancient green Subaru Outback at the fire hydrant gap. I lifted my brows as I looked from the car to him, at the way he proudly spun the keys around his finger.

"Very nice," I said, stepping back through the door long enough to grab my bag.

He took it and kissed my cheek, smiling widely at my approval. "Isn't it? I keep it in storage. I miss this car."

"When's the last time you drove it?" I asked.

He shrugged. "A while."

I followed him down the stairs, trying not to think about where we were going. Inviting Will had seemed like a great idea at the time, but now, barely a week later, I wondered how everyone was going to react— if I could keep my stupid grin to myself or my hands out of his pants. As I forced my eyes from his ass I realized the odds weren't looking good.

He looked unbelievable in his favorite jeans, a worn-to-perfection Star Wars T-shirt, and green sneakers. He appeared to be as relaxed as I was nervous.

We hadn't really talked about what would happen once we arrived. My family knew we'd been hanging out—it had been their idea, after all—but this, what was happening between us now, had most certainly *not* been part of the plan. I trusted Liv to keep our secret, because if Jensen knew the things Will had done to his little sister's body, there was a good chance there would be fisticuffs, or, at the very least, some horrifically awkward conversations. It was easy to keep that particular reality in check when we were here, in the city. But heading home meant being faced with the reality that Will was Jensen's best friend. I couldn't act the way I did here, as if . . . as if he belonged to *me*.

Will placed my bag in the trunk and moved to open my door, making sure to press me against the side of the car and leaning in for a long, slow kiss. "Ready?"

"Yeah," I said, recovering from my small epiphany. I *liked* feeling like Will belonged to me. He stared down at me and smiled until we both seemed to realize we had but a few hours in the car to enjoy being so unself-conscious about this comfortable intimacy.

He kissed me one more time, humming against my lips and sweeping his tongue gently across mine before stepping back so I could get in the car.

Walking around to the other side, he jumped in the driver's seat and immediately said, "You know we could take a few minutes, hop in the back? I could put the seat down to make it work for you. I know you like your legs spread wide."

I rolled my eyes, grinning. With a little shrug, Will turned the key in the ignition. The car started with a roar and Will put it in gear, winking at me before pressing the gas. We lurched forward, jerking to a stop only a few feet from the curb.

He frowned but restarted the engine and managed to pull out smoothly into traffic the second go-round. I snatched his phone from the cup holder and began scrolling through his music. He gave me a disapproving look but didn't comment, instead turning his eyes on the road.

"Britney Spears?" I asked, laughing, and he reached out blindly, attempting to take it from me.

"My sister," he mumbled.

"Suuuure."

We reached a light at Broadway and the car stalled again. Will coughed but started it, swearing when it stalled just a few minutes later.

"You sure you know how to handle this thing?" I asked, smirking. "Been a New Yorker so long you've forgotten how to drive?"

He glared at me. "This would be a lot easier if we'd had sex in the back first. Help me clear my head."

I looked out the windshield and then back to him, smiling, as I ducked beneath his arm and went to work on his zipper. "Who needs the backseat?"

CHAPTER SIXTEEN

I turned off the car and the engine ticked in the answering silence. Beside me, Hanna was asleep, her head resting away from me and against the passenger window. We were parked in front of the Bergstrom family home on the outskirts of Boston, which featured a wide, white porch wrapping around clean brick. The front windows were framed by navy shutters and inside could be seen the hint of heavy cream curtains. The house was large, and beautiful, and held so many of my own memories I couldn't even imagine what it was like for Hanna to come back here.

I hadn't been here in a couple of years, not since I'd visited with Jensen for a random summer weekend to catch up with his folks. None of the other kids had been there. It was quiet and relaxing, and we'd spent most of the weekend on the back veranda, sipping gin-and-tonics and reading. But now I was parked in front of the house, sitting next to my friend's sister, who had given me two rounds of stellar car head, the last one ending less than an hour ago with my hands white-knuckling the steering wheel and my cock so deep in her throat I could feel her swallowing when I came. She really was a natural with the oral skills. She thought she needed further instruction, and I was happy to keep up the ruse long enough for her to practice on me a few more times.

In the city, enmeshed in our day-to-day lives, it was easy to forget the Jensen connection, the *family* connection. The *they'd-all-kill-me-if-they-knew-what-we-were-doing* connection. I'd been blindsided when she'd brought up Liv because it had felt like such ancient history. But I would be faced with all of that this weekend: my brief history as Liv's former flame, as Jensen's best friend, as Johan's intern. And I would have to face all of that while trying to hide my infatuation with Hanna.

I put my hand on her shoulder, shaking gently. "Hanna."

She startled a little, but the first thing she saw when she opened her eyes was me. She was groggy and not quite conscious but she smiled as if looking at her favorite thing in the world, and murmured, "Mmmm, hey, you."

And, with that reaction, my heart exploded. "Hey, Plum."

She smiled shyly, turning her head to look out her

window as she stretched. When she saw where we'd parked, she startled a little, sitting up straighter, looking around. "Oh! We're here."

"We're here."

When she turned back to me, her eyes looked mildly panicked. "It's going to be weird, isn't it? I'm going to be staring at your button fly and Jensen will see me staring at your button fly and then you'll check out my chest and someone will see that, too! What if I touch you? Or"—her eyes went wide—"what if I *kiss* you?"

Her impending little freak-out calmed me immeasurably. Only one of us was allowed to feel weird at a time.

I shook my head, telling her, "It's going to be fine. We're here as friends. We're visiting your family as *friends*. There will be no public dick appreciation, and no public breast admiration. I didn't even pack another pair of button flies. Deal?"

"Deal," she repeated woodenly. "Just friends."

"Because that's what we *are*," I reminded her, ignoring the organ inside my chest that twisted as I said this.

Straightening, she nodded and reached for her door handle, chirping, "Friends! Friends visiting my house for Easter! We're going to see your old friend, my big brother! Thanks for driving me up here from New York, friend Will my friend!"

She laughed as she got out of the car and walked around to get her bag from the trunk.

"Hanna, calm down," I whispered, placing a soothing hand on her lower back. I felt my eyes move down her neck and settle on her breasts. "Don't be a lunatic."

"Eyes up here, William. Best start now."

Laughing, I whispered, "I'll try."

"Me, too." With a little wink, she whispered, "And remember to call me Ziggy."

———

Helena Bergstrom was such a good hugger she could have been from the Pacific Northwest. Only her softly lilting accent and dramatically European features gave her away as Norwegian-born. She welcomed me in, pulling me just past the front door and then into her familiar embrace. Like Hanna, she was on the tall side, and she had aged beautifully. I kissed her cheek, handing her the flowers we'd bought for her when we stopped to refuel.

"You're always so thoughtful," she said, taking them and waving us in. "Johan is still at work. Eric can't make it. Liv and Rob are here, but Jensen and Niels are still on the road." She looked past me, eyebrows drawn together. "It is going to rain, so I hope they all get here for dinner."

She rattled off her children's names as easily as she breathed. What had her life been like, I wondered, herding so many kids? And as each of them got married and had little ones of their own, this house would only grow more full.

I felt an unfamiliar ache to be part of it somehow and then blinked, looking away. This weekend had the potential to be strange enough without my new emotions thrown into the mix.

Inside, the house felt the same as it had years ago, even though they'd redecorated. It was still comfortable, but instead of the blue and gray décor I remembered from before, it was done in deep browns and reds with plush furniture and bright, cream walls. In the entryway and along the hallway leading deeper into the house, I could see that, redecoration or no, Helena still embraced her American life with a healthy smattering of life-affirming quotes masquerading as art on the walls. I knew what I would see farther into the house:

In the hallway, *Live, Laugh, Love!*

In the kitchen, *A balanced diet is a cookie in each hand!*

In the family room, *Our children: We give them roots so they can take flight!*

Catching me reading the one closest to the front door—*All roads lead home*—Hanna winked, wearing a knowing smile.

As feet tapped down the wooden stairs just to the side of the entryway, I looked up and met Liv's bright green eyes. My stomach dropped a little.

There was no reason for me to let things be weird with Liv; I'd seen her a handful of times since we'd hooked up, most recently at Jensen's wedding a few years ago, where we'd had a nice conversation about her job at a small commercial firm in Hanover. Her fiancé—now husband—had seemed nice. I'd walked away from the evening not thinking twice about where things stood with Liv of all people.

But that was because I hadn't considered that our brief fling had meant anything to her, I hadn't known she'd been heartsick when I returned to Yale after the Christmas holiday so many years ago. It was as if a huge chunk of my history with the Bergstrom family had been rewritten—with me as the flaky lothario—and now that I was here, I realized I hadn't done anything to mentally prepare for it.

As I stood stiff as a statue, she walked up and hugged me. "Hey, Will." I felt the press of her very pregnant belly against my stomach and she laughed, whispering, "*Hug* me, silly."

I relaxed, wrapping my arms around her. "Hey yourself. I think it's safe to say congratulations are in order?"

She stepped back, rubbing her stomach and smiling. "Thanks." Amusement twinkled in her eyes and I remembered that Hanna had called her after our fight, and that Liv probably knew *exactly* what was going on with me and her little sister.

My stomach twisted back into a knot, but I pushed past it, forcing the weekend to not be peculiar on every level. "Are we expecting a boy or a girl?"

"It's going to be a surprise," she said. "Rob wants

to know, but I don't. And so that means, of course, that I win." Laughing, she moved to the side to let her husband shake my hand.

We shared a few more pleasantries in the foyer; Hanna updated her mother and Liv on the latest news from graduate school, Rob and I spoke idly about the Knicks before Helena gestured to the kitchen. "I'm going to get back in there. Come on down for a cocktail after you've settled in a little."

I grabbed our bags and followed Hanna up the stairs.

"Put Will in the yellow room," Helena called.

"Was that my room before?" I asked, checking out Hanna's perfect ass. She had always been slender, but the running was doing really great things for her curves.

"No, you were in the white guest room, the other one," she said, and then turned to smile at me over her shoulder. "Not that I remember *every* detail of that summer or anything."

I laughed and stepped past her into the bedroom that was meant to be mine for the night. "Where is your room?" The question came out before I'd really considered whether it was a good thing to ask, and certainly whether I'd checked to make sure no one else had followed us up here.

She looked back over her shoulder and then stepped inside, closing the door. "Two doors down."

The space seemed to shrink, and we stood, staring at each other.

"Hey," she whispered.

It was the first time since we left New York that I considered this might be a horrible idea. I was in love with Hanna. How would I be able to keep that from showing every time I looked at her?

"Hey," I managed.

Tilting her head, she whispered, "You okay?"

"Yeah." I scratched my neck. "Just . . . want to kiss you."

She took a few steps closer until she could run her hands under my shirt and up my chest. I bent, pressing a single, chaste kiss to her mouth.

"But I shouldn't," I said against her lips when she came back for another.

"Probably not." Her mouth moved over my chin, down my jaw, sucking, nibbling. Beneath my shirt, she scratched my chest with her fingernails, lightly sliding over my nipples. In only seconds I was rigid, ready, felt the fever slide over my skin and dig down into my muscles.

"I won't want to stop at just kissing," I said, half-warning for her to stop, half-plea for her to keep going.

"We have a little time before everyone else gets here," she said. She stepped back far enough to unbutton my jeans. "We could—"

I stilled her hands, the cautious side winning out. "Hanna. No way."

"I'll be quiet."

"That isn't the only issue I have with *fucking* you in

your *parents' house*—during daylight, no less. Didn't we just have this conversation outside?"

"I know, I know. But what if this is the only time we'll be alone together?" she asked with a smile. "Don't you want to fool around with me here?"

She had lost her mind. "Hanna," I hissed, closing my eyes and stifling a groan as she pushed my jeans and boxers down my hips and wrapped a warm, tight hand around my shaft. "We really shouldn't."

She stopped, holding me gently. "We can be quick. For once."

I opened my eyes, looking at her. I didn't like to be quick ever, but especially not with Hanna. I liked to take my time. But if she was offering herself to me and we only had five minutes, I could handle five minutes. The rest of the family hadn't arrived yet; maybe it would be okay. And then I remembered: "Fuck. I don't have any condoms. I didn't pack any. For *obvious reasons.*"

She cursed, wincing. "Me, either."

The question hung between us when she looked at me, eyes wide and pleading.

"No," I said without her having to say a word.

"But I've been on the pill for years."

I closed my eyes, jaw tight. *Fuck.* Pregnancy was the only thing I'd really been worried about. Even in my wildest days, I'd never had sex without a condom. In the past several years I was tested for anything every few months anyway. *"Hanna."*

"No, you're right," she said, thumb sweeping over the head of my cock, spreading the moisture there. "It's not just about getting pregnant. It's about being safe . . ."

"I've never had sex without a condom," I blurted. Who knew I had a death wish?

She stilled. "Ever?"

"Never even rubbed around on the outside. I'm too paranoid."

Her eyes widened. "What about 'just the tip'? I thought every guy did just the tip as a point of habit."

"I'm paranoid and careful. I know it only takes one time." I smiled at her, knowing she'd understand the reference: I was an "oops" baby.

Her eyes darkened, moved to stare at my mouth. "Will? This would be your first time like this?"

Fuck. When she looked at me like that, when her voice got all husky and quiet, I was lost. It wasn't just a physical attraction between us. Of course I'd been attracted to women before. But there was something more with Hanna, some chemistry in our blood, something between us that snapped and crackled, that made me always want just a little more than I should take. She offered her friendship, I wanted her body. She offered her body, I wanted to hijack her thoughts. She offered her thoughts, I wanted her heart.

And here she was, wanting to feel me inside her— just me, just her—and it was nearly impossible to say no. But I tried.

"I really don't think it's a good idea. We should be a little more thoughtful about that decision."

Particularly if there will be other guys in your "experiment," I didn't say.

"I just want to feel it. I haven't had sex without a condom, either." She smiled, stretching to kiss me. "Just inside. Just for a second."

Laughing, I whispered, "Just the tip?"

She stepped backward and leaned against the edge of the mattress, pushing her skirt up her hips and shimmying her panties down her legs. She faced me, spread her thighs and leaned back on her elbows, her hips hovering at the edge of the mattress. All I had to do was step closer and I could push inside. Bare.

"I know it's crazy and I know it's stupid. But God, that's how you make me feel." Her tongue slipped out, pressed to her bottom lip. "I promise to be quiet."

I closed my eyes, knowing as soon as she said that, I'd decided. The more important question was whether *I* could be quiet. I shoved my pants farther down and stepped between her legs, holding my cock and leaning over her. "Fuck. What are we even doing?"

"Just feeling."

My heart hammered in my throat, in my chest, in every inch of my skin. This felt like the final sex frontier; how weird that I'd done almost everything except this? It seemed so simple, almost innocent. But I'd never wanted to feel anything as much as I wanted to feel her, skin to skin. It was like a fever, taking over my mind and my reason, telling me how good it would feel to sink into her for just a second, just to feel and that would be enough. She could go back down to her room, unpack, freshen up, and I'd jerk off harder and faster than I'd ever jerked off in my life.

It was settled.

"Come here," she whispered, reaching for my face. I lowered my chest, opening my mouth to taste her lips, sucking on her tongue, swallowing her sounds. I could feel the slick skin of her pussy against the underside of my cock but that wasn't where I wanted to feel her. I wanted to feel her all around me.

"You good?" I asked, reaching between us to rub her clit. "Can I make you come first? I don't think we should finish like this."

"Can you pull out?"

"Hanna," I whispered, sucking on her jaw. "What happened to 'just the tip'?"

"You don't want to feel what it's like?" she countered, hands sliding over my ass, hips rocking. "You don't want to feel *me*?"

I growled, nipping at her neck. "You are a fucking devious girl."

She reached down and moved my fingers away from her clit, and took hold of me, rubbing my length over and around her sweet, drenched skin. I groaned into her neck.

And then she guided me there, holding, waiting for me to move my hips. I shifted forward, and back again, feeling the subtle give of her body when the head of my cock slid just inside. I moved deeper, the tiniest bit into her, just until I felt her stretch around my shaft and I stopped, groaning.

"Fast," I said. "Quiet."

"I promise," she whispered.

I'd expected warmth, but I was unprepared for *how* warm, how soft, how fucking *wet* it would feel. I was unprepared to feel dizzy from the feel of her, the sensation of her pulse beating all around me, muscles fluttering, of her tight hungry sounds in my ear telling me how different it was for her, too.

"Fuck," I grunted, unable to stop from moving all the way into her. "I don't . . . I can't fuck like this yet. It's too good. I'll come fast."

She held her breath, hands gripping my arms so tight it hurt. "It's okay," she managed, and then let out her breath in a gust. "You always hold out so long. I want it to feel so good you can't last."

"You're so evil," I hissed and she laughed, turning her head to capture my mouth in a kiss.

We were propped at the edge of the bed, our shirts still on, my jeans around my ankles and her skirt bunched at her hips. We'd just come upstairs to put our things away, freshen up, get situated. It was so *bad* that we were doing this here, but somehow we were hardly making any sound, and I convinced myself that if I could keep my wits about me, maybe I could fuck her slow enough to keep the bed from squeaking.

But then I realized that I was *inside* her, completely *bare,* in her *parents'* house. I almost came just looking down at where I was buried inside her.

I slid almost all the way out—reveling in how wet I was from her—and inched back in, and then again, and again. And *fuck,* I was ruined. Ruined for sex with anyone else, ruined for using a condom with this girl.

"Executive decision," she whispered, voice hoarse, breaths coming out in sharp spikes. "Forget the running. We need to do this five times a day." Her voice was so faint I pressed my ear to her lips to hear what else she might say. But all I could make out in my haze of sensation were whispered broken sentences with words like *hard,* and *skin* and *stay inside me after you come.*

It was that last idea that did me in, that made me think about coming inside her, kissing her until she grew fevered and urgent again and then growing hard with her tensing all around me. I could fuck her, stay there, and fuck her again before falling asleep inside her.

I moved harder, holding on to her hip, finding that perfect rhythm that didn't jolt the bed frame, didn't bounce the aluminum headboard into the wall. The pace where she could still stay quiet, where I could try to hold on until I got her there . . . but it was a losing battle, and it had barely been a few minutes.

"Oh shit, Plum," I groaned. "I'm sorry. I'm sorry." I threw my head back, feeling my orgasm barreling up my legs, down my spine, coming too soon. I pulled out, jerking my cock hard in my fist as she reached between her legs, pressing her fingers to her clit.

Footsteps sounded just outside in the hall, and my eyes flew to Hanna's to see if she heard it, too, just a split second before someone pounded on the door.

My vision blurred and I felt myself starting to come. *Fuck. Fuuuuuck.*

Jensen yelled, "Will! Hey, I'm here! You in the bathroom?"

Hanna sat up abruptly, eyes wide and wild with apology but it was already too late. I closed my eyes, coming in my hand, on the bare skin of her thigh.

"Just a second," I wheezed, staring down at where I still pulsed in my grip. I bent over the bed, leaning one hand on the mattress for support. When I looked up at Hanna, she couldn't seem to tear her eyes away from where my release landed on her skin, and—*fuck*—all over her skirt.

"I'm just changing. I'll be right out," I managed, my heart feeling like it was about to pound out of my body with the sudden flush of adrenaline that pumped through my blood.

"Cool. I'll meet you downstairs," he said, his footsteps retreating.

"Shit, your skirt . . ." I stepped back, scrambling to get dressed quickly, but Hanna hadn't moved.

"Will," she whispered, and I saw the familiar hunger darken her eyes.

"Fuck." That was too fucking close. The door wasn't even locked. "I don't . . ."

But she leaned back, pulling me over her. She was so completely unconcerned about her brother walking in, seeing us. And he *had* left, hadn't he?

This girl made me insane.

My heart still racing, I bent down, pressing two fingers inside her and sliding my tongue over her pussy as she let her eyes fall closed. Her hands went in my hair, her hips rocked up to my mouth, and within only seconds, she started to come, lips parted in a silent cry. Beneath my touch, she shook, hips rising from the bed, fingers pulling my hair tight.

As her orgasm subsided, I continued slowly moving my fingers inside her, but kissed a gentle path from her clit, to her inner thigh, to her hip. Finally, I rested my forehead against her navel, still struggling to catch my breath.

"Oh God," she whispered once her hands had eased their grip on my hair, and she slid them up and over her breasts. "You make me feel *crazy.*"

I pulled my fingers from her and reached to kiss the back of her hand, inhaling the scent of her skin. "I know."

Hanna remained still on the bed for a quiet minute and then opened her eyes, gazing up at me as if she'd just come back to her senses. "Whoa. That was close."

Laughing, I agreed, "*Very* close. We should probably

get changed and head downstairs." I nodded to her skirt. "Sorry about that."

"I'll just wipe it off."

"Hanna," I said, stifling a frustrated laugh. "You can't go downstairs with a giant jizz stain on your *skirt*."

She considered this and gave me a goofy smile. "You're right. I just . . . I kind of like it there."

"Such a twisted girl."

She sat up straight as I pulled my pants up, and she kissed my stomach through my shirt. I wrapped my arms around her shoulders, holding her to me, and just reveling in the feel of her.

I was so lost in love with this girl.

After a few seconds, the sun passed behind a cloud outside, dimming everything a little, beautifully, and her voice rose out of the quiet: "Have you ever been in love?"

I stilled, wondering if I'd said it out loud. But when I looked down at her, she was only glancing up in open curiosity, eyes calm. If any other woman had said this to me after we just had a quickie, I would have felt the hot flush of panic and the itching need to extract myself from the situation immediately.

But with Hanna, the question seemed somehow appropriate for the moment, especially given how reckless we'd just been. In the past several years I'd grown, if anything, overly cautious about when and where I had sex, and—Jensen's wedding aside—rarely put myself in situations that would ever require a quick exit or explaining. But lately, being with Hanna made me feel slightly panicked, as if there were a limited number of times I would be able to feel her like this. The thought of having to give her up made me nauseous.

There were only two other lovers in my life for whom I'd ever felt something deeper than fondness, but I'd never told a woman I loved her before. It was weird, and at thirty-one I knew this omission made *me* weird, but I'd never felt the weight of that strangeness until just this moment.

I grew hyperaware of every blasé comment I'd made to Max and Bennett about love, and commitment. It wasn't that I didn't believe in them; I just had never been able to relate, exactly. Love was always something I'd find at some vague point in the future, when I was somehow more settled or less adventurous. The image of me as a player was very much like the deposit of minerals on glass over time; I hadn't bothered to care it was forming until it was hard to see past it.

"I'm guessing not," she whispered, smiling.

I shook my head. "I've never said 'I love you' before, if that's what you mean."

Though Hanna would have no way of knowing I said it to her, silently, nearly every time we touched.

"But have you ever *felt* it?"

I smiled. "Have you?"

She shrugged, and then nodded to the door to the

Jack-and-Jill bathroom that I was pretty sure adjoined Eric's bedroom. "I'm going to go clean up."

I nodded, closing my eyes, and slumping down after she left. I thanked every lucky power in the universe that Jensen hadn't just walked in. That would have been a disaster. Unless we wanted her family to know what was happening—and I was pretty sure that since Hanna still wanted this to remain friends-with-benefits—we would have to be *way* more careful.

━━━━

I checked my work email, sent a couple texts, and then pulled myself together in the bathroom, with some soap, water, and vigorous scrubbing. Hanna met me in the living room, wearing a bashful smile.

"I am so sorry," she said softly. "I don't know what got into me." She blinked, putting a hand to my mouth just as I started to crack the obvious joke. "Don't say it."

Laughing, I looked behind her into the kitchen, making sure no one was close enough to hear. "That was awesome. But holy shit it could have gone *very* wrong."

She looked embarrassed, and I smiled at her, making a goofy face. Out of the corner of my eye I caught sight of a little ceramic Jesus statue on an end table. I picked it up, holding it between Hanna's breasts. "Hey! Look! I found Jesus in your cleavage after all!"

She looked down, cracking up and started to shimmy a little, as if letting Jesus enjoy this most perfect of locations. "Jesus in my cleavage! Jesus in my cleavage!"

"Hey, guys."

When I heard Jensen's voice for the second time today, my arm flailed, hand flying away from the vicinity of Hanna's tits. Feeling as if I were watching it happen in slow motion and somewhere outside my own body, I flung the Jesus statue as quickly as I could, only realizing what I'd done when it landed on the hardwood floor several feet away from me, bouncing and exploding into a million little ceramic pieces.

"Oh, shiiiiiiit," I groaned, running over to the massacre. I kneeled down, trying to pick up the biggest shards. It was a worthless effort. Some of the pieces were so small they could be characterized as dust.

Hanna bent over, wheezing in laughter. "Will! You broke Jesus!"

"What were you *doing*?" Jensen asked, kneeling to help me.

Hanna left the room to get a broom, leaving me alone with the person who had witnessed much of my early-twenties bad behavior. I shrugged at Jensen, trying to not look like I'd just been playing with his little sister's breasts. "I was just looking at it. I mean, at the statue, and seeing what it was. And looking at the shape—of *Jesus*, I mean."

I ran a hand over my face and realized I was sweating a little. "I don't even know, Jens. You just startled me."

"Why are you so jumpy?" He laughed.

"Maybe the drive? It's been a while since I was behind the wheel." I shrugged, still unable to look at him for very long.

With a pat to my back, Jensen said, "I think you need a beer."

Hanna returned, and shooed us away so she could sweep the shards into a dustpan, but not before giving me a conspiratorial *holy shit* look. "I told Mom you broke this and she couldn't even remember which of her aunts gave it to her. I think you're fine."

I groaned, following her into the kitchen and apologizing to Helena with a kiss on her cheek. She handed me a beer and told me to relax.

At some point when I'd been upstairs fucking Hanna, or maybe when I'd been madly washing her scent off my dick and my fingers and my *face*, her father had arrived home. *Jesus Christ.* With some clarity away from naked Hanna and a closed bedroom door, I realized how insane we had been. What the fuck were we *thinking*?

Looking up from where he'd been digging in the fridge for a beer, Johan came over to greet me with his own brand of warmth and awkwardness. He was good at eye contact, bad with words. It usually meant that he ended up staring at people while they scrambled to come up with things to say.

"Hi," I said, returning his handshake and letting him pull me into a hug. "Sorry about Jesus."

He stepped back, smiled, and said, "Nah," and then paused, seemed to reconsider something. "Unless you've suddenly become religious?"

"Johan," Helena called, breaking our moment. I could have kissed her. "Honey, can you check the roast? The beans and bread are done."

Johan walked to the oven, pulling a meat thermometer out of the drawer. I felt Hanna step beside me, heard her clink her water glass to my beer bottle.

"Cheers," she said with an easy smile. "Hungry?"

"Famished," I admitted.

"Don't just stick the tip in, Johan," Helena called out to him. "Shove it all the way in there."

I coughed, feeling the burn of beer as it almost came out my nose. Cupping my hand over my mouth, I urged my throat to open, to allow me to swallow. Jensen stepped behind me, slapping my back and wearing a knowing grin. Liv and Rob were already sitting at the kitchen table, bent over in silent laughter.

"Holy shit, this is going to be a long night," Hanna mumbled.

———

Conversation looped around the table at dinner, breaking into smaller groups and then returning to include everyone. Partway through the meal, Niels arrived. Whereas Jensen was outgoing and one of my oldest friends, and Eric—only two years older than Hanna—was the wild child in the family, Niels was the middle child, the quiet brother, and the one I never really knew. At twenty-eight, he was an engineer with a prominent energy firm, and almost a carbon copy of his father, minus the eye contact and smiles.

But tonight, he surprised me: he bent to kiss Hanna before he sat down, and whispered, "You look amazing, Ziggs."

"You really do," Jensen said, pointing a fork at her. "What's different?"

I studied her from across the table, trying to see what they saw and feeling mysteriously irked at the suggestion. To me, she looked as she always had: comfortable in her skin, easy. Not fussy with clothes, or hair or makeup. But didn't *need* to be. She was beautiful when she woke up in the morning. She was radiant after a run. She was perfect when she was beneath me, sweaty and postcoital.

"Um," she said, shrugging and spearing a green bean with her fork. "I don't know."

"You look thinner," Liv suggested, head tilted.

Helena finished a bite and then said, "No, it's her hair."

"Maybe Hanna's just *happy*," I offered, looking down at my plate as I cut a bite of roast. The table went completely still and I looked up, nervous when

I saw the collection of wide eyes staring back at me. "What?"

Only then did I realize I'd called her by her given name, not Ziggy.

She covered smoothly, saying, "I'm running every day, so yes, I'm a little thinner. I did get my hair cut. But it's more. I'm enjoying my job. I have friends. Will's right—I *am* happy." She looked over at Jensen and gave him a cheeky little grin. "Turns out, you were right. Can we stop examining me now?"

Jensen beamed at her and the rest of the family all mumbled some variation of "Good," and returned to their food, quieter now. I could feel Liv's smile aimed at my face, and when I looked up from my plate, she winked.

Fuck.

"Dinner is delicious," I told Helena.

"Thanks, Will."

The silence grew, and I felt silently *inspected*. I'd been caught. It didn't help that Jesus' tiny decapitated porcelain head was watching me from the sideboard, judging. He knew. Ziggy was a nickname as ingrained in this family as their father's crazy work hours, or Jensen's tendency to be overprotective. I hadn't even known Hanna's given name when I'd gone running with her nearly two months ago. But fuck it. The only thing I could do was embrace it. I had to say it again.

"Did you know that Hanna has a paper coming out in *Cell*?" I hadn't been particularly smooth; her name came out louder than any other word but I went with it, smiling around the table.

Johan looked up, eyes widening. Turning to Hanna, he asked, "Really, *sötnos*?"

Hanna nodded. "It's on the epitope mapping project I was telling you about. It was just this random thing we did but it turned into something cool."

This seemed to steer the conversation into less awkward territory, and I let go of the little extra breath I'd been holding in. It was possible that the only thing more stressful than *meeting the parents* was *hiding everything from the family.* I caught Jensen watching me with a little smile, but simply returned it, and looked back down at my plate.

Nothing to see here. Keep moving along.

But during a break in the chatter, I found Hanna's eyes lingering on me, and they were surprised and thoughtful. "You," she mouthed.

"What?" I mouthed back.

She shook her head slowly, finally breaking eye contact to look down at her plate. I wanted to reach under the table with my leg, slide my foot over hers to get her to look back at me, but it was like a minefield of non-Hanna legs under there, and the conversation had already moved on.

———

After dinner, she and I volunteered to wash the dishes while the others retired to the family room with a cocktail. She snapped me with her dish towel and I flung soap suds at her. I was on the verge of leaning close and sucking on her neck when Niels came in to get another beer and looked at us both as if we had traded clothes.

"What are you doing?" he asked, suspicion heavy in his voice.

"Nothing," we answered in unison, and—making it worse—Hanna repeated, "Nothing. Just dishes."

He hesitated for a second before tossing his bottle cap in the trash and heading back to the others.

"That's twice today we've almost been busted," she whispered.

"Thrice," I corrected her.

"Nerd." She shook her head at me, amusement lighting up her eyes. "I probably shouldn't risk sneaking into your room tonight."

I started to protest but stopped when I caught the sly grin curving her lips.

"You're the devil, do you know that?" I murmured, reaching out to glide my thumb across her nipple. "No wonder Jesus didn't want to be in your cleavage."

With a sharp gasp, she smacked my hand and looked over her shoulder.

We were all alone in the kitchen, could hear the others' voices trailing in from the other room, and all I wanted to do was pull her into a kiss.

"Don't." Her eyes grew serious and the next words

came out shaking, as if she couldn't catch her breath: "I won't be able to stop."

━━━━━

After staying up for a few hours to catch up with Jensen, I finally headed to bed. I stared at the wall for an hour or so before giving up on waiting for the quiet padding of Hanna's feet from down the hall or the creak of the door as she snuck into my room.

So I drifted off and missed it when she actually did slip in, get undressed, and climb naked under the blankets with me. I woke only to the feel of her smooth, bare body curling around mine.

Her hands ran up my chest, mouth sucking at my neck, my jaw, my bottom lip. I was hard and ready to go before I was entirely conscious, and when I groaned, Hanna pressed a hand over my lips, reminding me, "Shh."

"What time is it?" I murmured, inhaling the sweet smell of her hair.

"A little after two."

"Are you sure no one heard you?" I asked.

"The only people who could hear me at this end of the hall are Jensen and Liv. Jensen's fan is on, so I know he's asleep. He can barely stay awake for ten seconds once that thing starts."

I laughed because she was right. I'd been his roommate for years, and I hated that fucking fan.

"And Rob is snoring," she murmured, kissing my jaw. "Liv has to fall asleep before him or else his snoring will keep her awake."

Satisfied that she'd been sufficiently stealthy—and that no one would be likely to knock on the door again while we were making love—I rolled to my side, pulling her close.

She snuck in for sex, clearly, but it didn't feel like all she wanted was a quick fuck. There was something else there, something brewing beneath the surface. I saw it in the way she kept her eyes open in the darkness, the way she kissed me so earnestly, each touch offered tentatively, as if she were asking a question. I saw it in the way she pulled my hand where she wanted it: over her neck, down across her breasts, coming to rest over her heart. It was *pounding*. Her bedroom was only a few doors down the hall; she wasn't winded from the effort. She was worked up over something, her mouth opening and closing a few times in the moonlight, as if she wanted to speak but couldn't find air.

"What's wrong?" I whispered, lips pressed to her ear.

"Are there still others?" she asked.

I pulled back and stared at her, confused. *Other women?* I'd wanted to have this conversation again a hundred times, but her subtle evasion had finally worn down my need for clarity. *She* wanted to date around, didn't trust me, and didn't think we should try to be exclusive. Or had I misunderstood? For *me,* there was no one else.

"I thought that's what you wanted?" I replied.

She stretched to kiss me; her mouth felt so familiar already, molding to mine in the easy rhythm of soft kisses that grew heated, and I wondered for a fevered beat how she could ever imagine sharing herself with anyone else.

She pulled me over her, reaching between us to slide me across her skin. "Is there a rule about having unprotected sex twice in a day?"

I sucked on the skin below her ear, and whispered, "I think the rule should be that there *aren't* any other lovers."

"So we break that rule then?" she asked, lifting her hips.

Fuck that. Fuck that noise.

I opened my mouth to protest, to put my foot down and tell her I'd had enough of this circular nondiscussion, but then she made a quiet, hungry sound and arched into me so that I slipped all the way inside her and I bit my lip to stifle a groan. It was unreal; I'd had sex thousands of times and it had never, *ever* been like this.

I tasted blood on my lip and fire beneath my skin wherever she touched me. But then she began to circle her hips, finding her pleasure beneath me, and I felt the words dissolve from my mind.

I'm only one man, for Christ's sake. I'm not a god. I

can't resist taking Hanna now and figuring out every-thing afterward.

It felt like cheating; she wouldn't give me her heart but she'd give me her body, and maybe if I took enough of her pleasure, stored it up, I could pretend it was more.

It didn't matter at the time how much I might regret it later.

Chapter Seventeen

It had never been like this, ever. Slow. Almost so slow that I wasn't sure either of us could get there, or that I even cared. Our lips were only millimeters apart, sharing breaths and noises and the whispered pleas to *Feel that? Do you feel that?*

I *did* feel it. I felt every one of his stuttering heartbeats under my palm, and the way his shoulders shook above me. I felt the unformed words on his lips, how he seemed to be trying to say something . . . maybe the same something I'd been skirting around since I snuck into his dark room. Even before that.

He didn't seem to understand what I was asking.

I'd never expected it to be so hard to put myself on the line. We'd made love—what felt like the true meaning of the phrase earlier; his skin, my skin, nothing else between us. He called me Hanna at the dinner table. . . . I don't think anyone had ever said that name out loud in this house before that. And even though Jensen—Will's best friend—was in the other room, Will had stayed with me to do dishes. He'd given me a meaningful look before I headed to bed, and texted me good night, saying, In case there's any question, my bedroom door shall remain unlocked.

It seemed like he was mine when we were in a room full of people. But here, alone behind his closed door, it was suddenly so unclear.

Are there others? . . .

I thought that's what you wanted.

The rule should be that there aren't other lovers . . .

So we break this rule then?

. . . Silence.

But what was I expecting? I closed my eyes, wrapping my arms tighter around him as he pulled almost all the way out and then slid slowly back inside, inch by perfect inch, and groaned quietly in my ear.

"So good, Plum." His hips rolled over me, one hand sliding down my ribs and back up to cup my breast and simply hold it, his thumb sweeping over the tight peak.

I loved the deep, molten sounds of his pleasure, and it helped distract me from the truth that he hadn't given me the words I'd wanted tonight. I'd wanted him to say, *There are no other women anymore.*

I'd wanted him to say, *Now that we're doing this without protection, we don't break that rule, ever.*

But he'd been the one to open this conversation before, only to have me shut it closed. Was it true that he really wasn't interested in being more than friends-who-fuck? Or was he unwilling to be the one to start the conversation again? And why was I being so *passive*? It was as if my fear of messing things up with him had stolen all of my words.

He arched his neck back, groaning quietly as he slid in and out of me, achingly slow. I closed my eyes, pressing my teeth into his neck, biting down, giving him every bit of pleasure I could think. I wanted him to want me so much that it didn't matter that I was inexperienced or unsure. I wanted to find a way to erase the memory of every woman who came before me. I wanted to feel—to *know*—that he belonged to me.

I wondered for a sharp, painful beat how many other women had thought the exact same thing.

I want to feel like you're mine. I pushed on his chest so he had to roll off me and I could climb over him. I'd never been on top with Will, not for sex, and looked down at him, feeling unsure, guiding his hands to my hips. "I've never done this."

He gripped his base with one hand and guided me over him, grunting as I sunk down. "Just find what feels good," he murmured, watching me. "This is where you get to drive."

I closed my eyes, trying different things and struggling to not feel foolish in my inexperience. I was so hyperaware of this earnest feeling pulling my ribs tight, I wondered if I moved differently, more clunky, less carefree and sexy. I had no idea if it felt good to him.

"Show me," I whispered. "I feel like I'm doing it wrong."

"You're perfect, are you fucking kidding?" he mumbled into my neck. "I want to last all night."

I grew sweaty, not from exertion but from being so wound up I thought I might burst from my skin. The bed was old and squeaky; we couldn't move the way we were used to—roughly for hours and using the entire mattress and frame and pillows. Before I realized what was happening, Will lifted me off him, carried me to the floor, and sat up beneath me so I could lower myself back onto him. He went so much deeper this way; he was so hard I could feel the press of him in some unknown, tender place. His open mouth moved across my chest and he ducked his head to suck and blow on my nipple.

"Just *fuck* me," he growled. "Down here you won't have to worry about the noise."

He thought I was worried about the creaky bed frame. I closed my eyes, rocking self-consciously, and just when I thought I would stop, tell him this position wasn't working for me, tell him I was choking on words and unanswered questions, he kissed my jaw, my cheek, my lips and whispered, "Where are you right now? Come back to me."

I stilled over him and rested my forehead on his shoulder. "I'm thinking too much."

"What about?"

"I'm nervous all of a sudden, and I just feel like you're mine only for these little bits of time. I guess I don't like that as much as I thought I would."

He slid his finger under my chin and tilted my face up so I had to look at him. His mouth pressed against mine, once, before he told me, "I'll be yours every second if that's what you want. You just have to tell me, Plum."

"Don't break me, okay?"

Even in the darkness I could see his brows pull together. "You said that before. Why do you think I would break you? Do you think I even *could*?" His voice sounded so pained, it plucked at something raw and taut in me, too.

"I think you *could*. Even if you didn't want to, I think you could now."

He sighed, pressing his face into my neck. "Why won't you give me what I want?"

"What *do* you want?" I asked, shifting so that my knees were more comfortable, but in the process, I slid up his cock and back down. He stilled me with forceful hands on my hips.

"I can't think when you're doing that." Taking several deep breaths, he whispered, "I just want *you*."

"So . . ." I whispered, running my hands into the hair at the nape of his neck. "Are there going to be others?"

"I think *you* need to tell *me* that, Hanna."

I closed my eyes, wondering if that would be good enough. I could tell him I wouldn't date anyone else, and I imagined he would agree to the same. But I didn't *want* it to be up to me. If Will was going to do this, to be with one person, it had to be something that wasn't negotiable for him—it had to be him wanting to call it off with the others because of how he felt for *me*. It couldn't be some loose decision, a maybe-maybe-not, a whatever-you-decide.

His mouth found mine then, and he gave me the sweetest, most gentle kiss I'd ever felt from him. "I told you I wanted to try," he whispered. "You were the one who said you thought it wouldn't work. You know who I am; you *know* I want to be different for you."

"I want it, too."

"Okay then." He kissed me and our pace started again, small thrusts from him beneath me, tiny circles from me on top. His exhales were my inhales; his teeth slid deliciously over my lips.

I'd never felt so close to another human in my life. His hands were everywhere: my breasts, my face, my thighs, my hips, between my legs. His voice rumbled low and encouraging in my ear, telling me how good I felt, how close he was, how he needed this so much he felt like he worked every day just to get back to me. He told me being with me felt like being home.

And when I fell, I didn't care whether I was awkward or jagged, whether I was inexperienced or naïve. I cared only that his lips were pressed firmly to my neck and his arms were wrapped around me so tight the only way I could move was closer to him.

———⌁———

"You ready?" Will asked Sunday afternoon, slipping into my bedroom and pressing a quick kiss to my cheek. The majority of the morning had played out this way: a covert kiss in an empty hallway, a rushed grope session in the kitchen.

"Almost. Just packing a few things Mom is sending home with me." I felt his arms fold solid around my waist and I leaned back, melting into him. I'd never noticed how much Will touched me until he couldn't do it freely. He'd always been tactile—small brushes of his fingers, a hand lingering at my hip, his shoulder bumping against mine—but I'd grown so used to it, so comfortable, I hardly noticed anymore. This weekend I'd felt the loss of every one of those small moments, and now I couldn't get enough. I was already debating how many miles we'd need to put between the car and this place before I could tell him to pull over and make good on his offer to take me in the backseat.

He pushed my ponytail out of the way as his lips

moved along my neck, stopping just below my ear. I heard the tinkling of his keys in his hand, felt the cool metal against my stomach where my shirt had ridden up the tiniest bit.

"I shouldn't be doing this," he said. "I think Jensen's been trying to corner me since brunch and I don't really have a death wish."

His words cooled my blood and I stepped away, reaching for a shirt on the opposite side of the bed. "Sounds like pretty standard Jensen," I murmured with a shrug. I knew it would be weird for my oldest brother—hell, it would be weird for Will and me, too, when the family knew about us—but all morning long I'd been replaying the previous night in the guest room. I wanted to ask him in the light of day: *did you really mean it when you said you wanted only me?* Because I was finally ready to take the leap.

I zipped my bag, started to lug it off the bed.

He reached around my body, grabbing the handle. "Can I take that?"

I felt the heat of him, the scent of his shampoo. When he straightened he didn't step away, didn't move to put distance between us. I closed my eyes, felt myself grow dizzy with how his proximity seemed to suck all the air out of the room. He tilted my chin and pressed his lips to mine, just a slow, lingering touch and I moved toward him, chasing the kiss.

He smiled. "Let me get this stuff in the car and we'll get out of here, okay?"

"Okay."

He brushed his thumb over my lower lip. "We'll be home soon," he whispered. "And I'm not going to my apartment."

"Okay," I said again, legs shaking.

He grinned, lifted the bag, and I watched, barely able to stand, as he left the room.

Going downstairs, I found my sister in the kitchen.

"Leaving?" Liv asked, rounding the counter to hug me.

I leaned into her, nodding. "Is Will already outside?" I glanced out the kitchen window but didn't see him. I was anxious to get on the road, to say everything in the light of day where it couldn't be ignored.

"Think he went out back to say goodbye to Jens," she said, walking back to the bowl of berries she'd been rinsing. "You two sure are cute together."

"What? No." Cookies cooled on the counter and I reached for a handful, tucking them away in a brown paper sack. "I told you, it's not like that, Liv."

"Say what you want, Hanna. That boy is smitten. Frankly, I'd be surprised if I'm the only one who's noticed."

Beginning to feel warm, I shook my head. Pulling two Styrofoam cups from the cupboard, I filled them with coffee from a huge stainless steel carafe, adding sugar and cream to mine and cream only to Will's. "I think pregnancy's mottled your brain. That's not what this is about." My sister wasn't an idiot; I'm sure she heard the lie in my voice as plainly as I had.

"Maybe not for you," she said with a skeptical shake of her head. "Though I don't really buy that one, either."

I stared blankly out the back window. I knew where Will and I stood . . . at least I thought I did. Things had shifted over the past few days and now I was eager to define this relationship. I'd been so afraid to give it limits because I thought I wanted more room to breathe. I thought it would upset me to hear how he slotted me into his schedule as conveniently as he did other women. Lately, my desire to avoid the conversation felt more about keeping my own heart caged than about how free he was with his. But it was a useless exercise. I knew we needed to have the full conversation now—the one he'd tried to have before. The one we'd touched on last night.

I would need to put myself out there, take a risk. It was time.

A door shut loudly somewhere and I jumped, blinking back to the coffee I was still stirring. Liv touched my shoulder. "I have to be big sister for just one minute, though. Be careful, okay?" she said. "This is the infamous Will Sumner we're talking about."

And that, right there, was reason number one I was terrified I was making a mistake.

With coffee and snacks for the road in hand, I made the rounds and said my goodbyes. My family was scattered all over the house, but the only two I couldn't seem to find were my brother and my ride.

I headed out front to check the car, the gravel path crunching beneath my feet. I neared the garage and stopped as voices filtered out through the cool morning air, above the birds and the creaking of the trees overhead.

"I'm just wondering what's going on between you two," I heard my brother say.

"Nothing," Will said. "We're just hanging out. Per your request, I might add."

I frowned, remembering that old saying about not eavesdropping because you probably won't like what you hear.

"Is 'hanging out' code for something?" Jensen asked. "You seem awfully familiar with her."

Will started to speak but paused, and I stepped back a bit to make sure my long shadow wouldn't be visible to anyone standing in the garage.

"I am seeing a few people," Will started, and I could just picture him scratching his jaw. "But no, Ziggy isn't one of them. She's just a good friend."

I felt like I'd been dropped in ice water, goose bumps spreading along my skin and despite knowing he was just following the rules we'd agreed on, my stomach dropped.

Will went on: "Actually, I am . . . interested in

exploring something more with one of the women I'm seeing." My heart started to hammer, and I was tempted to step forward, and keep him from saying too much. But then he added, "So I feel like I should end it with the other women I'm seeing. I think for the first time I might want more . . . but this girl has been cagey, and it's been hard to take that extra step and just cut off the old routine, you know?"

My arms felt like limp noodles and I leaned against the gate, steadying myself. My brother said something in reply, but I wasn't really listening anymore.

⁘

To say the atmosphere in the car was merely tense was laughable. We'd been on the road for almost an hour and I'd barely strung together more than two words at a time.

Are you hungry?

No.

Temperature okay? Too warm? Too cold?

It's fine.

Could you put this into the GPS?

Sure.

Mind if we stop for a bathroom break?

Okay.

The worst part was that I was pretty sure I was being bratty and unfair. With what Will said to Jensen, he was only following the rules that I'd put out there. I'd never really expected him to be exclusive before last night.

Open your mouth, Hanna. Tell him what you want.

"You okay over there?" he asked, ducking briefly to catch my eyes. "You're being awfully monosyllabic."

I turned and watched his profile as he drove: his stubbly jaw, his lips curled up in a smile just knowing I was staring at him. He let his eyes dart my way a couple of times, reaching for my hand and squeezing it. It was so much more than sex. He was my best friend. He was the one I wanted to call *boyfriend*.

The idea of him being with other women this whole time made me faintly nauseous. I was pretty sure that, after this weekend, he wouldn't be with them again since—*Jesus*—we'd had sex without a condom. If that didn't warrant a serious discussion, I didn't know what did.

I felt so close to him; I really felt like we had become something much more than friends.

I pressed my hands to my eyes, feeling jealous and nervous and . . . *God,* just so impatient for us to figure it out *now*. Why was it easy to talk to Will about every feeling I had but the ones we needed to declare between us?

When we stopped at a gas station to refuel, I distracted myself by going through the music on his phone, building the proper sequence of words in my head. Finding a song I was pretty sure he hated, I smiled, watching him hang up the pump, walk back to his side of the car.

He climbed back in, his hand hovering with the key perched in the ignition. "Garth *Brooks*?"

"If you don't like it, then why is it on your phone?" I teased. This was good, this was a start, I thought. Actual words were a step in the right direction. Ease into the conversation; prepare a soft landing and then jump.

He gave me a playful sour look, as if he'd tasted something gross, and started the engine to pull away. The words cycled through my head: *I want to be yours. I want you to be mine. Please tell me you haven't been with anyone else in the past couple of weeks, when things seemed so good with us. Please tell me that hadn't all been in my mind.*

I opened his iTunes and started scrolling through his music again, looking for something better, something that made my mood lighter and more sure of myself, when a text message flashed across his screen.

Sorry I missed this yesterday! Yes! I'm free Tuesday night and I can't wait to see you. My place? xoxox

Kitty.

I don't think I took a breath for an entire minute.

Turning off the screen, I sank lower into my seat, feeling like someone had reached down my throat and pulled my stomach inside out. My veins flushed hot with adrenaline, with embarrassment, with anger.

Sometime between fucking me without a condom at my parents' house yesterday afternoon and kissing my neck this morning, Will had messaged Kitty about getting together on Tuesday.

I looked out the window as we pulled away from the gas station and got back on the road, dropping the phone gently into his lap.

A few minutes later he glanced at his phone before wordlessly putting it back down.

He had clearly seen Kitty's message, and he didn't say anything. He didn't even look *surprised*.

I wanted to climb into a hole.

We arrived at my apartment but he made no attempt to come upstairs. I carried my bag to the door and we stood there awkwardly.

He pulled a stray hair from my cheek and then quickly dropped his hand when I winced. "You sure you're okay?"

I nodded. "Just tired."

"I guess I'll see you tomorrow?" he asked. "The race is Saturday so we should probably do a couple of longer runs early in the week and then rest."

"That sounds good."

"So I'll see you in the morning?"

I was suddenly desperate to hold on, to give him one last chance, a way to come clean and maybe clear up a huge misunderstanding.

"Yeah, and . . . I was wondering if you wanted to come over Tuesday night," I said, reaching out to place my hand on his forearm. "I feel like we should talk, you know? About everything that happened this weekend?"

He looked down at my hand, moved so his fingers could twist with mine. "You can't talk to me now?" he asked, brow furrowed and clearly confused. It was, after all, only seven at night on a Sunday. "Hanna, what's going on? I feel like I'm missing something."

"It was just a long drive and I'm tired. Tomorrow I have a late night in the lab, but Tuesday is open. Can you make it?" I wondered if my eyes were pleading as much as the voice inside my head was. *Please say yes. Please say yes.*

He licked his lips, glanced at his feet and up to where his hand was holding mine. It felt like I could see the actual seconds tick by and the air felt thick, almost solid, and so heavy I could hardly breathe.

"Actually," he said, and paused as if he was still considering, "I have a late . . . thing, for work. I have a late meeting on Tuesday," he babbled. *He lied.* "But I could make it during the day or—"

"No, it's fine. I'll just see you tomorrow morning."

"You sure?" he asked.

My heart felt like it had frozen over. "Yeah."

"Okay well, I'll just"—he motioned to the door over his shoulder—"go now. You sure everything's fine?"

When I didn't answer, and just stared at his shoes, he kissed my cheek before leaving and I locked up, heading straight for my room. I wouldn't think of another thing until morning.

⌐⌐⌐⌐

I slept like the dead, not waking until my alarm went off at five forty-five. I reached over to hit the snooze button and lay there, staring at the illuminated blue dial. Will had lied to me.

I tried to rationalize it, tried to pretend it didn't matter because maybe things weren't official with us, maybe we weren't *together* yet . . . but somehow, that didn't feel true, either. Because as much as I'd tried to convince myself that Will was a player and couldn't be trusted, deep down . . . I must have believed that Saturday night changed everything. I wouldn't feel like this otherwise. Still, apparently he was fine hooking up with other women until we sat down and made it *officially* official. I could never be that cavalier about separating emotion from sex. The simple realization that I wanted to be only with Will was enough to make me faithful.

We were entirely different creatures.

The numbers in front of me blurred and I blinked back the sting of tears as the snooze alarm broke through the silence. It was time to get up and run. Will would be waiting for me.

I didn't care.

I sat up long enough to unplug the clock from the wall and then rolled over. I was going back to sleep.

———

I spent the majority of Monday at work with my phone off, not heading home until long after the sun had gone down.

Tuesday I was up before my alarm and down at the local gym, running on the treadmill. It wasn't the same as the trails at the park with Will, but at this point, I didn't care. The exercise helped me breathe. It helped me think and clear my head, and gave me a brief moment of peace from thoughts of Will and whatever—*whoever*—he was doing tonight. I think I ran harder than I ever had. And later, in the lab, when I had barely come up for air all day, I had to leave early, around five, because I hadn't eaten anything other than a yogurt and felt like I was going to fall flat on my face.

When I got home, Will was waiting at my door.

"Hi," I said, slowing as I neared him. He turned around, shoved his hands in his pockets, and spent a long time just looking at me.

"Is there something wrong with your phone, Hanna?" he asked finally.

I felt a brief pang of guilt before I straightened, meeting his eyes. "No."

I moved to unlock the door, keeping some distance between us.

"What the fuck is going on?" he asked, following me inside.

Okay, so we were doing this now. I looked at his clothes. He'd obviously just come from work and I had to wonder if he'd stopped by here before going to meet . . . *her*. You know, to make the rounds and settle things down before stepping out with someone else. I wasn't sure I would ever understand how he could be so wild about me, while fucking other women.

"I thought you had a late meeting," I murmured, turning to drop my keys on the counter.

He hesitated, blinking several times before saying, "I do. It's at six."

Laughing, I murmured, "Right."

"Hanna, what the hell is going on? What did I do?"

I turned to face him . . . but chickened out, staring at the tie loosened at his neck instead, his striped shirt. "You didn't do anything," I started, breaking my own heart. "I should have been honest about my feelings. Or . . . lack of feelings."

His eyes went wide. "*Excuse* me?"

"Things at my parents' house were weird. And being so close, almost getting caught? I think that was the real thrill for me. Maybe I got carried away with everything we said on Saturday night." I turned away, fidgeted with a stack of mail on a table and felt the crackling, dried layers of my heart peel away and leave nothing but a hollow shell. I forced a smile on my face and gave him a casual shrug. "I'm twenty-four, Will. I just want to have fun."

He stood there and blinked, swaying slightly as if I'd hurled something at him heavier than words. "I don't understand."

"I'm sorry. I should have called or . . ." I shook my head, trying to shake the sound of static in my ears. My skin felt hot; my chest ached like my ribs were caving in. "I thought I could do this but I can't. This weekend just solidified that for me. I'm sorry."

He took a step back and glanced around like he'd just woken up and realized where he was. "I see." I watched him swallow, run a hand through his hair. As if he'd remembered something, he looked up. "Does this mean you won't run on Saturday? You've trained really hard and—"

"I'll be there."

He nodded once before turning, walking out the door, and disappearing, probably forever.

CHAPTER EIGHTEEN

There was a hill near my mom's house, just before the turn down the driveway. It was an uphill followed by a blind downhill curve, and we'd learned to honk whenever we went over it, but when people drove it for the first time, they were never aware of how tricky it was at first and would later always tell us how crazy that turn was.

I supposed my mom or I could have put up a curved mirror at some point, but we never did. Mom said she liked using only her horn, she liked that moment of faith, where she knew my schedule and she knew the curve so well she didn't need to see what was ahead in order to know it was clear. The thing was, I was never sure whether I loved or hated that feeling myself. I hated having to hope the coast was clear, hated not knowing what was coming, but I loved the moment of exhilaration when the car would coast downhill, clear and free.

Hanna made me feel this way. She was my blind curve, my mysterious hill, and I'd never been able to shake the lingering suspicion that she'd send something the other way that would crash blindly into me. But when I was with her, close enough to touch and kiss and hear all of her crazy theories on virginity and love, I'd never felt such a euphoric combination of calm, elation, and hunger. In those moments, I stopped caring that we might crash.

I wanted to think of her brush off tonight as a glitch, a scary curve that would soon straighten out, and that my relationship with her wasn't over before it even started. Maybe it was her youth; I tried to remember myself at twenty-four and could really only see a young idiot, working crazy hours in the lab and then spending night after night with different women in all manners of wildness. In some ways, Hanna was such an older twenty-four than I'd ever been; it was like we weren't even the same species. She was right so long ago when she said she always knew how to be a grown-up and needed to learn how to be a kid. She'd just accomplished her first immature blow-off with a complete lack of clear communication.

Well done, Plum.

I'd put Kitty in a cab and returned to work around eight, intent on diving into some reading, and trying to get out of my own head for a few hours. But as I passed Max's office on the way to mine, I saw that his light was still on, and he was sitting inside.

"What are you still doing here?" I asked, stepping just inside the room and leaning against the doorway.

Max looked up from where he'd been resting his head in his hands when I walked into his office. "Sara's out with Chloe. Just decided to work a bit late." He studied me, mouth turning down at the corners. "And I thought you left a few hours ago. Why are you back? It's Tuesday . . ."

We stared at each other for a beat, the implied question hanging between us. It had been so long since I'd spent a Tuesday night with Kitty, I don't think even Max knew exactly what he was asking.

"I saw Kitty tonight," I admitted. "Earlier, just for a bit."

His brows pulled together in irritation, but I held up a hand, explaining: "I asked her to meet me for a drink after work—"

"Seriously, Will, you're a right toss—"

"To *end* it, you ass," I growled, frustrated. "Even though things with her were always meant to be casual, I wanted her to know they were done. I haven't seen her in forever but she still checks in every Monday to ask. The fact that she even thinks it's a possibility made me feel like I've been cheating on Hanna."

Just saying that name out loud made my stomach twist. The way we had left things tonight had been a mess. I'd never seen her look so distant, so closed off. I clenched my jaw, looking over at the wall.

I knew she'd been lying; I just didn't know *why*.

Max's chair creaked as he leaned back. "So what are you doing here? Where is your Hanna?"

I blinked back over to him, finally taking in his appearance. He looked tired, and shaken, and . . . not at all like Max, even at the end of a long workday.

"What's with you?" I asked instead of answering. "You look like you've been through the wringer."

Finally he laughed, shaking his head. "Mate, you have no idea. Let's collect Ben and go grab a pint."

———

We got to the bar before Bennett did, but not by much. Just as we sat at a table in the back, near the dartboards and the broken karaoke machine, Bennett strode in still wearing his crisp dark suit and a look of such utter exhaustion I wondered how long the three of us would manage to remain conscious.

"You sure are making me drink a lot on weeknights lately, Will," Bennett mumbled, taking a seat.

"So order a soda," I said.

We both looked at Max, expecting his usual semi-serious and barely intelligible rant about the blasphemy of ordering a Diet Coke in a British pub, but he just remained uncharacteristically quiet, staring at the menu and then ordering what he always ordered: a pint of Guinness, a cheeseburger, and chips.

Maddie took the rest of our orders and disappeared. We were back on yet another Tuesday night and, just as before, the bar was almost empty. A strange quietness seemed to ring our table. It was as if none of us could get it up tonight to bother shit-talking.

"Really, though. What's up with you?" I asked Max again.

He smiled at me—a genuine Max smile—but then shook his head. "Ask me again after I've had two pints." Grinning up at Maddie as she put our drinks on the table, he gave her a little wink. "Thanks, love."

"The text from Max said we are convening at Maddie's for a girls' night out," Bennett said, and then took a sip of his beer. "So which of Will's women are we discussing tonight?"

"There's only the one woman, now," I murmured. "And Hanna ended it earlier tonight, so I guess technically there are *no* women." Both men looked up at me, eyes concerned. "She said, essentially she didn't want this."

"Fuck," Max murmured, rubbing his face in his hands.

"The thing is," I said, "I *think* she's full of shit."

"Will . . ." Bennett cautioned.

"No," I said, waving him off, and feeling a surge of relief, of realization as I thought more about it. Yes, she'd been pissed tonight at her place—and I still had no idea why—but I remembered how it felt making love on the floor this weekend, in the middle of the night, and the hunger in her eyes like she didn't just want me, she was starting to *need* me.

"I *know* she feels this, too. Something happened between us this weekend," I told them. "The sex has always been fucking amazing, but it was so intense at her parents' place."

Bennett coughed. "Sorry. You had sex at her *parents'* place?"

I chose to believe his ambiguous tone meant *impressed,* so I continued: "It was like she was finally going to admit there was more between us than just sex and friendship." I lifted my water glass to my lips, took a sip. "But the next morning, she snapped closed. She's talking herself out of it."

Both men hummed thoughtfully, considering this. Finally, Bennett asked, "Did you two ever decide to be exclusive? I'm sorry if I'm not following the map of this relationship very clearly. You leave a very treacherous path of women behind you."

"She knew that I wanted to be exclusive, but then I agreed to keep it open—because that's what she wanted. For me, she's *it*," I said, not caring whether they gave me a mountain of shit for being so whipped. I deserved it, and the funniest part was I *relished* being claimed. "You guys called it, and I have no problem admitting you're right. She's funny, and beautiful. She's sexy and she's fucking brilliant. I mean, she is *completely* it for me. I have to think today was just a bump in the road or else I will probably go on punching walls repeatedly until my hand is broken."

Bennett laughed, lifting his glass to clink it against mine. "Then here's to hoping she comes around."

Max lifted his glass, too, knowing there wasn't really anything he could say. He winced a little, apologetically, as if this was all somehow his fault simply because he'd wished lovesick misery on me only a couple months back.

After my little speech, the silence returned, and the weird mood with it. I struggled to not be pulled under. Of course I was worried I wouldn't be able to win Hanna back. From the first moment she slid her fingers beneath my shirt in the bedroom at the party, I'd been ruined for anyone else.

Hell, even before then. I think I'd been lost in her the second I pulled the wool cap over her adorably rumpled bed head on our first run.

But despite my certainty that she had lied about her feelings, and that she did feel something for me, doubt crept back in. *Why* had she lied? What happened between our obvious *lovemaking* and when we got into the car the next morning?

Bennett interrupted my downward spiral with his own misery: "Well, since we're letting out all of our feelings, I guess it's my turn to share. The wedding is driving us both mad. Everyone in our family is traveling to San Diego for the ceremony—I mean *everyone*—step-great-aunts and second-cousins-twice-removed and people I haven't seen since I was five. The same thing on Chlo's side."

"That's great," I said, and then reconsidered when Bennett slid his cool gaze to me. "Isn't it good when people accept your invitation?"

"I suppose it is, but many of these people weren't invited. Her family is mostly in North Dakota, and mine is all over Canada, and Michigan, and Illinois. They're all looking for a reason to have a vacation on the coast." Shaking his head, he continued: "So last night Chloe decided she wanted to elope. To cancel all of it, and she's so hell-bent on it that I'm afraid she is going to call the hotel and cancel and we'll be thoroughly fucked then."

"She wouldn't do that, mate," Max murmured, roused from his uncharacteristically quiet mood. "Would she?"

Bennett's hands slid into his hair and curled into fists, his elbows planted on the table. "Honestly, I don't know. This thing is getting *huge,* and even I feel like it's spiraling out of control. Everyone in our family is inviting whoever they want—as if it's just a big free party and why not? It's not even about cost at this point, it's about space, about having what *we* wanted. We were imagining a wedding of about a hundred and fifty. Now it's close to three hundred." He sighed. "It's just one day. It's a *day.* Chloe is trying to stay sane but it's hard on her because there's only so much I . . ." He laughed, shaking his head, and then sat up to look at us. "There are only so many details I give a shit about.

For once in my life, I don't need to control everything. I don't care what our colors are, or what wedding favors we choose. I don't care about the flowers. Everything that comes after is what I care about. I care that I get to fuck her for a week in Fiji and then we'll be married forever. *That's* what matters. Maybe I should just let her cancel it all and marry her this weekend so we can get to the fucking."

I opened my mouth to protest, to tell Bennett that I was sure every couple went through this kind of crisis, but the truth was, I had no idea. Even at Jensen's wedding—where I'd been the best man—the only thing keeping me going during the ceremony was the thought of taking the two bridesmaids to the coat closet to bang. I hadn't paid particularly close attention to the more sentimental emotions of the day.

So, I closed my mouth, rubbing a palm across it and feeling a dose of self-loathing sweep over me. *Fuck*. I already missed Hanna, and being with my two closest friends who were so . . . *situated* made it hard. It wasn't that I felt I needed to catch up to some milestone of theirs; I simply wanted that comfort of knowing I could go out with my friends for an evening and still come home to *her*. I missed the comfort of her company, the way she listened so carefully, the way I knew she said whatever came to mind when she was around me, a thing I noticed she didn't do with anyone else. I *loved* her for being so wildly her own self— so fierce and confident and curious and smart. And I missed feeling her body, taking pleasure from her, and, *fuck,* giving *her* pleasure unending.

I wanted to lie in bed with her at night, and bemoan the ordeal of planning a wedding. I wanted it all.

"Don't elope," I said, finally. "I realize that I know shit about any of this, and I'm sure my opinion means nothing, but I'm pretty sure *every* wedding feels like a complete clusterfuck at one point or another."

"It just feels like so much work for a single day," Bennett mumbled. "Life goes on so much longer beyond this one slip of time."

Max chuckled, lifting his glass, and then reconsidered, putting it back down on the table, before he started laughing again, and harder. We both turned to look at him.

"You *were* acting like zombie Max," I noted, "but now you're creepy clown Max. We're all sharing here—I've had my heart stomped on by Hanna, Bennett is wrestling with the age-old crisis of wedding planning madness. Your turn."

He shook his head, smiling down at his empty pint. "Fine." He waved to Maddie for another Guinness. "But Ben, you're here tonight only as my mate. Not as Sara's boss. Understood?"

Bennett nodded, brows pulled together. "Of course."

Offering a one-shouldered shrug, Max murmured, "Well, lads, it turns out I'm going to be a dad."

The relative quiet we had been enjoying seemed like roaring chaos in comparison to the vacuum that now existed. Bennett and I froze, and then exchanged a brief look.

"Max?" Bennett asked, with an uncharacteristic delicacy. "Sara's pregnant?"

"Yeah, mate." Max looked up, cheeks pink and eyes wide. "She's having my baby."

Bennett continued to watch him, probably assessing every reaction on Max's face.

"This is good," I said carefully. "Right? This is a good thing?"

Max nodded, blinking over to me. "It's bloody *amazing*. I just . . . I'm terrified, to be honest."

"How far along is she?" Bennett asked.

"A little over three months." We both started to respond in surprise but he held up his hand, nodding. "She's been stressed, and she thought . . ." Shaking his head, he continued: "She took a test this weekend, but didn't know until today how far she was. But today, when I was out at meetings . . . we had an ultrasound to measure the baby." He pressed the heels of his hands to his eyes. "Bloody hell, *the baby*. I just found out Sare's pregnant, and today I could see there's a fucking *kid* in there. Sara's far enough along that the ultrasound technician guessed it's a girl but we won't know for sure for a couple months. It's just . . . unreal."

"Max, why the fuck are you out with *us*?" I asked, laughing. "Shouldn't you be at home drinking sparkling cider and picking out names?"

He smiled. "She wanted some time away from me,

I think. I've been fucking unbearable the last few days, wanting to remodel the bloody apartment and talk about when we're getting married and all that shite. I think she wanted to tell Chloe. Besides, we've got a date planned for tomorrow." He stilled, his brows pulling together in concern when he said that. "But now that this day is over, I'm just *beat*."

"You're not worried about this, are you?" Bennett asked, studying Max. "I mean, this is unbelievable. You and Sara are going to have a *baby*."

"No, it's just the same worries I'm sure everyone feels I imagine," Max said, wiping a hand across his mouth. "Will I be a good dad? Sara's not much of a drinker, but did we do anything in the past three months that could hurt the baby? And, with my giant spawn growing in there, will little Sara be okay?"

I could barely hold back. I stood, pulling Max out of his chair and into a hug.

He was so in love with Sara he could barely think straight when she was around. And although most of the time I gave him endless shit about it, it was a pretty amazing thing to behold. I knew without him ever having to say it that he was ready for this, ready to settle down and be the devoted husband and dad. "You'll be amazing, Max. Seriously, congratulations."

Stepping back, I watched as Bennett stood, shaking Max's hand and then pulling him into a brief hug.

Holy shit.

The enormity of this started to sink in and I all

but collapsed back into my chair. This, here, was life. This was life beginning for us: weddings and families and deciding to step up and be a man for someone. It wasn't about the fucking jobs we had or the random thrills we sought or any of that. Life was built from the bricks of these connections and milestones and moments where you tell your two best friends that you're about to have a child.

I pulled out my phone, sending Hanna a single note.

You're all I can think about anymore.

Chapter Nineteen

When I was little, I'd drive my entire family insane by not sleeping for days before any holiday or big event. Nobody understood why. My exhausted mother would sit up with me night after night, begging me to just go to bed.

"Ziggy," she would say. "Honey, if you go to bed, Christmas will get here sooner. Time goes faster when you're asleep."

But it never seemed to work that way for me. "I can't sleep," I'd insist. "There's too much in my head. My thoughts won't slow down."

I'd spend the countdown to birthdays and vacations wide awake and anxious, pacing the halls of our big house while I should have been asleep upstairs. It was a habit I'd never outgrown.

Saturday wasn't Christmas or the first day of summer vacation, but I was counting every day, every minute as if it were. Because as pathetic as it sounded, and as much as I hated that I was looking forward to it, I knew I'd see Will. That thought alone was enough to find me up every night, wide awake at the window, recounting the streetlights to his building.

❧

I'd always heard the first week after a breakup was the hardest. I hoped that was true. Because getting Will's message on Tuesday night—*You're all I can think about anymore*—was torture.

Could he have texted the wrong number by mistake? Or did he say that because he ended up alone, or because he was with another woman, but thinking of me? I couldn't exactly be angry, and my initial self-righteousness over the prospect of him texting me while he was with Kitty faded quickly; I, too, had texted him when I was on my dates with Dylan.

The worst part was that I had no one to talk to about it, really. Well, I did, but I only wanted Will.

The sun had dipped low in the sky on Friday night as I walked the last few blocks to meet Chloe and Sara for drinks.

I'd tried to put on a brave front all week but I was miserable, and it was starting to show. I looked tired. I looked sad. I looked exactly how I felt. I missed him so much that I felt it with every breath, felt each second pass since I'd last seen him.

The Bathtub Gin was a small speakeasy in Chelsea. Visitors were greeted with an everyday storefront, the words STONE STREET COFFEE stenciled across the top. If you weren't sure what you were looking for, or happened to pass by during the week when there wasn't a crowd of people lined up outside, you might miss it. But if you knew it was there, illuminated by a single, glowing red bulb, you'd find the right door. One that opened up to a Prohibition-era club, complete with dim lighting, a steady hum of jazz, and even a large copper bathtub at the center.

I found Chloe and Sara sitting at the bar, drinks already in front of them and a gorgeous dark-haired man at their side.

"Hey, guys," I said, sliding onto the stool next to them. "Sorry I'm late."

The three of them turned, looked me up and down before the man said, "Oh honey, tell me all about the man who did this to you."

I blinked between them, confused. "I . . . hi, I'm Hanna?"

"Ignore him," Chloe said, sliding the menu across the bar to me. "We all do. And order a drink before you talk. You look like you could use it."

The mystery man looked appropriately offended and the three of them argued among themselves while I scanned the various cocktails and wines, picking the first thing that seemed to fit my mood.

"I'll have a Tomahawk," I told the bartender, noticing in my peripheral vision the way Sara and Chloe looked to each other in surprise.

"So it's like that, I see." Chloe motioned for another drink and then took my hand, leading us all to a table.

In all reality, I'd probably just hold my cocktail for most of the night and absorb the comfort afforded by the *option* to get completely hammered. But I knew I wanted to race tomorrow, and no way was I going to run hungover.

"By the way, Hanna," Chloe said, gesturing to the man currently watching me with curious, amused eyes. "This is George Mercer, Sara's assistant. George, this is the adorable and soon-to-be-drunk and/or facedown-on-the-table Hanna Bergstrom."

"Ah, a lightweight," George said, and nodded to Chloe. "What in the world are you doing with this old boozehound? She should come with a warning label for girls like you."

"George, how would you like my heel up your ass?" Chloe asked.

George barely blinked. "The whole heel?"

"Gross," Chloe groaned.

Laughing, George drawled, "Liar."

Sara leaned forward, elbows on the table. "Ignore them. It's like watching Bennett and Chloe, but they'd both rather screw Bennett than each other."

"I see," I murmured. A waitress placed our drinks

on the table and I took a tentative pull from my straw. "Holy *crap*," I coughed, my throat on fire.

I downed almost an entire glass of water while Sara watched me, appraising. "So what's happening?" she asked.

"This drink is so *spicy*."

"Not what she meant," Chloe said bluntly.

I looked down at my glass, tried to focus on the tiny specks of paprika floating along the surface and not the hollow feeling in my gut. "Have you guys talked to Will lately?"

They each shook their head but George perked up.

"Will Sumner?" he clarified. "You're banging *Sumner*? Jesus hell." He motioned to the waitress again. "We're gonna need another glass, lovely. Just bring the whole bottle."

"Actually, I haven't talked to him since Monday," Sara said.

"Tuesday afternoon," Chloe volunteered, pointing to her chest. "But I know he's had a crazy week."

"Uh-oh," Sara said. "Didn't he go home with you for the holiday?"

George sucked in a breath. "Yikes."

And now I was *that* girl, the one with the breakup story I didn't even want in my head, let alone as something to share over drinks. How did I explain that things had been perfect that weekend? That I had believed everything he said? That I had fallen in—I stopped, the words hardening like concrete in my thoughts.

"Hanna, honey?" Sara reached forward to set her hand on my forearm.

"I just feel like an idiot."

"Sweetie," Chloe said, her eyes full of nothing but concern. "You know you don't have to talk about it if you don't want to."

"The hell she doesn't," George snapped. "How are we all supposed to make his life appropriately horrible if we don't know every sordid detail? We should probably start at the beginning and work our way to the horror, though. First question: is his cock as epic as I've heard? And the fingers . . . are they truly quote-unquote magical?" He leaned closer, whispering, "And rumor has it the man could win a watermelon-eating contest, if you know what I'm saying."

"George," Sara groaned, and Chloe glared at him but I cracked a smile.

"I'm sure I have no idea what you mean," I whispered back.

"Look it up on YouTube," he said to me. "You'll get the visual."

"But back to the part where Hanna is *upset*," Sara said, eyes playfully stern and fixed on George.

"I just . . ." I took a deep breath, hunting for words. "What can you tell me about Kitty?"

"Oh," Chloe said, sitting back in her chair. She glanced at Sara. *"Oh."*

I leaned forward, brows drawn together. "What does 'oh' mean?"

"Is this the . . . I mean, is Kitty *one* of his . . ." George trailed off, waving his hand meaningfully.

"Yeah," Sara said. "Kitty is one of Will's lovers."

I rolled my eyes. "Do you know if he's still been seeing her?"

Chloe seemed to be considering her answer carefully. "Well—I don't *officially* know of him ending things with her," she said, wincing a little. "But Hanna, he adores you. Anyone can—"

"But he's still seeing her," I interrupted.

She sighed reluctantly. "I honestly don't know. I know we all gave him a hard time about not ending things, but I can't . . . for a fact, I mean, say that he ever stopped seeing her."

"Sara?" I asked.

Shaking her head, Sara murmured, "I'm sorry, honey. I honestly don't know, either."

I wondered if it was possible for a heart to break by fractions. I'd been sure I'd heard it crack when I'd read the text from Kitty. Felt another piece break with his lie about Tuesday night. And all week, I'd felt bruised, felt every tiny shard as it fell away until I wondered what could possibly still be beating in my chest.

"I'd overheard him talking to my brother about wanting to be serious with someone but being afraid to end things with the others. But I figured, maybe he just meant *officially* end them? Things seemed really good with us. But then Kitty sent him this text," I said. "I was playing with his phone and she replied to a message he'd obviously sent her about getting together Tuesday night."

"Why didn't you confront him?" Chloe asked.

"I wanted him to tell me himself. Will has always been all about honesty and communication, so I figured if I invited him over for dinner Tuesday he'd tell me he was going to be with Kitty."

"And?" Sara asked.

I sighed. "He said he had a *thing*. A meeting that night."

"Ouch," George said.

"Yeah," I mumbled. "So I ended it right there. But I did it really badly because I had no idea what to say. I told him that it was getting too heavy, that I was only twenty-four and didn't want anything serious. That I didn't want this anymore."

"Damn, girl," George sang quietly. "When you want to end things, you dig a hole and drop a bomb in it."

I groaned, pressing the heels of my hands against my eyes.

"There has to be an explanation," Sara said. "Will doesn't say he has a meeting when he's going to be with a woman. He just says he's going to be with a woman. Hanna, I've never seen him like this before. *Max* has never seen him like this before. It's clear he adores you."

"But does it matter?" I asked, my drink long forgotten. "He lied about the meeting, but I'm the one who said we should keep it open. It's just that open for me meant the *possibility* of someone else. Open for him was more of the reality already in hand. And all along he was the one pushing for more between us."

"Talk to him, Hanna," Chloe said. "Trust me on this one. You need to give him a chance to explain."

"Explain what?" I asked. "That he was still seeing her, per the rules I'd initially set? Then what?"

Chloe took my hand and squeezed it. "Then you hold your head high and tell him to fuck off in person."

I dressed as soon as the first hint of light appeared outside the window and walked the ten blocks to the race in a nervous haze. It was held in Central Park and the entire circuit went for just over thirteen miles, snaking through trails and paths in the park. Several local streets were cordoned off to support the sponsor trucks, tents, and herds of people, both racers and spectators.

This was real now. Will would be there and I would decide to talk to him or just leave things the way they were. I didn't know if I could handle either choice.

The sky had just started to brighten and a chill

hung in the morning air. But my face felt warm, my blood hot as it raced through arteries and veins, through my heart that beat too fast. I had to focus on pulling every breath into my lungs, pushing it out again.

I didn't know where I was going, or what I was doing, but the event seemed well organized, and as soon as I neared the location, signs directed me to where I was meant to check in.

"Hanna?"

I looked up to see my former training partner, my former lover, standing at the registration table, watching me with an expression I couldn't quite make out. I'd hoped my memory had exaggerated how striking he was, how overwhelming it was to just be near him. It hadn't. Will held my gaze, and I wondered if I would start laughing uncontrollably, cry, or maybe just run away if he got any closer.

"Hi," he said finally.

Abruptly, I held out my hand as if he should . . . what? Greet me with a handshake? *Jesus Christ, Hanna!* But I was committed now, and my trembling hand remained suspended between us as he looked down at it.

"Oh . . . we're . . . going to be like this," he mumbled, wiping his palm on his pants before gripping my hand in his. "Okay, hey. How are you?"

I swallowed, jerking my hand away as soon as I possibly could. "Hey. Good. I'm good."

This was comically bad, and it was the kind of bad I wanted to dissect with Will and only Will. I suddenly had a million questions about awkward post-breakup protocol, and whether handshakes were always a bad idea or just now.

Bending robotically, I signed my name on some line and took a packet of information from a woman seated behind the table. She was giving me instructions I barely comprehended; I felt like I was suspended underwater.

When I finished, Will was still standing there, wearing the same nervous, hopeful expression. "Do you need help?" he whispered.

I shook my head. "I think I'm good." It was a lie; I had no idea what I was doing.

"You just need to go to the tent over there," he said gently, reading me perfectly as always and putting a hand on my arm.

I pulled back and smiled stiffly. "I got it. Thanks, Will."

As the silence stretched on, a woman I hadn't even noticed at his side spoke up. "Hi," she said, and I blinked over to see her smiling with her hand outstretched. "I don't think we've been formally introduced. I'm Kitty."

It took a moment for the pieces to come together, and when they did, I couldn't even contain my shock. I felt my mouth fall open, my eyes go wide. How could he possibly think this was even remotely okay?

I looked from her to Will, who, I quickly realized, seemed as surprised as I was to find her standing there. Hadn't he seen her approach?

Will's face could have been at the dictionary entry for *uncomfortable*. "Oh God." He looked back and forth between us for a flash before murmuring, "Oh, shit, um . . . hey, Kitty, this is . . ." He looked to me, his eyes softening. "This is my Hanna."

I blinked to him. *What had he said?*

"Nice to meet you, Hanna. Will has told me all about you."

I knew they were speaking but the words didn't seem to penetrate the echo of that sentence repeating over and over again in my head. *This is my Hanna. This is my Hanna.*

It was a mistake. He was just uncomfortable. I pointed over my shoulder. "I've got to go." Turning, I stumbled away from the table and toward the women's tent.

"Hanna!" he called after me, but I didn't turn back.

I was still a bit foggy when I handed over my information, got my race number, and walked over to an empty spot to stretch and lace up my shoes. At the sound of footsteps, I looked up, already dreading what I would find. Seeing Kitty standing there, it was worse than I thought.

"He's really something," she said, pinning her number to the front of her shirt.

I lowered my eyes, ignored the fire that flared low in my belly. "Yeah, sure is."

She sat on a bench a few feet away and began peeling the label from a bottle of water. "You know, I never thought this would happen." She shook her head, laughing. "All this time and he's always used the *It's not you. I just don't want more with anybody* excuse. And now? Now that he finally ends things, it's because he *does* want more. Just with someone else."

I sat up, met her eyes. "He ended things with you?"

"Yeah. Well," she said, considering. "This week was the *official* end but we hadn't really seen each other since . . ." She looked up at the ceiling of the tent, considering. "Since February? And he'd been canceling on me ever since."

I didn't know what to say.

"At least I know why now." I must have looked completely dumbstruck because she smiled, leaned in a little bit. "Because he's in love with you. And if you're as amazing as he seems to think you are, you won't blow this."

⌐══════⌐

I don't remember crossing the park to where the other runners were gathered. My thoughts were hazy and jumbled.

February?

We had only been running then . . .

. . . March—that's when Will and I actually started sleeping together. . . .

Tuesday night . . . so he could end things, face-to-face.

Like a decent human being, like a good man. I closed my eyes when the full force of the realization hit me: he told her all of this even *after* I broke up with him.

"You ready for this?"

I jumped, surprised to see Will standing next to me. He put a hand on my arm, offering a tentative smile. "You okay?"

I looked around, as if I could escape somewhere and just . . . *think.* I wasn't ready for him to stand this close or talk like we were friends again, to be *nice.* I had such an enormous apology to make, and I still had an angry earful to give him for lying. . . . I didn't even know where to start. I met his eyes, looked for any sign there telling me that we could fix this. "I think so."

"Hey," he said, taking the smallest step closer. "Hanna . . ."

"Yeah?"

"You're . . . you're going to do great." His eyes searched mine, heavy with anxiety, and it made my stomach twist with guilt. "I know things are weird with us. Just put everything else out of your head. You need to be here, head in the race. You trained so impressively for it and you can do it."

I exhaled, felt the first flare of pre-race, non-Will anxiety.

Kneading my shoulders, he murmured, "Nervous?"

"A little."

I saw the moment he switched into trainer mode and I took some small level of comfort in it, grabbed on to this splinter of platonic familiarity.

"Remember to pace yourself. Don't start off too fast. The second half is the worst and you'll want to keep enough in the tank to finish, okay?"

I nodded.

"Remember, this is your first race and it's about crossing the finish line, not where you place."

Licking my lips, I answered, "Okay."

"You've done ten miles before; you can do thirteen. I'll be right there so . . . we'll do this together."

I blinked up at him, surprised. "You can *place*, Will. This is nothing for you—you should be in the front."

He shook his head. "That's not what this one is about. My race is in two weeks. This one is yours. I told you that."

I nodded again, numb, and couldn't look away from his face: at the mouth that had kissed me so many times, and wanted to kiss *only* me; at the eyes that watched me intently every time I said a word, every time I'd touched him; and at the hands that were now braced on my shoulders and were the same hands that had touched every inch of my skin. He'd told Kitty he wanted to be with me, only me. It's not like he hadn't said those exact words to me, too. But I'd never believed them.

Maybe the player really was gone.

With one last, searching look, Will dropped his hands from my shoulders, and pressed his palm to my back, leading me to the starting line.

⸻

The race started at the southwest corner of the park near Columbus Circle. Will motioned for me to follow and I went through the routine: calf stretch, quad stretch, hamstring. He nodded wordlessly, watched my form and kept in constant, reassuring contact.

"Hold it a little longer," he said, hovering over me. "Breathe through it."

They announced it was time to begin and we got into place. The crack of the starter pistol burst through the air and birds scattered in the trees overhead. The sudden rush of hundreds of bodies pushing off from the line melded into a collective burst of sound.

The marathon route began at the circle and followed the outer loop of Central Park, arching around Seventy-second Street and back to the start.

The first mile was always the hardest. By the second, the world grew fuzzy at the edges and only the muffled sound of feet on the trail and blood pumping in my ears filtered through the haze. We hardly spoke, but I could hear every one of Will's footsteps beside me, feel the occasional brush of his arm against mine.

"You're doing great," he told me, three miles in.

At mile seven, he reminded me, "Halfway done, Hanna, and you're just hitting your stride."

I felt every inch of the last mile. My body ached; my muscles went from stiff, to loose, to on fire and cramping. I could feel my pulse pounding in my chest. The heavy beat mirrored every one of my steps, and my lungs screamed for me to stop.

But inside my head it was calm. It was as though I was underwater, with muffled voices blending together until they were a single, constant hum. But one voice was clear, "Last mile, this is it. You're *doing it*. You're amazing, Plum."

I'd almost tripped when he called me that. His voice had gone soft and needy, but when I looked over at him, his jaw was set tight, eyes straight ahead. "I'm sorry," he rasped, immediately contrite. "I shouldn't have—I'm sorry."

I shook my head, licked my lips, and looked forward again, too tired to reach out and even touch him. I was struck by the realization that this moment was probably harder than all the tests I'd ever taken in school, every long night in the lab. Science had always come easy for me—I'd studied hard, of course, I'd done the work—but I'd never had to dig this deep and push on when I'd have liked nothing more than to collapse onto the grass and stay there. The Hanna that met Will that day on the icy trail would have never made it thirteen miles. She would have given it a half-assed try, gotten tired and finally, after having rationalized that this wasn't her strength, gone back to the lab and her books and her empty apartment with prepackaged, single-serving meals.

But not *this* Hanna, not now. And *he* helped get me here.

"Almost there," Will said, still encouraging. "I know it hurts, I know it's hard, but look," he pointed to a grouping of trees just off in the distance, "you're almost there."

I shook the hair from my face and kept going, breathing in and out, wanting him to keep talking but also wanting him to shut the hell up. Blood pumped through my veins, every part of me felt like I'd been plugged into a live wire, shocked with a thousand volts that had slowly seeped out of me and into the pavement with every step.

I'd never been more tired in my life, I'd never been in more pain, but I'd also never felt more alive. It was crazy, but even through limbs that felt like they were on fire, and every breath that seemed harder than the last—I couldn't wait to do it again. The pain had been worth the fear that I'd fail or be hurt. I'd wanted something, taken the chance, and jumped with both feet.

And with that last thought in mind, I took Will's hand when we crossed through the finish line together.

CHAPTER TWENTY

Several yards off to the side of the finish line, Hanna walked in small circles, then bent down and cupped her hands over her knees.

"Holy shit," she gasped, facing the ground. "I feel amazing. That was *amazing*."

Volunteers brought us Luna bars and bottles of Gatorade and we gulped them down. I was so fucking proud of her, and I couldn't hold back from pulling her into a sweaty, breathless hug, kissing the top of her head.

"*You* were amazing." I closed my eyes, pressing my face to her hair. "Hanna, I am so proud of you."

She froze in my arms and then slid her hands to my side, simply bracing there, her face in my neck. I could feel her inhaling and exhaling, could feel her hands shaking against me. For some reason, I didn't think it was only the adrenaline from the race.

Finally, she whispered, "I think we should go get our things."

I'd oscillated so wildly between confident and wrecked all week, and now that I was with her, I didn't particularly want to let her out of my sight. We turned to head back toward the tents; with the race snaking through Central Park, the finish line ended up only a few blocks from where we'd started. I listened to her breathing, watched her feet as she walked. I could tell she was exhausted.

"I'm guessing you've heard about Sara," she said, looking down and fidgeting with her race number. She pulled out the pins, took it off, and looked at it.

"Yeah," I said, smiling. "Pretty amazing."

"I saw her last night," she said. "She's so excited."

"I saw Max on Tuesday." I swallowed, feeling so fucking nervous all of a sudden. Beside me, Hanna faltered a little. "I went out with the guys that night. He has the expected look of terror and glee."

She laughed, and it was genuine, and soft and—fuck—I'd missed it.

"What are you up to after this?" I asked, ducking so she'd look up at me.

And when she did, it was there, the something I knew I hadn't imagined from the weekend before. I could still feel her sliding over me in the dark guest room, could still hear her quiet whisper-beg, Don't break me.

It had been the second time she'd said it, and here I'd been the one left broken.

She shrugged and looked away, navigating through the dense crowd as we drew nearer to the starting line tents. Panic started to well in my chest; I wasn't ready for goodbye yet.

"I was probably going to head home and shower. Get some lunch." She frowned. "Or stop for lunch on the way home. I'm not sure I have anything edible at my place, actually."

"Old shopping habits die hard," I noted dryly.

She gave a guilty wince. "Yeah. I've been sort of burying myself in the lab all week. Just . . . good distraction."

The words came out rushed, pressed together with how out of breath I felt: "I'd really love to hang out, and I have stuff for sandwiches, or salads. You could come over, or . . ." I trailed off when she stopped walking and turned to face me, looking bewildered and then . . . *adoring*.

Blinking away, I felt my chest squeeze. I tried to tamp down the impossible hope clawing up my throat. "What?" I asked, sounding more annoyed than I meant. "Why are you looking at me like that?"

Smiling, she said, "You're probably the only man I know who keeps his fridge so well stocked."

I felt my brows pull together in confusion. This had caused her to stop walking and stare at me? Cupping the back of my neck, I mumbled, "I try to keep healthy stuff at home so I don't go out and eat junk."

She stepped closer—close enough to feel a loose

strand of her hair when the wind blew it across my neck. Close enough to smell the light scent of her sweat, to remember how fucking amazing it felt to *make* her sweat. I dropped my gaze to her lips, wanting to kiss her so much it made my skin ache.

"I think you're amazing, Will," she said, licking her lips under the pressure of my attention. "And stop smoldering at me. There's only so much I can take from you today."

Before I could process any of this, she turned and moved toward the women's tent to retrieve her things. Numbly, I went the opposite way, to get my house keys, my extra socks, and the paperwork I'd bundled in my running jacket. When I emerged, she was waiting for me, holding a small duffel bag.

"So," I started, struggling to keep my distance. "You're coming over?"

"I really should shower . . ." she said, looking past me and down the street that led, eventually, to her building.

"You can shower at my place . . ." I didn't care how I sounded. I wasn't letting her go. I'd missed her. Nights had been almost unbearable, but strangely, mornings had been the worst. I missed her breathless conversation and how it would eventually fall away into the synchronized rhythm of our feet on pavement.

"And borrow some clean clothes?" she asked, wearing a teasing grin.

I nodded without hesitation. "Yes."

Her smile faded when she saw I was serious.

"Come over, Hanna. Just for lunch, I promise."

Lifting her hand to her forehead to block out the sun, she studied my face for a beat longer. "You sure?"

Instead of answering, I tilted my head, turning to walk. She fell into step beside me, and every time our fingers accidentally brushed, I wanted to pull her hand into mine and then pull her to me, pressing her against the nearest tree.

She'd been her old, playful self for those short, euphoric moments, but quiet Hanna reappeared as we walked the dozen or so blocks back to my building. I held the door for her as we stepped inside, slipped past her to push the up button for the elevator, and then stood close enough to feel the press of her arm along mine as we waited. At least three times I could hear her suck in a breath, start to speak, but then she would look at her shoes, at her fingernails, at the doors to the elevator. Anywhere but at my face.

Upstairs, my wide-open kitchen seemed to shrink under the tension between us, caused by the residue from the horrible conversation on Tuesday night, the hundreds of unspoken things from today, the simmering force that was always there. I handed her a blue Powerade because it was her favorite, and poured myself a glass of water, turning to watch her lips, her throat, her hand around the bottle as she took a deep drink.

You're so fucking beautiful, I didn't say.

I love you so much, I didn't say.

When she put the bottle down on the counter, her expression was full of all the things she wasn't saying, either. I could tell they were there, but had no idea what those things might be.

As we rehydrated in silence, I couldn't help but try to covertly check her out. But the secrecy was wasted. I could see her lips curl into a knowing smile when my attention moved over her face, to her chin, and down to the still-glistening skin of her chest, the hint of her breasts visible beneath her skimpy-ass sports bra— *fuck.* I'd so far managed to avoid looking directly at her chest, and now it pulled a familiar ache through me. Her chest was my happy place, and I wanted to sit down and press my face there.

I groaned, rubbing my eyes. It had been a terrible idea inviting her up here. I wanted to undress her, still sweaty, and feel the slide of her on top of me.

Just as I was pointing over my shoulder to the bathroom and asked, "Do you want the first shower?" Hanna tilted her head and grinned, asking, "Were you just looking at my chest?"

And because of the ease, the comfort, the fuck-ing *intimacy* of the question, anger flared in my blood. "Hanna, *don't*," I bit out. "Don't be the girl who plays head games. Barely a week ago you basically told me to get lost." I didn't expect it to come out like that, and in the quiet kitchen, my angry tone bounced around and surrounded us.

She blanched, looking devastated. "I'm sorry," she whispered.

"Fuck," I groaned, squeezing my eyes closed. "Don't be sorry just don't . . ." I opened my eyes to look at her. "Don't play games with me."

"I'm not trying to," she said, quiet urgency making her voice thin and hoarse. "I'm sorry I disappeared last week. I'm sorry I acted so horribly. I thought . . ."

I pulled out a kitchen stool, sinking down onto it. Running a half marathon didn't exhaust me as much as all of this did. My love for her was a heavy, pulsing, living *thing,* and it made me feel crazy, and anxious, and famished. I hated seeing her stressed and scared. I hated seeing her upset at my anger, but even worse was the knowledge that she had the power to break my heart and had very little experience being careful about it. I was completely at her fumbling, inexperienced mercy.

"I miss you," she said.

My chest tightened. "I miss you so much, Hanna. You have no idea. But I heard what you said on Tuesday. If you don't want this, then we have to find a way to be friends again. Asking me if I'm checking out your chest doesn't help us move past all of this."

"I'm sorry," she said, again. "Will . . ." she started and then the words fell away and she blinked down to her shoes.

I needed to understand what had happened, why everything had crumbled so abruptly after we'd made wildly intimate love only one week ago.

"That night," I started, and then reconsidered. "No, Hanna, *every* night—it was always intense like that with us—but that night last weekend . . . I thought it all kind of changed. *We* changed. Then the next day? And the drive back? Fuck, I don't even know what happened."

She moved closer, close enough for me to pull her by her hips to stand between my legs, but I didn't, and her hands fumbled at her sides before falling still.

"What happened was I heard what you said to Jensen," she said. "I knew there were other women in your life, but I kind of thought that you had ended things with them. I know I'd avoided talking about it, and that it wasn't fair of me to want that, but I thought you had."

"I hadn't 'officially' ended things, Hanna, but no one has been in my bed since you pulled me down that damn hall and asked to touch me. Fuck, not even before then."

"But how was I supposed to know that?" She dropped her head, stared at the floor. "And hearing what you said to Jensen might have been okay—I knew we needed to talk—but then I saw the text in the car. It popped up when I was picking out music." She stepped closer, pressing her thighs to my knees. "We'd had unprotected sex the night before, but then I saw her message, and it seemed like . . . like you were trying to hook up with her right after. I realized that Kitty still expected to be able to be with you, and I'd been trying—"

"I did *not* have sex with her on Tuesday, Hanna," I interrupted, my blood racing with panic. "Yes, I texted her asking if we could meet, but it was so I could let her know things were over between us. It wasn't like—"

"I know," she said, quietly cutting me off. "She told me today that you haven't been with her in a long time."

I let this sink in for a minute and then sighed. I wasn't sure I wanted to know what Kitty had told Hanna, but in the end, it didn't matter. I didn't have anything to hide. Yes, as someone who values being up front with people, I should have ended things cleanly with Kitty as soon as I told Hanna I wanted more, but I'd never lied to either of them, not once. I hadn't lied when I told Kitty so many months ago that I didn't want to dive into anything deeper. And I hadn't lied to Hanna only a month ago when I told her I wanted more, and only from her.

"I was just trying to stick to *your* rules. I wasn't going to bring up the relationship thing again because you'd determined I was incapable of it in the first place."

"I know," she said quickly. "I know."

But that was it; her eyes searched mine, waiting for me to say . . . what? What could I say that I hadn't said already? Hadn't I laid it all out enough times?

With a tired sigh, I stood. "Do you want the first shower?" I asked. Things were so weird between us, and even when we were still virtual strangers, running together that first, freezing morning, it hadn't ever been this way.

She had to step back to let me move past her. "No, it's okay. Go ahead."

———

I turned the water as hot as I could bear. I wasn't sore yet from the run—probably wouldn't get too sore anyway—but with the stress of wanting to make love to Hanna and wanting to throttle her at the same time, the hot water and the steam felt amazing.

It was possible she wanted things to be how they'd been before: sex, as friends. Comfortable without expectations. And I wanted her so intensely I knew how easy it would be to fall back into that, to enjoy her body and her friendship in equal measure, to never need or expect it to grow deeper.

But it wasn't what I wanted anymore. Not from anyone, and especially not from her. I soaped up, closing my eyes and inhaling the steam, washing away the race and the sweat. Wishing I could wash away the twisted mess inside.

I heard the faint click of the shower door only a split second before cold air bit across my skin. Adrenaline slid into my veins, pumping through my heart, filling my head with a wildness that made me dizzy. I pressed my hand to the wall, afraid to turn and face her, and feel all my resolve melt. There was only a fraction of me I knew would be able to hold back. The rest would give her anything she asked for.

She whispered my name, closing the door and stepping close enough for me to feel the press of her naked breasts against my back. Her skin was cool. She ran her hands up my sides, over my ribs.

"Will," she said again, moving her hands to my chest, and down over my stomach. "Look at me."

I reached down, gripping her wrists to keep her hands from moving any lower, low enough to feel how hard I was with just this small bit of contact. I was like a racehorse, held back by a single, flimsy gate. The muscles in my arms tensed and jumped; holding her at her wrists was to restrain myself as much as it was to keep her hands from my skin.

Leaning my forehead into the wall, I remained still until I was sure I could face her and not immediately take her in my arms. Finally, I turned, adjusting my grip on her wrists.

"I don't think I can do this," I whispered, looking down at her face.

Her hair was loose, and the wet strands clung to her cheeks, her neck, her shoulders. Her brows were pulled together in confusion and I knew she didn't understand my meaning. But then she seemed to hear me, and a bloom of humiliation spread across her cheeks and she squeezed her eyes shut. "I'm sor—"

"No," I said, interrupting her. "I mean can't do what we did before. I won't share. I don't want this if you still want to date other men."

Hanna opened her eyes, and they softened, her breath picking up.

"I can't fault you for wanting to experiment," I told her, my fists curling tighter around her wrists at the thought, "but I won't be able to keep my feelings for you from deepening, and I won't want to pretend we're just friends. Not even with Jensen. I know I'd take whatever you'll give me because I want you that much, but I would be miserable if it was only sex for you."

"I don't think it was ever just sex for me," she said.

I let her wrists go, studying her face and trying to understand what she was offering.

"When you called me *your* Hanna earlier," she began and then paused, pressing her hand to my chest, "I wanted it to be true. I want to be yours."

My breath formed a brick in my throat. Beneath the delicate skin of her neck, I could see her pulse thrumming.

"I mean, I *am* yours. Already." She stretched, eyes wide open as she carefully took my bottom lip between hers, sucking gently. She lifted my hand, pressed it around her breast and arched into my palm.

If what I felt now was even a small taste of the fear she'd felt all this time that I'd hurt her, then I suddenly understood why she'd been so skittish for so long. Being in love like this was terrifying.

"Please," she begged, kissing me again, reaching for my other hand and trying to pull it around her. "I want to be with you so much it's making it hard to breathe."

"Hanna," I choked, bending involuntarily, giving her better access to my lips, my neck. I curled my hand around her, rubbing my thumb over her nipple.

"I love you," she whispered, kissing down my chin, to my neck, and I squeezed my eyes closed, heart pounding.

When she said this, my resolve shattered and I opened my mouth, groaning when I felt her slide her tongue inside and go over mine. She moaned, clawing at my shoulders, my neck, pressing her stomach into the hard line of my cock.

She gasped at the shock of the cold tile on her back when I turned her, pressing her into the wall, and then gasped again when I ducked and lifted her breast to my mouth, sucking hungrily. It wasn't that my fear was gone; if anything, hearing her say she loved me was infinitely more terrifying because it brought hope along with it: hope that I could do this, that *she* could, that both of us could somehow navigate blindly through this elusive *first*.

I returned to her mouth, feeling wild now, lost in the fever of her kisses and knowing without having to ask that some of the water on her cheeks wasn't from the shower. I felt it, too, the dissolving relief, followed immediately with a fiery need to be inside her, to be moving in her, feeling her.

Reaching down, I cupped the back of her thighs, lifting her so she could wrap her legs around my waist. I felt the slick warmth of her sex, and rocked there, pressing just inside and out again, falling in love all over again at her raspy, impatient sounds.

"Never done this before," I murmured into the skin of her neck. "I have no fucking idea what I'm doing."

She laughed, biting at my neck and gripping my shoulders tightly. Slowly, I pressed into her, stilling when our hips met and knowing in an instant that this would be over fast. Her head fell back against the tile, landing with a quiet thud, and her chest rose and fell with sharp, jagged breaths.

"Oh my God, Will."

Pulling out, I whispered, "Do you feel it, too?"

Hanna hiccupped, begging me to move, pressing into me as much as she could, trapped between the wall and my body.

"That isn't just sex," I told her, sucking along her collarbone. "This feeling that it's so good it almost hurts? It's been like this every single time I've been inside you, Plum. That's what it feels like when you do this with someone you're fucking *insane* for."

"Someone you love?" she asked, her lips pressed to my ear.

"Yeah." I pushed in and pulled out again faster, knowing I was so close I would need to take her to my bed, suck on her pussy, and then fuck her again until we both collapsed. It was too intense, and as soon as I started moving I knew I wouldn't ever get used to the feel of being inside her without anything between us.

I jerked against her, relishing her sounds and whispering my apology into her neck over and over. "It's too intense . . ." All of it was overwhelming: the feeling of her around me, her words, and the understanding that she was really mine now. "I'm too close, Plum, I can't . . ."

She shook her head, nails biting into the skin of my shoulder, and pressed her lips to my ear. "I like when you can't hold back. It's how I always felt with you."

With a groan I let go, feeling myself spiral down

down

down

pressing deeper and harder until I could hear the gentle slap of my thighs on hers and her back on the wall, and felt my body flush warm and wet, coming inside her so hard my shout echoed sharply off the tile all around us.

I don't think I'd ever come that fast in my entire life and I felt both euphoric and mildly horrified.

Hanna pulled my hair, silently begging for my mouth on hers but after only a small kiss I slipped from her with a groan, and fell to my knees. Leaning forward, I spread her with my hands and sealed my mouth around the soft rise of her clit, sucking. I closed my eyes and groaned at the sound of her sweet moan, the feel of her sex against my tongue. Her legs shook—exhausted from the run, probably also exhausted from the rough treatment I'd just given her against a wall—and I slid my arms between her thighs, spreading her legs and lifting her so her thighs rested on my shoulders and my palms gripped her ass.

Above me, she cried out, her arms grappling wildly for something to hold on to, and finally she settled for clutching my head with her thighs and reaching down, bracing her hands on the top my head while she watched me with wide, fascinated eyes.

"I'm so close." Her voice wavered, hands shaking where she gripped my hair.

I hummed, smiling into her and moving my head slowly side to side as I sucked. I'd never done this before and felt so much like I was *loving* someone, making love in every way I possibly could. My chest warmed intensely when it occurred to me: this was our beginning. Right here, partially hidden by the steam of the shower, was where we clarified everything.

I could see the moment she started to come, the hot flush bloomed on her chest and spread upward, reaching her face just as her lips parted in a gasp.

I'd never get tired of this. I'd never tire of *her*. With the most possessive pleasure I'd ever felt, I watched as her orgasm rocked through her, pulling a scream from her throat.

Stopping when her thighs went lax, I carefully slid my arms from her, easing her down on shaking legs. I stood, staring down at her for a beat before she slid her arms around my neck and stretched to hold me.

She was soft and warm from the heat of the water and seemed to melt in my arms.

And it was so fucking different. It had never felt like this—like I was completely connected to her—even when we were in our most intimate moments as "just friends."

Here, she felt like mine.

"I love you," I whispered into her hair, before reaching to the side for my soap. Carefully, I washed every inch of her skin, her hair, and the delicate skin between her legs. I washed my orgasm away from her body, and kissed her jaw, her eyelids, her lips.

We stepped out and I wrapped her in a towel before pulling one around my own waist. I led her into the bedroom, sat her on the edge of the bed, and dried her, before urging her back onto the mattress.

"I'll bring you something to eat."

"I'll come with you." She struggled against my roaming hands, tried to sit up, but I shook my head, bending to suck her nipple into my mouth. "Just stay here and relax," I whispered against her skin. "I want to keep you here in bed all night long, so you're going to need to eat first."

Water from my hair dripped onto her naked skin and she gasped, eyes wide, pupils spreading inky black in the soft gray of her irises. She slid her hands to my shoulders, trying to pull me down and, *fuck,* I was ready to go again . . . but we needed food. I was already starting to feel woozy.

"I'll just throw something together."

———

We ate sandwiches, sitting naked on the bedspread, and talked for hours about the race, about the weekend with her family, and finally, about how it had felt when we thought things had ended between us.

We made love until the sunlight faded outside, and then slept, waking in the middle of the night starving for more. And then it was wild, and loud, and exactly how it had always been when things were best with us: honest.

For the moment, I was sated, and reached for my bedside table to find a pen. Curling around her, I put her tattoo back on her hip—*All that is rare for the rare*—hoping that I could be that rare thing, a recovered wildness, a reformed player, that Hanna deserved.

Epilogue

The flight attendant walked past, snapping the over-head bins shut with decisive clicks before bending to ask, "Orange juice or coffee?"

Will asked for coffee. I shook my head with a smile.

He patted my knee, palm up. "Give me your phone."

I handed it over, but complained anyway: "Why do I need wireless? I'm going to be asleep the entire flight." Never again would I let him book 6 a.m. flights from New York to the West Coast.

Will ignored me, entering some code into a tiny box on my phone's Web browser.

"If you haven't noticed, I'm sleepy. It's *someone's* fault that I was kept up all night," I whispered, leaning into him.

He stopped what he was doing, turning to smolder at me. "Is that how it happened?"

A thrill ran from my chest, down my belly, and between my legs. "Yes."

"You didn't come over after lab, a little . . . worked up?"

"No," I lied.

His eyebrow rose, a smile curling half of his mouth. "And you didn't interrupt my preparation of the very romantic dinner I was planning for you?"

"Me? No."

"And pull me down onto the couch asking me to 'do that thing with my mouth'?"

I held my hand to my chest. "I would *never*."

"It wasn't you who then ignored the delicious smells coming from the stove and pulled me to the bedroom and asked for some very, *very* dirty things?"

I closed my eyes as he leaned close, grazing his teeth over my jaw and murmuring, "I love you so fucking much, my naughty, sweet Plum."

Images from the night before pulled me deeper into the hungry, achy place I practically lived in anytime I was near Will. I remembered his rough hands, his commanding voice telling me exactly what he wanted me to do. I remembered those hands tugging my hair, his body moving over mine for hours, his voice finally low and begging for my teeth, my nails. I remembered the weight of him collapsing on me, sweaty and exhausted and falling asleep almost as soon as he found his release.

"Maybe that was me," I admitted. "It was a long day working in the safety hood, what can I say? I had a lot of time to think about your magical mouth."

He kissed me and then returned to my phone, smiling as he finished what he was doing and handing it back to me. "You're all set."

"I'm still going to sleep."

"Well, at least if Chloe needs you, your phone is working."

I slid my eyes to him, confused. "Why would she need me? I'm not in the wedding."

"Have you met Chloe? She's a fearsome general that could conscript you at a moment's notice," he said, gripping the back of his neck in the way he did when he was uncomfortable. "Whatever. Just sleep then."

"I have a feeling about this trip," I murmured, leaning into his shoulder. "Like a premonition."

"How uncharacteristically spiritual of you."

"I'm serious. I think it's going to be amazing, but I also feel like we're in a giant steel tube headed toward a week of insanity."

"Technically airplanes are made of aluminum alloy." Will looked over at me, bent to kiss my nose, and whispered, "But you knew that."

"Do *you* ever have a feeling about something?"

He hummed, kissed me again. "Once or twice."

I stared up at him—at the familiar dark lashes and deep blue eyes, at his five o'clock shadow at six in the morning, and at the goofy smile he'd been wearing since I woke him up—*again*—four hours ago with my mouth on his cock.

"Are you feeling sentimental, Dr. Sumner?"

He shrugged and blinked, clearing a bit of the lovestruck gleam in his eyes. "Just excited to go on vacation with you. Excited for the wedding. Excited that our little gang is having a baby soon."

"I have a question about a rule," I whispered.

He leaned in conspiratorially, whispering back, "I'm not your dating coach anymore. There are no rules, besides that no other guy touches you."

"Still. You know about these things."

With a smile he murmured, "Fine. Hit me."

"We've only been together two months, and—"

"Four," he corrected, always insisting I was his from that very first run.

"Fine. Have it your way, four. Is it bad form after only four months to tell you I think you're my forever?"

His smile straightened, his eyes moving over my face in that way that felt like a caress. He kissed me once, and then again.

"I would say that's incredibly *good* form." He pulled back to look at me for a long, heavy beat. "Sleep, Plum."

My phone buzzed on my lap, startling me awake. I straightened from where I'd been asleep on Will's shoulder and blinked, looking down at my phone, where a text from him lit up my screen. Beside me, I could almost feel his smile.

I read the text: What are you wearing?

I squinted sleepily at my phone as I typed, A skirt and no panties. But don't get any ideas, I'm a little sore from what my boyfriend did last night.

He made a sympathetic clucking noise beside me. That brute.

Why are you texting me?

He shook his head next to me, sighing with exaggerated weariness. Because I can. Because modern technology is amazing. Because we are 30,000 feet in the air and civilization has progressed to the point I can beam a filthy proposition to you from a satellite in space to a flying "steel tube."

I turned to look at him, eyebrows raised. "You woke me up to ask me what I'm wearing?"

He shook his head, and kept typing. In my lap, my phone buzzed.

I love you.

"I love you, too," I said. "I'm right here, you nerd. I'm not texting a reply."

He smiled, but kept typing. You're my forever, too.

I stared down at my phone, my chest suddenly so tight it was hard to breathe. I reached over my head, adjusting the airflow of the nozzle aimed at my seat.

`And I might propose to you soon.`

I stared at my phone, reading this line again, and again.

"Okay," I whispered.

`So give me a heads-up if you won't say yes, because I'm mildly terrified.`

I leaned back on his shoulder and he dropped his phone into his lap, wrapping his shaking hand around mine.

"Don't be," I whispered. "We've totally got this."

Acknowledgments

By the time we started working on this book, we'd only known our editor, Adam Wilson, for eight months, but together we had already released two books (*Bastard* and *Stranger*), with four more scheduled in the same year. This type of publishing schedule for a new author-editor combination is a bit like summer camp: everything is wild and goes by in a blur, and relationships don't have the luxury of the normal slow easing-in, getting-to-know-you time. As with anything else in life, sometimes those intense experiences work, and sometimes they don't, but with Adam we've been so profoundly lucky. When we finally met in July, we just knew: he is *our people* and is absolutely our brand of crazy (or very convincingly pretends to be because we send him both metaphorical and real cupcakes). Working with him has been one of the best experiences either of us has had, ever, and we can't wait to see what we get to do together next.

When we were first going through the query process, we read probably a hundred blog posts that emphasized the importance of finding an agent that clicks for you. It's not about finding an agent, everyone said, it's about finding the right one. In truth, Holly Root is not only the right agent for us, she's also one of the best people we've ever known. Without her, these books would never have found the perfect home with Gallery, or with Adam. She still says she knew from the very first time she spoke to him about the project that he would be a perfect fit for us. It's these types of relationships that make us feel eternally grateful.

But it's also the involvement of our beta readers— Erin, Martha, Tonya, Gretchen, Myra, Anne, Kellie, Katy, and Monica—that makes us realize that the process of writing is so much more than putting words to paper; it's also finding your community of people who will help you battle the crazy on the bad days, and help you celebrate the awesome on the good ones. If you've ever sent your work to someone to read, you know what a vulnerable experience that can be, and to every one of our readers who has helped with the *Beautiful* books, thank you for so perfectly balancing support with criticism. Sorry that we've killed some of your brain cells. Anne, thanks for the Nietzsche and the kick-ass line about him. Jen, thank you a million times over for the promo and cheerleading. Lauren, thank you forever for running the *Beautiful* social media, and being excited for every cover, excerpt, and email. We love you all.

We're erecting (hee! we said erecting!) a billboard in honor of our fabulous S&S/Gallery Books home. THANK YOU, Carolyn Reidy, Louise Burke, Jen Bergstrom, Liz Psaltis, the wonderful art department, Kristin Dwyer (we are kidnapping you soon), Mary McCue (SDCC next year, no choice), Jean Anne Rose, Ellen Chan, Natalie Ebel, Lauren McKenna, Stephanie DeLuca, and, of course, Ed Schlesinger for laughing at Hanna's jokes. You've all made us feel like we're family. We get a pullout couch in the offices, right?

Writing isn't a nine-to-five job, or a Monday-to-Friday job. It's a job you do whenever you have a slice of time, and it's also the job that is a slave to inspiration, so if you lack even a tiny slice of time (typical), but you have a flurry of ideas, you drop everything to get those thoughts down before the fickle bastards disappear. Sometimes that means running away to the computer while dinner is boiling on the stove, and sometimes it means that the husband takes the kids to a movie or the zoo or on a hike so that Mommy can get something done. But regardless, writing is a process that requires a lot of patience and support by everyone in the writer's life, and for that, we make loving heart eyes at the loves of our lives, Keith and Ryan. And our children: Bear, Cutest, and Ninja, we hope you someday realize how patient you've been, and how that patience means we now get to spend a lot more time with you. Thanks to our family and friends for putting up with the crazy: Erin, Jenn, Tawna, Jess, Joie, Veena, Ian, and Jamie.

And last but certainly not least, writing these stories would mean nothing without the amazing people who read them. We're still blown away when you tell us you stayed up all night reading, or pretended to have the stomach flu to steal a few hours locked in a bathroom because you couldn't put down our book. Your support and encouragement means more to us than we could ever hope to convey. Thank you. Thank you for continuing to buy our books, for loving our characters as much as we do, for sharing our sense of humor and dirty minds, and for every tweet, email, post, comment, review, and hug. We hope we get to hug each and every one of you one day.

Bennett would like to see you all in his office.

Lo, you are so much more than a co-author, you're my best friend, the moon of my life, the chocolate to my . . . you see where I'm going here. I love you more than all the boy bands and glitter and lip gloss combined.

PQ, you look so pretty today! I love you even though you make me pee myself laughing. In fact, I love you more than I love Excel, GraphPad, and SPSS combined. Is your collar tingling?

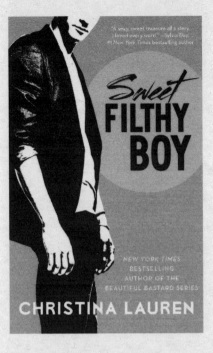

A sexy, sweet treasure of a story. I loved every word." —Sylvia Day #1 New York Times bestselling author

Sweet
FILTHY
BOY

NEW YORK TIMES
BESTSELLING
AUTHOR OF THE
BEAUTIFUL BASTARD SERIES

CHRISTINA LAUREN

Turn the page for a sneak peek of
Sweet Filthy Boy

Book One in the
Wild Seasons series
from Christina Lauren

ONE NIGHT STANDS ARE
SUPPOSED TO BE CONVENIENT.
FORGETTABLE. REGRETTABLE, EVEN.
THEY AREN'T SUPPOSED TO BE
WITH SOMEONE LIKE *HIM*.

Harlow orders fries before dropping her shot into her beer and downing it.

She pulls her forearm across her mouth and looks over at me. I must be gaping because she asks, "What? Should I be classier?"

I shrug, drawing the straw through the ice in my glass. After a morning massage and facial, an afternoon spent at the pool, followed by a few cocktails, we're all more than a little tipsy. Besides, even after chugging a beer with a shot in it, Harlow *looks* classy. She could jump into a bin full of plastic balls at McDonald's Playland and come out looking fresh.

"Why bother?" I ask. "We have the rest of our lives to be sophisticates, but only the one weekend in Vegas."

She listens to what I say, considers it before nodding firmly and motioning to the bartender. "I'll have two more shots and whatever that monstrosity is that she's drinking." She points to Lola, who's licking the whipped cream from the rim of a hideous, LED-flashing cup.

He frowns before shaking his head and says, "Two shots of whiskey and one Slut on a Trampoline, coming up."

Harlow gives me her best shocked face but I barely have time to register it before I feel someone press up behind me at the crowded bar. Large hands grip my hips only a split second before "There you are" is whispered hotly—and directly—into my ear.

I startle, turning and jumping away with a gasp.

Ansel.

My ear feels damp and warm, but when I look at him, I see the same playful light in his eyes he had last night. He's the guy who'll do a ridiculous robot dance to make you laugh, who'll lick the tip of your nose, make a fool out of himself for a smile. I'm sure if I tried to wrestle him to the ground, he'd let me win. And enjoy every minute.

"Too close?" he asks. "I was going for seductive, yet subtle."

"I'm not sure you could have been any closer," I admit, fighting a smile as I rub my ear. "You were practically inside my head."

"He'd make a horrible ninja," says one of the guys with him.

"Oliver, Finn," Ansel says, first pointing to a tall friend with messy brown hair, stubble, bright blue eyes behind thick-rimmed glasses, and then to the one who spoke, with short-cropped brown hair, dark backlit eyes, and what I can only imagine is a permanently cocky smirk. Ansel looks back at me. "And gentlemen, this is *Cerise*. I'm still waiting for her real name." He leans in a little, saying, "She'll have to give it up sometime."

"I'm Mia," I tell him, ignoring his innuendo. His eyes trip down my face and stall at my lips. It's precisely the look he would give me if we were about to kiss but he's too far away. He leans forward, and it feels like watching an airplane fly ten feet from the ground for miles, never getting closer.

"It's nice to put a face with all the man shouts," I say to break the thick sexual tension, looking around him to Oliver and Finn, then point to my wide-eyed friends beside me. "This is Lorelei, and Harlow."

They exchange handshakes, but remain suspiciously quiet. I'm not usually the one meeting guys in situations like this. I'm usually the one pulling Harlow back from hooking up on a table within minutes of meeting someone, while Lola considers beating up any guy who dares speak to us. They may be too stunned to know how to respond.

"Have you been looking for us?" I ask.

Ansel shrugs. "We may have gone to a couple of different places, just to peek."

Behind him, Oliver—the one in glasses—holds up seven fingers and I laugh. "A couple?"

"No more than three," Ansel says, winking.

I spot movement just behind him, and before I have a chance to say anything, Finn steps up, attempting to yank Ansel's pants down. Ansel doesn't even blink, but instead asks me, "What are you drinking?" and simply grips his waistband without looking even a little surprised or annoyed.

As if I can't see a considerable amount of gray boxers.

As if I'm not staring directly at where the distinct bulge in the cotton would be.

Is this what boys do?

"It's nice to see you in your underwear again," I say, struggling to restrain my grin.

"Almost," he clarifies. "At least my pants stayed up this time."

I glance down, wishing I could get another eyeful of his toned thighs. "That's debatable."

"Last time Finn did that, they didn't. I beat his road time this week and he's been trying to get me back ever since." He stops, brows lifting and seeming to only now hear what I said. He leans in a little bit, asking in a soft, low voice, "Are you hitting on me?"

"No." I swallow under the pressure of his unwavering attention. "Maybe?"

"Maybe if my pants go down, your dress should

go up," he whispers, and no sentence *anywhere* has ever sounded so dirty. "To level the playing field."

"She's way too hot for you," Finn says from behind him. Ansel reaches back, putting a hand on Finn's face and moving him farther away. He nods to my drink, wordlessly asking what was in my now-empty glass.

I stare back at him, feeling the strange warmth of familiarity spread through me. So *this* is what chemistry feels like. I've felt it with other performers, but that kind of connection is different from this. Usually chemistry between dancers diffuses offstage, or we force real life back in. Here with Ansel, I think we could charge large appliances with the energy moving between us.

He takes my glass and says, "Be right back," before glancing at Lola as she steps away from the others. She's watching Ansel like a hawk, with her arms crossed over her chest and stern mom-face on full display. "With a drink," he tells her good-naturedly. "Overpriced, watered-down alcohol, probably with some questionable fruit. Nothing funny, I promise. Would you like to come with me?"

"No, but I'm watching you," she says.

He gives her his most charming smile before turning to me. "Anything in particular you desire?"

"Surprise me," I tell him.

After he walks a few feet away to get the bartender's attention, the girls give me exaggerated *what the hell* stares and I shrug back—because, really, what can I say? The story is laid out right in front of them. A hot guy and his hot friends have located us in a club, and said hot guy is buying me a drink.

Lola, Harlow, and Ansel's friends make polite conversation but I can barely hear them, thanks to the booming music and my heartbeat pounding in my ears. I try not to stare down the bar to where Ansel has wedged himself between a few bodies, but in my peripheral vision I can see his head above most others, and his long, lean body leaning forward to call out his order to the bartender.

He returns a few minutes later with a new tumbler, full of ice and limes and clear liquid, offering it to me with a sweet smile. "Gin and tonic, right?"

"I was expecting you to get me something adventurous. Something in a pineapple or with sparklers."

"I smelled your glass," he says, shrugging. "I wanted to keep you on the same drink. Plus"—he gestures down my body—"you have this whole flapper girl thing going on with the short dress and the"—he draws a circle in the air with his index finger near my head—"the shiny black hair and straight bangs. And those red lips. I look at you and I think 'gin.'" He stops, scratching his chin, and adds, "Actually I look at you and think—"

Laughing, I hold up my hand to stop him there. "I have no idea what to do with you."

"I have some suggestions."

"I'm sure you do."

"Would you like to hear them?" he says, grin firmly in place.

I take a deep, steadying breath, pretty sure I'm in *way* over my head with this one. "How about you tell me a little about you guys first. Do you all live in the States?"

"No. We met a few years ago doing a volunteer program here where you bike from one city to another, building low-income housing as you go. We did it after university a few years back and worked from Florida to Arizona."

I look at him more closely now. I hadn't given much thought to who he is or what he does, but this is far more interesting than a group of asshole foreign guys blowing money on a Vegas suite. And biking from state to state definitely explains the muscular thighs. "That's not at all what I expected you to say."

"There were four of us who became very close. Finn, Oliver, me, and Perry. This year we did a reunion ride, but only from Austin to here. We're old men now."

I look around for the fourth one and then raise my eyebrows at him meaningfully. "Where is he?"

But Ansel only shrugs. "Just us three this time."

"It sounds amazing."

Sipping his drink, he nods. "It *was* amazing. I dread going home on Tuesday."

"Where exactly is home? France?"

He grins. "Yes."

"Home to France. What a drag," I say dryly.

"You should come to Paris with me."

"*Ha*. Okay."

He studies me for a long beat. "I'm serious."

"Oh, I'm sure you are."

He sips his drink again, eyebrows raised. "You may be the most beautiful woman I've ever seen. I suspect you're also the most clever." He leans in a little, whispering, "Can you juggle?"

Laughing, I say, "No."

"Pity." He hums, smiling at my mouth. "Well, I need to stay in France for another six months or so. You'll need to live there with me for a bit before we can buy a house Stateside. I can teach you then."

"I don't even know your last name," I say, laughing harder now. "We can't be discussing juggling lessons and cohabitation quite yet."

"My last name is Guillaume. My father is French. My mother is American."

"Gee what?" I repeat, floundering with the accent. "I wouldn't even know how to spell that." I frown, rolling the word around in my head a few times. "In fact, I'm not even sure what letter it begins with."

"You'll need to learn to spell it," he says, dimple flashing. "You'll have to sign your new name on your bank checks, after all."

Finally, I have to look away. I need to take a break from his grin and this DEFCON-1 level of flirtation.

I need oxygen. But when I blink to my right, I'm met with the renewed wide-eyed stares of my friends standing nearby.

I clear my throat, determined not to be self-conscious about how much fun I'm having and how easy this all feels. "What?" I ask, giving Lola the *don't overreact* face.

She turns her attention to Ansel. "You got her talking."

I can feel her shock, and I don't want it to consume me. If I think too much about how easy I feel around him, it'll rebound and I'll panic.

"This one?" he asks, pointing at me with his thumb. "She doesn't shut up, does she?"

Harlow and Lola laugh, but it's a *yeah, you're insane* laugh and Lola pulls me slightly to the side, putting a hand on my shoulder. "You."

"Me what?"

"You're having an instalove moment," she hisses. "It's freaking me out. Are your panties still on under there?" She bends dramatically as if to check.

"We met last night," I whisper, pulling her back up and trying to get her to lower her voice because even though we stepped away, we didn't move that far. All three men are listening in on our exchange.

"You met him and didn't tell us?"

"God, Mother. We were busy this morning and I forgot, okay? Last night they were partying across the hall. You would have heard them, too, if you hadn't had enough vodka to kill a horse. I walked over and asked them to quiet down."

"No, that wasn't the first time we met," Ansel interjects over my shoulder. "We met earlier."

"We did *not*," I insist, telling him with my expression to shut it. He doesn't know Lola's protective side but I do.

"But it was the first time she saw Ansel in his underwear," Finn adds, helpfully. "He invited her in."

Her eyebrows disappear beneath her hairline. "Oh my God. Am I drunk? What's in this thing?" she asks, peering into her obnoxiously flashing cup.

"Oh stop," I tell her, irritation rising. "I didn't go into his room. I didn't take the gorgeous stranger's candy even though I really wanted to because hello, look at him," I add, just daring her to freak out even more. "You should see him with his shirt off."

Ansel rocks on his heels, sipping his drink. "Please continue as if I'm not here. This is fantastic."

Finally—mercifully—Lola seems to decide to move on. We all step back into the small semicircle the guys have made, and drink our cocktails in stilted silence.

Either ignoring or oblivious to the awkward, Ansel pipes up. "So what are you all celebrating this weekend?" he asks.

He doesn't just speak the words, he pouts them, pushing each out in a little kiss. Never before have I had such an urge to touch someone's mouth with my fingers. As Harlow explains why we're in Vegas, drinking terrible shots and wearing the world's slut-tiest dresses, my eyes move down his chin, over his cheeks. Up close I can see he has perfect skin. Not just clear, but smooth and even. Only his cheeks are slightly ruddy, a constant boy-blush. It makes him look younger than I think he is. Onstage, he would remain untouched. No pancake, no lipstick. His nose is sharp, eyes perfectly spaced and an almost intimi-dating green. I imagine I'd be able to see the color from the back of a theater. There is no way he can possibly be as perfect as he seems.

"What do you do when you're not riding bikes or juggling?" I ask, and everyone turns to me in unison. I feel my pulse explode in my throat, but force my eyes to hold on to Ansel's, waiting for his answer.

He plants his elbows on the bar beside him and anchors me with his attention. "I'm an attorney."

My fantasy wilts immediately. My dad would be thrilled to know I'm chatting up a lawyer. "Oh."

His laugh is raspy. "Sorry to disappoint."

"I've never known an attorney before who wasn't old and lecherous," I admit, ignoring the looks Har-low and Lola have trained on the side of my face. At this point, I know they're counting how many words I've said in the last ten minutes. I'm breaking a per-sonal record now.

"Would it help if I said I work for a nonprofit?"

"Not really."

"Good. In that case I'll tell you the truth: I work

for the biggest, most ruthless corporate firm in Paris. I have a horrible schedule, really. This is why you should come to Paris. I'd like a reason to come home early from work."

I attempt to look unaffected by this, but he's watching me. I can practically feel his smile. It starts as a tiny tug in the corner of his mouth and grows the longer I pretend. "So I told you about me, what about you? Where are you from, *Cerise*?"

"I told you my name; you don't have to keep calling me that."

"What if I want to?"

It's really hard to concentrate when he's smiling like that. "I'm not sure I should tell you where I'm from. Stranger danger and all."

"I can give you my passport. Will that help?"

"Maybe."

"We can call my mom," he says, and reaches into his back pocket for his phone. "She's American, you'd get on fantastically. She tells me all the time what a sweet boy I am. I hear that a lot, actually."

"I'm sure you do," I say, and honestly, I think he really would let me call his mother. "I'm from California."

"Just California? I'm not an American but I hear that's a pretty big state."

I watch him through narrowed eyes before finally adding, "San Diego."

He grins as if he's won something, like I've just

wrapped this tiny piece of information up all shiny and bright and dropped it into his lap. "Ahh. And what do you do there in San Diego? Your friend said you're here celebrating graduation. What's next?"

"Uh . . . business school. Boston University," I say, and wonder if that answer will ever stop sounding stiff and rusty to my own ears, like I'm reading from a script.

Apparently it sounds that way to him, too, because for the first time, his smile slips. "I wouldn't have guessed that."

I glance to the bar and, without thinking, down the rest of my drink. The alcohol burns but I feel the heat seep into my limbs. The words I want to say bubble up in the back of my throat. "I used to dance. Ballet." It's the first time I've ever said those words to anyone.

His brows lift, his eyes moving first over my face, then trailing down my body. "Now that I can see."

Harlow squints at me, and then looks at Ansel. "You two are so fucking *nice*."

"It's disgusting," Finn agrees under his breath.

Their eyes meet from either side of me and hold. There's some sort of silent acknowledgment there, like they're on the same team—them against us— each trying to see which one can mortify their friend the most. And this is when I know we're only about an hour and a half from Harlow riding Finn reverse-cowgirl on the floor somewhere. Lola catches my eye and I know we're thinking the exact same thing.

As predicted, Harlow lifts her shot glass in Finn's direction. In the process, much of it slops over the side and onto her skin. Like the classy woman she is, she bends, dragging her tongue across the back of her hand before saying to no one in particular, "I'm probably gonna fuck him tonight."

Finn smiles, leaning closer to her and whispering something in her ear. I have no idea what he's just said but I'm sure I've never seen Harlow blush like this. She reaches up, toying with her earring. Beside me, Lorelei groans.

If Harlow looks you in the eye while she takes her earrings off, you're either going to be fucked or killed. When Finn smiles, I realize he's already figured out this rule and knows he's coming out on top.

"Harlow," I warn.

Clearly, Lola can't take any more, because she grabs Harlow's hand to haul her up and out of her chair. "Meeting of the minds in the ladies' room."

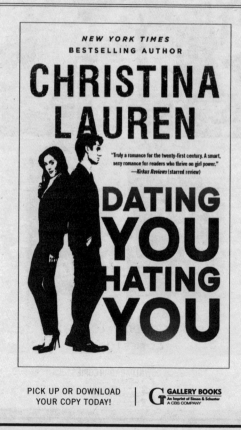